The Writings of M. T. Vasudevan Nair

The Writings of M. T. Vasudevan Nair

Mist & The Soul of Darkness

Kaalam

Kuttiedathi and Other Stories

Orient BlackSwan

THE WRITINGS OF M. T. VASUDEVAN NAIR

ORIENT BLACKSWAN PRIVATE LIMITED

Registered Office
3-6-752 Himayatnagar, Hyderabad 500 029 (A.P.), INDIA
E-mail: centraloffice@orientblackswan.com

Other offices
Bangalore, Bhopal, Bhubaneshwar, Chennai, Ernakulam, Guwahati, Hyderabad, Jaipur, Kolkata, Lucknow, Mumbai, New Delhi, Patna

Kaalam
First Published 1998 by Orient Longman Private Limited.
Reissued 2010

This collection first published 2010

ISBN : 978-81-250-3963-1

Lasertype in Adobe Garamond 11/13
by Eleven Arts, New Delhi

Printed in India at
De Unique, New Delhi

Published by
Orient Blackswan Private Limited
1/24 Asaf Ali Road
New Delhi 110 002
E-mail: delhi@orientblackswan.com

Contents

Kuttiedathi and Other Stories

MT and the Art of Artlessness

Practising artists rarely demonstrate a flair for the theory of art. They often avoid the academic vocabulary that one uses in theorising about art. To be 'artful', one might say, is to shun theory. If talking about the theory of art is to be somewhat 'artless', M. T. Vasudevan Nair is to be treated as artless in his practice as a writer. On the other hand, he can also be regarded as 'artful' in his approach inasmuch as he is enormously conscious of the complexities of the craft of fiction and can indeed talk authentically about them. He is one of the few fiction writers of his generation who have talked and written at length about the art of fiction writing in the form of letters, lectures, essays and book-length studies.[1]

MT, as he is known, has also been greatly consistent in his theory of art across time. He is not enamoured by fashions in theory. A perusal of *Kathikante Panippura* [The Storyteller's Workshop, 1963], his early treatise on fictional theory, read in conjunction with his recent lectures and essays on the topic would reveal that MT's views on the art of fiction have undergone little change over the years. His practice of fiction writing, on the other hand, has gone through enormous changes. 'Artless' again is the term that one might find handy in describing his views, given their underlying theory of reading that sees no major breach between reality and its fictional representation. An artless attitude to writing would suggest that one looks upon

[1] Apart from the several lectures and interviews that discuss the theory of art, MT has published three books in Malayalam that can be described as theoretical in orientation. They are *Kathikante Panippura* (Trichur: Current Books, 1963), *Hemingway: Oru Mukhavura* (Trichur: Current Books, 1964) and *Kathikante Kala* (Kottayam: DC Books, 1984).

literature as a transparent carry over of the problems of the real world to the world represented in fiction. One is moved almost spontaneously to creative expressiveness when one is overawed by the power of one's emotions. The gap between emotional turbulence and its expression, in this view, is too small to allow for any mediation worth mentioning.

It is useful to begin any discussion of MT's fiction with a reference to his theory of writing because outwardly his fiction seems almost transparent and unmediated. It is artless, both in the sense of 'being guileless' and 'making no pretence to art'. When MT started writing his narratives in the fifties of the last century, the story writing tradition in Malayalam was controlled largely by the ideology of what could be called 'renaissance fiction', which modelled itself on the social realism of such nineteenth-century European writers as Mauppasant, Balzac, Zola, Flaubert, Dickens and Chekhov. The writers who practised this kind of fiction were using the fictional medium to make a point or two about society. They belonged to the generation of Malayalam writers who were attempting to fictionalise across the public life of Kerala a generation earlier. Providing a formal shape to the experience of the renaissance was for them also a way of coming to terms with its social and political energy. A number of writers, including Thakazhi Sivasankara Pillai, Ponkunnam Varky, Kesava Dev, Vaikom Muhammad Basheer, K. Saraswati Amma and Lalitambika Antarjanam participated in their own individual ways in this great creative upsurge. Aside from the fact that all these writers inherited the social renaissance ideology of placing an abstractly conceived *man* at the centre of the scheme of things, each of them seemed to be distinctively individualistic in expressing his/her response to the world. But their seeming artlessness was what bound them together as writers of fiction. The artlessness had behind it the conviction that fiction represented a spontaneous and unmediated translation of experience from the plane of the worldly to that of the literary. The writer's creative genius arguably was all that was needed for this translation.

MT certainly shared this conviction and, unlike his renaissance predecessors, also chose to theorise on it. His preferred theory of creativity corresponded with that of the social realists who looked upon literary works as the creations of individuals whose invisible presence in the works would invariably be felt by the readers. Flaubert, the author of *Madame Bovary*, had once drawn a parallel between the artist and God, the supreme creator, and had suggested that like the Almighty, the artist in his creation should never become visible, but should make sure that the work is animated by the author's unseen presence. In his theoretical work, *Kathikante Kala* [The Storyteller's Art, 1984], MT quotes Flaubert with approval and remarks that the writer's pervasive, but invisible presence in the story is what transforms it into a well-written creative piece. A good work of art should appear almost artless.

In short, while it was their artlessness that characterised the writing of the renaissance fictionists, MT's intervention was aimed at transmuting this artlessness into an artistic virtue by integrating the form of the short story with a new sense of the craft of fiction. A few writers of the earlier generation like Karoor Nilakanta Pillai, S. K. Pottekkat and Uroob [P. C. Kuttikrishnan] as well as some of MT's own contemporaries like Madhavikkutty and T. Padmanabhan had already started moving in this direction with their path-breaking stories that probed the intricacies of the human mind. Indeed what MT did through his short and long fiction of the fifties and sixties was to draw the attention of the reader to the inner life of the individual whose voice had seldom been heard in renaissance fiction. His fiction delved deep into the dark recesses of the individual mind and shed light on its hidden aspects that no one before had suspected to exist. The human mind and the psychology of the individual were relatively new inventions for Malayalam fiction, and it was primarily MT who helped invent them through his cleverly crafted tales that told the stories of lonely, angry and alienated individuals fighting a society that was falling apart, a society that is on the verge of disintegration—this in a sense would neatly sum up the thematic kernel of much of MT's early fiction.

Though MT has diversified into other themes in the course of his development as a writer, 'outsider' figures battling it out with society have continued to fascinate him all through his fictional career. Right from his earliest short stories included in such collections as *Ninte Ormaykku* [Remembering You, 1956] and *Iruttinte Atmavu* [Creature of Darkness, 1957] and the early novels *Nalukettu* [The Feudal Household, 1958] and *Asuravithu* [Demon-seed, 1962], MT's major concern has been with fictionalising the strife and anxieties of individuals who are the victims of a system over which they have no control. This is true of most of his characters starting with Appunni, the central character of *Nalukettu*, the celebrated novel that launched the writer firmly on the literary horizon, to P. K. Venugopalan Nair, the journalist protagonist of 'Kadugannava: Oru Yatrakkurippu' [Kadugannava: A Travel Note, 1995], a short story written much later. Even Bhima, the hero of *Randamoozham* [The Second Turn, 1984], his reworking of the Mahabharata story of the Pandavas, can be read as the tale of an alienated outsider caught in the pressures of a family feud. Much of all this indeed is a reconstruction of what he felt, experienced, remembered and fantasised as the member of a joint family in a village in the Malabar region of pre-Independence Kerala. The autobiographical element in MT's fiction cannot be mistaken, and as he states in a note prefixed to a recent translation of *Nalukettu*, the stories that he wrote even before *Nalukettu* had an autobiographical slant about them, with anecdotes he had heard from his mother and grandmother about older members of the family appearing in them in disguised forms.[2]

But as the contents of this collection indicate, MT's fictional world is peopled not merely by alienated individuals from ex-feudal families. His thematic range is too diverse to limit his characters to societal freaks. It might indeed be facile to imagine a prolific writer like MT, who has authored ten novels, twenty-three short story collections, a full-length play and a number of screenplays and miscellaneous writings, and has also directed a few important feature films, to be narrow in his thematic focus. The themes that are fictionalised in his short stories and novels include, apart from an individual's psychological tension arising from the break-up of feudal family bonds, the conflict between village and city life, infidelity in marriage, hypocrisy in human relations, nostalgic recreations of the past, jealousies and petty rivalries in inter-personal relationships, the distance between the dream world and the real, psychological traumas and the grace of the elders in the family. All these of course are related to the general ambience involving the members of a society in transition. MT himself recognises this in

[2] M. T. Vasudevan Nair, 'Author's Note', in' *Nalukettu*, translated by Gita Krishnankutty (New Delhi: Oxford University Press, 2008), p. x.

the course of elaborating the organic connection between the epic-inspired *Randamoozham* and the imaginatively constructed earlier fiction, thus:

> I have dealt with the theme of family breakdown and the fate of men involved in it in my earlier novels against the background of my village. The only difference here is that in this novel [i.e., *Randamoozham*] I am narrating the story of the family of an older period.[3]

The artlessness in MT, then, is related to this thematic ambience, which would link his fiction to the village of Kudallur on the banks of the river Bharatappuzha where he was born in 1934 into a family that had witnessed the vicissitudes of the social transformation that he was to fictionalise. Several of his characters like Appunni [*Naluketty*], Sethu [*Kaalam*], Velayudhan [*Iruttinte Atmavu*], Govindankutty [*Asuravithu*] and Bhima [*Randamoozham*] share facets of MT's personality and his past. One would find it difficult to disentangle the 'narrative self' in some of the novels and short stories from the 'personal self' of the writer. The names of the protagonists of some stories are either a shorter form of the author's name [Vasu in 'Kuttiedathi'] or a rhyme word [Kesu in 'Bandhanam']. But this does not make his characters replicas of his self. The magic of his writing endows them with an otherworldly charm, so that the environs of the village and the ambience of the feudal household turn into something entirely different. That is why to the question whether the protagonist Appunni of *Naluketty* is a replica of his self, his answer is an emphatic 'no'.[4] This could with equal force be said of such other protagonists as well.[5]

It is in endowing the themes and characters with a constructed otherworldly air that the artfulness of MT operates in his fiction. In the short story 'Bondage' ['Bandhanam' in the original], included in

[3] M. T. Vasudevan Nair, *Randamoozham* (Trichur: Current Books, 1984), p. 300. (Translation mine)

[4] See Nair, 'Author's Note', *Naluketty*, p. xi.

[5] MT makes a similar disclaimer on behalf of Sethu, the protagonist of *Kaalam* too. See his interview with Vanajam Ravindran, 'Conversation with M. T. Vasudevan Nair,' *Wordsmiths*, ed. Meenakshi Sarma (New Delhi: Katha), p. 207.

this collection, the narrator Kesu is a young business executive who shifts his residence to the city in order to carry on his secret liaison with his paramour without the knowledge of his innocent wife who lives in the village. The conflict between the city and the village indeed is a staple theme of MT's fiction. But in this short story he is in a sense also constructing a metaphor for the art of fiction through the character of Kesu who is presented as an embodiment of guile and artfulness. The author describes the marital infidelity of Kesu in terms that can metaphorically be translated into the language of art theory. To be artful is also to be deceitful. Art is a lie, as art theorists are never tired of repeating, and MT seems to be talking about the balancing of artlessness with artfulness when he sketches the character of Kesu in the following terms:

> It was easy to make a lie work. His face would shine with honesty when he told one. Nature had endowed him with the mask of a calm face and eyes filled with innocence.

To tell a lie with an air of artlessness, then, is to be artful. This in fact is the pivot of MT's fictional technique. Expressive realism is the term that one might conveniently use in describing this pivot, which invites attention to the word magic that the writer invokes in order to impart to his fiction the quality of verisimilitude. This involves a perfect union of the form of fiction and the material that the writer has collected from the life around him. Only a shrewd craftsman can achieve this union, and MT, the artist of the artless, achieves this with remarkable competence. He knows that one has to go on chiseling at the words and images in a short story, just as a poet fine-hones the poem, before one can arrive at the perfect form that would convey to the reader the story's closeness to life.[6] Look at the short story 'Kuttiedathi' or the slightly longer story *Iruttinte Atmavu* [The Soul of Darkness]. Both narrate, almost artlessly, experiences in the

[6] In the interview noted above, MT refers to the attention that he pays to the craft of fiction in the following words: 'Structurally it [i.e., the short story] is closer to a poem. You go on chiseling it, removing unwanted portions, till you finally get the exact form.' Vanajam Ravindran, 'In Conversation with M. T. Vasudevan Nair,' p. 205.

life of individuals who appear to emerge from a familiar background. In both the experiences are narrated in a language that is carefully contrived and with the eye of an artist who does not miss out on the minutest details that hold the thread of the stories together.

A closer look at the form of *Kuttiedathi* and *The Soul of Darkness* (included in this collection) would illustrate how the contrived narrative structure of the two stories provides for the effect mentioned above. Although the similarity in the girl/boy-next-door images of Kuttiedathi and Velayudhan in the two stories might not go unnoticed by the sensitive reader, there is nothing common in the form or the content of the two stories on the surface. Closer scrutiny, however, would reveal important connections underneath. Indeed it is not difficult to describe the central characters to be both abnormal in certain respects. Kuttiedathi is somewhat abnormal in regard to her physical attributes and Velayudhan is greatly so in regard to his mental attributes. They are true to life as individuals who suffer from disadvantages that render them lesser beings in the eyes of the society. Dark-skinned Kuttiedathi with a big mole on her earlobe is spurned alike by her suitors, her family, and her own mother. Only the young narrator, Vasu, her cousin, has any communication with and sympathy for Kuttiedathi. Central to the story indeed is a conflict between the social norm and its breach symbolised by the character of Kuttiedathi. Kuttiedathi who can throw stones at mango trees and even climb them, who does not care for the restrictions imposed on her movements by her family and who ruins the family's reputation by falling in love with Appunni, the low caste, is the picture of a woman who dares to question the norms of behaviour prescribed by society. She falls out with the society that tries to curtail her freedom and chooses the course of suicide to bring her travails to an end.

The structure repeats itself in *The Soul of Darkness* where mentally challenged Velayudhan is hated by almost everyone in the family. Velayudhan finds comfort only in the presence of Ammukutty, his pretty cousin. As in the case of Kuttiedathi, society imposes restriction on the movement of Velayudhan: 'It was an unwritten law that he should not be seen anywhere in Uncle's portico.' The area of free space where Velayudhan can move about becomes increasingly curtailed as the story progresses and towards the end we see him in chains, in a state of total captivity. He tries to resist bondage, but when he realises that he is going to lose Ammukutty forever, he begs to be enchained. It is in fact a kind of spiritual suicide that he craves when he asks to be put in chains toward the end of the story. Velayudhan is Kuttiedathi's male counterpart, transplanted in a new environment. It is significant to note that all his younger cousins address him as 'Kuttiettan' ['Elder brother Kutty', the male form of 'Kuttiedathi', 'Elder sister Kutty' in Malayalam]. It is through the agency of the craft of fiction that this transplantation is effected.

Two longer works included in this collection are *Manju* [*Mist*, 1964], a novella, and *Kaalam* [Time, 1969], the novel that fetched for its author the Sahitya Akademi award for the best creative work in Malayalam in 1970. *Mist* indicates that MT cannot be considered a mere chronicler of the disintegration of the feudal family system, but that the mental landscape of the individual in turmoil is his real theme. It narrates the story of the long and unending wait of Vimala, a teacher in a boarding school in Nainital, for elusive Sudhir Kumar Misra, a researcher in international studies, with whom she had an affair when they met briefly in the snow-clad mountain ranges of Kumaon a few years earlier. The novella can be regarded as MT's first important foray into the world outside the precincts of the feudal Nalukettu. Though Vimala can be read as remotely connected to such characters as Appunni, Sethu and Govindankutty of the earlier novels in being somewhat alienated from the public world, what distinguishes *Mist* is the consistent use of the metaphor of mist to unravel the emotional tangle in the central character's mindscape. It is perhaps with this novel that Malayalam has for the first time started looking closely at the complex activities of the individual mind. Vimala digs deep into the interior of her mind to unravel feelings, emotions, memories, dreams and fantasies that lie dormant in the misty world of the unconscious. The conscious mind can only capture them vaguely. Through a deft interplay of the conscious and the unconscious, MT sets off in *Mist* an interior monologue that also proclaims that the way a story is narrated would invariably converge on what is narrated.

The lessons that MT learnt from *Mist* seem to have been put to practical use in the composition of all his later works, including

Kaalam, the novel that returns to his pet theme of the collapse of the feudal family, but with an awareness of its impact on the psychology of the people involved in it. It was suggested at the beginning of this introduction that though MT's views on the art of fiction have remained unchanged over the years, his practice of fiction writing has undergone enormous changes. *Kaalam* indeed proves this, but more than *Kaalam* it is some of his short stories of the later period that provide definite clues to the change. 'Kadugannava: A Travel Note', one of the more recent of MT's short stories included in this collection, is significant in this regard. The worth of this story in a certain sense lies in the fact that it is written in the form of a travel diary of a journalist who visits strife-torn Sri Lanka on receiving an invitation to attend an international seminar. This discursive distinction indeed is important in considering the progress of a writer who has been schooled in the tradition of expressive realism. We recognise the artistic value of the long and interesting distance that MT has successfully traveled in his journey from his early fiction to 'Kadugannava'. The real significance of 'Kadugannava' arises from the boldness with which it organises the discursive material at its disposal. There are no pretensions here about the formal coherence of the short story genre or anxieties about having to keep certain materials out the narrative in order to maintain the structural sanctity of the short story form. The unarticulated intertextual relations that the story invokes might even allow it to be placed in the discursive realm where fiction and history combine to produce experiences that are universally valid.

P. P. Raveendran

Mist & The Soul of Darkness

Translated from the Malayalam by
Gita Krishnankutty

Contents

Foreword

This book presents in English translation two significant stories written by M. T. Vasudevan Nair, one of the leading living writers of Malayalam fiction. 'Irutinde Atmavu' (*The Soul of Darkness*) is a long short-story, first published as a book in 1957. It was immediately acclaimed as a masterpiece by readers as well as critics. The story depicts the life of a mentally retarded young man in a matrilineal Nair joint family who suffers physical abuse and imprisonment under the callously unsympathetic eyes of his family. The story is etched on a small canvas to reach a dramatic finale.

'MT' (as he is popularly known throughout Kerala) started his writing career as a chronicler of life in the joint family of the matrilineal "tarawad" in Kerala and its crumbling feudal status. It is a milieu he describes with intimacy and feeling. However, he showed he could wing out of the confines of the tarawad into the wide world outside in 'Manhu' (*Mist*), the other novella included in this book.

'Manhu' is set in Nainital. It revolves round a teacher, Vimala, keeping vigil for a lover who deserted her nine years ago. The story is hauntingly told with the mountain mist as a metaphor for the emotions that weave in and out of the lives of the characters.

Both these stories have been made into Malayalam feature films. 'Irutinde Atmavu' received a special National Award, and 'Manhu' was directed by MT himself. MT is a writer who has mastered the medium of cinema. He has directed four feature films in Malayalam apart from a documentary and a teleserial. His first directorial venture *Nirmalyam,* based on a short story of his own, received the President's Gold Medal. He is also an accomplished screenplay writer whose services are much sought after by Malayalam film producers. His screenplays have received innumerable awards at state, national and international levels.

The two novellas presented in this book with totally different backgrounds exemplify the author's versatility and literary craft. His three seminal novels on life in the matriarchal family in Kerala are *Nalukettu*, *Asuravithu*, and *Kaalam*. His epic novel *Randamoozham* (*The Second Turn*) published in 1984 retells the story of the Mahabharatha from the point of view of Bhima, the hefty Pandava prince. The very boldness of the attempt would have daunted most writers but MT emerged to wide critical acclaim. His subtle craftsmanship has been highly appreciated by readers as the response amply demonstrates (two reprints within three months). No one in Kerala were therefore surprised when MT received the Jnanpith Award in 1995. MT is not a person to rest on his laurels, and he continues to touch upon new vistas of understanding the interplay of human emotions.

When this book was published by Orient Longman more than two decades ago in their Sangam Paperback series, it was part of a pioneering effort to bring out English translations of classic modern fiction in Indian languages. Response from readers was not very encouraging back then, as I personally know from my service with the company, but the scenario is vastly changed in the nineties and translations from Indian languages are now in great demand. Many leading publishers are bringing out more and more such works.

V. Abdulla

Mist

One

She had nothing to read. There were books piled untidily on the rack that was just within reach if she lay in bed and put her hand out. She had read all of them at some point of time or another. Idly, she turned the pages of the last one she had taken out. It was the story of a beautiful woman who had sold her graceful body to buy herself a kingdom. She read a few pages. And felt bored. She tossed the book on the mattress and lay back with her eyes closed.

The cold was creeping in through the thin slats of the closed window. It was the rhythm created by the mingling of innumerable faint sounds that made the silence audible. She realised the truth: that a state of soundlessness did not exist. Otherwise, one could say that there was silence everywhere now. Silence was a kind of music. Dust crumbled from the old ceiling, making a soft rustling sound. Dry twigs snapped somewhere in the distance. And crickets chirped.

Wasn't it on nights drenched by the Thulam rains that you heard the sound of crickets from the numbed areca-nut palms? But on the Kumaon hills, they chirped in broad daylight. She had taught zoology for nine years and still did not know the habits or habitats of crickets!

In the silence of the Kumaon hills, the crickets chirped in the daytime ...

Phylum Arthropoda, that was it... which class?

God! What silly thoughts these were!

The enveloping mist flowed into the room and drowned the music of silence.

She woke up hearing a knock on the door.

How long had she been dozing? The mist had not crept into the room. It was her eyes which were at fault—a faint screen of sleep had slid down over them.

She heard the knock again.

The polished wooden floor was very cold.

She opened the door expecting it to be Amar Singh. It was Rashmi Vajpayee.

The other children had left, some the evening before, some that morning. She realised Rashmi was the only one left.

'I'm leaving, Teacher-ji.'

'Good.'

Rashmi's dark green woolen coat was unbuttoned. Rashmi with the big black tilak on her forehead and dimples. Her eyes were dancing. She wore a *kameez* patterned with flowers as large as the palm of the hand. She was big for her age. It must have been because she was conscious of this that she had left her coat unbuttoned even though it was snowing.

'Is there a bus now?'

After all, she had been entrusted with the responsibility of forty-three girls.

'There is … until Haldwani.'

'And from there?'

Was it just an idle thought, or was some idea playing hide-and-seek in Rashmi's eyes? Her black eyelashes kept fluttering in an unnatural manner.

'From there—from there, there's another bus, Teacher-ji. A connecting bus. Pitaji, my father, has already sent someone to meet me.'

A flush rose to Rashmi's dark cheeks and disappeared like lightning.

'Um, all right.'

Vimala stepped out on the veranda and saw the young man standing under the arched entrance to the portico, his back turned. He was reading one of the papers attached to the mesh-covered notice-board on the wall.

'Who is that, Rashmi?' she asked in a very casual voice.

Rashmi's reply came after a split second, 'Um… my older brother.'

Vimala saw the young man's face when he turned around. Grey eyes. She wanted to ask, from where did your older brother get those grey eyes? But when she saw Rashmi Vajpayee's eyes as she stood there with the light flickering up and down her face, she saw a pitiful plea in them.

'You can go.'

'Namaste, Teacher-ji.'

'Namaste!'

The girl walked a few steps down the veranda, turned around and smiled with greater self-confidence.

'When are you going, Teacher-ji?'

'Tomorrow.'

She could answer that now without even thinking. It was a question they always asked her at the beginning of the vacation. And when they came back, they would ask:

'When did you get back, Teacher-ji?'

Sometimes, she did not answer. If the question was repeated, she would say,'Yesterday.'

Amar Singh, the *chowkidar*, would hear what she said. Nothing would move on that face, creased by the lines and scars of old age.

The vacations slipped by between tomorrow and yesterday. The springtimes of many years ...

Some of the children must have found out that Vimala-ji never went home for the vacation. But none of them had asked her, ever. Such a relief.

The Bhotia boy in his black trousers and shirt hoisted the leather suitcase on his back and went out. The young man with the pale yellow skin and grey eyes followed him. And behind him, Rashmi Vajpayee with her head bent.

Would Rashmi go home that night? There was a direct bus only at seven thirty in the morning. She suddenly thought of the tourist bungalow in Haldwani. The flush on Rashmi's cheeks, the flames glowing in her eyes, were a celebration of the moments to come.

Exercising the authority of a resident tutor, she could, if she wanted, send Girijashankar Vajpayee a telegram. 'Rashmi left on the three-thirty bus for Haldwani.'

A family swept by a hurricane and a pale trembling girl—she could easily imagine the scene. But Vimala decided to do nothing.

She stood watching Rashmi as she hurried down the footpath with the young man in brown boots. When the dark green of her coat disappeared behind the cluster of birch trees, Vimala said resentfully to herself, 'Don't assume that you fooled me, child!'

The girl had become a woman at sixteen.

Vimala went back to her room. It was in utter disorder. In the morning, she had resolved to fold the saris lying heaped on her suitcase and on the clothes-stand. Fine white motes of dust that kept flaking off the worn ceiling spattered the floor and table. The paper flowers on the stand in the corner had grown faded and crumpled. The battery company's calendar with a picture of the sun on it still marked the month of January. What was the date today? The eleventh of April.

The new year stood frozen, unable to move.

She opened the window. The cold air rushed in eagerly, embraced her, then hovered guiltily in the room.

There was a Nepali boy who worked near the cottage on the hill, just beyond the boundary of the boarding house. The cottage was one of those built by a contractor from Almora for the tourists who came for the season. It used to be called 'Chandrakanth' until the owner died. When his young son took charge, he changed the names of all the cottages. In the year that Vimala had arrived in the boarding house, 'Chandrakanth' had become 'Golden Nook.'

The sky was a pale grey. Thin streaks of mist dived playfully into the pine forests in the distance. The hills that lay beyond the woods and apple orchards had been cleared and lay bare. In December, she used to open the window every day in the afternoon and look out for a while. Wherever she looked, she could see a thick layer of fresh snow.

The days regularly wrought changes in a green and white world. In the end, all that remained would be patches of white here and there, like clouds that had fallen down, memories of a winter that had not quite melted.

Chaithra afternoons—when, after months, the hillsides were bathed in a gentle warmth. When the sun came out, silver streams could be glimpsed on the hillside, where the snow had melted... brooks gathered from yesterday's tears.

The sky cleared even as she watched. The gentle sunlight spread slowly over the hillside. The moist leaves of the huge birches lining the footpath in the valley gleamed softly.

In a distance where snow and cloud lay intertwined, the grey peaks of the mountains took shape.

This was the only one of the twenty-three rooms in the boarding house that enjoyed this blessing: when the sun came out in the afternoon, she could see the snow-capped mountain peaks take shape through the window. The well-known room Miss Pushpa Sarkar had occupied. She had stayed there for three years. Vimala had seen her just as she was leaving after having handed in her letter of resignation. Somebody had introduced them to each other on the veranda.

From the day she had joined work at school, she had been hearing about the dreadful Pushpa Sarkar who had dared to welcome a young man to her room in the boarding house in the dead of night.

Was it about this emaciated young woman with her protruding cheekbones that they had said all these things? That was the first thought that struck Vimala when she saw her.

Vimala had been afraid. How would this dangerous woman react to the girl who had come to insinuate herself into her place after she had been forced to resign and then been thrown out?

'Take my room, it's the best one.'

She had spoken without a trace of unease, and then turned back after walking a couple of paces.

'You can take my advice on this matter, you will not have any cause for regret.'

That had been nine years ago. God, nine years!

Where was Pushpa Sarkar now? The Home Science teacher, who came from Izzatnagar, used to revive memories of Pushpa Sarkar from time to time. Three marriages, court cases, occasions when she had run away. The last Vimala had heard of her, she had changed her religion.

Before Pushpa Sarkar, there had been the fifty-year-old Miss Bhatt, whom Vimala had never met.

And before that…

While the mountain ranges gleamed and faded as snow fell over them, the faces glimpsed between the slats of the window changed.

Outside, after months, a bright evening was taking shape.

She thought she would go out.

She closed and latched the window. From among the saris cluttering the stand, she chose a pale yellow one with glittering red leaves scattered over it. The gold on the border of the red blouse had dimmed. Never mind, she thought.

As she stood before the mirror, she tried, as usual, to console herself. She looked less tired. Her face was less pale. The mirror was fixed to a corner where there was not much light. So the grey strands which appeared in her hair from time to time were never properly visible in it.

Her heart always throbbed wildly when she looked at the mirror from a spot where the daylight shone bright.

Was it to comfort her that the old woman who helped her in the kitchen had said that the Madrasis who came from the plateau went grey very quickly on these snow-covered hills?

There was no oil on her face, it looked very dry. She dabbed some talcum powder on it, rubbed Vaseline on her lips. Her blackened lips now had the hue of clotted blood. She reached out for the blue coat on the hanger, put it on, went out and locked the door.

Amar Singh was seated on the steps outside the portico, smoking a *hookah*. He was barefoot and wore khaki trousers and a shabby, knee-length shirt the colour of filth. His sweater, full of holes, was not buttoned.

'Amar Singh, I'm going out.'

'Ji.' Exhaling smoke through his mouth and nostrils, he raised his tired grey eyes.

'I'm just going for a walk.'

'Ji.'

She went down the steps.

The footpath began to wind down the hill just outside the gate of the Golden Nook. If you crossed the stone-paved track meant for horse riders, the footpath rose higher. It was fun to look out from the spot where the path fanned into a semicircle, just above the grounds where the *pahadis*, the mountain folk, performed the Ramlila once a year.

A lake that had fallen down between the hills. On both sides, the red roofs of the town. The road that circled the lake in two strands. Through the trees you could see the huge wooden hoardings across the lake.

The faint April mist hanging over the lake and the town drifted like a daydream seen sometime in the distant past.

Two

You feel as if you're standing on the topmost layer of the world. Around you take shape the waves of the mosquito net that has been pulled down to hide your modesty from the daylight filtering in through the closed slats of the bedroom window. The snow covered peaks over which the red-tinted evening light plays mark the limit of your vision—the boundaries of a country that has never been remembered with love. The cool air has the fragrance of green leaves and wet earth.

A moment at the end of winter.

A moment… a moment of life.

'This moment took its place long ago on the footpath of time'—Sudhir Kumar Mishra, 19 May 1955.

Running, gasping for breath, your feet unsteady, you arrive here at last. At the moment that had been marked for you ages ago.

Three

The path was deserted. A young man wearing a blue shirt stood painting, in one of the paved shelters that stretched down from the shores of the lake into the water.

Boards that said—Wet paint. Beware—hung from the shining lamp-posts.

The city was getting ready for the month of May. It was trying to erase the grey lines of old age before the unknown tourists arrived, touching up a face whose colour had faded with usage over the passage of time.

Most of the boats lay asleep, tied to stakes on either side. Ducks waddled around, pecking, on the shores where white sand could be glimpsed. One of the multicoloured lifebuoys that had drifted down with the waves swayed to and fro, entangled in the branches of the trees that slanted down into the water.

Vimala sat on a rough cement bench looking at the empty lake.

The world around her seemed to be waking up from sleep and getting ready for someone, its face completely unenthusiastic. Vimala could read the heart of the city. They could understand each other.

Vimala had always looked contemptuously at the little city when it roared and laughed in May, flinging colours and scents everywhere.

For whom did the city do this?

Considering they had been companions who had known each other for nine years, she had never actually expressed this question.

She saw a boat setting out from Tallithal. It was full of children.

The huge bells of the temple of Naina Devi pealed.

When she had lived in Kerala as a child, she used to go to the temple every Tuesday and Friday. She had to cross the fields, walk over a sand-covered path and climb into the lane to get to the temple. *Karaveeraka* bushes covered with a profusion of yellow flowers lined both sides of the lane. She could still see the pebble-covered lane before her and remember the lengths of yarn trailing over the yards of the weavers' huts on the roadside. Coming back from the temple courtyard littered with pieces of broken tiles, she would stand next to the Adiyal's fence and gather coralnuts.

It was the period when Father was looking for a job in some faraway place. Often, when he came home, no one made him welcome. Having quarreled with his family and having left his maternal home, he no longer had a place anywhere.

She would never go back there now.

Was the temple with the dilapidated kitchen area still there?

She would never go back to the thatched house that stood high above the areca nut grove.

Father had always thought of the village where he had been born with intense dislike.

'Who do I have there?'

Who was there in his village who knew the apple orchard in Almora, the house Father owned there and the position he had achieved as a researcher on potatoes?

Maybe it was true.

Amma could not bear to think of her village. How would she endure the climate?

But was that the fault of the climate?

While Father lay groaning under the blanket, Amma would sit before the mirror, making up her face. It was then that Amma would hold forth, to no one in particular, about the frightfulness of the climate in her village.

Maybe Amma was afraid. What if Father changed his mind at the last moment?

The climate!

It must have been because the weather inside the house was growing steadily hotter that she set out everyday saying she was going to Mrs Chakravarthy's house. Obviously she had to go past Alfred Gomez's gate to get to Mrs Chakravarthy's house!

Seated in the *mandapam* like this one near the Boat Club, built to extend into the water of the lake opposite the Alka Hotel, she had once tried to recall the village.

...I can't remember.

...Nothing at all?

...It was sixteen years ago, Sudhir. Sixteen.

A clear night in May. The trees in the distance hung down like screens of blue smoke.

...As for me, I can recall everything that happened from the time I was five. Try and remember.

It was like picking out individual strands, trying to remember. Sounds and colours came back. The ferryboat that smelled of cashew oil. The sheaves that slanted down into fields where grasshoppers leaped. The rolling sound of the water-carrier that irrigated the fields. The thudding of the drums at night from the huts of the Harijan folk.

'Come on, tell me.'

Her mind murmured, don't, don't insist, Sudhir. This is all I have to remember, these few moments. Let me live in this second, when words reeking of cigarette smoke rub against my cheek.

'Sixteen years, my God! We must go there one time. Are you prepared for an adventure?'

Two tourists from North India turning up in Kerala, in her village—Mr and Mrs Sudhir Kumar Mishra.

'I want to see your place. I've been to most parts of India. I've seen Europe, South East Asia and Ceylon. I want to see Kerala. Where I live, green is not a cool colour. Women bring drinking water from three miles away. It's a disgrace that I, who have written a thesis on international relations, have not seen all of India.'

'What do you say, Vimala?'

What can I say?

These moments are all I want.

'All right, let's go.'

Don't say let's go, we must go.

'Certainly.'

To wander like strangers over the lanes and fields she had run around in as a child!

Mr Sudhir Kumar Mishra.

Mrs Vimala Mishra.

The silver tips of the mountain peaks became invisible. A blanket of mist tinted pale blue descended from the hills into the valley like another cloud. The colourful lifebuoy entangled in the creepers freed itself and drifted away.

She got up and began to walk over the path circling the temple, near the Mallithal ghat.

The sand-filled outer compound beyond the circular *mandapam* was deserted. A few people were gathered in front of the cinema theatre at the far end. When she came up to the jetty, the oarsmen in the slumbering boats suddenly grew lively.

'Coming, Memsaheb?'

'Just four annas, Memsaheb!'

They were all inviting her. The familiar *Mayflower* lay apart from all of them.

The *Mayflower*! What a beautiful name!

The *Mayflower* too showed traces of the passing years.

This was not Pratap, the old boatman. A young fellow with yellow teeth was seated on one of the red cushions, smoking a *beedi*. He stared, his chinky eyes full of laughter, making no attempt to coax her into his boat. As she walked down to the sandy bank, the chinky eyes opened wide, its grey depths full of expectation.

When the boatmen surrounded her, she was afraid that one of them would grip her hand and try to drag her in.

She took two paces forward towards the *Mayflower*. The boy threw his *beedi* into the water and vaulted out. He brought the boat to a stop. She sank down quietly on a cushion that could seat two people.

The boy began to row. As the boat left the shore behind, she gazed curiously at the *Mayflower*'s new boatman. Coppery hair, grey eyes, a rounded face pitted with innumerable brown spots.

'Where's Pratap?'

'He died, Memsaheb.'

'When?'

'Four years ago. The owner leased the boat to me last month. Pratap's younger brother was thrown out when he cheated Bhatt-ji of his money.'

'Hmm...'

After a while, she asked, 'What is your name?'

'Buddhu, that's what people call me.'

He smiled a foolish smile.

A faint smile touched Vimala's lips. It must have been the foolish smile that exposed his yellow teeth that had earned him his name.

'Some people call me 'Gora Sahib' as well, for fun.'

'Gora Sahib?'

'Yes, Memsaheb. My father was a white man.'

'Really?'

'Yes, Memsaheb. I've never seen him. My mother told me.'

'What does your mother do?'

'She died.' He pointed to a spot in the distance. 'The year that building was built. It must be six or seven years ago.'

As the oars moved rhythmically, its splashes grew louder, reminding her of the depth of the water.

'Aren't you a teacher in the girls' school, Memsaheb?'

Surprised that he had recognised her, she nodded in assent.

'I've seen you.'

'Hmm...'

He continued to ply the oars slowly, in silence.

'Where is your father?'

'I don't know. But I'll find him.'

'His name?'

'I don't know, Memsaheb. Amma was with him only for a week. But there are ways to find him.'

A picture took shape in her mind. Seventeen or eighteen years ago.

How old would this boy be? Certainly not more than eighteen.

Seventeen or eighteen years ago, in May, one of the pimps in the area brings a young girl to the house of a white man who had arrived by the lake.

They cannot speak to each other. The hunter finds its prey…

Here was one of the memories of the white man's pleasant stay—this boy seated in the boat, with his grey eyes, his coppery hair and a pock-marked face.

A sliver of light glimmered on the eastern side of the lake. The bevy of ducks pecking one another below the dilapidated temple on the western slope looked like foam floating on the blue expanse.

'The season will start late this year, won't it, Memsaheb?'

'Umm…'

'There were fewer white people last year. Wonder what it will be like this year!' He said almost to himself.

'I have a feeling I'll see him this time, my…'

She was amused to note that he found it difficult to complete the sentence. She finished it for him: 'Pitaji!'

A flush ran over his face. 'Hnh! Dinnu at the bus-stand—his aunt read my palm and said so.'

There was a gleam of expectation in Buddhu's eyes as he rowed, his head bent to one side, gazing at the middle of the lake.

'What will you ask him when you see him?'

'What is there to ask? I won't ask him anything. I just want to see him, that's all.'

Vimala could not bring herself to smile. She felt as if a lump of snow was melting inside the valley of her heart.

… I don't want anything. Just to see him…

Would this boy who laughed and talked so foolishly understand if she said to him, I too just want to see him, Buddhu. Nothing more.

The lights came on in the houses in the marketplace and on the hillside. The huge light on the dome of the *mandapam* opened its eye, diffusing a milk-white radiance. The pine forests were beginning to turn into shadows.

They were near the jetty now.

'Shall I park the boat now, Memsaheb, or go around one more time?'

'No.'

The boy steered the boat towards the platform made of wooden planks that jutted from the steps into the water.

She stepped out of the boat.

She groped inside her bag for an eight-anna coin and extended it to him. When she saw him delve into the inner pocket of his shirt, she thought he was looking for change.

'Keep it. The rest is for you to have tea.'

He smiled, showing all his yellow teeth. What he took out of his pocket was a leather purse.

He extracted a piece of paper from it carefully and said: 'Look, Memsaheb!'

It was not a piece of paper, it was a picture. A faded brown photograph marked by the passage of time with spots just like the ones on his face. By the light of a lamp burning by the river, she saw the image of a young white man seated on a horse, wearing breeches and a pullover. She stared at him for a minute.

When she handed the picture back, he said in a low voice: 'This is the secret of how I'll find him, Memsaheb! I've not told anyone about this.'

The bus stand was deserted. Bhotia porters in black shirts, with ropes bundled on their backs sat hunched up here and there, keeping watch, looking like messengers of death.

Even without turning around, she could see the sharp eyes of the soldiers standing near the veranda of the post office. She began to walk slightly faster.

Between the pine leaves, in the yard of the boarding house, a lamp on its high post could be seen flickering like a weeping star at the point where the road branched off upwards from the path on the west.

Four

She had a sense of relief once she crept in and nestled under the quilt on her string cot. One more day was coming to an end.

She felt more tired than usual. And when she closed her eyes, she thought she would fall asleep sooner than usual. But this was not just sleep, she felt she was falling into a bottomless abyss. Not only her body, but her bed, the room, the entire building, seemed to be gently sliding down from the summit of a peak like a wisp of cotton wool.

Suddenly startled awake, she lay with her eyes open. If she closed them, she kept sinking deeper and deeper into the abyss...

The mind was like an agile, restless monkey, springing from branch to branch. Otherwise, what reason did she have to think of Rashmi at that moment?

Hurtling through the dark hours, her eyes peered into one of the three rooms in the Haldwani travellers' bungalow. There were so many other things she could have thought about.

From somewhere along the shores of the lake, the sounds of drumbeats, pipes and ululations came to her ears through the closed window.

The *pahadi* mountain folk must be having a wedding procession. Petromax lamps, the bridegroom on a horse, wearing a turban and a silk tunic, a sword tucked into his waist and his companions—a scene she had witnessed many times took shape in her mind.

Somewhere on the hillside, the bride would be waiting in a small house among the pine trees, straining her ears to find out whether the band was approaching, while the minutes fell around her like hailstones.

The whole world would be waiting.

Buddhu the boatman would be asleep in the bus stand or at the gate of mansion, clutching a worn leather purse tightly to his chest. His 'Gora Sahib' was sure to come someday.

He was sure to come…

I, you, we have all been waiting aeons…

Snow kept falling and melting on the rocks of time. Huge slabs of snow melted and froze into a thick crust.

We are all waiting…

She felt a surge of affection for Buddhu with his yellow teeth and freckled face. Those who had heard his story would have laughed at him mockingly.

She could understand him. Because, every April, she too hoped that a dream she had lost nine years earlier would come alive again.

When the valleys began to prepare for the tourists coming from everywhere, a murmur would stir in a corner of her heart that she kept firmly hidden.

She tried to convince herself—I am not waiting for anyone.

Who was deceiving whom?

When the apple trees in the orchard blossomed, when the snow on the slopes melted and the peaks in the distance took clear shape in the bright sunlight, she would think—look, another spring on the Kumaon Hills!

Now, she no longer paid attention to the changes nature wrought around her.

One night, she heard a clamour outside. She listened carefully, they were sounds of celebration.

Holi ganga saagar me
Paar ganga saagar me
Holi hai…

So another Holi was here.

'Bibiji, it's Holi the day after tomorrow,' Amar Singh reminded her in good time about the *baksheesh* she owed him.

The nights waited now to hear the footfalls of the tourists.

Time had stagnated like the water of the lake.

Those who had come after years must be saying, this place looks the same as when we saw it long ago.

What changes had there been in nine years? You who run away from life, you will not be able to make them out. For there are grey streaks hidden among your dark strands of hair. And there are dents and deep cracks on the green paint of the lamp-posts.

Even the name of the rock where we used to sit, feeling as triumphant as if we had conquered the topmost peak in the world, has changed.

When I fall gradually into the abyss of darkness, God, there are white clouds floating around me…

The sound of horses' hooves moving over the stone-paved path.

The man who kept horses was dark-skinned. The heavy pockets of his filthy woollen coat hang down. He had a round cap on his head, a muffler wound around his neck. A white horse and a brown one.

'I want this white horse.'

'Your choice.'

'Syce, what's his name?'

'Hers, not his. You teach zoology and you don't know that!'

She hung her head in shame.

The syce said, 'Moti.'

He spoke in a low voice, 'The horses in this region have only one name, Moti.'

They tethered the horses at the top of the hill, walked on and came to a small temple. Many tourists in the temple courtyard had cameras slung around their necks. The bells hanging on the iron bars clanged. Most people were praying.

'Let's go in there and see.'

It was a clear morning. The odour of smoke hung in the air.

'Have you ever come this way?'

'No.'

'Do you know the name of the path?'

She looked down at her feet, unable to suppress a smile. She knew the name, but did not say it.

'A pretty name! Lovers' Track!'

The rock looked like a broken arrow piercing the breast of the sky.

'I wonder why people haven't given the rock a name...'

Where the lovers' path ended...

'The Rock of what should it be called?'

Names were carved here and there on the rock: 1953. Meena-Kishore.

P. (The drawing of a heart pierced by an arrow) S.

'A young couple I met in the hotel yesterday told me about this place.'

It was frightening to stand on the pointed tip of the rock and look out. The apple orchards looked like little squares. The world had carved out these isolated corners into the slope of the rock for couples who came to listen to the music of their hearts...

'Old names fade out and new ones appear.'

A faint breeze and mellow sunshine. He spoke of the cities he had visited. And of various other things. Jim Corbett ... a Vice Chancellor ... the autobahn ... a kissing game.

She had met this man who talked incessantly five days earlier. Was it only five days ago that he had smilingly asked her the time by the lakeside? Was it that morning that she had had to sit beside him in the bus? It seemed more than five years ago...!

On top of the Capitol, under the closed window, she lay underneath the quilt while the eyes of the city gleamed brightly, her head on his thick wrist, wanting to cry out—I am not alone, not alone!

Do you know, tourists don't go up the rock anymore? One day in June, a young girl climbed right up the pointed peak and jumped off. The slopes where couples used to tumble and roll, their arms wound tight around each other, grew deserted. Someone hammered the words—'This way to easy death'—onto a stone at the spot where the path made a turn. And drew a skull and crossbones under it.

And so the rock earned a new name: 'The Devils' Track.'

From the top of the rock which brushed the sky into the bottomless abyss...

Five

Amar Singh brought two letters.

Whenever the letters came, her heart would throb wildly, no matter how hard she tried to control herself. It was unbelievable—even after nine years, when she opened the envelope and unfolded the paper...

The purple letters would dance: 'My dear Vimala!'

Every time Amar Singh came back from the post office, a magical world of hope would rise up before her in seconds. And then dissolve like a bubble.

One was a postcard from Babu. He wrote in Hindi, generally. Babu and Anita could not read or write Malayalam.

Skimming over the last two or three sentences, she understood the gist of it: 'So as soon as you get this, you must send me twenty-five rupees, Didi.'

She thought of the house in the middle of the potato fields, fifty-three miles away. Her family lived just three hours away: her father, her mother, Babu, Anita.

When they were at home, Vimala and Anita used to sleep in the small bedroom next to the dining room. The rope cot in the storeroom nearby was Babu's, but it usually lay empty at night. As soon as darkness embraced the house, Babu would open the front door and slip out. He would go to the shop near the dak bungalow and play cards in a room upstairs that was enveloped in the fumes of ganja. Amma knew this. When she went to the dining room to drink water and turned on the light, its glow would reach the storeroom. But she would pretend not to see the vacant bed and go back.

'Is Babu asleep?'

'Mm…'

'So early?'

'Mm...'

Amma could not say anything else. Because, every time she looked into her son's piercing eyes, she barely managed not to show her fear.

There was always a threat in Babu's eyes.

Once…

It was when college was closed. Father was in the bathroom.

'I want fifty rupees.'

'I don't have any money.'

'You have to find it. I need it urgently.'

'Ask Father. Is it I who bring money in?'

'If you don't give me the money…' He paused for a second.

Amma's silence was suffocating.

'Just give me a letter. I'll get it from Mr Gomez.'

'Babu!'

All she could hear were her own heartbeats as mother and son sized each other up. She sank, exhausted, onto the settee in the drawing room.

Amma went in. She heard her opening and closing cases. In a little while, she saw her younger brother go out, looking triumphant.

Father would be lying with his eyes closed on the large double bed at the side of the big bedroom. He would close his eyes even if he was not sleeping. His eyelids would twitch when he heard footfalls. He found it difficult to open his eyes.

It always hurt her to hear him speak. Slurred, unclear words.

The week before, Amma had written—he cannot speak at all now. His only movement is a fluttering of the eyelids.

He had been bedridden for two years. Whenever she stood near his bed, she would think that death would be a blessing to him. The father she had admired had died years ago. She would see in her mind's eye the image of her father, slim and tall, in a cream coloured suit, a felt hat on his head, twirling a cane.'Father had not been merely the head of the family, he had been an emperor. He sat in a huge carved chair like a throne in the dining room. No one was allowed to touch it. Whenever she passed that way, she always looked fearfully at the chair.

Father did not like any noise when he was at home. The odour of tobacco would waft through the house from his pipe. Everyone would speak in low voices.

When she rested in the afternoon after lunch, Amma was afraid to close her eyes. What was the time? Unless she started at three thirty, coffee and snacks would not be ready by the time Father came back from his walk at four thirty. He would come straight to the dining room and sit down, not even bothering to change. If the table was not covered fully with food, a whirlwind would be unleashed.

She used to be terrified of sitting down to eat with Father.

'Where is Vimala? Where is Babu?'

'...It's too early for them. Let them eat later.'

'Vimala, Babu! Come and join me!'

If her glass overflowed, if she belched or sneezed, Father's naturally flushed face would grow redder. He would not scold. But his look always scared her.

Anita had said once: 'We must go to Kerala, Father.'

'Why, is your grandfather there?'

Anita's eyes filled with tears.

She had never heard Father speak of Kerala with affection.

She had always been scared of Father.

She used to be frightened even to write to him. He always insisted that she write in English. Every letter she sent came back with the mistakes underlined.

There would be a warning as well: You must remember that I am spending my hard-earned money to educate you.

But that was all long ago. There was no need for anyone to be scared of Father now. He could not even get up from bed. Only his eyes held vestiges of the old flames.

She had gone home about four months ago. She had felt fed up after staying just one night and had left by the morning bus.

She and Father had been alone in the house in the evening. As she stood by his bed, she saw him struggle to say something.

'Don't speak, Father. It will tire you.'

For the first time, she saw helplessness in his eyes. A good-for-nothing village lad had married a girl from a wealthy household—the story of an adventurous act she had heard many times in her childhood. He became the accountant of an estate, then a postmaster. After which he sold her mother's wedding chain and disappeared. The next they heard of him was that he was studying somewhere in Madras. She could understand why he had quarreled with his eldest sister after he got married, made over his share of the property to her and left his maternal home.

The man who had experienced so much in life lay in bed now, as helpless as a snake that the cowherds had mercilessly twirled and flung away.

She could not bear to stay long in that room. She went out through the outer veranda to the edge of the yard.

Amma had left as usual saying she was going to Mrs Bhatnagar's house. In a glittering sari, her lips stained a filthy red with lipstick, her hair, smeared with Loma hair oil, a patchy black and brown. It always disgusted Vimala to see her go out, all dolled-up.

Her younger sister was at the gate. She too made herself up elaborately every evening. Maybe she needed to. Pradeep Chandra Sharma, the doctor's son, would be lurking somewhere on the roadside in his leather jacket.

Until the day when people had found Father in the bathroom in the Club and brought him back, supporting his weight in their hands, no one used to even step into the courtyard.

Now her younger brother Babu spent his time smoking *bhang* with the *pahadis* and gambling. And her younger sister exchanged love letters through the servant Bir Bahadur. Amma had no time for anything. She struggled with her attempts to keep the ageing process at bay, filling her wrinkles with creams and powders, dyeing her hair.

Was Father aware of all this? He must be. Those sharp, piercing eyes had taken on the role of his slurred tongue.

One evening, at dusk, Dr Menon and Mrs Menon had come from Muktheshwaram in their jeep to enquire about Father's illness. There had been no one at home except Vimala.

Mrs Menon asked, 'Vimala, where's Mami?'

'She's gone out somewhere.'

She found it difficult to meet Mrs Menon's eyes. She must have heard about the pleasure trips Amma went on with Gomez.

Lying on her bed at night in the midst of the family, she could not sleep. What a family!

I hate it, I hate it all.

In March, Babu came to the boarding house once. Holi was round the corner. Amma had sent him to remind her.

Anita had written: Didi, you must come.

She sent her brother back saying she would come. She wrote to her sister: I'm terribly busy, so I won't be able to come just now.

She knew that one morning Babu or the servant, Bir Bahadur, would come and knock on the door.

'What is it?' she would ask.

'Father died. Or, Sahib has left all of us, Bibiji.'

One day…

May that good fortune soon come to her father, who lay listening to the foundations of his empire being shattered, she thought.

Six

The second letter was from Shanta, the science teacher. She was going to resign from her job. Her marriage had been fixed. She had met her fiancé in the railway station.

She must keep the date in mind. And send a telegram. Codes eight, fourteen and seventeen. The telegraph department kept ready several lifeless formulae for such occasions.

The inmates of the boarding house were escaping one by one...

A cold wind blew all day. She decided not to go out. She sorted out the things lying scattered around the room. While putting a sari away in her suitcase, she saw the pink sweater with musical notes embroidered on it in black lying at the bottom. She had never worn it. They had bought it the day before he left, from the shop in Mallital belonging to the old man with the dyed beard. She had chosen it herself.

'Will you choose a really nice sweater?'

'For whom?'

'For a girl.'

He had given her a wicked look, probably to find out if there was a flash of jealousy in her eyes. The old man himself had got up to display everything before them.

It was the first time she had seen a sweater with musical notes embroidered on it. It was a pleasant colour too.

'That's a pretty one.'

'You like it?'

'I don't know whether the girl who's going to get it will like it. But I do.'

'That's fine. After all, you approve of it, Vimala.'

It was she who had carried the plastic bag in which it was wrapped.

They walked straight to the cinema hall and went up to eat in the restaurant upstairs that was part of it. A student of hers who was in the ninth standard was seated with her family at the table next to theirs. The child came up to them, saying, 'Namaste.'

She would spread the news among her companions now. Vimala-ji has a boyfriend with blue eyes and hair that falls over his forehead! It was the students who had spread rumours about Pushpa Sarkar's lover right through the town.

Although she had not needed to, she introduced the girl to him. 'My student. This is my cousin, he's here for the season.'

She could recall all of it very clearly. Did they still have the same red cushions? She had never gone back to that restaurant that only rich people patronised. Did they still serve cassata ice cream with white wafer-wings inserted in the centre to their customers?

The human bodies inside the cinema hall and their breath made the air mildly hot. They sat next to each other, right at the back. It was a story about slaves who dived in the deep seas for pearls. Pretty girls wearing flower garlands around their necks danced in a group. When the hero kissed the moist lips of the girl with the coppery skin, they clasped each other's fingers tight.

'Lucky guy!' he murmured in her ear. His breath, which had the odour of cigarettes, brushed her cheek.

While saying goodbye to him at the turning to the boarding house, she handed over the plastic cover with the sweater in it.

'That's for you,' he said.

She was confused. Her immediate reaction was to say she did not want it.

'I… for me…' She could not say anything.

'I bought it for you. Good night.'

Walking back alone, she said to the cold wind whistling through the bushes, 'Thank you. Thank you for everything.'

She saw the yellow sunlight spreading over the courtyard of the boarding house, opened the windows and looked out. Two porters were carrying luggage into the Golden Nook. So this year's visitors had arrived.

Last year there had been an engineer from Delhi and his family. Nine children between the ages of three and sixteen. The neighbourhood had been very noisy until they left.

The year before, it had been a Brahmin couple on their honeymoon.

Suddenly, she felt that the weather outside was beautiful. Her decision not to go out weakened.

She met Amar Singh as she went out. He was returning from the market. He moved aside respectfully and held out a letter. Yet another letter in the evening post!

She looked at it, her heart thudding.

Ah, it was from Rashmi Vajpayee. As Amar Singh walked past her, she realised why he had been unusually respectful. The stench of arrack.

Walking on, she read the letter:

> Respected Teacher-ji, I reached home last night. I had no problem at all on the way. Pitaji conveys his namaskars. Rashmi.

The address was the Ramnagar one. She could not help smiling when she saw the postmark. Haldwani!

She could imagine the triumphant look on Rashmi's face as she gave the servant in the travellers' bungalow the letter that morning, before she left for the bus stand.

I have forgiven you. After all, you earned yourself a night that you will always remember.

Turning away from the path she generally took when she climbed up and down the hill, she walked over the slope and came to a dilapidated shack. Monkeys played among the bushes and trees. She sat down on an uneven heap of broken stones that resembled the skull of a demon with its protuberances and depressions. From where she was seated, she could have a glimpse of only one side of the lake.

She saw the spiral staircase of the hotel beyond the boat club. There was a figure standing on the terrace. An isolated human form beneath the vast sky.

The hotel had changed hands three times, its name as well. But the circular pillars and the wrought iron basket chairs would be the same.

Years later, when Rashmi walked past the travellers' bungalow in Haldwani as a wife and mother, she would probably peer in through one of the windows with secret delight.

Her first sin, the pain of having the veil of her womanhood pierced for the first time, the first time she knew bliss, ecstasy…

From where she stood, could she see the window on the right, near the spiral staircase that led to the terrace?

Seven

A floor carpeted in red. Cigarette smoke and Paul Anka's voice, smooth as silk, wafting on the air.

When she opened the door, a look of disbelief and astonishment appeared on the face of the young man in the tight-fitting red sports shirt.

'Oh, my God!'

'What is it?'

'I thought you wouldn't come.'

He moved a circular wrought iron chair shaped like a basket towards her and said, 'Sit down.'

Her eyes wandered over the room. Records were scattered over the carpet. There was a heap of books on the table and a camera in a leather case on its stand.

The singer was concluding his song:

Put your head on my shoulder
Whisper in my ear, baby
Words I want to hear, baby...

He had talked for hours in the pleasure boat on the lake, under the shade of the pine trees, on the Lovers' Track. But the man who had woven those endless garlands of words was very silent now.

She had nothing to say. Something heavy seemed lodged in her throat. When the needle of the record player crackled to a stop, the silence in the room almost exploded.

The silence was unbearable. He made an effort to say something. Meaningless words. And yet they seemed to imply many meanings. His voice was harsh. She tried to smile, a smile that was not her own.

He held out his hand and gripped her fingers to lift her up. The blood rushed to her face. Currents of pain springing from her trembling feet coursed through innumerable veins in her body.

Words and sounds seemed very distant. 'Come.'

All that remained was a memory as vague as the unidentifiable spot where a stone sinks into the centre of widening ripples—of expert fingers running over her body as she lay with her eyes shut in the faint light which crept furtively into the room through the closed window.

She had known this would happen.

'Don't, I can't bear it.' Her voice was feeble.

'It's nothing…' When she tried to open her eyes, she thought that those shining blue eyes dimmed for a moment as if a film of oil had descended over them.

Pain. She twisted in pain, biting her lips, her arms entwined around his neck.

I must not weep. At this moment when I surrender everything I have, I must not weep…

My mind is a valley into which mist floats down. My very own valley. At this moment when you dissolve completely into me, I must not weep.

Aeons later, when she opened her eyes, he asked her, his moist lips pressed against her cheek, did it hurt?

She could not say anything. She could laugh, she could cry. Her whole body burned. She was afraid to get up. She lay with her eyes closed and watched stars flowering in the clear May sky. Far away, a cloud drifted, like a white handkerchief that someone had set afloat on the wind.

Hoisting herself sideways up to the edge of the bed and balancing herself with one hand on the ground, she reached out to restart the record player and was overcome by acute embarrassment. She pulled at the quilt, to cover herself, and saw three bright spots of blood on the sheet.

A woman's voice began to sing about '*beautiful days and lonely nights.*'

He lay on his side and held out his hand, beads of perspiration running down his chest.

'Vimala!'

She forced her throbbing eyelids to stay closed. In her mind was a vast volume of things she wanted to say to him. But her throat felt parched.

I am no longer myself.

Her voice froze on her trembling lips. Her body had no weight at all. It drifted here and there like a sliver of cloud floating in the sky, like a white handkerchief someone had set afloat in the hurricane that swept the valley…

Eight

The street lamps she could see at the corner of the lake dimmed. The daylight would last for a long time yet.

When the humming voice behind her suddenly stopped, she turned.

'Memsaheb!'

It took her a moment to recognise the boy grinning broadly, displaying all his teeth—Buddhu.

'Why didn't you come to the lake today, Memsaheb?'

'Oh, just like that.'

'Do you come and sit here every day?'

'Sometimes.'

'Come for a boat ride every day, Memsaheb. You need give me only three annas.'

'All right.'

She stood up.

'The season has begun, Memsaheb. There's a special bus come from Delhi.'

That's the way it was. People kept coming every day. And then one day, you would hear them say, the season has begun! And as you watched, the valley would come alive…

'They're all our own people.' Was he disappointed because there were no foreigners?

'Why are you here, Buddhu?'

'One of my oars is broken, Memsaheb. Someone told me there's an old oar in Annu's house, over there.' He pointed to a spot below China Peak.

She began to walk away and he asked, 'You're going, Memsaheb?'

'Yes.'

'Are you going away because I came and spoke to you, Memsaheb?'

'No. It's getting late.'

Buddhu followed, a little distance behind her.

'Can I ask you something, Memsaheb?'

'What?'

'They say the white people have left our country. Is it true?'

She suppressed a smile when she noted the anxiety on his face.

'They're not telling the truth.'

'Yes, that's what I said. Would anyone go away, leaving such a beautiful country?'

Satisfied, he walked away and she heard him humming behind her again.

Amar Singh was lying on the bare floor below the concrete steps, snoring. He must have gone again to one of the huts on the hill and drunk his fill of arrack. He had been very happy for a week. What amazed her was that the tips the children who were going home had given him had lasted so long.

He enjoyed this kind of freedom only during the vacations. It was a rule Vimala had imposed from the time she became a resident tutor. If he felt the urge to drink while the children were at school, he had to bring the school gardener to stand in for him and take the evening off.

Amar Singh became more respectful when he had a drink. If he had too much, he would begin to weep and tell stories of his past—how his wife had run away, how his son had thrown him out of the house, how his son-in-law had hacked his daughter to death and gone to jail. On days when he could afford to buy all he could drink, he would pass out on the steps or on the ground.

She had heard the story of how, when a resident tutor came looking for him one morning in the portico, Amar Singh was not there. Then she saw his coat and trousers hanging on the wire fence. She called out to him again and then realised that it was Amar Singh himself who lay folded over the wire fence, not just his clothes!

A plate of wheat *chapatis* and vegetables had been left covered for her on her table in the room. And milk in a thermos flask.

She felt hot, having climbed up the hill. She opened the window and saw the lights coming on in the Golden Nook. Pulling off her sweater, she stood at the window. A man was seated on the veranda, near the pots filled with withered plants, both hands pressed to his forehead, his feet resting on a stool. She wished she knew who this year's guest at the Golden Nook was. He was a Sardarji. He looked like an old man.

He had placed his turban on his lap. The hair he had combed into a knot over his head cast a peak-shaped shadow on the yard. He was so still that it seemed as if someone had propped up a dead body on the armchair.

Minutes later, the human statue moved. When he raised his head and leaned back, Vimala moved away from the window and closed it. She heard the sound of a one-stringed *iktara*. Was it the same man playing? If it was, how expertly the thin fingers were moving on the single string!

Her mattress seemed as limp and cold as the body of a reptile.

The voice had to be the Sardarji's. A husky voice. She listened attentively.

Uddhi uddhi vethili aar kaaga
Lambhi layi ve udaari
Jaa aakheem mere naahi noo
Gori manon kyon bisaari

It was an old Punjabi folk song.

It made her think of the tired face of a young Punjabi girl walking idly among thick piles of harvested sheaves of maize in the hot afternoon sunshine as comfortably as if it were moonlight, twirling the rope she used to bind the sheaves.

She had always looked at brawny Punjabis with their matted hair, long beards and the reek of onions with disgust and an unreasonable fear. But she liked their songs. While studying in the college in Agra, she had had a Punjabi friend named Amrita who had sung many love songs to her. They seemed to her like daydreams blossoming in the eyes of rough young village lads.

The husky voice and the mournful sobbing of the *iktara* floated out from beyond the wall:

Dilka tukda main kaagazbagaavam
Ungaliya katta kaani
Akhaam daa kajjala mai shaahi banaavam
Hasuaam daa paani aa paani

Vimala felt her eyes filling with tears.

O crow, fly far, far away. Ask my beloved why he has forgotten me...

She reproached herself—after all, a woman of thirty-one should not feel so vulnerable listening to a folk song.

She heard the voice of the village girl lost in oblivion:

Dilka tukda main kaagazbagaavam...

Using a bit of my heart as paper, cutting off a finger to fashion a pen, dissolving mascara in my tears to make ink, let me write you a message!

The Sardarji's fingers seemed to strike into her heart. She thought she would read something in order to divert her attention. Flipping through the books on her shelf, she came upon a collection of poetry. Its cover had come off being in constant use. There was a signature scrawled in purple ink across the first page: Sudhir Kumar Mishra, January 1955.

On most of the pages, there were lines underlined in purple ink. Here were his favourite four lines, she had heard him repeat them over and over again innumerable number of times:

I am tired with my own life and the lives of those after me
I am dying in my own death and the deaths of those after me

The haunting notes of the one-stringed *iktara* still wafted through the cold night air.

The tourists who arrived for the season in the Golden Nook affected the life she lived in her room in many ways. The year before, there had been the clamour of children day and night. And the year before that, it had been the eloquent silence of a newly-married couple. The bride had had *sindoor* in the parting of her hair and a large *tilak* that almost filled her forehead. They had been there a month, staying inside the cottage day and night, rarely going out even for a walk. She would see their shadows beyond the curtains, coming close together, then drawing apart. Their voices were never heard outside.

To spend thirty days looking only at each other's faces, among all those noisy tourists who ran around to have a look at the lake and the snow-covered peaks of Naida Devi! Maybe it was possible because they had created a beautiful world for themselves within the closed doors of their room.

Once an old man and a young girl of seventeen or eighteen had come to stay there. Vimala had thought they were father and daughter. It was Amar Singh who had found out that the girl was the old man's bride.

While time stagnated in this room that Pushpa Sarkar had made notorious, innumerable faces appeared and disappeared in the Golden Nook.

The Sardarji's *iktara* had ceased.

Was he alone?

Whether he was an old man or a young man, was he alone?

Alone… alone…

Nine

Have you slept on the slopes of the Himalayas on a cold night? With only the loneliness of the next night to brood over? Whether it is November or May, the doors and windows are always closed. All around are walls paneled with wooden planks insensitive to cold or heat. If you wake up with a start at night, nothing of the world is visible. No sky. No stars. No earth-shadows, no treetops in the pallor of moonlight. Mist-coloured windows, dim windowpanes, eyes which have forfeited their vision of your world.

I am tired with my own life and the lives of those after me
I am dying in my own death and the deaths of those after me...

Listening to the echoes of the *iktara*, she fell asleep.

Ten

She heard Amar Singh laughing as she entered the portico in the morning and saw the Sardarji standing on the steps, talking to him. He was not as old as he had seemed when she saw him through the window. He could have been anywhere between forty and sixty. His glum face was full of lines and wrinkles. Dark nights slept in the depths of his eyes. A dark scar almost covered his forehead. Suddenly overcome by disgust, she almost went back inside.

'Namaste, Teacher-ji.'

Vimala turned. 'Namaste!'

'The *chowkidar* tells me that you read a lot of books.'

Vimala gave Amar Singh an annoyed look. Instead of sweeping the veranda clean in the morning, had he been telling this man who had come from nowhere about her habits?

She did not say yes or no.

'Would you mind lending me some books? I bought a few on the way here, but devoured them all in three days.'

A smile touched her face when she heard his expression. She had to say something, so she said, 'I have very few good books.'

'I read whatever I come across. A catalogue of medicines, a railway guide, a telephone directory—anything!'

Vimala could not help laughing.

He wore a shirt that was too big for him and trousers that were too wide. When he spoke, the black stubs of his worn, widely-spaced teeth looked repulsive.

'Let me see.'

While coming back from the bathroom, she peered into the kitchen. The fire was just being lighted. She walked through the veranda at the end of the hall. Looking through the arch, she saw Amar Singh and the Sardarji in the garden. The Sardarji was caressing the geraniums.

The last two weeks, she had not written to anyone. Letters to which she had to send replies lay piled up in her drawer. She had better write them today.

Dear Shanta, I am so happy to hear that you are getting married. You must let me know the exact date… Dear Amma, I am doing well. Hope all of you there are keeping well… Dear Shirin, I have been ill and in bed for a month. This is why my reply has been delayed…

She chose four or five books from the bookshelf. Three novels, the biography of an artist and the confessions of a Hollywood actor.

Amar Singh brought buttered toast and coffee on a walnut-wood tray on which the carvings had worn off. He moved the books stacked on the table to one side, put the tray down and asked, 'Are these for the Sardarji?'

'Yes, give them to him.'

'He is a good man. He speaks Hindi and Pahadi with equal fluency. He asked when he saw me, "Aren't you Amar Singh?"'

'Had he met you earlier?'

'He seems to have stayed in this cottage about eighteen years ago. What a memory!'

'Hmm...'

If she were to show interest, Amar Singh would start talking about his adventures in the days gone by. Of how strong he had been in his youth, of how he had been stabbed during a brawl, of how he had once played the role of Sriram Maharaj in a performance of the Ramlila.

'I think the Sardarji is a very rich man, Bibiji.'

She was irritated. 'Are you his accountant?'

'It's not that, Bibiji. He came from Delhi by taxi. Three hundred rupees, when he could have come by bus for eight!'

'Let those who have money spend it. What's it to you?'

She gave Amar Singh some money to buy stamps and sent him off. As usual, he reminded her: 'Write the letters and give them to me, Bibiji. I'll stick the required stamps and post them. That way, I can save an outing!'

She had known Amar Singh for quite some time. He would tear up the letters and throw them away and buy *bhang* with the money meant for the stamps. Since this was common knowledge, he was not offended if people distrusted him.

She closed the door and sat down to write her letters. Amar Singh suddenly shouted from outside, 'Bibiji, come quickly.'

The postman was waiting outside in his khaki clothes, a blanket wrapped around him. 'There's a phone call for you, Bibiji.' He added a clarification, 'A trunk call.'

Her heart thudded. She froze for a moment, then went in for her shawl.

'Amar Singh, I'm not locking the room.'

'All right, Bibiji. Will you buy the stamps yourself?'

She went out hurriedly, not answering him. When she had descended the hill and reached the level road, she slowed down. Something was going to happen to her life.

A familiar voice calling from somewhere distant. She closed the door of the public call office and picked up the receiver very, very slowly, her mind extremely calm.

'Who is it?'

Babu's voice. 'Babu!'...

'... What!'

'Yes, this morning. Yes, Didi... at five-thirty.'

She stood for a moment outside the post office at a spot where the paving stones were rough and uneven. Mellow sunshine. A beautiful morning for the tourists. Behind her, the bus stand roared.

How quickly this place that had lain wrapped in sleep had woken up! Huge groups of tourists, Bhotia porters hovering like vultures over piles of suitcases and hold-alls, the combined tumult of cycle-rickshaw drivers and hotel agents bidding for clients...

Yes, at five-thirty this morning.

But nothing has happened to me.

Waves of colour and sound rippled around her. A thousand unfamiliar faces. Were the eyes of a young girl she had met nine years ago among them? Dark eyes that looked as if they were lined with *kajal*, eyes that shone blue-black beneath the hair that lay disheveled over her forehead…?

Where was Buddhu? That bald man in shorts, was he a white man? Where's the picture, Buddhu? Amongst the boatmen who crowded the jetty trying to catch customers, was there a searching pair of eyes belonging to a boy who had the picture of a Gora Sahib in his pocket?

Vimala walked on. God, there's something wrong with me. I am not even able to cry.

She realised that her footsteps were not unsteady. No stream of sorrow was descending into her heart.

Early this morning, at five-thirty, my father died…

She had imagined that, confronted with the news of death, she would sway as helplessly as a blade of grass caught in a whirlpool. But nothing was happening. There was nothing in her heart except a deep calm.

Sardarji stood behind a neatly-trimmed bush at the turning near the Golden Nook, his eyes gleaming.

'Who is your guest, Teacher-ji?'

She did not understand.

'The *chowkidar* said you had a trunk call. Who is visiting you?'

'Death, death is my guest,' she wanted to shout, at the top of her voice!

He noticed her silence and the glint of mischief went out of his eyes. She looked boldly at him as he stood there looking faintly bewildered.

She hoped her voice would not falter, 'No one came. Someone went. My father.'

She had feared while returning from the post office that the sense of calm that had deepened with every step she took would be shattered in a second. I must not weep, she thought. Somewhere around her eyes, she felt an ache as if roots were giving way.

How long they seemed—the minutes it took her to get to her room!

Eleven

She had presumed that a house where death had taken place would be crowded with visitors. Her face paled as she climbed up into the veranda. Albert Gomez stood by the pillar, holding himself erect, wearing an impeccably pressed suit, his hair greying at the temples. He was smoking a cigarette in a gold-coloured holder. He had the air of someone who had just come out of a dance hall to relax and get a breath of fresh air. Making an effort to look sympathetic, he smiled and murmured something. She could not help looking annoyed. It was his sympathetic expression that she could not bear.

So he had come on the pretence of sharing their sorrow! It was a fortunate day for him today.

She felt uneasy as she entered the drawing room, as if great swarms of bees were buzzing through her head. Four or five people were distributed over the settee and chairs. Babu stood in a corner, chewing his nails.

Placing her airbag on the table in the dining room, she went into the small bedroom. Nothing seemed clear to her. Bees buzzed faster inside her head.

In the faint light, she saw Amma seated on the bed, leaning back against the wall. There were a lot of women with her. No one moved. Pale smiles gleamed around her. There was a stir in the cold atmosphere when Anita came and hugged her, weeping. When her tear-stained face sank into her shoulders, Vimala stroked her back and said softly, 'Don't cry, child, don't cry.'

Some of the women spoke to her. She could not find the words to respond to them.

Someone came up with his hand on Babu's shoulder and said to her, 'Vimala, come,' in Malayalam. She felt very relieved.

It was Menon Saab.

'Should we inform anyone in Kerala?'

'I don't know.'

'What's the point? It will take them five days to get here. We can't wait that long.'

Mr Gomez arrived at that point. 'So, Mr Menon…?

Mr Menon ignored him. His wife, Mrs Menon, knew the secret of Amma's evening walks. It had probably reached Mr Menon's ears as well.

'Is there anyone else we have to wait for, Vimala?'

Who did they have to wait for?

Mr Gomez was the last person to leave after the cremation. When he came into the room to say goodbye to Amma, Vimala went out. Let him console her in whatever way he wanted to, she thought.

Anita came up behind her as she stood on the outer veranda gazing at the drain that led the dirty water out of the kitchen. Shadow, the dog, chained to the pillar, sniffed at her feet.

'I'm leaving, Miss Vimala,' Gomez's voice came.

Her only response was to incline her head. She could feel Anita's tear-filled eyes on her.

The buildings belonging to the Potato Research Department lay scattered over the hill slopes. The building which housed the room where her father had worked looked the tallest. He had ruled over the empire below that red roof for years.

Her distress grew as night fell.

That night, none of them entered Father's bedroom.

Bir Bahadur served dinner and came and called them. But no one ate.

All of them slept together in the small bedroom without turning the light off. Anita wound her arms around her and Vimala felt it was more out of fear than sorrow. Vimala had gone to bed dreading that it would be a night when sleep would evade her, but, contrary to her expectations, she fell asleep very quickly. Snow fell steadily, making everything invisible. Delicate waves, drifting here and there.

She was floating… no not floating, she was gliding in a pleasure boat that carried a swan with outstretched wings on its prow. At first, it was Buddhu who rowed. But when he spoke, it was no longer Buddhu. The clean-shaven face on which pale green shadows lay was not Buddhu's. Bluish veins throbbed on the face and hair lay untidily over the forehead.

'Don't, don't steer the boat that way.'

'Why?'

'It's a whirlpool. You have to throw coins into it.'

'There are better uses for money.'

'They say that those who do not believe in God will drown there.'

'Are you afraid to die?'

Life was in bloom wherever one looked and it was impossible to think of death.

There was no fear in Buddhu's eyes even when the boat spun on the surface of the whirling current. Buddhu's face changed again. It wasn't his face any more, it was the one on which blue veins throbbed.

The edge of the boat seemed to touch the sky as it spun around. Suddenly, it went down, deeper, deeper… And now…

Amma!

'Vimala!'

'Amma, did you call me?'

'What is it, child?'

'Nothing.'

Her eyes suddenly filled. She wanted to hold her mother tight in her arms.

She closed her eyes again. Babu ground his teeth in his sleep and made meaningless sounds. Anita's arms tightened around her.

Standing in the yard, she saw the first bus of the day leaving. The buses stopped just below the house, in front of the small row of shops that was the bazaar.

The next bus was at eight-thirty. As she picked up her bag and went out, Amma asked, 'So what are you doing?'

'I'm leaving.'

'Can't you stay here a few days at least this time, Didi?' Babu's voice was resentful. She did not say anything.

Bir Bahadur came out of the kitchen, picked up her bag and walked out ahead of her. She patted Anita lightly on the back and went out.

With the bus pulling out, she was finally at peace with herself. She was going back to her world. Her own world. She could listen to the footfalls of the travelers who came from arid lands in search of mountains, lakes, mists, snow and the cold. Footfalls around her tomb.

Twelve

The posts to which the street lamps were fixed shone a bright green. Broad black and white stripes lined the zebra crossings.

If you stood near the lake, you could hear the sound of the horses' hooves as tourists galloped over the high mountain path to China Peak. Someone was fishing near the stone steps on the western side of the lake, from where, in the cold winter months, she used to gaze out at the deserted silence. Couples in brightly-coloured woolen sweaters walked over the path, holding hands. The odour of tobacco and outbursts of laughter tore piercingly through the air.

Seated on a little island made by a lawn lying between the path and the lake, Vimala watched a flock of ducks. They were fighting for the groundnuts that one of the tourists in a passing boat had thrown to them. Someone called out loudly from a boat that passed close by the bank, 'Namaste, Memsaheb!'

Buddhu. His yellow teeth shone. His passengers were a girl wearing huge rings in her ears and two young men. They turned to look at her.

'The season has started, Memsaheb!'

The trail left by the *Mayflower* lay like the tail of a comet on the surface of the water. A bald, dark-skinned man with a camera slung around his neck came and stood a little distance away, whistling, his hands tucked into his pockets. His stare pierced her sharply like the hook at the end of a fishing rod.

She turned and walked away. She crossed the road, skirted the two wide circles of lawn and walked up the footpath paved with stones.

She was coming this way after a long time. Once the city filled with tourists, this path and the area around the rocks would lie deserted.

How quickly people lost interest in things. Once, it used to be lovers who walked along this track, their faces close.

She stopped when she reached a spot where one slope ended and another began. She was short of breath after the climb. The temple was close by. The thickets which swarmed around it half hid it from sight. The old *pujari* was smoking a hookah, seated under a brass bell which had lost its tongue, suspended from an iron bar. In the old days, all those who went by used to offer the deity money. Every day, the *pujari* must certainly be cursing the young girl who had jumped from the top of the rock and died. The temple was asleep now, so was its god.

Hearing someone gasping loudly behind her, she turned to look. The Sardarji stood there, his hands pressed to his chest, his pale face flushed a bright red.

'The old horse has come to the end of his days!' Laughing and gasping at the same time, he asked, 'Going up, Teacher-ji?'

'Um…'

'I'm coming too. Let me just get my breath back.'

Generally, she did not like anyone accompanying her on this lonely footpath where memories slumbered. But she did not say anything. He followed her as she started to walk on.

He pointed to a tree among the thickets that looked as if it was centuries old and asked, 'Did you see that tree, Teacher-ji? There used to be so many fallen flowers under it in the old days! Have you heard, there's a story that the serpent that lies coiled around Shiva Bhagavan's neck comes out of the hole under the tree once a year, so that devotees can see it?'

She shook her head to say no.

'Now that people don't care about Bhagavan, who would bother about His serpent? Hm?'

He did not speak again until they reached the rock. She noticed his eyes wandering all around as he climbed, puffing and grunting, his breath coming in short gasps. By the time he reached the top, he was drenched in perspiration.

'Bear with me, Teacher-ji. Let me sit down for a while.'

He sat down. She gazed at the valley. In the cool breeze, strands of hair began to escape from her rounded chignon.

'Sit down, Teacher-ji.'

She sat down on a tall rock not too far away, her legs hanging down. Behind her, the black rocks jutted into the sky like a distorted temple *gopuram*.

'How old was your father, Teacher-ji?'

'Fifty-eight.'

He grunted. 'Hmm… I will not try to express my sympathy. Who can sympathise with whom?'

Turning her eyes away from the dark blue of the wooden huts in the valley, she looked at him. It seemed to her that the eyes of this man who sat there smiling, stroking his rough grey beard, were wandering through the innermost recesses of her heart.

'Death is a clown with no stage sense, isn't that so, Teacher-ji?'

She smiled painfully.

'I've not thought about it.'

'It's true. You can note it down somewhere and quote it as a sentence spoken by an unknown thinker.' Amused by his own joke, he burst out laughing.

He got up and said, walking over the uneven rocks, 'Many names have been erased by time…' Running his hands over the letters carved on the rock, he murmured, 'It was good that I did not carve my name here at that time.'

She was curious. Why hadn't he? She raised her eyes.

'At least I don't have to sigh over it now. If you don't mind my asking, Teacher-ji, where is the souvenir of your first visit here?'

Saying nothing in answer, she sat with her eyes riveted on the ground.

He said, as if to change the subject, 'Why do people seek out places suited for suicide as spots for lovers to meet? Maybe because life should be destroyed at the very spot at which it blossomed. Have you ever been to Madarihatt in Assam? There is a rock exactly like this one about two miles from there. How many couples have carved their names on it and added hearts pierced by arrows!'

She nodded to let him know she was listening attentively. It seemed as if he took great pleasure in talking.

'There is a pleasant dak bungalow near it. If you spend a night there, you can really hear the music of the forest. Yes, there is music in a forest. Rain and the wind have their own language and music.'

Gasping, he pressed the wisened fingers of his left hand on his chest and said in a much lower voice: 'I want to go one more time. But I wonder whether my guardian will allow me to…'

'Well…'

'I am now walking through all the places where I once traveled. Like the accountant at headquarters checking the stocks at the end of the year.'

When he laughed, the years seem to slide off him. His delight was like a child's.

'Teacher-ji, how long have you been here?'

'Nine years.'

'Hm… when you first came to climb this rock, you weren't alone, were you?'

She did not answer.

'I was not alone either. But it was many, many years ago.'

He bowed his head and closed his eyes. 'I was twenty-three years old then. Do you know which is the best time in a man's life? Take it from me, when he is twenty-three!'

He had a justification for this. Twenty-five was a turning point. You felt that you were a young man who had attained maturity. At twenty-four you could see the imminent turning point right before you. Between eighteen and twenty-two, vestiges of adolescence still remained. But twenty-three!

'The person who gave an adjective to describe those of your race who are seventeen forgot all about us!'

The minutes sank once again into a current of silence…

'Why don't you say something, Teacher-ji?'

'What can I say?'

'Something. I used to be like this, in the old days. I talked mostly only to myself. Now I can talk to anything. To rocks, trees, lamp-posts… It is a blessing, to be able to talk, Teacher-ji. Isn't it?'

'Maybe.'

The shadows on the slope of the hill grew longer. Mist flowed into the bottomless abyss beneath the rocks like a pale blue blanket.

'Let me climb up the rock.'

She wanted to tell him not to. It was risky for a feeble man like him to try to climb right up. However, she did not say anything.

He struggled to climb up. She could hear him breathing loudly, making a sound like the wind hissing through bellows full of holes. She saw the blood rush to his face and sweat bead his forehead even in this biting cold.

He stood on the sharp peak and looked down. His baggy trousers flapped noisily in the wind. She was afraid that, even as she looked at him, he would be blown away like a wisp of cotton.

'Teacher-ji!' He shouted, to drown the sound of the wind. 'Have you seen the face of death? Look!'

She looked fearfully at the man who stood against the fading light, smiling, one hand raised. Death hovered around his feet with a gaping mouth.

She wanted to scream—come down! But she controlled herself. Struggling even harder than when he had climbed up, he came down.

On the way back, they did not speak. She walked slowly, two paces behind him. He kept enthusiastically humming a line from a Punjabi love song over and over again. He stopped at the gate of the Golden Nook and so did she.

'Thank you!'

'For what?'

'For another happy evening. Thank you, Teacher-ji. My thanks to God, to the world.'

A happy evening...? Was Sardarji making fun of her?

'What are you doing tomorrow evening, Teacher-ji?'

'I haven't decided.'

'May I borrow an evening of yours? Today was a boon that fell into my lap. We can go on a boat ride.'

She was convinced that this stranger was taking liberties with her. The more she tried to distance herself, the closer he kept moving.

'I am not asking for all your evenings, Teacher-ji. Just tomorrow.'

She said, 'Let me see.'

'I'll come to the gate of the boarding house to fetch you.'

Neither saying yes nor no, she walked towards the wire fence.

'One moment, please!'

She slowed down.

'You must not lose your sleep thinking of the dead. There are so many people on this earth who are still alive.'

Amar Singh was repairing the tubelight in the portico.

'It's very late, Bibiji.'

'Um.'

'You shouldn't walk alone on the slopes, Bibiji.'

Spluttering and hissing, the light began to burn.

'You can walk whenever you like, at dusk or at midnight, around the lake, there's nothing to be afraid of. It's within Naina Devi's line of vision.'

'What about the hills?' she asked mockingly.

'It's not a joke, Bibiji. Have you heard of Chandan Singh?'

Vimala did not show any interest. Amar Singh must be getting ready to launch on a long narrative.

'He was a real villain. He had two swords tucked into his waist. It must have been about forty years ago. At the time when they were performing the Ramlila on the maidan beyond the dak bungalow. The fellow was coming back dead drunk when he saw a woman in a burkha at the gate of the bungalow. "Who are you?" he asked. People in that area generally quaked with fear when Chandan Singh's name was mentioned. The woman did not say anything. He went closer and lifted the burkha.' Amar Singh made appropriate gestures—'Teeth like this. Eyes as big as...! A tongue a yard long. He gave a yell. The fellow died three days later.'

Amar Singh had forgotten that he had told her the same story when he had described how his grandfather had died fighting a tiger!

The books that she had lent Sardarji had come back to her room. There was a note written in English on top—'Thanks. I saw only devils and angels in these. Do you have any stories about human beings in your collection?' His handwriting was beautiful, completely out of keeping with his physical appearance. He was a strange creature.

They had spent a lot of time together. And spoken of many things. But the boundaries of a casual acquaintance still lay between them. He had not said anything about himself; nor had she asked.

"Death is a clown with no stage sense. Anon."

Death—a body shrouded in a white cloth. A pale face with protruding bones. Closed eyes.

The sound of horses' hooves moving continuously over the mountain path grew fainter, then faded out. A wild bird fluttered its wings around the high lamp-post in the courtyard, then dived into the shadows of the night.

She lay on the mattress with her eyes closed and tried to pray. The soft strings of the *iktara* wafted in through the dead heart of the walls.

Thirteen

A man had invited her to go with him for a walk in the evening. This was the first thought that came to her mind in the morning. A man from somewhere. An ugly man who looked older than he was.

There had been days when she had waited all dressed up for evening to arrive. Days when she had looked arrogantly, scornfully, at the girls who passed by.

The Sardarji would arrive below the portico in the evening, stroking his grey beard. She felt neither insulted nor happy.

But, when evening came, Amar Singh did not turn up saying, 'Bibiji, Sardarji is asking for you.' The emotion of waiting grew more intense. Were the moments beginning to tremble in the grip of anxiety?

She heard footsteps on the verandah. Yes, it was Amar Singh.

'Bibiji, here's a note. Sardarji gave it to me.'

She read it: 'Forgive me. The companion who is my guardian has ordered me to rest today. I have no alternative except to obey him. The loss is mine.' There was no name below, only an illegible scrawl.

What she felt was not distress but a childish insistence—she felt she had to feign the pleasure of a tourist and walk around the lake, go for a boat ride.

Four or five boats lay at rest on the sand of the boat jetty. She did not see any of the boatmen she knew. Let Buddhu come, she thought, let him earn a fare of six annas because of her.

'Come, Memsaheb, come…' She shook her head, pretending to be a casual visitor who had come to enjoy a view of the lake. The pavilion and the sand-strewn yard were filled with people. Music floated out of the theatre—a film song that sounded like cats mewing and dogs howling.

'Picture postcards. Ten for two rupees!'

A hawker came up to her, glanced at her face and went away. He must have guessed she was not a tourist who had come to enjoy the season. How would he have guessed? Was it written in her greying hair, on the lips that had blackened with the vaseline she smeared on them, in the valleys of her shadow-filled eyes? A woman imprisoned by the years in the tomb of the hills!

She heard someone call out from a boat that had come to rest below: 'Come, Memsaheb, come…' It was Buddhu inviting her with a bright yellow smile, his chinky eyes filled with laughter. As she climbed into the boat, all the bells of the Naina Devi temple sounded in unison.

The Mayflower was all decked up again. The swan's beak and wings had been newly painted.

'What's the season like, Memsaheb?'

'Good.'

'There are more people this year, aren't there?'

'Yes.'

'There are lots of white people in the Lake Hotel.'

Vimala was silent.

'Do you belong here, Memsaheb?'

'No.'

'Are you from faraway?'

'Hmm...'

'Madras?' he asked, with a pleased smile at having found her out. She nodded assent.

'Ah, a Madrasi teacher. I've heard about them.'

'Hmm…'

'Don't you ever visit your place, Memsaheb?'

'I do.'

'When?'

'Sometimes.'

Buddhu steered the boat from the middle of the lake towards the shore, then circled around the lake. With a loud, foolish laugh, he said, 'Lots of white sahibs keep coming. Our man is the only one who's never to be seen.'

Letting go of one oar, he patted the spot on his chest where he had put away the leather purse and said firmly, 'This time he'll come. He's sure to come.'

All of us are waiting, Buddhu, every year. And so is this town. In the meanwhile, the days go by. Like bubbles scattering as the oar falls. You have the likeness of a white man to wait for. Someone else maybe waiting for a face with blue veins that twitch.

Whom does the town wait for, Buddhu,' with its lamp-posts newly painted, its pavements striped white and black?

Do you pray, child? Do you believe in God? Whom are you looking at, over the bowed heads listening to the huge bells that peal out from the temple of Naina Devi as she sits alone in the valley, performing penance?

'Did you say something, Memsaheb?'

'No.'

'What are you thinking about, Memsaheb?'

What I'm thinking about is...

There was a girl who used to come to the house-boat on the Dal Lake, selling walnut figurines. Her eyes were wider than the sky in the month of *Vaishaka*. No, this is not a poem. I am telling a story. When stories flow out of the soul, they become poetry. What did I say? A young girl. A dream I had dreamt for years in front of me. When I saw the girl the houseboat cook brought me as a companion for a fee of ten rupees—no I don't feel bad now, speaking of it. I have already told you the stories of those nights. The past no longer makes me feel ashamed. I see only you before me. Everything you own is dear to me. You fragrance surrounds me all the time like a halo... what did I say? A companion for one night. The essence of my dreams in front of me. No, not in front of me. My dreams lie under my feet, blood spurting from them.

The beauty of the bodies lying on the bed vanished in a second. I can tell you everything now. I am not a nineteen-year-old lover. Nor are you a schoolgirl.

Do you want to hear something else? Excuse me if I am vulgar. It was in the days when I was a college student. I felt I was in love with a girl who was my neighbour. Day and night, I thought about her. What would her body be like? Her face? I wanted all of her. I acknowledge once again that I did wrong. I told you, didn't I, that I have been pure from the moment we met? Ah, my beautiful neighbour. Entreaties and reconciliations. Then, finally, life fulfilled in a moment. If a seed of my own being took shape in her...Nothing would matter—challenging the whole world, I would—proclaim: she is mine! And then, when she gave herself to me, I would ask, are you scared? And she would reply, I am wearing my diaphragm! The blood-stained corpses of dreams!

You have never disappointed me. Far and near, in or out of your clothes, I worship you...

'Memsaheb!'

Oh, it's nothing, Buddhu. May you have the good fortune to meet that white man, your father.

If only we could see... standing on the peak of time, moving aside the screen of years, of generations, if we could see, we could have said—on this day, in this street, at this time, you will meet your white sahib.

That meeting was not an accident, Vimala Devi! Twenty-one-year old Vimala Devi, beautiful, with light blue hair on her upper lip, meets twenty-nine-year old, young, hot-headed Sudhir Kumar Mishra, early morning on 3 May, 1955, in a bus. It had been written on one of the pages in the great book of time that this would happen, even before we were born. It was to arrive at this moment that I had been wandering all over the country. It was for this that your father had severed his bonds with his own village. And it as for this that the sorrowful Mr Gomez became your mother's lover and you quarrelled with your mother and left home to work for your living. This was no ordinary event, Vimala Devi! It was the crucial moment when your life began to be fulfilled.

Buddhu stopped rowing and sat back, smiling at her. The *Mayflower* drifted over a spot where creepers snaked into the lake.

'Let's go back.'

He grinned, showing his yellow teeth and took up the oars.

'Memsaheb, your mind is somewhere else.'

'I was thinking...'

'So was I.'

'Who were you thinking about, Buddhu?'

'About my mother...'

'And about the white sahib...'

He laughed again, his foolish laugh.

'Would he have left too, Memsaheb, when the white men left our country?'

We can see nothing beyond this lamp-post, Buddhu!

'No, he would not have left.'

'Why?'

'He was fond of your mother, wasn't he? So he would have been fond of this place as well. He'll come ... he'll come back.'

She felt very tired. Here was the wooden bridge again. And the boat jetty. The porters who looked like messengers of Death. The path she had trod for nine years. The drowsy *chowkidar*, plunged in the ecstasy of *bhang*. Wheat *chapatis* and *dal*. A cold mattress.

She did not hear the sound of the *iktara* that night. She opened the window and looked out. There was a light in the Golden Nook. The *iktara* was asleep. And with it slept the heart of the Punjabi girl who had asked the blackbird to strum a message to her lover on its slender single string, telling him of her sorrow.

She closed the window.

If only we could see...

Fourteen

There was a letter in the morning post. People who did not know her well would have assumed it was her handwriting, her younger sister's was so like her own. She ran her eyes over it.

Vimala Didi, I can't go on living here. May I come and stay with you, Didi? Babu Ettan came home drunk yesterday and had a huge fight with Amma. He threatened to beat up Bir Bahadur. Please come. Otherwise I will come and stay with you.

She tucked it into the heap of letters in her drawer.

What had happened to Anita? Had Pradeep Chandra Sharma gone away? Or was she clearer in her mind now?

Amar Singh asked for some time off that evening. A relative of his who lived three miles away was dying. He would visit him and return before dusk, he promised.

She stood in the yard, below the portico and saw Sardarji walking up from the Golden Nook towards the gate. She thought he would go down the hill. But he came straight up to the fence.

'Good evening!'

'Evening!'

'How was the boat ride yesterday?'

'Who told you I went for a boat ride?' She looked at the long fingers holding onto the concrete pillar supporting the thorny fence.

'I could guess, couldn't I? I can read your whole mind if I want, like an open book. You generally like to stand apart from the crowd and watch. Although you don't like a boat ride when the lake is crowded, you accepted when I invited you. But I didn't turn up. So you must have set out, obstinately determined to do at least ten rounds by yourself around the lake.' He raised his eyes questioningly as if to ask, 'Right?'

'Let me smoke a cigarette. I don't want anyone to see.'

'Why don't you want them to see?'

'What I meant was that I don't want my guardian to see.'

Inhaling the cigarette with relish, he said, 'He and I are always at loggerheads.'

'I haven't met your guardian.'

'You never will. That's what makes him special.'

He strolled along the side of the fence, staying close enough to talk.

'Teacher-ji!'

She turned to him.

'Shall I tell you a joke?'

She waited attentively.

'I like you. For no special reason.'

She saw a flush appear and disappear on his withered, distorted face and felt distressed.

'There's nothing to be upset about. I won't waylay you or write you love letters. I won't do anything. I like you… just like that… without imagining any kind of relationship between us.'

The words were cold. Without emotion or appeal. He seemed to expect no reply either. She was devastated. She realised she had to say something. Trying to sound natural, she said, 'You… you don't even know who I am.'

'That's how it should be. I can find out your entire background by asking other people. Hundreds of details. When they all come together, there will be a thousand roots and branches and leaves in the picture. And you yourself will be only a speck…'

Taking a last puff of his cigarette, he flung it far away with a feeling of satisfaction.

Who are you? From where have you come? She had so many questions to ask about this man with his withered face, the ugly black stain on his forehead and a gleam in his eyes.

'Oh yes, Teacher-ji, I have a request.'

She made ready to listen to it in silence.

'You must laugh every now and then. Otherwise you will forget that great accomplishment.'

'I… I am not crying after all.'

'I feel disgusted when I see you crying. But I feel bad when you make an attempt to smile…'

He looked at his watch. 'Time for my medicine. My guardian is someone to be scared of!'

She watched him hurry away, his loose trousers flapping. Was he mad?

The dusk had begun to deepen. She turned on the dome-shaped light in the courtyard. She was afraid to sit all alone in that huge building in the pale darkness. She wondered how much longer it would take for Amar Singh to come. Walking around the veranda she pressed the switches on the alternate stone pillars.

She went to her room and flipped through her books. Covers she was tired of looking at. She was fed up.

During the day, it drizzled a number of times. The wind was icy cold. Seen from the semicircle of the stone built at the spot where the road made a turn on the slope of the hill, the distant peaks turned into curls of smoke. Now and then, the sound of horses' hooves could be heard on the mountain path.

Unusually, the mist came down by noon, spreading like a veil over the lake.

Tiny drops of water clung to the wind that began to screech by evening through the clefts in the hills.

After days, the murmuring of the *iktara* wafted out, followed by Sardarji's feeble voice.

When she opened the window a little, the cold wind rushed in, making her shiver. Through the mist, the gleaming panes of the Golden Nook shone a pale yellow.

Ungaliya katta kaani…
Akkham da kajjalamain…

The sound of the *iktara* rose, triumphing over the roar of the wind. In the freezing air, the Punjabi girl's sighs spread goosebumps over her.

Was the Sardarji's guardian asleep today? How come he had allowed the Sardarji to sing? She closed and bolted the window and lay down.

In the morning, someone started to knock rapidly on the door before she woke up. Waking with a start, she asked, her heart beating wildly, 'Who is it?'

'It's me, Bibiji.'

She opened the door. Amar Singh stood there rubbing his eyes.

'What is it?'

'The Sardarji wants to see you.'

'So early?'

'He wants to take leave of you.'

Not pausing to adjust her crumpled clothes, she wrapped a shawl around herself and walked through the veranda into the portico. The cold fingers of the wind caressed her face.

He stood in the courtyard in the half-light of dawn.

'Forgive me for disturbing your sleep, Teacher-ji.'

'It doesn't matter.'

Her voice was rough with drowsiness.

'I'm leaving, Teacher-ji.'

She was distressed, not sure how to respond. Finally, she said, 'We'll meet again.'

He smiled. 'I do not have the courage to say that, Teacher-ji. Four months at the most, that is what my guardian says.'

It seemed as if layers of sleep were slipping down from her eyes.

'Well, even that means something gained for me. I should thank God for it. A year is the time limit for this type of cancer. These four months have been given to me as a bonus!'

He laughed as if amused by his own words.

She did not say anything.

'Namaste, Teacher-ji. May all good things come to you!'

'Namaste.'

He walked a few steps and turned. She stood at the same spot.

'The evening I asked to borrow still remains. Don't forget!'

He laughed aloud and walked away, dragging his feet.

Two porters followed him carrying his luggage. But where was his companion?

She met Amar Singh as she came back through the veranda to her room. His face was wreathed in a smile.

'Sardarji is a very rich man, Bibiji. Do you know what he gave me as a tip? Ten rupees!'

'Amar Singh, where is his companion?'

'Companion? He was alone, Bibiji.'

She shut the door.

Fifteen

She stood on the stone steps by the lamp-post from which the paint had faded, looking at the lake in which the heavily overcast sky had fallen asleep.

The precincts of the temple, the sand-covered yard and the temple *mandapam* lay deserted.

She watched the boat with a swan's prow coming to rest below her with three *pahadi* boys seated in it. Buddhu smiled at her, his yellow teeth gleaming. He anchored the boat.

'How quickly the season finished, Memsaheb!'

'That's right.'

'No one came.'

She repeated, in a troubled voice, 'No one came.'

'We'll wait for next year, right, Memsaheb?'

Not paying attention to her reply, he repeated, 'Yes, next year…'

Unsure whether Memsaheb was showing the interest she should, Buddhu patted his skin-coloured jacket and asked rather loudly, 'He'll come for sure, won't he, Memsaheb?'

She nodded.

As the boat moved away, she gazed at the long snaky trail it left on the water and murmured, 'He's sure to come.'

The Soul of Darkness

One

He felt very frightened as he crept out of the room. At the door, he peered into the hall. Achuthan Nair was fast asleep. He waited for a minute, hesitating. It was so funny to see the lump in Achuthan Nair's throat moving up and down when he snored. The areca nuts he had tucked into his waist were about to roll off. When he looked at those huge, hairy arms and the fat, disgusting fingers, his first reaction was one of anger. Wasn't it that hand that, yesterday, at dusk... was it yesterday? Or several days ago?

Velayudhan stroked his neck. It still hurt. One day, he had to chop that hand off, without anyone seeing him do it. He had to keep a hatchet ready. Then, while Achuthan Nair was asleep with that rough, hairy hand resting on the floor, one day he would creep up stealthily and chop it off at one stroke!

The man deserved that. Why did he hurt people so badly?

Yesterday...was it yesterday? Or many days ago? He had been brought to the western veranda to be given a bath. For quite some time, Achuthan Nair had been giving him a bath. Velayudhan Nair did not like this at all. Was he a child, to be bathed by someone else? He had grown up, he really had. When he had been Gopi's age, he had bathed in the river, at the spot next to the *kuruthiparambu*, the sacrificial enclosure. Amma used to give him a bath at that time.

He was a grown man now. Muthassi, his grandmother, often said, 'He's twenty-one years old now, a young man. What a misfortune!'

Velayudhan knew she was speaking about him.

And yet, Achuthan Nair would drag him along for a bath. Three huge copper pots would be filled with water and kept ready. The water would be poured over his head from a small brass pot with a broken rim. One day, Achuthan Nair had sat him down on a low wooden stool next to the full copper pots and gone to fetch the little brass pot. An idea had suddenly occurred to Velayudhan. How would it look to have a small river flow along the western veranda? Big vessels with sails made of matting and small fishing canoes would start to go along it. He would be able to watch everything through the little window in his bedroom. Catfish would swirl through the water during the heavy rains in mid-Edavam. He could fish in the river as well, if he wanted to, through the little window in his bedroom.

He emptied out the water from the three copper pots into the channel that ran along the wall. He was watching the reddish, mud-streaked water flowing along when Achuthan Nair called out, 'Velayudhan!' He did not actually call out, he yelled. Velayudhan looked at him, terrified.

'Such impudence!'

Velayudhan did not say anything. Fire seemed to be spewing from Achuthan Nair's eyes. Velayudhan had just lifted up a pot to cover Achuthan Nair's head when the first blow fell.

'Don't hit me, please don't…' he could not help crying out aloud.

Muthassi, his grandmother, arrived at the edge of the veranda. Behind her were Valiamma, who was his aunt, and Gopi.

Dabbing her eyes with the tip of the towel she had wrapped around herself, Muthassi said, 'It's a sin in God's eyes, Achuthan. Don't you know he's not normal?'

'Did you see what he's done, Kali Amma?'

Valiamma muttered, 'No remedy's better than beating him up! It's all because of his impudence.'

Muthassi dabbed her eyes again and murmured, as she always did, 'It's our misfortune, our misfortune…'

Velayudhan tested his neck again, stroking it once more. The pain was still there.

Ayyappan had a very sharp hatchet. Velayudhan decided to take it from him when he came that evening after work to the gate of the storehouse to collect his wages. Then, while Achuthan Nair slept with his Adam's apple rolling up and down his neck, one single stroke! The fun would begin in the morning.

'This is not madness, it's sheer insolence!' Achuthan Nair would shout, and as he tried to thrash Velayudhan, he would find his hand was missing. While he ran around the house, frantically searching for his hand, Velayudhan would die laughing!

Velayudhan went through the hall into the northern room, the *vadikkini*. Muthassi was asleep on a grass mat by the open window. It was disgusting to look at Muthassi's body. It seemed as if it was covered with scales like those of a fish.

But he could not be angry with Muthassi. She never scolded him. Or hit him. Everyone else at home used to hit him, even Gopi and Sankarankutty, who were just children. Children did not usually hit their elders.

Luckily, Valiamma was not downstairs. Her room was upstairs. In the afternoons, once Valiamma, Gopi and his father went upstairs, they took a long time coming down again.

It was very dark in the southern room, the *thekkini*, even at noon. Only a tiny circle of light fell into it through the top of the open courtyard in the *naalukettu*. Wooden chests filled with grain and big bamboo baskets stood in the corners. Would there be evil spirits lurking in that darkness? What if Uncle himself was hiding there? If he was, he would certainly have a palm-leaf stalk with him. Uncle always enjoyed thrashing Velayudhan with it. But how could Uncle hide there if there were evil spirits? He thought of Uncle as he stepped into the front veranda. What if he was waiting there with a thick palm-leaf stalk?

One of these days, he must kill Uncle! If Uncle ever saw Velayudhan in the front veranda, he would call out in a voice that shook the rafters: 'Achuthan!' Achuthan Nair would come running. There was a rule that Velayudhan should not be seen in the front veranda. Whenever Achuthan Nair grabbed his hand with his bloated fingers, Velayudhan would feel disgusted. It felt repulsive, like treading on a frog. Achuthan Nair would never hit him in front of Muthassi. He would attack him only after they reached the northern side of the house.

Moving behind the door, he peered through a gap in the window. There was no one in sight. Uncle should not catch sight of him. Or

Sankarankutty either, because, if he did, he would call out, 'Father, there's Velayudhan!' The same thing would happen if Uncle's wife, Ammayi, saw him. No, she would not call out to Uncle. Instead, she'd say, 'Hey, Achu Nair, look who's come out here!' Sometimes, she would ask him directly, 'And where is His Majesty proceeding?' He couldn't bear to look at the white patches on her lips, they made him feel nauseous. He would collect a whole lot of pebbles from the top of the hill and the moment she started to call out 'Achu Nair!' in her singsong voice, he would stuff them in her mouth.

And what would he do with Sankarankutty? He would aim a blow at his shaven head with the grinding stone!

It was days since he had stepped into the yard. His eyes hurt when he looked out, the glare of the red, hot sun was so strong. Once the sun went down, Uncle would pace up and down the courtyard until dusk fell.

Vestiges of the patterns drawn with rice flour during the Onam season still lay on the cow dung-smeared ground. They had been traced around the clay image representing *Thrikkakara appan*. Once, when he had come to the front portico to look at the *Thrikkakara appan* image, Achuthan Nair had grabbed his neck and shoved him out. Uncle had been seated there, talking to his respectable friends, none of whom were supposed to catch sight of Velayudhan.

Picking up a bit of tinsel paper lying in the yard, Velayudhan walked to the western side of the *pathayappura* and stopped to drum lightly on the wooden water receptacle leaning against the wall. His aunt's calf lay munching something under the mango tree that poured a canopy of shade over the ground. A doubt occurred to Velayudhan as he stood in the cool patch of the shade.

What had he been thinking about?

He would go for a walk, just like that. Achuthan Nair was asleep. And Uncle was upstairs. It was a good opportunity. The *mana*, the residence of the Namboodiris, was just beyond the southern gate. He was afraid to go that side. Karineeli would be there, seated among the bushes in their compound, picking lice from her hair that was spread wide over her back.

Bhagavathi, may I never have to face Karineeli... She sucked the blood of babies and threw their dead bodies into the well. Would she hurt grown-ups as well? He had grown up, he had really grown. If he didn't bow his head when he went through a door, it would hit the door-frame—he was that tall! And a rough, thick stubble had appeared on his face. He ran his hand over it. How itchy it was! He was a grown man now, but what would he do if he came face to face with Karineeli? People said Karineeli always came rushing along like a hurricane, one breast thrown over her shoulder, hitting her chest... May there never be an occasion where he would meet her!

But, what if she came when he was all by himself? If he had a piece of banana pith with him, he would be all right. She would run away in fear if he flung it at her. Who had told him this?

Edathi, who lived in Father's house, had told him. Very, very long ago. He still remembered though. Was it when they were playing in the sand by the river at the time when he was a little boy wearing a red *konakam*?

Was it Devaki Edathi who had told him? Or was it Amma? Amma was no longer alive. She was buried in the earth, among the wild undergrowth that lay beyond the cluster of palmyra trees. Or was it when Amma was seated in the veranda with Meenakshi Edathi who had a torn earlobe that they had told him this?

Or was it Ammukutty who had told him? A crow flew down at that moment and settled on the calf's back. Crows were sly rogues. They had only one eye. Velayudhan knew all this. He still knew the rhyme he had learned as a child, '*kakkakkuyile, karin kuyile...*' He knew so many things. In spite of which, whatever he said and whatever he did people would say, 'He's not right in his mind—it's the fruit of his past lives.' Or, 'Just as well the old lady's gone. At least she didn't have to see all this.'

Velayudhan had realised that all these people were against him.

Someone called out to him softly as he watched the crow peck at the calf, 'Kuttiettan!'

He was startled—could it be Karineeli? But Karineeli would not call him 'Kuttiettan'. How stupid he was! He turned around and saw that the lower window of the *pathayappura* was open. Ammukutty was there, holding the wooden bars.

Not Karineeli, Ammukutty. Still, he had been frightened at first. He burst out laughing when he thought about it. He was such a fool!

His eyes fell on her fingers, reddened with henna, the colour of ripe, red Madagascar plums. Her hair lay scattered over her gleaming yellow blouse. As he stood looking at Ammukutty, she called him again, 'Kuttiettan!' Velayudhan was at a loss for words. He did not want to take his eyes off her cheeks, the colour of a reddish mango.

'What are you staring at, Kuttiettan?'

'Um…mmm…'

'Why have you come down to the yard?'

'Um…mmm…'

'Don't walk about outside, Kuttiettan.'

He raised his eyes slowly. When they met Ammukutty's, he was confused.

He could glimpse her stomach under the yellow blouse.

He felt quite shy.

'Before Achuthan Nair sees you…' Ammukutty began to say. Velayudhan forgot all about Achuthan Nair's rough, hairy arms. What if he just touched those reddish fingertips at the window…

'How did the skin on your knees peel off?'

He did not answer. Those reddish fingertips… like ripe, red Madagascar plums...

'Why did they thrash you yesterday?'

He did not respond to that either.

'What are you thinking about?'

Ammukutty turned her head to listen—was Uncle coming?

Velayudhan was still wondering, what if he touched… just once…?

'Kuttiettan, you'll soon be well.'

'Um…'

'You must obey Achuthan Nair.'

'Um…'

'If you don't, he'll hit you.'

'Um…'

'Why did you scream at night, the day before yesterday?'

'Um…mm…'

He felt sad when Ammukutty took her hand away from the window. She turned her back to him, loosened her *mundu* at the waist, shook it out, retied it tightly and placed her hand on the window again. He was relieved. Very, very nervously, he asked her, 'May I touch you just once, Ammukutty?'

Velayudhan saw a tender smile blossoming on Ammukutty's face. Gopi and Sankarankutty always laughed at him when he spoke. But Ammukutty's smile was never mocking. He wasn't sure why, but when he saw Ammukutty smile, he felt like crying.

He touched her fingers gently.

Ammukutty watched him nervously. 'You'd better go away, Kuttiettan. Achuthan Nair might come, or someone else.'

He did not move.

'Please go away.'

She seemed troubled. He continued to stand where he was.

He watched her climb the stairs to the *pathayappura*. He went out through the western gate into the lane, humming a tune. Her yellow blouse and, scattered over it, the wavy hair that fell over her shoulders. Her cheeks, the colour of reddish mangoes. How pretty Ammukutty was! Velayudhan loosened his *mundu*, which had been folded at the knee and tucked up. He looked at himself. He felt ashamed. His body was the colour of muddy water, so filthy, smeared with dirt! When he stroked his face, it was covered with stubble. The next time Govindan, the barber came, he would not try to avoid him.

There was not a trace of dirt on Ammukutty's body. Her black-bordered *mundu* was a pristine white. When she stood at the window, he had caught the fragrance of incense and screw pine flowers. Velayudhan raised his hands to his nose. Oh! the stench of fowl droppings! He felt nauseous. When he touched her fingers, he must have soiled them.

Ammukutty would have felt disgusted. If Ammayi had seen him touch her, that would have been the end of it. So many people would have thrashed him!

May all their heads explode, he thought—Uncle's, Achuthan Nair's, Ammayi's, Valiamma's and Sankarankutty's as well. Sankarankutty always made fun of him, laughed loudly at anything he did. If there were children around, he would cry out to them, 'Look, this Velayudhan is crazy!'

May his head explode as well!

Ammukutty never made fun of him, never hurt him. Bhagavathi, may all good things come to her.

There were dense bamboo thickets on both sides of the lane. The serpent shrine was below them. Creepers lay entwined in it like snakes. There was no need to be afraid now, since it was daytime. At night devils danced and played there, chewing on chunks of fire.

The lane ended at the slope of the hill. Cherumi women were drawing water there, from the well under the mango tree. Velayudhan avoided looking in that direction. 'Where are you going, Cheria Thamburan?' one of them asked. He did not reply. Why did she want to know? Was it because she wanted to tell Uncle, or send for Achuthan Nair?

With all his force, he flung a stone into the evenly shaped pit dug out of the clay on the roadside. Then he slowly climbed up the hill.

A cherumi girl drawing water said to her companion, who was rubbing oil into her child's hair, 'Why do they let him wander around outside?'

'That boss of his must be sleeping.'

Velayudhan paid no attention to them. He kept climbing without looking back. The *kannanthali* bushes on the hillside had all withered. The huge rock on the hillside looked like a wart on its belly. Velayudhan climbed up on it to gather the palmyra seeds scattered over it. What an amazing sight it was that he saw when he looked down from the crest of the rock! The serpent shrine lay below him and beyond it, the areca-nut grove. Between them, he could glimpse the tiled roof of his house. To the east, in the distance, were fields that had gone dry. On the other side was the red, clay-coloured road. The river, flowing beside a sandy bank, lay beyond. Memories surfaced in Velayudhan's mind when he saw the river bank. Memories of cucumber vines sprawling over the sand, cheruman children bringing cattle to the river to give them a bath, fishermen tying palm-leaves to ropes and dragging them across in their boats and Amma saying, 'Don't get out of the boat, child. There are octopuses in the water.' Wasn't it Amma who had said the octopus had a thousand heads?

He suddenly wanted to do somersaults on the sand. Achuthan Nair would not allow him to, nor would Uncle. No one ever allowed him to do anything. Muthassi was the only person who listened to him. But then, she would always say, 'You can do all that, Velayudhan. Just get well first.' Whatever he said, the reply was the same, 'Get well first'.

'It's all of you who are ill...don't make me say things...'

He must kill all of them, he thought, and set fire to that huge house. Then everyone would die. But no, Ammukutty must not die. When everything was burnt to cinders, only the two of them, he and Ammukutty, would be left. But how would they stay there alone? The whole house would be full of ghosts... the gatehouse, the *naalukettu*, the *pathayappura*. Muthassi knew all about the ghosts. Long ago, they had been senior members of the household. The one in the gatehouse was Uncle Chathu. At night, he had eaten a chicken that his niece had cooked for him and died, screaming for water. The chicken had been poisoned! No one had gone to him when he screamed. You could hear the screams of a man dying of thirst from the gatehouse even now. Velayudhan used to spend all night straining his ears to hear them.

When everything was burnt to ashes, they would find the copper pot in the *pathayappura*, filled with rupee coins and gold coins. If he were to have plenty of gold, he could build a big house on top of Tanni hill at the spot where the cheruman, Chathappan, had built a hut. A huge house, like a palace, with coloured windows bright with flowers, walls covered with paintings, golden dishes... a house as high as the sky.

Wait and see, it would all catch fire one night. The whole place would be in flames that licked up everything with their red tongues. He, Velayudhan, would pick up the copper pot filled with rupee coins and gold coins and walk quickly up to the top of Tanni hill. After that, he would swagger around like a prince, wearing gold-bordered clothes. Ammukutty would be dazzled!

What if he set fire to the place tonight? First of all, to the *pathayappura*? Uncle had to be burned first. Uncle had brought Achuthan Nair to stand guard over him and threatened to chop off his legs if he ever went out. Uncle had thrashed him with a palm branch once, just because he had placed a hand on Sankarankutty's shoulder—a branch thicker than Achuthan Nair's hairy arm!

Uncle would run wildly around all night, searching for the copper pot. But no one would find it. No one knew where exactly Uncle Thassan had buried it, not even Uncle Thassan himself!

Muthassi had told him that it had happened a long, long time ago. She did not remember exactly when. It was at the time when Muthassi's grandmother had been a little girl wearing only a red *konakam*. Uncle Thassan had made money selling paddy. Gold coins were the currency at that period. Uncle filled a copper pot with the coins and buried the pot in the yard. Then he became insane. He could not remember where he had buried the pot. Balancing an axe on his shoulder, he kept digging up the earth around the house. Finally, he died.

Even now, you could hear the sound of the axe hitting the ground. Velayudhan would lie awake all night listening to it. After dusk, he was scared to look at the *pathayappura*. Uncle Thassan would have set out with his axe... Poor Uncle Thassan! He was mad. They said you forgot everything if you went mad. Velayudhan had forgotten nothing, he remembered everything very clearly. He remembered Amma. He even remembered how they had buried her at a spot just beyond the cluster of palmyra trees. He remembered going to school with Ammukutty when he was a small boy. And how he had stood at the window and watched through the wooden bars when the mapillas beat a mad dog to death. When he went out, he had seen blood on the courtyard smeared with cow dung. He had felt sorry for the dog. It had been mad. But did they have to beat it to death because it was mad? When the wasps' hive was disturbed and they flew out over the fields, Velayudhan had panicked and hidden in the fields, among the paddy sheaves ready for harvesting. Ammukutty had been with him at the time. She had been a very small child then, not as pretty as she was now.

So many things had happened! He could remember all of them, so he was not mad. Certainly not. And yet, Sankarankutty, Gopi, Malu who lived next door—they all kept saying he was mad! It was they who were mad—they, their mothers and fathers. He must kill all of them, kill these people who made up stories just to craete trouble for him.

He needed a really sharp hatchet.

A little black kid who had been grazing among the *kannanthali* bushes put its head out and bleated softly. Velayudhan was startled. He climbed down the rock. Was it really a kid? He looked around again and did not see it. Could it have been Karineeli in the form of a kid? He glanced all around fearfully. Were there forms, black as the dark night, gathering here and there in the glittering sunlight? It seemed to him that the black rock nearby was raising its head, tossing it.

The darkness was slowly disappearing and darkness was flowing down the hillside. The darkness was full of fire-eating devils. As he stood there helplessly, gasping for breath, his eyes closed, he heard a voice come out of the darkness, 'Velayudhan!'

A rough hand touched his shoulder.

'Don't kill me... don't kill me...' he said terrified.

'Velayudhan!'

'Don't kill me... don't!' he repeated.

Shutting his eyes tight, he plunged through the darkness, still screaming, 'Don't kill me!'

Two

When the darkness moved away from his eyes, moonlight was playing hide-and-seek in the banana grove outside. It was pitch dark inside the room. He sat up on his mat and felt his forehead burning with pain. He leaned against the wall. There was no sound anywhere, nor any movement. Something moved among the shadows outside and black forms lurked here and there among them. But he was not afraid since he was inside the room. How could devils get in through a tiny window?

A sliver of sky was visible among the leaves of the papaya tree, and stars that were as pretty as the glass globes used to decorate the canopies over beds. As he looked at them, the bright stars suddenly became dark. Could there be black stars? He pressed his head on his knees. When he closed his eyes, small red and black bubbles burst from them and blossomed out…

He waited for light to filter through the room. Once it was daylight, the black shapes would run out of the clusters of banana trees and thickets and go off to hide elsewhere.

He tried to find out if Achuthan Nair had woken up and suddenly felt a surge of uncontrollable anger. The door had been locked from outside! This was unusual.

'Open the door,' he called out.

There was no answer.

He called out in a louder voice, 'Open the door!'

Nothing happened.

He kicked the door furiously, again and again. Let it shatter, he thought. The door opened.

Achuthan Nair came in, followed by Uncle. It scared him to see both of them together. Perhaps one of them would hold him tight and the other would thrash him. What were they going to do? If only he had a hatchet. One swing and both heads would fall down. He would hide the heads. He would not give them back even if they came asking for them. He stood with his eyes riveted to the ground, not looking at their faces.

Uncle said, 'I don't want to soil my hands, *eda*.' Achuthan Nair scratched the thicket of hair on his chest and said, 'If you act insolent, I'll churn your bones to water. Let me catch you going out again…'

'Don't let me hear a sound from you. If I do, I'll call the police and hand you over to them.'

I must chop off the policeman's head, thought Velayudhan.

'If I could get hold of a hatchet, I'd chop off your head,' he muttered softly. Uncle drew back a little and asked, 'Achuthan Nair, will he start attacking people?'

'He's just showing off.' Achuthan Nair looked at Velayudhan, rolled his eyes and said, 'If you try any tricks, I'll box your ears.'

'It's better to keep him locked up,' Uncle suggested.

Achuthan Nair locked the door and went away. After that, the door remained locked. Achuthan Nair took him out every morning and evening. Just for a short while. Velayudhan hated walking next to him, their shoulders rubbing.

Achuthan Nair was the only person who entered the room.

Now and then, he would hear Muthassi's voice beyond the door. 'It's all our misfortune, our misfortune…'

In the daytime, Velayudhan liked to sit near the small window on the western side. From there, he could see the banana grove, the papaya tree in the yard and the goat-shed. Gopi, Sankarankutty and the Thekkeppat children usually played under the papaya tree. Sometimes, they would come up to the small window, make faces at him and run away.

Once, Sankarankutty threw a stone at him and it hit his back. He had his revenge the next day, with a bell-metal tumbler. He was delighted to hear the sound the bell-metal made as it fell on a stone surface.

A scream arose outside. In a little while, Achuthan Nair opened the door and came in.

'If you harm the children, I'll make soup of your bones.'

Velayudhan thought, if only I had a hatchet…

'Will you try your tricks again? Do you want to go with the police?'

'I'll chop off your head, Achuthan Nair.'

'What did you say, rascal?'

Velayudhan muttered again, 'I'll chop off your head.'

'Have your fill then.' Achuthan Nair raised his hairy hand.

'Don't thrash me, don't…' Shrinking into a corner of the room, licking his lips that had the salty taste of tears, he beseeched in a voice like a moan, 'Please, don't thrash me…'

'Didn't I tell you to shut up?'

'Don't thrash me, don't…'

Muthassi kept saying, from outside, 'What a misfortune!'

When Achuthan Nair left, Velayudhan went back to the window, sobbing.

Gazing at the afternoon sun outside, he felt that darkness was flowing into the banana groves.

Afternoon sunshine, then darkness, appeared and faded in turns. When darkness gathered, he was afraid. What if arms stretched out through the dark, reaching out to him through the small window? Of devils that chewed on chunks of fire, or of Karineeli in flight, her hair wild and disheveled?

Velayudhan hated the night and the dark. He generally spent all night sitting up, leaning against the wall, listening carefully. Could he hear the sound of a stone hatchet hitting the ground? Was some thirsty person calling out for water from the gatehouse?

Tears fell on his dirt-smeared chest. He could not bear to look out, it was so painful. The afternoon sunlight was fading and darkness was flowing in, the darkness that nurtured fire-eating devils. He turned his face to the wall. He did not want to look out. Something was moving outside. He glanced cautiously over his shoulder.

A shudder ran through him. Her hair lay unbound over her shoulders. Was there fire in her mouth? Something tinkled—the bells on her feet?

He heard a soft voice. 'Kuttiettan!'

He lay with his face pressed to the ground, terrified.

'Kuttiettan, it's me...'

Fear and pain mingled in his whimpering voice. 'Don't kill me, don't...'

The small window was covered with a piece of palm-leaf matting.

Only the faint slivers of light that filtered in through the slits in the matting relieved the darkness now. As the days went by, the darkness in the room ceased to frighten him. He knew the black shapes lurking in the corners would not kill him. They had become his companions, whispering a hundred things in his ears.

He had many things to say to them as well. He was going to find the copper pot that Uncle Thassan had buried. He was going to build a mansion on top of the Tanni hill. He would sit on the seventh floor and watch the sandbank and the river over which boats glided.

At times, he saw eyes peering through the slits in the palm-leaf matting. He heard many voices.

'That young *thampuran*'s destiny...!'

'Just as well his mother died without having to witness all this.'

'Imagine, a grown-up man—what a pity!'

He did not want to listen to any of it.

He kept watching the little circles of light fall on the wall like rupee coins. He talked to the black companions who hid in the dark corners of the room.

One day, when Achuthan Nair brought his food on an iron plate, he threw up in front of Velayudhan. He left the plate outside the room, locked the door and went away. When he came back, he had a thick tamarind branch in his hand.

Velayudhan noticed the stick only when Achuthan Nair came right up to him and asked, 'Will you do it again? How many times I've told you that you must call me if you want to shit?'

The first blow fell on his shoulder. Velayudhan did not weep as he usually did. Anger blazed in his heart, in his eyes.

'Do you think you're going to burn me to death with your eyes?'

Another blow fell.

'Will you do it again? I'll cure you of this madness.' The tamarind branch twirled through the air.

'Will you repeat this?'

Hearing the commotion, Muthassi came to the door and Valiamma behind her.

Muthassi said in an unsteady voice, 'Don't, Achuthan. It's a sin in the eyes of God.'

'He's just being impudent, Kali Amma.'

Valiamma made her habitual proclamation, 'There's no better remedy than thrashing.'

Uncle arrived by this time. At the door, he covered his nose with his hand. Achuthan Nair explained what had happened. Velayudhan was taken out every morning and evening. Despite that, he had soiled the room. 'It's come to a point where we can't even lock him up in a room!' he said.

'What shall we do now? How can we live here if things go on like this? How can we even eat without wanting to throw up?'

'Why not lock him up in the room on the north?' suggested Uncle.

'It doesn't have a door. What if he turns that into a latrine too? It's too near the kitchen as well,' Achutan Nair replied.

Achuthan Nair thought it over, then whispered something in Uncle's ear.

Muthassi, who was standing near the door, blinking her rheum-filled eyes rapidly, overheard what he said. 'What a misfortune that I should have to see this happen with my own eyes.'

No one paid her any attention. She slowly crept away.

Velayudhan did not eat that day. He heard bits and pieces of the discussion Uncle and Achuthan Nair conducted in low voices outside the room. They had decided to kill him. They must have poisoned the rice they brought him. Like the poison that had killed the old uncle who died in the gatehouse, screaming for water—it had been mixed into the chicken-rice they gave him.

Velayudhan's whole body burned.

He flung the rice and vegetables that were in his iron plate on the ground. Ayyo! It was then that he saw that the floor was completely covered in shit. When had this happened? He could not help throwing up.

There was a sound behind the piece of matting that covered the small window. If only he had a hatchet! Achuthan would be waiting behind the window. Waiting to kill him. Two eyes peered through the slits in the palm-leaf matting.

Leaning back against the wall, full of fear, he said, 'I won't do it again, I won't...don't kill me.'

'Kuttiettan,' someone called very softly from outside.

'Who's that?'

'Don't you know, Kuttiettan. It's me, Ammukutty.' Ammukutty indeed! Ha, ha! He was amused. He made faces at the voice.

'Kuttiettan...'

He heard a stifled sob and imitated it perfectly. Then he burst into laughter that shook the walls. He heard the feeble voice call out again. He sprang up, gripped the bars of the window and shouted, 'I'll chop your head off!'

No, there were no sounds now. He was relieved. People kept tormenting him like this for fun. He stood holding on the window bars for a long time, until a gentle breeze began to blow in through the slits in the matting. It felt so pleasant when the cool air brushed against his burning shoulders. He felt very tired. Suddenly, he wondered—who had called out to him some time ago?

What was it that he had heard? Nothing seemed clear. He could not remember anything. It seemed as if he was groping in the dark for something he had lost.

The voice wafted to his ears again, 'Kuttiettan!'

Could it be true? His eyes filled with tears.

Picking up a shard of a broken earthenware pot, Velayudhan crouched on the ground and sketched the shape of a ladder. The slivers of darkness were slowly fading from his eyes.

Where was he now?

He glanced around. He was lying in the shed with a sloping roof that was attached to the northern side of the house. He felt a terrible throbbing in his head when he stood up. His legs hurt. When he moved, something jangled on his foot. A chain had been entwined around it. Bending down, he examined it. One end of it was fixed tightly to the wall. The skin on his ankle was red and raw where the chain had scraped against it. Who had wound this chain around his foot?

Velayudhan tried to remember when he had been brought to the shed. Who had done this to him? Were they teasing him for fun?

The floor was muddy and dirty. How filthy everything was!

He tried to remember. Nothing was clear. The events that must have taken place were as blurred as if seen through a mist. In the midst of all the confusion, a question kept surfacing over and over again. Were human beings ever chained up like dogs?

He had been ill. That must have been why he had been brought here. Still, were human beings ever put in chains like dogs?

Outside, the sun had set. In the *poovan* banana grove in the yard, a squirrel was drinking honey. Velayudhan watched him spring lightly from the tip of one leaf to the next, and bite open the outer peel of the banana flowers. He could hear sounds in the kitchen. If only someone would come out. They must have brought him to the shed because they thought he was ill. If someone came out, he could say, there's nothing wrong with me now, nothing wrong. Take off this chain.

Were human beings usually chained up like this?

Someone opened the kitchen window that opened onto the well and began to draw water. The pulley creaked. It must be Valiamma. Velayudhan called out, 'Valiamma, Valiamma…' There was no response.

Whom should he call out to? What strange people they were. There was nothing wrong with him, nothing.

He looked down at his body, covered with grime, and felt disgusted. Then he looked at himself again and was terribly ashamed. There was no *mundu* around his waist. If someone saw him, what would they think? Let no one see me, he prayed. He was not a small child, to go around without clothes. He had grown up, he really had. His rough beard rubbed against the skin of his neck, making it itch. And yet, to have no *mundu* around his waist… Velayudhan crouched on the ground. He must get hold of a *mundu*. But whom could he ask? Not Valiamma. He called out to Gopi repeatedly, in a loud voice. Please, let no one else come before he put on a *mundu*.

Someone came to the shed and asked, 'What's the matter?'

'Don't come in, please don't. Where's Gopi?'

'It's me, Gopi.'

Gopi wore striped red trousers and a shirt. He looked very smart.

'Why do you keep calling my name?'

'Bring me a *mundu*.'

'So you can tear it, right? No.'

'I won't tear it, Gopi. Bring me one quickly. Before anyone comes.'

Gopi hesitated.

'You're a good boy, aren't you? Please…'

Gopi went away and came back with a sparkling white *mundu*. Velayudhan was happy. The *mundu* was so clean.

'Will you tear it?'

'Tear it. Why?'

'If you're going to tear it, I won't give it to you.'

'Give it to me, Gopi. If anyone sees me like this…'

Gopi threw it to him from a safe distance.

Once he had draped the *mundu* around him, Velayudhan was relieved. It didn't matter if anyone came that side now.

'Who chained my foot to the wall?'

Gopi did not answer.

'Ask them to take the chain off.'

Gopi's only response was a gentle smile.

'Take it off, *eda*. Am I a dog?'

Gopi turned and walked off.

Was there no one who would come and take off this chain? He tried calling out to Muthassi. Then Valiamma. No one answered. No one would listen to him. He heard the clip-clop of wooden clogs in the courtyard. Uncle came and stood in front of the shed. Velayudhan stood up respectfully. It was not right to sit down in Uncle's presence.

'What is it, *eda*?'

Velayudhan was silent.

'Yes…?'

'Please take this off.'

'So that you can attack people again?'

'Why have you chained me up?'

'Because you're so impudent. Let me see if we can cure your madness.'

Uncle stomped away, his clogs clip-clopping loudly.

Velayudhan pondered—what impudence had he displayed? He had been ill but now there was nothing wrong with him, nothing at all. He wanted to proclaim it loudly—'There's nothing wrong with me. I'm not mad!'

He was very upset. Would no one come and take this chain off? Tears choked his throat. Would no one come? No one?

He kept gazing out helplessly. He could see the reddish sky through the leaves of the tamarind tree at the edge of the compound and wedged against it, a morsel of cloud painted black and red. He brushed the perspiration off his forehead, then stroked his foot. The chain jangled softly.

Fighting down tears, he thought over it all again. What had happened?

He had been ill. They had all said so. There's nothing wrong with me now though. Let me go… He leaned against the worn, ant-eaten pillar. He had been entirely naked a little while ago. Who would have seen him like that? Would Ammukutty have gone that way?

Ammukutty—if only he could see her. But she would be repulsed by him. His body was covered with dirt. If only he could look at his face. His beard had grown very long. When he scratched his matted hair, dust and dirt spattered around him.

There was never the slightest trace of filth on Ammukutty. If you stood next to her, there was a scent of herbal oil and screw pine flowers.

What if she saw him now…?

A secret he had guarded very closely came to mind when he thought of Ammukutty. No one knew it. Nor would he ever tell anyone. Once, they had sat close to each other under the mango tree in the outer yard, waiting for ripe mangoes to fall down. And he had reached out and bitten her cheek! She had lost her temper, pinched and scratched him. They had been children at that time. Now they had grown up so much!

So many things had happened since that day. Many of them were blurred images—like a closed door and a small window covered with palm-leaf matting. What had happened in that dark emptiness? When had this chain appeared on his foot?

'Kuttiettan, you'll soon be all right.' The soft voice floated on the air.

He had been ill. That's what all of them had said. Was it true? He wept, his face pressed between his legs. His tears upon falling on the sore spots bruised by the chains, felt like stings. Still, he felt comforted. He was completely cured now.

'There's nothing wrong with me. I'm not ill.'

He cried out loudly, 'Let me go, please let me go!'

No one came. Had no one heard him? Human beings were not usually chained. He was not a ferocious dog, after all.

'Let me go! Let me go, I say!'

He looked out hopefully from the edge of the veranda. Someone was peering over the wall. Was it Sankarankutty? Yes, it was.

'Sankarankutty!'

Sankarankutty came out from behind the wall.

'Come closer, Sankarankutty.'

Sankarankutty shook his head.

'Come closer, let me ask you something.'

'You want to beat me up, don't you?'

'No, I don't, Sankarankutty. I won't beat you up,' Velayudhan's voice was unsteady.

Sankarankutty still hesitated.

'I won't do anything to you.'

Timidly, Sankarankutty moved forward a bit.

'I've been told not to come here.'

'Who told you?'

'Father.'

'Who chained me up, Sankarankutty?'

Cowering in fear, Sankarankutty gave Velayudhan a look.

'Who?'

'Father asked the blacksmith to bring the chain.'

'Try and take it off.'

'No, I won't.'

'There's nothing wrong with me, Sankarankutty. Please take this off.'

'No, no, Kuttiettan. You're mad.'

Struggling not to weep, Velayudhan said, 'No, I'm not mad, Sankarankutty.'

Who would come and take this chain off? Muthassi would do it. At least, she would understand him. Or Ammukutty...

'Sankarankutty, go and call Muthassi.'

Sankarankutty clapped his hands and laughed loudly.

'Please call her.'

'You're mad, Velayudhan! Muthassi's dead!'

Velayudhan was shattered. What hurt more than the grief at Muthassi's death was the thought of the many things that had come to him in the darkness and he had not known. Many days and months... The chain jangled again.

Who would take this chain off? No one would listen to him, no one.

Velayudhan lowered his voice and whispered, 'Sankarankutty, call your Oppol, your elder sister.' Ammukutty would understand when he told her he was no longer ill.

'Don't you know that Oppol and my mother have gone away to Amma's house?' There was no mockery in Sankarankutty's expression, only pity.

'When did they leave?'

'It's been days. I went too. I just came back yesterday, with Father.'

'When will they come back?'

'They won't come back right now.'

'Why?'

'Don't you know? Oppol is getting married next month?'

Velayudhan did not ask any more questions. He had not known any of this. He had been sick. A closed door. A small window covered with palm-leaf matting. A rough, hairy hand.

'Kuttiettan, you'll soon be all right.'

It was now that he needed to see her. Ammukutty, there's nothing wrong with me. But she didn't know that. Wouldn't she come back, ever?

A woman came to the shed with rice and vegetables in an iron plate. Standing at quite a distance from him, she pushed the plate towards him. An elderly, bare-breasted woman with protruding teeth. He had no idea who she was. All the same, he said to her, 'Please take this chain off for me.'

She gave him an intimidating look. 'You must first be in your right mind.'

'There's ... there's nothing wrong with me. Let me go.' The woman spat noisily through her protruding teeth and went away, her expression stern and unrelenting.

He heard a commotion inside the house and recognised Valiamma's voice. She was scolding Gopi. 'He'll tear it to shreds now, won't he? Why did you give him a clean *mundu*?'

'It's the only one I could find, Amma.'

'What's the use of finding fault with you? It's you who's mad, not Velayudhan!'

Velayudhan longed to cry out, I'm not mad, Valiamma!

He was hungry. He gulped down most of the rice on the plate.

Darkness was slowly filling the banana grove. Someone was walking among the banana plants carrying a long stick with a sickle fastened to its tip. All he could see was the top of the stick. The sickle sliced off a banana flower. His mouth watered at the thought of the honey inside the flower. Ammukutty did not like the honey, what she always wanted was the white stamen hidden inside the flower. Janaky of Thekkepat liked the stamen too. Whenever they got hold of a flower, they would fight over it...

'We'll toss a leaf to decide who gets it.'

'Let me toss it.'

'No, let Kuttiettan do that.'

He would pluck a leaf and ask, 'Heads or tails?' Ammukutty would stand still with her eyes closed until the leaf fell, saying she was praying to Bhagavathi. She must be in her mother's *tharavad* now. Why had she gone there? She had always lived here, from the time she was a child. He remembered the lane scattered with the tiny seeds of the Indian liquorice, speckled bright red and black. He had visited Ammayi's house with Amma. There were so many liquorice plants growing by the boundary of the compound that the sand in the lane was always covered with seeds. The house was by a canal. He tried to recall it—a room with pretty coloured glass globes hanging from the ceiling, and a deer's antlers on the wall took shape in his mind. What would Ammukutty be doing there now?

Maybe she had just come from her bath and was standing below the grinding stone on the northern veranda, running her fingers through the strands of her outspread hair. Would she never come back here?

If only he see Ammukutty once more. She would not come back here after she got married. If only he could see her... Velayudhan rubbed his itchy back against the wall. The chain on his foot jangled. If he could somehow get the chain off, he could escape from the shed. He tried tugging at it. All that happened was that his fingers started to hurt. Would it never come off? Would no one come and take it off?

Valiamma passed by the shed on her way to tether the goat. He called out to her timidly. She did not even turn around to look at him.

Gopi and Sankarankutty were seated in the portico intoning their prayers. 'Nama Shivaaya…'

When the bare-breasted woman came to take the plate away, he pleaded with her, 'Won't you take this chain off for me?'

'Why, so that you can attack people again?'

He wiped his moist eyes and looked up at the sky. It was the colour of gleaming wet hair. Searching as far as his eyes could reach, he could make out only a single pale star flickering faintly.

The children finished chanting their prayers and he heard Uncle's voice reading the Ramayanam. Light streamed through the window of the northern room into the yard in front of the shed.

Lanterns moved to and fro inside the house. Vessels clattered in the kitchen. No one would come this side now. He said softly to the darkness, 'Let me go, let me go.' He wondered, wouldn't there be someone in the neighbouring house? Someone who would take the chain off his foot?

He attempted to shout loudly, 'Ayyo! Amma!' A lamp appeared at the edge of the veranda and a voice cried out, 'Velayudhan!'

'Let me go, let me go…'

'Shut up and lie down, or I'll beat your bones to pulp!'

The lamp disappeared.

The sounds and movements inside the house gradually died down. The light that had pierced the darkness in the yard also faded. Once again, he tugged at the chain on his foot. If only it would loosen, he would be free. After that, whoever came to torture him would meet his death.

Ferocious dogs were kept chained up. But human beings…if only he could loosen the chain. All he needed was for one link to snap, just one link.

They kept saying he was mad. It was they who were mad! Otherwise, would they torture people for no reason at all?

'There's nothing wrong with me. I'm not mad.' He tugged at the chain repeatedly, not giving up even when his fingers hurt.

Short of breath, he lay prone, gasping, his eyes closed.

When he opened his eyes, he realised he had been dreaming. Muthassi had often cradled him on her lap when he was a child and told him the story of the prince who had discovered a ruby. A demon had chained up a princess in a mansion under a huge lake, with a chain that fire could not melt nor metal cut through. An old woman who came to collect firewood in the forest gave the prince a dagger over which she had cast a spell in the form of a *mantram*, a divine incantation. When the prince chanted the *mantram* and pointed the dagger at the chain that bound the princess, it crumbled to pieces. The prince and princess climbed on white horses and rode off to a seven-storeyed mansion on top of a hill covered with *kannanthali* flowers.

Velayudhan opened his eyes at that point. There was no mansion, no ruby, no white horses. A faint streak of the moonlight flowed into the shed. Shadows drew patterns in the courtyard. He had to think for a moment before he knew where he was. He moved and the chain jangled. Furious, he pressed his feet against the wall, gripped the chain tight and yanked it with all the force he could muster.

If only one link would give way, just one.

'Amma!' He fell backwards. The chain had snapped. When he stood up, he felt as if his entire body had been smashed into little pieces. He limped down to the courtyard. With each step he took, the links in a length of the chain that still remained wound around his foot jangled. He went down the steps, pushed open the door of the gatehouse and stepped out.

In front of him lay a field. Walking over a high path that stretched out over the field like its spine, he thought to himself—where would he go now? The most urgent need he felt was to get away as far as possible from that shed. If they found him in the morning, the chain would be around his foot again. He had to go away, it did not matter where. The chain jangled softly in tune with the rustle of the paddy sheaves in the breeze. A dog whined pitifully from the southern bank. It must be a dog that had been chained up, he thought.

Thanks to the faint light of the moon, it was not difficult to see where he was going. Above him, the sky looked very pale. The tinkle of the chain kept breaking the night's frozen silence.

The field ended where the road began. He climbed onto the road through screw pine bushes. The river ran alongside.

In the morning, when they came, they would discover that the dog named Velayudhan was no longer lying chained up in the shed. The thought made him want to laugh out loud. But they would certainly come looking for him. He had to escape before they caught up with him. Where could he go? No one would believe him or listen to what he had to say.

He murmured to himself, 'I'm not mad. I'm not ill.'

'Kuttiettan, you'll be all right.' It was Ammukutty who had said that.

Dear Ammukutty, there's nothing wrong with me. She was the only one who was sure to believe him.

The road was wet, maybe because of the dew. He had forgotten when he had last come this way last. It was years ago. He walked past a row of closed shops and the mosque near the ferry.

He felt no fear as he went past the forest of creepers and the banyan trees where they said devils lived. Above him, the sky kept growing brighter and light was gradually creeping into the shadows around. He stopped for a while, near a stone platform on which wayfarers rested their loads. The east was turning reddish. Where was he now? Catching sight of a little island in the middle of a field, he recognised the spot. There was a mapilla school on the island. Beyond it, at the edge of the field, was a large pond and a small temple. He used to go there every month to worship, with his mother. A folk play had been staged once, in the field in front of the school where bull races were usually held. A bluish mist enveloped the field. Velayudhan stepped down into it. As he walked along, the chain tinkling at every footstep, he saw a dark figure coming from the opposite direction with a yoke balanced on its shoulder. The figure stopped in front of him.

'Who's there?'

Velayudhan did not reply. He hesitated a moment, then took a step forward. The man flung the yoke on the path and sprang into the field. Ignoring him, Velayudhan walked on. It felt good when the mellow sunlight touched his limbs. Standing straight up in the middle of the field which stretched well beyond his line of vision, he looked all around him. Cherumi women coming that way with earthenware pots on their heads jumped down as soon as they caught sight of him and fled into the fields, ripe for harvesting.

'A madman, a madman...' He heard hoots and cries behind him and quickened his pace. Was it him they were chasing? A field where young paddy shoots were being cultivated for transplantation lay at a slightly higher level. As he climbed into it, the sharp leaves of the screw pine tore at his feet, bruising them. He entered a lane and heard the uproar behind him growing louder. However, people coming from the side opposite him did not bar his way and this was a relief. Each person who came face to face with him simply moved out of his path and ran away. He felt sad, not afraid.

'I'm not mad, I'm not...'

Behind him, people shouted, 'A madman, a madman!'

At the end of the lane, he stopped for a while and put his arms around a huge stone that stood upright. He felt exhausted. He was about to walk on again when someone roared from the back, 'Stay there, you!' Here was a big-built man with a turban on his head and a grey moustache.

'I told you to stay there! I've caught bigger villains than you and tied them up,' he said.

Velayudhan gasped, 'I'm not mad, I'm not.'

'I'll cure you of your madness!'

Twirling a bamboo stick that he had kept hidden until then behind his back, the man came towards him. Terror blazed like a fire in Velayudhan's heart. The stick was going to fall on his head.

He picked up a huge, rounded stone from the ground and raised it threateningly. The man retreated and Velayudhan walked on.

The lane led to the hill. The path going up the hill was steep, but Velayudhan climbed it hurriedly. At the top of the hill, he saw the *pala* tree under which the *talappoli* festival was always held and the small temple built of red laterite next to it. He remembered the spot very well. If you went downwards from the *pala* tree, you would come to a cashew garden. Beyond that, was a lane and the canal... Bright red-and-black liquorice seeds would be scattered on the ground by the gate of the house that stood on the side of the canal.

Dear Ammukutty, I am not mad...

The hillside was deserted except for a huge black bull that was wandering over it.

When Velayudhan's feet sank into the grass, little drops of water kept spurting out. There was not a soul around. He would be at peace here.

By the time he reached the *pala* tree, his knees felt as if they would collapse. He sat down on the stone platform built around the tree. A cool breeze blew, making him want to close his eyes. His back ached agonisingly. He lay down, pressing his face into the wet grass.

He woke up from his slumber with a start, with a feeling that something had fallen on his back. He sat up and saw a group of cowherds some distance away, carrying prods and wearing umbrella-hats. They were staring at him. Another stone hurtled towards him, fell in front of him and ricocheted over his head.

Velayudhan got up nervously, the chain on his foot jangling.

The little group followed him as he started to walk. Stones kept being pelted at him. Dragging the chain over the rocky path, he ran down the slope. He turned and looked back as soon as he reached the lane.

A loud cry escaped him, 'Amma!' He wiped his forehead and saw blood on his hand.

'Catch him, catch him!'

'Here he comes! Move away, everyone!' He climbed down into the field and saw people fleeing in all directions. A little child standing by the roadside screamed, 'A madman! He'll attack you, move away!'

There was an uproar behind him again. Keeping to the edge of the field, Velayudhan reached the bank of the canal. He entered the lane, thickly bordered with trees on both sides and saw tiny speckled bright red-and-white seeds scattered over the ground. He remembered all those times he had played in this lane as a child. Then he saw the wall of red laterite and the house, crowned by a wooden statue of Hanuman holding himself ready to take a leap. His heart thudded rapidly. It was there that Ammukutty lived.

All he wanted was to see her. 'Ammukutty, I'm no longer ill. There's nothing wrong with me now, nothing,' he wanted to tell her. He climbed the steps to the house.

A child sat in the courtyard, on the platform built around the *kuvalam* tree, making a ball out of palm leaves. The large courtyard, coated with cow dung, lay bathed in mellow sunshine. Standing in front of the massive house, Velayudhan looked around him. The little boy picked up the ball he was making and ran inside.

Ammukutty! Wasn't Ammukutty there? He took a few steps forward, keeping to the edge of the yard.

He saw a woman hanging wet clothes on the clothesline. The chain jangled softly. The woman turned to look at him.

For a moment, Velayudhan was stunned. He looked at her face.

'A…a..Ammukutty!'

The woman flung the clothes that lay over her arms on the ground, sprang up to the veranda and shouted loudly, 'A madman! A madman!'

He wanted to say, it's me, Ammukutty. I'm not mad. But his tongue refused to move. He called out again, 'Ammukutty!'

But she had rushed into the house and disappeared. A cacophony of voices moved from within the house to the portico.

'A madman…!'

'Get me a stick and go inside!'

'A madman!'

Velayudhan did not wait any longer. Running his tongue over his lips, he found they tasted salty from the blood dripping down his forehead.

Dragging the chain on his foot, Velayudhan ran out of the gate. Although he was exhausted to the point of collapse, he ran with the speed of a cyclone. Behind him, he heard the rattle of tin cans. Hoots and cries followed him unceasingly. He rushed through the gatehouse into the courtyard of his house and saw Uncle seated in the portico with two men. They all got up, startled, hearing the sound of the jangling chain.

Velayudhan waited for a while, holding on to the wall. He watched Uncle take down the stick he kept between the rafters and come down to the yard. His tired, blurred eyes ran over his own body and he realised that he had lost the *mundu* he had been wearing around his waist.

He limped to the veranda and fell down. Uncle and his companions came up and stood around him.

Gasping for breath, Velayudhan stammered, 'I am mad. Put me in chains.'

Glossary

Ammayi	Uncle's wife
Bhagavathi	Goddess; usually Durga
Cheriambran	Young master. Formerly, Hindus belonging to the backward caste used to address male members of the higher caste as 'Thampuran'. 'Cheria Thampuran' was colloquially shortened 'Cheriambran'
Cheruman	Man belonging to a backward community called 'Cherumars'
Edathi	Elder sister, sometimes suffixed to a name as in Devakiedathi
Ettan	Elder brother, sometimes suffixed to a name as in Velayudhettan
Karanavar	Eldest male member of the family who would be head of the matrilinear joint family in Kerala
Konakam	A long piece of material used to cover the genitals; can be made of cloth or a tender palm-spathe
Kuruthiparambu	An enclosure erected in order to perform a special puja called the 'kuruthi sacrifice', dedicated to the Mother Goddess
Mana	The residence of a Namboodiri, a Kerala Brahmin

Mundu	An ankle length piece of cloth worn around the waist by men and women in Kerala
Naalukettu	A house built around a rectangular courtyard which is open to the sky; the word also refers to the courtyard itself
Onam	The most important festival in Kerala; also a harvest festival (According to legend the festival commemorates the annual visit to Kerala of Mahabali, the demon king, who was banished to the underworld by Vishnu)
Pathayappura	The wing of a house, usually two-storeyed (The word also means the place where grain is stored, but in the context of the story, it's really a separate wing of the house)
Pulaya	A man belonging to another backward community, the 'Pulayars'
Pulayi	A woman of the Pulayar community
Talappoli	A procession of young girls who carry platters with lighted wicks, flowers and rice arranged on them
Tharavad	The extended Namboodiri/Nair household; in the case of Nairs, the extended matrilinear household
Thampurankutty	Young master (See *Cheriambran* above)
Thekkini	The southern wing of the naalukettu
Thrikkakara appan	Clay image of Vishnu kept in the courtyard of the house during Onam
Vadikkini	A room in the northern wing of the naalukettu, adjacent to the kitchen, to which women have free access
Valiamma	Mother's elder sister
Vettuva	People belonging to a backward community in Kerala; they are professional coconut-pickers

Kaalam

Translated from the Malayalam by
Gita Krishnankutty

And when I woke, the marrow
Out of my bones ran out
that you were the friend I
                                        dreamt for
But not the dream I woke for
And so I put this down for
Doubt for doubt.

—Ezra Pound

Translator's Preface

Born in 1934 in the village of Kudallur in the Palakkad district of Kerala, M. T. Vasudevan Nair (known affectionately as M.T. to his friends and readers) grew up against a backdrop of lush paddy fields, with coconut and areca nut palms dipping and swaying in the winds, heavy with the fragrance of mango and jackfruit, in the vicinity of the river he loved, the Bharatha Puzha, which is believed to have nurtured some of Kerala's finest writers and poets on its banks. Kudallur provides the setting for much of his work. Its changing seasons, the rhythms of its agricultural cycle and the dreams and hopes of its people have never ceased to offer him rich material.

The youngest of four boys, M. T. longed passionately from the time he was very young to be a writer. He recalls repeatedly in many articles and interviews a childhood incident that left a deep impression on him. While he was still a schoolboy, he was sent one day to a neighbouring village to fetch a handwritten copy of Changampuzha's well known poem, *Ramanan*. It was lent on condition that it would be returned the next day. The boy brought it home and watched with astonishment while his brothers and sister-in-law sat up all night copying it out. "All this passion and hard work to copy out a poem?" he mused.

He began to read Malayalam poetry himself—the works of the great triad Vallathol, Kumaranasan and Ulloor; he also read Balamani Amma, G. Sankara Kurup, Changampuzha, Idassery, Vylopilli. He was fascinated to discover that the words they used were familiar to him, only the arrangements were new and magical. Mesmerised by the verses he read and learnt by heart, he took to wandering over the hillsides, chanting them aloud.

He went on to devour all the short stories that he could lay his hands on, stories by Basheer, Thakazhi, Lalithambika Anterjanam, S. K. Pottekkat, Karoor Neelakanta Pillai, Keshavadev. These writers became his heroes—he would cut out their pictures from magazines and paste them on the walls of his room. His desire to join their ranks grew rapidly.

M. T. began to write at the age of fourteen. He sent the stories he wrote to all the magazines that he could find the addresses of, his only problem being to somehow get hold of the three quarters of an anna that he needed to despatch them by post. In 1953, he won a prize for a short story competition organised by the weekly *Mathrubhumi* for his story "Circus Animals" (Valarthumrigangal). He never looked back after that.

M. T. has always said that the short story is his favourite literary form. He has eighteen short story collections to his credit. "In a short story you can almost achieve perfection. Structurally, it is closer to a poem. You go on chiselling it, removing unwanted portions till you finally get the exact form."[1] He continues to experiment with this form and some of his finest short stories, "Sherlock" and "Stone Inscriptions," for example, have appeared in this decade. If a tendency to sentimentalize mars some of his earlier work, his later prose is very finely honed, elegantly crafted and disciplined. Ayyappa Paniker points out that there are few writers whose style and craft have changed so much and so effectively within a lifetime.[2]

However, M. T. has not confined himself to short stories. He has written eight novels, all of which have been widely read and appreciated in Kerala, a play, and several successful screenplays. He was one of the first writers in Malayalam to invest fiction with a dimension that moved beyond the description of character and event and gave greater importance to thought and emotion, that examined the human mind and analyzed its secret desires and longings. His protagonists, both in the novels and the short stories, are generally outsiders, isolated from family and society, victims of circumstance, introspective and often full of self-loathing.

Kaalam (1969) is his sixth novel. It describes the life of the protagonist Sethu from the age of fifteen to thirty, the inexorable movement from a dream-filled, ambitious youth, confident that it can reach out and possess the whole world, to a maturity where material and social success go hand in hand with an overwhelming sense of disillusion and a tragic consciousness of failure. Although the novel is not strictly autobiographical, M. T. confesses, "Sethu of *Kaalam* is a lot like me. I share with Sethu his emotional experiences and the situations he has been through."[3] Many of the characters in the novel were a part of the life of his village as well.

Written in lyrical prose, the novel captures the changing moods and seasons of the landscape of M.T.'s childhood. The river, a mute witness to every crisis in Sethu's life, mirrors his journey from adolescence to an adulthood empty of hope and love. At the end of the novel, it lies as parched and dry as his own heart. Marked by his experiences, the river is transformed from the rippling surface over which the ferry boat had carried Sethu to his new life as a college student into a stretch of dry sand, "dreaming of floods," which he must cross in order to return to the meaningless existence he has carved out for himself in the city as Sethu Mudalali. M. T.'s sensitive portrayal of Sethu, of his capacity to analyze himself and his ability to realize what is happening to him at every instant, the fine portraits of the multitude of other characters and the evocative images of the Kudallur landscape give the novel its emotional intensity and a remarkable richness of texture.

The disintegrating matrilinear tarawad system of the Nairs of Kerala, its conflicts and problems, its petty rivalries and burning jealousies, which were part of the background that M.T. grew up against, furnished him with an inexhaustible fund of material. The sambandham system of marriage followed by the Nairs, in which men entered into contractual relationships with their wives and visited them in their houses, was still in force when M.T. was a child. To an outsider, it may not be immediately clear that the men in Sethu's household are visiting husbands who do not form strong or lasting bonds with their wives and children. His father, for example, is deeply attached to his own sisters and their children—an attachment that Sethu's mother detests both for its own sake and also because she believes that it influences him to give his sisters' children the greater part of his earnings. Sethu's own relationship with his father is ambivalent and unsatisfactory, he is haunted by the feeling that his father does not appreciate him and is reluctant to help him. His father's house, Pushpoth, where his paternal aunts live, and where he can go only as an honoured guest, symbolizes a happiness and security that he cannot attain at home, that he covets deeply and contrasts resentfully to his own dilapidated house with its chipped floor, its worm-eaten wooden pillars and its total absence of comfort.

Sethu's aunt, Cheriamma, has two visiting husbands. The first terminates his relationship with her when he stops visiting her regularly; the second moves into her household after taking his share of his own tarawad property and is obviously regarded as something of a parasite. Madhava Ammama, Sethu's uncle, moves briefly to Vadakkethu when he marries Devu, only to return to his sisters when things start to go badly there. However, Sethu's brother Parameswaran brings his wife home, but both move out when his mother quarrels with her daughter-in-law. They are representative of the new generation, Sethu's generation, which finally breaks away from the joint family system.

The real protagonist of the novel is kaalam itself, the ceaseless flow of time that shapes Sethu's life, alienating him from everyone and everything he loves and carrying him from one mistake to the next. The word "kaalam" holds within it a deep consciousness of the present, the past, and the future and an implicit awareness of the unrelenting passage of time. The title of the novel has been left untranslated because "time," the nearest English equivalent of "kaalam," suggests neither its complex connotations nor its infinite span.

The novel has forty-one chapters which are divided into seven sections. The first five sections deal with Sethu's life as a college student, his hopes and aspirations. In the sixth section, he searches for a job and finds one with great difficulty, only to lose it. The seventh and final section unfolds the stages of Sethu's transformation into Sethu Mudalali. Except for the third and fourth sections, where the perspective shifts from Sethu to his uncle Madhava Ammama, the rest of the novel revolves steadily around Sethu. Moving backward and forward in the time span allotted to each section, the novel sometimes concentrates on short periods marked by great intensity of feeling and sometimes condenses long periods into a single chapter. In the last part of the novel, for instance, the events of nine years flash rapidly through Sethu's mind when he returns to his house after a very long absence.

In *Naalukettu* (1958) and in *Asuravithu* (1960), M.T.'s other long novels of the earlier period, the protagonists avenge themselves on their families and on society for the sufferings they have endured, but Sethu of *Kaalam* misses fulfilment in every aspect of life—with the three women he loves and betrays, in all his personal relationships with the members of his family or with friends and colleagues, in his career which forces him into a pattern of action he detests. He is bitterly conscious of each successive failure but is never able to extricate himself from its unhappy consequences. In spite of all this, perhaps because of his tendency for relentless self-analysis, he emerges in the final instance as a person who somehow manages to keep his dreams alive even when he knows for certain that he cannot achieve them. It seems possible then to hope that the poem trapped in the morning sunlight shimmering on the parched river, struggling to find words, as Sethu leaves home for the last time, may still take shape.

1. "Vanajam Ravindran in Conversation with M.T. Vasudevan Nair," in *Wordsmiths*, ed. Meenakshi Sarma, Katha (1996), 205.
2. M. M. Basheer ed. *Kathayum Porulum*, Current Books (1996), 146.
3. "Vanajam Ravindran in Conversation with M.T. Vasudevan Nair," in *Wordsmiths*, ed. Meenakshi Sarma, Katha (1996), 207.

Kinship Terms

Achan	:	father
Amma	:	mother
Ammama(n)	:	mother's brother
Cheriachan	:	father's younger brother or mother's younger sister's husband
Cheriamma	:	mother's younger sister
Edathi	:	elder sister
Ettan	:	elder brother
Muthassi	:	grandmother
Oppu	:	elder sister

Part One

Night.

Grasshoppers, asleep in the newly sprouted shoots of karuka grass at the edge of the rain-drenched field, wake up startled at the sound of footsteps. They brush against my calves as I walk and rustle softly, evoking a memory that my troubled heart cannot define. When had I last heard this familiar, happy sound?

Scent of wet earth and the grey dark. It suddenly occurs to me that darkness and the night have a scent. The paths picked out by the men who came to spray the fields are full of pools of stagnant water which still reflect an overcast sky, even though the rain has stopped.

The flaming torch ahead lights our way.

I can hear the old cheruman gasping as he walks behind me carrying my tin trunk and mattress. The murmur of the river grows clearer as we leave the fields behind and climb onto the rough country road.

We stop and listen to the river ripple beneath the ferry boat, which is anchored to a stake on the shore. A river of darkness, with an endless stretch of half-light above. Do I hear train wheels roar over the trembling steel railroad bridge on the farther shore?

The ferryman, a sleep-dazed shadow, emerges from his hut. He knows the train timings by heart.

Is this the four thirty train? I dare not ask. For I am no longer an ignorant little boy. I am sixteen years old and on my way to college in a city fifty-three miles away, where a sultan once built a fortress. I am a young man now; I grew up in the space of a night.

(A night that has stayed undimmed in my memory all these years, as vivid as the sight and smell of fresh blood.)

The ferryman hangs his smoky, soot encrusted lantern over the boat and begins to bale out water with a palm spathe. I hear a pigeon coo inside my heart, a solitary temple pigeon that had descended on the tiled roof at dusk.

The river, the ferry boat.

The river I have crossed so many times to go to the eye doctor's house, the temple, the cucumber fields. And the ferry boat that still waits for me, after all these years.

Will the cheruman hold the tin trunk steady on the boat's seat? I don't want it to slip and fall when the boat moves. But I dare not say, "Chathappa, hold the trunk carefully, don't let it fall."

I place my hands firmly on the plank behind me and balance myself so that my clean, starched mundu, folded and tucked above my knees, does not get wet. The huts on the deserted shore begin to take shape in the morning light.

Cold water seeps into our footprints as we walk over the wet sand. I wish we could walk faster. Do I hear the steel bridge clatter? Embers fall from the torch and burn out on the moist sand. The worn railroad track flashes silver in the soft darkness.

I feel more frightened than happy.

Ammaman strides ahead, swinging his huge hands, his mundu folded and tucked above his knees, a towel wound around his head. He turns and calls.

"Hurry up, boy."

His voice is unnecessarily loud. They always talk too loudly, the grown-ups—Amma, Cheriamma, Ammama, that rare visitor, Parameswara Ettan—so that I never recall their faces, only their loud voices.

Careful now, there are sharp fragments of stone scattered over the sleepers on the railroad track.

Suddenly, I forget the four thirty train, the red signal lights, the city I had been trying so hard to imagine yesterday. I know it is foolish to feel sad, for I am not really going away. No, this uneasiness in my heart is not sorrow. And my eyes smart only because . . . yes, because the sweat makes the oil from my hair dribble into them.

The memory of the infinitely soft rustle of the grasshoppers moving through the field suddenly comes to mind. They sound exactly like press studs snapping open on a blue blouse.

Why had I not remembered earlier? As I walk faster over the sleepers, I accuse myself with all the fervour of a sixteen-year-old—why, why, had I not remembered earlier?

1

Sethu washed his face once more, sprinkled the last handful of water from the copper pot on his face and neck, came back to the eastern verandah and sat down with his back against the pillar.

Outside, the afternoon sun blazed. It was unbearably hot. An occasional breeze that strayed through the areca palms seemed laden with flames. If only the floor had been swept and mopped with a wet cloth, he could have lain on it. But it was dirty, cracked, and full of dust.

It was not yet time to go to the post office. Perhaps there would be a letter from Achan today. Parameswara Ettan had promised to send thirty rupees a month. If Achan sent the rest, he could go to college. Ettan had refused to write and ask Achan. Amma had written. Achan's reply had been full of complaints: he was ill, the work on the estate was not as lucrative as it used to be. Sethu had read the letter out to Amma and then gone through it again. No, it said nothing about him, Sethu. He had enclosed a letter of his own along with Amma's reply. That was nine days ago. Letters from the Anamalais usually took only two days to come.

If you watched from the hillside, you could see the mail train crossing the bridge. Sethu always made sure the red mailbox was on the train before he left for the post office. Even so, he often arrived there earlier than the local runner with corn-infested feet who brought the mail from Kuttippuram.

He would sleep till four. It was pleasant to lie with his head against the railings, where Amma slept during the summer.

He could not bear to look out. Flames seemed to hang over the fields. The sand beyond was white hot and he dared not keep his eyes on it for more than a minute.

They had hoped it would rain for Vishu, but it had not rained even for the talappoli festival at the Srirankara temple, later in the year. Cheriamma said she had never seen such a hot summer all her life. She said so every year, and always predicted that people would be scorched to death. Nobody ever died though.

"Sethu, have you seen Padmu?"

That was Cheriamma, from the verandah above.

"No."

"Wretched girl, she'll fall into a tank or a well one day. Children should be obedient. Wait till I get my hands on her."

Cheriamma would begin now to describe all the ways in which she would punish Padmu. He said,

"She must be playing next door."

Cheriamma slapped Padmu for the most trivial reasons and hit her with anything that came to hand. Whenever she quarrelled with Amma, she usually took it out on Padmu. Not that Amma cared. Padmu would sob until she was out of breath and then Amma would tell Sethu to take her away. "If she dies, there'll be no one except me to haul her body away."

Hours later, Cheriamma would give Padmu an oil bath and smear her forehead with vibhuti. She would take her on her lap, caress her and cry.

Cheriamma would pace up and down the verandah, her shabby undergarment visible beneath an inadequate little towel wrapped around her waist. She never wore a rowka in summer, preferring to leave her breasts uncovered. She would not go in even if there were visitors. Sethu often thought to himself angrily, wretched woman, why did she have to stay on the verandah half-clothed?

Even Madhava Ammama did not dare say anything to her. After all, he was younger than Amma or Cheriamma, so they did not have to listen to him.

Cheriamma said, "I left a fan here this morning. Where is it?"

Sethu did not answer. She had not asked him directly. All she needed when she began to talk was someone in her vicinity.

"There's not a soul to help me. Only plenty of people to torture me."

Cheriamma wiped her discoloured lips and spat into the courtyard. She was ready for a fight. "I had to ask a hundred people before Chathappan's son finally brought me a spathe to make the fan. Now everyone wants it!"

Sethu maintained an angry silence. Amma complained, to no one in particular, "I'm not allowed a little rest even in the afternoon."

Cheriamma shook out the last of the snuff from the bottle tucked in at her waist, inhaled it, wiped her nose and laughed contemptuously into the sunlight.

"Can't open my mouth, can I? Everything I say is wrong. Kalyani is the abandoned one, she has no one to speak for her. Tell me, boy, did I say anything wrong? All I said was that I left a fan here and that I can't find it now."

Sethu turned away, unwilling to play the role of a witness. When would he escape from all this?

Amma would not give in. Sethu went down the steps and walked up to the fence. Devu called out from the illam compound,

"Sethu, is Madhavettan there?"

"No."

"Tell him that Kunhathol wants to see him when he comes back."

It was Madhava Ammama who looked after the affairs of the illam, now that Kunjan Namboodiri had died. He had the areca nuts plucked and sold and collected the paddy from Govindan, the tenant-farmer. Kunhathol had great faith in Madhava Ammama. She knew he would not cheat her. And he seemed happy with whatever she gave him now and then.

Cheriamma complained that Madhava Ammamma never gave her even a quarter anna for snuff, in spite of what he made from the banana garden and his earnings as the manager of the illam.

Amma always defended him, "He's a man, after all, he needs money for his own expenses."

Sethu listened. Was the quarrel over? No. Amma had moved into the verandah, ready for battle.

What if he picked up a fallen palm spathe from Kunhathol's compound, made a fan with it and threw it into the verandah? No, it would not stop them. Both women loved to quarrel. Amma always won—after all, it was she who ran the household. Which meant that Padmu would surely be beaten today.

When Cheriamma's husband was alive, she had squabbled with him all the time. He used to sit like an ascetic, wearing a small mundu that barely covered him decently and stroke his beard and listen to her. He was Cheriamma's second husband. The first one was Kandulikkaran Krishnan Nair. He had had a sambandham relationship with her for two years.

Amma often accused Cheriamma. "A woman should stand in her man's shadow."

"And are all the noble ones who lived in their man's shadow prospering now? Don't provoke me." Cheriamma would retort. What she implied was that my father gave everything he earned to his nephews and nieces.

Actually, Cheriamma's husband, Krishnan Nair, had not been rich in those days. He used to take over the tenancy of an empty plot of land once the paddy had been harvested, and sow sesame seeds in it. Or bid for pieces of land near the river that had not been entrusted to tenant farmers and grow cucumbers in them. Amma had thought well of him, he was considered to be the sort who cared about his family. And she had had proof of this when Parameswara Ettan was a child. He had fallen ill once and nearly died. Vaidyan Kudumundukkaran could do nothing for him. Everyone thought he would die. Krishnan Nair had crossed the river at the dead of night and brought a washerwoman from five miles away. She was old and blind, could hardly walk and seldom went anywhere. But Krishnan Nair had persuaded her to come home. They arrived at daybreak and as soon as the old woman placed some herbal medicine on the child's forehead and chest and began to chant mantrams, Ettan had opened his eyes.

We lost touch with Krishnan Nair when he stopped visiting Cheriamma. All we knew was that he had left the village. After Cheriachan surrendered his property to his nephew and came to live with us, we once heard that Krishnan Nair was in business in Pazhani and that he had sent his sister five hundred rupees.

A pujari who had gone from our village to the temple at Pazhani for Thaipooyam told us that Krishnan Nair had done well for himself and made money, that he had a wife and children.

Krishnan Nair came to the village five years ago, a few days before Parameswara Ettan's wedding. Achan was at home. Madhava Ammama and Ettan had gone to Kunnamkulam to buy clothes.

A man in a blue shirt and a gold bordered veshti opened the gate. Krishnan Nair.

He had white stone earrings in his ears, gold chains on his neck and left wrist, huge rings on his fingers. An image of Krishna playing the flute was tattooed on his arm. Amma grew very agitated. There was a small commotion to serve him tea and snacks.

Achan and Krishnan Nair had much to tell each other. Amma came to the front door from time to time to join the conversation.

"Is Appu Nair at home?"

"He was here a while ago." Only Sethu had observed Cheriachan go to Vadakkethu.

When he was leaving, Krishnan Nair asked Amma, "Where's Kalyani Amma?"

Sethu thought Cheriamma would stay inside, nursing Padmu. But she had come, with Padmu on her hip, pulling her grey hair back over her left ear. Sethu saw her make an effort to smile.

"Are you all right?" Krishnan Nair bared his gold teeth in a smile, his hand on the door.

Cheriamma made a sound of assent. Her smile, as faded as a flower that had been used for the Onam decorations and then swept into the rubbish heap, stayed fixed on her face.

"I'm going back tomorrow. I thought I'd come and see all of you before I left."

Sethu saw Krishnan Nair place something in Padmu's hand. A five rupee note. As he said goodbye to Achan, he asked Sethu,

"Which class are you in?"

"Sixth." Sethu never forgot the fragrance of the new, uncreased five rupee note which Krishnan Nair gave him.

Amma waited on the verandah, fumbling in her betel leaf box, until Krishnan Nair left. Then she said, "However rich he's become, he's not forgotten the past. He has a good heart."

We saw Cheriachan dragging his stout frame through the fence, gasping for breath, his eyes on the ground.

Amma said, "It's all a matter of destiny, don't you see? She's younger than me, but what's the use? Her foolishness brought about her misfortune. She could have lived like a queen. A queen."

Cheriamma stood on the inner side of the door, like a forgotten creature, running her hands through her hair. She did not say a word, or look at Amma.

Achan scolded Amma, "There he is. Keep quiet."

"Sethu". That was Cheriamma.

The verandah was quiet. Amma seemed to have lost the battle. Cheriamma came up and whispered, "Are you going to the post office?"

"Maybe."

"Get me snuff for half an anna. I don't have any money." Sethu hoped Amma had not heard. It would start another quarrel. Amma hated women using snuff; it made her furious.

Where would he find a half anna? He said nothing to Cheriamma. She stretched out on the verandah, leaned her head on her elbows and spat into the yard.

He saw two people coming across the field towards the house. Who could it be, at this time of day? Parameswara Ettan? His heart sank as he made out one of them. Haridas! God, no!

His first thought was of Cheriamma, lying in full view without a rowka, her breasts uncovered and her undergarment showing.

"Cheriamma, someone's coming."

"Who?"

"A boy who was at school with me, and someone else."

"That's nice."

He dared not ask her to go in. Swallowing his embarrassment, he waited while Haridas came up the steps. When he realized that his own mundu was worn and dirty, he could not even manage a smile.

"It was difficult to find your house, Sethu."

"You could have dropped me a card."

"This is Chandrettan. We came to Gopi Menon's house and thought we would drop in on you since you were in the neighbourhood."

There were no chairs downstairs. Where would they sit?

Haridas's white poplin shirt was wet with perspiration. Haridas placed his hand on Sethu's shoulder and said, his eyes full of laughter, "Didn't I say I would give you a surprise one of these days?"

"Come, let's go upstairs."

Cheriamma raised her head, then lay down again.

They went upstairs. The easy chair which was usually on the verandah had been folded and put away. He invited them into the room, "Do sit down." They sat on the wooden ledge of the window in the dingy room. Dust and rubbish had been swept into a heap and left on the verandah. Sethu felt disgusted.

He would show Amma, if she boasted again, "It's not easy, keeping a mansion like this clean." Mansion indeed!

He thought of Haridas's pretty, tiled house. Potted plants on ledges beyond the iron gate, a jasmine bower in the courtyard. Chairs arranged around a circular table in the front room and a crocheted tablecloth with the designs picked out in colours. Haridas had introduced him to his mother. She wore a starched mundu of pristine white with a black border. Haridas's eldest sister had served them tea and sliced mangoes in a white porcelain plate.

He had dropped in at Haridas's on his way back from a debating competition. He had not won a prize that day. But the sweetness of Haridas's welcome still lingered in his mind.

He excused himself and ran down. It was shameful—he had pretended that his father was an important official who sent home huge sums of money every month, that his house had a big nalukettu, a four-pillared inner courtyard, that he even had a room of his own.

Cheriamma was no longer in the verandah. Good. He stepped inside. Where was Amma? He asked Padmu, who came in trailing a coconut shell tied to a string. "Where is Valiamma?"

"Don't know."

He made a face at her.

"Cheriamma, where's Amma?"

"Look in the kitchen."

"She's not there. Cheriamma, I have to give my friends tea."

"Your mother runs the house, child. I only eat what I am given. And I don't complain if I get nothing. Who am I, after all? If I had just the interest now on the petty cash I used to have, I could have bought my own soap and clothes."

"Please, Cheriamma, can you make me some tea?"

"With what? Your mother locks up the tea and sugar."

It was futile talking to her. He went out in search of Amma.

God! Don't let Haridas hear.

Amma was at the Vadakkethu fence, talking to Ammayi.

"Amma, I have visitors, my classmate Haridas and his brother. Please make some tea quickly."

Amma said, "There's no milk."

"Amme!" He was on the verge of tears.

"What can I do if there's no milk?"

He ran next door and spoke to Sumitra. She went to fetch the goat she had let out to graze. He rushed back to the kitchen.

"Amma, what shall we give them to eat?"

"Your head. Get out, boy. You're lucky you don't have to starve. And you think I'll make little snacks for you whenever you want?"

Why did Amma have to talk so loud? He ran up the stairs. Haridas and his brother were at the door.

"Hari, you're not leaving?"

"Yes, we must."

He said with an effort, "Stay and have a cup of tea."

Haridas's brother answered, "We have a couple of places to go to."

He could not bring himself to insist. They hesitated for a moment in the courtyard. Padmu was playing on the verandah.

"Where is your mother, Sethu?"

"In the kitchen, I think. I'll call her."

Chandrettan came to his rescue. "Let's go. Tell your mother we had to leave."

He walked with Haridas across the fields and along the road. It was the first time he had come out without a shirt on.

Chandrettan walked ahead of them.

Haridas asked, "What do you do with yourself during the vacation? I saw TKP the other day."

Sethu tried to smile. "Which college will you go to?"

"Let me wait for the results."

"Oh come on, of course you'll pass. I can't go to college even if I pass. We don't have the money."

They stopped by the canal. Sethu said, "So long, Das. I'll write."

"You must. I'll tell TKP I saw you."

Sethu walked back. The field was white hot beneath his feet.

When he reached back home, he felt furious with the whole world. He wanted to pull down the old thatched house with its chipped beams. A great tarawad indeed! He imagined Haridas describing his visit to Sethu's house to his friends.

"Sethu." Amma called out. "Padmu, tell Sethu I want him."

He did not move.

A little later, Amma came up with two brass tumblers of tea. "Here you are."

He hid his hurt and resentment and said, "They've gone."

Amma left a glass of tea beside him and went down. He poured it on the ground.

How would he ever face Haridas again?

They had become friends the year Haridas repeated his tenth standard. Haridas had curly hair, a mischievous smile and was always late for class. He took snuff, scoffed at the teachers and was often sent out of the class. Once, when he sat down next to Sethu, he had noticed a collection of Changampuzha's poems amongst Haridas's books and asked to borrow it. That was how they got to know each other.

They soon became friends, the most intelligent boy in the class and the naughtiest one. They went together everywhere. To the temple festival at Kallathoor. To meet Colonel Lakshmi, who had fought with Subash Chandra Bose. Haridas had brought the news that she was expected at a meeting nearby. Haridas was a year or two older than Sethu. If you looked hard, you could see the faintest shadow of a moustache on his lips.

Haridas recited poetry beautifully. So did Parukutty.

Parukutty, with the big, black pottu on her forehead, always came to school with a crowd of girls. She was the leader and the prettiest among them.

Haridas once showed him a letter. "Want to know who wrote it?"

"Who?"

"TKP."

"Who's TKP?"

The letter, which ran into four pages, was signed T. K. Parukutty.

Haridas began to come to school early. Sethu lived four miles away from school and found it hard to come early. However, at Haridas's insistence, he would gulp down his kanji and rush to school by nine. Class Ten B was one of the new classrooms upstairs. He would wait outside until he saw Parukutty come out of the girls' common room. Pretending she was going to the toilet, she would walk into the classroom and talk to Haridas, while Sethu kept watch on the verandah to make sure no one saw them.

Parukutty pronounced the consonant "sh" as if it were a "s." This was most noticeable when she recited poetry. But none of the boys laughed at her, because she was Parukutty.

One day, when Haridas had not come, Sethu heard someone call him as he went past the girls' common room.

It was Parukutty. He felt inexplicably happy.

"May I borrow your Physics notes?" she asked.

It was not a surprising request, for he was the brightest in class and always had the highest marks, although he was the youngest. That night, he copied the notes into a new notebook by the light of an oil lamp and covered the book with a sheet from an ancient calendar advertising Vinolia soap, that had hung on his wall for ages. He gave it to Parukutty with a great sense of achievement the next day.

He wondered whether to tell Haridas about it on Monday, but did not. He treasured this secret between him and Parukutty, a secret that Haridas did not share.

Sometimes, he looked at Parukutty timidly in class. She was so pretty and when she walked, her long skirt trailed on the ground.

One day Haridas said to him, "Parukutty is ill." She had typhoid. Haridas told him later that Parukutty would not come back to school. She did come once though, to collect her certificates. Sethu saw her from a distance. She had cut her hair, the long, swinging plait in which she used to weave red flowers, and cropped it short like a boy's. His heart ached. He turned away before she saw him.

He said to Haridas that day, "Parukutty had borrowed my Physics notes. Can you get them back for me?"

"She gave them to me long ago. I forgot."

Had her hair grown again? He had not dared to ask Haridas today.

"Who threw this tea out?" Amma asked.

He did not answer. He went upstairs and put on his shirt.

He heard her shout, "Why throw it away? Who are you angry with? I know you wanted me to produce tea and snacks. But it's sixty rupees your old man sends me to feed all of you. Ah, I'd like to know what you would have done without me."

She would start now, about her efficiency, her superiority, the respect that the women of the neighbourhood had for her. He hurried away before she could begin.

2

"Sethu, have you forgotten what I asked you for yesterday?"

"What?"

"I wanted snuff for half an anna."

Sethu did not answer. He was trying to figure out how to get hold of two annas for himself. And here was Cheriamma reminding him again.

Cheriamma sighed, "People don't care for you if you don't have anything of your own."

He had heard that Cheriamma had lived a comfortable life until Cheriachan gave up his rights to the family property and came here. But ever since Sethu could remember, Cheriachan had had financial problems. He would listen silently to whatever Amma and Cheriamma said.

He died one summer, a summer exactly like this one. Sethu had been in the eighth class at the time. The examinations were over and he was at home. It had been the first time he saw death.

Before that, Cheriamma had lost two babies as soon as they were born. But he had been at school on both occasions. On one occasion, he had heard Cheriamma moan in pain when he woke up in the morning. Her baby was due and Sethu was sent to fetch Chummukkutti Amma, the midwife. Amma and Paru Ammayi from Vadakkethu kept scolding Cheriamma because she would not lie down and insisted on pacing up and down the hall. "Go and lie down, wretched girl," said Amma, "I've had babies as well."

Ammayi from Vadakkethu gave Sethu his kanji that morning. When he went to fetch his school bag from under the stairs, the floor was wet, as if a pot of water had been overturned on it.

"The waters have broken. Why hasn't the midwife come?" Sethu ran away quickly.

He listened carefully for the baby's cry when he came back from school that evening. Amma and Ammayi did not speak to him. No kanji had been cooked. Cheriachan called him, "Come, Sethu."

They went out together. Cheriachan had just won a case against the Irimbiliyath family and received some money due to him as interest. He had notes and coins tucked into his waist. He bought Sethu tea and snacks. On the way back, Cheriachan stopped outside Kandunni's house saying he would be right back. Sethu stayed outside and blew up big leaves from the castor oil plant. Cheriachan came out after a long time, wiping his chin and spitting from time to time as he walked. His round face with the grey stubble had grown red and he smelt of arrack.

"Come on." Cheriachan seemed unsteady on his feet. He said, as they crossed the fields, "Your Cheriamma had a baby boy, but it died."

Everyone liked Cheriachan. When he wanted to marry for the third time and Cheriamma's name was proposed, no one in the family had anything against the fifty-year-old bridegroom. He was the karanavar, the senior most member, of his tarawad and owned a shop facing the Ariyambadath temple. But his business failed and his nephews decided to divide the family property. A dispute arose and Cheriachan surrendered his rights to the property in return for a settlement of three thousand rupees. Then he came to live here. He lent the sum out to the Irimbiliyath mapillas and lost both capital and interest. He filed a suit and pawned first Cheriamma's, then Amma's jewels to pay for the legal proceedings. He won the case, but the sum he received was hardly enough to pay off the debts he had accumulated.

Parameswarettan always gave Cheriachan a rupee or two to buy betel leaves whenever he came home. Cheriamma resented this. Cheriachan would get up early in the morning to escape her recriminations, go to the river and pray till the sun grew hot. After that, he would smear his forehead and chest with vibhuti, come home and pace the verandah. After lunch, he always went to Vadakkethu.

Since she was distantly related to us, all of us called Paru Amma of the Vadakkethu house next door Ammayi. Even Amma, who was older than her, called her Ammayi.

Devu or Sumitra would spread a mat for Cheriachan and he would stay at Vadakkethu until someone called him home for dinner. Ammayi sometimes gave him a cup of tea. She liked to have him there, for her household had no men of its own.

Cheriamma found fault with Padmu for this as well. "Can't your father stay in his own house? Why does he sit in their verandah, to shoo away the crows and chickens?"

The children—Devu, Sumitra and Unni Namboodiri—always played in Ammayi's yard. Cheriachan like to sit quietly and watch them play.

It was at dusk one day that Sethu saw death. Cheriachan had been ill for a month. Sethu heard a scream and ran downstairs.

He saw the sightless eyes open wider and wider. The face seemed to have altered in shape.

Amma asked him to take Padmu away to the illam or to Vadakkethu. But he lingered, staring at Cheriachan's dilated pupils, listening to his laboured breathing.

"I said, get out." Sethu dragged the uncomprehending Padmu away. Even before he reached the areca nut grove, he heard Cheriamma wail. He held Padmu close to him, shivering, and the little girl suddenly began to cry.

They sent word to Cheriachan's house, but no one came. They waited until midnight, then Madhava Ammama said they could go ahead with the cremation. Traditionally, an older person had to be burned with wood from a mango tree, but their sole mango tree still yielded fruit and no one wanted it cut.

Sethu slept at Ammayi's house that night. Sumitra fed Padmu, put her to sleep and then served Sethu.

"I wonder what Edathi is doing at your house," she said. Devu and Ammayi were still at Sethu's place.

Sumitra teased out the tangles in her hair by the light of the oil lamp and gathered it tightly into a knot above her head. She put Padmu to bed with Karthiyayani, who was a year older than Padmu, and told Sethu to sleep as well.

Sumitra and Sethu were the same age, but she suddenly seemed like a grown woman with responsibilities.

Sethu slept on a mat in the hall. He no longer thought of Cheriachan's white eyes widening fearfully. Instead, his mind went back to the time when he and Sumitra used to walk over the hill to school, chaperoned by Devu. Even when she was in the fifth, Sumitra had not worn a blouse. That year, she had stopped coming to school.

They used to stop at the illam fence on their way back from school, leave their books and slates under a tree and worm their way through the gap in the fence to look for fallen mangoes in the illam compound. Bamboo thickets and big trees were clustered there in such profusion that it was dark even at noon.

Only Unni Namboodiri was brave enough to go there to pick up the fallen mangoes. On days when he found a lot, he would give Sumitra and Sethu some. They would creep back through the areca nut grove, taking care that Kunju Namboodiri did not see them. When they got to the fence at the gate on the southern side, they would find Devu waiting with a cross look on her face.

Once he was in the ninth and had moved to the high school four miles away, Sethu had no longer gone looking for mangoes again, although he sometimes went to the old haunt. Now, children never went there at all. They avoided the place because Kunju Namboodiri had been cremated near it. It had become overgrown with shrubs.

For many nights, Sethu had dreamed of Kunju Namboodiri's cremation and woken up with a start. Even when he walked under the jnaval trees in daylight, he felt uneasy although he had forgotten Cheriachan's eyes very quickly. It was Sumitra who had persuaded him to go and watch Kunju Namboodiri being cremated. They had found a place on the rocks, under the jnaval tree. At first, the smoke and the crowd had obscured everything. When the breeze blew away the smoke, they saw Unni Namboodiri with a kindi of water in his hand, the end of his mundu drawn between his legs and tucked behind in ritual fashion.

Sumitra asked, "Do you think Unni Namboodiri would have cried?"

How can a child not cry when its father dies?

But Sumitra was sure he did not cry. Kunju Namboodiri used to beat his son everyday while he taught the boy to chant the Vedas in the bathing shed near the tank. The sound of his blows could be heard in the house. Afterwards, Unni Namboodiri would walk away, the flesh on his oversized body quivering, his face showing no trace of tears.

"Here comes our Hidumban," Madhava Ammama would say. "How many verses did you chant today?"

Although his body was covered with bruises, Unni Namboodiri would bare his big teeth in a grin. Madhava Ammama would tease him, "Eat a black cat, Tirumeni, then the blows won't hurt you."

No, Unni Namboodiri would not cry because his father was dead.

When the areca nut palms in the illam bent over, the children used to swing on them. Once, a palm fell down trapping Unni Namboodiri's hand under it. He pulled his hand out and scrambled up, and everyone saw nails hanging down from two crushed fingers. Even then, he had bared his big teeth as usual in a grin.

Unni Namboodiri sprinkled water, circumambulated.

The crowd fuelled the fire with long sticks of wood and palmyra branches. Sethu suddenly thought of a description of Hell which he had heard as a child, of how the messengers of Yama, the God of Death, threw chunks of flesh into the fire and toasted and fried them.

Sumitra gripped his shoulder and pointed, "Look, Sethu, look." Something in the shape of a huge black ape hung from one of the branches held out to stoke the fire. Sethu saw it for only a minute.

"They're his intestines."

He screamed and fled, leaving Sumitra behind. She had teased him for days, calling him a coward. Often, as he fell asleep, the thing like a black ape would come into his mind and he would wake up, terrified.

The mail train was on the bridge. Relieved, Sethu welcomed the end of another long, hot day of waiting. He pretended he was going for a dip in the illam tank. If he was lucky enough to run into Unni Namboodiri, he could ask him for two annas. But this was the season of temple festivals and Unni Namboodiri was probably at one of them. He loved to ride on the temple elephants. They paid namboodiris eight annas for doing this. But what Unni Namboodiri enjoyed more was being able to sit on an elephant's back as long as he pleased.

If he handled Unni Namboodiri well, he could coax two annas out of him. Which meant he could buy three postcards and Cheriamma's snuff.

Devu was at the tank, washing out the lees of the oil from the big flat bell-metal uruli. She told him that Unni Namboodiri was not at the illam. No one knew when he would be back. He came and went as he pleased.

"I came looking for the goat and saw Kunhathol making fresh oil. How could I refuse when she asked me to help?"

Devu talked like an old woman. Ever since the maidservant at the illam had been dismissed on the charge of having stolen rice, Devu went regularly to the illam to stable the cow, wash vessels and mop the floor. Neither she nor her mother would admit that she worked there. They pretended that she went to help Kunhathol because the latter was growing old.

Sethu heard the rope and pulley creak as he passed the well and saw Kunhathol there. She reminded him of the picture in the Ramayana of the rakshasi who guarded the captive Sita, with her earrings swinging in elongated earlobes, her rough voice and the dark shadows under her eyes. She was fair skinned and thin and her face frightened him.

"Sethu, where has Madhavan gone?"

"I don't know."

"He didn't come this side yesterday."

It was said that once they were ten years old namboodiri women never looked boys in the face. But Kunhathol was different. She talked directly even to Madhava Ammama.

"Did you get through your examinations?"

Sethu stopped. "I don't know yet."

When she sent Unni Namboodiri back to the fourth standard for the third year in succession, Kunhathol had asked Sethu to keep an eye on him. She used to ask him how things had gone after every examination they took. Unni Namboodiri had stopped coming to school after three months. But Kunhathol always said, "Lakshmi's son Sethu is very bright, he'll do well."

Kunhathol said now, "I've been meaning to ask you to bring the music box, Sethu."

"It's out of order. I'll bring it as soon as it is repaired."

Madhava Ammamma had won the gramophone in a raffle. He managed to get hold of some old records. At first, he would not allow anyone else to play them. Kunhathol always asked for "Kalayami sumate bhoosuramoule." She liked "Lakshmithaipe Murare" as well. When Sethu went over to play her the songs, she always gave him a glass of tea and jackfruit chips. She never allowed him to wash his glass and invert it as was the custom. "The girl will wash it when she comes."

He had turned back once as he was leaving and seen Kunhathol take the glass away herself.

Unni Namboodiri had been the only child who survived after she lost five babies in succession. People used to remark sadly, "His mother did not deserve such a cruel fate." Kunhathol was very generous to anyone who asked her for money or food. And yet, destiny had been unkind to her.

People said Unni Namboodiri was mentally retarded, but Sethu did not believe this. He had to use all his wits to coax an anna out of Unni Namboodiri.

Tea was never made at the illam in Kunju Namboodiri's lifetime. He used to come secretly to Sethu's house for a glass of tea. He would bring a packet of betel nuts and give it discreetly to Cheriamma; the tea was in return for this. Cheriamma would ask the cheruman to sell the betel nuts for her and buy snuff with the money.

Sethu put on a shirt, combed his hair, wiped his face with his hand and asked Amma hesitantly,

"Do you have two annas to spare, Amme?"

"What for?"

"I have to send a letter."

"To whom?"

He cursed himself for having asked.

"How many correspondents do you have? Get out now."

He felt something choke his throat. He swallowed hard and went out.

3

There were no letters at the post office for him. He waited while all the letters were sorted and stamped in the hope that his name would be called out. The postmaster came out at last and began to read the list of names, peering through his steel-rimmed glasses. Most of the letters were from the army.

He did not ask whether there was a money order. He hovered around after everyone had left, making sure the postmaster saw him. No, there was nothing for him.

He felt ashamed when he walked back empty-handed, day after day. Once, he came across advertisements inviting requests for free catalogues in a magazine that Parameswara Ettan had left behind. He took four annas from Amma's money box and wrote for them. He was happy for a week. Catalogues addressed to "P. K. Sethumadhavan, Padinjarapattu House" arrived everyday from jewellers' shops and pharmacies. He treasured the wrappers with his name and address on them.

A mile to walk back. The sand was still hot beneath his feet. He kept to the shade of the screwpine bushes. As he turned from the road onto the big field, he saw Unni Namboodiri squatting at

Ammayi's gate, grinning vacantly, opening and closing a five-cell torch.

His first reaction was shock. Had Unni Namboodiri really become soft headed because everyone said he was? He thought of Kunhathol making offerings at the Thriprangot temple so that her son should be right in the head.

He heard a laugh. It was Sumitra, gathering karuka grass near the fence."Is the festival over, Unni Namboodiri? Did you earn a lot of money going on the elephant?"

Unni Namboodiri smiled and held out the torch he had bought at the festival. "Six rupees! You can see very far when you switch it on."

Unni Namboodiri's speech was jerky. Sumitra told Sethu that Unni Namboodiri had been invited to the talappoli festival at Kalladuthoor. Unni Namboodiri smiled shyly, tucked the torch under his arm and walked away.

"Poor fellow!" said Sethu.

"Don't waste your pity on him. He can be smart enough when he wants."

Sethu did not know what she meant.

"Why do you think Kunhathol sent away the servant woman?"

"Because she stole rice."

Sumitra laughed and shook the earth off a bundle of karuka grass.

"Unni Namboodiri is not an innocent little child!"

Sethu walked home full of vague doubts. Amma was seated in the verandah with her legs stretched out, chewing betel, supervising Devu while she swept the front yard.

"No letters?"

"No."

"Hmm." Amma chewed silently. "It's two months now since he sent money. How can I go on? And Parameswaran is like his father, he doesn't care."

Devu asked, "Aren't Parameswara Ettan and his wife coming?"

"Why let strangers know how bad things are with us?"

Sethu went up, took off his shirt and lay down. The sky was the colour of copper. A soft yellow radiance lay over the courtyard. Thunder rumbled now and then and a faint breeze had begun to blow from the western hills.

The twentieth of April. Two months more and he could escape.

When Parameswara Ettan came back from college, he had been a different person. Sethu had been astonished when he opened his box. There were so many shirts, all ironed and faintly scented. Sethu had never worn an ironed shirt. The mapilla who had moved into the room next to the tailor's had an iron. He ironed starched shirts for half an anna. When Sethu suggested it to Amma, she said, "You don't need to be so stylish."

He heard Devu leave. Amma said to her, "Tell your mother to come and sleep here tonight."

Ammayi and her children often slept at Sethu's. Amma would stay up late and liked to have someone to talk to.

Footsteps sounded in the corridor. Cheriamma. She asked from the door, "Where are you, child? I've a bad headache."

"They had run out of snuff in Musaliyar's shop."

Cheriamma looked at him angrily, not believing what he said.

"They'll get some tomorrow. He shook out the jar to show me."

Cheriamma went away.

He heard Padmu chant her prayers and realized it was dusk. He went down and walked up and down the yard.

"Aren't you having a bath, Sethu?"

"No."

"How will you sleep in this heat if you don't have a bath?" In summer, Sethu slept on the floor in the front verandah, and Madhava Ammama on the wooden ledge.

Madhavammama came back late. He said that Govindan the tenant-farmer had brought the paddy to the illam very late that evening. Govindan was becoming impossibly arrogant, Madhava Ammama muttered.

Govindan's sons were in the army. And he had taken over a number of tenancies. You could buy paddy from Govindan only if he wanted to sell. It was futile to threaten him, he had money on his side, and strong young sons.

Amma, Cheriamma and Ammayi from Vadakkethu chattered noisily until Madhava Ammama came. No one would have thought looking at them then that they quarrelled with each other all day. No matter how sleepy she felt, Padmu would sit near the oil lamp, listening to them.

When Madhava Ammama came out after dinner with a wet towel around him, and lighted a beedi, they would lower their voices.

"Padmu, get me some water." It was always Devu who ran to fetch the water for Madhava Ammama.

Sumitra came out with a lamp, her hair tightly knotted above her head and sat down close to Amma. Sethu sat in the dark, leaning against the pillar. Sumitra had her mother's fair skin. Devu was said to be the image of her dead father. Devu looked comical. Her huge ears seemed to wave as she talked. Tall and dark, bony arms covered with hair, Devu reminded Sethu of the black cow which had fallen into a ditch and died during last year's monsoon.

Ammayi always maintained that Devu was much smarter than Sumitra and that she was good with the vegetable and wood accounts.

Amma took pride in the fact that the Vadakkethu women consulted her about all their affairs. It was Amma who had suggested that an opening be made in the fence between the houses.

Amma asked one of the children to spread Sethu's mat for him. Devu brought one and asked Madhava Ammama who was seated on the steps, smoking.

"Aren't you going to sleep, Madhavetta?"

Madhava Ammama grunted something that might have meant yes or no.

A silent flash of lightning illuminated the courtyard and the verandah.

Madhava Ammama said, "I'm going out, sister. Get me my umbrella."

"Where to, at this hour?"

"It's going to rain. If we sow tomorrow morning, we'll need Maimunni's calf. I'd better arrange for it now, everyone will want it."

Amma began to extol his efficiency and his devotion to the family as he disappeared into the darkness. At forty, Madhava Ammama was very hardworking. He did not chew betel, or drink. He had an excellent reputation. When Achan came home last, Amma had broached the subject of Madhava Ammama's marriage. But Madhava Ammama had said, "Sister, I can't get married now."

Amma said to everyone, "He's turned forty, but he won't listen to us." Most people realized that Amma was secretly happy about this, for she always added, "This devotion to the family will last only till he has a family of his own."

A gust of wind blew a trail of dust into the verandah. Lying on his mat, Sethu saw the sky through the areca nut palms, overcast with clouds and fitfully illuminated by lightning. It was going to rain.

Then he heard the faint swish of rain melting into the roar of the wind that tore through the areca nut palms. Sumitra came out with an oil lamp. "Sethu, are you asleep?"

He sat up at once.

"It's going to pour. Your mother asked if you'd like to sleep inside."

No. He loved to sleep here while the rain splashed noisily between the pieces of thatch hanging down unevenly from the roof, and the thunder crashed.

Sumitra smiled into the smoky flame of the lamp and Sethu suddenly thought, how beautiful she is! He had not realized it till now.

Sumitra placed the lamp on the threshold, sniffed her kerosene stained hands, rubbed them on her hair and sat down. Vaguely uneasy, Sethu watched her as she sat in the shadow. Her red glass bangles glittered.

Sumitra stared at the rain and asked, "When are you going next to Kumaranalloor?"

"I have to go and collect my certificate." His heart raced as he said it. How could he be so arrogant and presume he would pass? Bhagavathi, forgive me!

"Can you buy me red chandu for four annas?"

"I don't know."

Inside the house, Devu laughed loudly and Ammayi hushed her.

A gust of wind blew the lamp out. Sethu moved closer to Sumitra in the dark. He longed to touch her wrist, with the glass bangles circling it. Her clothes smelt faintly of washing soap. He hardly heard what Sumitra said. He felt uneasy and afraid. Sumitra seemed so distant! They had gone to school together, been in the same class, but she suddenly seemed older. He finally plucked up the courage to touch her fingertips. He was afraid she would pull her hand away, but she only smiled and said, "That's a steel ring, child. I bought it from the Chettichi."

He held her fingertips tightly and tried to smile back.

"People like us can't afford gold rings, can we, Sethu?" She took the lamp and went in. Sethu sat with his head bent, perspiring profusely, his heart racing.

He grew calmer as the roar of the first rain of the monsoon started. Large raindrops splashed on the thatched roof. A thousand isolated sounds merged into a vast symphony. Branches split with a soft crash. The old walls shivered as the thunder rolled in on them from the distance.

What would Amma say if the mud walls crumbled in the force of the rain? This great mansion!

This broken hovel, with its propped-up roof of thatch, its ghost-filled attic, its rooms that were dark even at noon—a mansion indeed!

He closed his eyes, trying to recapture the image of Sumitra's face in the coppery radiance of the smoking lamp.

4

Koyassan Mapilla of the ration shop subscribed to a newspaper. A boy from Anakkara who delivered soap brought it on his bicycle everyday.

Sethu went to the shop well in time on the day the results were expected. The boy was unusually late. He managed to grab the newspaper before the salesman in the shop put it away. There was a vast sea of numbers. His eyes found it at last, 51931. He checked again, to make sure. Yes, it was there alright. 51931. He had written down a lot of numbers but remembered only Haridas's. Haridas had failed.

He whistled as he walked home, feeling that he had conquered the world. If only someone would stop him on the way and ask; he wanted to tell everyone the news. Parameswara Ettan was at home when he got back. Amma was in the verandah talking to Appan Nair who had bought the house on the hill from the Chettis who made pappadams. He was trying to convince Amma that luck and a good horoscope were far more important than education. "Our Sivayi Pankunni Nair's son failed his tenth, didn't he? He's very rich now. If good fortune is written on your forehead, you don't need to pass a single examination."

Parameswara Ettan had failed the intermediate examination three times and worked in a bank near his wife's place now. Ettan had moved away to a corner of the courtyard, as if he was not interested in Appan Nair's arguments.

Amma and Cheriamma knew that Sethu had gone to find out his results. He had expected them to rush up to him when he came back.

"Where have you been, so early in the morning?" At least Appan Nair had thought to ask him.

"To check my results."

"Did you pass?"

Irritated, he grunted, "Hm."

"Do you have the first rank?"

"I don't know. The mark lists have not come."

Parameswara Ettan came up to them slowly, tearing a mango leaf into little shreds. "Have you sent for an application form for admission to a college?"

He nodded, not looking at Parameswara Ettan. Each time Ettan had failed, there had been a scene at home. Amma had defended him, "It's not that he's stupid. Or that he hasn't worked hard. His horoscope says it's a bad time now."

Sethu stomped up the stairs, threw off his shirt, came down. He ran out, up the hill. Obviously, his family did not think that the fact that he, Sethumadhavan, had passed the examination was an important event.

When he came down the hill, he saw the cheruman children catching crabs by the canal. The old mango tree which belonged to the illam was about to fall into the fields, since the earth at its roots had been washed away. As children, Unni Namboodiri, Sumitra and Sethu used to take turns to sit under the tree to catch the mangoes as they fell, before the cowherd boys could get at them. The mangoes were stringy, but large and very sweet. They used to fall into the seedling beds. The children had to vault over the fence, grab the fruit and run back. If Raghava Kurup, who owned the fields, or one of the workers saw them, they would be severely scolded.

"What are you doing here, Sethu?"

Sumitra. She wore a red silk blouse and a new, unbleached mundu. Seeing that Sethu had noticed them, she said, "I went to the temple this morning." The sandalwood paste she had smeared over her forehead was almost dissolved in sweat.

"Where are you going?" he asked.

"I went to borrow a hatchet from carpenter Raman, but he was not there. The other wretch will never give it to me."

She seemed taller, maybe because she had worn her mundu down, covering the ankles. Sumitra told him how crowded the temple had been; how her eyes had smarted with blowing on the firewood while cooking jaggery-rice.

"Parameswara Ettan is here, isn't he?"

"Yes."

"Is he going back today?"

Parameswara Ettan and Amma must be discussing his future now.

"Yes." Parameswara Ettan rarely came home, now that he was married. And he never stayed the night.

Sumitra's arms and neck were such a beautiful colour. He looked at his own arms which were dark, almost black. He felt too shy to even smile at Sumitra. He was embarrassed whenever he saw his large teeth with the gaps between them in the mirror. He could never keep his prickly hair neatly combed.

Sumitra walked along casually, reaching out to pluck seeds from the kongini bushes on the roadside. He was sure she was not aware of his presence. He would never come out again with his mundu tucked up like a small boy's. She obviously did not think of him as someone who had passed his tenth. No one did.

"I'm going away soon to Palghat, to college."

At the turn of the path, Sumitra said, "I'm going to look for my goats." She clambered up, holding on to the bushes, and disappeared into the jnaval grove. He stood where he was, not sure why she had taken no notice when he told her he was going away. He followed her. His legs smarted where thorns grazed them. He quickened his pace, trying to catch up with her and noticed a long weal on his leg.

Beyond the jnaval grove was a hill covered with rocks. It was a big hill and the whole countryside was visible from the top. Sumitra was nowhere to be seen. He came down again and heard her call out to the goats.

It began to drizzle. The rain gathered force as he came down the hill. He ran down the path and took shelter beneath a clump of bamboo. But the rain was too heavy. He took refuge under the teak tree. It had begun to pour steadily. He heard footsteps splash through the muddy water flowing down the hillside. There was a small sheltered area under a cluster of branches that stood clear of the river. Sumitra ran towards it, cursing the rain.

She wiped her hair and face and said, "What a nuisance. My mundu is completely dirty."

She was soaked. Her wet blouse clung to her skin. He pretended not to notice when her wet arms brushed against his ribs.

A gust of wind moved the leaves above them and dislodged water by the potful.

The rain grew heavier. Sumitra called him to follow and ran towards a little cave that had taken shape when that part of the hillside had been dug out to make bricks to repair the road. The goats were huddled there. She pushed them out and crept in. Sethu followed, trying to avoid stepping on the goat droppings. If they stood up, they would bump their heads. Water mixed with clay coursed down the slope over the cave.

They could see the bean patch in the kitchen yard of the illam and the pounding stone from here.

He stood quietly, his heart beating fast.

She said, "Do you remember being afraid and running away when you saw Kunjan Namboodiri being cremated?"

He smiled. Why had she thought of that now?

He looked at Sumitra from the corner of his eye as she crouched on the ground, scribbling on the wet clay with a twig. He tried to get closer to her but she moved away and asked, "Why are you pushing me?"

He did not reply. He said very softly, "You're all wet, Sumitra." He drew his finger gently down the back of her wet blouse. She did not move. He put his hand on her shoulder and thought he felt her tremble. Slipping his left hand around her neck, he tried to embrace her, but she sprang up. Her eyes, wide as the sky, almost blinded his vision.

"What are you doing, Sethu?"

He got up, still holding her obstinately, mumbling something indistinctly. He did not dare look at her. His head brushed against the wet earth above. The odour of sweat and wet sandalwood was strong in his nostrils.

It was his moment of victory. Her struggling body lay quiet in his arms, which had suddenly grown strong. Her face lay tucked into his neck. Waves of heat and cold coursed alternately through him as he broke away from her.

The old Sethu once more, he looked timidly at her face and could not believe what he saw. There was a soft, moist smile in the eyes that had so recently held fire and, instead of trembling with anger, her lips quivered shyly.

They stood there listening to the sound of the rain diminish.

"It's stopped raining." She vaulted onto the path and ran away. Sethu lingered, trying to capture the scent of sandalwood.

When he walked home through a fine drizzle, he felt that his heart was brimming over with joy like a field overflowing from the Thulam rains.

Amma asked, "Where were you?"

He did not answer. He wanted to tell the world, I, Sethu, embraced Sumitra today.

Parameswara Ettan's leather bag was not upstairs. He must have left.

He did not find it difficult to get through the long, hot days, waiting for his interview card. He began to listen for Sumitra's voice. He would sit by the railings upstairs and call out softly if she passed by. She would stand in the courtyard and look up at him.

He felt too shy to talk to her in front of the others.

And now he was about to leave.

The old tin trunk had been cleaned with a cloth dipped in kerosene. Four shirts, four mundus. Two of the shirts had been tailored when he was in the eighth. Made of coarse, thick, striped material that reminded him of pillow cases, they looked as if they would never tear.

Parameswara Ettan had come the day before. He could not go with Sethu, he had no leave. Madhava Ammama would take him. But Parameswara Ettan had gone alone to college, thought Sethu.

Achan had sent a hundred rupees. Parameswara Ettan had calculated that they needed fifty rupees more. It was Madhava Ammama who had suggested asking Kunhathol. They had just sold some paddy and she would have the cash. She would not refuse if they asked.

He heard Sumitra's voice outside. He closed his trunk and peered through the window. She disappeared around the corner of the house. He waited until she came back and whispered, "Sh."

She shaded her face from the sun with her hand and looked up.

"Come here."

"Why?" Her voice was soft, but he thought she sounded nervous.

"Come on."

She looked around doubtfully.

He called loudly, "Sumitre, I've spread my towel out on that wall. See if it's dry."

"Yes it is." Her voice trembled.

"Bring it here."

Her footsteps on the stairs sent a shiver through him. His heart beat very fast as she came into the room.

"When are you leaving, Sethu?"

"On the early morning train." He placed his hand on her shoulder and said, "Sit down."

"No, I'll stand."

"Sit down, please." He caught her hands and made her sit down. She trembled violently. A hurricane tore through his mind.

"No, no."

He paid no attention.

"Sethu!"

For the first time in his life, he forgot to be shy. Sumitra twisted in his grasp as his burning fingers ran over the flesh at her waist, tender as a banana stem.

He listened to her go down the stairs, heard her voice outside the kitchen and slowly got up. The oil from her hair had made indistinct patterns on the ochre coloured floor. He traced his initials in them: PKS.

He went to the window as her footsteps receded.

No one has the right to touch Sumitra now.

Only I can touch her.

I, Sethu.

Part Two

1

The small, two-storeyed house had sixteen rooms and had been acquired as a hostel only recently. The main building was exclusively for senior students. There were two other hostels some distance away. Sethu was pleased when the warden said he would give him a room in the hostel called "Premakumar." It was a dilapidated place and the floor was always covered with dust blown in by the traffic that roared past it on both sides. Nevertheless, the name teased his imagination and stirred a lingering fragrance through his mind.

Who was Premakumar? No one knew, not even the old watchman Nagu. The owners lived in some distant place.

When timber lorries from Mannarghat rounded the corner, the screech of brakes and the scrape of tyres often startled Sethu out of sleep. This had once been someone's home and Premakumar must have been the son of the family. Had he woken up like this as well, when the lorries roared past, and tried to recall the image of a young girl, her face beaded with perspiration?

At dusk, the students stood on the verandah and looked at the street, the pulsating artery of the town. Sethu asked himself, was this really the city he had dreamed of, lying on the window ledge at home? At night, when the street was empty and yellow circles of light lay around the lamp-posts, Sethu loved to gaze at the crossroads, wrapped in a dream-like mist.

In the evening, after class, students were not allowed out on the verandah. All the same, they gathered there to watch girls pass by. Bicycles and horse carriages would go past, flooding the road with colour. The young men stood smoking behind the round pillars, praying that one of the girls would look up for just a moment.

Sethu never went to the verandah unless it was empty. He felt awkward about meeting students who would recognize him.

When he arrived two months ago he had been nicknamed "Earrings" because he had been the only boy who wore them. He had worn his little earrings with the red stones for as long as he could remember and had never dreamed that they would be used against him. One Sunday, a group of boys rushed in from the main hostel carrying mugs of water mixed with soot. Someone warned him, "The seniors are going to duck us." Some of the boys were dragged towards the well. Closed doors were kicked open. Sethu did not understand what it was all about. He panicked and ran to the warden's house. Gasping for breath, he said, "The seniors have attacked our hostel." When the warden asked for names, he gave them. He tried not to look hurt when the warden told him coldly that he would look into the matter.

He delayed going back as long as he could. When he finally reached the hostel, everything seemed deceptively calm. But his room-mate Swamy said, "They know." The boy with the red stone earrings had betrayed them. He took off the earrings and, with Swamy's help, hid them at the bottom of his trunk. He tried to convince himself that no one would recognize him, but they came for him at night. They stripped him, hung a garland of slippers around his neck and carried him in a procession around the rooms. He did not cry until they freed him. The pain in his throat became a lump that choked him.

The boys now standing in the verandah might have forgotten him. But he was reluctant to face them all the same.

The girls' hostel was a furlong away. Two of its upstairs windows could be seen from near the three round pillars in the verandah. Shadows moved behind the yellow curtains at night. The boys gathered outside Sethu's room to look at them as soon as the warden finished his rounds.

A woman's shadow.

Malini? No, that's Leelavathi.

Want to take a bet?

How will we find out?

Balakrishnan from Payyanoor had an idea. He exhausted an entire box of Bengal lights each night so that Malini, the shadow behind the yellow curtain, could see his face in their flare.

Balakrishnan, Ganapathy and Sivasankaran formed a little group. They scaled the walls at night to go to the cinema, pursued the girls on bicycles, and smoked. Sethu could not afford these luxuries, so he stayed aloof and decided to be good.

His room-mate, Swamy, was the son of a rich merchant. But Swamy was very careful with his money and kept meticulous accounts in a little pocketbook. Sivasankaran had to try for a whole week to get Swamy to treat him to a cup of tea. He succeeded at last and Swamy wrote in his notebook, muttering angrily to himself, charity— one anna.

Sethu was sent sixty rupees from home on the second of every month. After he paid his hostel dues and the laundry charges, he barely had ten rupees left to manage on for the rest of the month. He wrote to his relatives without actually mentioning money. Dear Sankarankutty Ettan, I hope you are well. I joined college in June and am staying in the hostel. If only one of them would send him some money. They were all happy to know he was in college and some of them even wrote to say so. But that was all.

One Saturday, as he came downstairs, he heard the hostel peon, Ramakrishnan, arguing with someone. A group of students were gathered near the gate around a shrivelled woman clothed in rags. She had a dirty, dark-skinned baby at her breast. The boys nudged each other meaningfully as she nursed the baby unashamedly, fondling it while it suckled her withered nipple and talking all the while to Ramakrishnan.

She was from Kozhinjambara and her Malayalam had Tamil inflections. She had already walked nine miles in search of the baby's father. When she had gone to the workshop he had mentioned to her, they had told her that no one by that name worked there.

He suddenly thought of the heroines of the novels which Haridasan had lent him.

Oh God, Sumitra!

- Tell us, wretch, we'll make you tell us.

- You won't? You slut! You won't?

What if Ammayi tied her to the pillar and whipped her, to make her tell them? He shuddered. His mind wandered when he tried to study.

The men of the Padinjarakalathil family had always had an excellent reputation. Sethu was so quiet, so intelligent. And yet, he had done this!

Swamy studied for two hours every evening, from eight to ten. He would then push the two small tables they studied at together, hang a mosquito net over them, tying its corners to nails on the walls, say his prayers and lie down on this improvised bed. He usually got up at five. Sethu slept late and never got up before seven.

The hostel boys managed to collect a whole rupee for the woman from Kozhinjambara to which Swamy's contribution was an anna. While noting the sum down at night, he said, "Looking for him in a workshop indeed! It's a lie. She should have been slapped for her impudence."

Sethu did not say anything. As soon as Swamy went to sleep, he spread his mattress on the floor and turned off the light. He tried not to think about Sumitra. He heard the roar of the lorries on the road as they approached and then receded.

He thought of the time when the villagers had gathered around the tank where a cherumi's corpse had been found floating. He had been in the fourth class at the time. He fell asleep and dreamt of the dilapidated tank surrounded by screwpine bushes, at the edge of the field, and the corpse floating in it. He woke up with a start and wondered what the time was. His body was bathed in sweat and he could hear his heart racing wildly. The street lights flickered through the iron window bars.

He tried to erase Sumitra from his mind and think of all the girls in his class. Most of them were grown-up. The youngest was Shyamala Nair, who still wore a skirt. He had noticed her the very first day, when the names were called out from the attendance register.

Three hundred and sixty—Sethumadhavan.

Savitri, M.

Savitri, P. R.

Somasundaram.

Shyamala Nair. Large, bright eyes dominated the small face.

The boys talked animatedly when coming back from class. Malini stared at Kunhikrishnan all the time. Nalini always smiled at Chandran. Achamma laughed whenever Rajan said something funny. No one mentioned Shyamala. Sethu said a prayer. Hidden desires can turn into prayers. If ever anyone takes notice of me, let it be Shyamala. He wanted her large eyes to look at him once, at least once.

The day Sivasankaran's money order came, he invited Sethu for coffee. Swamy refused to go with them, so there were only the three of them, Sivasankaran, Prabhakaran and Sethu. Sivasankaran liked to eat biriyani once a week. He was a football player and believed in body building.

They went to the Madras Cafe. Sethu said he did not want biriyani, or chops.

"You're a vegetarian?"

"Yes." It was a lie. Sivasankaran would pay today, but Sethu would have to pay next week.

In his high school days, his mouth used to water whenever he saw meat being served in Balan Nair's hotel. A plate of mutton with the meal cost an extra four annas. The fat old man who sold mats at the local market on Wednesdays always ordered two plates for himself. Sethu used to watch the old man enviously. His mouth would water every time he thought of the flavour and aroma of the coconut fried in the oil used for cooking the chicken that had been sacrificed for the Bhuvaneswari puja.

Controlling himself, he said, "Just a tea for me."

They sat in one of the little cubicles marked out by faded glass panes. Sivasankaran gave the order and went to wash his hands. He came back and whispered, "Shyamala Nair is in the next room."

"Who else?"

"Lots of other people."

Prabhakaran said, "Her father is an advocate."

Sethu cursed Sivasankaran for eating so slowly and with such relish. He wanted to be outside when Shyamala left, wanted her to see him leave Madras Cafe.

They heard the voices of boys in the next room.

Sivasankaran paid, bought a cigarette for himself and asked Prabhakaran whether he wanted one. Prabhakaran hesitated, then bought one too.

"There's no point asking Sethu."

"But I want one." Sethu spoke with confidence but felt that Sivasankaran did not believe him. Sethu went into the street, spitting out the cigarette fumes he could not swallow and saw Shyamala leave with her companions. Maybe they were relatives. They got into a car parked near the lamp-post. A fat man with glasses drove it away. None of them looked at the boys.

Sethu coughed and spluttered, but did not throw away his cigarette. In the hostel someone asked where they had been.

"To town."

"Shopping?"

"No. To the Madras Cafe," said Sivasankaran. Sethu was proud to be part of the group.

Swamy asked him at night, "So you smoke?"

"No."

"Lies. You smell of cigarettes."

Embarrassed, he admitted, "I smoked one. But I won't make a habit of it."

Swamy thought well of Sethu because he spent his free time in the library and did not keep bad company or use bad language. But what would Swamy and the others say if they knew what would happen when he went back home?

He lay awake at night, cursing himself. He had not thought of anything like this the day Sumitra came up to his room. How could he find out whether a sixteen-year-old could father a child? Whom would he ask?

A week later, there was a letter from Parameswara Ettan. In an envelope. Parameswara Ettan seldom wrote letters. Had Amma written to him and . . . ? He went to a deserted corner of the verandah and opened the letter with trembling hands. Oh God, forgive me this once. I'll never do it again. Forgive me for the sin I committed!

He breathed normally only when he had finished reading. His heart steadied in the calm after a violent hurricane. The letter was about next month's fees. Achan could spare only sixty rupees. Could he find out from the office whether he could pay in two instalments? Hoping to see you at Michaelmas.

Of course they knew. They were waiting to get at him when he went home at Michaelmas.

He felt sorry for having been so foolish. How silly of him to have thought that all the beauty in the world was contained in

Sumitra. He had realized how wrong he was when he saw the riot of colours splashed on the balcony of the Pavilion Hall.

2

The Onam and Michelmas holidays coincided this time. Swamy decided to take his trunk home, so Sethu was able to borrow his leather bag. He packed freshly laundered shirts, mundus and a few books. He left on Friday night while the others were still celebrating the start of a fortnight's holiday. It was the first time they were going home after they had joined college.

Sethu pretended to laugh and joke with his friends. He played carroms, and smoked the cigarette they were given after the feast. All the time, he wondered what would happen when he reached home in the morning. Hiding his uneasiness, he stayed with the others, afraid to be alone.

Maybe I won't come back.

He would go away to a place where no one knew him. He was tired of running away from familiar faces.

Man was first prevailed upon to commit a sin by the serpent. When he had looked out through the railings upstairs, the serpent's hood had fanned out in the recesses of his mind. Standing on the uncovered station platform open to the icy wind that hurtled down the western mountain pass, he could not help thinking of the story from the Bible.

He imagined himself being heroic. Don't touch her. It was my fault, Amme.

You!

Yes, I. He would go up to her as she stood with her head bent, tears running down her cheeks. He would take her hand and lead her into the great wide world. He would say to her in his heart, so that only she could hear, I will always be with you.

But he only had to think of Parameswara Ettan's or Achan's face for this bright image to dissolve into darkness like a path visible only during a flash of lightning.

A bell rang. The platform suddenly came alive. There were students going as far as Kasaragode. They whistled, smoked and talked loudly in the mixture of English and Malayalam that identified them as students.

Sethu shrank from the jostling, pushing, kicking crowd in the train. Latecomers were being shouted at, those who had come early and secured good seats were delighted with themselves. People cursed as they dashed against steel trunks which got in their way.

Raghavan Nambiar from Cannanore had managed to secure a few seats by spreading a big towel over them. He invited Sethu to share one. An old man squatted near the bathroom. Sethu pretended not to see the woman who stood next to him, leaning on the window, and hoped that none of those who had studied the poem "Chivalry" in class were around.

Wierd images kept pace with the rhythm of the moving train. The air was full of the stale smell of sweat, beedi smoke and human breath. Balakrishnan from Payyanoor had wedged himself among the straw baskets and steel trunks in the luggage rack above Sethu. He and Nambiar talked late into the night.

The train hissed and panted its way through the darkness like some giant reptile. Sethu watched sparks fly through the window and melt into the night. The woman he had seen earlier was asleep on the wet, dirty floor littered with orange peel. The glass shade of the flickering lamp swung loose. He watched the moths which circled the bulb.

The train would arrive at the station at five thirty. He tried to see himself as a young man returning to his village from a city forty-five miles away.

The station platform, dimly lit by glass-shaded kerosene lamps, was deserted. He was lucky, none of his friends had woken up. They might have asked him his address. He could not bear to think of any of them dropping in. He still remembered the shameful experience of Haridasan's visit from long ago.

He waited on the cement bench until the darkness paled into daylight, feeling very sleepy.

The ferryman recognized him. "Home from school?"

He did not bother to explain the difference between college and school.

It was the first boat of the day and was full of vendors who had come to sell their goods in the local market. He was relieved there was no one who knew him. On its return journey he was the only passenger. The breeze felt cool. The fields lay ready for the harvest.

His heart started to beat faster as he neared home. He summoned up all the courage he had to enter. The old cherumi was sweeping the yard. Amma was seated on the verandah, teasing out the strands of her hair, her betel box beside her. Madhava Ammama sat on the steps, cleaning his teeth. The carpet of flowers laid out the day before for the Onam season had dissolved into the moist cowdung and the flowers lay scattered, disgustingly dirty.

He put his bag down, afraid to look at Amma. He was sure she would explode. Was this the calm before the storm?

"How many days' holidays do you have?"

The fresh breeze that blew over the fields cooled his thoughts as well. He sat down on the the verandah ledge, breathed normally and said, "Two weeks."

He heard the sound of goats' hooves. "This way, little kid, or I'll. . . . " Sumitra's voice. She herded the goats through the western courtyard and noticed Sethu only when she was right outside the house. She came in smiling.

Sumitra pulled down the upturned end of her mundu from her waist and asked, "Have you just come, Sethu?" She did not look like the sorrowful heroine he had imagined. She was the same Sumitra he had seen in June. But she seemed unusually reluctant to meet his eyes. She said to Amma,

"Hasn't Sethu grown taller?"

Sethu smiled. He was sure she had noticed his collar, still stiff after a night's journey, and his cuffs, turned up at the elbows. For the sake of saying something, he asked when Onam was.

Amma said, "Friday. Parameswaran has written that he is going south." To his wife's place, of course.

"We haven't harvested. I don't know how we'll find the money to celebrate Onam. We can do without a feast ourselves, but we have to feed the cherumans and their families the day after Onam. How can we do away with old customs like that? Madhavan." Amma turned to Madhava Ammama who was cleaning his teeth noisily on the other side of the verandah. Feeling nauseated, Sethu took up his bag and went upstairs. At the door, he looked back. Sumitra's eyes were following him.

3

Parameswara Ettan left soon after the Onam lunch. He had come on the morning bus. Amma said angrily, "He can't stay away from her even for a minute, the oaf."

Lying upstairs, he could hear the Onakkali songs from the illam. He had not taken off his shirt after lunch even though he had been sweating. The day after he arrived, Amma had scolded him for wearing a shirt in the house, but he had taken no notice. She had not mentioned it since.

He tried to whistle a tune,

Chale jaana nahi naina milaake.

He had seen only one film in the three months he had been in college. "Badi Bahen." Kunhikrishnan used to whistle some of the songs in it. Kunhikrishnan had seen "Vazhgai" nine times. He had stolen a poster of Vyjayanthimala from some place in town and hung it in his room. He wanted to look at her face first thing in the morning and last thing at night.

Sethu had seen Ammayi and Devu go to the illam earlier in the evening. In the old days, Kunhathol used to teach the women Onakkali dances and songs. Amma, Cheriamma and Ammayi had all gone to her when they were young. Kunhathol still invited the children in the neighbourhood to dance for Onam and Thiruvathira. She gave the adults betel leaves and buttermilk. In the old days, everyone who came to the illam during the Onam season used to stay for the feast, and people came from as far as five miles away. Madhava Ammama said that since Kunhathol was now dependent on the goodwill of her tenant, Govindan, for her annual subsistence, people were no longer interested in coming a long way just for betel leaves and buttermilk. But as Onam drew near, Kunhathol still asked everyone she met to come over to the illam.

Sethu saw a flash of white move around the corner, near the path to the illam. Yes, it was Sumitra.

He hurried down and walked casually around the yard in the hot sunshine. He pretended to himself that he did not want Sumitra to see him.

Madhava Ammama leaned against the pillar, smoking a beedi. Cheriamma came out. "Where's that wretched girl? She's going to have fever now, running about in the sun after an oil bath." Sethu had seen Padmu run towards the illam, but he kept quiet.

He went upstairs again and saw Sumitra pass by. Maybe she was on her way to the illam. She paused under the neem tree and looked up. She wore an unbleached mundu with a black border. Her face was flushed. Her blouse with the blue flowers seemed too tight for her. Had she grown taller since yesterday?

Madhava Ammama was serving lunch to the old mapilla boatman. Amma would be there as well. In spite of this, he waved boldly to Sumitra. She smiled into the sunlight and walked towards the illam fence.

He felt sleepy. But what if he missed Sumitra when she came back?

Who was that, coming through the banana grove, towards the fence? Yes, it was Sumitra. She looked straight up at the railings, smiled and walked quickly on. Madhava Amamma asked her, "Why did you come back, Sumitra?"

"The bitter gourd has been left out to dry in the courtyard and there's no one at home."

Sethu's drowsiness cleared at once. There was no one at Vadakkethu. He set off for the areca nut grove as if he was going for a walk in the compound. When he came to the broken fence outside Vadakkethu, he looked around to make sure no one saw him. The courtyard was deserted. He cleared his throat and went in. Sumitra was near the bean patch, her hair spread out over her shoulders.

"Where's Ammayi, Sumitre?" His voice was rough.

"They're all at the illam. I came back because the bitter gourd had been left out to dry."

He climbed into the verandah.

"Shall I bring you bananas and chips, Sethu?"

"No." She went into the house and he followed her. It was very dark. His eyes were blinded, coming in from the bright sunlight. He waited, trying to get used to the darkness. Sumitra opened the door of the southern room and the bolt screeched as it moved, startling him.

He prayed no one would see him now, Sethu who was so good, who never smoked beedis or went to teashops.

Light filtered into the little room through the rounded bars above the window ledge. Old mattresses were heaped on the cot. There was a big box on the floor. An earthenware pot hung from the ceiling. The odour of worn, oil-stained clothes and incense hung in the room.

They stood close to each other, not talking. When she closed the window, it was pitch dark. Starched cloth rustled as it was ripped away. A mingled smell of sweat, sandalwood and melted camphor closed in on his consciousness.

"Who's that?" Sumitra's frightened voice startled him. Someone coughed outside. She pressed her fingers on his trembling arms and got up. He lay half conscious, his eyes closed. A buzzing noise, like that of bees, filled his ears.

Sumitra came back smiling.

"It was Madhavettan. He wanted the bucket."

"Has he gone?"

"Yes."

He grinned foolishly as they stepped out into the bright yellow sunlight. She smiled at him with a touch of scorn.

"This will last only till you go away, isn't it? Afterwards, you'll forget."

"What an idea!" he said, without meeting her eyes. He could not bring himself to say, "I won't forget." He reached the areca nut grove with a sense of relief. Her huge, kohl-rimmed eyes had made him feel insignificant.

She called out, "Wait."

He stopped. What was she going to say?

"Don't worry, I just wanted to make sure there was no kohl on your face." He waited, as if he needed her permission to leave.

"Go on, then."

When he walked home through the cool, shaded garden, he felt no sense of victory. His mind was still filled with the confusion that had taken hold of him when he looked into Sumitra's shining eyes.

4

People were seated all over the maidan, on the concrete benches and on the grass. At four, they would start to play film songs over the loudspeakers. Sethu loved the few moments before the mercury lamps came on, when human forms moving in the shadow of the fort became indistinct shapes in the waning sunlight. They were the moments when he could hear the vague murmurings of his own heart.

Behind him lay a tomb that belonged to history.

They found a place away from the crowd, on the southern side of the fort, from where they could see the marks made by the cannon balls. Sethu had been inside the fort only once. The first thing that had caught his attention had been the old trees and their tired branches trailing on the ground. When he walked around the red-painted jail, he had heard the footsteps of the prisoners through the mesh-covered ventilators. Later, he had heard blows and the sound of screams. He had come out quickly, trembling with fear.

Prabhakaran threw stones into the moat and asked,

"What are you thinking about?"

"Mm."

College would reopen tomorrow. Many of the students had not yet returned. When he had gone for a walk in the afternoon, Sethu had seen a letter addressed to him, P. K. Sethumadhavan, in the letter box in front of the old-fashioned tiled office building.

It had arrived four weeks ago and was from Haridasan. From Vishakapatnam, where he was working on a ship, the INS Jalaja. His food and uniform were free and he earned sixty rupees a month. After a year they would increase his salary. Haridasan had described his first voyage, from Bombay to Vishakapatnam. There was a postscript underneath the long letter. Our TKP is married. To an agent dealing in rolled gold. I saw him. A horrible creature. He limps like a rheumatic buffalo.

Sethu told his friends about Haridasan. Events from his high school life seemed to belong to a distant past. Last year seemed so long ago!

Sivasankaran boasted about a daring feat he had performed during the Onam break. A Muslim girl lived in a thatched hut next to his house. One night he had cut the ropes that held the thatch in place with a blade and entered her hut. It was pitch dark. He did not know that the girl slept next to her mother. Groping in the dark, he found the mother's foot! She cursed the cat in her sleep. Everyone laughed. Sethu tried to laugh too.

Rajan from Cherpulasserry wanted to become a doctor. His father's brother was an influential executive in Madras. All Prabhakaran needed was a BSc after which he would do Textile

Technology in Benaras. His uncle, who was a dyeing master in one of the big Ahmedabad mills, had advised him to do a course in Textile Technology.

They asked, "What did you do in the holidays, Sethu?"

Achan had come the day before Onam and stayed four days. Sethu wanted a watch and had gone up to the gate with him to ask for one, but had not done so in the end. So there was nothing he had achieved in the vacation. He smiled and said, "I read. There was nothing else to do."

"That's not true."

If he closed his eyes, he could hear the crackle of unbleached cotton falling away from the skin and breathe the odour of incense in the dark room.

He kept quiet.

"You don't have to pretend, we know. How many m's do you have at home?"

"M's?"

"Maidservants."

Sivasankaran was the son of a wealthy landowner in Ottappalam. What did he know of people like Sethu?

"Two," he lied.

"How old are they?"

He had to tell another lie to cover up the first one, "Old, very old."

"And don't they have any relatives at home?"

"No."

"Indeed. I don't believe there's anyone who has not been initiated by a maidservant."

Sethu smiled foolishly. His companions accepted this as an admission of guilt. He hid his astonishment and listened to Sivasankaran and Prabhakaran talk with a casual air.

"I persuaded my sister to give me fifty rupees."

"I went to Guruvayoor in my uncle's car."

"I took away two shirts from my brother's box."

When they got back to the hostel there was a message to say that the warden wanted to see Sethu.

A big built rough-looking young man with a moustache stood outside the warden's house. "This is Krishnankutty," said the warden. "You'll have to share your room with him." Sethu realized only then that the young man was a student. Krishnankutty waited quietly.

"You have a corner room, don't you? We used to put in three students there." The warden made sure he had no excuse. Sethu consented and came out. He cursed his bad luck as he hurried away. Krishnankutty caught up with him in front of the soda factory.

"May I come with you?"

Sethu did not reply.

"I was in a lodge till now. It was so noisy, I couldn't read at all."

"Which year are you?"

"First. History." Krishnankutty had stayed at home for five years after doing his SSLC and then decided to come back to study.

"All I need is a place for my box and books. I can sleep in the common room or the verandah." His voice sounded gentle, though he looked rough.

Most of the hostel students stayed aloof from him but Sethu learnt to like and respect the taciturn and studious Krishnankutty. Krishnankutty usually went for a walk in the evenings. If there was a political meeting, he listened to the speeches. Otherwise he walked three or four miles along the railroad track. One evening he invited Sethu to go with him.

They walked towards the river which had narrowed to a stream that tumbled over the scattered, misshapen rocks.

Sethu felt he had to say something. "Sivasankaran and Prabhakaran are going to Coimbatore tomorrow afternoon to see Tara Singh fight."

Krishnankutty asked unexpectedly, "Do you want to be like them?"

The severity of his tone made Sethu feel small. He did not know what to say. Krishnankutty's eyes had narrowed to slits. "I detest those who like to show off that they have money. They think they are princes. They will know what life is like when they go out into the world in four years' time. Why don't they try to understand?"

Sethu said nothing.

"What use is it to be the leader of a handful of students in a hostel or in class?"

Sethu felt uncomfortable. "I."

"I'm not talking about you. I just don't think poverty is something one should be ashamed of."

"We are not rich," said Sethu.

Krishnankutty's father had a coconut plantation and land that yielded five hundred paras of paddy. He could have become part of the fashionable set in college with just the proceeds from the sale of the coconut palm branches that fell down on the ground. Sethu was astonished to know that he had worked in the Rural Credit Society in his village for four years to make enough money to pay for his studies.

Krishnankutty gazed at the little structure that had been built in the middle of the river, amongst the rocks, for a sanyasi. Before Sethu could ask, he said that all he wanted was to take a BT degree and go back to his village as a schoolteacher. He had fallen out with his father because he was in love with a girl of whom his father disapproved.

His father drank heavily, Every evening, he would drink with his friends. The house was as noisy as a market-place till mid-night. "It seems a mark of prestige for rich people like him to behave like that."

"And your mother?"

"She's been mentally ill for nine years now. An incurable condition. She had to be shut up in a room. The maidservants run the house."

Sethu imagined the scene as Krishnankutty described it. The son would be summoned before the group of drunken people. "Here he comes, my beloved son. Mambat Sivaraman Nair's son chooses to fall in love with a woman who works in a princely household!" The son had to stay and listen. Otherwise there would be outbursts, protests, the clatter of crashing china and neighbours would come to find out what was wrong, while the mother, who usually sat praying like an ascetic, would tear her clothes and scream. Rather than provoke all of this, the son would give in quietly.

Krishnankutty escaped to the girl's house whenever he could. He said, "I don't think I am in love. I think of the little house with its mud walls, its thatched roof and its soot-smeared floor as a refuge. It is my father and his friends who made my going there a crime.

"Does it surprise you, Sethu, that I talk about my father this way? When I was a child, he was a God to me. I used to feel so proud when people pointed to me as Sivaraman Nair's son. I began to realize the truth as I grew up. My father has a bell in his room upstairs. The maidservants know which of them is being summoned for two rings, which for three. While one of them is there, the others cannot go up."

Sethu stared silently at the darkening river in order to avoid looking at Krishnankutty's resentful face.

One day, Krishnankutty had confronted his father and moved out of the house to an unused room at the top of the gatehouse. When he went to the girl's house that evening, he said, "I will marry you as soon as I can support you, if you are willing." Her paralysed father, who lay holding pigeons close to his body to bring warmth to his limbs, heard what he said. The girl said nothing.

She was not beautiful or educated. She had left school after the eighth class. She began to visit him often, in his room above the gatehouse. Even at night.

"I've never touched her, although there were many occasions when I could have done so. We talked a lot, that was all." Krishnankutty's voice sounded like the murmur of a deep forest stream.

"I think of her often now. Her letters make me feel restless. Is this love? I do not know. You write poetry in the college magazine. Tell me, is this love?" Sethu made an effort to smile.

Krishnankutty seemed to be at peace as they walked back to the hostel over the railroad tracks. He even attempted to whistle lightheartedly. But Sethu felt restless and uneasy. He thought, I must go to Krishnankutty's wedding, wherever it is and say to his wife, when he introduces her to me, "I've known you for years."

He had realized what a happy experience it was to fall in love and get married at Parameswara Ettan's wedding. Ettan had remained cool and unruffled, although he was the centre of attention. Pretty, fair, Sarojini Edathi loved his brother! Sethu had felt a great respect for him. Parameswara Ettan was very dark.

Sarojini Edathi was Achan's niece. Achan and his relatives had approved of the match but Amma was against it, since she had never been on good terms with Achan's family. Amma's justification was that Achan had given all the earnings from the tea estate to his nephews and nieces. Amma said that Achan's relatives prayed earnestly for Amma and her family to fall ill. When they were all at a relative's wedding, Amma had been coerced into giving her consent for Parameswara Ettan to marry Sarojini Edathi.

Sethu remembered only two women who were at that wedding. One was the bride, the other was the girl who later became his sister-in-law. He loved her, in her blue saree with the silver flowers.

When she came to his house as a bride, it was Sethu who used to go with her to the river. He would look for fallen jnaval fruit that were not crushed and take them to her. He loved to watch her little white teeth, like grains of fine rice, bite into the ripe flesh and turn purple.

When he was in the eighth, Amma and Edathi Amma had a quarrel. Amma started it. "I know that women from Thrissur have an evil reputation."

Sarojini Edathi's voice, usually so soft, grew high with anger.

Amma went on, "You wretch, the only reason I consented to the marriage was because I did not want a woman to hang herself or jump in a well because of my son. Out of kindness. Not because the sorceress from Thrissur impressed me. And people respect me, so they don't ask why my son's wife, who is eight months gone . . . . "

Cheriamma begged her, "Softly, Edathi." Parameswara Ettan and his wife moved to a rented house near the bank where he worked the very next day. Sethu had been resentful of his mother for sending his sister-in-law away. She used to wash his clothes with 501 soap and fold them neatly so that there were no creases. The scent of talcum powder and perfumed chandu had flowed away from the house with her.

He imagined Krishnankutty starting life with the girl he loved.

Entering the road at the railway crossing, they saw groups of girls going back from the temple to the hostel. Their faces were indistinct in the dusk. Krishnankutty asked,

"What are you thinking about?"

"Nothing."

"Are you wondering why I told you all this?"

Sethu grunted noncommittally.

"I have to talk about it sometimes, otherwise I'm afraid my very features might change. I know that constant tension has already given me a cruel look."

Suddenly, the street lamps came on. They looked pale in the dust-laden air, as if they had been startled into wakefulness.

Krishnankutty asked, "Have you never been in love?"

Had he been in love with Sumitra? When he was returning after the Onam holidays, he had seen her waiting for him in the banana grove near the gate of Vadakkethu. He was busy picking his way carefully over the slippery, muddy fields. Had it been painful to walk farther and farther away from her?

He replied, in as expressionless a voice as he could manage, "No."
Although he knew in his heart that he did not want to lose Sumitra.

Krishnankutty took his books and went to the common room. Sethu borrowed an inland letter from Swamy and sat down to write to Haridasan. The hot April afternoon when he had said goodbye to Haridasan by the canal seemed years ago. There was much to tell him. He had not met Haridasan when he went to school to collect his certificates. He must write to him about college and classes, how he had thrown up after dissecting his first frog in the Natural Science practical session, about his friends and the poem he had written for the college magazine.

But in the end all he wrote was, "Dear Haridas, I received your letter and am glad to know you've started on your new job. College life is not bad. Let me know if you are coming home." He had thought of Haridasan as a friend from whom he would never be separated. Long ago. Did he really hope that Haridasan would go on writing to him? He tried to convince himself that he did.

5

The icy December wind of the Thiruvathira season tore down the narrow mountain pass, making the palms shiver. The nights were cold. And the days blazing hot. Sethu did not go home for the holidays. He wrote to Amma that he had special classes which he could not afford to miss. He had to eat out since the college mess had closed down.

He dreaded the thought of the summer vacation. He could forget everything else as long as he stayed in this hostel in the big town, a part of its noise and confusion. It was like hiding in the little cave dug out of the clay of the hillside, sheltered behind the heavy screen of rain, listening to the roar of the wind and the rain outside.

But when he got home he discovered to his astonishment that he had become a respected member of the household. Tea was sent up to him morning and evening. It touched his heart to see Padmu come up the stairs balancing the big bell-metal glass carefully in her hand so that the tea would not spill. Padmu had grown taller this past year. And she had become wary of him.

One day, she said timidly, "Sethu Etta, I need a cloth umbrella."

"Don't you have one?"

"Only an old palm leaf one."

So Sethu Ettan had grown up. Padmu was sure he would get her what she needed. She must have asked Amma and Cheriamma already, and one of them would have said, "A cloth umbrella indeed!"

If only I had an umbrella, Sethu thought, I could have given it to her. He knew he could never save the six rupees it cost. Still, he said,

"I'll get you one."

As he walked through the fields that evening, he saw Sumitra's younger sister, Karthiyayani. She was carrying packets wrapped in teak leaves. He went up to her.

"What is there in that stomach of yours?" he teased.

The nine-year-old stood shyly, her short towel barely covering her rounded abdomen. With her narrow, half-closed eyes and protruding stomach, she reminded him of the Chinese doll in the hostel warden's room.

"Where's your Sumitra Edathi?"

"Edathi is at Tirur."

"Tirur?"

"Kunjummalu Amma took her there."

Things became clearer when he heard Amma and Cheriamma talk to each other at night. Kandankulangara Appunni Menon had married a wealthy woman from Tirur. When she went home to have a baby, she had taken Sumitra with her. Ammayi made sure that no one would misunderstand the situation.

"I sent word that no one from our tarawad would ever work as a servant, even if we were starving. Then the lady came herself, big stomach and all, and said to me, would I ask her to be my servant? If you send Sumitra with me, I'll treat her like my younger sister. She's very fond of Sumitra. And it's only for ten days. Though Madhavan didn't like the idea one bit."

Sethu was taken aback to know that Appunni Menon had asked Madhava Ammama for permission. Why Madhava Ammama?

He found that the opening in the fence between his house and Ammayi's had been closed. He stood hesitating at the fence, soap and towel in hand. Amma saw him return and said,

"We've filled in that gap in the fence."

He did not ask why. Amma told him. "Cattle and goats stray in all the time. After all, people can always use the gate."

Cheriamma said to him, "Were you going for a bath, Sethu? The water at Vadakkethu is not good. Ten steps from here and you're at the river. The water there is excellent!"

Ammayi and her children did not come over as they used to.

Amma and Cheriamma talked about Sumitra going away with Kunjummalu Amma in a tone of contempt. They spoke ill of the Vadakkethu family to everyone.

When had this change taken place?

And then things began to fall into place. "He's a grown man, isn't he? And we are his older sisters. We can tell him once, twice, not more."

So Madhava Ammama was behind it. He was at Vadakkethu all the time. He looked after their affairs. Amma and Cheriamma were convinced that the Vadakkethu women had lured him there with a magic potion. Otherwise how could a man who used to turn his face away when even their names were mentioned have changed so much?

Sethu went to the river that evening for a bath. When he thought about Sumitra, he was filled with an unreasonable anger. The Kandankulangara Menons were rich. The villagers pawned their jewels and vessels with them to borrow cash or paddy. And he had heard that Kunjummalu Amma's tarawad at Tirur was an ancient, titled one.

The house must be huge. With deserted corridors and dimly lit rooms. At dusk, the bathing sheds near the tanks would be full of darkness. There would be young men in the house. College students, men with jobs. And Sumitra slept in that house. He would show her when she came back. Why had she gone away to stay with strangers? The more he thought about it, the angrier he became.

If he sat upstairs above the front verandah, he could hear what Amma and Cheriamma said to the village women who came to the courtyard to gossip. They discussed all the village scandals with Andoor Ummuttu Amma, old cherumi Kali and Beepathumma, the fisherman Muhammad's wife. If Amma or Cheriamma were by themselves, each would describe the other's atrocities as well. Cheriamma would talk of Amma's unkindness and Amma of Cheriamma's evil mind. Ummuttu Amma brought a new earthen pot one day and said, as she was leaving, "And when is Madhavan Nair going to begin his sambandham?"

Cheriamma said, "We can't make out what's come over him, Ummuttu. He used to get up and go away every time we talked about marriage. If Edathi tried to tell him that they are not strangers after all, that they need a man in the family, that they're our cousins, he would fly into a rage. Even the sound of her name used to make him furious. And now they've won him over completely with their chicken curry and their cups of tea and all the fuss they make over him."

Amma interrupted, her voice shrill with anger, "It makes my flesh creep to say it. He refused to listen when I coaxed him. Now they behave as if he belongs to them. Edathi Amma pretends to wheeze and look weak, but she knows what she wants."

Cheriamma added, "And the best bunch of bananas goes to Vadakkethu now."

Ummuttu said, "Madhavan Nair would be an excellent catch for anyone. The manager of the illam. He does the work of four. Did you hear, Chathu Nair's daughter, Janaki, has a secret lover."

Madhava Ammama came home very late. Sethu found it hard to believe when he first heard that Madhava Ammama really wanted to marry Devu with her huge ears, her bony face, hairy arms, and thick eyebrows.

Madhava Ammama ate silently and sat smoking in the verandah for a long time, leaning against the worn, cracked pillar. Sethu looked at him wonderingly. He was very dark. His hair, rough as coconut fibre, was growing thin and patches of white showed here and there on his scalp. He seldom smiled. The air whistled through the gaps in his big teeth when he spoke.

Devu did not work at the illam any more. Amma and Cheriamma thought that Madhava Ammama had asked her to stop.

"Where do you want to sleep?" Sethu was startled to hear Madhava Ammama's voice suddenly come out of the darkness.

"Upstairs or downstairs?"

"Upstairs."

Madhava Ammama spread the mattress kept folded on the wooden ledge, lit another beedi and came out. Sethu went in.

How could Madhava Ammama have changed so much?

Part Three

1

Madhavan threw the stub of his beedi over the wall and stood up.

He watched the shadows of the banana trees dance like living beings and thought he would never be able to sleep. The old wooden boards creaked as Sethu moved around the room upstairs.

He should have asked for some drinking water. He had thought of it when his sister brought the mattress out but had not said anything to her. Somehow, his sisters made him feel ashamed. They seemed to be brimming with unasked questions.

He thought of the time last year, around Onam it was, when he hid behind the thorn bushes near Sumitra's house so that Sethu could not see him. He saw Sumitra leave her house as he was giving the ferryman lunch and then noticed her return. He went into the compound as soon as the ferryman left, paused for a while near the coconut saplings that he had planted when the rains started last year and patted the earth around them firmly into place with his foot. When he finally reached the courtyard of Sumitra's house, he had felt afraid for the first time in his life. His throat went dry and his legs trembled. Had he cleared his throat loudly enough? The door opened. He tried to compose himself. He glanced at Sumitra's face for only a moment, then he began to stare at the branches of a medicinal tree that grew near the goats' shed. Sumitra asked,

"What is it Madhavetta?"

All he could think of was to ask for the wooden water carrier used to irrigate the field, but Sumitra said it was not there. He hesitated for a moment and left. Sumitra must have thought him such a fool—the month of Karkatakam was over, they had stopped irrigating the fields and the apparatus had been dismantled.

It seemed to him just yesterday that Sumitra had been a little child, running around in a shabby red konam, her face smeared with mango juice. Yet, when he saw her now, he felt confused and never knew what to say. He cursed himself. No one had seen him go out or come back, not even Sethu. By the time he got back home, the cherumans had bundled the rice they had been given into packets and left.

He heard the women talk to each other in the kitchen and thought of how foolish he had been.

He did not want to go out again. They would be playing cards in the room over Appu Nair's shop, as they usually did during the Onam season. He decided not to join them. He lay down on the wooden ledge outside and tried to sleep. Someone called from the yard. He opened his eyes. Sankunni's man had come for the dried pepper. What a nuisance! They had discussed it just yesterday.

"Padmu!"

It was so noisy, no one heard him. He called louder.

"What is it?"

"Give me the balance. There's a man come for the pepper."

"You took it to the illam the other day and didn't bring it back."

There was no one he could send to the illam now. Would Sethu go? Madhavan had often called him to help in the past. But the boy thought no end of himself, now that he had finished school. No, he would not ask him.

He told the man to wait and set out himself.

There was a crowd of women on the northern verandah of the illam. He stood uncertainly behind the pounding shed, under the withered mandaram tree. Kunhathol noticed him, and came down, "Yes, Madhavan?"

It pleased him that he was no longer regarded as a stranger at the illam, now that he looked after its affairs. Kunhathol never used a condescending tone to him, never treated him as if he were only a manager. She talked to him directly, without reserve. When he settled accounts with her after the areca nuts and bananas were sold, Kunhathol would push aside a heap of notes and coins and say, "Madhavan, put this away." He did not draw a regular salary. Kunhathol did not know how to keep accounts and Unni Namboodiri was not interested anyway. Still, Madhavan had never once thought of taking even a five rupee note for himself.

"Can I have the balance, Kunhathol?"

"It must be in the front verandah or under the stairs. Ask Unni to find it for you."

He crossed the muddy vegetable beds and avoided looking at the women doing Onakkali dances in the yard. Was that Sumitra's voice?

That fool Unni would be stretched out on the wooden seat in the verandah, replete after the Onam feast. The rascal! He hated the sight of him. He should have been Kunhathol's mainstay in her old age. Instead of looking after the areca nut palms, he spent his time wandering around on the backs of elephants. Of course, if someone else confronted the tenant farmer Govindan, on behalf of the family, extracted some paddy from him and put it away in the granary, Unni Namboodiri was ready enough to eat it.

The goats lay on the front steps, chewing cud. Unni Namboodiri was not to be seen. The door of the inner room was open, so Madhavan peered in. The balance was not there. Perhaps Unni Namboodiri was asleep in the thekkini? No, there was no one there. Whom could he ask? They were all so busy.

He found the balance under the stairs. As he went back through the dark corridor, he heard voices behind the door of the southern room. He waited a moment, listening. The door opened slowly and he made out a face with bony cheeks and large ears.

Devu!

He had no time to move away. He saw a scream freeze in her throat. As she crept forward and passed by him, the door opened fully. Teeth stained with betel juice gleamed in the dark. Unni Namboodiri's voice seemed to come from a great distance, "What is it, Madhava?"

He left without answering. Skirting the noisy crowd in the northern yard, he hurried home, his tightly curled fists trembling with fury.

Kunhathol called out to him but he did not respond. He only walked faster.

2

All day a fire smouldered inside him. He screamed at an old cherumi who was picking up areca nuts from the ground and chased her away, threatening to break her legs if he ever saw her there again. She muttered something angrily, running her hands through her tangled hair.

He shouted at Sankunni's man who was still waiting, "Go and tell the old fool I've no time today. What a day to have chosen! I can always find another buyer if Sankunni doesn't want the pepper."

His sister scolded him, "Just when we have so many expenses. Why can't you weigh out whatever there is and get the money for it?"

"Don't try to teach me how to do things. If you're so efficient, why can't you do it yourself?"

She mumbled something and went in. She must have been surprised. He had never shouted at his elder sister before. The younger sister came up to him as he was going out.

"Are you going out?"

"No, I'm coming in."

"What's the matter with you? I only asked because I wanted you to bring me snuff for half an anna if you're going out."

On his way to the bazaar, he kept asking himself, should he tell Devu's mother at Vadakkethu?

He thought of Devu with a feeling of disgust. Of her bony frame and black hairs bristling over her arms. He was not really concerned about her though. What worried him was that she would bring the Vadakkethu family a bad name.

"Didn't you hear, at Vadakkethu?"

"You know, where our Madhavan Nair. . . ." He added, fearfully, "Whom has he married?"

"The Vadakkethu. . . ."

"You mean our. . . ." He could not think beyond that point.

He sat down on the platform outside Veerankutty's tea shop and gazed at the people passing by.

"Will you have tea, Madhavan Nair?"

"No."

Nanu Nair, the manager of Kandankulangara, remarked, "You didn't come to play cards today."

"I fell asleep.

"I stopped playing when I lost four rupees."

Fishmongers who had spread out their catch in front of Bappu's shop some distance away screamed to attract buyers. The bazaar was coming alive.

Veerankutty knew that Madhavan Nair liked fish.

"There's good veloori today."

"Ah!" He continued to stare at the chameleons entangled on the fence across the road even as they separated. He recognized the figure walking over the fields even at this distance. Unni Namboodiri. He thought Unni Namboodiri would hurry past when he saw him. But he stopped and grinned, displaying all his reddened teeth. He looked like a sacrificial goat waiting to be thrown banana peels. A short, clean towel ineffectively hid bits of his scab-covered body. He held a long torch in his hand. Madhavan cursed him silently, "The rascal!"

Appukuttan called out, "Where to, Unni Namboodiri?"

"Nowhere in particular."

"If you want to taste good bazaar tea, Unni Namboodiri, you must drink mapilla tea."

Madhavan pretended not to notice Unni Namboodiri looking at him through the corner of his eye.

Veerankutty urged, "Come on, Unni Namboodiri, don't worry. Madhavan Nair won't tell on you. Will you, Madhavan Nair?"

Unni Namboodiri stood where he was, playing with the torch.

Madhavan got down from the platform, lit his beedi at the fireplace and left.

It was very noisy in the room above Achu's shop; they were obviously still playing cards. Someone had spread out straw to dry on the stretch of road beyond the shops. These people thought the public road was like their own yard. By the river, he heard the sound of axes hitting the roots of the banyan tree that had fallen down in the gale in Karkatakam.

People were sure to ask him questions if he hung around the shops. He suddenly wanted to distance himself from everyone. He went down to the fields. The big path was wide enough here for vehicles. It led to the Kandandulangara gatehouse. Two fields more and he would be at the Vadakkethu gate. He kept his eyes on the ground.

Did someone call out? No, it could not be. Then he heard distinctly, "Madhavetta, can you come this way?"

Sumitra was standing on the steps that had been freshly smeared with cowdung. He thought she would come down into the field if he did not go up. So he walked towards her gate.

She looked as if she had just had a bath and changed out of wet clothes, as she stood teasing out the tangled strands of her hair. Her arms, which were the colour of a faded banana stem and her neck with the black thread around it still looked moist.

"Amma said we have to make an offering to the gulikan tomorrow. She asked if you could come home."

He did not know what to say.

"We promised the offering when the goats fell ill. It's been arranged for tomorrow."

He was tempted to ask, do you need me when you make an offering to the gulikan at Vadakkethu? He stared at the muddy water collected in the footprints between the stumps of paddy in the field below. How could he refuse? He could not offend Sumitra.

"I was just about to send Karthu to call you when I saw you."

So she had seen him come down into the field as she stood in the courtyard, and recognized him from that distance.

He looked at her again and suddenly became aware of his hairy chest and tucked-up mundu. When he went next to Kumaranalloor, he should buy himself a few sleeved vests, he told himself.

"Shall I call Amma?"

"Tell her I'll come."

He waited for a minute, wondering whether Sumitra would say something more. As he turned to walk away, she asked,

"You didn't buy any fish today?"

"But it's Tiruvonam."

"You brought us narimeen last year, the day after Onam."

Aboobacker had brought two of them, huge ones, in return for having arranged for him to lease a small bit of land near the illam to grow tapioca. When sliced, they had a whole pot full. His elder sister had sent across four slices to Vadakkethu through Padmu.

He told himself as he changed direction, I'm not going to Aboobacker's, I'm going to have a look at the banana grove. There were five clusters of bananas that had been too unripe to cut down. He examined them, then took the long way back home, past Aboobacker's. Aboobacker had gone to Kuttippuram that morning. A net was lying in the yard. He asked Aboobacker's son,

"Don't you catch any narimeen these days?"

"I heard there were some on the northern side of the river."

"Hm."

He thought of the koothu last year at Ariyampadathu, as he walked to the illam. The seventh day's koothu. They were going to act the killing of Indrajit. Nanu Nair and Achu had told him that evening that they were going.

"Are you coming?"

"Let me see."

After dinner, he had decided to go. He put on his shirt and asked for the torch. Edathi Amma from Vadakkethu was in the kitchen. She asked,

"Where are you going, Madhava?"

They had come to sleep at his place.

When he told them he was going to Ariyampadath, they wanted to go with him. He cursed himself for having told them. Achu and the others would have left. He had to wait till the women and children got ready. He felt embarrassed, walking in front of them with a torch.

They spread the mat they had brought under the banyan tree in front of the koothambalam. Madhavan did not sit down. He looked for his friends but did not find them. Feeling tired, he came back. Some of them were asleep on the mat. Edathi Amma was dozing. She moved aside to make place for him.

Pests! Was it for this that he'd dragged them here? It irritated him to see them all lying there, fast asleep.

He leaned against the banyan tree, stretched out his legs and listened to the koothu performer's rhythmic, skilful word-play.

When the heavy sky cleared for a minute, he was surprised to see Sumitra lying asleep near his feet. She seemed like a marvel he had never seen before. Her breath moved in gentle waves over the bluish leaves and branches on her blouse.

He no longer heard the poet-performer's chant. Sumitra lay like a princess in the little island of light amidst the darkness. And he was her strong bodyguard, keeping watch over her.

That was the first time he had wanted to look at Sumitra without her being aware of it.

He heard someone washing clothes as he reached the illam. And a child crying continuously.

Kunhathol must be in the kitchen. Good. There was no one in the northern courtyard, where the women had danced that morning. He cleared his throat.

"Who is that?"

"It is me, Madhavan."

Kunhathol opened the door from the kitchen to the verandah and stood half hidden behind it.

"Did Govindan say anything about the rest of the paddy, Madhava?"

"I haven't seen him. I'll ask again."

"Instead of the usual two hundred paras he brings in Chingam, he's brought only fifty. It's going to be difficult if things go on this way."

He waited quietly. How was he to broach the subject?

"You must have lunch here tomorrow, Madhava."

Yes. He always had lunch at the illam the day after Onam. And Kunhathol always threw a five rupee note into his hand when he came away, "It's to buy new clothes for Onam. Unni doesn't know how to choose. Get something really nice."

He hesitated. Through the blackened railings, he could see the flames in the kitchen flare up and die down.

"There's something I'd like to say."

He wondered whether his voice sounded unusually rough. The dark circles below the eyes in Kunhathol's withered face seemed to deepen.

"What is it?"

The half-framed phrases in his mind splintered into bits.

"You must get Unni Namboodiri married."

Kunhathol's face brightened. "Yes I've been wanting to talk to the namboodiri at Kizhakkiniyath about it."

"Whoever arranges it, the sooner the better. Otherwise." He checked himself.

"What is it Madhava? Tell me, whatever it is."

Her voice sounded more hurt than anxious.

"Nothing."

He curbed the words that bubbled on the surface of his mind and said, "Let's see if he will look after the affairs of the illam at least when he's married."

He left at once. Midway down the garden he turned and looked back. Kunhathol stood with her hand on the door like a shadow that had taken refuge in the darkness.

He thought angrily, the illam would be destroyed, the mapillas would encroach on the land. He prayed that the old woman would die before that happened.

As a child he had heard the story of Varahamoorthy's curse, of how he went around carrying red-hot copper vessels to burn people's faces and a mattress soiled with menstrual blood to pollute their souls. He would dig the earth with his tusks and make tanks out of the spots where the illams stood.

Unni Namboodiri's illam had once stretched they said, from carpenter Raman's place to the upper boundary of the Kandankulangara property. It had been reduced now to one-fourth its former size.

The mapillas now ran a weaving factory in one of the illams on the banks of the river. The namboodiris who lived in the illam on the hill had been the wealthiest landlords in the region. A property dispute and the legal proceedings that followed had drained them. They had been forced to demolish the new outhouse and divide the proceeds from the sale of the tiles and the wooden rafters amongst themselves.

And here? Madhavan felt that Unni Namboodiri was the destructive seed of Varahamoorthy's curse in his own illam.

His mother had told him when he was a child that all the lands and fields in the countryside had belonged to the namboodiris of the Panniyur Gramam. They had prospered by the grace of Varahamoorthy's blessing. The folk of Shukapuram tried to take this grace away from them, but did not succeed. Then they engaged spies, who covered the idol of Varahamoorthy with a red-hot copper vessel in order to subdue its power. But the vessel exploded. The priest then placed a cloth soiled with menstrual blood on the idol to help the Shukapuram folk. It was then that Varahamoorthy had leaped out, shouting "Despicable ones!" Now his curse was taking effect.

The wind had died down. Wildcats bared their teeth in the overcast sky.

Madhavan tried to sleep and tossed and turned restlessly.

Because he went to Vadakkethu once in a while, everyone said, contemptuously, "He's there all the time. What on earth has happened to him?" Even his sisters thought he went there because he was consumed with desire for the one with the lean, bony face and the disgusting black hair on her cheeks and lips. He was furious with them.

It was the emaciated, asthmatic Edathi Amma of Vadakkethu who had started the rumour.

-Madhavan sent us a bunch of nenthran bananas.

-Madhavan says.

-Madhavan, Madhavan, Madhavan!

She would sit on the verandah and call out to Devu, "Give him a mat, Devu."

Devu never came out. His blood boiled when they hinted that she was too shy to face him.

"Things have changed after all," Sumitra teased, breaking off the little white chillies that grew near the fence and tossing them into the ends of her mundu. For a moment, he forgot that Devu was behind the door, waiting for him to say something while she mixed a tablet into the juice of herbs.

They were sure to lose patience and broach the subject one day.

"Madhava, I've been wanting to talk to you for a long time."

"About what?"

"We can't go on like this. Everyone wants to know when it's going to be."

"What are you talking about, Edathi Amma?"

"About Devu."

And then . . . it would all explode like the sudden gusts of wind . . . that broke out in Thulam. Wait and see, he said to himself.

3

Ever since Unni Namboodiri's marriage had been decided, people talked only about Karakkattu Mana, an illam which lay to the east of the village. It was as if the bored villagers had suddenly come upon a treasure.

Unni Namboodiri was lucky. His mother's goodness had brought him good fortune even though he was a simpleton, said Amma. An illam with a large income. They still had elephants.

Sethu overheard Sankunni the trumpet player describe the Karakattu elephant to Madhava Ammama.

Unni Namboodiri came to Sethu's house as soon as his marriage was fixed.

"What's the news, Unni Namboodiri?"

Unni Namboodiri smiled and kept his eyes on the ground, his mouth full of betel leaves.

"How much money are they giving you?" asked Cheriamma.

"Two thousand."

"Did you see the anterjanam?"

"Of course not!" Unni Namboodiri was not interested in such things. He said the deity had been carried on the Karakattu elephant's back at the Thirumanthamkunnu temple festival last year. Unni Namboodiri had been riding on the back of Kollengode Ayyappan at the time.

"He won't move an inch, no matter how many fireworks there are. And he's never hurt anyone."

Madhava Ammama had just got back from the illam. "Have you seen the Karakkat elephant, Madhava? He's really something to look at."

Madhava Ammama grunted non-committally.

"I believe he goes straight into the shed when he's in rut!"

Madhava Ammama gazed into the jnaval grove and said, "Even animals have brains, only Unni Namboodiri doesn't have them."

Unni Namboodiri laughed. He played with his torch, switching it on and off. He carried it with him even during the day.

Cheriamma tried to advise Unni Namboodiri. Once he was married she said, he should attend to the affairs of the illam, not go around festival grounds on elephant back. The anterjanam was from a good family, he should not make her suffer. Unni Namboodiri grinned vacantly. When he left, Cheriamma asked Madhava Ammama,

"Will they really give a dowry of two thousand rupees?"

Madhava Ammama pretended not to hear.

Cheriamma was irritated. "You're the chief manager of the illam, aren't you? That's why I asked."

"I don't know, I didn't ask. Why don't you go and find out if you're so interested?" And Madhava Ammama walked towards the hill, where the cherumans could be heard cutting firewood all day for the feast.

Besides the other namboodiris, two nairs had to go with Unni Namboodiri. Kunhathol had asked Madhava Ammama to go, but he had said he would send Narayanan Nair and Sankunni.

"I can't leave the place. There are so many things to attend to."

The illam was full of people the day before the bride was brought home. Someone said, "They have elephants and wealth enough at Karakkat illam, but they're getting rid of a bride whom no one wants."

"So what's what it is. I was wondering who would give this idiot a dowry of two thousand rupees."

Amma tried her best to persuade Sethu to go for the wedding feast, but he did not want to go. "There'll be such a crowd. I can't be bothered with all the pollution rules of these namboodiris."

"But the old lady came up to the fence two or three times to invite you."

He was adamant. Amma went so far as to threaten him with a Brahmin's curse.

And so he went, with great reluctance.

The garden was full of cheruman families waiting for the common feast. The nair women who had come with the bride chattered loudly in the northern courtyard. The nair men ran around organizing the feast. Sethu went to the front verandah, silently cursing his mother. Catching sight of Kandankulangara Chinnan Menon and his son, he went up to them. There was a crowd of namboodiris on the verandah, talking loudly enough for the whole world to hear. Pots and other cooking vessels clattered in the thatched shed on the southern side.

Madhava Ammama was the chief supervisor. He came up to Chinnan Menon "It won't be long now. I've made all the arrangements."

Sethu thought about the new bride from Karakkat. Someone had come home yesterday and said that she was short and waddled like a duck, that people had nicknamed her Ovuthangi, she who supports the trough. Who was it who had first thought and then named her after the ugly figure under the mouth of the stone trough in the Siva temple, through which the thirtham flowed?

Someone had been asked to give the signal as soon as the bride's party crossed the river. Madhava Ammama had arranged for a group of nair women to welcome them with ululations. Madhava Ammama was everywhere.

Chinnan Menon said to his son, "Let's go, Unni. If we wait for the namboodiris to finish lunch, we'll have to starve till the evening."

One of the helpers said, "It's not everyday that you have to do it, it's just this one time." Sethu thought that he probably had not recognized Kandankulangara Menon.

The namboodiri women and children had to eat first, then the namboodiri men. The nairs who had been invited could eat only in the third lot. Sethu decided to leave with Chinnan Menon and Unnikrishnan but Madhava Ammama appeared at that moment.

"Come, Menon, and both of you. I've arranged for a few leaves to be laid on the thekkini floor before the crowd comes in. Is there anyone else?"

The thekkini was usually reserved for the namboodiris. This was the first time the custom had been broken and a few distinguished nairs allowed to eat there. As they came out after their meal, ululations echoed in the air. Unni Namboodiri had arrived with his bride.

Sethu walked back across the field with Menon. Menon asked, "Which class are you in now?"

"I'm doing my Intermediate."

Amma wanted to know all about the feast. The wedding at the illam had been the only topic of conversation for the last nine days. And now it was over.

Sethu went upstairs and stood by the window, looking out. The ululations had died down. The feast must have begun.

He wrote a long letter to Krishnankutty.

I realize what boredom means. Each day starts exactly like the one before and ends like it as well, each tomorrow promises to be the same. He wondered whether he should add that even Sumitra was no longer at home. The sentence lingered in his mind for a moment, then he dropped it.

He posted his letter and browsed through old newspapers in the ration shop. He knew there would be no letters for him, but he waited all the same until the postman came and Velayudhan Master read out all the addresses. He walked over the paddy seedling beds to the broken-down temple.

Its god was asleep.

He suddenly wanted to write a poem to the god who lay dreaming of old times, when puja was performed and naivedyam offered to him. Young girls walked past carrying gleaming brass pots of rice and bundles of firewood, their long, wet hair fastened at the tip in a little knot, a sandal paste mark on their foreheads. The pradakshinam pathway was covered with tangles of grass and buffaloes grazed there, with periodic snorts and grunts of satisfaction. He sat down on the stone pillar that was half buried in the sand.

Elusive words fluttered through his mind like chattering sparrows. He realized that the cheruman children who were playing dice in the dilapidated prayer hall were staring at him and got up, feeling self-conscious.

"Are you going, Cheria Thampuran?"

He pretended not to hear.

"Throw us a beedi, Cheria Thampuran."

"In the glow of a thousand little earthen lamps."

No. The thoughts of the god who lived now on memories of the past refused to be trapped in words.

And the image of a young girl, eyes glowing with the radiance of a thousand lamps, would never find a place in the thoughts of a god.

He reached home as it began to grow dark. Padmu brought the lamp out and lit the three wicks which faced west on the front steps.

Nanu Nair came in, joined his palms before the lamp and smiled at Sethu. Amma was on the verandah, fumbling in her betel box.

"I've been wanting to come over. I thought I would talk to you when I came this way for the wedding feast."

Amma closed her betel box and waited silently. Sethu walked up and down the courtyard a couple of times and stopped near the crumbling wall.

"I'm not a fool, Nanu Nair." Amma's voice rose suddenly. Cheriamma rushed out, anxious not to miss anything. She had just finished her bath and was still knotting the ends of her rowka.

"I know what is happening, I've got eyes and ears."

Who was Amma angry with?

"These things should be done at the right time. You're older than he is, it's up to you to think it over and decide."

Sethu realized that they were talking about Madhava Ammama. He felt embarrassed when Amma repeated her grievances against him. He was always at Vadakkethu, drinking tea and talking to them.

"Just think of it, he even ate there on that little Karthu's birthday."

Cheriamma chimed in, "Don't we have a little girl here as well? But no, she wasn't invited. Only he was."

If there was good fish in the market, it always reached Vadakkethu.

Amma warned Cheriamma. "Keep quiet. I'll do the talking."

In order to provoke Amma, Cheriamma promptly changed sides. "He's forty years old after all, and knows his mind. If he wants to start a sambandham there, let him. Do you know, Nanu Nair, it was Edathi herself who kept on at him to visit them in the first place?"

"I'm not denying that, am I? It's true that I did. I thought they were harmless, that they had no one to help them. It wasn't that I thought much of them. I just pitied them."

"And has that changed then? They're still harmless and have no one to help them. Even now."

"That's what you don't realize. They have trapped Madhavan. It makes me mad to see them behave like Urvashis. If he starts a sambandham there now, they won't walk on the earth anymore."

"Look," said Nanu Nair. He cleared his throat and spat. He got up, moved his mat nearer Amma, lowered his voice and said,

"Madhavan is not moving in the direction you think."

Amma concealed her surprise.

So Madhava Ammama had sent Nanu Nair as his messenger, to get his sisters' consent. Achan could always be informed in a letter. And the Vadakkethu family could be asked to decide on a suitable date.

Cheriamma expressed the thought in Sethu's mind. "So Madhavan wants it. How can you blame a man for that?"

"But what does he see in her? She had no looks at all to boast of, the wretch."

"It's not the older one he's interested in."

"Then?" Had his voice joined Amma's and Cheriamma's? Sethu checked himself.

"There's the second one."

"Who, Sumitra?"

"I don't know what she's called, Sumitra or Kaikeyi."

The soft breeze that had wafted through the areca nut palms into the yard suddenly ceased. No one spoke. Sethu waited, listening to his heartbeats.

He felt relieved when he heard Amma's voice after what seemed to him endless days and nights.

"My God! What's happened to him?"

"I spoke to him. They won't like it either, giving away the younger one while the older one is still unmarried. Do you know what he said? That he can get Devu a husband."

Sethu pretended he had not heard anything and quickly went past them upstairs.

It was dark, but he did not ask Padmu for a lamp.

He lay down on the window ledge, full of resentment and blind revenge.

An enemy, a rival in Madhava Ammama! With his yellowed teeth, the stench of beedis, his black, hairy body.

He had pitied him once. But Madhava Ammama seemed like a rakshasa now. The rakshasa of his childhood stories, brandishing a spiked club and standing guard over an inaccessible stone fortress.

He went to bed feeling helpless and angry. He would never be the prince arriving at the door of the fortress with the seven magic stones that would release the princess. Never.

He thought of Sumitra lying on the ochre floor, her sandalwood coloured skin, her moist parted lips and her closed eyes.

It hurt him to think that she knew nothing of this danger, shut away in Appunni Menon's wife's house in Tirur.

It was the first time he had tasted the bitterness of jealousy, the anger and hurt of love that only an eighteen-year-old can understand.

He remembered how Sumitra used to follow him like an inimical shadow when he ran round the mango groves and jnaval trees as a little boy, his shorts with the broken buttons tucked into his waist thread. She would pick up a crushed mango with her witlow-covered fingers and hand it to him lovingly, and he would feel disgusted. She used to bathe in the bathing ghat next to his, wearing a faded red konam. If she came up to him, he used to move away. And then one day he had come upon her on the hillside and the years had dissolved. She was no longer the inimical shadow, she had become the beautiful princess of the fairy tale who had broken out of a curse.

After that, she had grown distant, and moved away from him. And he had been afraid even to call out her name in his hoarse voice which had just begun to break.

When life became a dream and she the world, he had waited outside. The little enemy of yesterday who had turned into a woman overnight was growing away from him and he could only watch resentfully.

There was no one he could speak to. No one would be interested in the dreams of an eighteen-year-old.

The palms seemed to wield iron clubs in their huge hands. He shuddered.

4

The night crept by slowly. Early morning, he heard the bleating of goats outside. He shook off his sleep and got up.

Yes, it was Sumitra's voice.

He gripped the window bars and listened. Amma asked coldly, holding her anger in check,

"So, when did you get back?"

He did not make out her reply. He rubbed the sleep from his eyes and hurried down only to find that Sumitra had gone up the hill with her goats.

Amma must have been surprised to see him up so early. Ever since he had come home from college, he had grown used to lying in bed till the sun became really hot. Padmu, who always got up with Cheriamma, was in the yard, following the old cherumi with her little broom and dustpan. He shouted at her for no reason,

"Go in, girl, don't make the place dirty." She looked at him, her huge eyes filled with fear, and walked away slowly.

He did not bother to have a wash. He wiped his face with the end of his mundu, ran his fingers through his hair and quickly went up the hill.

Sumitra's goats were looking for fresh stalks in the thickets. The old mother goat with full udders gave Sethu a baleful look and moved off. Sumitra was not to be seen. Nor did he look for her. He wanted to come upon her by chance. He walked past the clump of jnaval trees, down the lane and wandered right up to the palms. Then he turned and walked back to the compound near the illam which belonged to a mapilla. He had fenced it to grow root crops. Sethu picked up some stones, threw them at the goats and returned home.

Since the Vadakkethu fence had been closed, he would have to go round the fields if he wanted to see Sumitra.

I don't want to see anyone, he said to himself. Sumitra means nothing to me.

He sat upstairs reading till it was time for lunch, listening all the time for her voice.

It always distressed him when Padmu came and called him for lunch. After all, it was not so long ago that he used to watch Parameswara Ettan eat rice with resentment and hurt, knowing that he himself would be served only kanji. Now that he had grown up, rice was cooked for him every afternoon and the kanji bowls for the others would be set out only after he had finished his meal. If Padmu passed by while he was eating, the rice would taste of pebbles and Sethu would not be able to eat anymore.

He often thought of what Krishnankutty had said, that poverty was not a crime. But Amma and Cheriamma were always trying to hide that crime from him here.

My friend, I have become a stranger in my own house for no reason I can think of.

Everyone in the house prepared for an afternoon nap, mopping up their own bits of floor. He went out again towards the hillside in the afternoon sun.

He could see a portion of the Vadakkethu courtyard and the floor of their dilapidated cowshed if he stood in the shade of the palms near the Brahmarakshasu shrine.

He would summon her there by an act of will.

He remembered something he had learned in class. If human beings prayed for centuries to divine images made of stone or wood, their faith would invest the lifeless statues with a sacred power.

Whether it was the strength of his faith, or the acuteness of the electrical impulses in his brain he did not know—Sumitra came up the gravel path, sweating in the hot sunshine. He wanted to laugh in the arrogance of his victory.

"What are you doing here, Sethu?"

"Nothing."

"We're redoing the floor of the thekkini. I'm going to get the polishing stone from Paru's."

Had she put on weight? The red edging of her yellow satin blouse was soaked with sweat. She walked on and he called out to her.

He wanted to ask her about the big house in Tirur. About the people who lived there. Was the little gold chain with links shaped like beaten rice lying flat on her throat a gift from Kandankulangara Menon's wife?

He fumbled for words.

"When are you leaving, Sethu?" she asked, and he found his chance. "Are you in such a hurry for me to leave?"

Sumitra laughed, ignoring his reproachful tone.

"What is there to laugh about?"

She shook her head, still laughing.

"Though you're in college and all, you're still a baby, Sethu."

He burned with anger.

"I heard about Madhava Ammama's wedding."

But no, Sumitra did not look guilty, as he had thought she would.

"Oh yes, I know."

"Why does Madhava Ammama come so often to your house?"

"Who knows?"

"I'm sure it must be to see you."

Sumitra laughed loudly again. She walked a few paces, turned, spat and came back wiping her chin. He thought her eyes looked moist.

"I'll die of laughter, Sethu, listening to you."

He drew himself up and stared at her, willing his eyes to tell her, look at me and see if you can laugh.

"I thought you might have left by the time I got back. Karthu told me you were still here."

"When is the wedding?"

Sumitra seemed to be confused for a moment. Then she said calmly, her smile unchanged,

"Soon. You'll come, won't you?"

He wanted to shake her by the shoulders and ask, what did you see in that black-skinned man with his yellow teeth who smells of beedis? But he walked away, his head bent, as if it had been a casual encounter. He knew she was behind him. She called out to him as he turned into the lane.

"Look, Sethu."

He stopped, but did not look back.

"It won't be a grand wedding, but you must come."

He did not reply. He hurried away, murmuring the lines of a poem by Changampuzha which described women as the root of all destruction.

He sat upstairs and watched the daylight grow dimmer and another night creep up. He had finished one of the two books he had taken from the college library. He started on the Hardy novel. When he got to the part where the wife was about to be sold, he heard Amma and Cheriamma talking animatedly downstairs.

"What star was it yesterday? Put on water for tea, Padmu. And give Sethu Ettan the almanac."

Sethu came down. Pankutty, the son of the vettuvan who stayed in the little thatched hut in Achan's compound had come.

"Sarojini has had a baby girl Sethu, yesterday evening at six thirty. The star can't be Pooratam then, it has to be Uthratam."

Sethu consulted the almanac. To Amma's relief, it was Uthratam. "Pooratam is not a good star. We'd always be worried about its evil influence."

Cheriamma was instructed to make tea and uppuma. Amma called Sethu inside, "Do you have any money, child?"

Sethu was irritated, "From where?"

Amma murmured, "I have to give him at least five rupees, don't I, when he brings news of a childbirth? I'll send Padmu to the illam. Give me a clean, washed mundu if you have one, to give Pankutty."

He began to argue with Amma and she hushed him, "Sh . . . softly, don't let him hear. I don't want a very new one, just something that's not too old."

Amma walked up and down restlessly until Pankutty had eaten and left with his five rupees and a clean, washed mundu.

While he had dinner that night, Amma said, "Why don't you go there tomorrow?"

"Where?"

"To Achan's house. If no one goes to see the baby, they'll blame me."

"You go, Amma."

Amma stayed silent for a moment. "Hm . . . that's all I need to do now. You have nothing to do, Sethumadhavan, why can't you go?"

He had been to Achan's house only once, after Parameswara Ettan's wedding, five years ago.

He thought of Nalini Edathi, Valia Oppu and Cheria Oppu and suddenly wanted to go. Amma went out early morning and managed to borrow ten rupees from somewhere but he still pretended he was not interested. Even when she instructed him to give the midwife a rupee, he complained, "What a nuisance all this is!"

But secretly, he wanted to show his father's sisters that the little boy of five years ago with his thick striped shirt and oil-streaked face had grown up.

As he set out with a packet containing his clothes, Devu called from the gate, "Where to, Sethu?"

"To Thrissur."

He did not look that side. He did not care whether Sumitra heard or not.

As he hung onto the iron railings of the ferryboat amongst the fishmongers and the porters, sweating profusely, he thought about Nalini Edathi.

Nalini Edathi had been in the tenth when he went there five years ago. She had gone to Cannanore for a teachers' training course but had not completed it. The family had heard that she had fallen in love with a Christian boy who was her classmate. Edathi Amma had been the first to know. Parameswara Ettan had gone to bring her back but she had refused to come. He had overheard whispers that she had run away to live with the Christian boy. Achan had been sent for by telegram, so that he could get her married when she came home on vacation. But Nalini Edathi would not come back. Achan and Parameswara Ettan had gone and brought her back by force. Achan had ordered that she be shut in her room. There was no wedding. Afraid that his niece might run away, Achan had appointed a watchman. And after that no one talked about Nalini Edathi. Sethu had often wanted to ask Edathi Amma about her, but Edathi Amma had not mentioned the existence of a younger sister.

Loud-voiced Nalini Edathi always wore a big pottu and bangles from wrist to elbow and could whistle like a boy. Sethu had loved watching her embroider coloured flowers on lengths of off-white material.

After they passed the big heap of rocks, the broken-down temple and the tile factory and the road began to wind upwards, he called out to the conductor to stop. But the conductor, busy exchanging witticisms with the commuters in the seats at the back while he scratched himself obscenely, his trouser leg lifted, paid no attention and continued his attempts to amuse the passengers.

The kind driver stopped but only when they reached the foot of the hill. Sethu escaped from that pit of hell.

5

Here was the familiar lane, slippery with sand, and the great banyan tree. Coconut palm branches, coconut shells and banana stems lay heaped under the banyan. He used to run through the peon's house whenever he came back from the bathing ghat in the temple at dusk, to avoid the banyan tree, because black magic was often performed there.

It was a big house. He was proud of the way it lay spread out in the middle of the coconut grove. The branches of the mango tree in the courtyard reached right into the upstairs verandah with its black wooden railings.

This was not his house, though. He was a visitor here.

As he crossed the empty courtyard and climbed into the verandah, someone called out, "Who is it?"

He moved aside to make way for the woman who came in with a heap of dry clothes she had gathered from the clothesline.

"It's Sethu, isn't it? God! I didn't make you out at first!"

Nalini Edathi.

She looked much thinner and the borders of her mundu and veshti were worn and faded.

Cheria Oppu came out. He was happy to see his father's sisters; they were so dignified. They had their baths in the ghat of the kovilakam every morning and wore clean white clothes and sandal paste marks on their foreheads. He felt so ashamed of Amma and Cheriamma who wore short little towels under which their shabby undergarments showed.

"So now you've become a big person, going to college and all. Still, you could visit us now and then."

"Where's Valia Oppu?"

"She's gone to have a bath. Give me that packet now." Nalini Edathi took the paper packet he had with him and brought him water to wash his feet.

Valia Oppu came back.

"Have you seen the baby?"

The dark little room was heavy with the smell of Dettol and wet clothes.

Edathi Amma raised her head to ask, "Why didn't Amma come, Sethu?"

"She said she would come later, with Ettan."

The woman who looked after the baby brought the child out, wrapped in a dirty cloth. It seemed to him that its half-closed eyes were afraid of the light.

"Look who's come. It's Sethu Ammaman!"

"Where are Unni and Shyamala?"

"They've gone with Ettan. I won't have a minute's rest if they stay here," said Edathi Amma. "Is the upstairs door open, Amme? The folding chair has been put away. Its supporting rod is under the cot."

The room upstairs was Edathi Amma's. Nalini Edathi pushed the closed windows open.

"Sit down Sethu. Did you come by bus?"

He saw himself in the big mirror as he stood at the window holding on to the squared bars. A big framed photograph of Ettan and Edathi Amma hung above the other window.

Valia Oppu came up with mangoes in a silver plate and tea in a bell-metal glass.

Nalini Edathi took off the blanket that lay over the cot and shook out the mattress.

"Where's Ravi?"

"He's gone out. He'll be back soon."

Cheria Oppu's son Ravi and he were the same age. They used to be childhood friends. Ravi called Sethu Ettan because Sethu was three months older.

Nalini Edathi had changed a lot in five years! She had lost so much hair that her scalp showed in places. Her arms, which used to be covered to the elbow in coloured glass bangles were bare. She was as faded as a flower bed soaked in rain, and choked by wet sand.

"I wanted to write to you ever since I knew you were in college."

"Didn't you ever go back and write your exams, Nalini Edathi?"

Nalini Edathi gripped the panel of the door, bent her head and tried to smile.

"Exams! I'm too lazy now to even note down the number of clothes I give to the washerwoman. It's all over."

Sethu did not say anything.

"When you finish your studies and begin to work." Nalini Edathi turned her face away. "That's what I wanted to write about. It occurred to me suddenly one day. Edathi feels ashamed to take me with her. If you ever need someone to come and look after your children one day, you must send for me."

Sethu stood very still. She went out with the old sheet and pillow case. When she came back with fresh ones, he was still at the window.

"Don't worry, I'm not mad or anything like that. Do you wear trousers to college, Sethu?"

"I don't have trousers."

"It's Easter today, I saw in the calendar. When I was in Cannanore. . . ."

She stopped speaking and looked as if she wanted to shake something out of her mind. "What nonsense I've been talking. Sit down, Sethu."

He heard a shout from downstairs, "Sethu Etta!"

Ravi had arrived. He heard the stairs and the boards of the ceiling tremble as Ravi bounded up.

Ravi surprised him by having grown much bigger than him. The collar of his striped shirt, made by the village tailor, was too broad. He was bathed in sweat. His shirt was unbuttoned and the dirty vest underneath showed. He looked a bit of a boor. Sethu noticed that Ravi still wore his big red-stone earrings.

Sethu shrank away when a heavy hand fell on his shoulder.

"I'm taller than you, Sethu Etta." They stood next to each other to see who was taller. Ravi opened Sethu's parcel and examined its contents. He brought the clean, ironed shirts to the window and asked the price of each.

"Will you pass this time?"

"I'm fed up of studying, Sethu Etta. I'll kill the headmaster if he doesn't promote me this time. We have the cinema here now, near the river. Do you see many films in Palghat?"

"Sometimes."

"We'll go this evening."

"What is playing?"

"Gulebakkevali.' I heard it's good. There's a fight with a tiger."

"We'll think about it."

"What's there to think about?"

Ravi sat on the bed and talked about school. All he wanted was to somehow get through the tenth. He was the only son, and there was so much work at home. There were coconuts to be plucked and they grew tapioca by the sea.

Ravi went out again after they ate. He had to supervise the drawing up of water by a wheel for irrigation. He had to count the palm branches that had been cut down before buyers came for them. He said he would be late coming back.

Valia Oppu and Cheria Oppu came and talked to him by turns. Nalini Edathi brought him tea in the evening, and then settled down on the floor by the door. It distressed him to see her sit so quietly, with her head bent and her fingers running restlessly through her hair. She looked up with interest when he described the fort Tippu Sultan had built on the outskirts of the town he lived in now. The familiar gleam came back to her eyes when he told her the story of the secret underground passage which led out from the fort.

Long ago, there had been a military chief in charge of the fort, who had a lame daughter, a beautiful girl. She could not walk without help. Sardar Khan sighed whenever he saw his daughter who spent her days and nights playing the sitar. A prisoner came to the fort once. One night, she managed to get hold of the key to the secret passage and she somehow hobbled to his cell and helped him escape. They were caught and shot dead by the sentries. The passage had remained sealed from that day.

When he finished the story, Nalini Edathi asked, "Is that true, or did you make it up, Sethu?"

"People say it's true, people who know its history."

Nalini Edathi fell silent again. She leaned back, closed her eyes and then opened them again after a while, as if she had been asleep.

"What was the name of the prisoner in the story?"

"I don't know."

"He was a Hindu, wasn't he?"

"Hm."

"Do you go for films, Nalini Edathi?"

"Films! What a thing! When I was in Cannanore." She stopped as if she had had second thoughts about what she was going to say.

He described the maidan outside the fort, where he spent the evenings. And the girls in his class. He longed to see her laugh as she used to.

Someone was coming up the stairs, someone with a very soft footfall. He heard the tinkle of glass bangles in the corridor.

"Nalini Edathi, aren't you coming for a bath?"

"Take this glass down, Thangamani."

The girl who came in looked timidly at him. She was slightly built and wore a light green skirt with a white blouse.

"Don't you know Sethu?"

She shook her head, biting on her glass bead chain. Did she mean yes or no? Sethu tried to give shape to a shadowy memory.

"Haven't you met Thangamani, Sethu? She's from Cheriamma's place at Pushpoth." She had come from Pushpoth that morning to make an offering at the Siva temple.

"Which class are you in?"

"Ninth."

When Thangamani went down, he asked Nalini Edathi whether Pushpoth Govinda Ammaman was still at Tiruppur.

He had been to Pushpoth once, as a child. His paternal grandmother's younger sister had been in difficulties after the family partition. Her sons had no jobs. Her eldest daughter had married a teacher in a mapilla school who earned a salary of ten rupees. When the proprietor of the school refused to pay him even this pittance regularly, he had quarrelled with him, left the village and became accountant to a Chettiar in Tiruppur. Later, he had found employment in a mill and began to make good money.

Amma preferred her mother-in-law's younger sister, Pushpoth Cheriamma, to her mother-in-law.

Everyone was terrified of Govinda Ammaman. He was a hot-tempered man even now. When he came home on holidays, he would begin to drink early in the morning. Even his children were afraid of him. But he always brought plenty of money every time he came home and spent lavishly, both in his own house at Tirumanayur and in his wife's house.

He used to visit Sethu's house in the old days. Amma used to make chicken for him and send someone secretly to buy arrack.

"Whatever people say, he's so meek and gentle with me," Amma would say after he left. Govindammaman always gave Amma some money as he was leaving. Sethu could still recall the scent of the one rupee note he had once given him.

But Govinda Ammaman had not visited them for many years now.

Achan had gone to Tiruppur looking for a job, when he lost his job in the Anamalais. He had stayed with Govinda Ammaman for a month. They had quarrelled before they parted. Achan had come back with scandalous stories: Govinda Ammaman had two young girls to work for him and didn't want his wife and children in the house.

Sethu had wondered whether Govinda Ammaman would send him some money if he wrote to him from college. But in the end he did not have the courage to write.

When Sethu had come here for Unni's anna prasanam, Oppu had come from Pushpoth. She had invited him to go back with her. "There are lots of children there."

He had hung his head shyly. Oppu asked Parameswara Ettan, "Shall I take Sethu with me?"

Ettan had said, "He has to come back with me today, he can't miss school."

So he hadn't gone then. He had been to Pushpoth when he was six years old. He remembered Pushpoth Cheriamma very faintly. She wore a gold sovereign on a thread around her neck and was twice his grandmother's size, although she was younger. She walked with difficulty. He remembered playing hide-and-seek with the children. He had heard that the house had later been demolished and rebuilt.

When he came down, Thangamani and Nalini Edathi had still not gone for their bath.

"Don't you want a bath, Sethu?" asked Valia Oppu.

"Later, at dusk."

"Go down to the bathing ghat at the kovilakam, the water is excellent there."

"No, I prefer the tank." He felt shy now about bathing in an open place, having grown used to the hostel bathrooms.

Cheria Oppu asked, "Shall I make you some coffee?"

"No, I just had some. Why hasn't Ravi come?"

"He'll come now. Do you like sweets made with dates, Sethu?"

Of course he did. After coming here, he felt he loved the whole world.

Cheria Oppu said, "We'll go to the temple after dinner; there's a niramala today."

"All right."

The white sand between the coconut palms glittered in the evening sunshine. Crows pecked at the fallen jackfruits under the trees near the northern fence. A faint breeze rippled through the palm leaves. He could hear the indistinct murmur of the sea in the distance. A pleasant restlessness stirred inside him.

The clock in the verandah upstairs chimed. Six o'clock.

Thangamani spoke to Nalini Edathi somewhere inside the house. What a soft voice she had!

"Deepam!" Sethu turned and looked at her as she stood holding the lamp high for him to worship. But he did not join his palms, it seemed an undignified gesture for a grown-up boy who went to college.

He saw the long vibhuti mark on her small forehead in the bright yellow radiance of the oil lamp.

She set lighted wicks in the shrines in the courtyard and returned to the house.

"Aren't you having a bath, Sethu Etta?"

"I'll wait for Ravi."

Nalini Edathi came in from the yard and sat down on the steps. "I have such a headache every evening. I can't sleep all night. Go and have your bath, Sethu. Cheriamma said you're going to the temple for the niramala."

"Yes, Cheria Oppu said we could go."

"Thangamani, get the soap and a towel for him, child."

He went in to take his shirt off. Ravi had come back by the time he came out again.

"Sethu Etta, I'm coming for a bath as well."

Ravi helped Pankutty, the son of the farmhand, unload the burden on his head, paid him and instructed him about next morning's jobs. He asked his mother and aunt to tell him the arrears in the accounts the mapilla coconut buyer had given. Sethu was amazed to see the ninth standard schoolboy behaving like the manager of a tarawad.

Ravi pulled off his clothes, rolled them and threw them to Nalini Edathi. Wrapping a towel around his waist, he swung his arms and began to do exercises. "Get me some oil, girl," he called out.

Sethu could not make out Thangamani's face behind the thatch screen, but he thought silently to himself, "The oaf, calling her `girl' like that."

They walked towards the river.

"How many years more do you have at college, Sethu Etta?"

"Many more. And I have to pass every year, you know."

"How can *you* fail, Sethu Etta? Impossible! I plan to start a shop. I've found two rooms near the Panchayat office. No office job for me."

"Why should you have an office job? You have coconuts and paddy. It's those who don't have such things who have to hunt for jobs."

"I'll come and see you when you're in an important position."

Sethu thought with panic, how far away that time is.

The only ghat in the river which was deserted was the one where the elephants were bathed. So they went down to it. The water was lukewarm and only came up to their necks at its deepest. They could hear the men of the kovilakam talking loudly as they bathed by the light of lanterns in the tiled bathing ghat nearby.

"How many are there in your class?"

"About forty, mostly kids. I feel so ashamed, Sethu Etta. I'm glad Thangamani is in the other division."

"Are there any girls?"

"A few. All horrid creatures!"

Sethu tried to turn the conversation to girls, but Ravi did not seem to be interested. He talked about the giant fish in the temple tank, and the bats that hung on the banyan near the gate of the kovilakam, easy targets for a gun. Now and then, he reminded Sethu that they were going for a film.

A lantern had been lit by the time they got back and leaves laid for dinner.

They walked in the yard after dinner and Ravi asked softly, "Do you smoke, Sethu Etta?"

"Hm?"

"I just wanted to know, that's all."

"Sometimes. They give us cigarettes after a feast in the hostel. But I don't make a habit of it."

"I'll bring you some tomorrow."

He did not say anything.

Cheria Oppu asked, "Aren't you ready, Sethu?"

"What madness, Amma, as if Sethu Ettan wants to go to the niramala in the temple. We're going for a film. Anyway, you can't go into the temple. We are still in the period of pollution, with a newborn baby at home."

"Don't try to teach me. We were not going in anyway. And how can Thangamani and I go by ourselves?"

Sethu said to Ravi, "Why don't you come with us?"

"Not me." Ravi whispered, "Let them go. We can go for a late night show."

In the end, he had to disappoint Ravi. He put on his gleaming, ironed poplin shirt. His mundu was quite clean, but he changed it anyway. He took a little talcum powder from Edathi Amma's table.

"Do you need any small change?" asked Edathi Amma when he went to tell her he was going.

"No."

"Take a torch with you."

Beyond the lane was a sandy track, and then a few shops and a couple of banyan trees. After that an empty road stretched through a coconut grove.

Cheria Oppu led the way, talking about Amma. Why didn't she visit them sometimes? At least to mollify the villagers? After all, she said, none of us have harmed her in any way.

He followed the beam of the torch, listening to the footfalls of the girl who walked at arm's length from him. She looked more grown up now, in her flowered half-sari, with her hair in two plaits. A faint whiff reached him from the strand of jasmines wound in one plait.

A group of women with flaming torches in their hands came in from the lane and joined Cheria Oppu.

"And who is this?"

"Sethu, my older brother's younger son. He's in college in Palghat. He just came in today."

Sethu slowed down and fell back. Thangamani did not seem to want to join the other women.

"Walk carefully, the road is full of stones."

Her eyes gleamed softly in the shadows.

He wanted to talk to her.

She seemed like a bud with all its sweetness folded within it.

This was poetry, surely.

The clouds moved away and the sky cleared suddenly. In the bright moonlight, the long shadows of the palms and the road smiled at them. The flowing moonlight was like a marvel, unbelievable.

Why did the thought of Sumitra come to him now? He scolded himself. Sumitra matters nothing to me. A beautiful girl who had emerged from all the poems he had ever read was here beside him.

As they crossed over the makeshift bridge of coconut trunks, he said, "Carefully, hold my hand."

Her fingers felt fragile. He caught a scent of talcum powder and jasmine.

He did not release her hand when they reached the other side.

Above them, the sky was clear, and a sea of moonlight flowed beneath. A distant thudding of drums from the temple sounded like the beats of a giant heart and grew louder and louder with every step they took.

He held her hand, savouring the scent of freshly opened jasmines and thought, I had been waiting for this moment all my life.

Had the world been waiting for me, with moonlight and fragrance and the thudding of drums?

For me, and for you?

6

The thought of leaving next day distressed him.

And so we have to part. Till we see each other again.

The fields and coconut groves were left behind, and the sandy track merged into the tarred road. As he waited for the bus with his paper parcel under his arm, he had a strong feeling of loss. He shrank into the smallest possible space in the bus in the middle of a disgusting stench of human beings and no longer heard the sounds around him. All he heard was the tinkle of bangles. The scent of jasmines and talcum powder flowed around him like moonlight by the river. His fingers held the memory of touch, the feel of her left shoulder.

He slid into a near-coma induced by the heat and the rocking of the bus. Each minute of the past few days swam before his eyes like bubbles distilled from the indistinct colours of sunset clouds.

And so we have to part, till we meet each other again.

A guest must always leave before the novelty of his presence wears off. Valia Oppu and Cheria Oppu had tried to persuade him to stay on. Edathi Amma had said repeatedly, "College hasn't started yet. Stay for a few days."

Nalini Edathi had hidden her sadness and murmured, "After Sethu came, I felt I had someone to talk to."

"I'll come again."

"Write sometimes. I've often thought of writing a letter to myself and posting it."

"I'll write."

Thangamani had wanted to leave the day after the niramala, but they had persuaded her to stay. She had stood undecided on the verandah, drawing her nails over the cement flower patterns on the pillars.

"It may not be as comfortable here as at Pushpoth, but we are your aunts after all," Cheria Oppu had chided her.

Sethu had waited anxiously near the window until he was sure she would stay.

Time was not a strangling curse here. Every moment was filled with hope. Could he hear soft footsteps in the kitchen and the corridor? When the women laughed loudly at the foolishness of one of the maidservants he could make out her soft laugh distinctly amongst the others. He felt a shiver of delight run through him when he ran his fingers over the folds of the skirt she had hung up to dry on the upstairs verandah.

This must be what they call love.

I can murmur to the world, I have a secret. I am in love with a fifteen-year-old girl who is like a poem.

I love you!

All of them sat talking late into the night in the kitchen. Valia Oppu dramatized everything she said. If she talked about Asharichi Paru, she would pretend to be a trembling old woman with a stick. Nalini Edathi always listened to everything quietly and appreciatively.

Sethu could not stop laughing at the story of how the watchman's wife had fought with her husband and jumped into the well. There had been very little water in it. Her husband Raman heard her scream, ran up and asked, "Is there a lot of water?" No. "Did you hurt your hands or legs?" No. Raman rolled up his mat and pillow, came here to the house, and said, "I'll sleep on the ledge in the pounding shed tonight. At least I can sleep peacefully for one night without having to listen to her cries and screams!"

He listened for the soft laugh from the darkness beyond the kitchen door.

Nalini Edathi brought a lamp upstairs. "You must be sleepy, Sethu."

"No, I usually sleep quite late."

He heard Thangamani's footsteps in the corridor.

"Not asleep, Thangamani? Come and sit with us." Thangamani sat down just behind Nalini Edathi.

"Is Ravi asleep?"

"I mopped the verandah for him. He likes to sleep on the bare floor."

Once, coconuts had been stolen from four palms at the edge of the compound. Ever since, Ravi slept on the front verandah with a five-cell torch and a stick beside him.

Nalini Edathi said. "Tell us the story of one of the films you've seen."

"I don't remember any of them."

Thangamani said softly, "You must," and leaned on Nalini Edathi's shoulder.

The lamp in the verandah outside grew dimmer as the wick burned low. Leaning against the wall, he stretched out his legs, drew on a cigarette and told them a story. About the prince who fell in love with a gypsy girl who danced by the roadside.

Nalini Edathi's responses grew fainter.

"She's fallen asleep."

"Go on with the story," Thangamani insisted. She took her hand carefully away from Nalini Edathi's shoulder so as not to wake her and came up to him.

"Have you heard the song, `Suhani Raat'?"

"No."

That was what the prince had sung, when he came for the tryst by moonlight. Sethu knew his voice was rough. He could not sing, he could not even recite a line from a song properly.

Still, he said, "It's a beautiful song.

'Suhani raat dhal chuki, na jane tum kabaoge.'"

By the time the villain had fallen on the unsheathed knife and the hero had escaped, Thangamani's slender fingers were in his grasp.

Nalini Edathi woke up with a start. "I fell asleep. It must be quite late. Go to sleep now, Sethu."

Nalini Edathi picked up the lamp and it went out. It was pitch dark.

"Be careful, Thangamani, when you go down the stairs."

The darkness gave him courage. She fitted neatly in the circle of his arms. He held her close as they walked to the staircase. Then he touched her shoulder gently and said, "Go to sleep now."

He stood in the dark as she went down. Outside the window, moonlight played on the sand with the shadows of the mango trees. He closed his eyes and breathed in the fragrance of burnt camphor, of sandalwood paste and soap that lingered around him.

He said goodbye to Edathi Amma at the door of her room. Thangamani was about to leave as well. His father's sisters urged him to visit them more often and Ravi went with him to the gate.

Thangamani was just behind him. The lane was covered with elanji flowers. He stopped at the steps leading up to the coconut grove at the end of the lane.

"I'll go then."

"When will you come again, Sethu Etta?"

"Soon."

"Come when you come home next."

"I will."

"I'll tell Amma that you've promised to come."

He reached home late in the evening. Amma looked displeased. "Why did you stay so long?"

He felt intensely irritated. Did he have to be shut in here all the time? He had escaped only for three days, after all.

As he sat in the dark verandah with its chipped floor and worm-eaten pillars, he was overcome by disgust. One could hear the ant-eaten wood disintegrate slowly all the time here. The unpleasant odours of wet clothes and damp darkness clung to every corner of the house.

No one had even had the good sense to light a lamp. Where was Padmu? She finally appeared with a smoky little kerosene lamp, which she placed on the threshold. He sat silently watching the twisted soot patterns it made on the wall.

He imagined Thangamani coming here, and the thought filled him with panic. Her Sethu Ettan's house!

"Bring me a towel, girl."

Padmu shouted something to his mother.

Someone was washing clothes in the illam tank. He went down to the courtyard. Cheriamma said to him, as she brought in the dry clothes from outside, "There's a crowd of women at the illam tank, it won't be free for quite some time."

Padmu brought him a towel and a soapbox which contained two worn chips of soap.

"Do you want oil?" asked Cheriamma, but he did not reply. A faint breeze stirred through the fields. It was not quite dark yet.

He walked a little way and stopped. The lights were coming on in the shops. He heard a cart creak along the road.

This time yesterday, he had been strolling under the mango trees, like a prince on whose commands the household waited. His heart had beat faster every time a particular footstep drew near him.

And now, after three days of freedom, he was back in prison.

It looked like rain. It started to drizzle as he reached the gate of Vadakkethu. Darkness descended suddenly into the areca nut grove.

The front verandah at Ammayi's was enveloped in darkness. A lamp glimmered outside the kitchen. Karthiyayani was seated near it, picking stones from rice.

"Is it Sethu Ettan?" He stopped. Sumitra came out with a lamp in her hand.

"When did you come, Sethu?"

"This evening." He moved into the verandah, out of the rain and ran the towel over his hair.

"Does Sarojini Edathi's baby look healthy?"

"Hm." He grunted non-committally.

Sumitra peered at him in the red glow of the lamp.

"Where's Ammayi?" Sumitra told him that one of Ammayi's cousins had started her pains and Ammayi and Devu had gone to help.

"Are there any proposals for Nalini Edathi?"

"I don't know."

He put everything else out of his mind and concentrated on the fact that Sumitra was alone.

"Do you want an umbrella?"

"No."

"Here, take the lamp then. Be careful when you walk. Just yesterday we saw a snake near the screwpine bushes."

He pressed her fingers as he took the lamp from her hand.

The lamp's feeble glow intensified the darkness around. He even felt a little scared as he passed by the screwpine thicket. The tank seemed a bottomless pit of darkness. It used to be a well once, they had deepened and widened it.

He screened the lamp so that the raindrops which spattered the steps of the tank would not break its glass, and went down to the water. He sat down on the washing stone and dangled his feet in the water. It was very cold. He wiped himself all over with a wet towel and climbed up. Suddenly scared that someone was watching him from the darkness outside, he blew out the lamp.

"Sumitre!" he called out, trying to keep his voice steady. "Sumitre, the lamp has gone out. Get me a match."

Drops of water fell steadily around him. Was it raining again, or was it water dripping from the acrea nut palms?

Maybe Sumitra had not heard him. Maybe she would not come, even if she had heard. She was not the old Sumitra anymore. She would soon enter his house as his uncle's wife. That was why she had looked at him with such contempt. She had had the same look when they had stood under the palms the other day and talked about the wedding.

He saw the glow of a lighted wick weave its way through the thick darkness. Was it Karthu? He didn't care if it was. All he needed now was a light. His own, he told himself, had gone out in the wind.

It was Sumitra.

He took the wick from her, pretended to burn his hand while he lit the lamp and dropped it.

The little island they stood in was suddenly enveloped by waves of darkness. He felt a hurricane tear through his ears as he gripped her brutally.

The darkness whispered, "Don't Sethu, don't."

"So you've grown arrogant now. Did you ever think of Sethu while you stayed in the big house in Tirur? Who gave you that gold chain? It's the smell of beedi smoke that you like, and yellowed teeth, is it?

"Don't, Sethu, don't." Leaning against the wet, moss-grown stone wall, she murmured, "Don't" over and over again, not really making any effort to free herself.

No, you won't be able to push me away.

The wind unleashed itself dementedly around them and its moan rose to a roar. The areca nut palms swayed like possessed women seated in front of a sorcerer with their hair streaming wildly. Needle-fine rain spattered them. The scent of wet earth was all around them.

He came to himself when he saw her eyes shining like gleaming fish in muddy water.

"My elbows are badly grazed." Tears and laughter were mingled in Sumitra's voice.

Soaked to the skin, they sat shoulder to shoulder on the steps of the tank. She was very quiet. He wanted to dry himself quickly and go away, but his left hand was imprisoned in both her hands. Her fingers made wet trails across his wrist.

He broke away from her and got up. She came to him suddenly, gripped his shoulder and said. "You want to hurt me, don't you?"

He stood like a coward, the strength drained from him. Her face sank into his shoulder and he felt her hot tears.

A lighted torch moved across the courtyard.

"Who is in the tank, children?"

It was Madhava Ammama's rough voice. He wanted to escape, fast. But Sumitra did not seem to have heard. He raised her face and saw that she was still crying.

Forgive me, Sumitre. But no, the words stuck in his throat. All he could manage with difficulty was, "I must go now. I'll see you."

He patted her cheek lightly, took his soapbox and hurried through the darkness. He jumped over the low half-wall into the fields. Until he reached home, he was afraid that someone was following him. At his own gate, he slowed down. He was drenched. He wrung out his towel and dried himself.

Suddenly, he hated himself. Thangamani, forgive me. He thought of the rivers of moonlight and of her long, slender fingers. And whispered to himself, Sumitra is nothing to me.

Before you, I am a god.

Still, the bitterness of having seen Sumitra cry for the first time hung heavily in his mind. No, I won't do it again, I promise.

Forgive me, all of you!

His heart and body seemed as limp as a pile of rags.

Sethu wanted to weep.

Part Four

1

Visitors began to arrive from early morning. The first to come were those who merely wanted to make a formal visit, have tea, chew betel leaves and leave. There was no way he could escape them. Even people who had avoided him until the day before came to exchange small talk.

Relatives began to pour in by noon. Madhavan could not find a hiding place, so he came and sat in the verandah with a wooden expression born of helplessness on his face. Another group arrived at the gate. Unnichiri Edathi, who had gone away in Muthassi's time when the family property was divided, and her children. Seventy-year-old Unnichiri Edathi held her long-handled palm leaf umbrella high over her head and walked erect like a man. She lived three miles away across the river and had come with her daughter and three grandchildren.

Narayanan Nair, who had come to help for the wedding, was busy cutting and stacking banana leaves at the other end of the verandah.

It was very noisy inside the house.

His eldest sister came out, "Where's Madhavan?"

He heard her but did not move.

The easy chair in the inner room creaked and his brother-in-law said, "I saw him here a while ago."

Don't worry, I'm not going to run away, he muttered angrily.

"Ah, you're sitting here then? What a thing."

What do you want me to do? Jump? Turn somersaults?

"Kavungal Chathu Nair hasn't turned up yet. Did you tell him?"

"I didn't see him." He kept his eyes on the gravelled courtyard.

"I sent word to him twice. How can Kunhukuttan manage the cooking by himself?"

He lost his temper. "What can I do about that?"

"Nothing. What do you care, anyway? True, we've invited only members of the family, but we have to give them a decent meal. And Parameswaran's father is here as well."

If he sat there longer, he would have to listen to his sister describe how hard she worked, how she had to bear the entire responsibility. He got up, pretending he had to attend to something important.

"Madhava!" That was his brother-in-law. "Have you arranged for a petromax?"

"No." It cost six rupees to rent a petromax. And the kerosene was extra. It was easy for his brother-in-law to give orders, lounging in his easy chair. He obviously wanted to make sure nothing was wanting.

There was more noise than actual activity. He stood at the edge of the yard, trying to convince himself that this was not his affair, that it had nothing to do with him.

"Where's Madhavan?" It was his younger sister. She sounded as if her nostrils were blocked with snuff.

"Come here, Madhava."

"What is it?"

"Open the storeroom and get me some areca nuts." She lowered her voice and muttered, "The wretches. They chew endlessly, like goats. I had just put out four bunches of betel leaves a minute ago and now there's nothing left." He opened the storeroom and took out the big jar for her.

As he walked away, he thought, all he had wanted was something very simple, but it has turned out as elaborate and crowded as Parameswaran's wedding, which he had conducted himself, and for which he had worked really hard. The invitees had been served in two lots. He had eaten only with the cooks, after everyone was fed, and he had stopped feeling hungry. This would be one more time when he would be famished, and would not be able to eat in time.

He suddenly remembered that Parameswaran's wedding had been much like this one. His sister had been against it at the beginning and had scowled angrily when it was fixed. But she had changed her attitude as the function drew near because she had wanted to show off that she was in charge.

His sister had agreed when he had told her that he did not want all the pomp and rituals. The Vadakkethu people wanted a simple wedding as well. A small group would come late in the evening and they would leave for the wedding after the lamps had been lighted. There would be an exchange of rings and the Vadakkethu family would prepare a modest feast, that was all. Even when his brother-in-law arrived four days ago, these had been the arrangements.

"What a waste, having a feast and celebrations. People stuff themselves and then complain there's not enough salt or spices in the food."

His sister said, "I've told Parameswaran's father and he's agreed that it will be a very simple wedding."

But by the evening they had decided to invite all their relatives. Members of the extended family lived across the river and on the other side of the hill. They could not be left out. "How can we forget our blood relations?" argued his sister. And then they decided to invite people to accompany the bridegroom to the bride's house. They justified this as well. "After all, as Parameswaran's father says, we don't have to go by bus or train to invite them. All we have to give them is a glass of tea."

He waited uneasily, listening, holding on to a rafter. The sharp odour of cheroots clung to his brother-in-law.

Unnichiri Edathi squatted on the floor, chewing betel.

"Hasn't Parameswaran come?"

"He's expected."

"What about the younger one? I forget his name."

"Sethu? He has to study, so he won't come."

"Madhava, what are you doing there?"

The old woman was sharp-sighted, though she was over seventy. She moved forward to look at him.

"You're doing a wise thing, son. They're not strangers and you can count only on neighbours for help. This marriage will bring you good fortune."

Good fortune! A wedding that would bring him good fortune, indeed!

He wanted to be alone. He could not go out. Everyone he met on the road would ask questions. And it would not be proper to sit in a teashop or the bazaar while preparations were going on for his wedding. The house was full of guests. A fire had been lit in the courtyard and the children were gathered around the big flat uruli placed over it in which uppuma was being made. It was only this morning that his sister and brother-in-law had decided that those who were accompanying the bridegroom had to be served something besides tea.

His sisters competed with each other to be everywhere, in the yard and the kitchen and the living room. They had decided to open the fence between the houses once again. Although they had been the ones to complain resentfully that Madhavan had been bewitched.

In the end—

"What have you decided, Madhavan?" He had detected anger and spite in her voice.

"I've made my decision, sister," he had said, not looking at her face. He had expected an explosion, but there had been only silence. His sister had said,

"Tell Achuthankutty Panikker that I need to see him tomorrow. We have to find an auspicious date. And it's only right and proper that you write to Parameswaran's father yourself today."

His sisters had taken on the entire burden of the wedding from that point.

He took a sip of the bitter tea which Padmu had brought. In the courtyard, someone was clearing his throat to attract attention. It was Vilakathra Kunhan, who had the right to carry the steel box containing the married couple's things.

The sun had gone down and the shadow of the verandah stretched to the compound wall.

"It's getting late, Madhava. People will soon start arriving. Go and have your bath, Madhava."

It was as if he was an irresponsible child again to be advised, scolded and ordered around.

He got up.

"Padmu, bring him a towel."

Unnichiri Edathi reminded him that he could not use oil today, his wedding day. The sastrams forbade it.

All right then, he would do everything according to the sastrams.

2

As he stepped over the stile he noticed someone in a white shirt and mundu in the field next to the banana grove. Yes, it was Parameswaran. Madhavan kept his eyes on the paddy seedling beds to avoid him.

He was relieved to see that there was no one at the river. At last, he could escape their mocking eyes. He stopped by the path which led to the river. What if he crossed over now, and went through the fields and the vegetable gardens to the bridge? Beyond it was the railway track which went on its endless journey to unknown destinations.

No, there was no escape now.

And he could not find fault with anyone, except himself.

He felt ashamed when he thought of how he had stood in front of Sumitra, feeling shattered, unable to raise the slightest sound of protest.

It was the day he had heard that river fish was being sold near the bathing ghats. On his way there, he saw Devu and her mother leaving the house. He bought the fish, wrapped it in a teak leaf and went home, his mind in a whirl. What if he went to Vadakkethu to see Sumitra? At first he thought, better not. She might think he had deliberately chosen a time when she was alone at home. But he was restless. Finally he went, hesitantly.

He knew there was nobody at the bathing tank, but he still called out to make sure.

Karthiyayani opened the door and brought a lamp into the verandah.

"So, you've shut yourself up in the house," he teased her.

"Edathi and Amma have gone to Vadakkumuri." He sat in the shadow, just outside the tiny circle of lamplight.

"Shall I bring you a mat?" He stared into the dark, straining his ears for the sound of footsteps.

"Bring me a glass of water." He dared not ask where Sumitra was. He drank a mouthful of the water she brought. Surely Sumitra must have heard his voice. Karthu went inside again.

He looked vacantly into the dark. Sumitra came out, "The tank is free now." She shook out her mundu, tied it tightly around her again, and stood leaning against the wall.

He was not sure how to say what he wanted. He had tried to talk to her so many times, but he always became tongue-tied when he came face-to-face with her.

She repeated, "There's no one at the tank."

He got up and waited for a moment in the courtyard as if he had forgotten something. Sumitra was about to go in, so he called quickly.

"Sumitre!"

"I've . . . well . . . been wanting to say something to you." He stopped and looked at her, drawing a deep breath. Her eyes gleamed in the shadows.

"Your mother knows, so do all my people."

Sumitra listened in silence.

"I thought you would have guessed as well."

"What is it Madhavetta?"

He swallowed hard.

"I don't understand, Madhavetta."

He took out a beedi and put it in his mouth. The first match went out. Sheltering the flame of the next with trembling fingers, he managed to light it.

He did not dare look at her face. He gazed instead at the smoke curling out of the lamp and said, "About the wedding." He felt as relieved as if he had finished telling her a long story.

"Oh, that! I know about that."

Oh God! A cool breeze seemed to touch the intense Medam heat.

He saw torches at the gate. Devu walked in front, waving a palm leaf torch and her mother followed. Should he go to the tank before they came in? Confused, he looked at Sumitra. Sumitra stood leaning against the wall, partly hiding the calendar picture of Krishna behind her. Was she smiling? Why did she not say something?

"Edathi and Amma have come. Aren't you having a bath, Madhavetta?"

He walked into the darkness, his mouth full of the bitter taste of dissatisfaction. He blamed himself for not having spoken clearly. He had not even given her a chance to say that she liked the idea.

He thought about it again as he lay on the ledge that night, waiting for sleep to overtake him. How clumsy he had been! Sumitra knew and so did her mother. Whose permission did they have to wait for now?

Next day they had to cut down leaf-manure from the jnaval trees for the fields. All the trees in the village were being cut down and sold, and it was hard to find leaf-manure now. If they were not closely supervised, the cherumans would take away the leaves stealthily for their own vegetable patches. He decided to go home when they broke off for their noon kanji. Sumitra's goats were grazing near the illam compound. She came down the lane opposite him.

Her heavily starched mundu crackled as it brushed her ankles. She placed a foot on a rock that had rolled into the lane during the Thulam rains, ran her fingers over the thorns on the fence and said, "I was looking for you, Madhavetta."

He felt as if fishes were leaping inside him.

"I wanted to tell you something." She plucked a leaf from the fence, rubbed it between her fingers and said, smilling, "We don't have men in our family, that's why I thought I would tell you."

He whispered, tell me anything you want.

"I like you, Madhavetta.'

He smiled, trying to control the happiness that surged through him.

"You'll listen to me, won't you? You won't be upset?"

"Upset?" He laughed out loud. "Tell me what you want, Sumitra."

"All of us want you to be part of our household."

He felt so light, he thought he would float away in the air like a wisp of cotton.

"I want you to, Madhavettan, I want you to . . . marry Edathi."

His right hand, which held the axe, trembled. He tried to keep steady as the ground spun beneath his feet. The breeze blowing through the bamboo thicket suddenly turned into a gale storming around his ears.

Only Sumitra's smiling face and her moist, parted lips remained clear in front of his eyes.

3

He was startled to hear hooting from all directions. He thought people were laughing at him, but then realized that they were children with oiled bodies playing on the sand before they had a bath. Women were coming down the path beyond the mapilla fisherman's house, probably from the southern side of the river. They walked along the banks, searching for a shallow spot, shouting at the children to behave themselves.

He finished his bath in a hurry—the guests must have begun to arrive and the bridegroom had no right to hide from them by the river. He went round by a marshy channel to avoid the women, cleaned his feet on the first bed of karuka grass he saw and climbed up from the river.

From the edge of the field he could see both the gates. The Embrandiri was coming from Vadakkethu. He must have been sent for to clean the shrine of the rakshasu and offer milk and water. Sumitra must have gone early in the morning to the temple to arrange it.

Sumitra had organized everything. As he walked on, thinking of all that had happened, he suddenly discovered a secret, a marvellous secret. It was not he who had given in, in a moment of weakness. Indeed, he had not actually consented at all. Sumitra had wanted this. And decided on it.

He had not dared to say anything to her in the lane. Wanting only to escape, he had run away and had realized only when he reached home that he had wanted to say a number of things.

Devu Edathi!

Sumitra did not know Devu Edathi. He thought of Devu standing in the dim light of the inner room at the illam, like a bad dream.

Do you want to hear, Sumitra? I saw, with my own eyes.

He thought of another night when he had not been able to sleep, when he had heard even the rustle of the dry banana leaves clearly. The darkness had been full of murmurs. The wind had grown stronger by morning. Cold had crawled out of the ground like a reptile and crept through him. Sleep had finally enveloped him like a fit of unconsciousness.

He had dreamed that he was drawing water for the areca nut palms from the tank. It seemed a bottomless tank, for even when he let out the entire rope, it still did not touch water. He decided to draw the bucket up but it was caught on something. Or rather, someone seemed to be trying to pull it down. He peered into the tank and saw a horrible shape surfacing in the water, clinging onto the bucket. Dripping wet hair covered its body. He slipped and fell in. The arms waiting for him below seemed to grow longer. As he came to the end of that interminable fall, he saw the creature's face, the long teeth protruding from a mass of wet hair. He almost collapsed. It was Devu's face!

He had tried his best to avoid Sumitra over the next few days, but he had not succeeded. She sought him out.

"I've told Amma."

"What?"

"That you're willing, Madhavetta."

"I . . . but." He had stood transfixed, his face black with anger. Sumtira came so close that she could touch him if she put out her hand.

"What are you thinking about Madhavetta?"

"I."

"Don't worry. I'm telling you, after all." Her eyes flashed. He wanted to stretch out his arms but they had suddenly grown heavy. She smiled and went past, her body almost brushing his, leaving him weak.

"So you've been having an elaborate bath today, Madhavan Nair." He made an effort to smile. People were seated on the mats spread on the verandah, having tea.

His sister brought him an unbleached mundu and a veshti with a thin gold border. "Parameswaran's father brought this for you to wear when you go to the bride's house."

He came out in his bridegroom's clothes. The younger of his sisters told him to light a wick to the household deity before he started.

The people crowded outside moved to make way for him. Krishnan Nair, who owned the teashop, teased him, "Why don't we cut across the garden? There's no need to go around by the fields, is there?"

Someone laughed. Sankunni said,

"It's only this one day that he has to take the trouble."

"Look who's here." His brother-in-law got up from his chair, "Do sit down."

Unni Namboodiri. Parameswaran came up to welcome him properly.

Unni Namboodiri stood scratching the scabs on his chest. He seemed reluctant to sit down. Sankunni pushed a grass mat towards him.

His brother-in-law sat down again and called out, "Madhava, what shall we give Unni Namboodiri? What about some bananas and a tender coconut?"

Parameswaran said, "Those days are over, aren't they, Unni Namboodiri?"

"Tea will be all right."

Madhavan went in and brought him tea and uppuma in a plantain leaf. "Please eat," he said, without looking at Unni Namboodiri's face.

They waited until it was dusk, chewing betel and smoking to pass the time. Their voices grew inaudible as he drifted into his own world. He no longer felt troubled. Courage flowed quietly back into him. He looked at Unni Namboodiri seated cross-legged on the ground sipping tea, and the knife-edge of enmity slipped back into its sheath.

There was nothing to be ashamed of. He was going to marry Devu of Vadakkethu. She was not good looking. But there was something else that no one knew. It wasn't Devu that mattered. He was going to be the master of the household where Sumitra lived.

He told himself that there was no need to be so timid before these people, who laughed and talked so loudly.

The teashop Nair's present wife had been his older brother's wife. The older brother had been poisoned and the younger one had gone to help the widow and her three small children. When she had had her fourth baby, he had accepted her openly as his wife. Surely, Madhavan Nair said to himself angrily, he did not have to be embarrassed before such a person.

As for Kuttappa Kurup, he probably thought himself handsome, in spite of having a face channelled and pitted with smallpox scars. Everyone knew why he had been appointed to supervise the Kandankulangara lands. There were people who had seen him turn back from his own door knowing that Chinnan Menon was inside. Oh yes, everyone knew these stories and laughed about them.

Padmanabhan's wife dragged a foot as she walked, like a buffalo with rheumatism. And Unni Namboodiri had brought home a frightful looking creature from a rich illam which owned elephants.

He suddenly realized that he had been staring at Unni Namboodiri all this time.

Padmu called from inside, "Deepam!"

"Make your obeisance to the lamp and we'll go. Hurry now."

They were all ready. He went down to the yard with them. His brother-in-law was busy giving everyone instructions.

He muttered disgustedly to himself, trying not to show he was upset. Here comes the bridegroom to the wedding pandal, his head held as high as the sky. The red heart of the earth thrills to his footsteps as he comes to wed Devu of Vadakkethu.

4

It looked as if it was going to rain during the day. The sleepy light would not open its eyes.

Madhavan looked at the courtyard, full of grey smoke, and thought of the night that had gone by. So he was a husband now and part of the Vadakkethu family.

When had he entered the poky little room, bathed in sweat? After the moment when they had set out for the bride's house, he had no clear idea of the sequence of events.

When had all the guests left? The house and compound were silent now. He heard footsteps in the outer hall and saw small oil lamps go to and fro.

"I'll hold a lamp for them. If they don't clean up at once, the cats and dogs will make a mess by morning." Sumitra's voice.

He stood by the window, looking through the bars into the darkness. It was very still and his shirt was soaked in sweat. He took it off and hung it on a nail, over the calendar of Krishna. He thought of Sumitra rushing around, busy with household chores.

The wedding rituals, the feast, being ushered into this room by Krishnan Nair and Nanu Nair—all had become hazy memories.

It had not been very dark when the bridegroom's party had reached the courtyard, and the lanterns had looked pale in the evening light. The rituals were over very quickly. There were just enough people to eat in two lots.

He heard Sumitra's mother's voice in the kitchen, "It's very late, girl. Don't you think we should try and get some sleep? We got up at cock-crow this morning."

He felt tired. He looked at the bed pushed against the wall, and the white sheet, longing to sit down. He took off the lid of the broken enamel cup and saw that it contained water. He swallowed a mouthful. Angrily, he remembered that he had left his beedis and matches somewhere outside. He was sure he could find them, but he felt reluctant to leave the poky little room.

An old woman croaked, "Imagine girls being so shy nowadays." She was one of the wedding guests. His heart beat fast when he heard murmurs at the door. He did not turn round. Were his legs trembling?

Footsteps. And more murmurs. The bolt grated with a mocking noise. He leaned his elbows on the ledge, cursing himself for having forgotten his beedis and continued to stare out into the dark.

He turned around slowly when he heard the tinkle of glass bangles and the sound of quick breathing. He could barely make out Devu's form in the shadows by the bed. When he had stood in front of the big oil lamp to tie the thali around her neck, all he had seen were the border of her red saree and the witlows on her toes. She had changed into a white mundu. She looked as if she was trying to shrink into the shadows.

He felt numb. She looked funny, he thought, cowering like a helpless insect. She moved from the shadows and placed a hand hesitantly on the bed. He looked at her contemptuously.

Ants swarmed over the ledge by the window. If he slept there, there would be a breeze at least after midnight. But it was impossible. It was full of ants and kerosene stains from the lamp.

The lights in the house went out one by one and mats were being unrolled. Someone snored. There was a clink of bangles and a yawn. Was that Sumitra?

He climbed into bed, ignoring Devu. He thought he would fall asleep at once, he was so tired, but sleep eluded him. He covered his eyes with his hands to shut out the light and did not open them even when he heard her moving around the room. The bolt on the inside of the door creaked. The room grew dark. He opened his eyes for a moment, then closed them again.

He pretended not to notice her creeping quietly into bed and moved closer to the wall.

When he next heard the sound of the door and opened his eyes, he was surprised to see that it was morning.

When had he fallen asleep?

He lay in bed for a while watching the grey light coming through the window. Then he went out. Karthu and the old woman were still asleep in the hall. He walked quietly to the front verandah. Crows pecked noisily at a stack of used banana leaves at the edge of the yard.

Sumitra had just come from her bath. She took a pinch of vibhuti from the hanging basket and asked, "Why did you get up so early?" She went in without waiting for an answer and came out again with his beedis and matchbox. Her mundu slipped a little as she put them down near him. Her wet footprints faded slowly as she walked away.

He squatted on the verandah and watched the noisy crows.

Sumitra came out again wearing crisp, dry clothes. She had brought him toothpowder and water in a gleaming bell-metal kindi.

"Will you have a glass of tea?"

He did not answer.

She brought him tea. "They're plucking areca nuts at the illam, aren't they? I saw Kumaran and Kandunni go that side."

"Hm." He drank his tea and lit another beedi.

"There's something I need from Chalisseri. When you go next month."

"What is it?'

She said, "There's no hurry. My earrings are broken. I wanted to get them weighed and exchanged for another pair. Some other time, not today."

Her mother came out. "Why are you up so early?"

"They'll come to pluck areca nuts at the illam."

He saw Devu behind the door.

"Give me my veshti, Sumitra."

Devu said, "Tell him breakfast will be ready soon. He can eat."

Sumitra ignored her, went in and brought him a clean towel. "Here you are. I'll fold your veshti and put it away. Your shirt is dirty. I'll wash it out."

He stepped into the courtyard and hesitated, wondering what to say.

"It's Friday, so there won't be fresh fish. But come in time for dinner anyway," said Sumitra.

"It will be late when I get back from Chalissery."

"That doesn't matter. We won't lock the gate till you get back."

She came up to the gate with him. "Try to come early, the moon is on the wane."

He was sure of one thing now, that Devu had no place at all at Vadakkethu. Eagerness spread through him like the morning sunlight. He called out from the gate in a tone of authority,

"Sumitre!"

She was by the coconut palms, but she hurried down to him.

"Get whatever you need from Vappu's shop and ask them to put it in my account. I'll settle it later."

"Hm."

"Then." No, there was nothing more he wanted to say. He strode on confidently, thinking that she would look very pretty if she had gold studs in her ears.

Did Devu wear earrings? He could recall only her hairy arms and a face with jutting cheekbones.

No, Devu would never dare stand face-to-face before him.

Part Five

1

It was Friday. If Thangamani had written the day after she received his letter, the reply would have arrived today. Her letter usually came on the fifth day after he wrote.

Sreedevi Amma was taking a Chemistry class. He not only had to listen, he had to write down what she said in his notebook as well. She scolded them often and treated them as a mother would, but they respected her. In spite of the sloppy way in which she wore her saree, and her oily face, the class would fall silent when she stood on the dais.

The aura of a romance clung to her and all the students had heard of it. Maybe the compassion it awoke in them lay behind the concern and respect they showed her. She was the daughter of a highly placed official. She had fallen in love with her father's chauffeur. He was married and had children. She ran away from home to live with him. They now lived in a dirty little house in the workers' colony in the lime quarries. She had children by him. No one had met her husband. His first wife, who stayed somewhere quite distant, came at the beginning of every month to Sreedevi Amma to collect money for herself and her children.

Sethu always felt that her eyes held a deep sadness which she tried to hide. He had heard that all her sisters had married rich men. He detested the man, her husband, who had deserted his wife and three children. It hurt him to think of this princess who had sacrificed her kingdom for love. He could only guess at the depths of her sorrow.

Every Friday morning, Sethu woke up full of hope. It was the day Thangamani's letters usually arrived. Her big, rounded, childish handwriting seemed to be full of life. He read and re-read each letter and put it away under a sheet of paper spread at the bottom of his trunk, feeling that it added to a store of accumulated treasure.

The first time he wrote, he kept his emotions in check and composed a very ordinary letter. My dear Thangamani, I hope you are well.

He was disappointed when no reply came. As disappointment turned to anger, her letter arrived. A letter that could have been written to a father, an older brother, an uncle. She had added at the end that she had finished writing it five days ago, but had not been able to get hold of an envelope. When he wrote next, he sent her a self-addressed envelope.

I thought you had forgotten me, Thangam, when I did not hear from you.

I'll never forget you, Sethu Etta. It hurts when you say that.

Had she written that line because she was childishly upset? He analyzed it over and over again.

His next letter began, "My dearest Thangamani" and went on, I am so lonely. Only I know how much I suffer. I want to stay aloof from the noise and bustle in the college and hostel. On sleepless nights, the memory of you is my only pleasure , Thangam.

A love letter. He was afraid after he sent it. What if someone else opened and read it? What if it fell into her father's hands, and he sent it along with a letter of his own to Achan?

Would she understand, would she make out the tone of the very first love letter he had ever written?

After the special class on Saturday, he waited in the verandah for Francis the postman. The afternoon sun blazed outside, throwing flames on the tarred road. He recognized the self-addressed envelope at once. The words danced before his eyes and rivers of moonlight flowed through the noon sunshine.

"Amma asked, when I was reading your letter, whose it was. When I said it was yours Sethu Ettan, she asked me to keep it behind the mirror for her to read. But I did not put it there and luckily, she did not ask again."

If Sreedevi Amma finished her class ahead of time, he could go to the hostel, check the mail and join the first batch for lunch. But she always went on for a few minutes after the bell rang and no one dared to protest.

He persuaded two students who were already being served to move down and make place for him in the mess queue. He hurried to his room after lunch. There were no letters, only a card that had fallen under the table. Achan's, come by the day's mail. He would return on the morning of the ninth, by train. There had been unexpected expenses because of Madhava Ammama's wedding. He would be able to send money only after he got back. He hoped Sethu was well.

Oh yes, I am well. Very, very well!

Achan had not written before he went home. Maybe he had gone by bus. There was a bus from Pollachi to Thrissur.

It was Parameswara Ettan who had written to Sethu about Madhava Ammama's wedding. Sethu had given in his name for a study tour and had to pay forty rupees. Parameswara Ettan wrote that it was impossible that month since he had to send some money home. You must have heard, he wrote, that Madhava Ammama is going to marry Devu of Vadakkethu.

He had wished he could go for the wedding. He imagined Madhava Ammama and Devu standing close to each other. And Sumitra, running around organizing things. Would she have looked at him with contempt if he had turned up? "You'll come, Sethu, won't you? We can't afford a grand wedding."

He realized now why she had had a mocking look on her face that day.

The thought of the tears he had seen glistening on her face in the darkness of the bathing ghat often troubled him. It had been the only time he had seen her look weak and helpless.

He tried to convince himself that it was not his fault but God's. It should have been Thangamani he met first. Sumitra would never have entered his thoughts then. He would not have felt now like someone who had lost his way.

But the memory of her tear-stained face haunted him. Whose fault was it?

He decided that night that he would go and meet Achan's train in the morning.

He did not feel like reading. He looked through "The Gardener" and tried to find images for two of the lines:

I kissed her and said, you are blind even as the flowers are.

'You yourself know not how beautiful is your gift.'

No, he could not fit the likeness of the blind girl to a flower.

He got up earlier than usual the next morning. The train would arrive at nine thirty. There were passenger trains from the village at nine thirty and eleven thirty. Achan's card mentioned only the date. It must be the nine thirty train. Achan had not asked him to meet the train.

He ran into a group of friends returning from breakfast at Krishna Iyer's. "Hurry up," they said, "Swamy's oothappams are very good today."

"I'm going to the station."

"Oh?"

"My father will be on the morning train."

Balakrishnan said, "Look, I need to borrow ten rupees. Won't your father give you something?"

He smiled and crossed the road. Waiting at the crossroads for a bus, he thought, everyone looks forward to a visit from a guardian—a father or an uncle. It meant they would get pocket money. Some guardians took their wards shopping. The lucky one's friends would politely keep away from him. And, as a reward for good behaviour, they would be taken to the Madras Cafe that evening.

Daniel John in room number eleven had acquired a small battery operated radio set when his father came to see him. His father had noticed that there was no radio in the hostel. The students in the common room had stood up respectfully and explained that they had requested the warden for one. Daniel's father said he had one in the car and asked Daniel to fetch it.

"Thank you, Papa!"

"It's alright."

It was Nambiar who had told Sethu about this; he had been in the common room at the time.

Sethu had watched enviously as father and son took leave of each other. Daniel's father worked in a British firm in Coimbatore. Sethu did not know Daniel very well. Someone had told him that Daniel's father had arrived in a huge Pontiac.

Daniel's father was six feet tall, well-built, fair-skinned and bald. He smoked a pipe and wore white trousers and a white slack shirt. The cleanliness of the reddish heels above the polished black Punjabi chappals caught Sethu's eye. They were uncreased and a bright pink—baby feet.

Nambiar told him later that Daniel's father had said when he hugged him, "You smell of cigarettes."

"No!"

"Don't bluff." He had pointed to the empty cigarette packets on the bookshelf. "Probably you buy them to decorate your shelf." He had smiled and advised Daniel, "Stick to one brand and eat well."

The visit was the topic of the day in the hostel.

Sethu hovered around the verandah when Daniel's father was ready to leave. Father and son talked to each other like friends. As he got into the driving seat, he asked Daniel something which Sethu could not hear. Daniel laughed. The engine came to life.

"So long." Sethu watched wonderingly as they shook hands. As the car moved away, he noticed Krishnankutty leaning on the low wall, looking at it. Krishnankutty tried to smile but could not eraze the scowl on his face. They looked at each other for a minute.

It was a mistake to have said he was going to meet his father. They would insist on knowing how much pocket money he had been given.

The bus was late. He heard someone say that the bus from Tirunellayi had broken down. They would have to wait another half an hour for the bus from Manapillikkavu. He tried to peer at the watch on the hand of a passer-by. Was it seven forty-five or eight forty-five? Had he counted wrong when the clock in the common room struck the hour? He had written to Parameswara Ettan and to Achan about a watch. Neither had responded.

He had heard that watches from Singapore were sold cheap, at eighty-five rupees each.

Krishnankutty had said that poverty was not a crime. But he realized how valuable eighty-five rupees could be as he prayed for a passer-by to hold his hand in such a way that his left wrist was visible. And when he walked out of the mess at night, his stomach revolting against the dried chapatis and the evil smelling radish sambar, he longed to have an anna and a half to spend on the bananas hanging before Ravuthar's shop.

The crowd at the bus stop increased. Women working in the tile factories hurried down the road speaking loudly in Malayalam tinged with Tamil inflections.

There was a stampede as the roar of the bus was heard. A number of trucks smelling sharply of beedis and tobacco went past. The bus came at last and he clambered on the footboard with four others, scared to death.

By the time he bought a platform ticket and crossed the overbridge, the train had come in. He rushed down the platform but did not see Achan. A porter told him that the train on the metre guage line was going to Pollachi. He must be in that, then. Pilgrims in ochre robes, carrying kavadis were crowding the doors. He found Achan in a compartment just behind the engine, sitting at the window with a newspaper. He was surrounded by a group of dark skinned Tamils and Chettichi women in bright red sarees, carrying brass water-pots.

Achan was engrossed in the newspaper. Sethu stood near the window uncertainly. From as far back as he could remember, Achan had seldom been at home. Sethu avoided him on his rare visits. He found it difficult to talk to him loudly, or call out "Acha" from afar.

Achan looked up suddenly. He folded his newspaper and asked, "Don't you have class today?"

He said, "No," although he did have classes.

Achan had not shaved before he set out. He stroked the grey stubble on his chin. His forehead creased and his eyes closed, he seemed immersed in thought. There were patches of fungus on his closely cropped head.

"When is your exam?"

"On December fifteenth."

"Um." They fell silent again.

His earliest memories of Achan were when he worked in the Nilgiris. Sethu used to wait eagerly for him to come home. He would stand next to him proudly as Achan sat in the easy chair with his embroidered red shawl around him. Achan smelled good as he walked by. Sethu had never tired of looking at Achan's glasses, Achan's chappals, Achan's shaving soap.

"When do you have to pay your dues?"

"Tomorrow."

"Um."

"Or by the twenty-fifth with a fine."

The boy selling tea repeatedly asked if they wanted some. Achan signalled no. As an afterthought, Achan asked, "Do you want tea?"

"No," he said, "I had tea before I came."

Achan mumbled, "So many unexpected expenses. I spent nearly sixty rupees on Madhavan's wedding. No one realizes that my income is not as good as it used to be."

Sethu pretended not to hear.

"I managed to educate one son and set him up in life. I should have retired by now. There was a time when I used to earn ninety rupees and send money to my mother and sisters as well as take care of my wife and children."

Were Achan's complaints directed at Parameswara Ettan?

A new group of passengers had come, bound for Palani, and were scrambling for seats.

He wanted to tell Achan that he never had money left over after paying his dues. But that would mean listening to Achan tell him how much he earned, how much he had to send to Amma and so on. He kept quiet.

He was relieved when the bell rang and the engine whistled.

Achan put his head out. "All right, then. Get along."

The sun was very hot. He waited near the market-place for the town bus, feeling irritated with himself. He should not have come.

He had only a rupee left. And he would have to change that as well, for the bus. Only a rupee for himself until his money came on the twenty-fifth.

He was drenched in sweat by the time he walked the two and a half miles to the hostel. Everyone had gone to class. The time on the tower clock was eleven. He did not want to go to class. He took off his shirt, changed his mundu, unrolled his mattress and lay down to read his library copy of *Leaves of Grass*.

He heard voices in the verandah and the sound of shoes. Balakrishnan and Daniel John were back from the first hour.

Balakrishnan came to the door. "You cut class?"

"I don't feel well. I have a headache."

They went away. Balakrishnan came back and said softly, "I wasn't joking. Give me ten rupees, Sethu."

"Why don't you ask someone like Daniel, who has money?"

"I don't want to. I don't know him all that well. Give me ten, Sethu. I'll return it to you when my money order comes."

"I don't have any money."

"You went to see your father, didn't you? What did he give you?"

Sethu kept his eyes on Whitman's verses and said, "He didn't come. He must have changed his plans."

"Bad luck." Sethu closed the door and lay down. And suddenly thought, surely there would be a letter from Thangamani.

His tired heart began to beat with anticipation. The postman was late.

Having something to wait for drove everything else out of his mind.

2

When he tried to recall Thangamani's house, what he remembered best were the glass windows. The images of the house and of its surroundings were vague.

There were new roads and shops. He remembered a bridge made of coconut tree trunks at the place where one turned off the road. He was a little anxious when he did not see it. He walked past the shops and asked a workman,

"Which way to Pushpoth?"

"Turn by the culvert into the field. It's directly east once you cross the field."

He retraced his steps, his eyes on the ground, feeling suspicious eyes darting around him like wasps. What did he want at Pushpoth, they asked. Going through the coconut grove into the field he saw a familiar clump of bamboos in the distance.

His uneasiness grew as he neared the house. True, he had waited months for this day. But only Thangamani had invited him. Did that give him the right to go there?

What if there were a lot of people when he arrived?

"Who are you? I don't know you."

"I." He imagined how he would introduce himself. How he would sit on the verandah, exchanging the cold formalities of small talk, have tea and leave. He blamed himself for not having thought of all this when he wrote to Thangamani that he would come.

He had packed three sets of clothes, a couple of books and borrowed a box camera. He tucked the leather bag under his arm, and opened the gate feeling helpless but determined to go ahead, come what may.

He tried to smile confidently and hide his nervousness. There was no one in the verandah. An old man was busy digging around the cucumber patch. His leather bag felt heavier and channels of sweat ran down his chest.

"Why are you standing there like that?" He was relieved to see Thangamani's mother come out, smiling.

He had seen her years ago but she did not seem to have changed much except that there was more grey in the hair over her ears.

He put his bag down and smiled, not quite sure what to say.

"Sit down, Sethu. The girl told me you would come, but I didn't really believe her."

"We had a students' meeting at Thrissur. A number of us had come." He made that up, reluctant to say that he had caught an early morning bus to come straight here.

Ten-year-old Unni ran in with a bandaged leg, wearing muddy shorts, his face stained with burns from cashew oil. He stopped warily by the pillar when he saw Sethu.

"Come along. Don't you know me?" He knew it was Unni who had been posting Thangamani's letters to him.

Unni came up confidently to Sethu, his body reeking of cashew fruits.

"It's Sethu," his mother said. "Remember, you've seen him at Valiamma's."

Unni nodded his head, sat down and began to twist the buckles on Sethu's bag. He ran his hands over it searchingly and his eyes lit up when he felt the edges of the camera.

Sethu had forgotten about Unni. He should have brought him something. When his mother went in, Sethu laid his hand on Unni's shoulder and asked, "Which class are you in?"

"Fifth."

He was sure that someone had come into the corridor. He stood up. Thangamani was at the door, smiling. He thought she had grown taller.

"So you were here, then?"

"Mm . . . I saw you from upstairs as you came over the fields."

Her voice sounded deeper. He saw her face flush, and her eyes dart fearfully at him.

"Did you get my letter?"

"Yes, the day before yesterday. I thought you would come in the afternoon. How many days' holidays do you have?"

"I have to be in college on Monday."

Unable to contain his impatience, Unni asked, "What is this, Sethu Etta?"

"It's a camera, I'll take a picture of you."

Unni took it from him and turned it over in his hand.

"Be careful. There's film in it, it might be wasted."

"Don't spoil it, Unni."

"What's wrong with you, Thangoppu? As if it will be spoilt if I touch it."

Thangamani's mother arrived with tea and jackfruit chips on a silver plate. She squatted on the floor to talk to him. She said she had almost forgotten what Sethu's mother looked like, it had been so long since they had met.

"I used to see Edathi Amma when she came over in the old days. Now she doesn't come. And I can never get away from here, I simply don't have the time."

Thangamani's mother used to live here with her mother, her older sisters and their children. Govinda Ammaman, Thangamani's father, had bought the house and compound when the family property was divided. Their mother now stayed with the eldest sister and sometimes came here to visit.

"I said we could divide the property after Amma's time, but no one would listen."

It was the eldest sister's husband who had first broached the subject of divisions. When there was a general protest, he had backed out. But then Govinda Ammaman took it up.

Sethu knew that Thangamani was in the corridor. His attention was concentrated on the faint movements he could make out behind the door. Her mother continued to talk about her husband's temper and his tantrums.

The land, she said, had been leased out to tenant-farmers and the two coconut groves were under the supervision of caretakers.

"He used to complain that he could not bear to spend even a few days amongst all the riff-raff here. And now look at me, alone with the children. He doesn't care to come even for two days in the year!"

He sent money every month. When she wrote that the blacksmith was selling his land, he had sent her money to pay an advance, and promised to have the documents registered on his next visit.

"But what's the use of money? He has no affection. When he comes, the first two days are peaceful, but on the third day there's a quarrel. He doesn't need a reason. I hear he's on bad terms with Sarada's husband."

Sarada, Thangamani's older sister, lived in Vishakapatnam. She was married to a man who worked for a shipping company.

Thangamani's mother mentioned the row Achan had had with Govinda Ammaman. "In the old days, your's was the first place he visited when he came on leave. You can never be sure when he's going to fall out with someone." Her voice began to tremble.

"Amma, isn't it time for your bath?" Thangamani called out, but she pretended not to hear. She talked about the oil-seller Paulose's son who had left the village looking for a job and finally arrived at Govinda Ammaman's place. Govinda Ammaman had found him a job in the mill. But he had been driven away in a month's time. He had come back to the village with scars all over his body. He had evidently been hit with a belt. The tales he brought back were the talk of the village.

"Sometimes, I think, why don't I go away with the two children when they have holidays."

Sethu watched dusk spread over the coconut grove and the field beyond.

"You'll want to have a bath, Sethu. Unni, take Sethu Ettan's bag upstairs."

Seated in the easy chair by the window at night, turning over the pages of an old magazine, he thought proudly that he was not a stranger here, but an esteemed guest. He listened to Thangamani move around in the next room. He could make out her footsteps distinctly.

She came up to the door to say something to Unni and he asked her reproachfully, "So you're terribly busy, are you?"

"What did you expect?"

"Have you eaten?"

"Um."

She had bathed and changed her skirt and blouse but the white half-sari with the blue flowers was the one she had worn earlier.

She brought him milk in a tumbler and stood for a moment between the armrests of the easy chair, her knees brushing his own. Sethu looked warily at Unni who knelt on the floor, chattering nonstop. Thangamani moved away, the edge of her long skirt touching his feet.

He heard doors being closed downstairs and the clatter of pots and pans. The old man who worked in the garden shook out his mat, coughing noisily.

Thangamani's mother came in, scolded Unni for being troublesome, and sat on the floor, her legs stretched out. Thangamani brought her the betel box and disappeared into the verandah. "Are you sleepy, Sethu? Spread the mattress for him, child."

"It's been spread already."

Unni unrolled a mattress for himself and lay down. He was asleep in a minute.

"Just the one boy and he's so disobedient. He's inherited his father's boorishness and temper. The only consolation is that he's not bad at studies."

"He's only a child. He'll be alright when he grows up." Sethu said, sounding grown-up and worldly.

They talked late into the night. Thangamani's mother was full of complaints against the husband who had given her a house, money, coconut groves, everything except affection. Last time he came, Sarada had been here with her husband and children and he had not spoken a word to Sarada's husband. After all, what harm had that man done?

"It's very late. You came just when I was longing to unburden myself, Sethu. After all, I have to tell someone these things."

It felt very hot when he blew the lamp out. He took off his vest. He heard them unroll mattresses in the next room. Thangamani talked softly to her mother. He reached out and opened the windows wide. The long shadows of the coconut palms made strange patterns in the faint moonlight.

He lay in the dark with his eyes open. Thangamani was only a few feet away, on the other side of the wall. Would she have fallen asleep? She said so much in her letters but was so quiet now.

He concentrated on a single thought and whispered to the darkness, Come.

Did he hear her snap her fingers on the other side of the wall? He cleared his throat to let her know he was not asleep, that he could not sleep.

As the darkness deepened, the clock in the corridor seemed to tick louder.

Amma would not like his having come to Pushpoth. Neither would Achan. As for Govinda Ammaman, he needed no real reason to start a quarrel. Even if people did what he wanted, he would be angry if they had not consulted him first, if he did not have a part in making the decision. Sethu thought that opposition could be a good thing to face. He would take Thangamani away from this house even if the whole world opposed him.

He did not know when he fell asleep. He woke up with a start and felt that someone was in the room. There was a soft tinkle of bangles. Thangamani!

It was fear rather than joy that took hold of him. He felt his heartbeats echoing loudly in the darkness. He sat up and glanced at Unni, fast asleep on the floor. He caught her hand and realized she was trembling. He was suddenly afraid of being caught like a criminal in a flood of light.

He said softly, "You didn't sleep?"

He held her close, unable to speak. Her thin wrists were now rounded. She was no longer the little girl he had held in his arms in Achan's house.

He thought, this is my temple, I am only a devotee here. He pressed his lips to her neck and cheeks, fragrant with the scent of sandalwood soap.

"Are you scared?"

"Why should I be?"

"What if Amma wakes up?"

"Hm." He could see her smile, even in the dark.

He wanted to say, "I've often thought at night about the time when you and I will be alone together. But now, it's enough that you're near me. I'm prepared to wait until you come into my room by right."

"When are you leaving?"

"Tomorrow."

Her voice was soft, but he could make out her anger and distress. "Why did you come, then? You needn't have come if you were in such a hurry."

"The day after then. But it's not enough, is it, if only you invite me?"

"Do you want Amma to invite you? She knows you write to me."

He stroked her shoulders.

She said, "We'll go to the beach tomorrow."

"Will your mother allow that?"

"We'll take Unni with us. I'll insist on going."

"It's so hot," he said, blowing on his chest. She wiped his forehead and neck with the edge if her half-sari.

"Your father won't approve of me." He thought of the lovers he had read about in poems and novels and said, "I don't have money. I have nothing. Rich young men will ask for you."

"And what if this is enough for me?"

"You'll regret it."

"Indeed?"

Unni turned in his sleep and muttered.

"Go to sleep now, Thangam." She said nothing, but her arms tightened around him. He was suddenly afraid. This was not Sumitra. This was Thangamani. No, he could not afford to be rash.

"Go to sleep Thangam. Your mother might wake up." He knew she would not understand, but still he said, "We must wait."

He led her to the door, and gently released her from his arms. He felt proud of himself when he came back and lay down.

Next evening, he dressed carefully to go to the beach. He wore the best shirt he had, powdered his face and moistened his thin moustache with his tongue. Satisfied, he took his camera and went out. Unni was in the courtyard. He guessed from her mother's look of displeaure that Thangamani had an argument before she got permission to go. She made an effort to smile and said,

"Come back before it gets late," and muttered, "As if she's a child to go off like that."

He was astonished to see Thangamani in a sari. She had done her hair in two plaits with shining gilt paper roses tucked into them.

Sethu hesitated when he saw an old man come in through the gate.

Unni explained that he was his mother's older sister's husband. He used to be a village officer.

"Who's this?"

Sethu smiled respectfully. Thangamani's mother introduced Sethu.

Thangamani signalled with her eyes, let's go. She went out with Unni and Sethu followed, feeling embarrassed.

He was relieved when they reached the road. "Your uncle will tell everyone now."

Thangamani said softly, so that Unni would not hear, "Let him."

They went through the coconut groves and fields and came to the sea where it was cooler. He thought Thangamani's face, flushed from the sunshine, was the colour of faded four o' clock flowers. He hated the way the sturdy young boatmen who passed by them stared at her.

The seashore was deserted. Waves coiled around their feet like little snakes and slipped away.

"Come on." He went down to the water and held out his hand. The dark-skinned people who lived in the huts on the seashore were looking at them. He ignored them and took her hand.

Thangamani cried out excitedly when a huge wave tore away the sand under their feet.

They sat close to each other on the warm sand. Brushing the sand off the gold border of her saree, Thangamani said.

"Amma didn't like my coming with you. She gave in only because I insisted."

"Shall I take a picture of you?"

"No, I won't let you."

"We'll see."

"I never come out well in pictures."

"I don't care. It's for me to look at."

He first took a picture of Unni. All the rest were of Thangamani. He prayed that he had understood what Balakrishnan had taught him about the mechanism of the old box camera a couple of days ago.

"You must tear up the ones that don't come out all right."

"Sethu Etta, you must blow mine up and send it to me," said Unni.

The sea turned from deep blue to copper. Bright yellow and red clouds streaked the grey sky.

Unni wanted to go back, "Let's go, Sethu Etta!"

Sethu wanted to stay there, gazing at her faintly smiling eyes and the beads of sweat on her upper lip. He got up reluctantly. They walked through the dim twilight. As they neared the house, it saddened him to think that the few hours when he had been her protector were nearly over.

He spent another night listening for her footsteps. Holding her body that smelled of sandalwood soap close to him and talking softly to her of the future, he told himself, "I am a god now."

He saw her reddened eyes as he said goodbye in the morning, and pain spread through him like a black cloud.

"Tell your mother I asked after her. And come whenever you're free, Sethu."

His eyes ached when he tried to smile. He turned back at the edge of the field and saw the flash of a blue skirt among the bamboo thickets.

3

Sethu had planned to go straight back to college and not go home on his way back. He had two and a half rupees with him and he could take a direct bus to town with it. But the bus which should have arrived at eleven thirty had not come even at noon. A vendor who sold booklets of folk songs and wooden clogs put down his tray of wares near Sethu and sat down to rest. It was from him that Sethu learnt the bus had broken down. The next one would come only at three. The bus to his village arrived as he waited, uncertain what to do. Tired of having been on his feet since morning, he decided to get in, if only to sit down.

Amma asked, as soon as he got home, "Where are you coming from, at this time of day?"

The tone of her voice warned him not to tell a lie. "Parameswaran came to Palghat looking for you and said you were not there."

"When did he go?"

"The day before yesterday."

Sethu thought for a moment, then said, "I had to go to Thrissur for a meeting. After that I went to a friend's house with him." Should he mention the boy's name, his family name, his father's occupation? And describe the house? No, Amma wouldn't be interested. Very casually, he added, "My friend lives close to Pushpoth, so I dropped in on the way back."

He did not look at Amma's face as he spoke. He thought she would stop frowning and ask him about Pushpoth. But all she did was to open her betel box and stare at it unconcernedly.

Sethu had not had lunch. Hunger spread through him suddenly like a flame.

He went upstairs, took off his shirt and vest and lay on the ledge, fuming. What would Amma have thought? It was the first time Parameswarettan had visited him. What an occasion he had chosen.

He took the camera out of his bag and fiddled with it. Padmu brought a glass of coffee and left it on the window sill. The glass felt sticky. It had probably not been washed properly. Specks of coffee floated in a liquid the colour of dirty water. He swallowed a mouthful. It had the filthy flavour of palmyra jaggery.

He heard Cheriamma ask Amma, "Who's that upstairs?"

"Sethu."

"Does he have holidays now?" Amma did not answer. He pushed opened the crumbling door of the makeshift bathroom, threw away the contents of the glass and left it on the ledge.

He did not feel like going out. He thought he would lie down. He tried to fix the images of the last two nights clearly in his mind and felt a pleasant laziness run through him.

At dusk he went down and walked in the yard. A lamp had been lighted and left on the steps. The flame flickered and died because there no oil. Madhava Ammama came in with a teak leaf packet and gave it to Padmu, "Take this in through the outside verandah."

Fish was never taken directly into the kitchen. Madhava Ammama sat down on the verandah, took out a beedi and asked,

"When did you come?"

"This evening."

Amma came out just as Madhava Ammama got up to leave. "Are you leaving?"

Madhava Ammama waited.

"Shall I serve dinner?"

"No."

"They sent for you from the illam a couple of times. Have you been there?"

Madhava Ammama did not answer.

"That poor young Kunhathol dragged herself to the fence, big stomach and all, to call you."

"So what can I do about that? I can't force Govindan to give them the paddy in his granary, can I? I'm not a paid employee. They have a sturdy young man there to look after their affairs, anyway."

"But we all know that Unni Namboodiri is quite useless."

Madhava Ammama did not say anything to that.

"I got them some petty cash twice from the areca nut transactions. I can't go asking for any again."

"But she is near her term. There'll be a curse on us if she starves."

"Give them charity then, if you're so concerned."

Amma gave her younger brother a long look and went in. Madhava Ammama left.

Amma muttered to herself, "The insensitive brute!"

Sethu realized that the opening in the fence between their house and Vadakkethu had been closed again.

He would have liked to see Sumitra. He wondered how the newly married Devu was. He would have to call her Ammayi now.

Cheriamma began talking to the old cherumi woman who had brought a bundle of drumstick leaves in a very low voice. Sethu realized that there had been a quarrel four days after the wedding.

"You tell us now, do we have to worship her, I and my sister, just because she's married to our brother? We cannot forget the past." Evidently, Padmu had called her "Devu Edathi" by mistake.

"It's like we have a mother-in-law!"

The river was full now, so the water would be muddy. There were no sounds from the illam tank. There was probably no one there. He asked for a towel. He was given one that had been washed and flung in a corner while wet, and it smelled dank. When he got to the illam tank, there was a someone in it. He sat down on a stone in the coconut grove. He could hear the indistinct voices of people going home from the market through the fields.

"Who is that?"

"It's me." Sethu stood up.

"When did you come, Sethu?" It was Unni Namboodiri.

"This evening. I was waiting for the tank to be free."

Unni Namboodiri squatted down next to him. "Have you finished your studies, then?"

"No, I've got another year. I have to write my BA examinations."

Someone came up from the tank murmuring prayers.

Sethu said, "The tank is free now." Unni Namboodiri walked with him.

Sethu was relucant to get into the water, so he started to wash out his towel. Unni Namboodiri squatted on a step above.

"You weren't here, Sethu, were you, when my mother died?"

"Valia Kunhathol died? I didn't know."

"Yes, in Thulam. I wasn't here. I was at the Amakkavu temple. They sent for me."

Sethu suddenly realized that he had not heard Unni Namboodiri's usual laugh. He could not make out Unni Namboodiri's face as he sat hunched up, stroking his spiky hair, but he felt he had changed.

"Why don't you become a doctor, Sethu?" Why had Unni Namboodiri thought that a good idea?

"It's very expensive. People like me can't afford it."

"Doctors earn a lot. For my wife's confinement. . . ." Unni Namboodiri's anterjanam had been in labour for four whole days. They had had to send three times in succession for the doctor, who lived all of six miles away.

"He's a Variar, the doctor, from Shukapuram. He asked me, do you want the child or the mother. The child was still born. And that Variar had to treat her for a long time."

Unni Namboodiri lit a beedi. Sethu saw that he looked like an old man.

Sethu had a quick dip. The water was very cold. Busy wiping his hair dry, he did not hear what Unni Namboodiri said.

"What?"

"What kind of job can you get with a BA?"

"I'll have to look around."

"What kind of salary, anyway?"

Sethu smiled at Unni Namboodiri's ignorance. "It depends on one's luck."

Unni Namboodiri grunted, then laughed his familiar foolish laugh. "You're lucky, all of you." He had a bath, came out of the water and said, "My torch is spoilt; the batteries have run down."

It was very dark in the coconut grove, so they returned by way of the illam. Sethu felt a sudden surge of compassion for Unni Namboodiri as they stood together in the courtyard and he used the old formula of respect, "Adiyan, is leaving tomorrow."

Unni Namboodiri scratched his head. "I believe the newspapers say that the tenant-farmers can take all the lands for themselves. Did you read it, Sethu?"

Sethu was embarrassed. "They can't take over completely. The landlords will have smaller incomes. Only the landlords with a lot of land will be affected."

"I asked the lawyer. He said it was no use going to court. What can we do if the government is on Govindan's side? I didn't know this was what Independence meant!"

Sethu waited quietly for a minute. "Adiyan must leave."

He thought of the dead Kunhathol as he walked through the dark. He could still remember her tired eyes lighting up as she stood in the shadows behind the door, listening to the gramophone play kathakali songs, her long earlobes swinging as she shook her head. What had she died of ? He had forgotten to ask Unni Namboodiri.

He overheard Amma and Cheriamma discuss the troubles at the illam. Madhava Ammama went there now only on the days when the areca nuts were plucked. He had paid an advance for the purchase of the Kandankulangara seedling nursery. He would have five hundred rupees' worth of tapioca to sell. Vadakkethu was going to be tiled. Cheriamma had heard about it from someone. When Amma came to know, she had exploded.

"Let him build their palace for them. The wretches used to live on others' leavings. Phoo!"

While Sethu ate, Cheriamma asked curiously, "Amma said you'd been to Pushpoth?"

"Um."

"What's up with them?"

He said, without looking up from his plate, "They're all right."

"Does Govindan Nair send them any money?"

"Maybe he does. I didn't ask."

"Is the eldest girl there?"

"She's in Vishakapatnam."

"There's one younger—what's her name now? She must have grown up."

The younger one whose name you can't remember. Ah, it's from her name that a whirlwind will burst in this house.

"I think she's in the tenth."

"And the youngest is a boy, the same age as my Padmu."

Sethu said, to change the subject, "I didn't know Kunhathol died until Unni Namboodiri told me."

"Poor thing, she went quickly without too much suffering. She was lucky."

At night, he spread his mattress on the ledge in the verandah. The night before, he had slept on a double mattress in the room with the glass windows.

The sky he could see now through the areca nut palms was not beautiful. He could hardly believe in the past two nights, the nights that had murmured so softly to him. Maybe they were a dream. But no, Thangam had lain here, in the circle of his arms. He could still feel her breath, faintly warm. Here, in his arms.

He decided to leave by the nine thirty train next morning. Amma was in the kitchen, slicing raw bananas into a winnowing tray.

"I'm going. I want to catch the nine thirty train."

"Um."

"Can you give me five rupees?"

Amma raised her head to look at him. Then she threw the knife down, wiped her banana-stained hands on her dirty mundu and went inside. She brought him three filthy one rupee notes. "This is all I have."

He took them and went out, bending his head so that it did not knock against the door. Amma said,

"We don't have money in deposits or a treasure to educate you. Remember the old man is working hard for you in some strange place."

He was furious. He asked angrily, "And what can I do about that?"

"If you go wandering around the countryside when you should be studying, you'll be a fit companion for your brother, I'm sure."

He fought down his anger and sadness. His mother's harsh words lingered in his mind like specks of dust. He had scored the highest mark in every examination in high school, although no one had asked this of him. At every annual function in school, he had gone up to the stage to receive his prizes. No one at home had cared about them. No one ever checked whether he had paid his fees or hostel dues on time, whether he had enough money to travel up and down.

The day after he reached college, he managed to see Krishnankutty alone. They went out for a walk. He had secrets to tell Krishnankutty now. But when they settled down in a corner of the maidan, in the shadow of the fort, he felt confused.

His joy was tinged with pain. He was in love. The world was against him. It was difficult to start describing it, but once he started, he had a lot to say.

"Who is against it?" asked Krishnankutty.

"My mother doesn't like it. My father doesn't know, but he will not like it either."

"And your brother?"

"He'll be against it as well."

"What about her people?"

"Her father is sure to object."

The imaginary pictures grew sharper as he talked. His love affair was being discussed by everyone in the family. He was now ready for anything. Her hard-hearted father might try to marry her to someone else. He felt inspired, delighted, by all these illusionary obstacles.

Krishnankutty listened attentively, gazing into the distance. "Tell me frankly," he said. "Are you serious? Or is this a passing fancy?"

Sethu's eyes were full of appeal. You too, Krishnankutty?

"Don't be upset. I've seen a lot of people your age confuse the two."

"Do you know, Krishnankutty, how many days it is since I slept soundly? I can't even concentrate on my studies."

Krishnankutty stood up. "Do you have faith in this girl?"

"Of course, a hundred per cent. But if she is forced."

Krishnankutty would not allow him to go on. "No, I don't want to listen. There's nothing for you to worry about."

It distressed him to think that he had not succeeded in arousing Krishnankutty's sympathy. They walked in silence. As they neared the hostel, Krishnankutty said.

"Let me tell you something Sethu. I never went in search of love. You can only imagine what my life was like. I needed someone to have faith in. I finally found her, this girl. I liked her." He stopped, as an acquaintance greeted them. When they were alone again, he went on, "You are a poet and everything you look at is tinted by the imagination. After all, it is often the image of the maidservant next door, a mother of three, seated on the pounding stone and combing out her hair, that inspires most of you to write words like `you are a dream in blue stone'."

Sethu kept quiet. At least the ruffian had admitted that he was a poet. That was a relief.

A week later, the letters arrived together, Nalini Edathi's and Achan's. He read Nalini Edathi's first.

"Ravi told me that you had come to Pushpoth. It made all of us very sad that you came so nearby and did not visit us. I know you'll come to Pushpoth again. Don't forget it was I who introduced you." Nalini Edathi's complaint did not distress him. It made him happy that she had guessed the reason for his going to Pushpoth. Let the whole world know, he thought.

Achan had written about the examination fees. He had repeated Amma's advice, "Don't go wandering around when you should be studying." He re-read the letter and was glad to acknowledge an enemy.

Achan had always been a stranger to him. The relationship between them was confined to the sixty rupees he sent Sethu every month and the accompanying letter recounting his problems.

When Achan came home once, he had shown him the prizes he had won for general proficiency and general knowledge with great pride. Achan had turned over the leaves of the prize books, put them on the arm of the chair and remarked, "How badly they bind books nowadays."

Although they had never said a kind word to him, they were quick enough to find fault with him now.

"Whose letter is it?" Krishnankutty asked.

"My father's."

"Any news?"

He did not answer. He stared at Krishnankutty. You don't believe me, do you? Wait and see. The battle has begun!

4

There was a house near the Aralikkara temple that Sethu had always admired as a high school student. It belonged to Chandrasekharan Master, who dragged a wasted foot as he walked. The house was on the banks of a small canal and big rocks lay behind it. Children who came with their mothers to the temple played on the rocks. Rows of plants with yellow flowers grew on the fence. The garden was not big, but it was pretty, with the tiled house set in the midst of areca nut palms laden with flowers and nuts, lovely and tender as young women. Whenever Sethu thought about a family of his own, it was the image of this house that came to his mind.

Sethu remembered with relief that he would soon finish his studies and be independent. Then he could have a house like that.

In the month of Edavam, the areca nut palms in its garden swayed in the wind like women with long hair. In Chingam, shadows lurked shyly between patches of moonlight. In Thulam, when the canal overflowed with the rains, you could sit on the verandah and watch the water bubble over the beds of karuka grass, listen to the bells from the temple, people talking near the temple tank.

"Thangamani, we must find a name for our house."

"You tell me."

"No, you must."

"Shall I? Kavita!"

When he sent the examination fees, Achan wrote, the question of my extension is still under discussion. Most probably, I will have to retire by the thirty-first of March.

Sethu's reading had been confined to poetry books from the library and Thangamani's letters. He became terribly nervous as the examinations drew near. He had not made notes. He did not have textbooks for Rural Economics and Public Finance. If he could manage a first class in the first or second part, he would at least get a job as a tutor in a college.

Thangamani wrote that her examinations would begin on March tenth. She was writing a government examination as well. In his reply, he wished her success, and wrote that he was going to work very hard over the next few days. It is your fault, Thangam, that I cannot concentrate. You disturb me when I read and when I try to sleep. I shall punish you severely for this when we meet next.

It made him happy to think of her smiling and squirming with pleasure when she read that.

He ended the letter, "Dearest one, won't you pray for me?"

As soon as the exams were over, the atmosphere in the hostel changed. Senior students had to say their goodbyes. Even those who normally kept aloof joined the others. It was hard to take leave of all the people he had met here. He felt he would never find such good friends again. Juniors whom he hardly knew wanted him to write messages and childish words of wisdom on the coloured pages of their autograph books. He wrote down addresses and gave his own to many friends.

When he came back from writing the last paper, someone said, "Balakrishnan is looking for you." He went to Balakrishnan's room.

Balakrishnan said nonchalantly, "I just waited for half an hour. These fools don't let you out before that. I'll make an attempt to do the exam in September."

"Why were you looking for me?"

"I've fixed up something for the evening. Don't go out."

"What is it?"

"I'll tell you in time. Don't tell Krishnankutty. He'll make a fuss."

Krishnankutty was busy stacking his books at the bottom of his trunk.

"Packing?"

"How have you done? Will you get a first?"

"I don't know. I'll pass."

"A third is no use at all. You can do a BT or find someone to recommend you for a job, that's all. Won't your father be able to get you a job on the estate?"

"He's going to retire soon."

"But he's sure to have contacts. If you're not going to study further, it's best to get into some white man's company."

Sethu did not say anything. When Krishnankutty went on his usual walk in the evening, he stayed back. Most of the students had gone out to celebrate. He found Aravindan and Daniel John in Balakrishnan's room. Balakrishnan closed the windows, bolted the door and took out a handful of small bottles from the cupboard, like the ones sold by medical salesmen in trains. There were five of them, with pretty labels. Sethu read—banana essence, strawberry essence, tomato essence.

"Not to worry, it's liquor."

"But there's a prohibition on." The first thought that occurred to Sethu was that it would be breaking the law.

"Prohibition doesn't apply to these, they're sold in all the shops. They're the best of their kind."

Daniel described the special qualities of many kinds of alcohol. There were frequent parties at his house. After two or three rounds, his father would invite him, "Pull up a chair and have a small."

Balakrishnan said, "Toddy is best for the body."

"Come to my place. I'll give you the best toddy."

Balakrishnan opened one of the essence bottles, poured out some and topped the glass with water from the mud water pot. He held out the glass to Daniel.

Daniel savoured a mouthful and said, "Fine smell. Not bad at all."

There was just one glass. Aravindan drank, filled the glass again and extended it to Sethu.

"Please, no. I've never touched it till now."

"Touch it now then."

Aravindan told him, "One sip of this and then two puffs of a cigarette."

Sethu hesitated, "No."

Balakrishnan said, "I wasn't interested in such things at all. A friend in my place insisted that we have a drink the very day they declared prohibition. Who is the government, he said, to decide what we should drink."

"But it's not good to make a habit of it."

Sethu looked at the pale yellow liquid which had the smell of lemon grass and said, "Give it to me."

But Balakrishnan snatched the glass, emptied it in a gulp and lit a cigarette. Sethu observed that no one seemed surprised.

"I'm against prohibition. The law cannot make Mahatma Gandhis of us."

Aravindan's eyes seemed to have grown smaller. The glass exchanged hands once more.

Balakrishnan seemed to be suddenly inspired. "My friend says, will the government feed you if you are starving? Will they undertake to give you a job when you finish your studies? They and their laws!"

Sethu felt distanced from them. He leaned his elbows on the quilt spread over the coir cot and listened. When Balakrishnan opened the last bottle of essence, poured the liquid into an ounce glass, mixed it with water and held it out, Sethu accepted it. It did not taste too bad. He drank half and gave Balakrishnan the glass.

"I've had enough. You drink the rest."

He took a cigarette from Daniel's packet. What a relief, he felt all right. He got up. "See you then."

Balakrishnan came out with him and whispered that Ramakrishnan the watchman had arranged for them to go to a place in Kalpathy that night. It would cost five rupees.

"Coming?"

"No."

"She's a brahmin, and young."

"I'm not coming."

He opened the window in his room, unrolled his mattress and lay down. What if his head began to spin? Krishnankutty came back. Sethu was surprised his head felt perfectly clear.

What would Thangamani think of him ? Her examination would be over now. Would she get through? If she scored high marks, she would insist on going to college. Sethu did not like the idea of her leaving the protective circle of home. He imagined how the boys would pursue her on bicycles, how they would watch as she came out of the ladies' hostel with her friends.

"What are you thinking about?"

He smiled. "Actually, I was praying."

"To pass?'

"No, that my girlfriend may not pass."

Krishnankutty stared uncomprehendingly. He explained. If she passes, she will go to college. What if she changes after four years in the city?

Krishnankutty laughed and declaimed, "Selfishness, is not thy name Sethu?"

The next day they said their goodbyes. When he went to Balakrishnan's room to get his address, he whispered to Sethu, "You should have come. It was very safe. That rascal Ramakrishnan could have told us earlier."

Krishnankutty and Sethu left together next morning. Their friends helped them load their luggage into a horse-drawn cart. Students who had finished their theory papers were still waiting to complete their practicals. Everyone looked gloomy as they shook hands, even those who were normally rough and insensitive.

He dropped Krishnankutty at the bus stand and asked, "When will I see you again?"

"Sometime. Maybe very soon, maybe after many years. Maybe we will never meet at all. These things are not certain."

"Oh come on, you're only forty miles away. We can always meet. I'll write."

Krishnankutty smiled. "I haven't met people who live four furlongs away for years."

Sethu did not know what to say.

"Good luck!"

"I do not believe in luck, so I will not wish you the same."

Krishnankutty groped in his pocket for change to give the jutka driver. Sethu said, 'I'll pay."

"No, we'll share. You need only give him eight annas now." Sethu watched angrily as he counted out the coins. They had shared a room for three years and told each other all their secrets. Did he have to render accounts for eight annas now?

As if reading his thoughts, Krishnankutty said, "I believe in affection. Let us not be indebted to each other. Eight annas is a debt, even between us."

Sethu stood uncertainly, not sure what to say. Krishnankutty laid a hand on his shoulder and said, "Go along now, don't miss your train."

The emaciated carthorse walked slowly over the road, on which the tar had begun to melt in the heat. Whipmarks lay like threads of blood on its back. The whip cracked threateningly and Sethu could see the black, wounded flesh quiver as it whistled through the air. With a courage born of helplessness, the horse refused to speed up and ambled along slowly, dragging its hooves.

5

He got down from the train at three thirty. Since he had written earlier to Amma, Thami the cheruman boy was at the station. He had the same big teeth and spiky hair and had grown bigger.

It was Thami's father who had carried his trunk to the station that rainy night four years ago. Sethu had heard that the old man no longer worked. He had become an oracle for the cherumans.

The river was an endless stretch of sand. There were stagnant pools of muddy water where the water's flow had been checked. Even with his sandals on, he could feel the heat of the sand. Thami walked unconcernedly over the burning sand carrying the tin trunk filled with books and clothes and the rolled-up mattress on top of it.

Achan was seated on the easy chair in the verandah. Sethu had always come back home with a sense of uneasiness. But this time he felt confident. I have become a man now, I am going to begin my life.

As he helped Thami put down the luggage, Achan got up from his chair, spat into the courtyard and said, "Didn't you write that your examinations would be over the day before yesterday?" Achan's tone implied, why did you stay on for an extra day?

"Yes, they were over."

The first person he saw when he went in was Cheriamma. "When did Achan come, Cheriamma?"

"Yesterday. He came on here after visiting his house. He doesn't have to go back to work."

They seemed to be happy that he had retired. They knew he had put by enough money. They could tile the roof now. Amma had always wanted a bit of land near the river so that they would have enough paddy through the year if the crops did not fail.

"Why should he stay in strange places and live a hard life? He's too old for that now." Sethu knew that what Amma really hoped for as she said this was a tiled roof and a bit of land near the river.

Sethu sat down on the window sill in the kitchen and said, "I haven't given Thami anything."

"Um, I'll give him something."

Amma poured the tea she had made for Achan into two glasses and held out one to Sethu.

"Padmu, take this to the verandah."

She moved the aluminium vessel to the corner, put the shabby old tins of tea and sugar on the shelf and sat at the kitchen door, scratching her arms. "Um, and isn't it gold, real gold, that he's brought home when he retired. I just pray that I don't say too much."

Amma evidently found it difficult to control her anger. "He's come after being fed and entertained by his sisters. I knew, even then."

Sethu provoked her. "He might have money in the bank. How would you know?"

Amma imitated Achan's tone and expression. "Why would I need wealth? I have two sons after all."

Cheriamma contributed a profound statement. "Fulfilment is a matter of destiny!" She had an example to illustrate this. Madhava Ammama did not have a job, but he could live on the tapioca and nenthram bananas that he grew. He had given Vadakkethu a tiled roof and their garden was full of newly planted saplings.

Achan's shirt and veshti hung in the upstairs room and the old leather case was on the ledge. Sethu tried to open it, but it was locked. It was then that he saw the half empty bottle under the cot. The inverted glass next to it smelt of alcohol.

He hurried down when he heard Achan come up the stairs, coughing. He stood aside on the stairs for him to go by. Achan paused and asked, not meeting his eyes.

"When will your results be out?"

"In two months."

The thought uppermost in his mind was that he no longer had a place where he could be undisturbed. He walked up and down the yard, feeling disgusted. Achan had come down again. Lying in his easy chair, he kept wiping his face with his towel and spitting into the yard.

"As if it's so easy to pay for a boy these days until he finishes his BA. So many rich people around, but how many of them educate their children? I didn't do all this in the hope that the children will be useful to me. I don't want them to feel that way."

The next time he spat, the spittle fell on the verandah. Sethu watched him, full of irritation and disgust.

Whom did Achan want to accuse? Him? Amma? The world?

"I had enough, educating one of them. If I'd used that money to buy a coconut grove, I would have been sure of a hundred rupees a month now."

"And your nephews and nieces would enjoy all of it. Why blame us," said Amma, who had just come to the verandah. Achan fell silent. He cleared his throat, blew his nose, got up, threw down his slippers from the rafters noisily and went out.

Sethu thought of the debts that Krishnankutty had talked about. He had kept accounts for all the money Achan had sent him. He told himself that he had to go through them. Father must have already exhausted his capital. An image of the moneylender Sait doing the rounds to collect his interest flashed through Sethu's mind.

He had boasted about his father to a lot of his friends. He thought uneasily of all those to whom he had given his address.

What if Daniel turned up here!

Hullo, meet my father.

This is my mother.

He moved into the southern room and called out to Padmu for a lamp. Amma said, "You've finished your exams, haven't you? It won't hurt you not to read for one day. It's not even three days since I bought a bottle of kerosene oil, and there's not a drop left."

Sethu lay flat in the dark on the creaky wooden ledge and muttered, "Home, sweet home!"

Part Six

He waits as the ferryboat creeps slowly over the river from the farther shore.

The thought suddenly occurs to him that the boat has always been on the farther shore every time he started on a journey. And whenever he got down from the train in the hot afternoon sunshine and came to the farther shore, the boat would be rocking gently on its moorings on this side.

Is it only here that this happens?

Does this happen only to me?

As he waits for the eastbound train, the porter says, the westbound train is due to cross here. He listens attentively for the bell. Good, it is the eastbound train that has been blocked. Bag on shoulder, he prepares to elbow his way in, only to see the train come in on the second line! He has to wait resentfully until the westbound train arrives, spits out a crowd of people, takes in another crowd and finally moves off.

My boat is always on the farther shore, and my train on the second line!

As he sits in the bus, hot and thirsty, waiting for the closed railroad crossing to open, it is the gate on the farther side that opens first. Exhausted, he waits for rows and rows of vehicles to pass. He tells himself, it is because I am in this bus that it so happened.

1

There were sounds of a quarrel one evening at Vadakkethu.

Amma said, "Wretches, they're at it again. There's no rest or peace for the neighbours."

It took Sethu some time to realize that it was a squabble. Devu's voice rose to a wail and Ammayi began to scream. Sumitra kept her voice down. After that he heard Madhava Ammama shout, "I'll kick out the whole lot of you."

The screams became sobs. Cheriamma stood at the northern door, listening and giving Amma a running commentary.

When all was quiet, Amma said contemptuously, "They're as bad as the cherumans. Only he would bother to look after them."

Sethu was afraid to go out. Everyone would ask, "Haven't you found a job yet?"

"I'm looking for one."

"In what field?"

He would answer, the Railways or the Customs, to escape further questions.

Everyday, he would stand at the door of the post office, craning his neck to find out whether any of the envelopes that the postman had stamped were official. He tried to look casual, careful not to show that he hoped the next name to be called would be his. Then he would leave pretending he had just dropped in while passing by. His face and forehead beaded with sweat, he would pray that no one would notice him. And as he walked home, keeping in the shade of the screwpine bushes, someone would ask,

"So Sethumadhavan, you haven't found a job yet?"

People had their own ideas about jobs. Most people were happy to hear that he was trying to get a job in the railways. It meant good money. If he became the station master at Tirur or Thanur, he could make a hundred rupees a day effortlessly. In the bigger stations, it was better to work in the goods or parcel section. He did not have to receive money directly. Bribes paid by those who came to book their goods were shared by all the employees. The villagers were full of stories of people who had made money in railway jobs.

He had been able to put people off until the results came.

He finally stopped going to the post office. If there was something for him, the delivery man would bring it next morning. A stream of letters came from his friends as soon as he got home, but had soon dwindled. Congratulatory messages had arrived as soon as the results were announced. Those who had passed wrote to him about their future plans.

The congratulations had not moved him. He had a second class in the first and second parts and a third in the subsidiary subjects.

Krishnankutty had passed but had only a third. There were no letters from him. Sethu thought of writing to him many times, but put it off. He would write to him, he thought, after he found a job.

Thangamani's letters came regularly. He needed four annas a week to reply to her. He had made a habit of sending her a self-addressed envelope, so he could not break it now. He would ask Amma for a rupee or two to send his application forms. He had to walk six miles to meet a gazetted officer or a doctor in a government hospital, who would attest the copies of his certificates. Amma usually gave him the money for his applications without any questions. Except once, when she asked.

"Wasn't it just the other day that you said you were going for a certificate?"

"That was another one."

She looked disgruntled, but did not dare protest since it concerned his career.

He saw Thangamani once after the results came out, when he went to see Achan about a job. Amma asked, "Is it for a post on the estate?"

"Mm."

Amma had no money to give him for the journey, so she sent Padmu to the illam. They had none either. The young Kunhathol herself had to borrow small sums from the women who came to the ghat to bathe.

Cheriamma suggested sending Padmu to Andoor Meenakshi Amma's house. Her guess that they were sure to have money since the mud pots they made were selling at better prices proved right.

Sethu had been worried that Amma would ask him to delay his going by a couple of days. He had already written to

Thangamani that he was going to see Achan and she would be expecting him.

When he reached Achan's house, Thangamani and Unni had already arrived that morning.

He knew that Nalini Edathi and Achan's sisters were watching him closely. So he kept away from Thangamani. In the evening, seated near the kuvalam tree, talking to Unni, he saw her near the pounding shed.

He tried to keep track of her as she moved around the house. A lucky chance suddenly came his way.

Valia Oppu grumbled, "I wonder whether there's oil in the lamp upstairs. It's not been cleaned for days. I suppose you have your usual headache, Nalini. Don't provoke me into saying something I shouldn't—Thangam, go and get me the lamp."

He said to Ravi, "I forgot, There's something I want to show you." Unni wanted to go up with him, so he asked him to get him the newspaper from Achan's room and went quickly into the house. He was lucky, no one was about. Valia Oppu was in the verandah, scolding Nalini Edathi. "You and your headaches! Who wants to see your gloomy face?"

He went up quietly and waited. The stairs creaked. Thangamani. She ran into his arms like a baby bird seeking shelter.

"Did you get my letter?"

"Yes, this morning. I started at once."

"I have to leave tomorrow."

"Won't you come home?"

"Not this time, Thangam."

"I've been waiting for so many days. You don't care for me, do you?" She sulked like a child. He thought her eyes were wet.

"It's because I can't come. Please understand, Thangam."

He stroked her shoulder and said, trying to make his voice sound sad, "Why give people a reason to talk? I'm ready for whatever they say about me, but if they talk about you." He gazed steadily at an invisible point beyond her, hoping that tears would come to his eyes.

They heard footsteps outside and quickly drew apart. It was Nalini Edathi.

He felt intensely irritated. She had come up as quietly as a cat.

"I have a headache. I'll lie down for a while." She brushed past Sethu and went into the room. He hurried downstairs without talking to Thangamani. He had only himself to blame. He should have taken care.

As he went into the courtyard wiping his forehead, Ravi asked, "Where is it, Sethu Etta?"

"What?"

He suddenly remembered the lie he had told Ravi. "I wanted to show you a photograph. But I think I've forgotten to bring it."

Achan called out, "Have you had a bath, Sethumadhavan?"

"Yes."

"You can sleep here."

In Achan's room. He did not say anything to that. Achan came down and began to pace up and down the courtyard. Sethu waited, leaning against the cement pillar, hoping he would say something.

"What happened to the job in Madras?"

"They haven't replied."

"Um."

He thought the topic was closed when Achan asked, "What job is it?"

"A tutor's post in the office of the Education Department of the Director of Public Instruction. If I get it and work for two years, I can do my MA privately."

"There are so many other good departments. Why don't you apply to them?"

Resentment flared up in him. When he had wanted to subscribe to an English newspaper, they had not allowed him. They had told him that Parameswaran would look at the newspapers and tell him if there was anything suitable. So he had had to wait every evening by the fields and waylay Krishnan Master of the Elementary School in order to have a look at his three-day-old paper for job vacancies.

After a while, he hinted to Achan, "Anyway there's no point these days in just sending an application. You need to know someone with influence."

If only he could get a clerk's job on a white man's estate. They started with a salary of at least a hundred and fifty. Surely Achan could write to someone he knew?

He had dinner with Achan. He kept his eyes on his leaf whenever Nalini Edathi passed by them.

After dinner, he sat by himself at the end of the verandah. Nalani Edathi came up to him. "Why are you sitting in the dark?"

"Just like that."

"Shall I bring the lamp this side?"

"No."

She sat down on the floor, below the open window. He knew she wanted to talk to him. He got up and said, "I think I'll go to bed early today."

"Why, aren't you feeling well?"

"I have a headache."

Nalini Edathi smiled. "I have a headache all the time. Amma says it's just my imagination. Cheriamma thinks it's an excuse to shirk housework."

Edathi Amma's room was empty, but they had spread his mattress in the outer room, on the floor, beside Achan's cot. Was it because Achan had told them to do so? Or had they made the decision because Thangamani was in the house?

Unni and Ravi slept on the front verandah. They invited him to join them.

A lamp had been lit at dusk before the picture of Krishna in Achan's room, and the odour of the burnt-out wick still clung to the room, mingling with a faint smell of alcohol.

Achan's cot creaked every time Sethu was about to fall asleep. He woke up with a start. Achan coughed constantly and called out, "Amme, Guruvayurappa!" or "Ah, my Gods!" Did Achan usually pray in his sleep?

In the morning, Sethu stuffed his clothes into his bag and said, "I'm leaving."

"Why are you in such a hurry? You can go tomorrow," said Achan, but his tone implied that he did not really care.

"There might be some information in the post."

Achan did not insist. He gave Sethu five one rupee notes and said, "I'll be there next week."

Nalini Edathi and his father's sisters asked him to wait and have breakfast before he left. He offered all sorts of excuses. He had to catch the nine thirty bus. He had to collect two certificates on the way and send them immediately by registered post.

He had tea and left as if in protest. As he walked through the lane he saw Thangamani beneath the papaya tree near the pounding shed.

2

Achan came home after a week. He asked, as usual, "What happened to your application?"

Which one? There had been so many.

"Nothing so far."

Appu Nair of Kunnathuparambil brought a bit of news. Narayanan Nair, the High Court Judge, was home on vacation. He was a kind person and had recommended many people to good positions. Appu Nair's older brother managed Narayanan Nair's affairs and would speak to the Judge on Sethu's behalf.

The Judge was his student when Achan had been a schoolmaster. Sethu had often heard Achan say so.

Appu Nair said, "Come home early one morning and go with Ettan. He'll do whatever is necessary."

Appu Nair and Achan talked about the Judge's good fortune, his generosity, his food habits. Sethu went up the hill and saw the train come over the bridge with the red mail box on it. The mail was late. Surely there would be something for him today, he hoped, as he watched the delivery agent Kuttinarayanan pass by each day.

He had sent applications to all the firms whose addresses he knew. He knew the formula by heart now and could write without thinking. "Having come to understand that there are a few vacancies in your company, I beg to. . . ."

Some of them, generally the British companies, sent printed regret cards. Only they had the kindness to put an end to the agony of waiting.

He walked through the jnaval grove to the rocks above. The stretches in the distance which had once been covered with grass were now marked out into sweet potato fields. A few isolated cattle grazed on the hillside, over which the last rays of the setting sun still lingered, making it impossible for darkness to take over. He came down the hill and began to walk home. By the jnaval trees, he met Sumitra.

"When did you get back from your father's?"

Sumitra looked darker in the dim light. Her blouse seemed too large for her.

"On Friday. Where are you going, Sumitra?"

"I went to Mani's. Her chit had matured. I have a half share."

He noticed black shadows under her eyes.

"I never see you these days, Sethu."

He did not reply. To change the subject, he asked, "What was the noise about?"

"It goes on all the time. It's just that you haven't heard it before, Sethu."

"Who is she quarrelling with?"

"I try my best to be patient. What can I do if Edathi is determined to start a fight? When she goes too far, I say something as well."

"What does Edathi have against you?"

"How would I know?"

Sethu kept quiet. She asked, "Don't you go to collect the post now?"

"Why should I?"

"I just asked, that's all. I often see you go. But even if I stand at the gate, you take no notice of me." She tried to speak casually but Sethu could make out the distress in her voice.

"I didn't see you, Sumitra."

"You wouldn't."

Darkness had settled in the bamboo thickets and the jnaval leaves.

"When will you get a job, Sethu?"

"I'm trying for one."

"Boys can always go away somewhere, they're so lucky." She walked ahead and asked, without turning around, "Shall I come with you, Sethu, when you get a job and go away?"

He could not see her face. Was she teasing him?

"Don't be silly."

"I'm serious. If you feel ashamed of me, you can always tell people that you took me along from the village to cook and clean for you."

He was disappointed with himself, because he could not laugh loudly and pretend it was a joke.

They walked in the dark, close to each other, without touching. Sethu stopped at the turning to his house. Sumitra was so near him. He caught the unpleasant odour of her sweat and of her hair that had been gathered into a knot before it had dried properly.

He thought with astonishment that Sumitra had once been the flame that blazed in his blood, his nerves, the pores of his skin. Now, standing next to her, he felt no excitement, nor did his heartbeats quicken.

He patted her shoulder as if to reassure her.

"I'll have to go."

She gripped the fingers of his left hand. "When will I see you again?"

"I'll see you."

"When?"

"I must find the time, child."

She would not release his hand. He walked with her, feeling uneasy. They went through the broken fence, and he made no attempt to free his hand. The old teak tree, shorn of its leaves, looked like the skeleton of a rakshasa. He took his hand away from her grip, put an arm around her waist and touched her cheek gently.

"It's dark Sumitra. Go home now."

Sumitra smiled. "I always knew that that was all you cared."

He could not bear to think that she had begun to understand him. He pulled her to him roughly, "What did you say, what?"

He murmured all kinds of meaningless words, not even sure she heard him.

When he pulled her down on the moist earth covered with dry leaves, she did not protest.

Raindrops that still clung to the rakshasa's skeleton from the morning's shower dripped on them. He was filled with cruelty, not excitement.

"Sethu, wait, there are thorns." He paid no attention.

A sudden wind ran wildly through the leaves, making strange noises.

He leaned against the worm-eaten trunk of the teak tree and said goodbye to her. He thought she would go away quietly into the darkness.

She rubbed her elbows, came close to him and peered, as if trying to make out his face in the dark.

"Why did you you come back so soon from your father's?"

"Just like that."

"You didn't go to Pushpoth?"

"Um."

"Of course you did."

"Um?"

"You think no one knows?

"Knows what?'

He was full of happiness. So Sumitra knew. She could not accuse him now of having deceived her. He felt as if he had been absolved from all blame.

"Do you do these things to Thangamani?"

"Don't talk like that!" He raised his hand as though to hit her. "It's very late, Sumitra. Now go along."

He hurried away without waiting for her. It took him some time to find the opening in the fence, in the dark.

He saw Achan in the courtyard and quickly went round by the south, pretending he had just come from the illam tank. Achan said,

"You had better get up early tomorrow. We can come back before it gets too hot."

"Where are we going?"

"Across the river, to see Menon. I don't want anyone to blame me for not doing my best."

He heard Achan's voice from the darkness in the southern room. "It's not enough that I educated him, now I have to find him a job as well. He expects me to do everything for him. Boys should be able to handle their own affairs. And be smart. No one hands out a job for the asking."

Sethu said to Amma, "Let Achan go by himself. I'm not going."

Amma drew herself up, ready to do battle. "Why waste good things on a dog? Shut yourself in your room with your silly books and squeeze out your pimples to pass the time."

Sethu pushed open the door angrily and went in.

3

Achan asked at the gate, "Have you taken all your certificates?"

"No, should I?"

Achan muttered something indistinctly. He said, "I'll go and get them."

He had already turned when Achan checked him, "Don't go back now."

Then Achan said rather sadly, resentfully, "You turned back anyway. Go and get them now."

He hurried up the steps, went in and took the envelope with the certificates out of the tin trunk. He told himself firmly that it was just a silly superstition that you should not turn back once you had set out on a mission. A foolish old saying. But when he remembered that it concerned his own career, he was afraid. He consoled himself— as if everyone in the world lived by such beliefs!

Patches of blue showed here and there on Achan's over-starched shirt. His long veshti with the black border kept slipping off his shoulder and he had to stop every ten yards to put it back. He walked very fast, the edge of his mundu and his umbrella clutched in his hand.

When Sethu had gone to bed, he had decided he would not go to meet anyone about a job, even if it were the governor himself. But his courage had gradually dwindled. What if he had arrived at fortune's door? The Judge's recommendation might open the way to new worlds. It would be foolish to be obstinate. There was nothing to lose. What if he regretted it later? He finally decided to go and meet the Judge.

As they crossed from the field onto the road, they met Madhava Ammama. He moved aside and asked Achan respectfully, "Where to?"

"Across the river."

Sethu thought Madhava Ammama looked a little more well-groomed. He wore a double mundu and a new vest obviously bought in the town, not the kind the local tailor sold. It had white silk seams at the sleeves and neck.

The river was quiet after the floods in Thulam. The ferryboat was on the farther shore. As they waited, people asked, "Where to, father and son?"

Sethu was embarrassed when Achan explained at length that they were going to see Judge Menon about a job. Why did he want to tell everyone this ? Nor did he stop there. He went on to tell them how he had taught Menon long ago.

Achan had worked in many places during the last thirty years. But he had remained a villager in his speech and attitudes.

The post master said he had been to the Judge's house before he became a High Court Judge. "He's so well off. They say he's built a mansion in Madras, a splendid place. There's nothing he can't do for you."

A man sitting on the culvert took up from that point. "You cannot accuse him of not helping the villagers. It was he who found our Sankunni's son Chathukutty a position. He's an ameen in the Ottappalam court now." Sethu had seen the old man in he vicinity of the post office, but did not know his name.

Anyway, Achan had laid the matter of his job open for the villagers to discuss.

One of them might ask what the envelope in his hand contained. If he told them, many of them would want to look at the certificates. Not one of them would understand what the certificates meant, but they would discuss the quality of the paper, the colours, the typed letters. He quickly slipped the envelope inside his shirt.

The ferryboat arrived and they crossed over. People waiting on the other side asked, "Where to, father and son?"

Unfortunately, there was no donkey. There should have been a father, a son and a donkey.

The river bed, used to cultivate vegetables in summer, was full of holes now filled with muddy water from the Thulam rains. The old pathways were covered with dirt. Sethu slowed down as they reached the field which had been ploughed for the summer crop. Achan was way ahead.

They went past the building in which Cheriachan used to have a shop. It looked the same except that the provisions occupied only half the space. The other half was a teashop. He saw a mappila with a rounded beard seated in front of the provisions. They passed the weavers' huts, came to the lane and crossed a number of unmarked compounds without walls or fences before they reached the temple. Achan took off his slippers, stood on the first stone step of the temple, tied his veshti around his waist, joined his palms and closed his eyes.

They could not see the temple from the dilapidated steps. A huge banyan tree obscured their view.

Sethu wondered, should he pray? He closed his eyes for a second. Bhagavathi, take care of me. That was enough. Faith was in the mind, the mind would prostrate itself.

Achan made sure he was behind and went on. They saw the big tiled gatehouse at the edge of the field after they had walked a mile. Achan turned and said, "That's the house."

People were clustered together in the courtyard. The sun had begun to get hot. Nambisan came out of the house, a tulasi flower tucked behind his ear, a big sandalwood paste mark on his forehead and a leaf cup in his hand. Achan asked, "Is he in?"

"Yes."

Huge crotons stood in pots on both sides of the pathway. Sethu felt that the eyes of everyone waiting in the cemented courtyard were on the newcomers. He suddenly felt afraid as they climbed into the verandah. The grey-haired man with spectacles stretched out on the easy chair in the room just beyond the verandah must be Judge Menon. The room was filled with people. Sethu kept behind Achan.

Achan stood at the door and joined his palms to make an obeisance. The boatsong he had learnt in the fourth class suddenly came to mind. "Clasping to his breast his fellow-disciple whose breast smelled of sweat." The lines from Ramapurathu Variar's poem on Kuchelan that Krishnan Master used to recite.

But this was not Achan's fellow-disciple, this was his student. Sethu waited impatiently for the Judge to get up, come and take Achan's hand and lead him inside. Maybe Judge Menon had not seen Achan properly. But Achan was standing right at the door, he could not have missed seeing him. Maybe he had not recognized him. Sethu moved towards the end of the verandah.

Achan continued to stand there hopefully with his palms joined. Then he slowly came back to Sethu. Sethu gazed at the garden. The people waiting outside must be watching him and Achan. He did not dare turn and look. What if there were other young men here who had come for a recommendation?

Steps led from the verandah to the eastern courtyard. The kitchen would be somewhere there, thought Sethu. He recognised the person who had just come out, the man with a stoop, wearing a knee-length towel. It was the manager, Govindan Nair. Achan saw him at last and went towards him, looking relieved.

Govindan Nair pushed a copper pot towards the door and came up to Achan. Sethu watched resentfully while they talked. Imagine asking this old, stooping servant for a recommendation. He made an effort to smile as they came up to him.

Govindan Nair asked Achan to sit on the bench in the verandah. Achan hesitated, but sat down when the other man insisted.

Govindan Nair spoke in a low voice, "People have been

streaming in since morning. It's only natural, since he comes only once in a way. I'll go and tell him." He scolded Sethu affectionately, "Why can't you sit down for a bit."

Sethu refused. He could avoid facing the people in the verandah if he stood near the bench. Some of them inched their way to this corner, had a look at them and went back.

A litter of puppies covered with dirt fought playfully with each other near the pit into which used banana leaves were thrown. They had just begun to open their eyes. A skinny mongrel lay near them with its eyes closed.

Sethu's vest was soaked in sweat. He took out the envelope with the certificates. It was wet. He opened the envelope carefully. The University certificate was dry, but the ink had spread on the conduct certificate his professor had given him.

The first time he had read the certificate, he had been ecstatic. He had gone to the professor's house late one evening to say goodbye. The professor was an asthmatic and always spoke in a soft voice which hurt Sethu. Master's younger daughter had brought him Ovaltine. Sethu had asked for a certificate. The professor had put on his glasses and asked his daughter for his letter pad. He had taken half an hour to write the certificate. When Sethu had returned to his room and read it, he had felt weak with delight. Brilliant, imaginative, a man of initiative and drive—he had been generous with words. He had not even forgotten to praise the style and expressiveness of the poems Sethu had written for the college magazine.

He had shown the certificate secretly to friends, and had felt very proud when he sent a true copy of it along with his applications. This is me!

He realized now that no one would have read it. It would have taken its place amongst the papers swept up by those who cleaned the managers' rooms and offices in big establishments.

Govindan Nair hurried out of the kitchen with two glasses of tea and put them down near Achan. "Here, have some tea. Five minutes more. Madhava Menon is with him, the lawyer from Ottappalam. As soon as he goes."

Sethu took the glass reluctantly and the tea spilled. He emptied it quickly and cleaned the pool of tea on the bench with the bottom of the glass.

The puppies had stopped playing and begun to suck the mongrel's flat teats as she lay on her side, her mouth open.

People went in and out. An old woman in a rowka came out and threw the strands of hair she had wound around her fingers into the yard. They waited, expecting Govindan Nair to come out any minute.

"What's the time?" asked Achan and Sethu realized it was the first time Achan had spoken to him directly since they left home that morning.

He was tempted to answer, I don't have a watch. Instead, he looked out at the sun and said, "It must be eleven."

As a student, he had never had enough money. He had always thought that he had shouldered a great burden and had nursed a resentment towards everyone because of it. He now realized that those were really days of happiness. As long as he had been a student, he had been able to hold his head high and give an answer when asked what he was doing.

"What are you doing?"

"My BA."

He thought of many things while they waited for the manager to appear. Of the speeches he had learned by heart for the High School Debating Society. The students of today are the citizens of tomorrow. Our future engineers, physicians and political leaders will take shape from this young generation.

Who had written all this for him?

Applause. To which he had listened, thrilled, at the school anniversary function.

The audience filled the space between the two sheds. The invitees were always in the front row. His heart beat rapidly as he listened to the headmaster read out the list of prizewinners from the temporary stage put up next to the verandah of the main hall.

Sixth Form. First Prize for General Proficiency, Sethumadhavan.

As he made his way through the cordoned path between the crowd of boys and girls, the students of Sixth A began to clap. And the others took it on until it spread into a steady rhythm like the beating of waves.

He returned and looked through his prize books, still listening to the list being called out.

General Knowledge, First: Sethumadhavan, Sixth A.

He received his prize and joined his palms before the President and the audience. The headmaster said, "Don't go back."

Versification, First Prize.

His friends cheered wildly as he climbed onto the stage once more. The applause echoed.

Pisharoty Master had collected students to start a handwritten magazine and said to them, "Sethumadhavan has a bright future."

He waited for the bright future to unfold.

All his college mates used to remark that Sethu was the only student who was not frightened by examinations. They could barely score thirty-five even if they pored over their books, while all Sethu needed was to turn over the pages.

You have a bright future.

Why don't you try for the IAS?

Govindan Nair was here again. "Come on, if we wait for everyone to leave, we'll waste your time and mine."

Father laid his umbrella on the bench, took off his slippers, straightened his veshti and followed Govindan Nair. Sethu tried not to betray his anxiety and embarrassment. There were three people in the big room besides the Judge. Sethu saw the Judge at close quarters for the first time. He wore a white half-sleeved shirt and had a towel over his shoulder. His lifeless eyes peered out from behind thick glasses.

"Yes?" He straightened up and looked at Govindan Nair and Achan in turn.

Achan stood with joined palms.

Govindan Nair introduced them. "They're my neighbours from across the river."

Sethu stood with his head bent.

Govindan Nair added, "He taught for some time in the Athirattakodu school."

Achan started to say, "I was your. . . ." Before he could finish, the Judge took off his glasses, rubbed his eyes and said, "What is it?"

"This is my son. He's done his BA. He hasn't found a job yet."

"Can't you do teachers' training?"

Sethu realized that the judge was addressing him. He did not answer. He made an effort to smile and look respectful.

"That's the best thing to do. Then you can get a job in Kerala."

Achan said, "It doesn't matter where he works. I have already retired." Sethu wondered whether he would begin to talk about his problems.

"It's not like old days. It's difficult to find jobs outside Kerala now."

"His marks are good. We've brought his certificates." Achan held out his hand for the envelope.

The judge wiped his face with the towel and smiled. "There's no use my looking at them. I don't have the authority to give him a job. And recommendations are not allowed."

Govindan Nair had already skirted the easy chair respectfully and gone in.

"All right, then, I'll keep it in mind."

He turned to the stout, bald man on his left and asked, "Then what was the immediate provocation?"

Sethu prayed that Achan would have the good sense to leave now, before the Judge asked them to leave. Thankfully, Achan joined his palms again to take leave.

Sethu was drenched in sweat when they came out. The faint breeze from the banana grove sent the blood rushing back to his face.

Achan put on his slippers and took his umbrella. Sethu did not look at his face. Govindan Nair came out from the kitchen with an air of satisfaction on his face.

"What, you're leaving?"

"Yes, we must go."

"No, no, it's time for lunch. Lunch is ready here by eleven. Please eat. No one will mind."

Achan ignored this invitation and said goodbye to Govindan Nair.

"Did you tell him everything?"

"Um."

"What does he think?"

Achan said indifferently. "He said he would consider it."

"That's enough then. That's all he usually says. But he always keeps his word. He's very fond of everyone who belongs to the village. I'll remind him again before he leaves tomorrow."

Sethu smiled at Govindan Nair and followed Achan.

The sun was blazing. Achan stopped near the temple once more and took off his slippers to go up the steps. Sethu walked on without waiting for him.

4

He had heard much about this town sixty miles away from home, but it was the first time he was here. There had been students from this place in college with him. He tried to remember who they were and looked at the faces of those who passed by without much hope.

There was a light drizzle. Stagnant pools of rain water from yesterday's showers lay stagnant in the potholes on the road. He moved aside to make way for vehicles carrying passengers who had arrived on the train. A passing horse cart splashed muddy water in all directions, but luckily it missed him. By the time the people who had been spattered began to scold the driver, the cart had already gone quite a distance.

He saw the board of a hotel just beyond the culvert. It said, Jubilee Hotel, Boarding and Lodging. It looked a modest place, so he went in. Yes, there was a room. The rent was two and a half rupees.

The room was a cubicle with asbestos partitions, hardly bigger than a box. The hotel boy spread a blue cloth over the dirty, oil-stained mattress. There was only one small window opening onto the tiled roof. He pushed it open. The shabby brown roofs of the city houses stretched as far as the eye could reach.

He had to appear for an interview next day. He had been asked to report at the Collectorate at nine.

How many times had he done this!

He had heard that more than a hundred candidates would be selected, so he was hopeful. The minimum qualification they had asked for was SSLC, so there would not be many applicants with a BA. They would pay a stipend of fifty rupees during the six month training period. After that he would get a salary of a hundred and five rupees. The interview card said that those who were selected had to leave at once for the farm. They had even enclosed a cyclostyled list of the things that had to be taken along.

A bucket, a broom, two pairs of khadar shorts, two khadi shirts, a bedroll, a big plate and a small one.

He had begun to regret the postage he had to spend each time he sent an application.

He had felt nervous and confused when the interview card came. If he got the job and did not accept it, there would be a scene. How could he refuse a government job!

He imagined visitors asking his parents about him.

"Where is Sethu now?"

"Where is the place? He told me its name."

"How far did he study?"

"He did his BA."

"What job is he doing?"

Achan might say, he's in the National Extension Scheme. Amma would not know, so she would say, "He's a rural service worker or something like that."

He had prayed with great fervour before an interview for a tutor's post in a college. His going to Madras had been quite an event in the village.

He had given charity to all the beggars at the station, thinking, may the force of their prayers support me.

He had written to his acquaintances in Madras, even to Daniel, who was doing his MSc in Christian College. Until the train reached the Central Station, he was nervous. He saw Daniel waiting for him with a sense of relief. Daniel had arranged for him to stay in the hostel as a guest and had taken leave from work next day. He knew every nook and corner of the city. He took Sethu to the DPI's office in a taxi, wished him luck and promised to be back in two hours.

There were more Telugu and Tamil candidates than Malayalis. The Director was a Malayali. There were candidates in full suits, in full shirts and gabardine trousers and shining ties. Some of them spoke English with an American accent. Sethu was too timid to talk to any of them. How many of them, he wondered, would have got a first? Although he had only a second, he had the consolation that he had scored fifty-seven per cent.

It was the first time he had worn trousers. He had bought a pair of cotton trousers the day before from Moore Market for seven-and-a-half rupees. And chappals for six rupees. He felt naked. What if his fly was open? His skin felt raw where the strap of the new chappals chafed against it. He looked enviously at the young men waiting under the trees and told himself that it was not important to wear a suit and a tie. A good director would be contemptuous of things like that. He would know that what a teacher needed were knowledge and simplicity, that only ignorant people dressed up fashionably.

The names were called out in alphabetical order.

His interview was at eleven. He opened the spring door nervously and his voice trembled when he said good morning.

They signalled to him to sit down.

Was this Menon, the Director? He reminded Sethu of Kurup the sorcerer from Kalladikothu, who used to come to his house often when he was a child.

He had been told that it was bad manners to place his elbows on the table. His chair had no arms and he felt his hands grow heavier since he had to keep them hanging down its sides. The light green paper lying on the table was his application.

"Certificates."

He held out the envelope.

What would they ask? Marlowe? Milton? Donne? He hoped it would be one of the modern poets.

The first question was, "How did you miss your First Class?"

He had not expected it at all. He could not answer. There had been no reason. He realized he had to say something.

"I don't know."

In the column marked talents and preferences, he had written that he wrote poetry.

"You write poetry?"

"Yes, Sir."

"About what?"

His palms felt moist. He could not speak.

"Tell me briefly about your latest poem."

God, if only he could think of a poem.

Ah, giver of happiness, when you come with the blue pleats of your skirt unfurled, my heart plays the music of flutes.

The serpents of grief hear, and gather around me.

No, he could not explain all that in English. He said, without looking up,

"The last one I did was a translation of a Tagore poem."

The Director pushed the certificates towards him and said, "That is all. You can go."

His head spun as he came out. They had not even glanced at the conduct certificate that his professor had written with such care.

He hurried down without looking at the candidates still awaiting their turn. Daniel was at the gate. He held out a cigarette and asked,

"How was it?"

"Not bad."

He lit the cigarette and felt his taut nerves relax. They wandered round the city and went to a Hindi film at night. They had dinner in a dimly lit restaurant where soft music played. Daniel told him about his new girlfriend. She had come to his hostel for dinner once with her cousin who was at Queen Mary's College. After that, they had met in church. They had talked to each other on the telephone a few times and now they met every Sunday. Many people had tried to bring him down to earth, but had not succeeded.

Bring him down to earth? Daniel's term was new to him.

He had a sense of relief when he said goodbye to Daniel and his friends and boarded the crowded Mangalore Mail, even though he knew he had to go back to the days of endless waiting for the postman.

And now here he was, with another interview ahead of him.

At least in Madras, Daniel had been with him for company. Here, he knew no one. He kept to the sides of the crowded streets, feeling a little scared. He was a total stranger here. The Collectorate, where he had to appear for the interview, was just a furlong away from where he stayed.

In the evening, he went to the beach. A long line of cars was parked near the footpath, under the casuarina trees. The wet stretch of sand was deserted. The wind blowing over the roaring waves was laden with drops of moisture. Was it at this spot that da Gama's yachts had glimpsed the shore? He had no desire to explore the city.

He had to ask his way twice to the hotel. The narrow room was dark, moist and smelly. He heard soda bottles being opened beyond the thin asbestos partition, and voices rising steadily in volume.

"Come on, try it, it's good."

"Um, um." That was a woman.

"Just gulp it down."

"I'll feel nauseous."

"Rubbish."

Raindrops splattered the tiled roof. The window banged shut in the wind, and then flew open again.

The rain grew heavier. As it rose to a roar, the sounds in the next room died down.

He thought of Sumitra and suddenly longed to see her. He saw her very rarely now. They quarrelled all the time at Vadakkethu. Sumitra and Devu, Sumitra and her mother, Madhava Ammama and Devu.

Madhava Ammama hardly ever came home these days. Sethu heard that there had been proposals of marriage for Sumitra. One of them had nearly materialized. The horoscopes matched. The boy's family liked the girl. But Madhava Ammama visited their house in Muduthala, came back and said it was not a suitable match.

The reason he gave was that the boy's mother and sister worked as servants for a rich family. Amma heard this and asked, "And what were the Vadakkethu women doing at the illam? Were they visiting?"

"That was in the old days. They're Madhavan Nair's wife's family now."

Amma and Cheriamma whispered in the kitchen, "He probably doesn't like the idea of another man living there." The whispers gradually became inaudible.

Sethu lay awake wondering why he could not concentrate on Thangamani. He had had a letter from her quite some time ago and knew she would be upset that he had not replied.

What could he write? That he had not achieved anything? That he would never enter a class in a city college as an eager tutor? That he would never write his MA privately, or become a lecturer. Nor would he write a thesis, be awarded an MLitt and have his picture in the papers.

5

All the candidates were gathered in the upstairs verandah of the Collectorate. Most of them wore khadar shirts. Sethu wondered whether some of them who had come earlier in borrowed gabardine suits to the DPI's office had turned up here in khadar shirts and mundus.

A fair, good-looking man came and asked him, "Aren't you Sethumadhavan?"

"Yes."

"I've seen you in Palghat, I used to come to the hostel with Aravindan."

Aravindan had been Sethu's classmate. Gopi was his relative.

"What is Aravindan doing now?"

"He wrote his exams in September and again in March, but didn't get through."

Gopi had done his SSLC and then worked in various places, in a cooperative store, a petrol bunk and a handloom society. They had all been leave vacancies.

"The Head Clerk told me that not many graduates have applied. So you stand a good chance."

Gopi knew everything about the job. A Grade One employee was paid a hundred twenty rupees. In the Higher Division Clerk scale, you had a chance of being promoted as a Secondary Education Officer or a Block Development Officer since fifty per cent of the recruitments were from the department.

Gopi moved from group to group. The crowd kept increasing. How many were there? Three hundred? Four hundred?

Gopi was very nervous. What would they ask at the interview?

Sethu stood at the end of the verandah. He could see the washermen washing clothes in the open maidan and policeman practising exercises in the courtyard of the building beyond.

Gopi wove his way through the crowd, took Sethu's hand and led him to a deserted corner. He whispered, "They will question us on the Five Year Plan."

"Who told you?"

"Never mind that. But I don't know a damn thing about this Five Year Plan. What is it?"

"I haven't studied it either."

"What is the difference between the first and the second Five Year Plan?

"I don't know."

"My God, we're finished."

Gopi questioned candidates who he thought were intelligent.

Sethu watched the multicoloured clothes flapping on the lines like festival flags and thought to himself, who cares, let them ask whatever they want.

Gopi came back beaming. "I've got it."

"Um?"

"Industry is the most important factor of the first Five Year Plan. The second one emphasises agriculture, cottage industries and the electrification of villages."

"Really?"

"What if they ask about the National Extension Scheme? Isn't it meant to accelerate village development?"

"Maybe."

"Go on, tell me what to say if they ask."

Sethu was irritated. Gopi seemed to imply that he wanted to keep information to himself.

"Come on now, tell me. I won't tell anyone else."

"If the National Extension Scheme is implemented, there will be electricity in all the villages, parks for the children, good roads, jobs for everyone—in short, our country will become a heaven. Milk and honey will flow through it. You can tell them that."

Gopi wondered whether Sethu was joking. No, he looked serious.

"We have a National Employment Scheme in our village. A handful of women rush about in a jeep. But of course I'll tell them what you said if they ask." Gopi began to repeat what Sethu had said.

They had begun to call people in. Gopi tried to find out from those who had finished what questions they had been asked. Gopi was called before him. He came back smiling.

"It's over!"

"What did they ask?"

"It was all in Malayalam. They asked how India's economic status can be improved. I reeled off a quotation from Gandhi. The only way the poor of India can progress is through agriculture. Agriculture that uses all types of manure. I think it's the Revenue District Officer who is conducting the interview."

They called Sethu's name at last. How long had he waited for this door to open! From between the stacks of yellowed paper that surrounded the table, tired grey eyes peered out at him as if from inside a well.

He had a feeling that all of them looked alike, bored and angry at once. Sethu did not feel as nervous as he had been in the Director's office.

"So you're a graduate?"

"Yes."

"Why did you apply for this job?"

Do you want to know? Because I could not find anything else. Because I had come to the end of my tether. Because I thought that if I get this job, I will earn at least fifty rupees. Because I wanted to escape questions about my attempts to find a job. Because I wanted to run away from my family.

"Come on, answer me!"

"I." He debated for a minute. "I wish to serve in the villages. I believe that the greatest service I can render to the nation is to work in undeveloped villages. Factors like starvation, unemployment, superstition. . . ."

Whose voice was this? He was back in the Debating Society in school. Did they want to hear more?

"I believe it is the duty of every educated person to lift our brothers in the villages out of the darkness in which they are sunk."

Their tired eyes focused slowly on him. He paused for a moment, wondering whether to go on. The officer said,

"All right. We will let you know."

He hurried out quickly, but Gopi caught up with him in the street.

"Wait, I'll come too. How was it? You must have done well."

"Yes, I did." Sethu smiled. They went back to the Jubilee Hotel.

It would be a real Gandhian life, said Gopi. No tea or coffee, no cigarettes. Prayers in the morning, then field work. Would they be asked to clean shit?

"I don't know."

"I heard that we might have to."

Gopi said, "I don't mind herding cattle, or digging, or drinking panakam instead of coffee or tea. But if they ask me to clean shit?"

"You have to do it then. Mahatma Gandhi said so, didn't he?"

Gopi's face, which had been bright and happy, suddenly darkened. He lowered his eyes and fell silent.

6

A list of train timings had been cut out from the newspaper and stuck near the counter. Sethu thought he would go to the station fifteen minutes ahead. He arranged for a rickshaw to take his luggage. He bought his ticket and went in only to learn from the chalked mark on the black announcement board that the number two mail was running sixty minutes late.

The platform was terribly crowded. There seemed to be more people waiting to receive incoming passengers than those travelling on the train. He asked the porter to put his luggage down by the bookstall. The old man walked contentedly away with the four annas he paid him. He felt he should have given him another four annas. Perhaps he had not really seen the coin that Sethu had placed in his shrivelled palm?

Porters were usually a dissatisfied lot. It was the first time Sethu had seen one who had not protested or complained. Maybe this fellow had never heard about the porters and jutka drivers in Olavakkode!

Two pretty girls in short dresses stood at the bookstall, leafing through the English magazines. They spoke in a convent-trained English accent. Their middle-aged guardian waited patiently some distance away, a folded ten rupee note held in his hand.

"You buy that. I'll buy a Denise Robins," said the one who looked the older of the two.

"Do you have *A Wounded Heart?*" She spoke Malayalam with the air of one committing a crime.

"Hurry up, girls," said the man, loosening his tie.

"One minute, Daddy!"

"Do you have *Lovers' Fate*? No, I've read this."

The salesman laid out all the Denise Robins novels he had, *A Flaming Heart, A Lonely Girl, The Ill-Fated Affair.* She did not want any of them.

"Any new book by Hermina Black?"

Sethu craned his neck to peer at the titles on the dusty spines of the paperbacks arranged behind the bookseller.

Someone tapped his shoulder. Gopi.

"What a fellow. I've been looking everywhere for you. I even wondered whether you had gone by bus." Gopi took a newspaper from the counter and browsed through it, pretending he was going to read it.

It was Gopi who had brought the news to the hotel the day before that the list of selected candidates had been put up at the Collectorate, and that Sethu's name was there.

Sethu had not been surprised. Only rejects from elsewhere had turned up here, after all.

Gopi was enthusiastic. "There are only forty on this list. The peon said there would be a second list. But I can't bear to think of their training programme. Damn! Do you think we can buy a bucket and broom after we get there?"

Sethu did not reply.

"Don't you think we can wait till we get there?"

"I suppose so."

"We'll buy khadar for the uniforms here, it's cheaper. We'll travel together."

"We'll see."

"Why are you lying down?"

He pressed his hands to his temples, closed his eyes and said, "I have a headache, I'll lie down for a while."

Gopi went away. Sethu wondered whether he should sleep for a while. All kinds of things seemed to be crawling over the pillow, which was as stiff as wood, and polished with oil and sweat too.

He got up, changed his mundu, put on a shirt and went out. The concrete road blazed in the sun.

My name is there, among all the lucky ones that have been chosen. The name that time had waited to enter on fortune's list! He wanted to laugh as well as cry. Here he was, with a day of celebration before him!

He hesitated in the Collectorate compound for a long time before going up to the verandah. Were any of the applicants around? He had come for the interview as if it was a casual matter. He made sure no one was about and went upto the notice board. Yes, his name was there for once, on the typed list!

He walked until it was dusk and he was hungry, then went into a Muslim hotel. There were no vacant tables downstairs, in the common dining area. He felt reluctant to sit at a table with strangers. The manager noticed him and said, "There's room upstairs."

There were small cubicles upstairs with partitions of coloured glass. The hall was deserted. Fans turned above the cubicles. The fat little waiter opened an empty cubicle and switched on the fan. The room was meant for four. The waiter wiped the table and waited for his order.

"What will you have?"

"What is there?"

Soda bottles were being opened noisily in the next room. The smell of liquor and slurred voices floated in from beyond the shoulder-high partition.

The boy removed the dirty handkerchief wound around his head, tied it on his neck and rattled off the names of various dishes. He was fleshy and blue-eyed. If he had worn clean clothes, he could have been taken for an Embrandiri boy. He reminded Sethu of Balan who used to hang around with the football players in College, whose nickname had been "Plymouth."

This was a day for celebration. Two cigarettes, then biriyani. He made a quick calculation—he had seventy rupees in all, including what he had borrowed from Madhava Ammama. Khader shirts, shorts, a bucket, a plate.

The boy asked with a meaningful smile, "Nothing else?"

"What do you have?"

"Country stuff."

The head waiter opened the half-door and asked, "Haven't you taken the order yet, Abu?"

The boy asked, "Soda, or iced water?"

"Iced water."

The boy brought him two cigarettes and a box of matches on a plastic plate. Sethu realized what he had meant when the big glass arrived and the stench of country arrack rose to his nostrils.

Taken aback, he said, "This?"

"It's only a quarter bottle." The boy would not leave. All right then, if that was what he wanted! His throat and palate burned with the first mouthful. Flames raced inside him.

He said, without looking up, "Bring the food."

The boy brought the biriyani and asked, "How was it?"

He emptied the glass of water in the wash basin, and pushed the glass towards Sethu, "Let me have a drop as well."

Sethu poured out half a glass gladly, it meant he had that much less to swallow. The boy drank it down in one gulp, wiped his chin and tossed his head.

Sethu asked, "Don't you have Prohibition here?"

The boy's blue eyes gleamed. His face was flushed. "The Inspectors are in the next room. They've already finished three bottles." He lowered his voice, "Didn't you come here with the lawyer the other day?"

Sethu did not answer. He picked up the onion slices soaked in vinegar from his plate and ate them. He held his breath, grimaced, drained the glass and felt better. He had not really tasted the disgusting odour. The boy went out and he began to eat. A fire blazed inside him and sweat broke out on his forehead. The first few mouthfuls nauseated him. His head felt heavier and his legs were unsteady. He washed his hands at the basin, wiped them on his hair and lit the second cigarette.

The boy brought the bill. Two-and-a-half rupees. He looked again to make sure. Yes, two-and-a-half rupees.

"A rupee extra for the other thing. It's not included in the bill."

Sethu placed five rupees in the saucer. The boy stood smirking, his elbows planted on the table. Sethu said angrily, "Get me the change."

He left a four anna tip and left. The neon lamps had come on and the city smiled at him. The streets had grown crowded. He kept to the side of the street, feeling unsteady. He wanted to get back quickly to his room and write to Achan, to Amma, to Parameswara Ettan. By the grace of your blessings, I shall now begin to eat the salt of the sarkar!

But when he opened the whitewashed asbestos door of his room, all he wanted was to pitch into bed. He thought about the letters. He had to write to Thangamani as well. It could wait until he reached the training centre.

He woke up only when Gopi knocked on the door.

Gopi finished reading the paper, hovered around the ladies' waiting room for a while and came back. "Let's go to the other side. Our group is there."

Sethu was still thinking of the night that had gone by. He had dreamed that he had a quarrel with someone. He could not remember the face.

The other side of the platform was crowded with boys bound for the training centre, seated on their bundles and boxes. There was a mountain of luggage—buckets, brooms, bedrolls of different types, boxes.

"Where's your box and mattress?"

"Near the bookstall."

"Let's bring it over here." Gopi brought the steel trunk and bedroll himself.

"The Mail is going to be crowded."

"There won't be room for all of us in a single carriage. We'll get in wherever there's space."

Gopi knew everyone and introduced them one by one to Sethu.

Nedungadi from Tirunavaya asked, "Aren't you a graduate? Why didn't you do a BT? You would have a higher pay scale."

Sankarankutty from Parappanangadi said, "I can't bear teaching. I could have got into the TTC if I tried. But it's such a bore."

Venkataswamy from Kozhijambara thought that a secondary school teacher's job near home would have been better than this. He had tried to get one for two years. You needed very good marks to be on the Government list. Otherwise you had to have a recommendation. And if you wanted a job in the training school run by the management, you had to pay.

A young man in a coarse khadar shirt said, "You can always get into a basic school."

"Indeed," said Nedungadi, moving from a mound of bedrolls to Sethu's trunk. "The basic school takes five hundred rupees as well. But they don't call it a bribe, they have some other name for it. My Valiamma's daughter paid to get into Minister Sankara Menon's son's school."

Sethu smiled, "You could call it a sambhavana, a gift for rebuilding the nation."

"No, no, sambhavana is in Malayalam. The Sarvodaya people would never use the word. They think people won't understand if you call cottage industries 'kutil vyavasayam'. They insist on calling it 'gramodyog'. What do they say for 'basic,' Master Ramakrishnan?

Sethu took a liking to Nedungadi, with his narrow eyes and a sandal paste mark from his morning bath still fresh on his forehead.

Ramakrishnan of the khader shirt said indifferently, "Nayi talim," and moved down the platform in order to spit and blow his nose.

Gopi muttered, "He's a Sarvodaya fanatic. They say his father is a Jeevandani."

"Well, what more can one give than one's life?"

"One could always do nothing. Or be lazy and go to sleep. Or commit a fraud."

Ramakrishnan came back ready for an argument. "I studied in a basic school. And I'm proud of it. This new fashion of turning out people who aren't fit for any sort of job. . . ."

Gopi interrupted, "Look my friend, what's the name of that drink in which they put coriander?"

Nedungadi knew. "It's called jappee. Mahatma Gandhi's special jappee."

"Ah, yes, jappee. Will Sarvodaya be destroyed if one drinks tea instead?"

Ramakrishnan would not give in. It was a drink suited to Indians. Many great men had praised it. Gandhi, Vinobha Bhave, Shankar Rao Deo, Kelappaji.

"Do you want to listen to a joke?" That was Nedungadi. "My village was a donated one. A lot of the villagers are jeevandanis. One of them, Kuttisankaran, after being a jeevandani for two years, sells arrack now. He's doing quite well. His house has been tiled and he has enough money. But that's not what I wanted to say. Shankar Rao Deo came to our place to receive the donation. Have you seen him?"

Controlling his irritation, Ramakrishnan said, "Yes, I know him. He visited us at home. My father knew him in Wardha.

"I'll tell you for the benefit of those who don't know. He wears only a mundu, no shirt. He shaves once in three months. He was supposed to stay with a man who had returned from Singapore, who had a latrine with a septic tank. Sarvodayas are forbidden to use them. He controlled himself for three days, and on the fourth, a pit was dug for him in the compound."

When all of them began to protest, Ramakrishnan changed his tone and laughed foolishly, "You'll find out when the training begins. You can play at being rich landlords until then."

"We'll see. There are quite a few of us, after all."

Many had doubts and fears about life in the training centre.

"It's only for six months, after that we'll be independent."

Venkataswamy was full of sympathy, "It's a pity graduates have to stoop to manual labour of the lowest type."

Gopi consoled Sethu, "We're the second batch, remember? Graduates stand a good chance of being promoted."

Thomas of Kunnamkulam invited Sethu for a cup of tea but he declined. "Come on, the train has not yet been blocked."

Venkatachalam and Nedungadi went along with them as well, and so did Ramakrishnan. Gopi teased him, "We'll see whether they'll give us jappee."

The train came finally after an hour and three quarters. The platform was suddenly crowded with people. Porters in dirty blue shirts with red turbans on their heads came out of their dens and surrounded the luggage like vultures.

An old porter came limping towards them. His blue shirt had faded to grey and his turban to ochre. It was difficult to believe that his lips had once been red. Scratching his face, where grey stubble grew in the furrows in his creased skin, he bared his decayed teeth in a smile and asked, "Shall I take your luggage in, mudalali?"

Before Sethu could answer, Gopi said, "No, there are enough of us."

Sethu felt sorry for the old man who waited for some time, his mouth still open in a pitiful smile, then limped slowly away into the crowd.

The train was more crowded than usual, and their group had to spread themselves over three compartments. Sethu found himself with Gopi, Ramakrishnan and Thomas.

"Where's Nedungadi?"

"In the last compartment."

There was hardly any space to sit. Gopi elbowed his way into a seat which he shared with Sethu.

So this was the beginning of his journey to his place of work. Sethu was not happy. An uneasiness like a black rain cloud that kept changing its shape moved through him. He rebuked himself. Six months. If you can manage on fifty rupees a month for six months, you'll have a career and be independent!

Gopi found one more person who was going to the training centre. He was tall and dark, with curly hair and glasses and the scar of a burn on his left cheek. Gopi kept asking him questions and he finally folded the copy of *The Hindu* that he was reading, took off his glasses, wiped them and sat up.

Gopi said, "Unni Narayanan is a graduate as well. You don't know each other, do you?"

Unni Narayanan asked, "Which college?"

Sethu told him.

He said, "I came there in fifty-one."

"I was there then."

Unni Narayanan had come for the Inter-collegiate Debate from Thrissur. That year someone from Thevara had won the first prize and Unni Narayanan had won the second. The following year he had won the trophy at Ernakulam.

Sethu asked, "Which year did you finish?"

He had been a year senior to Sethu.

"You haven't worked anywhere?"

"I tried, but nothing came through." The young man who had won trophies for his College in debating competitions fell silent. Then he said, "Actually, I've been thinking. They say two to three years' experience is essential for every job. But if no one gives you a job how can you have experience?" Unni Narayanan's eyes glinted behind his glasses.

"The only other way is to be born a lower caste, as a pulaya or a pariah. Unfortunately, I'm not one. Or you have to be a girl, a fairly good-looking one."

He asked, "Do you know Antony? He left our College and joined yours."

"The footballer?"

"Yes. We were classmates. He lived next door to me. He took three years to do his Inter and then came over to your college." Sethu had seen him. Someone had pointed him out admiringly when he was chosen as a University player.

Antony's photograph had been next to the poem he had published in the college magazine. He had been wearing a blazer with the name of the University on it and a dotted silk scarf around his neck.

"He is with Mafatlal now. All you need is to be good at sports, and you can earn a salary of seven hundred rupees. He will get an increment after the next season in Calcutta. His brother told me that all the clubs are fighting over who is to have him."

"Didn't he go abroad?"

He had played in the Indian team at Bangkok and came back a star.

Unni Narayanan seemed to grow more and more irritated when he described how Antony had risen high because he played football. Then he told Sethu about another one of his classmates who had barely managed to graduate. He was the Assistant Manager now in a white man's rubber estate. He had a salary of seven hundred rupees and four months' salary as bonus. And a jeep.

Sethu consoled Unni Narayanan, "It's just a matter of luck."

"Luck indeed! I know him well. He's an arch fool. He cannot write a single sentence in English without making mistakes. He fawned on his examiners and bribed them to get thirty-five per cent. His father worked in Singapore and his mother was a society lady. They wined and dined the General Manager of the estate and prevailed on the Labour Minister to recommend his name. What more did he need? It wouldn't have mattered if he was illiterate."

Sethu gazed at the backwaters, choked with scum.

"Didn't you try to do your BT?"

"It's not easy. I tried to work as an untrained teacher. Have you heard of Unni Krishnan Nair who is in charge of appointments at the District Board Office?"

"No."

"He won't relent even if the President recommends someone. He is the type who would have faced a firing squad in the white man's regime. Teachers who want a transfer have to go and meet him at home. If they are male, he accepts money. If I could have worked in a high school for some time, I could have done my BT. But how can one get in with people like him running things?"

There was a sudden silence in the compartment. Sethu remembered that there were other passengers as well. Unni Narayanan must have realized it too, for he opened his paper again. Sethu looked at the coconut groves and the fields rushing by.

Here I come, here I come, here I come.

The train gathered speed. He listened to the steady rhythm of the iron wheels, to the song they played on the rail track. He felt words take shape from the music. Here we come, to awaken the villages that are filled with darkness!

Thangamani must be asleep upstairs now, after lunch, on the clean floor in her house, her hair spread over the red cement.

He had to write to her. I dreamed of you, my darling, on my journey to freedom.

The train hooted with delight and broke into song once more, Here we come, here we come!

7

The well-known farm waited for them somewhere across the river and between the hills. His very first place of work. He felt happy when he saw the familiar line of the Western Ghats in the distance. Looking at them from atop the hill on the west of his house, from the railway track, from the downstairs verandah of the hostel, their indistinct shapes had always seemed to him like the boundaries of his life.

The train arrived at four. Gopi arranged for the luggage to be loaded on a handcart. The spirits of the tired young travellers suddenly rose as they walked in a procession behind the cart. It began to drizzle when they reached the bus stand. They took shelter under the sloping roofs of the little box-like shops on the roadside.

Sethu bought a half packet of cigarettes so that the owner of the shop on whose verandah he had sought shelter would not be displeased. He held out the packet to Unni Narayanan, who refused. He had never smoked, he considered it a luxury that he could not think about until he began to make money himself.

Unni Narayanan reminded Sethu of Krishnankutty, except that he had a kind expression, while Krishnankutty had always looked stern.

As he lit his cigarette from the wick hung on the bamboo pillar, he wondered whether Krishnankutty ever thought of him.

Gopi had found out that there were buses going every hour to their destination, the farm, and that one was due now. It started from the city and more than half the seats were vacant. There was a scramble for seats. It saddened and disgusted Sethu to watch his companions, who had all travelled together and who were bound for the same place, suddenly fighting with each other.

This is how we battle for standing space on the footboards. We hurt and kick each other so as not to be left behind.

Unni Narayanan had been thrown back. When he finally reached the door to salvation, the conductor said expressionlessly. "There are no seats left."

Those who had managed to get in shouted to Gopi for their luggage.

Gopi had loaded all the luggage and was practically drenched in the rain. When the door closed, he shouted an obscenity. Sethu said consolingly, "We'll go on the next bus."

Gopi, Unni Narayanan, Sethu and two others whose names they did not know were left behind. Sethu lit another cigarette and decided to wait on the shop verandah. But Gopi would not accept defeat. He argued with the conductor until he was given permission to stand in the bus. The others got in as well. They would have to hang on and balance themselves for thirty miles.

As the bus wound though the narrow streets, the town looked smaller than he had imagined. Most of the football players in college had been from here. Sethu peered out, bending his head, as they came to the railroad bridge.

The river, which had broken free from the hills, suddenly lay quiet here before the fearful sea.

Nedungadi moved aside and gave Sethu a little space to sit down.

The hills spread out from the farther shore. The uneven path, full of ruts, circled the barren hills. The wet path gleamed like a channel of sweat running down a cherumi girl's chest.

Large compounds lay beyond the village. Then came the cashew groves. There was the scent of moisture and old leaves in the air. Scraps of sunlight were lost in the patches of shade covered with dry leaves.

The dark shadows of the Western Ghats grew thicker and heavier between the clumps of the trees and over the bare hills. Shreds of cloud below dissolved into fine wisps of mist in the band of blue-black behind the range of hills.

They covered the distance rapidly. The bus stopped. All eyes turned to the gate. Here was the gate to the new life they had been waiting for.

Varika varika sahajare!
Veeraram yuvakkale!
Come, come my brothers,
Brave young men!

Sethu could not remember who had started to hum the famous marching song of the Communist Party.

Gopi became their leader again and rushed up to unload the luggage.

There was a huge board showing the name of the farm on the concrete pillars at the beginning of the red clay path and below it, a small one with the name of the training centre fixed to a wooden post.

Remember, right foot forward.

Everyone fell silent as they entered the gate. They put down the luggage on the verandah of the first building they saw. A few of them went in search of the office.

Chilli creepers climbed over the huge trees. Rows of yellow notice boards detailed statistics.

Those who had gone to look for the office returned, "All of us have to go to the quarters."

"Who said so?"

"Did you see the Director?"

"Where are the quarters?"

"Over there!" No one knew exactly where they were. They saw a man in a khaki shirt and turban come towards them, dangling a big bunch of iron keys. They were happy once more. Here was someone to show them where they had to go.

Sethu found it difficult to walk carrying his tin trunk and bedroll. They went through a papaya garden and a grove planted with coconut seedlings. The quarters were at the end of the path.

A long building with a tiled roof. The rough cement floor was marked in squares.

Khaki shirt turned. He said, "Four in each room."

Sethu went to the third room. It smelt of whitewash and varnish. When he opened the big window, the room was filled with white light. Unni Narayanan, Gopi, Venkataswamy and Nedungadi were all in the same room. When he heard there was place elsewhere, Venkataswamy left.

Sethu was hungry and very tired. None of them had had lunch. Sethu pushed his bedroll against the wall and sat on it.

As they assessed the room, the man in the khaki shirt came back. Unni Narayanan took the lock and key from him. Sethu called out to him as he left, but he did not hear.

"Hey!"

The peon turned, looking displeased.

"Don't you have chairs or tables or furniture of any kind?"

"No. The rules don't permit them."

Gopi went up to the door. "No beds either?"

"The order says you have to bring mattresses."

"We've got them. But what about cots? Do we have to spread the mattresses on this cement floor?"

The peon looked unmoved. "Those are the rules. You can talk to him yourself."

Gopi muttered, "Has Mahatma Gandhi said that even people with rheumatism cannot sleep on cots?"

There was a well nearby, and bathrooms. The Gandhian latrines were a furlong away. The dining room was visible from the verandah. The hall where classes would be held was next to the tall office building.

Gopi and Unni Narayanan went for a walk around the farm and Nedungadi for a bath. Sethu unrolled his mattress and lay down. His forehead felt hot and his head ached. The boys from the next room dropped in, but went away when he said he had a headache.

It grew dark very quickly and was unpleasantly cold. Someone turned on the light in the verandah and a ray of light came in.

The others came back and said, "We have to assemble at seven."

"What's the time now?"

"Ten to seven." They began to change and get ready to go.

"Aren't you going to change?"

Sethu got up and said, "I feel so tired, I just want to cover myself and go to sleep." Outside, the cold wind pricked like needles.

They fought for front seats on the mat spread in the hall. Sethu sat near the door. When the wind blew in raindrops, he shivered.

The dais was empty. There were framed pictures of national leaders on the wall with khadar garlands decorating them. Seven o'clock. As the waiting prolonged itself, there were angry mutterings that soon grew to a roar.

The round dial of the clock that hung next to the coloured picture of Gandhiji standing with folded hands showed seven thirty. Shoes grated on the verandah outside. Everyone got up. By the light of the bright bulb that swung over the dais, they saw a man in dark green khadar trousers and a brown bush-shirt. The Hitler moustache under his flat nose added to his ugliness.

"Sit down." Everyone sat down.

The man on the dais reminded Sethu of a cartoon he had seen in an advertisement.

He began in Malayalam. "From today, you are government servants."

Sethu placed his hand on his chest. Did he have fever? He shivered; it could have been the cold.

The responsibilities of a government servant, the amount of money the government would spend on this training scheme, the kind of discipline expected during the training period. Sethu tried to pay attention. He found the rough North Malabar accent amusing. His attention wandered. The rebuilding of the nation, Mahatmaji, the future of India, and finally, instructions.

They had to report to the field at seven thirty and there would be field work till noon. They were free after that and could go to the town to buy what they wanted. They had to be back before eight.

Sethu was famished. He regretted not having bought a plate when they reached the dining hall. There were others like him, however. One of the servants went out and brought big teak leaves.

They were given chapatis and steaming hot green gram dal. A young instructor announced, "Prayers first. Everyone has to take part."

He put back the dal.

Om sa ha nav avatu
saha nau bhunaktu
saha veeryam karavavahai.

May he protect us both
May he be pleased with us both
May we work together with vigour

He pretended to move his lips along with them while they intoned the invocation to the Kathopanishad.

Om Santhi! Santhi!

Sethu came back to his room, lay down and covered himself with a used mundu. He thought he would fall asleep at once. But he did not. Everyone was writing letters home. He pulled his tin trunk towards him, sat cross-legged and began to write. To Amma, Parameswara Ettan, Achan.

He knew he should write to Krishnankutty, Balakrishnan and Daniel. But what could he write? Dear friends, let me convey to you the happy news that I have arrived here in order to serve our villages.

He imagined Padmu stumbling through his letter, reading it to Amma. Cheriamma would arrive just as she finished. "Is it from Sethu? Read it again, girl!" And she would comment, "At least he's earning a living now."

Amma would be quiet, undemonstrative as usual, praying silently as she always did. She would say, "I must send four annas to the temple on Friday to have a flower offering, done on his star."

Achan would not talk about him at all. Parameswarettan might speak to Edathi Amma about him.

Everyone spread out their mattress. Sethu did not feel so cold now. He felt pleasantly lazy and his headache had gone.

It was very dark outside and nothing was visible through the indistinct outlines of the bushes. The western wind roared outside the closed windows.

"Shall I put out the light?"

"Wait." Sethu pulled out the magazine he had bought on the way and sat back against the wall to read.

Gopi warned him, "Lights out at nine, that's the rule."

Sethu pretended not to hear. He had just one cigarette left. He rolled it between his palms to warm it, then lit it.

He had not written to Thangamani. How would he begin? Maybe you are annoyed with me. I write this in the solitude of the night, far away on the hills, listening to the music of the darkness and the whirlwind.

Someone knocked on the door.

He said, "Come in," thinking it was one of his companions from next door.

He did not make out the person who came in at once. He looked closer at the bespectacled face with a muffler wound around it, the long-sleeved sweater, the tucked-up mundu. The Director!

Sethu threw his cigarette down and stood up.

"What is your name?"

"Sethumadhavan."

The others woke up and scrambled up hastily to their feet.

"Lights off at nine o'clock. That is the rule."

"I did not know, Sir."

"You are a government servant. Ignorance of the rule is no excuse."

Sethu kept quiet.

"Which school did you study in?" Sethu told him.

"Hm. Smoking is not allowed in the campus. You know that?"

"But this is my room, Sir. In the room. . . ."

The small thick moustache beneath the flattened nose quivered. He moved towards the door, turned and asked, "What did you say your name was?"

"Sethumadhavan."

The others crowded around him when the Director left, including their neighbours from next door.

"I told you, didn't I, to turn off the light?"

Sethu was irritated. "Get lost. What is this, Napoleon's military camp? Even there, you'd have rules like this only in wartime."

The others went away. He switched off the light and lay down, but could not sleep. He felt very uneasy. The cold of the cement floor crept in worm-like through the thin quilt.

He woke up startled just as he was about to fall asleep. A jackal howled somewhere. The wind had died down. Only the coconut palms rustled softly.

Someone shook him awake. The sky was so dark, he could not believe it was daylight.

"It's seven fifteen. Get up."

"Seven fifteen?"

He sat up, rubbed his eyes, looked out through the window and asked,

"Couldn't you have called me earlier?"

"I did, a hundred times."

As they left, they said to him, "Get ready quickly. We'll be in the mess."

He brushed his teeth, washed his face and changed hurriedly. The mess was deserted when he got there. He did not wait for coffee. Where did they have to report for field work? The servants in the mess did not know. Confused, he looked around, not knowing where to go, then ran to the office. The peon told him the way.

He cursed himself as he walked quickly. Why did he always find himself alone?

He was relieved when he caught up with them a couple of furlongs away.

The Director was there, as well as the Instructor who had led the prayers the day before. The Director stopped speaking as Sethu came up.

Sethu walked with his head bent towards the students. He heard the Director's voice, "Look here."

Surely he was not talking to him?

"I say, look here."

Sethu stopped, and realized that all eyes were on him.

"You can go." The Director turned to the instructor and said, "Mark him absent."

Sethu wanted to say something. I'm sorry, sir. From tomorrow. The words eluded him.

He walked away, his head bent. His eyes hurt, but anger drowned the pain. Three minutes! He had been only three minutes late. He had glanced at the watch of the last person in the row.

His friends came back at eleven to find him still in bed.

"Did you have coffee?"

"Yes."

No one mentioned the morning's incident. Many of them wanted to go to the city.

The peon came half an hour later. "Sethumadhavan is wanted in the office."

Sethu got up. Gopi whispered, "Don't answer back. It will be better if you apologize."

Sethu was amused. "It's a court martial, isn't it? They'll sentence me to death."

A car drove into the portico as he reached the office. A fair-skinned, fat young man got out and went in swinging his keys.

The peon said, "Wait till he leaves." He added, although Sethu had not asked, "He's Kunhappootty Mudalali's son."

He waited, leaning against the pillar in the verandah. Ten minutes, fifteen. When the young man came out, the Director was with him. Sethu moved aside. He was sure the Director had seen him. The Director got into the car with the young man and said to the peon, taking no notice of Sethu,

"Kunhikanna, I'm going to the quarters."

His friends came to find out what had happened. The peon said consolingly, "He'll be back soon."

Noon. Sethu asked the peon, "Where are the quarters?"

"He'll be back now."

"Call me when he comes. I'll be in my room."

The peon came in half an hour.

The Director did not look up when Sethu entered. He went up to the table and said softly, "Sir!"

"You know you are a Government servant?"

"Yes, Sir."

He stubbed out his cigarette in the ashtray and leaned forward. Sethu caught a faint whiff of liquor.

"If people like you cannot obey the rules here, you would have done better to stay at home."

Sethu trembled. "How did I go against. . . ."

"You know you are a Government servant?"

God, how many times?

"Who gave people like you degrees?"

Sethu could not contain himself. "Your old man!"

Sethu felt his arms grow stronger. The tall, thin figure before him trembled. After a moment's silence, the Director shouted,

"Get out!"

"I'd decided to go without your telling me."

"I said, get out!"

Sethu felt the blood race to his head as he went out. His eyes were blinded.

There were many people in the verandah. Their faces looked indistinct, but he was aware that they accompanied him to his room. He put his hands on Unni Narayanan's shoulder and Gopi's. "Help me. I want to leave at once."

He did not hear what they said. Someone packed his things. They walked with him silently in a sorrowful procession. No one spoke even at the bus stop. He attempted to smile as he put out his head and waved at them from the window.

"Goodbye!"

He closed his eyes as their faces moved away from his line of vision.

"Goodbye!"

Part Seven

The river has grown dry. He stands for a minute on the sandy bank, which looks different every time he sees it. There are no more streams of running water. He thinks, I am here again after so many years, on the banks of a river of time which flows endlessly.

Where is the broken-down Bhagavathy temple in which the cowherd boys used to play games with stones? He can still imagine it clearly, the worn wooden engravings, the mouldy tiles, the yali lying with its nose buried in the sand.

Rows of the boat-shaped instruments used to draw water move over the vegetable patches that have encroached on half the river. The tiled roof that could be seen as soon as one climbed the bridge is no longer there, nor the path bordered by tamarind trees covered thickly with creepers. On the banks of the river that waits for the Edavam monsoon, the roots of trees waiting for death grope in the emptiness like skeletal fingers.

The question he wants to avoid asking himself keeps teasing him: is it only I who have changed?

I have come back finally to the shores of this drained river of time.

He searches the faces of the people who pass him on the narrow path hopefully, waiting with mingled fear and delight for a memory to surface and for a smile to light up their shrivelled faces. But they lower their voices when they see him, a stranger, and raise them again only when they escape from the pall of silence that envelops him. He rushes anxiously towards the next group of human voices.

As he walks, panting and sweating over what seems like an interminable stretch of sand, the man carrying his tin trunk comes abreast of him. "They've started to build the bridge, Mudalali. Next time you come, you can take the car across the river."

He pays no attention and the man calls out again, "Mudalali."

"How many years is it since you last came, Mudalali?"

The rains have washed over this stretch of sand thousands of times since I last came.

1

He got up when the musical chime of the calling bell sounded twice. The summons was for him. The bell chimed once for Menon; twice for him.

He pushed open the flush door of the air-conditioned room. The Mudalali was seated with his legs on the window sill and an elbow planted on the table behind him, reading a letter. He took his legs down, swung around, and put the letter in his pocket.

"Is the cash balance right?"

"Yes."

"What about the thousand I took the day before?"

"I've put it in the suspense account."

He listened attentively: bills, letters of credit, overdrafts, accountable, unaccountable. As he turned to leave, the Mudalali called him back.

"Writer!"

He thought, I no longer have a name. The peon Menon called him Writer. Everyone else knew him as Srinivasan Mudalali's Writer.

The Mudalali was lost in thought. Running his fingers through his grey hair, he seemed to be trying to remember something he had forgotten. A faint smile spread over the face pitted with smallpox scars. His red eyes glittered with a suggestion of madness when he smiled.

"And how is the house, Writer?"

"It's fine."

"Where do you eat?"

"In a hotel."

"I'll send a boy from the warehouse to work for you."

His smile was a blend of gratitude and respect, as if to say, You are very kind.

He went back to his seat and sorted out the letters which had to be answered. He had a terrible headache. His eyes would not focus on the paper. Another late night was taking its toll.

He had been with Rajettan the night before till midnight, in a room of the third-rate hotel in which he usually stayed. He had first met Rajettan, the car broker, when he had come to see the Mudalali. Everyone called him Rajettan. Rajettan began to invite Sethu to his room each time they met somewhere. Sethu liked talking to him. He knew a lot more than car dealers normally know. He was interested in subjects like Eisenhower and Kruschev and Sputniks.

Rajettan had sent for Raman, a short, stout man with a face scarred by knife wounds.

"What do you have for us?"

He said to Sethu, "He's known as Acid Raman. He was in jail for three months. He came out the day before yesterday."

"We have first rate stuff, Rajetta."

"I don't want any. Give me a half bottle of the lowdown one."

The man turned, moved aside his mundu and took out a big bottle from the pocket of his shorts. "Take a full bottle, Rajetta. Then you don't need to keep calling for me."

Rajettan stopped talking about world leaders by ten. "Do you know Pappammal?"

"No."

"What do you know then, you BA fellow?"

He would grow familiar after half a bottle. Later, he would apologize.

Pappammal belonged to Coimbatore. Her permanent address now was "Delhi Hotel." Which meant that Pappammal kept her clothes, her mirror and her powder in a bundle in a small space under the outer staircase of the Delhi Hotel. A letter sent to that address would reach her. She had sent money orders regularly over the last fifteen years to her son Marimuthu, who studied in Coimbatore. Rajettan wrote the address for her.

When Sethu had finally got down from a rickshaw at midnight at the gate of the new residence his Mudalali had given him, he had felt as if floods were heaving through his stomach. He had held on to the pillar in the verandah, swaying, the bitterness of vomit clinging to his mouth.

"Menon, can you get me a lime?"

A young man in khaki shorts and a checked shirt came up the steps and asked Menon in Malayalam whether the Mudalali was in. Sethu was surprised. The visitor was a white man. Menon ushered him in respectfully, came back and said,

"That's Wilson Mudalali."

"Is he a sahib?"

"His father was. They have a huge coffee plantation in Wynaad."

The lime juice was refreshing. The sahib came out and said light-heartedly to Menon, "Spare a thought for me, Menon."

The Mudalali emerged from the office. "Are there any cheques to be signed?"

"No."

The garage doors grated on the cement tracks with an unpleasant sound. The jeep started. Sethu always recognised the Mudalali's jeep by the sound it made when the gears were changed at the turn in the road.

Menon looked out of the window, "It's the Mudalali who's driving today."

Menon spent most of his free time standing at the windows. The road was visible from the northern window, and the courtyard of the Mudalali's house from the southern one. Menon knew everyone who came to see the Mudalali, their profession and the make of their cars.

"There's Rarichan Mudalali's Impala. It's a later model than Hajiar's but the Mudalali's Benz costs more."

The office was at the edge of the compound, above the garage. If Sethu lay back in his chair, he could see the tops of the gulmohur trees in the yard. Once the noon mail had come and he had replied all the letters, he was free. He would lie back in his chair and watch the parrots quarrel on the branches of the trees or listen to Menon gossip.

Menon had been the first to greet him when he came here. With the sandalwood mark on his forehead and the two protruding teeth that made him look as if he was always smiling, he had looked a harmless person. So Sethu had made friends with him quickly. Karunakaran Writer, who had been pensioned from the PWD, had been in charge of the office. As thin and dried up as a slate pencil, he never smiled. The dull shortsighted eyes behind the glasses seemed full of unbearable sorrow.

One day Sethu had asked, "Are you feeling ill?" but he had not answered.

It was Menon who had found Sethu a place in the lodge by the smelly canal on the outskirts of the city. Menon moved freely between the office and the Mudalali's house. He looked older than he really was. Rajettan had told Sethu how Menon had gradually acquired control over the Mudalali. Sethu found it difficult to believe.

Rajettan said, "The Mudalali gave him a thousand rupees for his eldest daughter's marriage, you know."

Sethu did not let on to Menon what he knew about this gift. Rajettan had counselled him that it would be useful to be friendly with Menon.

The accountant, Nambiar, usually came at one o'clock. He worked part-time in many places. His Income Tax accounts were flawless. He had taken over from Karunakaran Writer. The Writer had been too clever. When he had sent a cheque for two thousand three hundred rupees to the Sea Breeze Hotel to cover a week's bills, he had scolded the hotel employee who brought the bills. The hotel owner had reported this to the Mudalali. When the Mudalali questioned him, the Writer had advised him like an old friend. Next day, the Writer did not come for work. Menon had related all this to Sethu.

"Did the Mudalali find fault with him then?"

"Oh no. All he said was, 'I'm not drinking the money your old man earned.' That's all."

Menon went out for lunch. Sethu got up, moved the curtain at the window and looked out. He had heard that the Mudalali's bungalow had been built during the period of the timber auction in Coorg. The rounded pillars in front were of gleaming rosewood that had stood the test of time. There were Venetian blinds at both the windows. A spotted tiger skin lay over the easy chair in the front verandah. A sleek Siamese cat dozed under the gulmohur tree.

He saw the old servant woman's shabby mundu and scaly feet behind the half-drawn Venetian blinds. And then pink feet in red slippers sinking into the red carpet in the hall. A yellow satin underskirt swirled under the gold border of an off-white saree.

His heart began to beat very fast when she came out to the southern end of the verandah, near the potted plants. Her movements were like those of a dancer performing before an invisible audience.

Mrs Lalitha Srinivasan!

Unknown to her, he watched her whenever Menon went out, with fear in his heart and a secret delight.

He could see her clearly now that she was no longer hidden by the Venetian blinds. The black blouse with the gold flowers embroidered on it tightened every time she neatened the unruly strands of her unoiled hair.

She looked prettier now than in the picture he had seen of her yesterday in a magazine, standing with a group of Rotarian wives wielding brooms during the clean-the-city week.

A bright red Standard drove into the portico. Because of the pillars he could see only the khaki-clad legs. He moved to the next window. It was Wilson Mudalali. He pulled out a handkerchief from his pocket and wiped his reddened neck. Sethu could not hear what he said. All he could see were the red chappals at the edge of the carpet.

Sethu went back to his chair as soon as Wilson Mudalali came out. There were no parrots today on the gulmohur.

He heard Menon clear his throat outside and the stench of beedis came up from the stairwell. Menon never smoked in front of Sethu.

Menon asked, as soon as he came in, "Aren't you going for lunch, Writer?"

He was famished, but a bitter taste still lingered in his mouth.

"Can you send someone for a cup of coffee and a banana?"

Menon went to the window. "Has the Mudalali returned?"

"No."

"I saw the car from Breeze parked here. Who was it?"

"Wilson Mudalali!"

"Hm. Wilson Mudalali loves to have a good time. Do you know how much money he spends when he comes up from the estate for a couple of days?"

Sethu hastily reminded him about the coffee, unwilling to listen to Wilson Mudalali's history. "If I could have my coffee. I'd like to leave as soon as Nambiar comes. I don't feel very well."

The telephone rang in the office. Sethu answered it. It was the Income Tax Officer. He had tried to reach the Mudalali at the club, the mill, at Sea Breeze. Where was he? "Is that Writer?"

He paused for a moment and said, "Yes."

"I need a car for an hour."

The Fiat was in the workshop. The Benz was used only for long trips. But he remembered the Mudalali's instructions. The caller's name was high on the list of people to be kept in good humour. So he said respectfully, "I'll send one."

The driver Appu was not in the garage. He usually dozed there when he was free or sat on the kitchen verandah talking to the maidservants.

Bougainvillea grew in profusion over the gate of the bungalow. The red Standard was still parked in the portico. He hesitated on the verandah and ran his fingers over the tiger skin on the easy chair. The drawing room was empty. He came out again and rang the bell.

He listened carefully, but there was no sound or movement. He wondered whether to go back and send Menon.

He heard Wilson Mudalali's voice, "I'll telephone."

"When?" A woman's voice.

Wilson Mudalali and Mrs Srinivasan emerged in front of him, parting the pagoda patterned curtains. He moved aside without looking at them.

The red car drove away. She waited near the curtains.

"The Income Tax Officer wants a car."

"So?" Her voice sounded harsh.

"I can't find the driver."

"Do you want me to drive it then?"

He felt only contempt for her, no irritation. Trying not to show his feelings, he turned back into the courtyard.

She called out, "Writer!"

He wanted to say, "I have a name," but her voice was gentle. She came out. She had changed into a black saree embroidered with gold and a gold blouse.

"The driver is not available. Please arrange for a private taxi."

Her full rounded face, lightly covered with pimples, was no longer angry and begged his forgiveness mutely.

"If the driver does not come in the evening, the car will have to be sent to the convent for the children as well."

The accountant Nambiar was in the office when he got back.

Just as he was about to leave in the evening, Menon said, "She's sent for you."

"Who?"

"The lady."

"She wants to see me?" He thought Menon was joking.

"She wants you to go there when you are free."

She came out as soon as he reached the verandah. "Come in." She invited him to sit down in the drawing room. He sat on the sofa opposite the huge mirror framed in elephant tusks.

She sat on the divan, pulled up her sari which was slipping down and swung her legs. He quickly withdrew his eyes, feeling it was wrong to stare.

"Aren't you a graduate, Writer?"

"Yes."

"I have to make a speech at the Baby Show next week. I can give you the points; will you write the speech for me? I can't manage Malayalam."

"Yes, I can do it."

"Not too many difficult words. My Malayalam is very poor. Or I'll write it in English and you can translate."

"All right."

He got up.

"Are you in a hurry? Have a cup of coffee?"

"No."

The children came in noisily. Red ties, dark blue dresses.

"Mummy, Sushma says."

"Go in now." Both the little fair-skinned girls ran in clutching their aluminum school boxes. The older one even had a mole on her right cheek like her mother. The dark little boy with the skinny face and dull eyes clung to his mother.

She got up. "Once they are back, there is utter confusion. We'll discuss it tomorrow."

She pushed back the hair on her forehead, smiled and asked, "What did you say your name was?"

"I didn't say. Sethu."

He smiled to himself and went out.

2

In the evenings, the streets were more crowded. The sound of people and vehicles drowned the stench from the gutters.

He went through the narrow lanes of the Anglo-Indian quarter and came to the street where pot-bellied Multani money-lenders sat cross-legged behind low tables. He had been walking for hours and longed to sit down.

Entering the street where provision lorries and trolleys lay in disorderly rows, he looked at the tiled shops on either side of the dusty road, thinking of the transactions running into lakhs of rupees that took place in them. Piles of rubbish lay on the edges of the road and the air resounded constantly with the obscenities of the cart drivers. He skirted a lorry unloading heavy bales of palm leaves, jumped over the yoke of a stationary bullock cart and came face-to-face with a young man coming out of one of the shops. He had a towel over his shoulder and a zipped bag under his arm.

Sethu could not believe his eyes. Swamy. Wasn't it Swamy?

Sethu hurried on, but could not help looking back. The other person was staring at him as well.

Swamy came up to him. "Weren't you at Palghat?"

Sethu had a deep sense of hurt. They had shared the same room for a whole year.

"Don't you remember me, Swamy?"

"Hullo, room-mate!"

They shook hands and made sounds of mutual delight. Sethu tried to remember forgotten formulae.

Swamy said, "I didn't make you out."

I don't blame you. Most people would not make me out, room-mate. I don't recognize myself!

"You've put on weight, Swamy."

Swamy smiled. He used to be as thin as a broomstick. He used to wear half-sleeved mull shirts and the tip of his tongue used to show between his lips even when he was not talking. He looked well-settled now, and prosperous.

They moved towards a lamp-post.

"What are you doing, Sethu?"

"I work in a firm."

He asked Swamy about himself in order to avoid being questioned. Swamy had stopped his studies after he finished his Intermediate and joined his father's business. His father had died two years ago and now he ran the business himself.

"Are you married, Sethu?"

He laughed foolishly. He had become an expert at this. "No, no."

Swamy said, with an apologetic air, "I have a one-year-old child. I did not know your address to send you a wedding invitation."

He did not tell Swamy, I have no proper address. A coffee estate in Wynaad, Hajiyar's petrol bunk, a gambling den at a carnival—he drifted like foam on a wave.

"Which way?"

"Nowhere in particular."

"I've parked the car beyond the market. Come, I'll drop you."

"No, I'll walk with you till there."

Swamy asked, "Care for coffee?"

"No." He wondered whether Swamy still kept accounts on what he spent for charity.

The black Fiat was parked just outside the arched gate of the market. Swamy started the engine and asked, "Can I drop you somewhere? I have to see Viswanatha Iyer, the wholesale tea dealer. He's my wife's uncle."

"It's all right. I have to go somewhere nearby."

"See you then. I'll write."

The Fiat made its way confidently through the undisciplined crowds on the road. Swamy must have felt as relieved as Sethu when they parted. They would not meet again, or write. They had put an end to an old bond forged six years ago with a polite exchange of words. When they met next time, they could pretend not to recognize each other.

He no longer wrote to anyone, nor did he receive any letters. Three months after he joined Srinivasan Mudalali's office, he had a letter from Parameswarettan. It had been soon after he ran into the mapilla, Aseesukutty, who worked in a teashop next to the provision store in his village. Maybe he had carelessly mentioned Srinivasan Mudalali's name to Aseesukutty, that must have been how Parameswara Ettan found out his address.

When Menon brought the post in and left it on the table, he always felt anxious. He would pray that there would be nothing for him. He had not opened the last latter which had come with Thangamani's handwriting on it. But he wrote a reply. "I am going away and do not know when I will be back. I was a good person once, the person you loved. All the doors of escape are open before you and you are free to decide." The words sounded meaningless when he re-read them, so he tore the letter up.

He stopped near the Gandhi statue in front of the Town Hall. Where now? He turned west, towards the sea, wanting to sit down somewhere by himself.

Young men sat on the stone benches next to the footpath, under the casuarina trees. He kept to the side of the road. Beyond the lamp-post, in front of the locked building belonging to a British firm, the crowd was thinner. Water had collected in pools after high tide. He watched the children dragging shreds of netting through the muddy water in order to trap fish.

Scooters and cars went slowly along the road. A speedboat raced over the water. The vague outlines of cargo ships were visible on the open sea beyond. A bearded madman, with a piece of sacking over him, leaned against the walls of the building opposite and called out to invisible powers.

Sethu realized that he had to eat somewhere and get home fast. Food had become a problem after he had moved to the house the Mudalali had found for him so far from the town.

When Nambiar had found him the house, the post office clerk who had shared his room in the lodge near the stinking canal had been surprised.

"Do you have to pay the rent yourself?"

"I don't know."

"I'm sure the rent is sixty, maybe even seventy rupees."

So the Mudalali had found him a house that fetched a rent of sixty rupees. And he had thought that kindness was only a myth! He could not believe that someone who lived in a house with high walls covered with glass peices, with Gurkhas and Alsatian dogs at the gate, knew the meaning of kindness. He had never read of kind-hearted Mudalalis.

"If I rent it out," the Mudalali had explained. "I'll never get it back when I want. I'm going to demolish and rebuild it when I'm less busy."

"Forgive me for having misjudged you, Mudalali," he said to himself.

Each time he wrote out cheques for the Mudalali's monthly bills, had them signed and sent them through Menon to be paid he had been shocked at how insignificant a commodity money could be. Hotel bills, club bills—the figures ran into thousands. The cigarettes alone came to two hundred rupees a month. Even though he knew that the Mudalali's bank balance multiplied by tens of thousands every time a truck took a log of rosewood to the Cochin harbour, he still felt astonished.

If only his forefathers had thought to plant a few trees on the empty hillsides, he had said once to Menon, instead of breeding bulls and fighting legal cases!

The little boys who had been fishing ran away. When the dirt settled, the blackish water shone like a mirror, and he could see the reflection of his face.

Every morning, he would look at his own face in the little folding mirror and think, the last two years have changed my features. The black dark of the nights when hunger had wiped out sleep had gathered into shadows under his eyes. His teeth were stained a dirty yellow. The frames of his glasses had become loose.

He felt that he could no longer smile, that his face looked more distorted when he tried to do so.

On sleepless nights, he thought of the dark room where he had experienced the odour of death. It was the day he had left the training camp. He had rented a room for a rupee and a half on top of an old dilapidated building and sat in it, thinking about death, while it drizzled outside.

Smoke blowing in from the kitchen downstairs clung to the room. The unpleasant smell of wet smoke, worm-eaten wood and crumbling walls had reminded him of a dead body. He took up a pen and paper. Whom should he write to first? Whom could he console? His fingers trembled as he held the pen.

The lights went out suddenly and the city was plunged in darkness. He leaned his head on the table and waited for the lights to come back. One of the servants who passed by had said they would not be back because a tree had fallen on a transformer and damaged it.

He put away his pen and went out. Brisk trade was being done in the shops in the bazaar by the light of candles and petromax lamps. He clung to the darkness like a shadow and walked on, beyond the seashore and the railroad bridge, towards the military camp. He sank down on the wet grass. A newspaper headline danced before his eyes. Dead body found in hotel room!

Red flames shone in open fireplaces near the culvert and the stench of burning rubber wafted on the wind. He heard low voices. Someone seemed to be coming towards him.

"Sh, sh."

He walked faster. Full of fear, his heart beating fast, he fled, thinking, I love life! I want to escape!

He heard footsteps behind him.

"You're going away?" It was a woman's voice. He hurried to the edge of the maidan to find out how to reach the road. She came up to him, her protruding teeth gleaming in the dark.

"Give us a beedi."

He gave her a cigarette. When he lit a match, he saw her round, pockmarked face and projecting teeth clearly. The red glow of the cigarette between her teeth reminded him of a fire spitting demon.

"Give me money for a tea, Mudalali."

He wanted to laugh. Mudalali, indeed!

He found a five rupee note in his pocket. She examined it unbelievingly while he walked on, laughing aloud.

"Don't you want me, Mudalali?"

He did not look back. He spent the rest of the night in the room that smelled of death, lying prone on the dirty mat and laughing to himself.

He had ten rupees left. In the morning, after he settled his accounts, he would have seven and a half rupees with which to start a new life!

"Writer."

Moopan, who had two boats of his own and held a contract to load and unload timber for the Mudalali, got down from his cycle.

"What are you doing by yourself, Writer?"

"Nothing. Where are you going, Moopan?"

Moopan invited him for a cup of tea and described the difficulties of building a house. He was going to invite everyone for the house-warming; the writer must come.

"Whatever people say about the Mudalali, he's a person who cares. He's helped me a lot." Moopan remarked that everyone who had joined the Mudalali had prospered.

"You're lucky, Writer. The Mudalali trusts you."

Moopan asked, as he left, "Is there anything I can do for you?"

"No, Moopan."

Fat Gujarati women dragged their chappals noisily over the cement path. The sea gleamed under the black sky like an open container filled with kohl. The lights on the cargo boats grew brighter.

Life began to flow through the black arteries of the city at night. Thousands of little sounds merged into an indistinct symphony. Prostitutes who had been asleep all day crowded around the municipal tap to get ready for their work. Brokers hung bits of sacking outside the shuttered shops to establish their place of business and waited, smoking.

Sethu walked slowly through the bustling crowds, feeling contented. He could wander among these people, crowded as densely as worms in an abscess and be sure no one would recognize him!

He had begun to love this city, with its overflowing gutters, its pockets of darkness, its foaming streams of people.

When he reached home, someone was waiting on the steps.

"Who is that?"

"Mm." It was probably the servant boy the Mudalali had said he would send. No, it was Menon, the peon from the office. Menon came up to him respectfully, "You're late, Writer."

"What is it, Menon?"

"Nothing."

Sethu noticed that the front door was open.

"Has the servant boy come?"

"What?" Menon was quick to prevent him entering. He said softly, "Sh. The Mudalali is inside." Sethu was surprised. Why was the Mudalali here?

"There's someone with him."

The Mudalali called out, "Who is that, Menon?"

"It's the writer."

There were no chairs on the verandah. All Sethu wanted was to sit down somewhere. The Mudalali invited him, "Come in, Writer."

Menon gave him a meaningful smile. The Mudalali was at the door of the bedroom, wearing only a mundu and smoking a cigarette.

"Come right in, Writer."

The room was filled with cigarette smoke and the smell of liquor. A young girl leaned against the wall. She wore a knee length white skirt and a green blouse.

The Mudalali sat down on the cot. "Sit down, Writer."

Sethu took the glass of brandy he held out.

"My friend. She's a nice girl, isn't she, Writer? What's your name, child? I've forgotten it again."

The girl shrank into the shadow of the saree hanging on the clothesline.

"Sarojini."

"Writer, this girl will stay here for two days. The servant boy will be here tomorrow morning. He will bring her food. Look here girl, this is our Writer. Now come and sit here. What a shy thing you are!"

The Mudalali screwed up his reddened eyes and said, "No one will suspect anything here. Tell the servant she's your relative."

Sethu kept quiet.

"Why are you playing with your glass? Come on, the Mudalali and the writer will drink together. What do you say, girl?"

The girl stood silently in the shadow, her head bent.

"Writer, tell Menon to let me know when the car comes."

Sweat broke out on Sethu's forehead as he left the empty glass on the table and went out. Where was Menon? Would he have to go to the gate and look for him? Ah, there he was, with a fresh cigarette at his lips. His breath smelt of alcohol. Menon seemed to be celebrating.

"You met her, then?" Sethu did not answer.

Menon offered him a cigarette. The unpleasant taste in his mouth lessened as he blew on it.

"You're lucky, Writer. It was I who thought of this place when she refused to go to a hotel."

He sat down on the floor and listened to Menon laugh and chatter, trying to fight down his anger. So that was what the Mudalali had wanted, when this little house surrounded by high walls fell vacant, a tenant who would not arouse anyone's suspicions. No one would wonder why the Mudalali's car was at the writer's gate. And Menon would hang around like a faithful watchdog.

Sethu suddenly wondered what Mrs Lalitha Srinivasan would be doing now. He remembered her seated on the sofa in her living room, her flushed and glowing face, her light-coloured eyes, her dishevelled hair. The radiance of her smile was still alive in him.

He felt light-headed. Here I am, waiting on the verandah of my own house for my bed to be empty. He felt no distress, only self-reproach and mockery.

"Writer!"

"Shut up!"

Menon was startled. "Writer!"

"Don't speak. If you do." He checked himself. When he saw fear spread over Menon's face, he smiled to himself.

Waves of heat began to course through his bloodstream.

3

The cry he heard in the distance turned into the roar of a train. He looked out of the window. Dismembered bodies, still alive, writhed in chains on the path next to the railroad track. He saw eyes blazing in the emaciated face of a little boy who was trying to break free of the chain piercing his leg. The roar grew and diminished.

Someone seemed to be shaking him awake. He sat up. The bright yellow light of the dusty bulb on the verandah went through his eyes like needles.

Still haunted by the distorted shapes he had seen, he asked, "Mm?"

"Go in and lie down, Writer, I'll come in the morning." Menon was leaving.

Sethu saw an old man curled up on a mat in the verandah. Where had he seen him before? Yes, he had been at the gate when Sethu came back.

"Close the door and go to sleep, Writer. The Mudalali has left." The smoky haze of sleep cleared for a second. So he was not alone in the house. He went in and switched off the verandah light. The corridor was dark. A yellow patch of light lay in the bedroom.

He found the room as disorderly as a third class waiting room just cleared of passengers. Greasy yellow bits of paper, morsels of bone, and empty soda bottles lay everywhere. The girl lying on his bed, fast asleep with her face turned to the wall, looked like a child.

He brushed grains of yellow rice off a chair and sat down. A bottle encased in fine silver wire, a quarter full, lay on the ground with an unopened packet of biriyani near it. He gazed at the yellowish-red liquid in the bottle and at the picture of the crown and grapes. Then he poured out a glassful of water from the earthenware pot on the floor and drank a mouthful.

What was her name? She had told the Mudalali when he asked.

"Sarojini." She did not answer.

"Sarojini."

"Um."

"Get up."

She moved closer to the wall. He raised his voice. "Sarojini!"

She sat up and rubbed her eyes. She wore an underskirt that had turned a faded yellow with repeated washing, and a blouse with red dots. She looked tired and a little frightened.

He thought of the image of a prostitute that he had cherished, culled from books and hearsay—moist, intoxicating eyes, a passionate presence that made one uneasy, naked surfaces.

She seemed vaguely familiar as she sat on the edge of the cot, looking at the floor. She brought to mind the country girls he knew who would walk through the village lanes carrying baskets of straw and bottles of oil.

"Have you eaten?"

"Um."

"Are you sleepy?"

She covered her mouth to hide a yawn, rubbed her eyes with the back of her hand and shook her head as if to say no.

"Where do you live?" She gave him the name of a village about seven miles away from the town.

He opened the packet of biriyani, but did not feel hungry enough to eat.

"Have you been to school?"

"Um."

"Till which class?"

"I failed in the seventh and didn't go any more."

"You have a family?"

She did not answer. He repeated the question. She said, "Yes."

She could not have been more than fifteen or sixteen. It could not have been very long since a man had first used her. He wondered who had brought her to this town.

He had been insatiably curious about prostitutes. As a child, he had often overheard people talk in low voices about a woman who lived on the northern bank of the river who knew how to lure men. In his last year at the elementary school, he had asked Vaidyan Govindan's son, Ramankutty, to point her out to him. He had to part with two of his pebbles and a snuffbox with a broken lid before Ramankutty would consent. They walked through the lanes, full of fear, and Ramankutty said, "Look!"

He saw her clearly, sitting with her legs stretched out in the verandah of her small house, combing her hair. Her red nose ring glittered. It was one of the great events of his life, seeing this woman who stood at the gate every evening like the yakshi under the coconut palm, waiting to ensnare men.

But it distressed him to look at this child, playing with the black rubber bangles on her wrists, thin as papaya stalks. He got up and laid his hand on her sweat-stained shoulder. She attempted a smile, hardly that of a prostitute.

"Get up." Somehow, he felt disgusted.

He threw his quilt down and said, "Go and lie down somewhere."

The unspoken question in her eyes irritated him. "I'm not being kind. Go and lie down."

He thought to himself, I've seen your face everywhere, in the taxis parked behind big hotels, in isolated travellers' bungalows, in dark lanes, in the marshes near the railway track. Nothing about you astonishes me!

He straightened the wrinkled sheet, turned over the pillow, which smelt of oil and cheap scent, lay down and covered his eyes with his hands.

"Turn off the light."

He saw her spread the quilt in the corridor. Seconds later, he heard footsteps and the clink of empty soda bottles. She was in the room. Was she trying to steal something from the pocket of the shirt he had hung on the wall? He turned quietly to look. There was nothing valuable in the room.

She went away and he heard the front door being opened. The old bolts creaked in spite of the care she took to be quiet. Maybe she was going away. Convinced that she had stolen something and was trying to run away with the old man who lay outside keeping watch, he got up. Her cheap silk saree still hung on the line. He followed her softly and heard her voice at the door.

"Achan, how can you sleep like this!"

The old man grunted and sucked his lips.

"Get up, Achan, come on." She shook him awake.

"What is it?" He was still half-asleep.

"Here, eat this."

He saw the old man open the leaf packet she gave him and eat greedily by the faint light of the municipal lamp beyond the wall. He hiccuped, stopped eating for a minute and asked,

"Did you eat something?"

"Um."

"When did the Mudalali say we can go?"

"He didn't say."

"Can you get me some water to drink?"

"Where can I get water?" Her voice was suddenly rough. "Don't create a racket. He's asleep."

Sethu went back to bed. He heard her close the door carefully and come back to the corridor.

He wanted to cry. He no longer thought of her lying so close by, just beyond the door, ready to give herself to him. Instead, he pictured her family, lying asleep on a torn mat in a little hut in her village. The younger ones would ask their mother,

"Where's Edathi, Amme?"

"She's gone with Achan."

"Why didn't Achan take us?"

"Shut up and go to sleep."

The mother would console herself thinking that now she could at least face her creditors.

The girl would go back after a few days and her mother would wash the nine rupee silk saree and put it away carefully. When she took the rolled gold chain off her daughter's neck and tucked it into the niche above the picture of Krishna, would she ask, "Where did you go?"

When the old man took a newspaper packet from his waist, coughing and grunting as he squatted on the floor, and handed the notes to his wife, would she ask, where did you take her? Who was it?

They would sleep contentedly that night, all huddled up together on the three mats, the father, the mother and the seven children.

Sethu heard a train hoot. He was not sure when he fell asleep. He woke up to the sound of water being drawn from the well. The quilt had been neatly folded and the mat was rolled up against the corridor wall. There was no one outside. He walked through the courtyard and came upon the man. He was not as old as Sethu had thought, he could not be more than fifty. The man waited uncertainly, scratching the grey stubble on his chin.

"Get a vessel from inside and buy tea for all of us."

He smoked a beedi while he waited for the tea, which the man brought him in a freshly washed glass.

Sethu went in to get a towel. She was in his room, in her saree, combing her hair in front of the mirror hung on the window. Ants crawled over the greasy bits of paper on the floor.

"Clean all this up."

She called out as he left, "Don't you have talcum powder?"

She looked uneasily at his angry face. He walked to the well without answering her.

He wanted to get away quickly. He washed his face, dressed hurriedly and combed his hair. She had had a bath and her hair, spread out to dry, trailed over the sheet on the bed. The glittering red silk saree did not suit her. He thought she would look pretty in a mundu, with a sandal paste mark on her forehead, and a mandaram flower wound into the tips of her hair.

Menon came in as Sethu left.

"Why are you off so early?"

"I have to meet someone."

Menon had something more to say, but he did not wait to hear it.

4

The beginning of another unpleasant day.

There was a time when he used to feel relieved when it was evening. Once he reached his den, he felt he could escape at least for a few hours. But now he had become a stranger in his own house.

Eleven o'clock. He stood at the window looking at the gulmohur trees. The Mudalali came in with one of his friends. Sethu took him some cheques which he signed without looking up. Sethu thought of how ready the man had been to share his most secret experiences with him the night before.

The Mudalali spoke only of office matters. Sethu's fear that he would talk about the house had been unfounded.

After Menon left, Sethu went back to the window. There was no one on the verandah. Disappointed that he could not see her, he was about to go back to his seat when the Benz rolled into the portico. Her butter-coloured saree with the broad red border matched the tone of her skin perfectly. She caught the pallu as it slipped and drew it over her shoulder. He went back to his seat as she entered the house.

There were two cars parked at his gate when he got back that evening. The number plates looked familiar, but he could not quite remember whose they were.

Why was he so afraid to come back to his own house? The old man sat outside, stroking the stubble on his face, looking bored.

"Who is in the house?"

The answer was indistinct.

A chauffeur came in carrying a canvas bag, in which bottles clinked.

"Do you have a beedi?"

Sethu spat into the yard and walked out without answering. Someone clapped and waved out to him at the petrol pump. "Writer!"

Rajettan stood next to an old Ford, waving his arms vigorously and arguing with a group of people. As Sethu approached, Rajettan said, "Look here, I have to go with the writer now. Don't waste my time, Pillai. Come on, close the deal, quickly."

Rajettan said to him, "You go on, I'll be with you soon." Rajettan caught up with him in a few minutes.

"Thank God, that's over. I've been at it three days and my throat is parched. I made a profit of a hundred and fifty rupees. May God help the buyer!"

They went to Rajettan's room, asking Acid Raman to keep watch outside.

"Whose car is KLC 8181, Rajetta?"

"Why?"

"Nothing, I just asked, that's all."

"It's the one Choyikutty sold to the DYSP. There's some patchwork on the body but the engine is in good condition." Rajettan knew the inside and outside of every car in the city.

Sethu could not keep his mind on what Rajettan was saying.

"What's the matter with you?"

"Nothing."

He emptied the second glass and went to the window.

"What do you want?"

He did not answer.

"What is it, Writer?"

"Don't call me Writer. That's the first thing I want. Then."

"Then?" Rajettan handed him the third glass. "What else?"

"I want a car. I want to drive up to Srinivasan Mudalali's house in my own car."

Sethu checked himself when Rajettan began to laugh. He went back to his chair and tried to put his scattered thoughts in order.

I stand on the terrace and play the fiddle like Nero as all the buildings around me burn.

He burst out laughing. What I want is. . . .

Rajettan's speech grew slurred. He put his head on the table and went to sleep. Sethu went out into the deserted street. The lights burned dimly and it had begun to drizzle. He walked home dragging his unsteady feet. The cars were no longer there. He leaned his hands on the moss-covered wall and threw up. As he spat out the bile and recovered his breath, someone called,

"Sethu Etta."

He turned, and made out who it was as he came nearer. Unni!

"Sethu Etta."

Sethu leaned his head on the wall and retched again. Unni laid his hand on his shoulder.

"Unni!" Unni stroked his back and he wept. He staggered towards the house holding on to Unni and asked, "Why did you come, Unni, why?"

"Thankoppu asked me to come."

Sethu sank down on the verandah. Unni had grown so much. How quickly children grew!

"I arrived at five thirty. They gave me your address at the office. I found my way here somehow."

There was no one on the verandah. He pushed the door open and stumbled in, nearly tripping over the old man, who muttered something in his sleep.

"Unni!" He went out again and saw Unni still standing outside, hesitating.

"Couldn't you have written that you were coming? I would have been expecting you then."

"Thankoppu wrote."

Her letter must have been among the ones he had thrown unread into the wastepaper basket.

Unni opened his bag and handed him a letter. He took it without looking at Unni.

"Don't you have class today?"

"It's Saturday."

What could he talk about? The little boy in shorts with cashew fruit stains on them was a young man now. He shrank before Unni's probing eyes.

"Come, let's go. You can't stay here." Holding on to Unni for support, he walked to the lodge on the main road, next to the Muslim hotel. The fat man at the counter with the checked towel wound around his head kept staring at Unni. Sethu wanted to kill him, though he could hardly hold himself upright.

He glared vengefully at the man while taking the key, as if to say, "Come on, if you want to die, come on!"

He fell asleep at once, feeling that he was slipping into a pit of darkness. He tried to hold on to the roots of consciousness, but kept sliding back into a bottomless abyss.

He woke up with the sun in his eyes. It took him a minute to remember where he was. The dark night detached itself from a dream.

Where was Unni? He asked the boy with the light grey eyes who was sweeping the verandah, "Did you see the person who was in the room with me?"

"The fair boy? He took his bag and went away early morning," answered the servant with a leer on his face. Sethu longed to slap him and felt ashamed of his cowardice. He could not hold himself up even in front of this silly boy.

He had a splitting headache. The house was empty and the corridor full of muddy footprints. Thangamani's letter lay on the floor. He bent down and picked it up with trembling hands. Fragments of glass were scattered over the floor and the air was laden with the smell of liquor. He lay down on his mattress, stained with the grime of countless dark nights and wept.

5

The letter was wet and smudged and tear stains had changed the shape of the words. She had asked, what did I do that was wrong?

It was my fault, Thangamani.

Once, his mind had been filled with thoughts of her. A sliver of moonlight gleaming through the shadows of the coconut palms, a faint fragrance of flowers wafting in on the breeze, a childish face glimpsed in a crowd—they all brought back memories of her. He had not cared that no one approved; it had only made him more obstinate. He had wanted to climb to the top of the world and shout, "You are mine, no one can keep me away from you."

He used to feel that he would explode with anger when he heard people discuss her marriage. When had that anger turned into a secret prayer? A prayer that she would soon be married, that he would stand somewhere where she could not see him and watch her go around the lamps in the pandal. He had hoped that he could go to her new home as a visitor, suppressing his own pain within himself.

He found it difficult to believe now that he had imagined all this. He spent days composing unwritten replies to her. Finally he decided to leave the city, go back and beg her forgiveness.

He would write, I am coming back to you at last. You will realize how wrong you were, to believe that human beings can live by their dreams. Do not curse me when you discover this.

Sunday. He detested Sundays, when the city was as still and sluggish as a snake shedding its skin.

It made him happy to think he could go to the office next day, settle accounts and leave. Who did he have to say goodbye to? To Rajettan. And the Mudalali. Should he go to the bungalow and see the Mudalali's wife? He had not written the speech in Malayalam after all. She had not asked for it. He decided he would go and see her once more.

He shaved, had a bath and changed. The sun had gone down. To console himself, he thought of the letter to Thangamani. He would write tonight, and make up for the long silence.

The shops were closed but the main roads were still crowded. Hawkers had established themselves outside the closed shutters of the shops, to sell calendars, peacock oil and siddha drugs. Groups of people were clustered around quack astrologers with parrots, and palmists.

The beach was deserted, maybe because it was wet after the rain and the sea had an angry look. He walked over the wet sand towards the sea. The waves dragged the sand from under his feet and he thought of how Thangamani had laughed that day, long ago.

It seemed to be raining at sea. Everything looked indistinct. The western sky was a blur of many colours, like a homam ground after the rituals, when the sacred drawings had been rubbed out.

He realized how long he had been walking only when the lamps were lit. Small oil lamps blossomed like little red buds in the thatched huts. He found his way back to a footpath, and came upon the Mudalali's Benz near the children's park. The children stood near the ice cream cart. The older girl looked grown up in a salwar-kameez. A ring flashed at the door of the car and its lightning gleam sent an answering glow through him. He turned, walked casually along the seashore and pretended to have come upon the car by accident. He stopped, looking surprised and respectful.

"Hullo!"

He smiled. The children had finished their ice cream and were counting the seconds it took for the decorative lamps to come on one by one.

"The Mudalali is not with you?"

"He's in Coorg." She opened the door fully and said, "Even if he had been here, do you think he would have bothered to take his family out to the beach? You should know his habits by now, Writer." She laughed, as if she did not want him to feel that she was finding fault with her husband.

"No activities today?" he asked.

She laughed again. "I'm fed up with social service. I'm trying to find a way to escape from it now."

"It's the first time I've seen you at the beach. Do you come often?"

"I hate it. Such a crowd, and the noise! The children insisted. I've been in bed all morning with a headache."

The children ran up noisily. She scolded them and sent them away. He realized how beautiful the English language sounded when she spoke in it.

"I like to park somewhere here and watch the sea when it rains. There's not so much noise then and less of a crowd."

She opened the door, got out, and stood looking silently at the overcast sky. The wind ruffled her hair.

"I like empty spaces. When we were in Jaipur, I used to take the car out without telling my father and visit the lakes and fortresses for which the city is known. I love to be by a lake or on a hillside by myself. Alone in the wilderness. My father would have been angry if he knew. Nobody understands that solitude gives you peace of mind." She looked unhappy and spoke rapidly to hide the trembling of her voice. She seemed to have lost all her confidence.

"Life is miserable here. Nothing to see, nowhere to go. And there's no one you can trust." She checked herself and went on, "Don't take it seriously. Do you want to hear something funny? A young girl came to me saying she was starving and I employed her in the house. She would not be more than fifteen, sixteen. I dismissed her this morning. See, you can't trust anybody." She emphasized the last word.

He kept quiet.

"Do you have a lot of friends?"

"No, I don't have any friends."

She sat on the cement parapet and talked about the north Indian towns where she had spent her childhood, about holiday resorts and people.

"Why don't you sit down?"

He sat down, a little away from her.

"Do you live alone?"

The question was unexpected. "Yes."

"How do you spend your time, then, say on Sundays like this?"

He smiled. "I read, or go for walks."

She told him she loved books, that she used to read a lot when she was in the convent at Cannanore and then at Queen Mary's in Madras. She had no time for anything now.

"Some people have an aversion to reading. Look at my husband. He does not even read a newspaper. I persuaded him to take me to a film during our honeymoon."

"People who are in big business don't have time for anything."

Her face suddenly hardened like stone. Then she calmed down and said,

"Yes, yes."

He paid no attention to what she was saying. Seated there against the background of the dark sky, her words seemed to break free of meaning and turn into music. The roar of traffic in front of them and the boom of the waves flowed into the distance.

"I wanted to go abroad, and I asked my father to try for a job in the foreign service, but he did not like the idea."

She asked him, "Why did you accept this job?"

He wondered uneasily whether he should tell her. He had been drifting around the city until he found a job as a part-time cashier in the hotel where he had met the Mudalali. The Mudalali had arranged for him to go as a witness in a fraudulent case. The proprietor of the hotel had vouched for the writer and the telephone operator as witnesses.

"Your name?"

"Sethumadhavan."

"Are you educated?"

"I am a BA."

"Your occupation?"

"Hotel clerk."

"Where were you on the sixteenth at dusk?"

"In the room next to the counter."

The case was dismissed. However, the Mudalali was impressed with the witness. He had described what he saw through the window exactly as the lawyer had instructed. He had seen the accused trying to prevent the Mudalali getting into the car. He had heard him use obscene words. Fearing that the accused might attack Srinivasan Mudalali, he and the PBX operator had rushed up.

The Mudalali had offered him fifty rupees. Instead of accepting it, he had said softly, "I need a job."

Trying to put the moments in the witness box out of his mind, he said, "I am leaving tomorrow."

"Where are you going?"

"Somewhere. I wanted to come and tell you before I left. I want to find another job, another city."

The children sounded the horn of the car. She got up. "Time went by so quickly."

She got into the car. "Which way are you going?"

"Nowhere in particular. I usually walk around a long time and then go home."

"I wish I could roam about like you. Come, I'll drop you."

"No. I. . . ."

"Oh, come on."

The little boy was in front and the girls at the back. He hesitated even when she switched on the engine.

"Get in. Little one, open the door."

The boy, who was playing with the plastic dog hanging over the dashboard, opened the door unwillingly and moved as close as he could to his mother.

The girls lowered their voices to a whisper. She braked at the gate of her house and sounded the horn. The old cook came out. The girls got out and slammed the doors.

"Get down, little one." Sethu got out first and took the child's hand. He shook it free and ran up the cement path to the house.

She asked the cook, "Has she left?"

"No, she said she would wait until the Mudalali got back."

Her voice trembled with anger. "Didn't I tell you to throw her out?"

The old man stood quietly, his eyes on the ground. She muttered something to herself.

"Get in."

"I'll walk home."

"Get in. I want to see that house. My property, I'm told. One day I may live there. Give me the key when you leave. I want to repair it and make it comfortable."

He started to open the back door but she reached out and opened the front one. She took the road skirting the beach, and speeded up, laughing. "Let me give you a ride in the Benz, Writer. This is your send-off party. You're leaving tomorrow, aren't you? I will see you off."

He shrank into his seat, feeling he had no right to be there. By the time they reached the town, the streets which had been crowded in the evening were deserted. Through the corner of his eye, he watched her delicate hands move effortlessly over the steering wheel.

They turned off the main road. She asked, "So how was the last party?"

"Which party?"

"Your party. Why is it you invite only the Mudalali for your parties?"

He was taken aback.

"Who were there?"

"I don't know."

"You are the caretaker. You should know." She added, "I get to know everything, even if it's later. Everything. There's nothing I don't know."

The streets seemed unusually dark. Perhaps some of the municipal lamps had gone out. He gave her directions. The house was in total darkness. He pointed it out to her. She seemed not to have heard, absorbed as she was in an invisible point on the steering wheel.

"Do you want to see the house?" His heart began to beat very fast when he realized that he would be the host now, not the person who kept watch on the outside verandah. He calmed down, somehow found the courage to go around, open the door of the car and ask, with a mixture of fear and cruelty,

"Aren't you getting down?"

He saw her troubled face for a second in the glow of the car light as she opened the door. He felt unsteady as they walked over the dead leaves piled in the courtyard.

"Careful, there's a step here." He held out his hand. The blood rushed to his face when he caught her soft hand in his trembling fingers. He let go of her hand in the verandah. The door took longer than usual to open. He switched on the lights and said, with the air of a host, "Come in, don't you want to see?"

He showed her the kitchen and the corridor. Then he opened the door of the bedroom. "This is the only room I use."

She began to go through the books in the wall cupboard with the broken door. For the sake of saying something, he asked, "When are you going to demolish this place?"

She ignored his question. "I lost a lot of my books, but I still have quite a number."

"I'd like to see them."

"When are you leaving?"

"I've not decided. Tomorrow, or the day after."

He stood quietly like a sentry guarding the women's quarters while she looked around the room. Suddenly, she said in English, "I can read your thoughts."

He pretended not to have any thoughts at all.

"Don't judge me, don't think I am spoilt and spiteful. The thing is, I am worried. It's been a very bad day for me!"

He held her hand to show her the way through the dark courtyard. At the gate, he suddenly lost control and began to speak in a language incomprehensible to himself.

This was a dream in which a princess had graced a shepherd's hut. I am a nobody. But I used to stand at the window and look out for you.

She tried to withdraw her hands, but he held them tight.

"I worship you!" He had often marvelled at how easily words came to him when he needed them.

He told her, as she got into the car, "I'm not leaving."

"Um?"

"I want to go on seeing you. Until now, I had nothing to dream about. Now I can wait for the princess to come again to the shepherd's dwelling."

The car roared away. Minutes later, he realized that he was standing alone at the gate.

When he lay down, he became aware that a haunting fragrance clung to his fingertips. The night blossomed around him like a flower through the memory of that fragrance and filled the world like a black lotus. He laid his head on one of its petals, listened to the music of the waves and slept.

6

He asked the driver to turn into the small one-roomed travellers' bungalow on the outskirts of the town. Anxious to establish the fact that he had been there many times with the Mudalali, the driver said,

"There's a big tourist home on the other side, it's more convenient."

He pretended he had not heard. The building was enveloped in darkness. It did not look as if anyone had stayed there recently, for the courtyard was covered with dead leaves.

The driver had to honk two or three times before the watchman shuffled out of the darkness. He waited till the watchman put on the light and opened the front door before he got down from the jeep.

The rough tiled floor was chipped and the cane on the chairs torn so badly that they could not be used. The mirror was foggy. The old Coorg watchman wore a tattered coat and a cloth around his head. He opened the cupboard, took out a sheet and spread it over the worn mattress. Then he picked up the earthen water pot, opened the bathroom door with difficulty and went out.

He stretched his legs out on the table and lit a cigarette. The driver came in.

"The tourist home is more comfortable. No one usually stays here alone." He smiled meaningfully, to emphasise "alone."

Sethu did not attempt to hide his displeasure. People had begun to talk to him now with great respect. Menon had been the first, then the employees when he went to the yard or the mill or the accounting department. This driver was the only one who had not fallen in line. Sethu had noticed it all the way here. Even when he answered the fellow in monosyllables, he had tried to be familiar. It had annoyed Sethu very much when he had picked up Sethu's matches from the seat to light his beedi. And here he was now, hovering arrogantly around the room.

He watched the curls of smoke from his cigarette freeze in the cold air and said, without turning his face, "Driver, take my case out of the car." He enjoyed seeing the man's face darken at his authoritative tone. Would he answer back? Go on, if you dare.

The man brought the box in and banged it on the table. Sethu thought contemptuously, wait and see, you're all just beginning to know how it will be!

There had been a lot of changes in the office, the mill and the yard of late. Was it after the Mudalali had started to send him for auctions, or before? Menon's sharp eyes saw everything. He certainly knew that Sethu often saw the Mudalali's wife at home. The first time he had felt a breath of scandal, he had been proud of himself. He longed for the moment when the news would reach the Mudalali's ears with a mixture of fear and delight.

When Menon rushed into his house one day, Sethu was prepared for the worst.

"The Mudalali is not well. He's in hospital."

The hospital yard was filled with cars. The Mudalali had fallen down in the bathroom at night. The servants had hurried up hearing his wife scream and found him unconscious. Someone said, "It's a stroke. He's paralysed." When he returned home a month later, one side of his body had become useless.

The watchman came in after filling the vessels in the bathroom with water and asked in broken Malayalam what Sethu would like to eat. He called out to the driver, "Take the watchman into town." He told the old man to get him something light, an omelette with bread perhaps, and gave the driver five rupees.

He got up and opened the window when they left. Wisps of mist floated over the treetops like memories. It felt much colder. He pulled down the sleeves of his shirt and lit another cigarette.

When they got back, he asked the watchman to give the driver something to sleep on.

"Yes, Mudalali."

He saw the driver look enviously at the second cot in the room.

A car drew up outside just as he was about to fall asleep under the old, smelly blanket the watchman had brought him.

There were voices on the verandah and then a knock. He got up and opened the door.

"Hullo!"

Karunakaran from Ollur, Muhammad Sait from Kochi and a third man whom Karunakaran introduced. "Iyengar, one of the biggest exporters in Madras."

"How is Srinivasan?"

"He's better." Sethu thought of the scene he had witnessed when he went to take leave of the Mudalali. He had been struggling to make his way to the bathroom using only his left hand and leg and holding on to a rope for support. He had driven away the servant who came to help,

"Get out, you son of a dog."

Illness had aggravated the cruelty in the Mudalali's eyes and the sharpness of his tongue. He spent his days on a mattress in a corner of the living room, holding pigeons close to him, as the ayurvedic physician had advised. In the evenings, he moved into the bedroom with the help of the servants.

"Why did you choose this place?"

"It's very quiet."

Karunakaran's eyes were bloodshot and his breath smelled of whisky.

While they drove along, they remarked to each other on the beauty of the Coorg women with their pallus pinned across their breasts. He joined their discussions on the feats they had performed at the recent auctions and said to himself, I belong with these people now, who deal in transactions that run into lakhs of rupees.

They dropped him back after midnight. He had only one thought in his mind, that if he held back from bidding at the auction next day, Iyengar would give him five thousand rupees.

Five thousand rupees!

At ten next morning, Karunakaran came up to him in front of the depot.

"You haven't forgotten what we told you last night, have you?"

"I don't forget so easily."

They shared out the money in the tourist home. The Sait said, "This is not over, we can't finish without Iyengar's bottle as well."

Sethu got up, intending to leave at once, but they persuaded him to stay and hinted at the possibilities the night offered. He managed to extricate himself. The envelope with the five thousand rupees lay inside his vest, next to his skin.

Roaring down the hill, he left. The jeep was not fast enough. He longed to get back to the city. He had begun to love the minutes he spent at the window of his house, looking at the gate through the slit in the curtains. When the car door closed, the doors of his heart would open, and then the moments would fall gently like petals from a faded flower to the beat of her high-heeled shoes on the cement steps. Lying in her arms, enveloped in scent and colour, he would feel the strength of a rakshasa flowing through his veins.

He had become very fond of the little house on the outskirts of the town. There were pale green curtains now at the windows, flowered drapes at the door, and blue-bordered sheets on the bed. The window screens caressed the room into a cool, soft darkness.

There was a record player which he could operate from the bed.

"I am going to give you something. A companion for you." She stood in her yellow satin petticoat, showing him how to operate it. A worker arrived from the yard and he went out to talk to him. The man remarked,

"I saw the Mudalali's car outside."

"Yes, I brought it." He glowered at the man, as if to ask, do you need more explanations, and the man left quickly.

He listened to her like an obedient student as she described pop singers.

"Pat Boone sings about a fool's paradise; Tony Brent, who sang "Dark Moon" was Indian."

"My pet, don't be so formal, call me by my name."

"I can't. It feels strange."

"You must. Call me, you girl. I like it."

He laughed.

"My pet. Aren't you my darling boy."

The silken strands of music wove a magical world around them. Until at last he was left with the scent of her hair on the pillow and the crumpled sheets. He would feel a pleasant ache when he was alone and begin to wait for the moment when he would hear her footsteps again on the cement path.

It was the third day after he got back from Coorg. A Sunday. He got up thinking, she's sure to come today. He came back from work by noon. The servant boy had cleaned the house, filled water in the bathrooms, put his food in the tiffin carrier and coffee in a flask.

He said, "You can go now. Come back at eight." The Mudalali had trained the boy to obey without asking questions.

He waited at the window, looking out at the gate, and saw someone who looked like the accountant, Pachukutty. He realized with a start that it was Parameswara Ettan.

Parameswara Ettan blew his nose noisily and came in. Sethu tried to smile.

"You've just arrived?"

"I came yesterday. She's not well, she's been admitted in hospital." "She" was Edathi Amma.

"What's wrong with her?"

"She's been ill for a couple of months now. She vomits all the time. She might need an operation."

Sethu pushed a chair towards him. Parameswara Ettan undid the buttons on his coarse bush-shirt and blew on his chest.

"Have you had lunch?"

"Yes. How do you manage your food here?"

"There's a boy who gets me food from the hotel."

He asked a lot of unnecessary questions about Edathi Amma's illness. Did she have fever? Or a stomach ache? He did not want to give Parameswara Ettan a chance to talk. Was the hospital comfortable? She was in a general ward now. She could have someone stay with her only in a special ward. Parameswara Ettan began to talk about the rates for special wards. He said,

"Don't worry, I'll arrange all that."

He sat down to eat but found he had no appetite. He felt troubled. Parameswara Ettan would soon ask why he never went home though he lived only sixty miles away. He made a pretence of eating, stacked the dishes and came out. Parameswara Ettan was looking through an old newspaper.

"Didn't Achan write to you?"

"I wrote yesterday. And sent money." He always wrote the same words on the money order. Letter follows. But he never wrote. As soon as he began to make money, he had started to send money orders, as regularly as one paid instalments to a merchant.

"Amma expected you every Sunday. I waited for you as well, two or three Sundays."

"I wanted to come, but the proprietor fell ill. I've been very busy. So many responsibilities, even on Sundays."

He became aware that he was talking disjointedly and tried to hide his confusion by lighting a cigarette. As he blew out the smoke he realized this was the first time he had ever sat down in front of Parameswara Ettan, and that he had even dared to smoke.

He moved the packet of cigarettes towards Parameswara Ettan who took no notice if it.

"It's a bad time for us. Amma is not well either. She's always in bed."

"Can't you take her to a doctor?"

"We took her to Moosa. And Doctor Lassar came home once or twice." Parameswara Ettan took off his glasses and wiped them. He took out a cheap brand of cigarette from his pocket, broke one in half and lighted it. Sethu felt a pang of pity. His brother had suddenly grown old over the last few years. The hair above his ears was grey. Disgusting scabs had formed on the patches on his head where his hair had dropped.

He became conscious of the silence and asked, "Which ward is Edathi Amma in?"

"Sixteen. It's upstairs, at the end of the corridor."

Sethu was tense. The car might come at any moment now. There was a meeting of the Mental Hospital Committee at two and she had said she would drop in on the way back.

"Where did you stay last night, Ettan?"

"I took a room in a hotel near the hospital. I thought it would be difficult to find your place at night."

If Parameswara Ettan did not leave now, he would miss seeing her. He went in, changed, came out and said, "I have to meet a buyer at the warehouse."

His brother got up.

"You can rest here, I'll get back quickly."

Parameswara Ettan answered as he had hoped he would. "No, no, I'll leave now."

"I'll come to the hospital as soon as I'm free." He locked the door. At the crossroads, he said, "Go straight on, you'll get a number nine bus. It will drop you right in front of the hospital."

He crept furtively back to the house like a thief. As he opened the door, he heard her car brake outside the gate.

7

The unpleasant odour of the hospital reminded him of unhealed wounds.

His sister-in-law lay on an iron cot with a red blanket upto her waist. Her face looked pale. Her tired eyes lit up when she saw him. He had expected her to find fault with him, but she seemed more hurt than angry. "I've been waiting since yesterday."

"It was only when Parameswara Ettan came that I knew." He examined the chart at the foot of the bed with the air of an expert. "We'll have you moved to a special ward. It's more convenient, I can come and see you whenever I am free. Don't worry, we'll arrange everything."

"I get news of you. So good fortune has come your way, then."

He smiled, "Oh, well."

"I don't need your money. But can't you write once in a while?"

He kept quiet. It seemed so long ago, the time when he had roamed over the hillside to find her little raw mangoes and jnaval fruit.

She asked him to sit down at the foot of the bed. "I want to stay with you for a day after I'm all right. I have so much to tell you."

"You'll feel better soon. You must stay with me for a few days before you return."

"It's the thought of the children that worries me."

Visitors were crowded around the beds and the ward had grown very noisy.

"It's nearly a month and a half since I went to your house. Not since Amma fell ill," she said.

She began to talk of the village and he suddenly felt distanced from the clamour in the ward. Edathi Amma told him about the thief who went to steal and fell into the well. Her eyes narrowed when she laughed.

"Did you know Madhava Ammama stays at home now?"

"No."

"He's bought Yousuf's provision shop. They say it's doing well."

"I heard that."

"You know that the Vadakkethu property has been divided?"

He had not known. Nor had he known about Madhava Ammama's shop. Yet he said, "Someone mentioned it to me recently."

"The little one, Karthu, is married. Her husband is in a workshop in Salem or Tanjore or somewhere like that. He's from Ummathoor."

And Sumitra? He fought down the desire to ask about Sumitra.

Sumitra and Devu had each taken their share, said Edathi Amma and separated. Sumitra lived by herself in a house she had built on the hill. Devu was at Vadakkethu. Madhava Ammama visited her sometimes, met the children and gave Devu some money.

Sethu found it easy to visualize the family quarrel that took place on a Sivarathri day as Edathi Amma began to describe it.

Madhava Ammama had opened a tea stall on the day the villagers celebrated Sivarathri. It was a profitable venture. Unni Namboodiri was appointed cook. Madhava Ammama slapped Unni Namboodiri in front of everyone because the idli batter had not been ground finely enough. Devu and the children were in the shop at the time. Devu intervened and Madhava Ammama hit her as well. That night, everyone heard Devu's screams from Vadakkethu. Madhava Ammama had walked out of the house.

He did not go back although Amma had tried her best to persuade him. Kandankulangara Menon had spoken to him on Devu's behalf, after which he went sometimes in the daytime, to see the children.

"Sumitra is ill as well. She has hysteria."

People said it was because she had built her house near the shrine of a Brahmarakshasu. One day, after a bath in the river, she had run across the fields, dripping wet, screaming. That had been the beginning. When they had caught her finally, at the edge of the field, she had been unconscious.

"Who does she stay with?"

"Whom does she have?"

Parameswara Ettan arrived with milk, bread and oranges, and scolded Edathi Amma, "Can't you hold your tongue even when you're ill?"

The bell rang and visitors had to leave. Parameswara Ettan said he would go out with him.

"Why don't you give up the hotel room and come and stay with me?"

"It's only two-and-a-half rupees and it's right next door. I'll stay there." Ettan invited him to his room in the little hotel.

"Come in. You're not in a hurry, are you?"

"No, no."

Ettan took off his shirt and sat on the bed. He had grown even more haggard than Achan.

"How much leave do you have?"

"Two weeks. If I extend it, it will be on loss of pay."

Ettan seemed about to say something. He lit another cigarette, in an attempt to hide his uneasiness.

"I've been wanting to write to you, but what's the use. You never reply."

Sethu felt himself grow smaller. He could offer no justification. He swallowed and sat quietly.

"What have you decided about the Pushpoth girl?"

"I'll think about it later."

"No one disapproves. If someone said something unpleasant earlier, don't take it seriously."

"We'll see."

"When?"

He avoided a direct answer and talked instead about how busy he was. He was going to start a business and needed capital. His mind was full of plans.

Ettan's continued to look at him expressionlessly.

"I'll come home soon."

"Mm." Ettan did not sound as if he believed him.

He got up and held out the hundred rupee note he had kept ready.

"Here, keep this with you. It's better to shift her to the special ward tomorrow."

"No, that's all right, I have enough for the moment."

He was not sure how to persuade Ettan to take the money.

"Really, I don't need it."

He folded the note and put it back in his pocket.

Walking through the crowded streets, he thought of Sumitra, alone in her hut by the Brahmarakshasu shrine. The noise and crowd around him faded and he saw the jnaval trees and hills of a lost world. He thought of the little boy with the torn shorts tucked into his waist thread, combing the hillside for a fallen jnaval fruit that was whole. He remembered how thrilled he had been when he finally found one and gifted it to Edathi Amma and watched a tint of violet spread over her pretty white teeth.

As he grew tired and his pace flagged, thousands of city sounds encircled him again, screaming.

8

The river had run dry. He walked over its parched bed, leaving the lost years behind and climbed onto the road.

New stone steps had been built at the bathing ghat. The thatched shed beyond the river had become a small tiled mosque.

The young sixteen-year-olds who passed by looked at him admiringly.

There was a high school now near the village. In the old days, children stopped going to school after the fifth class and helped in the fields or in the shops. He was sure everyone sent their children to high school now.

He felt contemptuous and a little sad, looking at the thinly pencilled moustaches behind the beedi smoke and the turned up collars. He imagined these village princes setting out with their certificates in search of a livelihood.

It seemed so long ago now, the time when the city had lain before him like a great secret, with its thousands of closed doors that would open by magic. He had waited, sweating and gasping, in front of its many arched gateways, watching other people go in and out with resentment and envy.

The first thing that caught his eye as he walked down the road was the ugly statue on the new tiled house by the river. Whose house had it been? The mapilla fishmonger's. Next to his hut there had been a double banyan that spread its shade over the road all day. It had been cut down. Bullocks freed temporarily from their yoke used to lie in its shade, chewing cud, their bells tinkling softly.

The path over the fields leading to the Kandankulangara house which had been broad enough to allow a bullock cart to pass was much narrower now; bits had been cut off on either side.

He did not read the new board by the roadside. The harvested fields lay shrivelled and dry, waiting for the Medam rains.

His heart began to beat faster when he reached the Vadakkethu gate. There was no one outside. Would someone catch sight of him through the gap in the areca nut palms?

The stone steps at the entrance to his house were chipped. A coconut palm had pushed its way through the corner of the blackened wall, overgrown with moss, and hung over the fields. The worm-eaten gateposts shook when he touched them. The house reminded him of a hunched up old woman with a shaven head basking in the sun with her eyes closed. He quickly ran up the steps. He had to bend his head so that it did not hit the rafters in the verandah.

A dark, emaciated girl came to the door and peered out.

Padmu! The little snot-nosed child whom he used to carry on his hip through the areca nut grove, with Cheriamma's shouts pursuing them!

"Come on, girl, where's Cheriamma?"

Her voice trembled with happiness. "Amme! It's Sethu Ettan."

Crows and chickens pecked at the reddish worms in the heap of dung near the wall. He stood with his hand touching the rafter and remembered how he used to reach out to it with his thumb every week to measure his height.

Cheriamma came out dragging her feet, wiping the spittle running out of her mouth with the back of her hand.

"Look who's here now. Do you remember us at all, child? It's been so long."

She leaned against the door and wept. He hurried to help the porter take his box down from his head.

Age had not changed Cheriamma very much. There were more red patches around her lips and she had grown greyer and thinner. There were red scars on her wrinkled feet as well.

"We've been waiting for you so many years, not just one or two." Her words were drowned again in tears. He went in. The whole house, the verandah, the outer and inner rooms looked much smaller than the images he had treasured of them in his mind.

Through her tears, Cheriamma lamented, "I don't have all that long to live now."

Padmu stood at the door with a pathetic smile. He said to her, with the authority of a family member, "Ask someone to take that box upstairs." He noticed that she had changed into a clean mundu. He gave her two rupees to give the porter. She said to her mother softly as she went out,

"Sh, keep all that crying for later. We have visitors."

Cheriamma calmed down. "Get him a grass mat, child," she said.

He came out to the verandah once he was sure that she had stopped crying. The easy chair usually placed there for Achan was missing. The lime used to repair the worm-eaten patches on the wooden seat had begun to peel off.

Padmu said hesitantly, "The screws of the easy chair have come out, it's not safe to sit on it."

The visitors had entered the courtyard. Narayanan Nair. Appu Nair. He did not make out Sankunni Nair immediately, since his protruding teeth had been extracted.

They greeted him with smiles, and spoke in voices full of respect.

"Ah, so you still remember the way home."

"What's the news, Narayanan Nair?"

Someone had seen Sethu from the road and made a guess, they said. Narayanan Nair had come to ascertain whether it really was Sethu.

"Do sit down. Bring a mat."

"No, no, I don't need a mat."

They sat on the chipped floor. Sethu leaned against the pillar and Cheriamma warned him, "Your mundu will get dirty."

Sethu did not take the mat which Padmu brought him.

"Why didn't you write that you were coming? Achan was here yesterday. He didn't tell us you would be here."

"I was free suddenly."

"Did you come by train or by car?"

"By car to the other side of the river."

"We need a bridge over our river. People like you go to so many places, meet so many highly placed persons, why don't you try to get it done?"

He pretended to be interested in what they had to say about the hot weather and the disease that had attacked the areca nut palms.

Sankunni said, "I walked with your father up to the road. He's not as healthy as he used to be."

Sethu started to talk about the city, the price of rice, the profit in the timber trade. When he ran out of subjects, Cheriamma hinted, in an effort to get him to herself,

"Why don't you have a wash and change? You've made a long trip."

The visitors asked whether he would be staying a few days.

"I haven't decided."

"Why don't you come along with us and meet everyone?"

"Later."

After they left, an old man hobbled in with a stick. Padmu said,

"It's Chinnan Menon."

Cheriamma sounded irritated, but he detected a note of pride as well, "You've hardly set foot in the house and the whole village seems to know!" She called out to Padmu to bring a mat. Kandankulangara Menon had to be treated with respect, after all. Menon hoisted himself up the steps with difficulty and asked,

"So, did you make me out?" Sethu smiled and invited him to sit down. Menon fanned himself with his mundu and said, "I have asthma. I consulted Dr Gopala Menon and he prescribed all kinds of medicines. But I can hardly sleep during the full moon period."

He asked Cheriamma for a drink of hot water. When he stopped gasping, he asked Sethu, "What are you doing now?"

"I have a small business."

"Timber?"

"Um."

"Your own, Sethu?" Sethu grunted.

"I've been asking your father to write to you. When I heard you were here, I thought I'd come myself."

Cheriamma was right. How quickly the news had spread that he was home!

"I'm not sure whether you've seen my youngest son. I didn't educate him. He failed his ninth, he's no good at studies. He's been idling at home for three years now, you must find him a job somewhere."

"A job these days. . . ."

Menon did not allow him to finish. "It doesn't matter what it is or where. You are," he paused for a moment. "You can manage it now. I couldn't possibly ask other people."

"Let me think about it."

"I'm the only one left in the tarawad. You must have heard that we had a partition in the family."

"Yes, I heard."

"I have to go across the river this evening, so I thought I'd come and see you at once. When can I send him?"

"Let me find out. I'll write to you."

Menon left. Cheriamma brought Sethu tea in a bell-metal glass. "He drinks all the time. That's why he fell out with his brothers."

The tea smelt of fresh goat's milk. He put the glass down. Cheriamma asked, "Do you want more sugar? Drink it up quickly before someone else comes."

He gulped down most of it, gave her the glass and lit a cigarette.

"We don't need your money." Cheriamma's voice trembled. "This is your place and you should remember we're all here for you. Do you realize how many years it has been? Not just one or two, child. Nine years! I've kept count."

Nine years.

He got up, afraid that she would start talking about the events of those nine years.

He went to his old room above the front verandah. Memories from the past slumbered in the faint light that crept hesitatingly through the rounded window bars. Were the verses and addresses he had scribbled on the wall still there? He would have to light the lamp to find out. The familiar musty odour of bell-metal stained with verdigris still clung to the room. He hung his shirt and vest on the foot of the bed, took out a towel from his bag and lay down on the wooden ledge.

Did the room look darker than before? Or was it because he was so tired that he could not see the smooth ochre coloured floor clearly?

He heard Cheriamma give Padmu instructions. Then she went to the eastern verandah to make excuses for him to someone waiting there.

"He's lying down. He had to leave the car on the other side of the river and walk. Come again tomorrow. Look, Thami, the Cheria Thampuran won't go away in a hurry, you can see him. Come later."

Cheriamma came slowly up the stairs. "So many people to see you, cherumans, mapillas!" She laughed, showing her blackened gums. "They all want something from you, they've heard you're minting money."

She added, "You're looking healthy enough."

She began to talk about her ailments. By evening, her feet hurt so badly she could not walk. She'd thought it might be rheumatism and tried massaging them with oil. Her digestion was not good, food nauseated her.

He listened, making a sound of assent now and then. Cheriamma fell silent and gazed out of the window for a long time, inhaling snuff and rubbing the end of her flat nose. Then she suddenly asked,

"When Parameswaran's telegram came, you were not there, were you?"

"No," he answered slowly turning his face to the wall.

He looked at her again and he saw her wipe her eyes. "We waited till the morning train arrived before cremating her, thinking you would come."

That cool May night. That day had started with a blazing sun.

He had woken up at nine in the hotel room with a heavy head. The sun had already become hot. The thought that they would give the verdict that day took shape in his foggy mind. The night before, he had blotted out the thought in drink before he fell heavily asleep.

It was the hotel where he had once worked as a part-time clerk. There were waiters who still remembered.

"Who is in number fourteen?"

"Sethu Mudalali."

He picked up the cup of coffee with unsteady hands, took a gulp and called Reception. "A large whisky."

The court would assemble at eleven. All his new found friends would come by ten to give him moral support.

Would she have slept? He wondered whether to call her and the telephone rang.

"How are you?" Her voice always soothed his taut nerves.

"I am all right." He said, to comfort her, "Don't worry about anything."

"Are you worried?"

He laughed lifelessly.

He had guessed that the registered letter contained the order for his dismissal when he signed for it. He had already vacated the house in expectation. He had read the letter with a sense of disgust and then telephoned her.

"I have a piece of good news. I'm no longer your husband's salaried employee."

She had warned him as soon as her brother-in-law had been sent for from Bombay. He and the lawyer had spent a whole day at her husband's bedside, conferring in low voices.

He was not perturbed when they served a charge on the grounds that he had embezzled large sums of money from the business. He woke up his lawyer at the dead of night and requested him to file a counter case, after calculating the amounts due to him for having removed certain files from the office and adjusted the figures. They owed him a lakh of rupees and part of the profits.

When they approached him for a settlement, he said, "He's the Mudalali, isn't he? Let him fight his case and win."

"The Mudalali will withdraw the case. You know the condition he's in. We're not sure whose fault it is. In the name of humanity."

He laughed aloud and they were shocked.

"Why are you laughing?"

"Nothing."

In the name of humanity?

"What are we to do?"

"Whatever you want. You can even decide that I am not human."

One night, he asked Lalitha, "Do you have the courage?"

"For what?"

"For whatever happens."

"I came here because I had courage. I thought I would not come but I could not stay away."

"File a suit then, if you have courage."

"For what?"

"Divorce."

Her face suddenly grew pale. He got up when the silence became unbearable and went to the bathroom to change. She was seated at the dressing table combing her hair when he came out. He looked at her reflection in the mirror for an instant and then withdrew his eyes.

She walked out to the dark lane where her trustworthy driver had parked the car. Her footsteps faltered now and then.

She called him unexpectedly that night. "I am ready."

"What?"

"I am ready."

Next day, she had listened with an expressionless face while the criminal lawyer explained what "extreme mental cruelty" and "incompatibility" meant.

Eleven o'clock.

He thought his nerves would break, they were so taut. The telephone rang. The lawyer's rough voice said, "It's going to take till one o'clock. Don't worry."

The sun blazed outside. The fumes of the duty free whisky that the peon of the merchants' Club had smuggled in coursed through his stomach. The lawyer called again just as he was slipping into unconsciousness.

"Congratulations! We've won."

He burst into laughter. Was it he himself he had to congratulate? He had told himself many times that this was the moment he had been waiting for his whole life.

The lawyer, who had a reputation for being able to change the face of truth, was offering him congratulations!

"You're congratulating me?"

He was suddenly aware that he had not achieved anything. Who had won, then?

The telephone rang again and he heard her tired voice.

"Are you happy?"

Happiness, pleasure—it made him laugh.

She insisted that they leave at once, she wanted to escape from everyone for a few days.

Parameswara Ettan's telegram must have come that evening. They had already checked into the well-known hotel near the garden on the river.

Standing on the private balcony of their third floor suite, she talked about the children. He had booked a trunk call to his office. When it came through, the clerk said to him,

"There's a telegram for you."

"From where?"

The young man seemed hesitant to reply. He said angrily,

"Open it and read it out."

"It's from your house, Mudalali. Mother . . . mother expired."

He put the phone down, moved aside the curtain dividing the living area from the bedroom and took a cigarette from the table. She came in and asked,

"What happened?"

"Nothing." He did not look at her face. He stood in the balcony, longing to weep, but his heart had hardened like rock.

"Your tea will grow cold," she called out.

He watched the crowds moving amongst the squares and circles of the garden in the artificial moonlight of the lamps. The news stood just outside his mind like a traveller in search of shelter—Amma was dead!

He went in and saw a look of reproach on her face. She had put on a new perfume and was rubbing Max Factor cream on her wrinkled eyelids.

He lit another cigarette, sat down and stretched out his legs on the low stool. She repeated, "Your tea is cold."

Was she finding fault with him?

"Pour it into the sink."

Had he sounded rude? She seemed more nervous than surprised. He noticed her lips trembling. What is it? What happened? Her eyes were full of unasked questions.

Nothing. I'm all right.

He lay on his half of the wide double bed, breathing in her perfume and asked himself, where was the thrill he used to feel when he heard her footsteps on the stone steps?

The mattress felt cold and so did her flesh. He closed his eyes and felt them smart with tears. He could still not cry then. Once, he thought he sobbed. He controlled himself and heard her soft voice,

"What is it, darling?"

Nothing. Nothing is wrong with me.

Her warm fingers ran gently over his chest and he drew away.

"Tell me, what is it?"

"Nothing."

Nothing. The dark night was nothing and the long path he had travelled was nothing. The delight he had experienced during those moments of waiting and the scent of the pillow, all was nothing. You are nothing, the facts and figures you gave me are nothing. This expensive hotel room and the symbol of the lion on the windscreen of the car are nothing. You will not understand. Nothing, nothing.

"Tell me, please."

"It's nothing."

The honeymoon that had not yet begun ended that cold night, on a pillow wet with tears.

The wasp that had been circling the parrot's cage doubtfully went back into its hive.

Cheriamma said,

"God was good to her in that she did not become a burden to anyone. All of us pray for that. All I want you to do, child, is to find a husband for this girl of mine. You know I think of you as my son. That's all I want from you. Once that is done, I'll have no worries left."

He sat very quiet.

"What is it, Sethu?"

"Nothing."

9

Padmu lighted the wick on the front steps at dusk. It glimmered faintly, like some half-forgotten grief, in the waning evening light. A child, probably from Vadakkethu, intoned its prayers mechanically. An old film song drifted in from the direction of the rosewood forest in the south. There must be a wedding in progress, he thought. The child at Vadakkethu stopped chanting.

He walked up and down the yard, Cheriamma said, "We can heat some water if you want a bath, and you can bathe by the well after dark."

She complained about the cheruman, Thami, who had still not made a screened shed near the well though she had told him to do so many times.

"I just need a wash."

The illam compound was enveloped in darkness. At first sight, the shabby house seemed deserted, then he saw a chimney lamp move behind the blackened bars of the kitchen.

The path to the illam was overgrown with plants and weeds. His heart turned over when a black form moved near the broken fence. Someone came towards him. He made him out when he drew close—Unni Namboodiri.

Unni Namboodiri had grown quite grey and looked like a man in his sixties. He wore a dirty towel that barely reached his knees.

"What news, Unni Namboodiri?"

"I just heard that you were here."

"Come and sit down."

Unni Namboodiri sat on the verandah near the stone steps. The wick had gone out.

Padmu brought a lamp. Sethu saw Unni Namboodiri's face clearly in its gleam and was suddenly afraid. The prickly stubble on his chin was completely grey, his teeth were worn and blackened and his straggly hair was as rough as coconut fibre. Anyone who met him on a lonely country road was sure to run away.

Unni Namboodiri darted quick looks at him from time to time and then lowered his eyes.

"Do you still go for temple festivals, Unni Namboodiri?"

"No."

He waited for Unni Namboodiri to talk, to burst as usual into loud laughter. But he was very quiet.

"How many children do you have Unni Namboodiri?"

"Three." He added after a moment, "They're all girls. I lost the only boy I had." A festival was celebrated in his wife's family temple after an interval of twelve years. Unni Namboodiri had sat right on top of one of the walls, with the child on his lap and his grip had suddenly loosened.

"I watched him fall. As he fell." Cheriamma was at the door. She said softly, "Amme, Mahamaye!"

An uneasy silence settled on them again.

Cheriamma asked, "Did you sell the mango tree which gives those delicious little mangoes, Unni Namboodiri?"

"Yes. They've given us fifteen and owe us ten more."

He guessed that Unni Namboodiri must have come to him for help and decided to give him ten rupees when he left. Unni

Namboodiri moved right up to him. He smelled of the earth, of betel leaves and sweat.

"When are you leaving?" he asked.

"I've not decided."

"Then." Unni Namboodiri hesitated and Sethu said, "Tell me, come on."

"If I come with you Sethumadhavan, can you get me a job somewhere?"

"Get you a job, Unni Namboodiri?"

"Yes."

Sethu smiled. "Who will look after the illam?"

Unni Namboodiri's laugh was not the foolish laugh of old. He seemed to be trying to hide the trembling of his voice.

"What is there to look after now? Govindan does not give us a single grain of paddy. And after we lost the areca nuts . . . it's all a mess."

Sethu wondered what to say. Unni Namboodiri said, "I don't mind cooking or serving."

He saw Unni Namboodiri's eyes glisten in the dark and took a quick step backwards.

"All right, Unni Namboodiri, we'll see what we can do."

Unni Namboodiri's black form dissolved into the darkness.

"They demolished everything, even the wooden storerooms, to sell the wood. His wife looks more miserable than a cherumi woman," Cheriamma said.

Cheriamma insisted he have a wash. "Will you eat now?"

"I'm not in a hurry."

"Madhavan comes very late. He says trade is best at dusk."

But Madhava Ammama came earlier than usual. He took off his creaking slippers and sat down, the keys at his waist clinking. He had put on weight. He wore a mill made T-shirt with a collar and had a towel with a red border over his shoulder. He lit his beedi with a lighter. Sethu noticed that one of his front teeth was missing.

"Why didn't you bring the children?" he asked.

The children? *His* children? They were waiting for another decree from the court. She must be wondering now how they should address him when they came home. He fumbled for a reply.

"I came away in a hurry. Just decided suddenly."

"I come there occasionally to buy provisions. But I don't know your place and since I always come back the same evening, I never have time to go looking for it."

Madhava Ammama took off his vest, asked for a towel and made his way towards the well.

"It's a terrible season. There's not a drop of water in the river."

He overheard Padmu ask Cheriamma softly whether to fry the pappadams whole or in bits. Cheriamma asked her to make an extra curry, a liquid coconut chutney and went into the kitchen with her.

This time yesterday, he had been at K. A. Menon's housewarming party. While listening to Menon talk in heavily slurred accents about the bombing in Rangoon he had been glancing at the sofa by the radio from time to time, trying to warn her silently.

That evening, when she had groped for the car keys on the table and thrown them into his hands, her eyes had been full of appeal. So he had asked, "Coming?"

"Do you want me to?"

She talked too much when her speech began to slur. There was a time when they used to talk endlessly. In the end, they would ask each other,

"What did we talk about?"

Nothing!

My God! So much time had gone by, and now?

Now, words had become brittle showpieces in a glass case, to be used only on special occasions.

The unpleasant memory of the first cabaret show conducted in the newly opened hotel in the city still lingered in his mind.

She said, "I'll come if you don't mind. Or I can tell Mrs Menon that I have a headache. Headaches are a blessing in disguise now, thank God!" The last few years had taught him to hide emotion behind a smile.

"Get ready."

On the way, she told him about the Menons. He was very wealthy and she was his second wife.

The house was beyond the city limits. The cold of the sea wind and the roar of the waves pierced his ears. The driveway was full of cars. She looked longingly at one of them and asked,

"It's an imported Morris Oxford. Whose is it?"

"I don't know."

She must have calculated its price in her mind.

Introductions and polite phrases were exchanged.

Mrs Menon was everywhere, a glass of gin in her hand. She could have been mistaken for Menon's daughter. The daughter, a sixteen-year-old, brought him a tin of cigarettes.

A sports car screeched to a stop outside and someone got out. Sethu glanced at his wife. Pleasure had ironed out the wrinkles on her face.

The tall young man who got out of the car had bushy eyebrows and reddish lips and wore a copper bangle on his hand. As if to emphasize his height, he bent his head as he came in through the door, forcing everyone's attention onto himself.

Menon introduced him. He was an engineer, newly appointed in a Marwari firm. Indrajit.

He went around, meeting everyone, and said, "Indrajit, yes. But I have to disappoint you. I am not Ravana's son." He sat down between Sethu and a doctor and lifted his glass. "Cheers!" Confidence overflowed from his words, his looks, his stance. Sethu felt jealous.

Glasses emptied and filled. Music flowed from the stereo players. The laughter grew louder. He kept an eye on his wife, even while listening to the man sitting next to him talk. Careful, careful.

She pretended not to see the warning in his eyes. Was the half-empty glass in her hand her second or third? On the pretext of getting himself a box of matches, he went up to her and murmured, "Careful."

She did not raise her head.

Mrs Menon knew how to make a party lively. "Circulate," she commanded. Everyone had to change places.

The Sindhi proprietor of the flour mill and Menon invited Sethu to go out with them for a breath of fresh air. Menon insisted that they take their glasses into the garden.

Menon animatedly described the swimming pool he was going to make. The indistinct murmur of the sea could be heard behind them, like the reverberation from a distant temple festival.

Someone whistled, "One, two, three, I love you," from the terrace.

Every time he reminded himself uneasily that it was getting late and tried to leave, Menon would tell him how young the night still was.

He finally escaped with Mirchandani's help. In the dining hall the middle-aged insurance broker was running his fingers over Mrs Menon's palm, reading it.

"Where is she?"

"Oh, don't be a pest. Leave her free." Her words were slurred. She could not hold her head up properly and it kept sliding on to the palmist's shoulder. Disgusted, Sethu went into the house. People were huddled in small groups.

"Did you see my wife?"

"Worried?"

Someone laughed. He stayed with them a couple of minutes, to prove he was not anxious, and slipped away.

He found her on the terrace. The hand with the copper bangle was wound around her shoulder.

He watched her coldly as she staggered down the spiral staircase, expecting her to trip and fall. If she lost her grip on the aluminum railing, she would collapse in a heap at the foot of the twenty-seven steps and a red stain would spread slowly over the ground.

He was startled when the car door slammed. Had he shut it himself?

He pretended not to hear her sobs.

They passed the fishermen's huts and the lighthouse and turned into the city. The frightened street lamps seemed to be fleeing behind them. He made a turn and came up against a high wall. He pressed his foot on the accelarator and began to laugh. The endless waves of his laughter merged with the screech of metal and tyres.

He heard fear in the silence beside him.

An isolated lamp-post that could not escape him toppled over and he hooted with laughter.

"You're mad."

"Yes, all of us are mad, this car and the lamp-post as well. Yes." He laughed again.

And so I reach your gate. The day always ends here. I go through the garden you fashioned so artistically, open the door and enter your bedroom. I stand by your cold mattress with all the futile anger of an impotent man, full of regret for the lost opportunity, the moment when the skidding tyres wailed and broken metal screeched.

There were no questions when the black and yellow taxi arrived at the gate in the morning. When the servant placed the suitcase he had packed in a hurry on the seat, he had waited fearfully to be asked. But no, he did not have to tell her where he was going.

Madhava Ammama came into the verandah, smearing vibhuti over his forehead. "Krishna, Guruvayoorappa, protect us!" He asked, "Why are you sitting in the dark?"

"Just like that."

He got up. Cheriamma called out, "Come and eat. I laid the leaves long ago."

Padmu followed them with the lamp.

Cheriamma said, "I could not get good fish. The cheruman boy hunted all over and brought a handful of veloori."

"I'll arrange with the fishermen tomorrow, if you are staying."

He did not answer.

He enjoyed the drumstick leaves cooked with dal and Padmu refilled his deep plate again and again. Although he did not want a second helping of rice, Cheriamma insisted. "Just a handful, with buttermilk."

After dinner, he walked in the yard. Padmu spread Madhava Ammama's mattress on the verandah. Cheriamma said, "Your mattress is spread upstairs, Sethu. Tell me when you're going to sleep and I'll send a lamp."

"A little later."

"Aren't you going to Achan's place?"

"Yes, I must."

"Achan isn't well at all. Why don't you go and see him sometimes?" She called out to Padmu, "Eat something, girl, and go to bed. I don't eat at night. I have terrible problems with my acidity."

Cheriamma sat on the floor and stretched out her legs. Madhava Ammama had begun to snore.

"I suppose you know that Pushpoth Thangamani is in Bombay."

He turned his face away, afraid that she would see it, even in the dark. He could hear his own heartbeats.

"Destiny decides for each of us. I heard she came home to have her second baby."

He walked unsteadily to the wall and stared into the banana grove, where darkness and the wind played with the leaves. He hoped Cheriamma would not say anything more. She sighed.

"Bring her and the children here some time. I want to see her."

"I will." His throat was parched and he spoke with difficulty. "I'll go to bed. Give me a lamp."

"Take the hurricane lantern. I'll light another one inside."

He went up, lowered the wick and lay down. Cheriamma brought water in a brass jar, left it on the ledge and waited, obviously to say something to him. He pretended he was sleepy.

Once he was alone, he put the lamp out.

It looked as if it might rain. He longed to hear the sound of raindrops on the banana leaves. But it did not rain. A jackal howled somewhere on the hillside.

A faint breeze blew through the little window. He lay in the dark with his eyes closed, hoping to feel calmer. Maybe he would sleep tonight without a tranquillizer. He decided not to think about nights when sleeping pills erased memories, or about the painful days when saws seemed to run through him.

It was years since he had been to the temple. He thought he would go in the morning. He had not prayed since he was a child. What would he pray for when he went to the temple?

There was nothing to pray for. He knew what he wanted, a second chance. "Please give me another chance."

He would always stand outside the closed doors of a temple, praying for boons that would never be granted.

Always.

One more chance!

He felt as if heavy rain clouds were weighing down his heart in the merciless Medam heat.

He turned over and opened his eyes. Moonlight fell through the little window. He sat up, full of gladness. The world was bathed in moonlight as far as he could see, like a marvel, a dream. The same moonlight that had woken him up years ago.

He sat up, leaned on the window sill and looked out. Thousands of white mandaram flowers seemed to have blossomed in the sky. The white moonlight gleamed through the undone tresses of the areca nut palms like a dream. A terrifying beauty flowed through the empty courtyard. Silver tendrils played around the shadows in the banana grove.

He felt sad that he could not see the moonlight raining over the dry sand of the river bed from here. Darkness hid the pala tree on the way to the illam. He thought of how the creepers moving in the breeze resembled the form of a rakshasi with tangled hair.

Amma's southern field was just above the spot he was looking at. Had the coconut sapling he had planted on the heap of earth there grown?

He remembered the stories he had heard as a child, and was afraid. The Gandharvan at the foot of the pala tree, Karineeli from Meleparambu and the Brahmarakhshasu from the illam would be setting out now, to walk in the moonlight.

Everytime he drifted into sleep, he woke up with a start.

One of the bottles in the little box in his suitcase contained tranquillizers, but he was reluctant to get up and search for it.

He chanted, "Arjunan, Phalgunan, Parthan, Vijayan." Famous names, and then "Kireeti." He chanted louder and louder, until he was comforted by the sound of his own voice.

The sound of a creaking door woke him up. He rubbed his eyes and opened them, to find it was day.

He went softly down the stairs. No one was up yet. Madhava Ammama had covered himself with his mundu and was still fast asleep.

He went up the hill by the path on the west. There were so many changes. Beds had been dug and prepared for tapioca in the place where the jnaval grove used to be.

On the other side of the parched river, slivers of light spattered the eastern sky like drops of blood.

The little semicircular cave where the goats used to take shelter in the rain had been here. Now that the hillside had been levelled and the path widened, it had disappeared.

The teak tree shorn of leaves that used to be by the bamboo thicket had been cut down. Wet leaves were heaped around its ant-eaten stump.

He saw the low mud walls and the thatched roof just beyond the palms. He felt quite calm as he entered the cowdung-smeared yard. When he saw the closed door, he suddenly wanted to call out her name.

He heard footsteps behind him and turned. Startled, he realised it was Sumitra.

She had just had a bath and had wrapped a wet, ochre coloured mundu around her. Water dripped from the ends of her thick, matted hair. The bones above her sunken cheeks jutted out. Her eyes opened wide when she saw him. When he looked away, she said,

"It is Pooyam today, I went to the river at dawn for a bath."

He was silent.

"Sit down."

She opened the door and went in. He continued to stand there, drawing his fingers along the platform outside the house.

She came out and asked, without a trace of emotion, "Why don't you sit down?"

Had she not made him out?

Her bluish lips seemed to be muttering something silently. The wide vibhuti stripes on her forehead showed clearly as the moisture dried. Drops of water still trickled from the tips of the tangles that stuck out through her untidily knotted hair. A pale glow flickered in her eyes above dark patches of shadow, faint as that of a wick lit at dusk.

"Sumitre."

For an instant, her lips stopped moving, then began their indistinct mutterings again.

"Do you live here alone?"

"God is with me."

Was she mocking him? He looked at her thin, chapped wrists and the bones jutting out beneath her neck.

"I heard that you were ill."

"It's a lie."

"Sumitre!"

For a second, her eyes looked vulnerable, in a face as pale as thumba flowers that had been trampled on.

The words that crowded to his lips froze and remained unspoken.

"Do you hate me?"

Sumitra laughed. An echo of the laughter he had heard years ago ran swiftly through his mind.

"I loved you."

Sumitra laughed agian.

"Love?" He lowered his eyes and heard her say, "Sethu has loved only one person, ever. And that is Sethu himself."

When he looked at her again, she smiled and asked, "Isn't that so?"

He did not answer.

Sumitra sat down near the wall and started to pray as if he was not there.

He cleared his throat. "If there is something I can do."

"Narayana! Narayana! Narayana!" Her voice grew louder.

He stood there quietly for a few minutes and then walked away, his head bent.

The morning sky was flooded with pale colours. The east looked as if it was spattered with blood.

On the farther shore, wagons with heavy loads went up the steel railroad bridge. The screech of the wheels tore into his ears above the roar of the railway track and the odour of wet logs.

10

Wisps of bluish mist floated over the dew-wet sand. His long shadow tried to keep pace with him as he walked along the deserted banks of the river in the gentle morning sunshine.

His tired footsteps lagged as he looked into the dazzling spires of light high above the trees and remembered how he had once wanted to write poems about the sunrise. About the morning sunlight blossoming like flowers through the crevices in old temple walls, and fingers of light prising open the eyes of invisible lotuses.

How did they go, those two lines he had scrawled in pencil on the wall of his old room? He could not remember. His mind was as empty as the parched river.

His feet kept sinking into the endless stretch of sand and each time he pulled them out, he thought helplessly that he could not remember.

The cheruman carrying his suitcase caught up with him.

In the distance, the steel bridge and the railroad track shivered. The river, his river, dreaming of floods even as it grew dry, lay behind him like a lifeless body drained of blood and movement.

Glossary

adiyan	:	term used by a person from a lower caste to designate himself/herself while talking to someone from a higher caste
ameen	:	an employee of the Civil Court
anna prasanam	:	a ceremony conducted when a child is fed rice for the first time
anterjanam	:	a namboodiri woman
Brahmarakshasu	:	the spirit of a Brahmin who died a premature or gruesome death
chandu	:	a coloured liquid used to mark the forehead
cheruman	:	one of the lower castes {masc.}
cherumi	:	one of the lower castes {fem.}
Chettiar	:	a merchant community
Chettichi	:	fem. gender of Chettiar
chunam	:	lime paste
deepam	:	a lamp
embrandiri	:	a Brahmin, usually a pujari
gulikan	:	an evil spirit that has to be propitiated
Hidumban	:	a rakshasa; a demon
homam	:	a ritual performed before a sacred fire
illam	:	the residence of a namboodiri
jenmi	:	landowner
kanji	:	rice served with the water in which it is cooked
karanavar	:	the head or senior most member of a joint family
karyasthan	:	manager
kasavu	:	gold thread, usually woven into a border

kavadi	:	bow-shaped wooden structure decorated with peacock feathers and flowers, carried on the shoulder as an offering by pilgrims going to Subramania temples
kindi	:	metal mug of bell metal, silver or copper, with a spout; used to pour water
konam	:	a narrow piece of cloth used to cover the genitals
koothambalam	:	a hall set apart in the temple for performances
kooja	:	a pot to hold drinking water
koothu	:	a dance-drama performed in temples
kovilakam	:	the residence of a princely family
kuvalam	:	a tree the leaves and flowers of which are sacred to Shiva
Mahamaya	:	one of the names of the Devi
mudalali	:	owner, proprietor
naivedyam	:	food offered to a deity
nalukettu	:	a sunken courtyard with four wooden pillars flanking it
nazhi	:	a measure, about one-third of a litre
niramala	:	an offering made in a temple in which the shrine is decorated with flowers
panakam	:	a drink made with water, jaggery and cardamom
para	:	a measure for paddy or rice, about thirteen litres
pathayam	:	a wooden structure to store grain; it can also refer to the room itself where the grains are stored
pottu	:	a mark made on the forehead
pradakshinam	:	ritual circumambulation of the temple
pulaya	:	one of the lower castes
rowka	:	a blouse, the ends of the which are knotted above the waist

sambandham	:	a contractual marriage relationship
sastrams	:	the scriptures
tarawad	:	a joint family
Thampuran	:	form of address for someone of a higher caste
thekkini	:	a room on the southern side of the house
thirtham	:	sacred water
tirumeni	:	form of address used for a namboodiri
Variar	:	a community that has duties and rights in the temple
Vishu	:	the Malayali New Year, in mid-April
yakshi	:	a female spirit that can change its form at will and exercise an evil influence
yali	:	a mythical lion-like animal; sculptures of the yali are often seen in the temples
yejaman	:	owner, master

List Of Malayalam Months

With Approximate Equivalents in the Gregorian Calender

Chingam	:	August-September
Kanni	:	September-October
Thulam	:	October-November
Vrischikam	:	November-December
Dhanu	:	December-January
Makaram	:	January-February
Kumbham	:	February-March
Meenam	:	March-April
Medam	:	April-May
Edavam	:	May-June
Mithunam	:	June-July
Karkitakam	:	July-August

Kuttiedathi and Other Stories

Translated from the Malayalam by
V. Abdulla

Contents

Foreword

The trend of progressive realism had just blown over when, with the coming of Independence, there was a shift towards greater subjectivity and inwardness in all genres of literature in Malayalam. There was a change of focus from generalised abstractions to felt authenticity in the perception and recording of social reality. A mood of introspection came in the wake of the writings of Karoor Nilakanta Pillai, S.K. Pottekkatt, Vaikom Mohamed Basheer and P.C. Kuttikrishnan (Uroob). The strident voice of Kesava Dev, and Thakazhi Sivasankara Pillai had mellowed, with the former raising the question For Whose Sake? (*Arku Vendi*?) and the latter turning away from beggars, peasants and scavengers to the love story of Pareekutty and Karuthamma in *Chemmeen*. Society was still there, with all its complicated political and economic tangles, but the individual or personal concerns of the members of the upper class or middle class or lower class came to be addressed by the writers. Karoor highlighted compassion and pathos as fundamental elements in the everyday life of his characters, cutting across class divisions. Basheer often poked fun at the behavioural style and vocabulary of the self-styled leaders, drawing attention to the down to earth man and woman. Uroob, in short and long fiction, provided a larger canvas for the private lives of individuals and families, but was sympathetic to the sufferings and struggles of man in society. It was during this interregnum that M.T. Vasudevan Nair and others of his generation entered the scene, particularly of short fiction, to draw the attention of the reading public to the loneliness and alienation felt by individual characters caught in a social transition. Individual human beings with their private agonies emerged replacing the social stereotypes of erstwhile fiction committed to grand ideologies and slogan shouting. The whisper of the soul became audible, which had earlier been swallowed or stifled by public oration and street-side chorus. The new trend immediately caught popular attention, since that came to be symptomatic of the early years of independence. Slogans were replaced by sobs; with a gentle touch of the romantic without excessive sentimentality, the new and young writers wound their way into the sensitive minds of the new generation readers. A remarkably fresh sensitivity was evoked by the new short story, which was soon echoed in longer fiction too. A quiet and un-proclaimed revolution was sweeping through the corridors of Malayalam fiction, which in a way had its impact on the senior writers as well. In a few years the modernist writers with existentialist leanings, questioning current assumptions, came upon the scene: among them may be mentioned Pattathuvila Karunakaran, Kakkanadan and O.V. Vijayan. Vasudevan Nair, however, steered his course away from philosophical obsessions and simplistic formulae about life and society, and has till date maintained his integrity by pursuing his own perceptions and his own style.

The ten stories collected here in English translation by the veteran and seasoned translator V. Abdulla constitute some of the most well-known stories of Vasudevan Nair, fairly representative of his opus. Spread over a broad span of time from 1962 to 2000, they reflect the built-in variety of his fictional concerns and the changing tones of his narration. A true artist careful about the generic nature of short fiction, he attends to the minutest details of his work here more than perhaps in his longer works. Being a novelist and a short story writer at the same time, Nair knows the difference between the two from the aesthetic point of view. What is perhaps passable in the bulk of a long narrative will not be overlooked or forgiven by the reader of short fiction. Here, the reader's focus is sharper than in the longer narrative; every word, every image, the rhythm of the language and the tone of the narrator, count. Nair proves an excellent craftsman in several of his short stories. He has effective control over the incidents described, but more remarkable than that is the close attention he pays to the choice of words, their sensuousness, their scent and their flavour. In stories where the events are not more important than the atmosphere conveyed, the lyrical element is predominant. Grief, resignation, helplessness, loneliness, isolation, nostalgia: these are some of the emotions most powerfully evoked by Vasudevan Nair as a master of short fiction. In the novels, perhaps, some of these may appear repetitious or belaboured, but within the controlled frame of the short story every word does its duty. There is tremendous economy. One word too many can easily spoil the ambience of a short story. Especially when the emotion is delicately evoked, there is no scope for elaboration or admixture of contrary sentiments. The poetics of the lyrical short story does not provide for laxity.

The earliest of the ten stories in this volume is "Kuttiedathi" (1962) and the latest is "Insight" (2000). The other stories in this volume were all written between these two dates. But it is difficult to say that they illustrate a linear development of the author's art or craft, each of them being a finished work at the date of its composition. As they cover nearly forty years of a successful career, it may be argued that together they constitute the high peaks of the author's creativity. Some of them like "Red Earth" are rather short, while some others like "When the Doors of Heaven Open" are fairly long. In the shorter tales the effort is only to evoke a single mood and the tone of narration does not change. Only one moment, one single context, is evoked in all its intensely sensuous power and passion. The central idea is not spelt out in so many words, but interiorised so that the reader has to get at that through indirect means. In "Red Earth" only a minimal space is devoted to the description of the event or its location; the emotional surge is impressionistically hinted at without straining after effect. A rich sense of ambiguity is slowly built up, by mixing fact with fantasy. The goddess of the legend, the ceremony that was disrupted, and the inner desolation of the locale are felt presences in the consciousness of the visiting lady tourist, to whom the whole enterprise takes on the dimensions of an oppressive experience. Within a minimal frame the story achieves its telling effect in a manner characteristic of the author. The same kind of artistry may be found in "Once Again in Search of a Refuge", where too the fleshy details are suppressed and the narration is kept to the bare minimum. The owner of the house, the manager, the neighbours, the maintenance workers etc. are there to provide the framework of the story, but the focus is on the mood of the loner seeking refuge. An unspecified locale, nondescript characters and expressionist sketching of people and objects help to suggest and evoke a certain mood of isolation and alienation without the aid of any incident as such to make the tale rooted. "Kuttiedathi", on the other hand, tells the sad story of an unmarried girl in an old taravad in decline, as told by a young boy, who is an eye-witness to the domestic tragedy leading to the suicide of the girl, but is too young to understand the nature and dimensions of the tragedy itself. The evil fate overhanging the erstwhile feudal Nair household in Malabar is a recurring theme in Nair's oeuvre, and he is an expert in the slow and sensitive delineation of the agonies of characters trapped in this situation. What with her dark complexion and the ugly wart disfiguring her, Kuttiedathi, as she is called by the boy, is earmarked for suffering and sacrifice. Her natural tendency to protest and prevail is offset by the conspiracy of circumstances, as it were. She ends up a victim of the socio-economic tensions of her milieu. A similar preoccupation on the part of the author with the tragedy inherent in the joint family system comes to the fore again in the longest story in this volume, "When the Doors of Heaven Open". The wry humour and irony built into this narrative about the death of the head of the family, which is expected by the relatives, but actually does not come off, since no one knows when the doors of heaven finally open, account for the elaboration of the story. Every relative had turned up, in spite of their heavy and busy schedule, but the patient did not oblige; he recovered to the consternation and relief of everyone assembled and now ready to leave one by one. The old man also understood their eagerness to leave, as nothing expected did happen and there was no need to stay any longer. His words sum up the denouement:

> Master cleared the phlegm in his throat and said softly: 'Are you listening? If I fall seriously ill again, don't send for the children. They've hundreds of things to do. No telegrams, no phone calls. Don't inform them till you're sure it's all over.

There is matter enough here for a novelette, but observing the unities of time, place and action, the author has tightened the structure of the narrative to close in on the focus. Vasudevan Nair knows where to end a story. His endings are generally subdued in tone, without high dramatics, but they make the reader look back once again at the casual beginnings of the narratives. Several of them are not along unexpected lines. Surprises are rare; normally he does not resort to clever tour de force. They story in its totality has its impact on the reader. Some stories may read like episodes in longer works of fiction but with a sense of finality. Some of them dramatise the tension in man-woman relationship. "Bondage", for instance illustrates a favourite theme of the author's, the pull in opposite directions, 'from one prison camp to another', as summed up at the end. "The Deluge" is narrated from the point of view of the suffering wife, who she discovers is cheated by her husband, who in turn goes about with his young secretary. The theme of marital infidelity is nothing new, but the surrealistic ending is especially effective here. In such stories an uncanny understanding of the psychology of women is displayed with delicacy and precision. The interior monologue of the central character is an effective technique in the absence of a hero to play the role of her counter-part. Triangular love relationship is a recurring theme in Vasudevan Nair's fiction, but it is given a subtle treatment in

"Insight", where the old woman gives a bit of advice to young Sudha to take her own bold decision in personal matters. True happiness does not depend on convention, but on one's own predilections. "The Sale" is another story that explores the loneliness syndrome of the business executive's life partner, left to fend for herself, when the boss is away on business trips for days on end. The stream of consciousness technique of narration helps to mix up ever so many disparate elements in the story. "Kadugannawa", subtitled "A travel note", is located mainly in Sri Lanka and is apparently about a journey in search of the past, but ends up without any discovery; all the same it takes on a metaphysical dimension in spite of the dense physical details of the trip to Kadugannawa and the search for the ancestor. Some stories highlight violence and cruelty. "The Enemy" in this selection, with its bizarre account of a visit to a jail, may come within this category. But in all of these stories as a rule the author cares to depict the subtle nuances of human emotions. The metaphors and poetic images strewn all over the narrative linger in the mind of the reader more than perhaps the situations, which invoke them. One may say that the reader's satisfaction is rooted in the artistic workmanship displayed in the small canvas of the short story as in a miniature painting. These features make Vasudevan Nair's short stories some of the best examples of lyrical narratives in Malayalam.

AYYAPPA PANIKER

Kuttiedathi

Valiamma, as I called my aunt, had two daughters, Kutti and Janu. Since they were older than me, I added *edathi*, elder sister, to their names, so they were Kuttiedathi and Januedathi to me. Kuttiedathi's real name was Malu and Valiamma called her that.

Januedathi was pretty and fair-skinned. Her arms, on which the veins showed blue, were as smooth as the tender core of the banana plant. If she came near you, you could smell the fragrance of sandalwood soap. Her *mundu* and blouse were always a sparkling white. But it was Kuttiedathi I liked more.

Kuttiedathi was dark-skinned. In Januedathi's opinion, you only had to touch her body if you wanted to apply collyrium to your eyes! The tips of two big teeth showed outside her mouth even when she was not smiling. If you held her hands, they were so rough, they felt like dry firewood. She always wore a dirty blouse with black dots. You never saw her wearing a mundu that was not stained with mud and soot. She smelt of soot, oil and clothes that were still damp because they had not been spread out properly to dry: odours that made you want to retch.

There's something I forgot: Kuttiedathi had a growth on her left earlobe, a fleshy protuberance as round and big as a pearl. I would gaze at it, fascinated, when she stood near me, or talked, or sat down to do her hair. It was I who always felt disgusted when she fingered it.

All the same, I liked Kuttiedathi.

No one else at home liked her. Valiamma scolded her whenever she caught sight of her. And always for the same reason: she was not disciplined, not modest. Valiamma would add an old saying to her tirade, that destructive weeds would turn any garden into a desert. And as if that was not enough:

'When you were born, even salt and water must have disappeared from the face of the earth!'

Perhaps because she was used to hearing this all the time, Kuttiedathi would laugh loudly. And that would infuriate Valiamma further. She would reach out for the thing nearest her—a kitchen knife or a wooden ladle—and brandish it, saying: 'Get out of my sight! My life was ruined from the moment this creature was conceived!'

Kuttiedathi hardly ever obeyed Valiamma. What she really liked was to play with me. We would sit behind the kitchen playing kothankallu, a game with pebbles, or she would dig into the earth and catch ant-lions for me. All this had to be done without Valiamma seeing us. We had to take care Amma didn't see us either. If Valiamma caught us, it was Kuttiedathi who was scolded, not me.

Valiamma would shout in a thundering voice: 'Malukutty!'

If there was no answer, the next shout would be: 'You wretched girl!'

'What's wrong with you, Amma?' Kuttiedathi would ask, annoyed.

'You're grown up now. Is it any wonder that no one comes to marry you?'

Kuttiedathi could not run around playing with me. It would harm her reputation, no one would come to marry her!

Valiamma would never scold me; she would advise me.

'Vasu, you're a boy, you shouldn't hang around with this girl.' She had a wise saying for me as well. Prosperity would not come to a house where people played games all the time.

Kuttiedathi could never sit quietly in a place. She quarrelled with everyone. Every day she'd return from the bathing tank after having done something mischievous. She'd thrown Anthurath

Meenakshi Amma's silver dish into the water! She'd beaten up Chummu Kutty! She'd splashed water on Mukami Amma, who was scared of water! The list went on like that. No matter how many times Amma and Valiamma told her not to, she'd draw water from the well in the month of Thulam, an inauspicious thing to do!

In the afternoons, Kuttiedathi would wander through the *illam* compound, go to Kali's hut and through Amina Umma's courtyard and then go back home. She could not wander around like that, she was a grown-up girl, of marriageable age! Valiamma told her so, so did Amma. Valiamma thrashed her with a tamarind twig until it broke. But Kuttiedathi would not stop wandering around.

Valiamma usually had a nap in the corridor after lunch. Amma would be in the northern room. Januedathi's room was upstairs. After lunch she would chew betel leaves, redden her lips, sit down on the window seat and sing the ballad, 'Sarojini's Cruel Deed.' She sang it softly. Januedathi could read and write. Whenever she quarrelled with Kuttiedathi, she'd say,

'Kuttiedathi, remember, I'm educated!'

Occasionally I went up to Januedathi's room. Whenever she was not reading her book of ballads, she would sit in front of the mirror, twisting her hair into curls and pressing them down over her forehead. If I touched her by chance, she would shout, 'The rascal has made me dirty!'

I could not touch her bed, or her song book, or the mirror placed on the big wooden box, or her *chandu* bottle or her collyrium container. Actually I went upstairs only to look at Januedathi's collyrium container. It was a lovely thing, with a little mirror the size of a quarter-anna on its lid. But the moment I entered the room, Januedathi would be alarmed. 'You scamp, stop it ... don't touch this, you brat ... you'll upset that now!'

Why couldn't she call me by my name? It wasn't 'scamp' or 'brat'! Kuttiedathi always called me my name. She would call me lovingly, stretching out the name: 'Basu-o!' I loved hearing her call me that.

The moment Kuttiedathi entered the room, Januedathi

would start shouting for Valiamma. Whatever Kuttiedathi touched, Januedathi would scream—according to her, Kuttiedathi ruined anything she touched. Valiamma would say, 'Isn't she younger than you, girl?'

Kuttiedathi had an answer to that: 'Am I not older than her?'

One day Kuttiedathi took a gold-bordered *veshti* off the clothesline and draped it around herself. Januedathi could not bear to look at her.

'You've smeared soot all over it. My God, what will I wear now when I go to Ariyambadath?'

Kuttiedathi held out her palms and asked, 'Where's the soot on my hands?'

Paying no attention, Januedathi screamed louder:

'Amma, she's dirtied my veshti all over!'

'What am I, a low-caste woman?'

'Who knows?'

'Look at this beauty!'

Kuttiedathi took off the veshti, crumpled it and threw it contemptuously at Januedathi's face. I said to myself, 'Well done. She deserves that!'

'What do you lose if I'm a beauty, Kuttiedathi?'

'Don't put on airs with me. I'll hammer your face till you're dead!'

Januedathi quietened down at once. If Kuttiedathi threatened to beat someone, she would.

'Come on, Basu-o.' Kuttiedathi caught hold of my hand and walked off.

We went straight to the mango tree north of the illam compound. Everyone at the illam would be asleep. This was the right time to throw stones at the mangoes.

'Shall we bring down some mangoes?'

'Can you aim stones at them, Kuttiedathi?'

'Why can't I?'

'Can girls throw stones at mangoes?'

'All right, watch out now!'

I was excited. I had thought only boys could throw stones

at mangoes and bring them down. I started to pick up the kind of stones she would need. She said:

'If we throw stones, we'll make a noise. We'll manage with sticks.'

If we made a noise, Kunju Namboodiri would come out and shout at us. He was very mean. He never allowed people to pick up even the mangoes that had fallen on the ground.

Kuttiedathi broke off some twigs.

'Step aside.'

I moved aside respectfully. Kuttiedathi took aim and threw the twig at the tree. How high it went! Even Thupran couldn't have thrown it that high. In those days, Thupran was the one who could throw the highest among the people I knew.

But no mangoes fell down. Kuttiedathi threw the stick again and again. The fourth time it caught on a branch. I looked at Kuttiedathi sadly. What would we do now?

Kuttiedathi was furious.

'Basu-o, climb up that *azhu* tree there. Tell me when that Namboodiri steps into the yard.'

I went up the short azhu tree obediently and kept watch. What was Kuttiedathi going to do? She looked around, hitched up her mundu, tied the ends firmly around her waist and started to climb the mango tree.

I hadn't expected her to go that far!

I stood on the top of the azhu tree and looked in turns at the front yard of the illam and the mango tree. Kuttiedathi was scampering up like a squirrel. Januedathi should see her now, I thought. All she knew was how to put a *pottu* on her forehead and read 'Sarojini's Cruel Deed.' She couldn't climb trees or pluck mangoes.

'Look, Basu-o!'

I saw Kuttiedathi sitting on a branch, swinging her legs and laughing. I couldn't help clapping my hands gleefully. Kuttiedathi plucked mangoes and threw them down at a spot covered by dead leaves, to muffle the sound.

At that moment I heard a laugh on the other side of the

clump of bamboos. I turned and saw Kutty Narayanan. Kuttiedathi pretended she hadn't see him.

'The girl climbed a tree! The girl climbed a tree!' he shouted. What was wrong with him?

But he was like that. Kuttiedathi came down the tree, unruffled. She pulled the ends of her mundu down and gathered the mangoes. Kutty Narayanan continued to shout:

'The girl climbed a tree! The girl climbed a tree!'

I prayed: 'God, don't let Kunju Namboodiri hear!' Kuttiedathi wrapped the mangoes in teak leaves, handed them to me and went straight up to Kutty Narayanan. She didn't say anything, she just slapped his face.

He deserved it. What if women climbed trees? Evidently he was wondering how to take revenge. Kuttiedathi must have realised this. She raised her hand and said:

'Stupid buffalo! Get away!'

Kutty Narayanan took her advice and ran.

However, the matter came up before Valiamma. There were two changes. One, Kuttiedathi had climbed the mango tree. Two, she had slapped Kutty Narayanan, a man!

'Malukutty, did you climb a tree?'

'I did.'

'You did, girl?'

'I did. So what?'

Frightened, I went close to Amma, pretending I knew nothing.

'You're a grown up girl. Do you know that?'

Kuttiedathi was silent.

'There are no elders in this house, but you must at least fear the pillars that support the roof.'

There was no reply to that either.

'I'll teach you to behave properly.'

Then came the sound of blows. One, two, three.

'Will you climb a tree again?'

One, two, three …

'Will you fight with boys?'

One, two, three …

I covered my ears with my hands and stepped into the yard. I couldn't bear it. When I went in after some time, Valiamma was in the courtyard of the *nalukettu*, leaning against a pillar, sobbing and talking to herself.

'Oh Guruvayoorappa! That a creature like this should have been born in this *taravad!*' Valiamma saw me standing there hesitantly and called out to me. I went up to her, full of fear. But she clasped me to her and wept.

'You're a boy, little one ... It's you who'll be the master of the house tomorrow.'

I extricated myself and went to Amma. Amma was wiping her eyes as well. Why had Valiamma wept? Not a day passed without her weeping. Amma explained: Valiamma has no one of her own.

Valiamma had no one. She had no money. My mother had a son. And my father sent her money every month.

It made Amma sad to think of Valiamma. When Amma talked about her, there would be a catch in her voice. One night she told me many things. Valiamma was Thazhevalappu Kuttan Nair's wife. Kuttan Nair was the head of a big joint family. He was a businessman. Valiamma used to stay at Thazhevalappu. When she visited her own house, she travelled in a palanquin.

Amma was a child at the time. She went to stay with Valiamma at Thazhevalappu. The Thazhevalappu folk made a gold necklace with a pendant for Amma. Valiamma stayed on the first floor of the main wing of the house. She never came downstairs. No one ever went against her wishes. The local people liked Valiamma. When she went to the tank for a bath, a person would walk in front of her carrying a large boat-shaped dish containing three measures of oil. The oil would be poured out for anyone who wanted it. On festival days, she would distribute clothes to those who needed it and money to the others.

'How generous she used to be with gifts!' Amma would say.

But Valiamma's prosperous times came to a sudden end. One night, Kuttan Nair came back from work with hiccups. While eating, he threw up. He died at midnight.

Kuttiedathi was three years old then. Januedathi was not yet a year old.

The next morning, Kuttan Nair's nephew took charge of the keys of the house. Even before the body was cremated, Valiamma was sent back to her house with the maidservant, Paru. Amma remembered her coming home with the two children, followed by Paru carrying a bundle of clothes.

'How generous she used to be with gifts, child! It's all her destiny!'

I stole a glance at Valiamma, sitting with her head buried between her knees.

It was then that I thought of Kuttiedathi. She was not anywhere downstairs. When I went upstairs, I heard a sob from the room used for the Bhuvaneshwari puja. It was dark there even in the daytime.

I entered hesitantly.

'Kuttiedathi ...'

There was no answer.

'Kuttiedathi ...'

I went up to her, put my hand on her shoulder and asked: 'Did Valiamma beat you a lot?'

'H'm...h'm...' she grunted, between sobs.

'Did it hurt very much?'

'H'm...h'm...' She shook her head to say 'no'.

'Then why are you crying, Kuttiedathi?'

Kuttiedathi put her arms around me, laid her cheek on mine and said, 'I won't cry.'

I lay with my head on her breast, wet with sweat and tears, and sobbed as well.

'Does Basu like Kuttiedathi?'

'Yes.'

'No one likes Kuttiedathi.'

Her tears fell on my face.

I often asked myself: did no one like Kuttiedathi? Valiamma scolded her, sometimes hit her. My mother scolded her too. And Januedathi hated her. Maybe it was because Kuttiedathi was dark-skinned. Or because she had that wart on her earlobe.

No one scolded Januedathi. They said a nice young man would come to marry her.

Valiamma liked Januedathi more. Whenever she went to Thirunavaya to have a dip in the holy river on new moon day, it was Januedathi she would take with her. Once, when Valiamma was going to Ariyambadam to see the *koothu* dance in the temple, Kuttiedathi wanted to go with her. Valiamma scolded her: 'Can't you stay quietly in your corner, girl?'

After that Kuttiedathi would never go with her even if she was invited. Valiamma asked her to go along when she went to see Vadekkathi Parvathy Amma's baby son, to visit Cholayil Valiamma when she was ill, to see the festival of lamps at the Ayyappan temple in Kalayakkalam. But Kuttiedathi refused to go. She said: 'Amma doesn't think I'm pretty enough to accompany her.'

If she heard her say that, Valiamma would lose her temper and begin to curse. 'You wretch, not even grass will grow where you stand!'

Kuttiedathi was not afraid of curses. Or even of evil spirits, not even the most troublesome of them, the Brahmarakshas. Being Kuttiedathi's disciple, I was very brave too. She had given me instructions on what to do if I encountered any spririts. If it was a Brahmarakshas, I had to throw a stone at it without turning back to look. For other evil spirits, I had to chant 'Narayana Namah!', Hail, Lord Narayana! Three times loudly. Narayana's name would drive away any evil spirit.

But I was afraid of the goddess Bhagavathi. Bhagavathi lived in the attic. You could not walk by the attic if you had been polluted by the touch of lower castes. You could not take fish that side. You could not lie down in front of the attic door. If you did anything that displeased the Bhagavathi—it was fearsome even to think of—the Mother Goddess would scatter seeds over you. This meant that you would catch small pox!

Only I could enter the attic. Tuesdays and Fridays, it was I who lit the lamp there and burned camphor. Little girls who had not come of age could go in and so could old women. Other women were not allowed to enter.

Once Kuttiedathi opened the door, went into the attic, drained out the oil from the lamp and rubbed it into her hair. Valiamma caught her doing this.

'You've polluted everything. What are you doing, Malutty?'

'Why Amma ... you know there's no oil at home.'

Placing her hands on her head in despair, Valiamma said: 'You'll ruin the place with your waywardness. What's the use of saying anything? The house is falling to pieces, that's all!'

Valiamma had a Namboodiri perform a purification ceremony the same day. In spite of this, she lived in fear the next few days, wondering what calamities would befall them.

Everyone believed that Bhagavathi had hidden away treasure in the attic. Appukutta Panicker would come, cast his cowrie shells and say: 'This house has a *Chovva,* the planet Mars. By Chovva here, I mean the Bhagavathi. She has great powers. She can turn a violent storm into a whiff of mist. There is treasure here. This is a taravad blessed with good fortune.'

One day, Kuttiedathi made preparations to get at this good fortune. She said to me, 'We must dig up the attic.'

I trembled. Imagine digging up the attic, where Bhagavathi dwelt!

'Don't be scared, boy. You keep watch. Let's find out if there's any treasure.'

The thought of the Mother Goddess scattering her seeds drained me of all strength.

'Bhagavathi's ...'

'Why would Bhagavathi need treasure?'

When I thought it over, I felt she was right. It served no purpose for the treasure to lie there, under the floor. While we could do many things with it. But would Bhagavathi let us go unpunished?

'Wouldn't it be a sin?'

'Who's going to take away the treasure, fellow? Treasure indeed! It's just a lie. We have to dig up the ground. And then, when that Panicker comes here again with his bag of cowrie shells, I'll show him ...'

Kuttiedathi's plans were not going to do anyone any good.

She was not even allowed to enter the attic. If women who had periods went in, everything would be polluted. And to dig up the floor of the attic! I could not sleep at night, thinking of it. But I couldn't tell anyone. If I did, Kuttiedathi would be thrashed.

Kuttiedathi decided to dig up the attic floor on the day Amma and Valiamma went to the temple. I had to keep watch. What if Januedathi saw? She would tell Amma. Then, in addition to Bhagavathi's punishment, Amma would punish Kuttiedathi as well.

'Januedathi will sneak on you.'

'I'll thrash her!'

I was convinced a great calamity would befall the house in three days' time. The Friday that was coming was a festival day. Kuttiedathi would be annoyed if I didn't keep watch when she dug up the attic floor. I was afraid of her.

But Kuttiedathi did not dig up the attic floor. The reason was that our uncle, Govinda Ammaman, came that morning. Amma and Valiamma put off their visit to the temple. I was relieved.

Govinda Ammaman was our great-uncle and the head of the joint family. He had moved away to live by himself after the property had been divided. He visited us once a month. It was his ancestral home, after all. Govinda Ammaman was very old and deaf as well. You had to talk to him very loudly. Whenever he came, he would sit in the portico for a long time. If Karuppan was working in the garden, he would call him and ask him to pluck a bunch of ripe areca nuts. He would give him two nuts as a present. Then he would ask:

'Karuppa, do you remember, this taravad once had one hundred and twenty-four members?'

Karuppan would answer in a loud voice: 'Yes, yes. The cattle shed used to be there, in front of the grain house. Your humble servant, Karuppan, was only as old as the young master at that time.' He would point to me as he said that.

Govinda Ammaman never tired of talking about the past. I'd heard so many times: the outhouse used to stand at the spot where banana and drumstick trees grew now. That pit there was made when the old kitchen well was filled up. There used to be a storeroom where Valiamma's hen-coop stands now.

He would step down into the front yard and walk up and down three or four times. Then he would lean over the wall, take a look at the grounds and say, addressing no one in particular.

'It's time the banana tree was transplanted.'

No one paid him any attention. It seemed as if he himself was not concerned that anyone should pay him attention.

'The roof has to be redone.'

If Karuppan was nearby, he would murmur assent.

'Karuppan!'

'Your humble servant is here.'

'Do you know, the master who taught the children lived there, in that room?' He would point to a room on the ground floor. 'All the Nair children in the neighbourhood came here to learn to read and write.'

Amma and Valiamma would have finished making lunch by then. I had often heard Valiamma say:

'The old man comes here only to have a square meal.'

Govinda Ammaman had no money. But he would never talk about it. He would talk of past glories all the time. After lunch, he would lie down on the verandah on a rush mat. Just before he left, he would fling a question into the house:

'Everything all right? Nothing special, is there?'

No one would answer.

'I'm going.'

Often, there would be no one around and he would take leave of the darkness in the house.

Sometimes, as he stepped into the yard, he would call Amma in a soft voice: 'Unnimaya, come here.'

Amma would go up to him.

He would whisper to her, as if he was speaking of some family matter. Amma would go in, return with an eight anna coin and give it to him. He would tuck it into a fold of his mundu at the waist and walk away, making a rat-tat sound with his stick on the ground.

Valiamma would scold Amma: 'Why do you give him money every time he asks? Don't you know it's all wasted in Pangodan's toddy shop?'

'After all, he's the head of the family,' Amma would reply.

The day the attic floor was to be dug up, Govinda Ammaman arrived early. As he climbed noisily up the steps, Amma called out:

'Malutty, bring water in the bell-metal pot.'

Kuttiedathi, who was busy thinking of how best to dig up the attic, cursed as she brought the water. Govinda Ammaman washed his feet, fanned himself with the towel and said, 'How hot it is, even in the morning!'

As usual, Amma asked from behind the door:

'You're coming from home, aren't you?'

'Yes, yes; it's so hot!'

'The children all right?'

'Quite all right.'

Having done her duty, Amma went to the kitchen.

Valiamma cursed. 'The old man has to arrive just as we think of going to the temple!'

Govinda Ammaman paced up and down the yard, came back and sat down. He called out:

'Is Narayani there? Tell her to come here.'

Valiamma came to the door.

'Kuttunnair had come from Perumannur yesterday. To talk about that other matter.'

Valiamma grunted.

'The boy has some land. His father's a Namboodiri. He owns a bit of land with about fifty coconut trees ...' Govinda Ammaman thought for a while, then asked: 'How old is the girl?'

'Malutty's nineteen. Janu will be sixteen in the month of Kanni.'

'Hm ... that's all right. They'll be here the day after tomorrow.'

Valiamma was anxious. She asked her elder brother. 'Won't you be here, *Oppa*?'

'Eh?'

Valiamma asked in a louder voice:

'I was asking, Oppa, won't you be here?'

'I'm busy. But how can I not come when it's so important? I'll be here.'

Valiamma said in an unsteady voice, 'Oppa, it won't go through unless you take an interest.'

'What fate decrees will happen. There's no use making a fuss before things are decided.'

When Govinda Ammaman left that day, Valiamma took a rupee from Amma and gave it to him. And she said to Amma:

'The old man's quite affectionate.'

I asked Amma when she was in a good mood, 'Are we having visitors?'

'Someone's coming to see your Kuttiedathi. A proposal of marriage!'

I searched for Kuttiedathi, found her and said, 'Someone's coming to marry you, Kuttiedathi.'

Kuttiedathi laughed and said, 'Go on, you scamp!'

'No Kuttiedathi, it's the truth. Amma told me.'

The day the visitors were expected, I was happy. Valiamma advised Kuttiedathi in the morning.

'Be quiet and well-behaved. Don't let them see your pranks.'

Kuttiedathi had a bath in the morning. She wore a freshly washed mundu with a coloured border and blouse with red and blue dots. She placed a large red round mark on her forehead with *sindooram.*

I made fun of her. 'Look at Kuttiedathi, what airs she's putting on!'

Januedathi chanted in a singsong voice, as if reading a lesson:

'Will the crow turn into a white crane if it bathes?'

Kuttiedathi did not scold her or slap her. Unusually, it was Valiamma who rebuked Januedathi. 'Get away! What a thing to say!'

Januedathi remarked, as soon as Valiamma went away: 'They can't but like you, Kuttiedathi.'

'Go on, say whatever you like!'

'You just have to take off the wart on your earlobe!'

I was certain Januedathi would get a slap then. But all Kuttiedathi did was look out of the window and say softly, 'Janu, wasn't it God who gave it to me?'

Three others came besides Govinda Ammaman. The reed mat with the picture of a tiger, borrowed from the neighbours, was spread on the floor. Coffee and snacks were served. While they were relaxing after coffee, I peered at them through the wooden bars of the window, taking care not to make noise.

Which one would marry Kuttiedathi?

Only one of them wore a shirt. He's the one, I decided, the one with the shirt.

Govinda Ammaman called out, 'Bring us water to wash our mouths.'

Valiamma seemed to have been waiting for that signal. She filled a small bell-metal pot with water, placed it in Kuttiedathi's hands and said softly, 'Go on.'

Kuttiedathi put the pot down at the edge of the verandah abutting the portico and came back.

They sat there a long time, talking. Then they left. Govinda Ammaman left with them.

He came again after a week. Valiamma ran up to him. 'What did they say?'

'It didn't work out.'

He went on. 'Says he saw the younger one. If it's her, he'll agree ...'

Valiamma was silent for some time.

'What do you say, Narayani?'

'It's not right, is it, to get the younger one married while the older one's still at home?'

'That's true. It's never happened in our family. All the same ...'

Valiamma wiped her eyes with the end of her mundu.

Govinda Ammaman said: 'We can't be so particular. If we can manage one, at least that's over.'

Valiamma thought it over. 'No, Oppa. Someone else will come along if it's in her destiny.'

I realised the one who'd worn a shirt had not liked Kuttiedathi. When I went upstairs, Kuttiedathi was sitting in the dark.

'Kuttiedathi!' I called out hesitantly.

'What is it, Basu-o?'

'Won't he come back?'

'No, he won't. No one will come.'

Govinda Ammaman came again next month with some other people. That day too, Kuttiedathi had a bath, put collyrium in her eyes and a sindooram mark on her forehead. She took out the mundu with the coloured border and the dotted blouse. And went to the verandah with a pot of water.

As soon as they went away, Kuttiedathi went upstairs and began to weep.

A few days later, there was Govinda Ammaman again. And with him were some more people. But Kuttiedathi's mood had changed.

'I'm not going to the verandah.'

'What?'

'No one need come to see me.'

'Malutty!' Valiamma ground her teeth.

'I'll not go, not even if you kill me!'

'Malutty! My little one! I've made an offering to the Goddess.'

'I won't go!'

'This will work out.'

Kuttiedathi's voice rose. 'Will you keep quiet, Amma, and go away?'

Valiamma threatened her: 'You wretch, at this rate you'll turn old and grey, sitting here.'

'Let me turn grey then!'

Valiamma and Amma took turns to coax her. But she would not agree.

Valiamma caught her by her hair and gave her a few blows on her head. Amma intervened. 'Edathi, there are strangers outside.'

Waiting for the water to be brought to the verandah, Govinda Ammaman called out again. Valiamma went up to the door and said in an unsteady voice, 'Malutty's having her periods.'

No sooner did the visitors leave than Valiamma caught hold of Kuttiedathi and began to thrash her. After putting up with it for a while, Kuttiedathi pushed Valiamma's hands away and said, 'Don't touch me!'

'I'll cure your insolence!'

'I'll get myself a length of rope …'

'Get it over and done with then!'

Valiamma dragged Kuttiedathi along the floor by her hair, then began to thrash her again. Amma intervened once more and caught hold of Valiamma's hands.

'Don't kill the creature, Edathi.'

'I'm going to die!' said Kuttiedathi.

'Let her die!'

Amma freed Kuttiedathi from Valiamma's grip. Kuttiedathi sat down on the western end of the verandah, leaned against the pillar and sobbed. I felt very sad. What a thrashing Kuttiedathi had got!

I went up to her and said, 'Kuttiedathi!'

'Get lost!' Kuttiedathi was angry.

'Kuttiedathi!'

'I told you to go away!'

I could not bear it. I sat down near her and began to weep. Kuttiedathi laid me down on her lap, stroked my back and said, 'Kuttiedathi's going to hang herself!'

Kuttiedathi mustn't die. If she died …

I said, 'No, you mustn't.'

'I'll hang myself from the beam one day. Only then will they learn …'

I lay with my head on her lap, silent, full of fear.

'Basu-o, go away!'

I didn't go away. Supposing I went away and Kuttiedathi hanged herself!

Valiamma did not talk to Kuttiedathi for days. Kuttiedathi would wander around the neighbourhood all day. She would come to the kitchen when it was time to eat. Valiamma would serve out something on a plate and say, 'Here, lick it up!'

Amma advised Kuttiedathi: 'You're a grown-up girl. You shouldn't loaf around like this.' Kuttiedathi paid no attention.

Januedathi gave her a nickname: 'The loafing officer.'

One day, there was a heavy downpour. Kuttiedathi didn't go out anywhere. In the afternoon, she called me and said, 'Go and get that mirror.'

While I was bringing her the mirror, Januedathi asked, 'Who's the mirror for, boy?'

'For Kuttiedathi.'

'Tell her to look well at her beauty!'

I scolded Januedathi wordlessly as I walked away with the mirror.

Kuttiedathi looked at her face in the mirror. She combed her hair with a broken comb, wiped her face with the edge of her mundu. She bent sideways, felt the wart on her earlobe and asked, 'Basu-o, will Kuttiedathi look prettier if the wart on her earlobe goes away?'

'Will it go?'

'It will. I'll show you a trick. Go and get the kitchen knife.'

I brought her the knife. She sharpened it against the stone ledge of the drain. She took the spittoon kept in a corner of the room, placed it near the bed and closed the door.

'Don't tell anyone ...'

What was this? I couldn't understand. Kuttiedathi lay down on her side on the bed and said, 'Move the spittoon a little nearer.'

I obeyed.

I watched, dazed, while Kuttiedathi moved the knife towards her ear. I trembled all over and placed my hands over my eyes.

'Am...mm...e!' When I opened my eyes, hearing Kuttiedathi cry out, I saw blood dripping from her ear. I screamed, 'Amme, come quickly!' Even as she pressed her writhing head into the pillow, Kuttiedathi gave me an angry look.

Amma, Valiamma and Januedathi came running. Kuttiedathi lay there, refusing to raise her head. There was blood on the floor, in the spittoon, on the bed, everywhere.

Valiamma kept saying, 'The wretched girl … the wretch …'

Amma prayed: 'Guruvayoorappa!' She wet a piece of cloth and pressed it to Kuttiedathi's ear. Valiamma sent Karuppan to Vannan nanu, the local medicine man, to get herbs to heal the wound.

It took nearly seven days for the wound to heal. I saw it when they peeled off the layer of herbal paste they had put on it. The wart had not gone. It hung down by a thin strand of skin. Kuttiedathi looked at it in the mirror only once. The next moment the mirror lay on the floor, shattered. I saw the tears coursing down her cheeks as she stormed noisily out of the room.

Kuttiedathi stopped talking, she hardly spoke even to me. She no longer called me when she went out in the afternoons. If I tried to go with her, she would say, 'Don't come!'

I did not have the courage to disobey her.

One day I had gone to the compound above ours to look for fallen mangoes. It was the middle of the afternoon. When I stepped into the lane, I heard Kuttiedathi's laughter from the serpent shrine. I was surprised to discover Kuttiedathi talking to Appunni.

Appunni was the son of an old woman who lived in a little house near ours. I hated him. I couldn't bear to look at his face. One of his eyes looked like a dead fish that had surfaced on the water. Appunni was a stone mason. He always wore a mundu the colour of red laterite.

Appunni hurried away as I walked up to them. Kuttiedathi asked me angrily: 'Why have you come here?'

'Why have you come, Kuttiedathi?'

'To perform your father's funeral rites!'

I was ready to cry. Hadn't she sworn at me? Kuttiedathi understood.

'Don't cry. I was only teasing you. Don't tell anyone, child.'

'I will! I'll tell everyone what you said about my father!'

'It was *my* father I was talking about. But it's not that. Don't tell them anything else.'

'What else?'

'That ... that I was talking to Appunni. Will you?'

'No.'

I didn't tell. I saw Kuttiedathi talking to Appunni many afternoons, standing behind the serpent shrine. One day Kuttiedathi said Appunni was a good man ... he had bought her glass bangles. She had hidden them in her soap box.

'Will you tell?'

'I won't.'

'I'll get you a rubber ball.'

'Where will you get it?'

'I'll tell someone to bring it.'

'Whom will you ask?'

'There's someone ...' Kuttiedathi put her arms around me and kissed my cheek.

It was dusk. I was seated on the verandah, leaning against the pillar, telling my prayers. Amma was busy in the kitchen. Valiamma was on the verandah cleaning the glass shade of the hurricane lamp. Karuppan came and stood at the gate, scratching his head.

Valiamma asked, 'What is it, Karuppan?'

'I've something to tell you, Mistress.'

'Tell me, Karuppan.'

'You mustn't misunderstand me, Mistress.'

'What is it, Karuppan?'

'This humble servant feels distressed to tell you. I saw something. All the Mistress need do is take heed of what I say.'

'What is it. Karuppan? What?'

'I saw the older young Mistress and that mason Appunni talking to each other. It didn't look proper to me.'

'She's betrayed us!' Valiamma sprang up as if she'd been stung by a scorpion. 'Guruvayoorappa! What calamity will this wretched creature bring upon us!'

Valiamma went in and roared in a voice like thunder: 'Malutty!'

Kuttiedathi appeared.

Suppressing her tears. Valiamma said, 'At least until I'm taken out to be cremated ...' She could not complete the sentence.

'What is it, Amma?'

'You ... haven't you ruined the family's reputation?'

'What are you saying, Amma?'

'What business have you talking to that Appunni?' Kuttiedathi did not say anything. Valiamma gave her two resounding slaps on each cheek. Then screamed:

'Speak. You slut!'

Kuttiedathi did not say anything.

'We'll have to listen to unspeakable things because of you. If you step into the yard from now on, you'll be dead!'

Kuttiedathi rubbed her cheeks and went upstairs not even crying. While Valiamma muttered, 'There may be no men here, but you must respect at least the wooden pillars that hold up our family house.'

After that, Kuttiedathi was not permitted to go out of the house. She lay in one of the rooms upstairs, talking to no one. She would answer no questions. She would not come and play with me.

One evening at dusk, Kuttiedathi was seen at the fence talking to someone. It was Januedathi who saw her. Januedathi said slyly, 'I saw you.'

'What if you saw me?'

'You should be ashamed, talking to low caste people ...'

'Don't try to improve my morals.'

They continued to argue and Januedathi brought up the incident of Kuttiedathi having cut off the wart on her ear. She called Kuttiedathi a black creature. Januedathi was about to be given a slap when Valiamma rushed up.

'What are you doing, you wretch, at this auspicious twilight hour?'

Januedathi wept as she told her: all this was because she had seen Kuttiedathi standing at the fence, talking to a man. Was that her, Janu's fault?

Valiamma placed her hands on her head and sank down on the floor in despair. Amma muttered, 'The family will be disgraced.'

Valiamma suddenly picked up a broom that was lying in a corner and began to hit Kuttiedathi all over her body with it.

'Either change your ways or die!'

I thought she would kill Kuttiedathi and, terrified, I wound my arms tightly around Amma.

'Speak up, you wretch! Will I have to listen to such things again?'

Blows rained on her again.

'Don't hit Kuttiedathi,' I said to my mother, crying.

'She deserves it, the slut!'

Kuttiedathi did not cry. She held on to the door and writhed as the blows rained on her.

More blows.

'Will I hear such things again?'

Another blow.

'I'll die ...'

'Die then, wretch!'

'I'll take my life ...'

'Die, you wretch!'

The broom came apart and the broomsticks scattered. Valiamma screamed, fell on the ground and began to wail loudly.

I had buried my face in Amma's breast. When I looked up, I saw Kuttiedathi still clinging to the door and murmuring, with her eyes closed: 'I'll die ...'

There was neither sound nor movement in the house that night. Kuttiedathi lay on her face on a mat in the corridor.

Valiamma did not eat. Amma called Kuttiedathi to eat, but she said she did not want anything. Januedathi said she too did not want anything in that case. Neither did I. Amma tried to persuade me to eat. I would not. Unexpectedly, Amma gave me a slap on my thigh. I was waiting for a reason—bursting into tears. I ran and fell on Kuttiedathi's mat. Kuttiedathi asked in a tired voice: 'Did you eat, Basu-o?'

'I don't want anything.'

Amma came up and asked me to go to sleep. I said angrily, full of bitterness, 'I'm sleeping here.'

Kuttiedathi held me in a tight embrace.

I heard the front door and the kitchen door being shut. The lights went out. I could not sleep. I felt Kuttiedathi was awake as well. Lying close to her, I could hear her sobbing. Lying in the darkness with my eyes wide open for a long time, I called softly: 'Kuttiedathi!'

'Go to sleep.'

'Did it hurt a lot?'

'No. Go to sleep.'

I snuggled against her breast, wet with tears.

'You must be a good boy, Basu. You must look after Amma and Valiamma.'

I grunted. Kuttiedathi's fingers beat a tattoo on my back.

'Sleep, little one. Sleep ...'

Gradually, my eyes closed.

I woke up with a start as day broke, hearing the sound of wailing. Rubbing my eyes. I sat up and saw Amma and Valiamma weeping, their hands on their heads. Januedathi was crying too, holding Valiamma close. Frightened, I looked around. Kuttiedathi's body swung from the rafter at the end of a rope.

Bondage

From a distance, he had seen the railway gate lying wide open. But by the time he reached it, it had closed. He stopped the car and silently cursed with no one particular in mind. His resentful eyes followed the gateman who, unconcerned, not even looking at his car, was going to close the gate on the opposite side.

He could not even hear the sound of the train. He looked at his watch. It was twenty past six.

He had wanted to start early. It was Saturday, so he had been free in the afternoon. But he had felt like taking a nap after lunch, although he knew it would ruin his evening. He had gone to bed at two thirty the night before and woken up at five thirty. However late he went to bed, he always woke up at five thirty. It had become a habit, a relic of childhood when he had been frightened of even the wooden pillars in the house. When he woke up, he had stood at the window, his eyes misted with distress. He had seen the bright yellow sunlight fade and a light drizzle begin to fall, becoming a downpour in minutes. How quickly nature's emotions changed!

He had toyed with the idea of not going. Spending a Sunday in the city meant having the entire day with Miss D'Souza. As he listened to the sweet, sad melodies of "When the swallows fly back to Capistrano," "Black Moon" and "April Love", the softness and fragrance of her body would make him heady.

But when he remembered that he had let three Saturdays go

by while the darkness of many moonless nights melted into the circles around his pregnant wife's listless eyes, he decided to go.

It was in a spirit of sacrifice that he stepped into the car. He had set out on his journey and had to reach home as fast as possible. He always felt he was in a hurry to get there.

He would be reluctant to start, would cook up excuses for not going from the shadowy corners of his mind and line them up before him. But when he finally decided to go, he would suddenly feel impatient. His wife was waiting for him, his little daughter was waiting. He had to rush, leaving behind the twisting roads and teeming crowds of a city that became noisy at dusk.

Someone called out from the car parked next to him: 'Hello, Sir!'

He turned. It was the tile factory owner he had met when he arrived last year in the city.

'Hello!' He waved and smiled.

He did not hear what the man said because of the roar of the approaching train. He might have asked, 'Are you going home?' He nodded, smiling feebly. It could mean yes or no.

It was a goods train which moved as slowly as boring days and nights succeeding each other. The frightening screech of the wheels over the iron rails seemed to crash into the stone embankments on either side.

The gate opened after an age had gone by. Behind him was a sea of vehicles and pedestrians. If the car didn't start now when he switched on the engine ... he started it with a warning. The little car had obeyed him like a slave the last seven years. But it had showed signs of trouble of late. The engine throbbed into life. It was very noisy. The shock absorbers had worn out.

He had a sudden doubt as he reached the city limits—did he need petrol? He had about seven or eight litres and had to go twenty-seven miles. What if he had difficulty on the return journey? He stopped at the next petrol bunk and put in ten litres. When he put his hand into his pocket to take out his purse, he remembered the medicine. The prescription had been in his wallet for days. Then he had put it away in the drawer of his table. If he wanted it now, he would have to go back four miles, open two doors and the drawer. No.

His wife would probably ask him when he got home, 'Did you bring Baby's medicine?' He would have to tell her some kind of lie. 'It's not available anywhere. Ask the doctor to give you a prescription for another tonic.'

It was easy to make a lie work. His face would shine with honesty when he told one. Nature had endowed him with the mask of a calm face and eyes filled with innocence. When he was a child, his mother used to tell her friends:

'Kesu is the most innocent of my children.'

Bharathi would not wonder why a tonic so commonly prescribed for children was not available in this great city. She believed everyone implicitly. Her life consisted of breathing in beliefs in many things. She believed that it had been a sacrifice on his part to marry her. She thought of him as a great man: in spite of having had every opportunity to marry a woman with beauty, he had made this sacrifice. Perhaps she also believed he loved her more than the coconut grove in its prime situated on thirty-two acres of land on the seashore. May the links of her faith never be broken, he thought.

Two people he knew waved to him from a stationwagon that came up from the opposite side. He had made acquaintances only after he came to this city. He had no friends. This had been the case even in other places where he had worked. He never associated with groups. He did not make much conversation. And so, in the eyes of other people, he was considered an innocent, a good person.

He could see a halo of dignity taking shape around him because of the way he kept aloof. He always appeared very simply dressed in clubs and at parties. He spoke little and with profound calm. All the same, he wove a web of magic with words effortlessly whenever he spoke at felicitations or farewell functions. At parties where expensive foreign liquor flowed freely, he would only drink lime juice, to keep the others company.

But, as soon as he reached his own room, he would take out bottles of cheap liquor from his waste-paper basket. Only his servant knew about them. He detested the boy, who had black, ugly lips, who walked awkwardly, like a mother hen, so that the corns on his feet would not scrape against the ground. He resented him because he had seen the other face of the great man who was so respected in the city's higher circles of society. With his ruddy, bloated face and drooping eyes, he was like a question mark, fearful and loathsome.

There were other question marks like him.

The car moved slowly. Sandy tracts lay on either side. Isolated, scraggy coconut palms flew back as he went along. He had not come far beyond the city limits, but there were no signs of human habitation. He saw an old man lighting the wicks on an oil lamp made of stone in front of a dilapidated temple.

The road was deserted. Occasionally, a bullock cart laden with coconuts came from the opposite side. Only two buses plied on this route.

He drove with his eyes glued to the road.

He suddenly thought of a Muslim colleague he had had in Bangalore. He had started driving at the age of sixteen. Cars were a part of his life. Yet, he was prone to accidents if he was alone in the car. He would think about all sorts of things and not concentrate on driving.

The metalled road ended at that point. The culverts beyond were made of the trunks of coconut palms. There were many potholes; the dispute between the panchayat and the community project officer on who should repair the road had evidently not been settled.

Light from the evening lamps glowed beyond the coconut groves. He could make out the gaps between the trees.

Thatched structures that were shops in front and dwellings for the family behind began to make their appearance. The people and the lights meant the beginning of the village bazaar.

A sudden drizzle came from nowhere. The lights in the shops, the people took on weird shapes through the dim windscreen at the back, spattered with water. The road had been straight after he left the city. It was only when he got to this point that he had to start honking.

He turned left in the middle of the bazaar and had to apply the brakes at once. A crowd had collected—it could be a pickpocket, a death, a brawl, a madman, anything. Cursing, he drew up on the side of the road. What a nuisance! Why did it have to happen right there? He waited, his fingers pressed over his eyes.

'You must be on your way home?' An old man. He had taken off the towel lying on his shoulder, was standing respectfully holding it in his hand.

He grunted in response.

'I had come to see you last week.'

'I didn't come home last week.'

'I've told them about it. Master, you must settle the matter between me and the youngster.'

He remembered—it was a boundary dispute between father and son. The man had come to him on a Sunday evening two months ago just as he was leaving.

'Can I come and see you tomorrow?'

'Yes, I'll be there.'

'When can I come, Master?'

'Make it in the evening.'

He said it deliberately, knowing he might leave by then.

He looked around to see if the crowd was dispersing and honked gently. People moved aside. What had drawn the crowd was something quite unexpected—a large fish.

'Master, is there something I can do for you?'

'No, nothing.'

'I'll see you then, Master.'

He knew it was not he who merited this position of respect. Many village disputes used to be settled in the courtyard of his wife's house. Her father had been wealthy and powerful. The man's achievements were pursuing him now.

Even after seven years, he felt like a stranger when he stood in front of the sprawling house set by the side of a vast coconut grove within high walls. The villagers treated him with respect. He used to feel embarrassed when people hovered in the courtyard, waiting for their disputes to be settled.

He would remember the image of a naked urchin shivering on a night of pouring rain, his arms wrapped around his shoulders, dreaming of a hearty meal of burnt vegetables and cold rice as he stood near the giant grinding stone on the verandah of the feudal mansion, where servant women were busily grinding herbs.

He had nursed only one aim that burned like a spark of fire within him when he left his grandmother's house, weeping, when he had fought for the small bits of coconut the oracle threw to the children. He walked away, hungry and ashamed that he had not got even one, to the leaky thatched hut into which the rain streamed in: his day would arrive, tomorrow if not today.

And the same aim had stayed with him, making his blood boil, when he had arrived in a strange new town with two pairs of khaki shorts and two blue checked shirts crammed into a gunny bag. He had forty-three rupees left over from the sale of the ancient gold coin he had stolen from his grandmother.

Life had begun then in right earnest. Writing accounts for a warehouse in the daytime, studying at night. That journey to success had astonished many people.

A self-made man.

The good man who helped him through college and allowed him to stay in his outhouse would tell his irresponsible son: 'Learn from him—effort always pays.'

He did not keep the silent compact he had had with the man.

He still remembered the wet eyes of that fair, slender girl.

You could call it cheating or ingratitude.

He had become a stranger to himself.

Goodness had always been an illusion for him.

He reached the spot where he had to turn off to the estate—a small road raised over mud flats in which coconut husks had been buried for softening. The smell of rotting husks always hung in the air. He had to drive carefully. The jeep in which Fernandes had come to see him once had overturned at this spot.

He glimpsed the wall in the distance. At the next turn the headlights would shine on the iron gates.

He honked softly, to alert Achuthan who would be in the watchman's shed. By the time he reached the gates, one of them had swung open. It was not Achuthan today, it was his talkative younger brother.

A cool breeze blew through the coconut grove. The air was always humid here, since they were next to the sea.

It was after he had got to know Miss Margaret D'Souza that the moist sea breeze had come to his aid.

He had stood before his wife one day with a tired face.

'What's the matter, aren't you well?'

'A breathlessness. I had asthma at night. Nothing serious.'

He seemed to be breathing with effort.

'It's a few days since this started?'

'Two or three.'

'Why didn't you consult a doctor?'

'No, I don't need to. I tell you, it's nothing.'

'You're always like this, you never look after yourself. You have to see a doctor tomorrow.'

She was full of complaints ... He would never attend to his own needs. She was sure he was working too hard. She was convinced he was travelling too much on the days he did not come home at night. He was probably not eating regularly during the day.

He finally agreed he would see the doctor the next day.

The next day: 'Did you see the doctor?'

'Yes. It's nothing serious. Just asthma.'

'Nothing indeed! Didn't he give you any medicine?'

'I'm taking some tablets.'

She believed the tablets he took at night were for asthma. The words printed on the bottle indicated that the tablets would prolong his pleasure at night. Her education in English had not gone beyond the tenth standard.

He would never get rid of the asthma as long as he inhaled the sea air while he slept. The doctor said he had to live in the city. How would that be possible?

'To hell with the asthma!'

'You mustn't say that. What is life without health?' she said agitatedly.

They could rent a house in the city and live there. But who would look after things here then? Almost twenty people worked here every day. If she left it all to the manager, she would be the loser.

'Your property'

'Ours!'

Mine.

That was true. Finally, she found a way out. He would have to move out until he was better. But he must come home often. He must not fail to do so. Her eyes were brimming with tears.

He thought it an achievement that his face did not betray his happiness.

Let me see that chap who wrote that woman was a problem to which there was no solution and rubbish like that, he thought!

He pretended to accept her suggestion with distress, to agree only because he did not want to disregard her pleas.

The roar of the sea came nearer. Being the monsoon season, the sea was rough. As the car climbed, the headlamps threw a beam of light on the small garden behind the wire fence. At this point, the headlights would always pick up Caesar's eyes and make them glow like emeralds, from where he lay on the verandah. It was a sight that never failed to give him pleasure.

The garage doors were open. By the time he took the car in, the servant Gopalan came running up with a hurricane lamp. He saw the man peering at the back seat. There were no parcels to be taken in.

It was still drizzling.

Caesar's loud barks reverberated in the wet air.

He called out, 'Caesar!' and the dog suddenly fell silent.

Insects fluttered around the petromax lamp hung in the verandah. As he climbed the steps, Caesar wagged his tail, growled and tried to break free of his chain. He went up to the dog and stroked him. He would usually open the packet of biscuits he had brought for Baby and give him one. But of late he had been coming empty-handed and the dog seemed to have realised it. Looking into his eyes, he thought he saw cruelty in them. All right, he seemed to say indifferently, let things go on as they are! Caesar had grown up lying on his lap and drinking milk from a feeding bottle. He was three months older than Baby.

He saw Bharathi come up to the door, look at him and go back. He looked at Caesar's face again. Nostrils distended, he was sniffing the air.

When he went up to him to stroke his neck once more, the dog gave an unpleasant growl, put out his tongue and breathed heavily. He took note of the long, large, curved teeth, the leashed strength of the huge body and quailed before the mistrust in his eyes.

Underneath the petromax lamp, the floor was littered with dead moths, singed wings and wriggling bodies.

He walked towards the door, calling: 'Baby, my little one!'

Bharathi came to the door and said, 'She's eating.'

He looked at his watch. It was ten past seven.

'So early?'

'It's not that early. Do you want coffee or shall I make Horlicks?'

'A glass of drinking water will do.' He put on as pleasant an expression as possible. Bharathi went into the kitchen, dragging her huge belly. She seemed to have grown weaker than when he last saw her. Her eyes were sunk deeper in their sockets. Her skin looked rough, as if it needed to be oiled.

He took off his shoes, put them under the bed and called out, 'Baby, little one, are you eating?'

He went through the corridor into the dining room, took the glass Bharathi brought and drank a mouthful. Baby had finished her meal. Naniyamma was helping her wash her hands. He had another mouthful of water and set the glass down on the table that was covered with a black plastic sheet. Baby came up to him, her large, dark eyes gleaming and a faint smile on her lips.

He remembered that he had not brought her medicine. He

caught the child's hand and went into the bedroom. Once he was sure Bharathi would not overhear, he asked: 'Do you have a stomach-ache these days?'

'No. Amma gives me medicine.'

'What medicine?'

'That one.' She pointed to the bottle of Ayurvedic medicine on the shelf.

He sat down on the cane chair holding Baby close to him and thought about all sorts of things. How he had never forgotten to fulfil Miss D'Souza's slightest wish. How memory had never played tricks on him when he tried to get hold of the things she said she liked.

He stroked his daughter's hair, his eyes closed. He had nothing to ask her nor did she have anything to tell him.

'Aren't you going to school?'

'Yes, I am.'

'Does the Master scold you?'

'It's not Master, it's Teacher.' She had told him that many times.

'Do you know all the poems in your book by heart?'

'While we were playing, Teacher taught us the bird's song.'

'What lesson are you learning now?'

'The Fishing Boat and the Precious Stone.'

'What?'

She repeated the title. He sensed Bharathi behind him. She had not asked about the medicine. Or why he had not come the last three weeks.

God! Had she begun to understand how things were?

Her silent look of helpessness disturbed him.

'Do you feel better now?'

He answered like a fool, 'Eh? What? It's not bad.'

'Do you have asthma at night?'

'It's not too bad.'

He spoke without looking up. A cool breeze was blowing through the window opposite. When it was open, the sea was visible. Beyond the barbed wire fence, the waves broke over the sand.

'Shall I close the window?'

'No.'

'Move over to the other chair. If you sit there in the breeze, you will catch a cold.'

He wanted to laugh and cry at the same time. He had often wished she would be a jealous wife, full of accusations and barbed words. He felt helpless before the hurt and faith in the sunken eyes this woman had.

He waited for her to ask why he had not come for the past three weeks.

'The General Manager came last Sunday.'

She did not ask, what about the Sunday before that one.

'I was afraid you were not well. I even thought of sending Gopalan to find out.'

'I wanted to make a quick visit but the car was in the workshop.'

'A man came for the coconuts even last week. I told him we'd sell only after you came.'

'Couldn't you have sold them?' he asked, grabbing at the chance he had been given. 'There's no point letting them go dry. And I don't have a minute to spare since it's the end of the financial year. We'll never get through everything in time unless we make the staff work even on Sundays.'

It was the distance of twenty-seven miles that protected the imaginary picture he always drew of his busy life in the city, with its pressure of work, its burdens, its responsibilities and the constant fear that he would fall ill.

'Don't you want a *mundu*?'

'Yes.'

Baby freed herself from his grasp and went in.

'Where are you going, little one?'

'I haven't given Caesar his food.'

Caesar and Baby were companions. The animal, which had the strength of an ox, never obeyed anyone's orders, but would listen to anything Baby commanded him to do. If he didn't allow Gopalan to chain him in the mornings, Baby just had to call out to him.

He changed into a mundu, wrapped a freshly laundered towel around himself and went to the portico. Baby was seated on her haunches, tickling Caesar's neck. The dog got up when he heard his master's footsteps.

'Caesar!'

The dog looked at him, then stretched its head out to Baby again. He said to himself that Caesar would be the first in this family to understand what he was like.

'Don't you give Caesar a bath these days, Baby?'

'Yes, on sunny days.'

It must have been the close association with Caesar that was making Baby more and more reserved. He felt that her mind was much more mature than that of a five-year-old.

He called out to Caesar again, but he did not move. He pulled the dog up by its collar. It opened its mouth wide, baring its cruel-looking pointed white teeth. He looked at the animal with an air of casual authority.

I'll teach you one of these days!

The mother called out to Baby from the kitchen.

He walked up and down near the portico steps.

'Father, your hot water is ready.'

He felt refreshed after he had a bath in lukewarm water.

His wife came in to say that dinner was ready. He was combing his hair. Whenever he looked into the mirror, he would secretly rejoice at his good fortune in having such a youthful-looking face.

Bharathi picked up Baby's mattress, which was folded and placed on one end of the bed, and spread it on the floor. When she bent down, she looked as if the weight of her huge stomach might topple her over. Her bones stood out on her emaciated body.

'Won't the maid come? You shouldn't be ...'

Bharathi did not reply. She was in her eighth month of pregnancy.

There were only vegetables for dinner. She put down a bowl of scrambled eggs on the table and said, 'There's no fish because of the rain.'

She turned the lamp around so that its shadow would not fall on the plates and came and stood next to him.

'You're looking run down.' She always said that life in the city had ruined his health.

He did not ask about her health. He had arranged for a woman doctor who lived five miles away to come and examine her once a week. There was a midwife living nearby as well.

'Did the doctor come?'

'She came this morning.'

'Write and ask your aunt to come.'

'I've already written.'

'I'll take leave from next month,' he said to comfort her.

He feigned an air of enthusiasm. 'The white man who's my new boss is an unpleasant fellow. If he doesn't grant me leave when I ask for it, I'm going to tick him off and walk out.'

He had already drawn for her a frightening picture of the Britisher who was his manager. He was always persecuting his assistant manager. He would never grant him leave or allow him to go out of town even on holidays. If he gave in even a little, the man would take advantage of it.

'Don't pick quarrels with him. We don't want trouble, that's all.'

'How will you manage things here without anyone?' Whose voice was that?

'The midwife comes every day. And Aunt Ammu is coming next week anyway. I can always send Gopalan if I need anything urgently.'

'H...m...m.'

'Just come here now and then, that will be a great comfort.'

He started to roll a big ball of rice for Caesar and she said, 'Finish that rice. I'll serve some more for the dog.'

'No.'

'Do you want some more mango pickle?'

'It's very good. No, I don't want more.'

He threw the ball of rice into Caesar's aluminium plate and went to wash his hands. When he came back, Bharathi had sat down in his place. Naniyamma was serving her rice on the banana leaf he had used.

Baby was in the inner room, looking at the pictures in an old English magazine.

'Isn't it time for you to go to sleep, little one?'

She closed the magazine, went up to her mattress and stood there uncertainly. 'Go to bed when you are ready,' he said.

He walked around the room, uncertain what to do or say. Maybe it was better to leave the child alone. He went up and drew a chair into the portico. In the faint light filtering through the coconut palms, he could see the waves, intertwined with each other like mating snakes, beating on the shore beyond the fence.

A long gleam of light from the revolving lamp in the lighthouse two miles away stretched out over the black expanse of the sea from time to time. They said it guided ships on the high seas.

On nights when he had sat here, listening to the roar of the sea and watching the waves rise and crash down on the shore, he had always felt he was in some unknown corner of the world.

Miss D'Souza would be seated in her well-appointed room now, reading. Or she would be immersed in the pathos of some sad song.

Miss D'Souza had written to him about her solitary nights. Her name, Miss D'Souza, would be typed in red at the top.

I always experience your presence in this room. When I open the drawer, your letters are there, your presents are in the almirah; even the records I listen to at night were ordered by you. The string of pearls around my neck, my best satin jacket: all these remind me of you.

When I lie down at night in the bedroom, I can see the marks your feet made on the wall in the glow of the lamp. Do you remember how I too placed my feet against the wall one night to make marks? I always see you in this room and in my heart.

My dearest darling, when will the doors of your house open for me?

Margaret D'Souza, this is my house. Those who will receive

you at the door will be my pregnant wife and my five-year-old daughter.

The husband who was going to marry her was the head of a family twenty-seven miles away—when the Goan girl learned this … he dared not think of it. He had never thought of it.

He shivered. He could see his fingers trembling as he held the window bars.

He must tear off this mask one day and tell Miss D'Souza the truth. He would then stand before Bharathi and declare: I am not the good person you think I am. I have never loved you.

From that moment, he could live as a free, simple man.

He prayed he would find the strength that day to describe the nights he had spent in a drunken stupor, the furtive moments when he had knocked at doors behind which pleasure was sold.

Bharathi came from the kitchen after her chores. In her hand was a glass filled to the brim with milk.

'Is Baby asleep?' he asked.

'Yes. Isn't it time for you to go to bed?'

Time moved so slowly here. By the time night started in the city, this village would be asleep.

Bharathi spread a white sheet on the bed, took down a pillow from a heap stacked on the almirah and placed it at the foot. Then she spread a large, thin mattress on the floor, near Baby's.

She went in again to give Gopalan and Naniyamma instructions. Milk the cow early. Keep the water boiling. Gopalan, go to the butcher in the morning and ask him to send meat and liver quickly.

Her keys jangled as she locked the storeroom. She lowered the wick of the small lamp in the anteroom.

'Why don't you lie down?'

He obeyed silently. A cool breeze wafted in through the window. The sea sounded now like the roar of a crowd in the distance.

She called out before she closed the front door: 'Gopalan, let Caesar off the leash.'

Caesar growled on hearing his name. He knew the vast kingdom of the coconut grove would now be his. As soon as he was unchained, he barked loud enough to frighten even the shadows.

'Shall I turn off the lamp?'

He grunted.

She stroked Baby and straightened her limbs. Then she turned down the lamp and lay down, murmuring, 'Guruvayoorappa, protect us.'

The light from the small table lamp in the anteroom shed its glow over this room.

Baby always slept on her side, curled up, and would not cover herself even when it was cold.

His wife and child were asleep an arm's length from him. The newest addition to the family moved inside his wife's swollen belly. He found it difficult to reconcile himself to these facts.

Nor could he quite accept the image of the lover who parked his car at a distance, walked like a shadow, hugging the edge of the road and knocked at Miss D'Souza's door.

All he could imagine was a scrap of palm leaf floating over many-coloured bubbles of water.

God!

He turned on his side. Bharathi would not be asleep. He longed to plunge into the depths of her silence.

Her thin figure had always evoked his sympathy. He felt her huge belly growing and enveloping her completely as he watched. She was not ugly. But he had never found the slightest element of beauty in her. She had not become a part of his life, not even at this moment, when she was carrying the difficult burden of a second child. Her presence had become painful to him. All he could feel for her was pity.

But when he thought of Miss D'Souza lying on her thick spring mattress, gazing at her footprints on the white wall

If Bharathi evoked pain, Miss D'Souza brought only delight …

There was something intoxicating about every part of

Margaret's body. Even hours after he had said goodbye and left her, her fragrance would linger in him. A kiss from her moist lips could gift everything a woman could possibly bestow on a man.

The rhythmic breathing of the mother and daughter filled the room. The roar of the sea beyond the closed window was like the beat of a great heart. The fragrance of Miss D'Souza's clothes, of her waving hair, wafted out of the empty air and crept towards him. He would write to Margaret as soon as he returned to the city. Forgive me, forgive me … Margaret would shudder when she learnt the truth behind the deception. There would be dark circles under the eyes of the unmarried woman past her prime, standing on the wet sands of the seashore.

Bharathi would forgive him. He had to write Margaret a detailed letter and come to the village on a month's leave. He would live here like a husband and father. By the time he went back, Margaret's anger or sorrow would have subsided. Perhaps he would not run into her after that. She would not find it difficult to get herself another companion.

Another companion beside her, listening to "Dreams that do not lie" and "Black Moon" … he could not bear to think of that either. He tossed and turned, full of resentment.

The doors of his house would never be opened to receive her. She did not know that he had no home.

And yet he could not even think of her giving another man pleasure.

Worlds of light and darkness danced before him as he closed his eyes. He woke up at five thirty in the morning and lay with his eyes closed for another half hour. Bharathi must have woken up at five. He got up when she brought him hot coffee. He usually lay in bed until seven on Sundays even if he did not sleep.

Baby was asleep. He got up, picked up his shaving set and soapbox. By the time he shaved, Naniyamma had got hot water ready for him. He had a bath and changed into the freshly-washed clothes Bharathi had laid out for him.

His breakfast had been prepared very early in the morning.

It was just six thirty. He sat down at the round table to eat and Bharathi came to the door. He thought her face looked very unattractive beneath the dishevelled hair.

The thoughts he had had at night must have been distant, meaningless dreams.

'Why did you get up so early?'

'I have to go.'

She was silent.

'I'll come this evening.' (Would he?)

Baby was up by the time he was ready to leave.

He picked her up, stood her on the table and said: 'Daddy's going. I'll be back this evening.'

Baby rubbed her eyes and clung to his shoulder.

'What shall I bring you, little one?'

'M…mm…m…' She did not really say what she wanted.

Perhaps the veils of secrecy with which he thought he had hidden his life had already slipped down before his wife, his daughter and Caesar, who had grown up on his lap. He was not prepared to accept defeat. He said firmly:

'Bharathi, I'll come in the evening. Is there anything I should tell the doctor on my way?'

'No.'

'Anyway, I'll see her. I'd forgotten there's a case coming up tomorrow. I have to see the advocate.'

He went down the steps. Caesar growled as he walked to the garage—he had forgotten to give the dog the usual share of his breakfast. He saw some emotion he could not identify in Caesar's eyes and turned and looked at the dog resentfully.

Gopalan opened the garage door and shouted to Achuthan to open the gate.

The air was thick with mist and drops of moisture. A cold wind whistled past his ears. The car flew over the sandy, deserted road. The machine, reading his mind, seemed to long to reach the city. He was not even aware of having passed the doctor's house.

As the wheels sped over the wet road, the home he had left behind faded in his memory. He glanced at the back of the car casually and saw the jar of *kadumanga* pickle, neatly wrapped. What a nuisance!

This road, filled with tired bullocks pulling carts laden with coconuts, dark-skinned women carrying loads of beaten husks on their heads, villagers with dirty towels covering their head and necks, led to the city ... He speeded up. The pitiful cries of a stray dog that had cut across the road faded in an instant. He could go as fast as he liked on this road, that lay soaked in the tears of the night. Towards gatherings of the rich on hotel lawns as soft as spring mattresses; towards company offices where he would be greeted with respectfully bowed heads and extended hands; towards home, where liquor bottles were hidden in the garbage bin and glasses reeking of drink in the bathroom; towards dark alleys with open gutters where pimps lurked, waiting to sell the pleasure of a moment.

Towards a mattress heady with the scent of French perfume, lying under a wall where footprints echoed the memory of a time when swallows flew back to Capistrano ...

From one prison camp to another.

The Enemy

As the bloodstained knife rose from the depths of his ribs like a tongue of fire to plunge in again, he pleaded: 'Don't kill me, Suleiman, don't kill me!'

'Die, you beggar, die!'

He stood waiting at the door until the last spasm of the writhing body stilled.

The picture of a murderer!

He wakes with a start in the middle of the night as the watchman taps on the walls to show him how attentive he is to his work. When he closes his eyes again to escape into the valleys of sleep, the bloodstained knife gleams in the darkness. The picture of a murderer. Another face beneath the white sheet on the mortuary table, over which spreads a red wetness. The face of death, with teeth bared and half-open eyes.

The car was going slowly. He sat silently in the front seat, saying softly over and over again in his mind, Suleiman, I can imagine you standing guard at the door with your knife raised, waiting for the final spasms to cease. I am coming now to see your face as it waits for death

In front of him, the rays of the afternoon sun danced over the melting tar like colourless shadows.

Behind him, Krishnankutty and Vasu kept talking. They asked him something every now and then in an effort to make him join in the conversation. Since he replied in monosyllables and grunts, they finally left him alone.

They were talking about the tough people who lived and died by the strength of their arms, the sharpness of their knives.

Death had never hurt him. The reason being, he had never loved life. He had stood under the casuarina trees one day imagining his mangled body washed up on the shore by the waves. He was then the sixth member living in a lodge for which five people shared the rent.

He had got up and walked out from the bench in the front verandah. In his stomach lay the smouldering ashes of a hunger that had burned a whole night and two days.

They had been days of hunger. Days when, short of money, he had walked sixteen miles to see an acquaintance who had not been there and trudged back in a half-conscious state. Later, they had become memories, amusing stories to relate at dinners.

He had not thought that a meeting which had taken place years ago would forge new relationships in his life.

He had gone into the room very reluctantly with an acquaintance.

The man was seated with his stockinged feet stretched out on the table. The fan whirred overhead. An expensive cigarette glowed between his fingers. He had said to himself contemptuously, 'Another money-bag!'

'Sit down.'

Introductions. 'Don't you know Abdul Razack, who writes for the magazines?'

The laughing eyes had wandered over his dry mop of hair, his shabby clothes, the stubble on his withered face.

He had felt uneasy.

'You're a philosopher? Will your thoughts satisfy your hunger?'

Those were the days when he used to spend time conversing with Howard Fast, Upton Sinclair and Christopher Caldwell in the public libraries. And here was this money-bag now! Hiding his resentment, he listened with indifference. When he got up to go, the man stopped him.

'Wait, I'm coming out too.'

Hours later, as he got out of the car at the gate of the lodge, the man had called out, 'Hey, Razack!'

Surprisingly, he had not resented the intimacy, the familiarity in that voice.

'Can't you work?'

'What sort of work?'

'Any sort. Nothing to pick and choose.'

'But I must first get a job ...'

'If you do, will you set your philosophical thoughts aside and work five hours a day, six days a week?'

He laughed foolishly.

A night when he did not feel the pangs of hunger. Inside, the card players were making a noise. It was years since he had lain flat on his back on the bench looking up at the sky. The same sky he had watched through the leaves of the casuarinas in the orphanage looked beautiful now. He saw stars blossoming in the expanse of blue.

At the back, Vasu was telling stories. Kunhamu was the chief of the toughs. There was no one who could confront him. Suleiman challenged him. They fought all the way from the Kallayi bridge to Mooriyad. Kunhamu took out three knives, but Suleiman knocked them all out of his hand. It was from that day that Suleiman became Suleiman Moopan, the leader.

The last meeting.

When Sahib drove through the crowded streets at frightening speed, he cautioned him: 'Slow down a bit.'

'Afraid? Didn't you once try to commit suicide?'

'You destroyed me. You made me work. You persuaded me to get married. Now life has made me its prisoner.'

When we reached the gate of the hotel, he was insistent: 'Come on.'

'I have to get home soon. My younger son has fever.' He opened the door hurriedly, got out and asked, with his hand still on the door handle:

'Lend me a hundred rupees.'

'Get lost!'

'I need it badly.'

'What about the two hundred you've already taken?'

'It's still there.'

'What do you do with your four hundred rupee salary?'

'Don't talk of this and that. Give me the money. I'll return it on the first.'

'Sure?'

'Sure.'

'All right, I'll write off the past. But I'll kill you if you don't give this to me exactly on the first.'

Sahib called out as he was going, 'Look, Razack, we're cleaning out the bathing tank tomorrow. Come for lunch.'

He thought about himself as he hurried to get home before eight. Those nights when he had wandered around in the light from the pale street lamps while the deserted city was fast asleep seemed so long ago!

The house on the edge of the gravel path where you turned left at the road. He always had a sense of wonder when he went in through the gate. My house, he thought! My family. He thought of the long line of children moving through the verandah of the orphanage into the kitchen, holding enamel plates in their hands. The nine-year-old with festering sores on his knees and cheeks would always be the last, pushed to the back in the crowd. At the age of sixteen, he had stepped into the street with a certificate bound in khaki cloth.

At the back, Vasu was relating another story.

Even the police were afraid of him. With his arm around the girl, he warded off their blows. There were six of them.

'Sir, you didn't hear about the incident?'

'H'm...m.' He grunted assent without turning around.

In the end they hit him from the back with an iron rod and he fell down. But they didn't let the girl go. The fellow had to take off the towel wound around his head and stand respectfully before the chief.

He was lying on the easy chair in the verandah and looking at his son doing his second standard lessons. His wife was inside, listening to the radio with the younger one, who had fever, lying on her lap, covered with a flannel shawl. She was singing softly, trying to echo the radio singer. Her long, slender fingers moved over the yellow shawl in time with the music.

The messenger of death had arrived gasping at that moment, borne on the wings of darkness.

The funeral procession moved behind the bier over the broad path dividing the fields. He stood at the edge of the compound staring at the water tank that was to have been emptied that day, at the fishes that had escaped death darting through the water. When the courtyard and the compound were finally emptied of people, he walked back through a coppery twilight.

The moonlight laughed from the window like a shameless whore. He felt as if he was lying on the mortuary table under a white sheet.

You stood guard at the door, Suleiman, with a bloodstained knife in your hand, looking at my writhing body. Throughout the night, to make sure I didn't escape death.

As the road approached the seashore, he felt cool, relieved. The remains of a dog that had been crushed to death under the wheels of a truck the previous day lay scattered over the road. Beyond the coconut grove, vultures satiated with dead flesh sat pecking at foul-smelling heaps. He held his breath to shut out the smell and looked at the gleaming sea.

The milestone marked another fourteen miles.

He could breathe now, the foul-smelling zone was over.

At the back, his companions were talking about jails. Krishnankutty, who had once been a political worker, had been in jail for a month in 1942.

Vasu said: 'I've never seen a jail. This is my first experience.'

He thought it was his first experience as well.

In order to ward off nightmares, he drew pictures of the enemy twisting and turning in agony over and over again in his mind.

He had never seen a courtroom. He went to the court one day, to see the enemy standing in the dock.

Many people were seated on the four or five benches meant for visitors.

It was not the courtroom of his imagination. The Judge sat writing in an enclosure behind brass railings. Behind his head, he could see the motto: *fiat justitia ruat coelum*, let justice be done even if the heavens fall.

He stood just beyond the door, behind the visitors.

The first person he noticed was the young man in the witness box.

The advocate was questioning him in a low voice. The witness answered softly as well. He could make out what they were saying only if he listened attentively. He thought of a courtroom scene in some movie, where everyone shouted.

That was when he saw the prisoner's dock. He was surprised—even though it was right in front of him, he had not noticed it earlier.

He first saw the prisoner from the back. Hefty arms. Huge fists, knotted with thick veins.

One of the visitors seated on the bench smiled at him in recognition. He moved to make place and invited him silently.

He felt that the accused, whose head was bowed, was peering intently at the young man in the witness box.

He saw him when he turned his head. There was neither fear nor shame in the narrowed eyes, the clean-shaven, heavy face. It looked completely wooden.

The man seated next to him pointed out the defense counsel who was behind the desk at the western end of the room. He had a sprig of *tulasi* tucked behind his ear, sacred ash smeared on his forehead and tired eyes. He looked at the old man vengefully, full of disgust.

He had heard stories about his legal triumphs. The man had retired after saving many criminals and more money than he needed. And he had come back now, to save the enemy!

When he was walking back through the grounds of the court, someone had stopped him.

'How is the case, Sir?'

'It's going on.'

'Swami is clever. Will he get him off?'

'Who knows?'

'He should be let off. Then we'll take care of him.' Who had said that? Hate had blazed in the eyes in the pock-marked face.

'The court might let him off but we won't!'

He wanted to say, 'Moideen, I'll be with you to see that.'

An appeal, a petition for mercy. He had arranged for news to get to him regularly. The week before, a friend in the court had come and told him that the date had been fixed. The eleventh of March. In the morning.

He had been telling himself ever since he started: Suleiman, I am coming to see your face as it awaits death.

The town which was well-known for its central jails and the children of white men's concubines. Krishnankutty told the driver the way.

The gate set in the huge wall was wide open.

Vasu said: 'The quarters are on the other side of the road. Do you want to take a look? We can call Jamal if he's there. He's a friend of mine.'

'No, I know the Jailer.' Krishnankutty got down from the car.

They came to the second wall.

Vasu said: 'The sanctum sanctorum. Hindus call it the garbhagriha.'

Sentries with bayonets stood in arched niches on either side of the massive iron gate. As Krishnankutty talked to them, he sat in the car looking at the enormous steel door. He knew Krishnankutty would talk too much. Don't you know who's sitting in the car? Abdul Razack, the famous ...

The small barred door set within the steel shutters opened.

'You can go in, Sir.'

He had to bend to enter. The door had been made small so that you had to bow down before the might of the law. He had heard that there was a board saying, "For each man what he deserves," in front of the Nazi concentration camps.

On either side under the high roof were two raised platforms with a small corridor between them. Guards off duty sat talking to one another on the cement platforms, smoking.

There were stairs going up on the left side. Krishnankutty spoke to the handsome guard standing there. They were given permission to go up.

There were only two chairs in the Jailer's office. A bell was rung for another chair and while they waited, Vasu made room for himself on the bench heaped with papers. 'I'll sit here.'

A dark-skinned, middle-aged man in coarse, faded khaki shorts and a loose vest made of the same material brought another chair. As he was leaving the officer said:

'Rama, ask them to send up four cups of tea.'

The Jailer said to them as the man left, 'He's a lifer.' Then added, in case they had not understood: 'A life sentence. Seven years are over. He has one more year.'

They listened, although they knew these things. When convicts have been imprisoned a long time and are thought to have mellowed, they are appointed as orderlies.

Vasu had a doubt to clear: 'Excuse me, Sir, don't these people have checked uniforms?'

The Jailer laughed. 'Only in the movies!'

He went on in an aggrieved voice: 'No one knows anything about our jails. People like you should come and look at them now and then. Things have improved quite a lot. Good food. Measured in grams. Mutton twice a week.'

He was amused. Welcome, my friends, welcome. Tasty food, good exercise. Come, everyone!

'In the Student Congress Movement in 1942 …'

No one paid attention to Krishnankutty's experience of jail. There were footsteps on the stairs. He looked at the face of the dark-skinned, middle-aged man as he placed the glasses of tea on the table. The veins above his jaws moved as if he was chewing something. There were little circular bald patches between the stubble on his scalp, the scars of sores.

The Jailer said, as we drank tea, 'Suleiman Moopan is here. The hanging is tomorrow.'

He felt a lump in his throat. He swallowed the tea with difficulty and said without showing any interest: 'Oh …'

'The murder case created quite a sensation in your part of the country.'

'Yes, yes.'

'What was the victim's name?'

He sat silent, rubbing his eyes with his fingers as the Jailer tried to recall the name.

Krishnankutty came to the forgetful officer's help.

'Do you want to see Moopan?'

The companions on either side of him must have exchanged meaningful glances.

'Yes, we do.' He added, by way of courtesy: 'If you don't mind.'

'It's a pleasure.'

The Jailer locked his table, got up and pulled his khaki shirt down.

'We'll walk around.'

When he walked past to go out, he saw the long, thin, red gash across his right cheek that looked as if a sharp thorn had grazed it.

'Come, I'll introduce you to the Superintendent.'

The Superintendent was in the next room. There was a board with his name and designation on the door.

The Assistant Jailer went in and talked to him, then invited us in.

A grey-haired man with a gentle face and gleaming eyes was seated behind the table. I thought to myself, didn't this man look like Ayyavu Iyer, the Mathematics teacher in the Orphanage High School?

When the introductions were over, he said: 'I thought we'd just step in and see you … we were passing this way …'

'Very nice of you.'

The Superintendent handed over the heavy bunch of keys that had been hanging on a large ring on the wall to the Jailer.

As they thanked him and moved out, the Jailer asked, 'Would you like to see the gallows?'

He looked at his companions for a moment.

'Yes, if you don't mind.'

The Superintendent took out a key from his table, opened the iron safe in the corner of the room and took a long key from it. He watched the Jailer take it from him reverently with some amusement.

The Superintendent smiled and said: 'This key is one of the things in the jail that we guard very carefully.'

The sunshine had dimmed. Everyone in the narrow office rooms upstairs and in the verandah was sweating profusely in the heat.

We walked past wooden shelves piled with coarse garments and went down the stairs.

The orderly moved aside to let us pass.

He asked the Jailer as he walked beside him, 'What was his crime?'

'Raman's? A double murder. His wife and her father.'

Walking by the edge of the garden at the end of the courtyard, the Jailer fondled the crotons that stretched their heads out through the wire fence and said: 'All this is the work of the inmates.'

He talked incessantly as they went through the weaving shed and the workshop. Assuming an expression of deep interest, he walked beside him. The inmates wove all the clothes they needed. Our carpentry section is a leading one. We supply furniture to all the schools.

Old grey buildings stood stooped inside the squares marked off by wire fencing.

He saw the prisoners crowded together in the grounds near the banana grove. When the Jailer drew near, they raised their hands silently and saluted him.

'They've all committed major crimes.'

They stopped at a spot where four paths branched off and the Jailer pointed out the hospital and the recreation room. He was gasping for breath. A row of young coconut palms above the roof showed off their full clusters of nuts proudly. He looked at the group of criminals. As the guard called out a number, each of them would move two steps forward, salute and repeat it.

The Jailer followed his glance and said: 'Did you see that old man? He's from Koratti. The fair-skinned stout one is a teacher. He murdered his wife. Look at that young man—no, not that one, the one behind the fellow with a moustache. He's the one ...'

The Jailer told them the story of how the man had killed his elder brother right in the middle of the road, taken his severed head straight to the police station and surrendered.

'Don't you want to see the kitchen? Come, come, that's a must! We give our inmates a larger ration than they would get outside.'

They saw a machine consisting of two receptacles, one inside the other, compress cooked rice into flat cakes. The Jailer asked for one of the cakes to be broken up and spread on the floor.

'Isn't that enough? What do you think?'

The Jailer told us about the old man working in the kitchen as we left. 'He was a troublesome fellow when he arrived. There was not a day when he didn't come to blows with someone. But after four or five years, everything mellows, doesn't it?' He laughed.

An empty dormitory. Raised cement platforms that served as beds. He remembered nights in the orphanage dormitory. At the head of each cement platform, above the rolled-up mats, calendar pictures of Hindu gods and the crucified Christ were stuck here and there.

On the way back, they saw prisoners bathing in open cubicles with low walls. The murmur of voices they had heard at a distance died down as they drew nearer. They could hear only the sound of water from the taps falling on the ground.

When they passed the hospital and the empty B-class rooms for prisoners and came to the banana grove on the south, he lighted a cigarette. He did not ask if it was allowed. The Jailer was talking about an incident that took place in Salem. A man had gone out in the evening with his wife for a walk. A prisoner who had just been released after serving his sentence stabbed him with a *bichuva*, a sickle, from the back. Fortunately he was wounded on the face, not on the neck.

'The people caught him. He was given five years—but in Coimbatore.'

He said with a sly smile, 'In four or five months I too got a transfer to Coimbatore.'

'What was his reaction when he saw you again?' asked Vasu.

Running his index finger over the thin red line that time had transformed his wound into, the Jailer smiled. 'Wasn't that why I worked so hard for six months to get a transfer? I know how to deal with tough fellows.'

He grew silent for a while, as if thinking of something.

'They understand only one language. And you can be sure it's not love!'

Yes, I understand.

He would have thought of his assailant, lying in the hospital. Then, when he finally received his transfer orders from Salem and caught sight of him in the distance, working in the labour ground, his heart would have filled with joy.

I too understand.

They walked on until they came to another gate in the wire fence. There was a small open ground in front, dotted here and there with withered bushes. They saw the huge globe of a light on the iron pillar in the centre. There were tiled buildings on both sides. Barred iron doors opened into the verandah.

'Cells for the condemned prisoners.'

A shudder ran through him when he heard the Jailer's voice.

He took another look. In the single cells, behind the barred iron doors, he could make out human figures.

'There are seven of them. Three of them are in the mercy petition stage.'

As we entered the courtyard, the guards on duty in the verandah saluted the Jailer.

The Jailer was replying to Krishnankutty's queries. The hanging was at four in the morning. That's a convention … yes, yes, definitely … I have to attend. Let me see.

I? Yes, quite a number.

He stood looking at the withered grass on the dry ground and at the base of the iron post.

'There, there, Suleiman is in number three.'

He summoned a mask of courage to his face and turned his eyes that way. The third door. The murderer, Suleiman.

He hurried behind the Jailer to avoid looking at the people who stood saluting behind the first two doors and climbed into the verandah.

He felt a sense of weightlessness in his trembling ankles. Someone seemed to be trying to break open the bars inside the cage of his heart.

'Well, Suleiman, do you know these people?'

'Razack Master, isn't it? We come from the same place.'

He tried to smile, standing next to the Jailer in front of the barred door. Moopan, under whose feet the earth used to tremble when he walked. The stubble on his face was overgrown and the face itself looked small. He looked completely changed.

Moopan smiled. One of his front teeth was broken.

The words he had thought up for this moment eluded him. He clasped and unclasped his fingers that were trembling helplessly and tried to smile. Moopan stood smiling behind the iron bars.

The Jailer said in a low voice, 'He is well-behaved. Very brave.' This was not a picture of the enemy—it couldn't be. This figure in the loose, coarse vest, the tapering shorts gathered at the knees, the broken tooth showing in a smile—it was so different from the one he knew.

'Master, is everyone well?'

Words still eluded him.

'Do you see Raghavan Nair? Are Rajettan and the others well?'

The words came at last with difficulty.

'Yes.'

'How's Mammukka's business?'

'Not bad.'

'Tell them all that I enquired about them.'

He saw Krishnankutty's face and Vasu's on either side of him. And heard the stillness with which they held their breath.

'Will you go back today?'

'Yes.'

'I'm so happy you came Razack Master.'

Silence spread around them again. The Jailer glanced at the empty cells on either side. The scraping of the sentries' shoes standing guard in the verandah was the only sound.

He read the mute appeal on his companions' faces. Let us go.

'I have people in Ponnani,' said Suleiman. 'They've agreed to take away the body and do whatever has to be done.'

The Jailer explained: The body would be handed over if there were claimants. Otherwise the burial could be arranged here.

The questions he had meant to ask lay silently in his mind. 'Why did you do it, Moopa, why?'

He said, with great difficulty, 'I'm going, Moopa.'

He held out his hand. When the rough palm extended through the bars lay in his, he did not think of the fingers in his blood-stained dreams.

Moopan asked: 'Won't it do if you leave after … the ceremony in the morning?'

He did not look at Moopan's face.

He had always prided himself on the wealth of his language, but he fumbled for words now. And said, feeling helpless:

'Have courage, Moopan.'

He withdrew his hand slowly. Moopan looked at his own hand for a moment, then pressed it to his forehead and said:

'My salaams … to all of you.'

For the first time, he heard Moopan's voice tremble and the sound of a sob that he could not control.

He stepped down from the verandah into the courtyard without waiting for the Jailer. Voices murmured salaams from behind the iron bars.

He thought, I am no one. No great man with the power to grant freedom.

The Jailer caught up with him and asked, 'Then you knew Moopan before?'

The smile on his tired face assented.

'You knew the murdered man as well?'

He replied to that too silently.

That death orphaned me—for the second time.

They were about to walk straight on. The Jailer said,

'One minute. Don't you want to see the gallows?'

Jamal, the Assistant Warden, who had come on duty at six, joined their group. He walked with Vasu a little behind them, talking softly.

They walked westward, skirting the area which had single cells to house murderers moved out of the mental asylum.

The Jailer kept explaining: lights burned all night on the verandah and the courtyard outside the condemned block. The sentries could see every movement the inmates made in each cell. When the door was opened at four in the morning and the prisoner was led-out, he would be surrounded by armed guards. There were people who had run away and attempted to commit suicide.

The prisoner's arms were tied behind him as soon as he was brought out. As they were led away, some of them screamed, cried out. Some would have to be dragged along.

'... Yes, yes, it can happen. There are prisoners who have torn their uniforms to make a rope and hanged themselves. When I was in Salem ... they can't do that anymore ... did you notice? The ventilators are very high. Besides, the guards can see what is happening inside right through the night.'

They stopped before another wall covered with moss. Heavy wooden doors with iron hoops.

'The gallows are here.'

He peered beyond the wall. When he was young, the mention of the gallows had always brought to mind the image of a machine that looked like a huge crane in the harbour, visible from every point in the jail. But all he could see here was a roof of faded tiles above the moss-covered wall.

The lock was wrapped tightly in cloth. Jamal unwound the

cloth carefully. The Jailer took out the long key from his pocket of his trousers and opened it. Pushing open the doors with difficulty, he reminded his assistant: 'Jamal, see that these hinges are oiled.'

It was dark inside. Shut away from sunlight, the air was dank and humid and had the odour of decayed flowers.

The Jailer, who could see even in the dark, turned on the light. In its faint yellow radiance, they saw before them the engine of death.

Consciousness faded into a kind of twilight. Words seemed to be crawling somewhere into the distance.

'There are executioners in the Poojappura Jail in Trivandrum. From families who are hangmen by tradition. Here we have to do it all ourselves.'

'How long will it take?' Was that Krishnankutty's voice?

'Simple. Here, Mr Razack, stand beside me. Look here, they are made to stand on this platform. The rope is slung from this beam. I'll show you.'

He took out the cord from the whistle on the shoulder of his khaki uniform and tied it to the crescent-shaped groove on the iron arm.

'This is the noose. Jamal, pull that lever. Look. Yes, when you operate the lever with your foot, the platform opens downwards like the twin panels of a door. Below, there's a pit ...'

There was silence around the machine. They followed the Jailer. He said with pride:

'In Poojappura, it is the executioners who make the rope. Here, we have it specially manufactured in Madras. It's very smooth. The executioners make rougher ropes. It takes longer.'

They saw the steps leading into the dark pit.

'Do you want to go down? There are steps.'

'No.'

'Two or three minutes. By the time you go down, it's all over.'

He gave them details, anxious to convince them how

efficiently it was done. 'Very simple. As soon as they are brought in, the head is covered with a hood.'

Then he gave them figures. About ... three minutes to bring them here from the cell. One minute to cover the head with a black hood, stand them on the platform and operate the lever. Altogether ... altogether everything would take about six or seven minutes.

'The body can be collected from that door.'

'Let's go,' he said to his companions, loud enough for the Jailer to hear.

'One second. Want to hear a joke? Last time—when was it, Jamal? The seventh. When we went down to the pit to look at the dead body, there was a snake there.'

'Wonderful!' he murmured.

'What?'

'Perfect arrangements.' Excellent planning. Bright lights in the yard and on the verandahs. High ventilators. Food tested and declared poison-free by expert doctors. Smooth ropes specially manufactured by mills in Madras ...

He exclaimed, sounding almost intoxicated with pleasure: 'Beautiful! Wonderful!' Then he turned towards the door fighting for breath, trying to hide the sobs rising in him.

He bent down and went through the wicket gate, shook the Jailer's hand, trying hard to smile and thanked him again.

As the car turned, they saw, between the high walls, the gravel path meant for the vehicle to go to the rear of the gallows and collect the body.

They drove the fifty-six miles back to the hotel on the seaside in silence. He got down and said goodbye to his companions in a monosyllable.

He tried to forget the hours creeping by amidst the crowd and bustle, the drunken, meaningless words.

When he collapsed on the bed, the clock was striking two.

Darkness thick as granite slabs closed in around him. A deep sleep almost like unconsciousness descended over him like a pall of black.

When he opened his eyes, struggling to breathe, he was startled to see his wife's frightened, tearful face.

He heard her voice, drenched in tears: 'What is it, what is it?'

His neck was being crushed. Holding it tight with both hands, he wept and said, pressing his face into his pillow:

'It was I who died, it was I who died.'

Red Earth

The granite slabs were still burning from the heat of the midday sun. The group of visitors hastily discarded their footwear and ran into the shelter beyond the large door.

He took a long time to remove his shoes. So she stood waiting in the afternoon sun, like a solitary flower in the last green patch left by the vanishing spring. She waited, feeling the heat from the granite slabs run up her bare feet. She had felt a thrill when the rough lips of the burning granite had first pressed against the cold soles of her bare feet. The thrill turned into an agonising pain which she tried to bear quietly. She laughed to herself recalling her new-found ability to talk to herself silently. Goddess Parvati had done penance amid the five fires. Is there a *pativrata*, a chaste woman, who cannot bear the mellow heat the noonday sun belches out?

He finally managed to get out of his shoes, wiped away the sweat gathered in the folds of his face and hurried towards her. But she would not go forward.

'Come, come, my feet are burning.'

He walked hurriedly into the temple so as not to be isolated from the group. She still lagged behind. She could hear the guide's echoing voice. A voice that matched his figure.

'In the distance, at the point where the three oceans meet the Goddess sat in meditation. From here in Suchindram the Lord saw the Virgin Goddess and was filled with love for her.'

On his forehead the sandal-paste mark had almost been washed away by sweat. She imagined he had been a demon's statue sleeping on one of granite blocks, that he had now come alive to join the tourists. His eyes, in which red veins stood out with clarity, strayed from face to face as he mouthed his well-memorised sentences.

Her companion tried to persuade her to join the group while she hung back. He read what was written on the boards at the base of the enormous figures and repeated it to her as if to a child.

'The Gods felt that the Virgin Goddess would lose her divine strength if she wed. They decided that the marriage should be prevented.'

Sweat glistened on the bare granite-like body of the guide. She recalled the sorcerer who had come in her childhood to their kitchen to melt down lead in order to perform an exorcism.

She pretended to identify the names on the boards when she realised that he was watching her through his thick glasses to see how she reacted.

'They decided upon the auspicious moment when the marriage rites should be performed, the hour of midnight. The Holy Sages could agree only upon that moment as the most auspicious. Lord Shiva, the bridegroom, set out to reach the point of confluence of the three oceans at the appointed time. Devendra came in the form of a cock and stood in his way and crowed. Thinking that the auspicious moment had gone by, Shiva returned disappointed.'

'Then what about the Goddess?'

The visitors turned round to look at her. She was surprised: was it she who asked that question?

'Look here; look at this.'

Whenever he spoke impatiently bubbles of spittle would come out through his lips.

'Then what about the Goddess?'

The red-veined eyes of the guide reached out over the visitors and hovered on her. The blood-red eyes were laughing.

'The Goddess snapped the wedding garland and threw away

the pieces. She tore the pandal apart. It is because the dishes made for the wedding feast that day soaked through them and changed their colour that the sands of Kanyakumari are red.

'Come, come here.'

He called again, open camera in hand. There was a foolish grin on his fat face as he beckoned to her as if asking her to come to a secret love tryst.

'Let's take a photo with this background. It'll be good. There, stand there. Move a little to the left; let me see.'

The visiting group had reached the Dance Hall. The echo of the guide's voice boomed. He was describing the windows that had been made so that the lovely women of the household could watch a performance without being seen themselves.

'Laugh, just once. Smile please.'

She looked with terrified fascination, over the heads of the tourists, at the face of the demon with the blood-red eyes.

'Ready. Smile please. Ready.'

She turned when she heard the click of the camera.

She saw the thick lips trembling and the disgusting white bubbles of spittle gather at the corner of his lips. He was always like this when he tried to conceal his anger.

She burst out laughing.

'You did not laugh then. You always laugh at the wrong moment.'

She had moved away and he found himself talking to the stone elephant with the granite ball in its mouth. She could not help laughing again.

The tourists trooped out. Some of them tipped the guide. Before she could say anything, he muttered: 'Money for this! Everyone knows these things.'

He found a seat quickly on the bus. She looked up at the upper deck of the vehicle. She sat on the extreme edge of the vacant half of the seat, taking care not to touch the brown shirt soaked in sweat.

The bus filled up. Their former guide climbed in as the whistle blew. He stood in front of them gripping the iron bars in his hand. Her companion seemed to have thought of something and, as if to amuse her, he said: 'You've only heard of the Negro. You can see one now.

She could not see the eyes with the blood-red veins running through them. He was gazing into the distance somewhere.

Her companion watched her feet beating time to the tune the young man in the front seat was playing on a mouth organ.

When they had gone far enough to hear the roar of the sea he asked, 'Tired?'

She nodded. It could mean yes or no.

'I have always liked the sea. We went to look at the sea when I first came to your house with your elder brother for the vacation. Do you remember?'

She sat with her eyes closed.

'You remember nothing. Not even the first time I saw you!'

She tried to smile.

'We all went together. You were a child then. You wouldn't remember.'

She looked silently at the trembling fronds of the palmyra trees on parched earth receding into the distance.

'You wouldn't remember. You were dressed in a long white skirt which trailed on the ground and a green blouse. Your sister was wearing a saree. You wouldn't remember.'

I remember. You walked down with the waves holding *chechi's* hand. You took her photograph. You wiped away the drops of water that the waves had splashed on her hair.

'You didn't step into the sea. You were afraid.'

I sat in the shade of the coconut palm. I wrote on the sand with my finger; "Sri Rama is a thief." I wrote it again and again. I thought a big wave would come to wipe it out and engulf you all. What I had written remained. No wave came splashing up.

When they saw the seat in the distance he said, 'Oh! How beautiful!'

'Who? My chechi?'

'What—Oh no, the sea.'

People who had come to see the sunset crowded in little groups here and there. They move their way back through them. By the time they reached the hotel he was panting.

She did not pay any attention to the directions he was giving the servant boy about the luggage. Twisting the window curtain fluttering in the breeze, she looked out at the sea. Red earth!

When they were alone he asked, 'These needless comments about your sister ...'

'I didn't say anything.'

'You'll never finish saying it. That's my affliction!'

His face reddened with an infusion of blood. Sweat streamed down in channels. She opened the suitcase and took out the bottle of tranquillisers. She dropped two pills on his trembling hand. He swallowed them and drank some water. Short of breath, he lay down on the bed.

As she changed her saree and started powdering her face she realised that his tired eyes were questioning her.

'I'll go for a walk.'

At the door, without turning back she repeated, 'Take rest. I'll be back after a stroll.'

She saw the guide sitting by himself on the cement bench on the path beside the sea. Although there was another path opposite, she took the one next to the bench. The Negro stood up suddenly like a demon with his head touching the sky. He joined his palms, 'Namaskaram!'

A voice that boomed; the penetrating odour of country liquor; his eyes were red flames. She paid no attention to him and tried to look as indifferent as she could. She walked on, her head held high against the breeze.

She sat on the edge of the path looking at the sand dunes in the distance and the red streaks in the sky above. The seashore was growing deserted. She dreamt of the pandal that was once put up there. Around her she saw scattered on the ground the decorations that had been torn apart, the ornaments that had been broken and flung away, the food that had been kicked over and stamped into the earth.

She was afraid to turn around and look. She had to find out whether there was a light in the window of her hotel room. Even if it was not to see whether the drunken demon seated in meditation on the cement bench had waken up.

The crunch-crunch of sand being stamped underfoot. The demon approached, the beedi tip glowing like a third bloodshot eye. The emptied seashore trembled beneath his feet.

Behind him, the light from the hotel room brightened. She pressed her elbows on the red sand and raised her face to the darkened sky. She listened attentively to the sound of the heavy feet sink into the sound as they come nearer and nearer. She lay with her eyes closed, as if all her strength had drained out of her.

Once Again in Search of a Refuge

Yet another journey in search of a refuge.

The river, again.

Long ago, there used to be a travellers' bungalow at the bend of the river, where it turned towards the village. The picture that memory drew held a heap of empty tar barrels at the edge of a yard overgrown with grass. The profusion of red flowers clustered on the oleander trees in the background reflected the rays of the setting sun even on the east. Long ago.

Looking at the spot from afar, the twilight red of the oleander flowers was missing. He could see the river at the turn of the path. What month was it? The days and months of the Malayalam calendar had dropped out of his mind long ago. There was water in the middle of the river. Below him, the ferryboat had left for the other bank. He was delighted—he had once grieved to see the river become an expanse of burning sand.

The ruins of the old temple lay among the overgrown thickets.

What was the name of those plants with tiny thorns and pale pink flowers that looked like ear-studs? He used to know their name, these plants that served as a fence. He had crept through them often, holding the thorns away from his body. My plants, he thought, my months, my times for transplanting seedlings ...

He walked down the road along the river bank. A

government jeep came from the opposite side. The red earth road had been tarred. There was no dust. A bus crowded with people going to the village overtook him.

Had he missed his way? The banyan tree was not there. The stone bench meant for resting headloads was not there either. There were no stray goats reluctant to come out of the fields at dusk.

Someone in the group watching the ferryboat crossed to the other side, came up to him and asked:

'Has Anita gone?'

He did not know what to say in reply. Who was Anita?

'There's no K.B.T. Someone said Anita would come a little early.'

It took him a few moments to realise he was talking about a bus.

'I don't know.'

He walked on, passing more unfamiliar faces and reached the small bazaar at the second bend of the river. It was then that the eastern sky growled. He waited near a shop which was closed and listened to the indistinct sounds. He heard low rumblings again in the sky.

'The northeast monsoon now, in the middle of the month of Vrischikam?' An old man gazing at the eastern sky asked, maybe of nature. No one answered, nor did the old man wait for a response.

The small lane grew dark. There were isolated lamp posts now and street lamps, but no one had lighted them. Pale flickers of yellow light gleamed here and there in the thatched rooms that served as shops.

He stepped onto the open verandah of the closed shop and leaned against the wooden planks. People walked in and out of the shops on either side, taking no notice of him.

He decided to walk on. Where did this road end? Tell me, where does this end?

He used to know, once. But the road had changed now. The river had changed. The faces had changed.

Three or four people who passed by in the gathering

darkness stopped and turned to look at him. They came up to him hesitantly.

He heard one of them say, it's a stranger.

'Who is it?'

He mumbled something indistinct.

'Where are you going?'

Without waiting for a reply, one of them said, there's no bus today.

He recovered a lost voice and words: 'I need a place.'

A place.

They stood aside and talked to each other in low voices. Then came forward.

'For strangers to stay ...'

There was silence again.

'There are no hotels here. It's not a town.'

'There's a travellers' bungalow four miles away.'

'It's full. I asked,' he said. Was there something peculiar about his voice? They seemed to be waiting wonderingly for his next word.

'What I want is a place to rent.'

'For how long?'

'For a few days. I can't decide by myself for ... for how many days exactly.'

Along with curiosity, there was a tinge of respect now on the villagers' faces.

'You didn't tell us what you do.'

Instead of answering, he made a vague sound.

A man who looked capable and confident came nearer. His narrow eyes pierced the darkness as he looked at the bag on his shoulder and asked:

'Your things?'

'They'll come.'

They began to whisper among themselves.

Disembodied voices.

-Must be the Salt Inspector. Must tell Kothamma to be careful.

-Oh no! Must be a C.I.D. chap. That case ...

-He's a stranger. Can't be trusted. These expert burglars nowadays

-Would thieves be so bold?

The villagers came nearer.

'You insist on a house? If it's a day or two …'

'I must have a house.'

The walls of a house around me. A floor to sleep on. Under the sky above, a small roof.

'Only the Eman's, the Master's, house is vacant. His manager just left.'

'Who's Eman?'

They were surprised.

'You don't know Dharman Mudalali? What a thing!'

Dharman. He had never heard of him. Appu, Appa, Appunni, Kutti Narayanan, Kutti Sankaran. The old names had changed.

Who was Dharman?

'You must have heard of the Master.'

He grunted, a sound that could mean anything.

'There can't be anyone who's not heard of him. He's so prosperous.'

Someone brought a lamp. From a shop nearby someone else brought an old bench that could seat two people.

'Please sit down'

He sat down and listened, showing no interest at all, as if they were talking about accommodation for someone else. Someone had seen the manager coming out from Chitran Tirumeni's outhouse. The first messenger they sent came and reported that he had told him about the matter. A little later, another messenger came, drenched in perspiration and said: 'He'll come. The manager will come.'

Then he didn't need to see Eman?

'You can see him later.'

The locals took the visitor's side and listed the shortcomings of the village. If strangers came, there were no hotels where they could eat. No place where they could sleep. The travellers' bungalow was always occupied by revenue or government officials. That was not all. There was the Anita bus service. There was not a day when it ran properly.

An unexpected question assailed him:

'Are you on duty, Inspector?'

He looked down and laughed silently from inside his sweat-stained, faded clothes. Inspector. Supervisor. Overseer. The villagers changed his position from time to time. They had all come to investigate. They were searching for unknown paths on soil that had changed its very face.

The villagers spoke for him, made efforts on his behalf.

And he waited.

It was not new to him, this kind of waiting, for someone who would come and tell him where to turn at a crossroad he did not know. And now he waited for a manager who worked for an owner he had never seen of a house he might rent.

A mongrel came running up from the south and sniffed at the people around. Then it came up to him, stood there uncertainly and ran off northward.

The manager came at last. He would have to face a lot of questions again ... The fear that he would have to fumble for answers was unfounded. The manager hurried towards him, taking long strides, his hurricane lamp tearing apart the darkness on the road. The knot of people moved away to show him respect.

The manager said to everyone there: 'I've got the key.'

They expressed their wonder: 'Really? We knew only you could pull it off.'

'He'd shut the place up after the village headman left, saying he wasn't going to rent it out anymore. How many people asked for it! Would he listen? Your things ...?'

The villagers answered: 'They'll come.'

'It must be infested with bats and mice and bandicoots upstairs. The ground floor won't be too bad.'

The villagers said: 'One person doesn't need much space.'

'When the things come, will the coolies know the way?'

He did not answer.

The villagers came to his help.

'We'll arrange with the shopkeeper here.'

Good.

He followed the glow of the manager's lantern. Four of the villagers went behind him. Someone chased away the mongrel that came sniffing at them again.

The paths cutting across the fields were wet. There were rumblings again in the dark sky. The darkness that had run away from the pale light of the open fields hovered in the yard they entered and in the locked house.

In the dim light, he made out the wooden door which had once had carvings on it. The manager opened it with an effort. The hinges creaked in pain.

'Wait. There must be a lantern inside.'

The manager went in with his hurricane lamp. There were sounds of more doors being opened inside. Then the stairs creaked. The manager brought out another lighted lantern and placed it in the porch.

'Your things?'

The villagers repeated: 'They'll come.'

'What about food?'

'I had some on the way.'

'The well is there,' said the manager, pointing it out. 'The bucket is by it.'

After what seemed to him like a very long time, he was alone. The dark house, the smoking lantern and the rusty key were in his possession.

He blew away the specks of wood falling down from the moth-eaten ceiling and lay down, his head on his elbow, gazing into the darkness outside.

The manager had promised to come again the next day to discuss the rent and other formalities. A vague meeting in some faraway space called tomorrow. Forget it, he thought. He had finally found a house. Bats upstairs, white ants which had eaten into the worn wood downstairs, crickets outside. All the same it was a house, the refuge he had imagined during his wanderings. Yes, my friends, a refuge for me as well.

In the morning, people gathered in the first teashop to open in the bazaar, to find out about the stranger who had just arrived. They waited for the manager to come and see the new tenant. It seemed he had not haggled about the rent. He had paid it in advance saying he did not want to be in debt. He was going to engage workmen to clean the house.

The manager went on. Our Eman's a loner. And harmless. But he's quite mad at times. Sometimes he'd say he didn't want any tenants, sometimes that he wanted to demolish the house and rebuild it. Sometimes …

The villagers agreed: 'The Master's always like that!'

People hovered around the rented house without going in. To see the new person who had come from another place. The yard had been cleaned. Workmen were planting karaveeraka saplings to form a higher fence at the edge instead of the old broken one. Watching the new tenant wring out the rag with which he had mopped the floor and spread it out to dry, they asked, hoping to strike up an acquaintance: 'Have your things come?'

'They have.'

He was relieved to see them go away with a satisfied smile. They had not asked when the things came or how.

He worked hard. He had to clean the cobwebs before the next batch of villagers came. And chase out the bats.

The workman who had gone to the market arrived with provisions and household articles.

When the palm leaf screens over the windows were lifted, light poured into the house. The musty odour of stale air slowly disappeared. He walked in and out of the house with a faint air of possessive pride.

The memory of the room he had slept in when he started on his journey had grown dim. He tried to recall it as he lay down, tired after working late. Pots of wet clay turning smooth as they rubbed against the spinning potter's wheel. The smell of burnt clay in the kiln. Fresh clay moulded in various shapes everywhere he looked. A floor smeared with cowdung. In the direction where drains filled with the stench of urine snaked towards the light, only smoking kilns could be seen.

It was from that room that he had started his journey. Over the years his footsteps, wandering over fallen leaves and dust, had left no impressions. After that—verandahs leaking with rain water, bamboo screens and benches stained with sweat and dirt, interminable paths, nightmares …

In the evening, he planted the rose cuttings the workmen had brought in the corner of the yard. He arranged the new pots and pans in the room that darkness had vacated for him. He gazed wonderingly at the pan boiling over the lighted fire.

At night, a lighted lantern and the Eman's manager arrived, cleaving the darkness.

'You're well?'

'Yes!'

'No trouble of any kind?'

'No.'

The manager expressed doubts about the wisdom of having the yard and compound cleaned. A place that belonged to someone else. If the Eman told him to, he would have to vacate. The manager advised him not to waste money.

When the manager left, he told himself confidently, I won't vacate, I won't give up the house.

He made friends with the people around. He could identify the yellow birds in the clump of bamboo near the fence. The little birds that pecked at the grass around the areca nut trees began to recognise him. What a wonder, weaver birds began to build a nest in a corner of the western room. One night he discovered that the chirp of the crickets in the fields had a rhythm of its own.

Once the villagers who came asked him:

'Have you decided how long you want the house?'

He said calmly: 'I am not leaving.'

They were shocked.

Someone who knew the Eman and the manager said: 'All the beams are rotten. It seems they want to rebuild the place.'

He grunted, concealing his uneasiness. Someone said:

'It's a place no one wanted. Now that there's a tenant, Master's being difficult!'

Before the rains came, the manager came and told him. The Eman is not going to thatch the roof. He says, let it leak and fall down.

The manager was reluctant to accept the advance rent. But he insisted on giving it.

The rains started. The wind whistled over the fields, then blew through the areca nut palms. The showers grew heavier and rainwater collected in the drains. The areca nut palms and banana plants shivered, completely drenched by rain.

He sat inside and watched fearfully as the rainwater seeped in through the cracks in the crumbling mud walls and gushed into the house. Was everything going to collapse, just like the owner wanted? Straw blew off the verandah. Water that was stained red poured through the gaps in the roof. He went out in the rain, made a paste of clay and water and tried to block the cracks in the walls. He lined up pots and pans on the floor to catch the water gushing through the roof. He mopped up the water that the wind had driven in.

Then the furious rain stopped. The last puff of wind lingered in the air like a child's whimper.

The manager came again. He did not smile or sit down. He wanted to say to this man who wore such a stern expression, look, I've plugged the leaks. I'm going to repair the roof. I'll see that this old house doesn't collapse. I'm not vacating it.

The manager sat there looking as if he was annoyed with someone, while he went out and called workmen from hutments in the next compound. They plucked leaves from the palmyra tree near the fence and thrust them into the gaps in the roof.

Sunshine still wet with rain spread around them.

The manager said without looking at him, holding out the balance of the rent: 'The Eman says you have to leave the house. Here, take this.' He did not take it.

'It's not my fault. That's Master's nature. He won't listen to anyone.'

The manager left the money on the seat and walked off. When he got to the gate, he turned.

'It's better you go. What else can you do? No one has ever gone against Eman's wishes.'

The villagers came. They would not look him in the eye either. But there was sympathy in their faces.

'We're sorry you're leaving. What can you do? It's the Master's house. You have to leave when he tells you to.'

The manager came again three days later. 'They're sending people to throw out your things and evict you. I don't know anything. I'm going.'

He went to the small inner room and bolted the door.

They would come, Dharman Mudalali's hired labourers.

He did not light a fire. Through the window, he could see the paths across the fields. He pulled the window shut.

He heard the lowered voices coming nearer and nearer and asked, with a start:

'Who is it?'

They were Eman's workmen.

He did not say anything. He swallowed hard.

He heard the sound of pots and pans being hurled out. Then the sounds of the house being broken up.

'We have nothing against you. We're doing what the Master told us to do, that's all.'

'We're tearing down the roof. Then we'll break the walls down. We'll smash the walls of the room you're sitting in last of all. You can sit there till Eman comes.'

'Will he come?'

'He will. If he says he'll come, he will.'

Another period of waiting. He peered out through the window. Pots and pans were scattered over the courtyard. Things he had collected on his travels. The fields were still empty. Perhaps … he made a wish. That the Master would change his mind.

I will call him Yejamanan, Master. I'll always call him that. I'll prostrate before him. Look, give me back my refuge. At least this final refuge that I found. I can't bear it. Travellers in soiled clothes, waiting endlessly. Rooms reeking with the odour of dirty bundles and sweat. Cold benches. The smell of burning kilns. I can't, I can't go back to them.

Muttering to himself, he paced the room within the four walls that still stood.

Look, clay-stained rainwater will no longer flow through the gaping roof. The rain and wind will not come through the palmyra thatch—just look.

He lay down, warning himself to stay calm. When the evening light faded, he shivered. Was darkness creeping in on him like the Yejamanan?

There was no place to run away to. Where were those sounds from? Were they hooves or human footfalls? Were they cattle returning home? He waited, a bundle wrapped in a filthy cloth clutched to his breast.

Somehow, when the fearsome sounds came nearer, he did not feel afraid. Heavy footsteps, coming up the front steps, then into the verandah.

He placed the bundle quietly on his head, closed his eyes and lay down. The doors wept as they were opened, showing the way in.

Come, Yejamanan, come.

The Sale

He had more or less learnt the topography of that huge city. It was not difficult to understand the instructions given on the telephone. He got off at the bus stop near the Siddhi Vinayaka temple, asked a few discreet questions to make sure it was the road leading westward to the seashore and walked along. When the woman's voice had asked on the telephone whether he was coming by car, Sunil Roy had said he was coming in a taxi—and accused himself of an unnecessary shred of false pride.

Any instructions given to someone coming in a taxi were of course applicable to those who came on foot as well. The soft voice of the woman had said in convent-accented English: 'A kilometre after you come on to Sea Face Road, you will see a high-rise building under construction on the right side. No one can miss it. There are large flats coming up there. Another five minutes and you'll see this building. The name is Sagar. Remember, Sagar. It's flat number nine on the fourth floor.'

'Your name?'

'That's not necessary. Flat number nine, Sagar.'

Since she was selling household goods, maybe a shred of false pride prevented her too from revealing her name.

It was farther than he had expected. Most of the buildings had names associated with the sea. Large old buildings in spacious compounds full of trees and ornamental shrubs. Finally, he saw the skeleton of a huge building with many floors on his right. There was a big crane on top of it, the labourers underneath looking like so many ants. He walked on and saw Sagar exactly where it should have been. If people had to be given directions, they had to be as accurate as this.

It was an old building. There was a Gurkha watchman on the ground-floor verandah, half sitting, half reclining, leaning on his elbow, looking very bored. He moved slightly and looked at the visitor, but said nothing.

The lift had gone up. He pressed the bell and waited. He could hear the machine creaking and groaning as it moved, tired of going up and down the spine of the old building. A middle-aged man with patches of leucoderma on his hands and lips opened the door and stepped out, a suitcase in his hand. Sunil thought he resembled Gopal Dutt, the cashier in the first newspaper office where he had worked.

When he got off at the third floor he saw three doors in front of him. Number nine was right in front and there was no board outside. Maybe the names of the residents on all the floors were displayed downstairs. He should have taken a look. In the science of buying and selling, it was useful to address a person by name. He thought of his old Sales Manager's study class. It was because he could not master that science that, fed up after five years of selling sewing machines, Sunil had gone back to the love of his youth, journalism.

He pressed the doorbell. Was he being inspected through the magic eye on the door? The small corridor outside was dark even in the daytime. Those who looked from inside would not see anything clearly.

As he wondered whether to press the bell again, the door opened slowly.

'I phoned a while ago. The name is Sunil Roy.'

The door opened fully. In front of him was a tall, slender woman in a blue saree with a touch of grey in the strands of hair over her forehead. Her very fair skin seemed to have a tinge of yellow.

'Please come in.'

It was the voice he had heard on the telephone.

'My God!' There was a sudden note of anxiety in her voice. 'Did you step on it? Did you?'

She bent down and picked up something. A small paper packet.

She explained: 'They're flowers for the puja. The maid servant usually brings it in. You didn't step on it, did you?'

'No.'

He followed her in.

'Just a minute. Excuse me. Do sit down if you want to.'

She opened a door on the right of the living room and went in. That must be the master bedroom. Was the master of the house performing a puja or having a bath?

How ugly the building looked from outside! And yet, once you were inside, the flat was beautiful! The venetian blinds had been pulled up and one of the shutters of the glass window lay open. A cool sea breeze blew in through it. The leaves of the money plants growing in brass jars swayed in the breeze.

Until now, Sunil had had only a vague idea of how to furnish a flat if he were to live in a big city one with someone of his choice. Here was an excellent model before him.

A sofa set upholstered in black leather. A carpet in the centre. A big heart-shaped glass-topped table and small round stools with little cloth covers on them. He looked for the price of the set. Maybe it was not for sale.

The experience of the two Sundays previous to this one had taught him that the articles for sale in large houses were usually kept aside. Cards with the price written on them would be hung on each piece, to avoid bargaining. You could take a look, buy if you wanted to or walk out.

He realised that she was not performing a puja inside but wrestling with a cupboard. To the right of the door through which he had come in was the kitchen. Its counter opened into the living room. Food could be picked up from the counter and passed onto the guests. The visitors would not see the ugly faces of the kitchen or the servant. It was not enough to have money, one had to know how to live in style: that was one of Father's golden dictums. Father had been contemptuous of the newly rich. He had derived the greatest amusement from decrying them. Even in his last days, when he did not have the money to buy the opium he needed to relieve his suffering, he would describe the courage he had displayed, wearing khadi when going for an interview before an English Sahib. While struggling to live on the salary of the forty-five rupees he earned as an elementary school teacher, he had secured a first class in the B.A. degree examination of the Calcutta University. He would talk of all this repeatedly to his companions.

The mistress of the house came back and said:

'One of the cupboards doesn't open. What a nuisance!'

As a matter of courtesy he asked: 'Have you lost the key? Is it for sale?'

'This is the key all right. I opened it even yesterday.'

'Can I help?' asked Sunil hesitantly. Not many people knew that this was not an act he put on: helping women, being at their service, had become a part of his character. Therefore little things he did were often misinterpreted. They would say it was not chivalry but chauvinism. Gowri went to the extent of calling it a masked male chauvinism.

'Please, will you?' She gave him the key.

'My husband sent in this advertisement just the day before yesterday. And then he had to go on a business tour. It's I who am in trouble now.'

She opened the bedroom door and showed him the cupboard. Sunil noticed the new air-conditioner. The key was bent because she had used force when the door would not open. He made an effort to open it, praying he would not fail.

'Sorry. It won't open.'

'Never mind.'

'Is there anything you need urgently in ...?'

'No, nothing like that.'

They went back to the living room.

The telephone rang. She picked it up and gave her number.

'Yes, that's right. Come and have a look. To tell you the price of each ... come and look at them, that's best.'

She put the telephone down and said: 'Now all sorts of

bothersome people will come and nothing will be sold. He put in the advertisement without telling me. Now I have to talk to everyone who comes. There have been telephone calls since six thirty this morning.'

Sunil Roy reminded her of what he wanted.

'The things for sale?'

'All these. The sofa set. The dining table. The bed. Everything's for sale.'

'You're leaving Bombay, are you?'

'Ahmedabad next. A promotion and transfer for my husband. What are the things you want?'

Sunil thought for a minute.

'The ad mentioned a typewriter.'

'Oh, that's gone. A man in this building came in the morning—actually, the servant from the next flat. His brother types petitions for a living. Poor chap!'

He wondered if she had given it away out of compassion. He thought unhappily that if he had started out as soon as he had read the *Times*, he would have got it cheap.

'It ... it was the typewriter I wanted.'

'It was a very old machine. He bought it when he got his first job.'

He was not interested in anything else. Still, for the fun of it, he asked: 'What will this sofa set cost?'

'This.' She thought for a while, scratching the top of her right ear. 'I wonder where that paper's gone ...'

She began to search for it. She said, 'I know, we should have noted down the prices on tags and hung them on all these things. That would have saved trouble for the buyers. But I didn't think anyone would buy anything. When I reminded him about the ad just as he was about to leave yesterday, I saw him scribble something on a piece of paper.'

She finally found the piece of paper between the pages of a book.

'Here it is. Let me see. Sofa set ... four thousand.'

He concealed his surprise.

'It was made to order when we were in Calcutta. We must

have spent much more than that. Still, will anyone buy it for four thousand? I doubt it. It's far too much, isn't it?' She spoke haltingly, slowly, then suddenly very fast.

'Isn't it?'

He essayed a smile. 'I think so.'

'Mr Parekh, my husband, thinks all this looks old-fashioned now. You're not buying it anyway, are you? Don't they all seem brand new?'

'They certainly do.'

'Are you from Bombay?'

'No, from Calcutta.'

'A Bengali?'

'Yes, Madam.'

He saw a sudden eagerness in her face.

'I like Bengalis. Most of my friends, my close friends, are Bengalis. And Calcutta—it's my favourite place. Whatever people might say, Calcutta is the best place in India. What does this Bombay have ...?'

He tried to smile. He remembered Calcutta had dealt him its share of wounds. He had arrived in Delhi, believing it was an escape. But that city too had not been behind the other in dealing him wounds—through his newspaper office, through Gowri. This was his third city.

'I've only been here three months.'

'You'll soon realise. Wait a bit. Bombay will suck the life out of you. Look, it was after I came here that my hair began to turn grey.'

She smoothed out the strands of grey above her forehead.

'They say those who have stayed in Bombay never want to leave it. I would be happy to run away even a day earlier. What's Ahmedabad like?'

He admitted his ignorance. 'I don't know. I've never been there.'

'I'm sure it will be better than this. My flat in Calcutta—how peaceful Lake Road was.'

He decided to offer a deserving word of praise:

'Isn't this a pleasant flat? The sea just beyond and a cool breeze.'

The telephone rang.

As she muttered, 'This nuisance will go on all day,' and walked to the phone, the doorbell rang. She appealed to him: 'Please!' Then said in broken Bengali, 'Must be a buyer. Please talk to them on my behalf.'

Was she using his mother tongue in order to take liberties with him? He was amused. Was the man who had come to buy an old typewriter going to play the role of the man of the house?

He opened the door and saw a short man with glasses in a white safari suit and a stout woman who had vermilion smeared thickly over the parting of her hair. Upper middle-class, he thought. Husband and wife. Maybe married couples began to look like each other over the years.

The husband asked in English, with no trace of a North Indian accent, 'Is this the place mentioned in the advertisement?'

Behind him, Mrs Parekh was describing the household articles. He thought the person on the other end of the line must be the sort that was insistent on knowing all the details.

He put on a salesman's smile and said, 'This is the place. Come in and see. Welcome.'

'What are the things?'

Drawing a half circle in the air that took in the sofa set and dining table, Sunil Roy said: 'All these.'

Mrs Parekh burst out laughing over the telephone. Covering the mouthpiece, she said to him in Bengali: 'When I said a thousand rupees for the bed, he asked what was so 'is-special' about it! Does he want to know whether there's something else that goes along with it?'

He had no desire to laugh. He invited the visitors into the living room.

Mrs Parekh spoke into the telephone again: 'I was laughing with a friend of mine. Come and have a look and buy it if you like.'

The woman who had come asked: 'You are Bengalis, aren't you?'

He nodded in assent. Their attention was on the dining table. An oval one that would seat eight. The chairs had high backs and carved legs.

'How much is it?'

Mrs Parekh moved to his side so that he too could look at the piece of paper in her hand. It was quite hard to read Mr Parekh's handwriting. A dining table, then 'eight chairs' in brackets—he was embarrassed to tell them the figure written against the words.

Mrs Parekh ran her index finger under the line. There were traces of nail polish on her fingers. She prodded him silently.

He said, 'Six thousand.'

The woman looked at the man with a twisted smile, as if she had just heard a joke.

The man gave Sunil Roy a look that seemed to bore into him and asked: 'Really?'

Since he did not want to admit defeat either in his role of salesman or as the temporary master of the house, he said very seriously: 'It's new. It was made to order a year ago. How much do you think it will cost to make a set like this now?'

It was the woman who replied. 'You may be right. But one comes to a sale to get things cheap.'

The husband asked, looking as if he was ready to listen to another joke: 'What do you want for this sofa set?'

With her eyes on the paper, Mrs Parekh raised the sum: 'Five thousand.'

He looked at her and realised she had not said it by mistake. The husband and wife moved to a corner of the living room for a whispered consultation, then came back. The woman took out a visiting card from her handbag and held it out to Sunil, saying:

'Our card. Please call this number if there is any change in the price of the dining table.' She smiled at Mrs Parekh, inclined her head and walked out, followed by her husband.

He looked at the card. Mr and Mrs Dharadher. Both were doctors with foreign degrees.

Mrs Parekh read the card and said: 'Doctors ... with their own clinic. Must be making plenty of money. With both being doctors, I wonder what their family life is like. They cannot hide any of the secrets of their bodies from each other, can they?'

Not able to find a direct answer, he said vaguely, 'Who knows?'

To make sure his role in the drama was over, he said, 'I'll go now.'

'Sit down,' she said. 'You spoke in an authoritative tone, like Mr Parekh. It's a godsend that you thought of coming here. I would have gone mad if I had been alone in all this confusion.'

He sat down on one of the seats near the glass window. On the seashore below, washermen were washing clothes on the granite slabs scattered here and there. The sea seemed to peer in at this point and go back. The expanse of blue tinged with black was calm. The line of water where the inner sea met the ocean seemed to him to have a metallic gleam.

As if to justify his sitting there feeling so relaxed, he said: Such a beautiful view.'

'Oh, it was the flat on Lake Road I really liked. I was never bored even if I was by myself for days. I've never been afraid in Calcutta.'

'What does Mr Parekh do?' he asked with a secret hope that this would be the beginning of an acquaintance with someone in a high position.

'He's an executive in Brett and Company. He'll soon be the Indian Director.'

He had heard of women of this class falling in love in order to escape the boredom caused by a combination of prosperity and laziness. Most of the stories took shape from malice. But he knew at least one artist who had made capital out of such a situation. Vipin, whom he had met in Delhi. The man had known well that even at forty-one, his face was lack-lustre, drained of blood and energy. Sunil took firm hold of his thoughts which had begun to run wild, trampling on the dead leaves of memory.

'What are you doing here?'

'Journalism.'

If she asked anything more, he thought he would tell her

the name of the newspaper whose management had agreed to consider his appointment at the beginning of the next month.

The bulge in her stomach was out of proportion to her tall, slender figure. When she stood beside him, he guessed she was at least an inch taller than he. Fifteen years ago, eyes that failed to conceal admiration and envy must have followed her every time she walked into a gathering.

'Where do you stay in Bombay?'

'Sion.'

'I've only heard of it. I don't know where it is.'

He hoped he would not have to tell her lies about the dark, unventilated room on the first floor of an old building that belonged to a grocer, next to a cemetery.

'You live with your family?'

After a minute's delay he said, 'No, alone.'

'Do you need anything else? A cupboard or a dressing table? There's a good writing table. Come, I'll show you. I had forgotten about it.'

She opened a door and he walked in. Another bedroom. It showed signs of having been used until very recently. A good writing table and chair. A number of old books lay on the table and prints of Abba and Osibisa were stuck on either side. A plastic board warned: 'A genius at work. Please be silent.'

He asked with a faint smile, 'Who is this genius?'

'My daughter. This was her room.'

'And now …?'

'She's in London. She went there on a scholarship to study business management. Then she married and settled down there.'

'You've only one daughter?'

'Yes.'

'When you are bored with Bombay, you can go to London for a change, to your daughter.'

He thought she had not heard him. And found fault with himself for asking her about things that did not concern him.

'Who knows whether she's in London now or somewhere

else! Her last letter was about the man she was going to marry. It's a year now. We had just arrived here.'

'Who is her husband?'

'A German. She had sent a photograph. It must be somewhere here.' There were a few books in the cupboard in the room. And a landscape of some foreign country on the wall. 'She was brilliant as a student. First rank, first prize in all the quiz competitions. Four hundred candidates wrote the exam and there were two scholarships. Deepa got one of them. Do you like the writing table?'

'It's good. But I doubt it will fit in my study.'

'Take it if you like it. Don't bother about the price. It's not on the list. Let it be of use to someone. Take it.'

She wrote "Sold" on the table with her finger in bold letters and signed below. The letters and signature showed clearly on the dusty wooden top. Sold.

Sunil Roy did not show his astonishment. The telephone rang again.

'I must sell all these off somehow, then get some sleep,' she muttered as she went out. He followed her.

He asked himself why he was hanging around here needlessly. And found the answer himself: he had escaped the bleakness of another Sunday of roaming around the streets in the area.

She was describing the sofa and dining table over the telephone.

'No, there are no electrical appliances. No, not that either.'

The doorbell rang again. Mrs Parekh stretched out her hand and signalled to him. He opened the door. A young man and woman who reminded him of married couples or lovers in advertisements. Both wore faded jeans. On the young man's bare chest was a tiny anchor on a gold chain. She came in with her hand on his shoulder.

Mrs Parekh put down the telephone and said softly: 'Show them around. I didn't offer you anything to drink. Tea or coffee?'

'Thank you, nothing now. Come in, please.'

'This is where the advertisement ...'

'This is the place.' Once again, he shook off his irritation at having slipped into this situation and donned a salesman's persuasive role. 'This is the dining table. And the sofa set. The four pieces on the other side go with it.'

'Do you have a cot?'

He looked at Mrs Parekh, ready to say, 'No.' She said, 'There's a double cot. And two singles. Come and see.'

This was certainly not the young man who had asked over the phone if there was anything special about the bed. This new bridegroom or lover was pretending a greater seriousness than was needed, probably to appear more mature than he really was before his companion.

He invited them to go with Mrs Parekh.

The young man tapped the double bed with his hand. The girl pressed the mattress down. She asked half in jest,

'Will you give us the mattress with the bed?'

'Of course. You can take the lot.' Mrs Parekh signalled to him to come out.

'What should I say they cost together? There's no price marked on the mattress.'

'Do you want to sell it?'

'Mr Parekh had decided to sell everything. And change all the old things.'

She laughed softly. Her voice trembled slightly: 'I'm the oldest.' The young man and woman had come out and were waiting anxiously to know the price.

'Two cots, two mattresses, pillows: two thousand five hundred for all of them together.'

She glanced at Sunil Roy as if to confirm she had calculated right. He turned his face away.

'It's far too much,' said the girl.

He wondered whether he should start a sales talk and the young man said:

'It's not that the price is too high. What we meant is we can't afford that.'

Mrs Parekh's face brightened.

'Right. You liked them?'

'Yes.'

'Will they do for you?'

'Oh yes, certainly.'

'How much can you give me?'

They looked at each other. The girl said: 'Five hundred now. The rest in six instalments.'

The young man corrected her: 'Not six, four. Four at the most.'

'If we can finish in four instalments ...'

'How much would that be totally?'

They were not the only ones to find Mrs Parekh's question surprising. Sunil Roy wondered how people could leave for Ahmedabad with debts they had to collect here. The young woman mustered enough courage to say with a smile:

'A thousand five hundred. That's all we can afford.'

Mrs Parekh said: 'Bring the money. And a truck or van. Offer accepted.'

The young people looked relieved, as if they had achieved a great thing.

'All right.'

As they moved towards the door, Mrs Parekh said, 'You must take them away quickly. With four Bombay Mills sheets as a bonus from me.' She heaved a sigh of relief as they left.

'A sale at last. May it be useful to them.'

She hurried inside as if she had suddenly remembered something, picked up a lipstick from among the cosmetics scattered on the dressing table, opened it and marked on the three pillows lying on the double bed: Sold. Sold. Sold. The telephone rang again. 'Please answer.'

He agreed to her request and picked up the phone.

'Eight-three-four-two-four-two?'

'Yes.'

'Yes, it's we who put in the ad. He hesitated a moment when the caller asked who was speaking, then answered: 'This is Mr Parekh's house.'

He followed Mrs Parekh's example and gave them a list. He invited them to come and have a look whenever they wished.

When he put the phone down, she said: 'It was God who sent you to me. God is with those who have no one of their own.'

He was beginning to enjoy this. He moved one of the stools to a spot where he could get a better view of the sea and the breeze blew better, and sat down.

'Tea?'

'No.'

'A drink? There's beer, whisky and gin here.'

He was embarrassed. 'So early? No.'

'With your permission.' She opened the cupboard near the dining table and took out the bottles. She poured out almost half a glass of gin, added cordial and took a large gulp. Glass in hand, she came and sat down facing him.

'Come on, talk. Say something about Calcutta.'

He smiled. 'What can I say? I lived there twenty-eight years. That's all.'

She gazed at some distant point in the sea and slowly sipped her drink.

He observed her attentively without her being aware of it. Dark shadows under her eyes. A moistness at the corner of her eyes, as if a drop of liquid had melted there. Her blue veins stood out on the fair skin of her arms. She looked at him suddenly and, to conceal his embarrassment, he asked:

'When will Mr Parekh be back?'

'Maybe tonight. Maybe tomorrow. He said he would call. Anyway, we managed a sale.'

She drank what was left of the gimlet in her glass, then said: 'His theory is that I do not have the capacity to do anything well. Not even to keep the servants in order or maintain laundry accounts.'

She stopped. He felt the gimlet had given her a sudden sense of well-being. Gazing at the sea, she asked: 'Which country would you reach if you went straight across the sea from here?'

It was the Arabian Sea. On the other side of it ... he tried to draw a map in his mind and failed. So he said: 'I don't know. Africa, perhaps ...'

'One should be able to cross over to the opposite shore whenever one wants, shouldn't one?'

He laughed.

Mrs Parekh looked at her empty glass and said: 'I grew up under the thumb of a very, very orthodox father. Even eggs and onions were forbidden in the house. After my marriage, when someone forced me to drink a gimlet at the first dinner party, I threw up. My husband scolded me when we got home that night for not being used to such things ...'

He looked at the shadows under her eyes as if to show that he was interested in the story of her life.

'Now he quarrels with me because I drink in the daytime. What is there to do in the daytime? Sit down doing nothing, then sleep a lot. Dinner parties at night.'

He moved into the role of an advisor and said, 'You can do a lot of things. Social work. Or you can take up a job.'

The doorbell rang again.

'I'll go.' She said as she was going out, 'Pour out another drink for me. Now you can have one too, can't you?'

He got up. But was not ready for a drink himself.

The newcomers were a bent old woman with a huge swelling on her neck and a small girl.

Mrs Parekh began to speak in Hindi and the old woman said in English: 'I am Mrs Kamath. This is my granddaughter.'

What she wanted was the sofa set. She walked around it, examining it attentively. Sunil was convinced that the old woman had seen much in her life. Her walk, her look, her speech, all of them showed remarkable self-confidence.

She used to live abroad. Her three children were abroad. She had lived with each of them in turn and was now back in Bombay. There were tenants in one half of the family house. She was going to stay in the other half.

Mrs Parekh said, 'My husband had marked the price at four thousand. I don't want four thousand. You can have it for three thousand five hundred.'

The old lady had a beautiful smile. Not one of her teeth was bad. 'Isn't that too much?' It was him she asked.

Mrs Parekh smiled. 'Auntie, what's your budget for a sofa set?'

The change in her attitude was obvious.

'I don't have a budget to speak of. The tenants give me some money. And I still get a bit of my husband's pension.'

'Still, there must be a figure in your mind.'

'No, there isn't.'

The old woman sat down on the sofa. Mrs Parekh sat down beside her, took the child by the hand and made her sit down too. She laid her hand on the old woman's shoulder and said softly: 'Auntie, that's a mistake. A mistake we women make. We don't have a budget for anything. No estimate, no accounts. That's why our men have to go to such trouble.'

She looked at Sunil Roy as if to ask whether she was right. He was confused, not sure what she had in mind.

Mrs Parekh continued to talk to the old woman and her granddaughter. 'Our men lose heavily in business. They lose at the card table. Their pretty secretaries land them in losses. None of this hurts their valour. But if we don't maintain our household budgets, they'd be shattered.'

There was a smile of sympathy on the old woman's face. Mrs Parekh took the child's hand and said to her affectionately: 'You must learn this when you grow up. Don't forget.'

Sunil Roy made his decision. To make up for lost time—what had he lost?—he would help himself to a drink and then leave. He walked to the liquor cabinet with his empty glass.

Mrs Parekh was talking very softly to the old lady, who seemed to be protesting from time to time. She took the old lady's hand and said something that sounded as if she was pleading with her. He heard the old lady say as if she was in a trance, 'Thank you dear, thank you, dear.'

She took her grandchild's hand and left.

He was immersed in mixing his gimlet. Mrs Parekh came up to him looking very happy. 'I've sold it! Nice old woman. I hope she keeps well and has many guests.'

He was about to add cordial to her gin but she gestured to him not to. She added some water to it herself, raised the glass and said formally, 'Cheers!'

'How much did you sell the sofa set for?'

'Don't ask. It's sold. It wasn't nice of us to have sent those doctors away. Where's that card?'

She began looking for the visiting card she had left on one of the stools. He swallowed a mouthful from his glass lest it spill over, went up to the window and looked out at the sea. Another meaningless day was creeping past him. He wanted to talk to someone. He had not come across a single friend who was worthwhile the last three months. It was then that he saw it—the huge advertisement on a page of the women's magazine lying open on top of the curio cabinet. Gowri, modelling a saree, with a bewitching smile. He felt no animosity towards Gowri for having escaped from the prison of wifehood she had been in with the senior subeditor Sunil Roy. Had Gowri's smile really been so bewitching? Gowri had become more beautiful when she became a model.

He was halfway through his drink when he heard her voice, delighted at having found the lost visiting card. Mrs Parekh picked up the telephone. 'Dr Dharadher?'

'Then put me on to Mrs Dharadher please.' She winked childishly to signal that the person she wanted was coming on the line.

'This is Mrs Parekh. What price can you offer for the dining table you saw? Tell me ... don't hestitate.'

The reply must have come after the other person thought it over for a while.

'Agreed. Come and take the things. You're welcome.'

She put the phone down and said, 'Grand! Simply grand! It's sold. The doctor is happy.'

He took out the crumpled packet of cigarettes he remembered having in his pocket. Luckily, there was one left. He lighted it and looked out at the sea, savouring the flavour of the gin.

Mrs Parekh came and sat down again facing him. A mild excitement coursed through his veins.

He wondered whether to talk about Gowri. He did not want anyone to tell him Gowri had been in the wrong. All he wanted was for someone to say *he* had not been in the wrong. Some disinterested third party.

Mrs Parekh said, 'You must come again. Even if we are in Ahmedabad. You're a journalist after all, you'll be paid for your time. You can interview Mr Parekh and write about him. Won't it make a good story, how a mere salesman rose to be a director?'

'All successes make amazing stories.'

'What is there left to sell? Please stay until everything goes. I'm alone, don't you see? It was God who sent you.'

'This sale … is it one of the amusements of the wealthy?'

His voice was quite serious.

'We have to sell everything and vacate the flat,' said Mrs Parekh, paying no heed to his question. 'Perhaps you can go to a little more trouble for me and do me one more favour?'

He was willing to hear what it was.

'Even after everything is sold, people are sure to keep coming. I will lie still on the floor here. Write some kind of price on a tag and tie it around my neck.'

He tried to smile and failed.

'It's not a joke. What figure will you write? You look to me like an intelligent person. What price will you mark? Tell me …'

He did not say anything. She leaned against an arm of the sofa and said, 'I didn't sleep last night. I could not sleep even after I took three Calmpose tablets. What price will you mark on the tag around my neck?'

The doorbell rang again.

Mrs Parekh said without opening her eyes: 'Sell anything you please. At whatever price they offer.'

He hurried to the door. It was a tall, lean man, with a skin as fair as a foreigner's. His moustache had been blackened with an eyebrow pencil, he had long, thick hair with a tinge of grey in it and blue eyes. There was a briefcase in his hand.

Sunil closed the door and the newcomer looked at him in surprise. Sunil said: 'This is the place. A cupboard, a sofa set and …'

The man asked: 'Who are you?'

Mrs Parekh sat up on the sofa. 'Welcome. I am Mrs Parekh.' She pointed at Sunil Roy and said, 'That is Mr Parekh. We are selling all our old things and going in for new ones. She prodded her own chest with her finger: 'You can name a price for everything including *this*.'

Sunil thought the visitor looked stunned.

Mrs Parekh began to laugh softly. The laughter grew louder and louder, became interspersed with sobs.

The visitor crossed the room in three or four quick strides, gave Mrs Parekh a sound slap on her cheek and said in a low voice:

'Learn to behave yourself. To behave.'

The laughter ceased and there was silence. The distant murmur of waves hovered outside.

Seeing another Sunday which had begun with faint expectations coming to an end, Sunil Roy opened the door quickly and went out.

He checked outside the door, to avoid making a mistake. Was there a packet of flowers? No, there wasn't.

When the Doors of Heaven Open

Kutti Narayanan could not help thinking how ill-fated a river was if the water in it should flow waist-deep even in the month of Thulam. If this was the situation now, the villagers were really going to suffer. But then, in all houses these days, men and women had begun to bathe in closed bathrooms. Even the Christian chap from the pump-house, who used to come to bathe in the river at this time, was not to be seen.

He finished his bath and was drying his dhoti in the breeze when Thami the cheruman came with a message: 'They've asked you to come at once. To Madhavan Thampuran's.'

The old man must have something for him to do. Maybe he wanted an offering to be made in the temple on the other bank of the river. Getting there was easy. Only three and a half miles. But the return trip! If it was an auspicious day, by the time the puja was over and he collected the *prasadam*, the sand of the river bed would have turned burning hot. He could not wear sandals because of his corns. And when he came back after the walk over the hot sand and gave the old man the prasadam, he would subject him to a spate of advice. He would remind him of all the sins he had committed on various occasions in life. Then, out would come twenty-five paise with a flourish, as if he was doing something great. It had in fact become a ritual to receive Madhavan Master's advice, his reprimands and the twenty-five paise.

Kutti Narayanan was annoyed to see Thami waiting on the river bank. The cheruman stood there as if he had brought a warrant of arrest to take him away.

'Get going, rascal, I'll come.'

'They said in the house that the Thampuran is worse.'

So he had been sent from the ancestral house. Couldn't the stupid fellow have told him earlier? A feeling of happy anticipation spread through him. Careful not to show it, he said, 'Walk along. I'll come straight there.'

So the schoolmaster Madhavan Nair's time had come at last. He made a mental calculation. Eighteen years older than he was. Master was seventy-two now. Seventy-two was a ripe age to die.

Kutti Narayanan was the most helpful man in the village of Kizhakkemuri. He was in demand wherever there was a birth or a death, a twenty-eighth day ceremony after a baby was born, the day a child was fed rice for the first time or during a wedding. Formerly, it was Kottilil Chathu Nair who had conducted these functions. It was he, Kutti Narayanan, who had attended Chathu Nair's death. But in Chathu Nair's time, customs and traditions had been strictly followed. Nowadays, when labour pains began, there was no need to send for the village midwife. Even the women of Kizhakkemuri had their babies in nursing homes. Wedding feasts did not have to be supervised. Were there men now who were bold enough to conduct a wedding in their ancestral home? Weddings were held in the Guruvayoor temple. There were no rituals for death anniversaries, no elaborate funeral rituals, no ceremonies for feeding a baby rice for the first time. All that remained were deaths. And even those were few.

As he wound his half-dry *mundu* around his waist, he made a mental calculation. It was a good thing Madhavan Master had decided to die. It must happen after sunset tomorrow, he thought. If he gave his relatives and near ones the chance to arrive as he drew his last breath before sunset the next day, it would be auspicious. There would be the right configuration of the zodiac signs: the conjunction of the eleventh and twelfth days after full moon, with the Thirovonam star in the ascendant. The moment when the doors of heaven would open.

There were only three of his children to come. His sister's children were right here. Since his children lived in distant places, the miserliness which was characteristic of the folk of Kizhakkemuri would not have affected them greatly. They would give generously when they left. It would be no empty boast to say no one knew as well as Kutti Narayanan how to make a person die neatly. There were rules for deciding when to close the eyes, when to tie up the mouth and so on. And then, it was no small matter to bathe and lay out the body and smear *vibhuti* on it. When Kutti Narayanan laid it out, smeared with vibhuti, the body would take on a dignity of its own regardless of how disreputable the dead person had been.

True, on days when he had nothing to do, he had to put up with the barbed words people threw at him. It was all his fate.

He had been a pupil in the fifth standard, the class taught by the Madhavan Nair who was awaiting death now. You learnt much more writing and arithmetic in those days in the fifth standard than the B.A. students of today did. When all the older members of his family died and he was left alone, he stopped studying. That was when he went astray. He had inherited land which yielded a modest quantity of paddy and fifty cents of areca-nut garden. He learnt to gamble. Since he found farming tiresome, he leased out the land to tenants. Then, maybe because the stars that presided over his life were unlucky, he developed a liking for the taste of toddy. It was because he was ill-fated that he was pushed into evil ways.

When he finished a bath in the river, he usually stopped by Kunhuamma's house, took a pinch of vibhuti from the basket hanging on the verandah and dabbed it on his forehead. Today, he felt he was entitled to go right into the verandah. Kunhuamma's daughter was nursing her baby.

'Where's your mother?'

'She must be around somewhere,' she said without looking at him.

Kutti Narayanan said solemnly, 'Call her.' Kunhuamma came out just then with a winnowing tray full of paddy.

'Kunhu Kutti Amma!' he cried, adding the word 'Kutti' as a mark of respect. 'Madhavan Nair is finding it difficult to breathe. I'm on my way there.'

Kunhuamma said philosophically: 'All of us have to die one day or the other.'

'I have to organise things there. Won't get even a drink of water until all the rituals are over. Give me a glass of good water.'

Although extremely miserly by nature, Kunhuamma fell into the trap. In the old days, Kutti Narayanan used to take a little ground sandal paste along with the vibhuti to smear on his forehead. She had complained that he was wearing out the lump of sandalwood and hidden it! The way she had brandished a broom and driven out her husband was another story. Kunhuamma felt unusually kind-hearted towards Kutti Naryanan, on his way now to preside over a man's death.

'Hey, children, give Kutti Narayanan a glass of tea. And two idlies if there are any.'

Kutti Naryanan waited, chanting his prayers. He called out to those inside: 'Whatever it is, bring it quickly. Everyone there will be confused, not knowing what to do. It's only at times like these that we can be of help.'

Three idlies came with the tea. They did not taste too good, the chutney had been diluted with too much water.

'I'll see you when I'm a little more free, Kunhu Kutti Amma,' he said by way of thanking her as he walked away. Smiling, he murmured to himself, 'I'm the only one who calls her Kunhu Kutti Amma. But does the black ogress show me any gratitude for it?'

Crossing the rice fields, he went along the old path bordered by screwpine bushes that had now become a road and climbed the hill. This hill, Thannikunnu, had once been barren rock. Now many houses had been put up. The Panchayat President had said a road would soon go through it.

Of late, he had been avoiding going to Madhavan Nair's,

dreading the climb. But of course he had to go if he was sent for.

The man who was about to die was a person everyone in Kizhakkemuri respected. He led a well-ordered life. He did not chew betel leaves, use snuff or smoke beedies. He had learnt about Kutti Narayanan's newly-acquired evil habits only when he saw him involved in a brawl in front of the toddy shop. Master had sent for him and rebuked him. 'What a pity! You were intelligent enough when you were a student. What's happened to you now?'

Master reminded Kutti Narayanan that he had been very good at arithmetic. People would respect a person only if he made something of himself, he counselled. What a lot of advice like this he had received at various stages of his life! All this had happened because of certain configurations of the planets. What could a small individual like him do against the planets that directed his destiny? A married life that lasted a month. Which God-forsaken hole was that bitch in now?

He was nearly at Master's house. Master was educated, a man of the world. It was his bad horoscope that had brought about his failure in life. The house was still unplastered. After the partition of the property, the kitchen block had been demolished, a bathroom and lavatory had been built for his convenience and even a small room to store grain.

During the floods the next year, the river had rushed by devouring half the garden. They had predicted heavy rains the following year as well. Yet another flood took away three quarters of the front yard. Fearing that the Flood of '99 would wash away the house itself, Master had sold the property to a Moplah Muslim for the price he named. It was the next year that embankments were put up to protect the river. They did not need to fear the floods after that. The Moplah family built steps going down to the river and could have baths in the river now like princes.

It was then that Master had built his house on the hill. By the time it had to be plastered, he had run out of money. Master stopped work on it, saying, let the children work on it at their convenience, and moved in.

There was no one to be seen. Kutti Narayanan said to himself, this is what is so special about the Kizhakkemuri folk. They're never to be seen when they're needed. Master's nephew, Achu, and the Christian chap, the Chettan who looked after the pump house, were on the verandah. Chettan had bought some land on the hillside and built a house. The man who had arrived to work in the pump house had become the owner of forty cents of land in four years' time. He wondered, would the salary the man earned for pumping water allow him to save that much?

Achu asked angrily: 'Hey, where were you? Gadding about when we needed you here ...'

'I was having a bath when I got the news, Achu,' he said and walked into the house. Achu's mother, Narayani Amma, Master's younger sister, who was seated near the bed, looked at Kutti Narayanan through her thick glasses. He thought it was Chakkama's daughter, Cheeru, who stood leaning against the wall.

Master lay with his eyes closed, breathing normally. Kutti Narayanan looked at him attentively.

'He makes out when he's called.'

Kutti Narayanan sat down beside him and stroked his forehead. He called softly: 'Master!'

'Master, it's me, Kutti Narayanan.'

Master's throat and lips moved as if he was trying to say something.

'There's phlegm in his chest, it's congested. Put a frying pan on the fire, child. Take out some rice bran and make two poultices, this size. Heat them moderately and hold them to his chest. He'll have some relief then from the phlegm.'

He said to the sister in a low voice: 'Otherwise he'll suffer when the real breathing trouble starts. Do you have Kasthuryadi tablets here?'

The sister didn't know what they had in the house. She'd arrived when she heard Master had fallen ill.

'If there aren't any, buy some. And boil some water with cummin seeds.'

He walked out.

Although Achu always scolded him when they met, the man knew his worth. Which was why he asked: 'What's his condition, Kutti Narayanan Nair?'

Kutti Narayanan thought deeply before he answered: 'Won't live to see the fourth day from now. We'll see what happens tomorrow or the day after.'

He made another calculation. 'Tomorrow night.'

He looked at Achu. Achu knew he never made mistakes about such matters.

Pump-house Chettan asked: 'Should we send for a doctor?'

'Buy some Kasthuryadi tablets when the Ayurvedic shop opens. We won't need anything else.'

'The doctor will come this way when he's going back from the dispensary. I telephoned him.'

Kutti Narayanan smiled wryly.

'Do we need the doctor? If it's to be a peaceful end, in my opinion, it's better not to poke needles into him. Have you informed the children?'

Achu grunted.

'Isn't his son in Coimbatore?'

'H'm...'

Chettan said, sounding astonished: 'He walked around the compound just yesterday. Read the paper and philosophised on things for quite a while. That's what the human condition is.' Master lived alone. After his wife died he had spent a month with each of his daughters. Then he came back here.

He used to have a woman at first to do the cooking. When a match factory was started on the hillside, she stopped coming to the house to work. His sister began to send him food from the ancestral house, but he said he did not want it. Chakkamma's daughter cleaned the house every morning and drew water for him. As for cooking, Master managed on his own.

It was only recently that his vision had become poorer because of cataract. Master knew if he went to Thrissur or

Kozhikode and had an operation done, his vision would be restored. He postponed it because there was no one to accompany him. Kutti Narayanan had said he would go along. But Master would not have it. 'No, you won't do. Let's wait till one of the children is free.'

That morning, Master had not opened the front door even when Cheeru had finished sweeping. Chettan had arrived just then. Master used to get the newspaper every day. The last three months, he had not been able to read the small print. Chettan would read aloud to him, then Master would talk about the news. Only after this would Chettan rub his body with oil, do his exercises and have a bath in the river.

Chettan looked through the window and saw that Master was asleep. He called out, there was only a groan. It was then that Chettan sent Cheeru to bring Achu and forced open the back door with a hack knife.

'If you ask me ...' Chettan looked at Achu and Kutti Narayanan, 'he should have gone in his sleep. That would have been fortunate.'

Achu did not say anything. There had been no need for the old man to live like a hermit, cooking for himself. He could have died in his ancestral house. These old fogeys would remain obstinate to their last breath!

Kutti Narayanan did not agree with Chettan. Die in one's sleep indeed! Death, like birth, was an important ceremony in life. An event to be celebrated, conducted stage by stage. To die without all that in one's sleep was a kind of deception. All those who had done good had to go through the different stages. They *would* go through them.

Pacing the verandah, Achu lit a cigarette. He was a member of the Panchayat. And a director of the Agricultural Cooperative Bank. A very busy man.

'I have a committee meeting at ten. The Block Development Officer will come this evening. A hundred things to do today.'

Kutti Narayanan said, 'You can go, Achu. There's no point staying here. Nothing is going to happen today. Come when you're free. I'll be here.'

Achu said: 'Let Amma be here. There are phones in all the places I'm going to. If you need me, tell them at the house. Malukutty will telephone me.'

Achu had been the first person to install a telephone at home. Even now, the Kizhakkemuri folk had still not come alive to the miraculous capacities of the telephone.

Achu went in, spoke to his mother and came out. As he was about to go, Kutti Narayanan reminded him: 'Bring the Kasthuryadi tablets when you come. If you can send them earlier ...'

'Send one of the boys for it.'

Achu took out a five rupee note from his pocket and held it out.

Kutti Narayanan calculated. Six Kasthuryadi tablets cost three rupees. Three would be enough for the present.

Chettan said he would have a bath, go to the pump-house and come back at once. Cheeru said the rice bran and frying pan were ready. 'You must be here. There'll be people dropping in. We'll have to serve some of them tea. Have some boiled milk ready. Get another half-measure from somewhere.'

Cheeru's mother Chakkama came into the courtyard. She worked on building sites, carrying headloads of quarry stones.

'Who are the stones being quarried for?'

'Assanaji's son.'

'Oh, the chap who went to Dubai. Has he come back?'

'It's quite some time since he came. He'll go back now only after the house is complete and the housewarming over. There are twenty people carrying stones!'

'Go to the bazaar and tell the *vaidyar* to send five or six Kasthuryadi tablets through one of the boys. It's urgent. We'll pay them here. Bring it yourself if you can spare the time.'

Chakkamma hesitated. 'It's very late.'

The local rate for transporting stones was twenty paise per piece, but these people had made it thirty. If they started early morning, they could move a hundred stones by dusk. But Chakkamma was not one to forget that she had worked for the family a long time. That's why she had sent Cheeru to work here in spite of her complaints. No one knew it was for just ten rupees a month.

'Let me see, Master.'

'It's not enough to say that. Do it.'

Cheeru reminded him, 'The frying pan is red-hot.'

'I'm coming. Chakkamma, you can send one of the boys.'

Chakkama said, 'Who's likely to be there at this hour ...?'

As Kutti Narayanan heated the rice bran, prepared a poultice and took it in, he thought: at least there are some people who haven't stopped calling the higher castes Master or Thampuran.

Achu noticed some people getting off the bus from Palghat at the bus stop near the ferry. Yes, they were Seethalakshmi and her husband. Achu was just paying off the taxi which had brought him back from the Block Office. He got into the taxi again and said, 'Go on. I'll get down at the ferry.'

By the time the taxi reached the ferry, Seethalakshmi and Padmanabhan had picked up their luggage and started to walk on. Achu asked the taxi driver to stop, got out, paid him and walked towards them.

'There was a meeting of the Block Committee. I'm on my way back after getting them to cancel it.

Seethalakshmi guessed the event had not yet taken place since they had met Achu on the road.

'I left the place just half an hour ago. You can't tell anything from his present condition.'

Padmanabhan asked, 'Can't you get a coolie here?'

'They've all gone to work. Give it to me.' He took Seethalakshmi's small suitcase from her. Padmanabhan walked on ahead.

'I was just starting my scooter when the neighbours said there was a long distance call. That was lucky—when we arrived at the bus stand, the fast bus was just about to leave.'

'I always find fault with the telephones for the delays. But luckily, I got through to every place I called very quickly today.'

Seethalakshmi asked as they walked along, 'Who's the doctor attending on him, Achuetta?'

'Our Govindankutty. He's quite adequate for cases like this.'

'What did he say?'

'What can he say? Uncle's quite old, after all.'

'And Vishaledathi? Have you sent ...?'

'She'll come. I spoke to her. She said she'd start at once.'

'What about Ettan?'

'He wasn't there. He'd gone to the station to collect someone. I spoke to Raju and said it would be best he comes by the West Coast Express.'

Achu described how he had broken open the door that morning. Wasn't it sheer obstinacy that made Uncle live alone like this? If something had happened at night, everyone would have got a bad name. He spoke of the important meetings he had cancelled that day because of this.

'I have to run around all the time. I spent forty-two rupees on taxi fares today. Haven't you got a phone yet?'

Padmanabhan lied. 'The office allotted me one long ago. But it hasn't been connected yet. They say they don't have a cable.'

A man coming from the opposite side saw Achu, got down from the field and stood there scratching his head. Achu said, 'Kumara, I haven't forgotten about you. Let all this be over—you've heard about Uncle's condition.'

Achu wished another ten people would come one after another like this. Seethalakshmi had not had much of an opinion about the Achu who had failed his tenth standard three times and was loafing around the village. Now they wanted Achu for every little matter in Kizhakkemuri. Recommendations for jobs. How many people had this B.Sc. qualified husband of hers been able to find jobs for? Achu went around in a taxi in order to save time and be punctual for appointments. He had managed to get two ministers to include Kizhakkemuri in their itinerary and given them receptions there. And who had seen to it that Government buses passed through the village and arranged for a telephone exchange to be opened there?

As they climbed the hill, Achu asked,

'The children?'

'They have class.'

'The older one,' it was then Achu remembered his name: 'Ravi—you could have brought him.'

'He has a scholarship examination tomorrow.'

'If one of the boys is here ...'

They understood what Achu meant. It was always a son who performed the funeral rituals.

'He needn't have stayed in the ancestral house if he didn't want to. One of the children would have brought him food three times a day. That wouldn't have been difficult for them. But what can one say if Uncle wouldn't allow that?'

Padmanabhan smiled. 'Uncle is quite unique. How many times we asked him to stay with us!'

'He stayed with us just a month. He wouldn't stay with Vishaledathi even that long. Hardly three weeks. He wouldn't have liked all those parties and dinners at her place.'

'He's always been like that. Apart from some trouble with his eyes, he's never been ill.'

Seethalakshmi remembered then: 'I had written to Father last month. There's a good doctor in our place now. He did cataract surgery and restored so many people's eyesight. I'd written about that.'

Seethalakshmi's heart beat faster as they neared the house. When she went in and saw her father, she could barely suppress a sob. She sat down near Achu's mother. When she had calmed herself somewhat she asked what was happening in the kitchen.

'Don't worry about cooking anything now. They'll bring food from the ancestral house.'

Narayani Amma gave Kutti Narayanan a look as if to say she knew nothing about this. He said, 'I've arranged all that.'

Padmanabhan and Achu came in with the doctor. He felt the patient's pulse and examined his heart and chest with a stethoscope. Then he checked his blood pressure. He went out, followed by Padmanabhan.

The doctor said, 'The pulse is rather weak and the blood pressure low. There's nothing to be done now.'

Making sure they were out of earshot, Padmanabhan asked: 'What's your opinion, doctor?'

The doctor hesitated. Seethalakshmi had edged closer by that time.

'He may continue to be in this coma for quite a few days. We can't say anything with certainty. Or the end may come suddenly without any change taking place.'

The doctor was about to leave. Achu, who had been standing apart, came up to him. 'Wait, doctor.'

Seethalakshmi saw Achu put his hand in his pocket and looked accusingly at her husband. Padmanabhan took out fifteen rupees and gave it to the doctor.

'Thank you, doctor.'

After he left, Padmanabhan asked Achu: 'Wasn't fifteen enough?'

'Ah, yes … fifteen or twenty. It's twenty for visits to the house. But in our case, it doesn't matter. The doctor stays in my outhouse.'

Padmanabhan took off his glasses, wiped them and said softly:

'Actually I thought everything would be over by the time we got here.'

Seethalakshmi agreed. 'I thought so too when we got the phone call.'

Kutti Narayanan, who was standing behind them, thought there was a hint of disappointment in both their voices.

He said with certainty: 'Wait for tomorrow night. It won't go beyond that. It's not the coma and full stop the doctor spoke about that matters. These things have a rhythm of their own.'

Padmanabhan sat down on the raised platform on the verandah and leaned against a pillar. He had thought, if they waited for Bhaskarettan, the cremation would be over by the morning at the latest. Then he could catch the direct bus at midday.

'Don't you want to change?'

'H'm…'

He knew Seethalakshmi was watching him intently.

'Kutti Narayanan has watched many people die.'

'H'm…' What was she driving at?'

He asked, 'Where have you kept the suitcase?'

He went into the house with his wife.

There was an old double bed in the unused room. Padmanabhan changed from trousers into a mundu and sat down on the bed, next to the rolled-up mattress.

Seethalakshmi closed the door and took off her sari. She said, as she folded it: 'Look at it, after just two washes!'

He looked attentively at his wife as she bent down in her under-skirt to take out a mundu and *veshti* from her suitcase. It was as if he was looking at a new person. A protruding belly, full of creases. Could women change so much in fifteen years? There were very few who did not change that much. Like Vanaja. No one would guess that Vanaja, the stenographer in his office, was a mother of four. She was probably a year or two older than Seethalakshmi. He had calculated that when he saw her date of birth once on some piece of paper. Her beauty lay not only in the way she wore a sari. There was not a single crease on her belly. A body that had withstood the onslaught of age.

Kutti Narayanan called from beyond the door: 'Do you want tea? Lunch will soon be ready.'

Seethalakshmi tucked the veshti into her waist and opened the door. 'No, nothing now, we'll just have lunch.'

Sweat had formed black blotches under the arms of her green blouse.

'What did you think of him?' asked Padmanabhan.

She did not know what he meant.

'I was asking about your father.'

'What, if as the doctor said, he lies in this condition for a long time?'

She opened the window and stood facing him, leaning againt the wall.

'When is the M.D. coming?'

He had answered the same question four times since they had left. He said irritably: 'Didn't I tell you in Malayalam? The day after tomorrow.'

'He'll arrive in the morning?'

'I don't know.'

She knew how important the visit was. That's why she was anxious. The Company was going to set up a new factory near Walayar. The person who would be responsible for the whole unit, the Project-in-Charge as he was called, would be nominated the day after tomorrow. Two hundred people were to be appointed for the new factory. The Project Officer would be responsible for making twenty-five per cent of the appointments from the local personnel. There would be no increase in salary—just a slightly higher allowance. But the authority it conferred ... The three kinds of pickle that were to be entrusted to the M.D.'s driver, apparently intended for the M.D.'s wife, were ready. And the special coconut oil from Guruvayoor for his mother.

'Won't he stay for a while?' asked Seethalakshmi hesitantly.

'I've asked for two rooms in the Guest House. He may leave for Ernakulam in the evening. Rajasekharan said he will not make a halt here. But he never tells the truth.'

'Can't we persuade him to have dinner with us?'

'That would be ...' He stopped, realising he had no business talking to her about office protocol. He had kept a secret to himself however. The retired I.G., Kumara Panicker, was a close friend of the M.D.'s. There would be a party for the M.D. at his house in the evening. Neither Natarajan or Sankara Pillai were ever allowed there. But he could walk in. The Black Label whisky he had sent Verghese to buy, a carton of Rothman's cigarettes ... once he knew the M.D. was not leaving, he would take them to Panicker's house and tell him: 'A relative of mine brought these from the Gulf. I have no use for either. Let them be here.'

Panicker might say, 'Good. Your M.D. is coming for dinner.'

Certain that it would not be accepted, Panicker might even extend a casual invitation.

He would reply: 'No Sir. Some other time. My colleagues in the office will say I am trying to curry favour. This is a time when so many proposals are being considered.'

While leaving, he would make an explicit offer. 'Sir, there's a cousin of mine coming from the Gulf next month. If there's something particular you would like, I can write and ask him for it.'

The retired I.G. already approved of his respectful behaviour. Nothing wrong in that. He would never repeat Natarajan's dirty tactics. Everyone in the company had heard from the Guest House watchman what Natarajan had offered the M.D. during his last visit. He had told himself firmly that even if Seethalakshmi had been younger and prettier, he would never have thought of that way.

But he had to be there the day after. It must be the authority to appoint fifty people that had attracted Natarajan and Pillai.

'I wonder whether Vishaledathi will come,' said Seethalakshmi to no one in particular.

Vishalam had to come from Alwaye. She had been to Japan the year before with her husband, apparently at the company's expense. Half the money Father had made on the sale of the house and compound by the river had been spent on Vishalam's wedding. Seethalakshmi had not realised the importance of this at the time. It was after she had had Ravi that Pangu Ettan had given her these accounts. Although Vishalam's husband had status and owned a car, it was Seethalakshmi's husband who had been of help to Father. Few people knew this. It was to Seethalakshmi Father had written when he needed a good sweater and a scarf.

Padmanabhan gazed at the thoughtful Seethalakshmi, running his fingers through his hair. He went out, stood at the door of the patient's room, took a look at him and went into the backyard behind the kitchen. The coconut palm saplings which had been planted there in pits had not yet grown and had a feeble look. Seethalakshmi followed him and stood just behind. He asked her:

'How many cents of land here?'

'I think about sixty.'

'Are there sixty?'

Master's distant relative, the deed writer Sankunni, crossed the fence at the back and came in.

'Ah, so you've come.'

'H'm...'

'I heard the news just now.'

Sankunni noticed Padmanabhan looking at the ill-grown saplings and remarked: 'Coconut palms will never grow on the hillside. They'll wither in the southern sunlight.'

'What's the price of land in this area?'

'Don't even talk about that! Koyassan sold four plots on the roadside for two thousand a cent. Isn't there a limit even for land on the roadside?'

'Wherever it's from, people have money.'

'How much would this land fetch, Sankunni?'

'This?' He glanced at the plot with the air of an expert. 'Would it be fifty cents?'

'Sixty,' Padmanabhan corrected him.

'And the house ... It costs quite a bit nowadays to build a house. Maimunni's boy bought Gopi's house and compound for seventy-five. And it was only thirty cents. It's a pity the area by the river was sold for a paltry sum.'

'Will it fetch a lakh and a half?'

Kutti Narayanan came to tell them that rice and vegetable preparations had arrived from the ancestral house.

'How is he, Kuttiarana?' asked Sankunni.

'There'll be a change when the stars change their position at night. I think the breathing may become difficult.'

Padmanabhan asked, 'Are you giving him *kanji* or glucose?'

'Just a ladleful of kanji water with great difficulty. After that he couldn't retain anything.' He looked hard at Seethalakshmi to find out whether she had understood the significance of what he had said. 'It's a sign that difficulty in breathing will soon set in.'

Sankunni went in. As Padmanabhan washed his hands on the kitchen verandah, Seethalakshmi was laying the banana leaves to serve lunch, while Kutti Narayanan was washing the ladle and the flat serving spoon for rice. Padmanabhan said, 'I'll have to go to the office the day after tomorrow. I have some very important work to do.'

Kutti Narayanan thought it over. 'The day after …' He made a gesture of helplessness. 'Can't say anything definite, Padmanabhan. The day of the week, the star, the position of the moon, are all auspicious from tonight onwards. It can take place any time after tonight. He lowered his voice and asked: 'Shall we ask Kunhikuttan Panikker to make calculations with cowrie shells?'

'No.'

'By God's grace, the rain has stopped. It was pouring when our Parakkat house grandmother died this time last year. What difficulty we had getting the firewood chopped and the body cremated.'

Padmanabhan sat down by himself to the meal. He asked Seethalakshmi, who was about to serve him: 'Where's Achu Ettan?'

'He'd said he'd go home for lunch. He has to telephone someone.'

'H'm…'

He and his phone calls, he thought! As soon as a telephone exchange came to Kizhakkemuri a year ago and Achu had a connection installed at home, he had made a long distance call to Padmanabhan's office in Palghat: 'Now it will be easy to let me know if there's anything important. Note down my number and ask Seethalakshmi to write it down at home.'

These villagers were so petty. The applications he had made for a phone in his residence had accumulated into a huge file and lay in the head office in Trivandrum. Few people knew that private companies were sometimes worse than government ones!

Seethalakshmi drew his attention to the fact that her father's sister had sent two kinds of vegetables for the meal. Well, these country folk could well afford two and three kinds of vegetables. All they had to do was pluck them from their compound. What did they know of the hardships of the salaried class?

If the death occurred after dusk the next day, he would not be able to go to the office the day after. The cremation would be over only by noon … He could phone the office from Achu's house. If the M.D. was halting for the night, he could reach

Palghat by dusk and meet him at Panicker's house or at the Guest House. He could not be in the office during the day because of this misfortune, so it would not be wrong to go and meet him after office hours. No superior officer would reprimand an employee who was mourning a death in the family.

It would be best if it occurred tonight. Or at least the next day. If the son from Coimbatore arrived soon, they would not have to keep the body until he came.

'What news of your brother?'

'He'll come.'

Padmanabhan continued to eat. Whether Vishalam came or not was no problem. But the rituals could not be conducted if the eldest son did not come. If he was busy, he could send his son. Or his son's son. And he could come and take part in the Bali ceremonies on the seventh or twelfth day according to his convenience. Padmanabhan would not stand for the cremation being delayed because Vishalam or her husband had not come. He was ready for a row over this if it became necessary. Although he was not an executive trained in Japan, his job had responsibilities.

It was Ravi's scholarship examination that had led to all this trouble. But for that, he could have sent Seethalakshmi with Ravi. Then he could have come at his own convenience for the fourteenth or sixteenth day ceremony and there would have been no bother. When he had heard what Achu said on the telephone ... anyway, did these country bumpkins know how to speak clearly and sensibly on the telephone?

Padmanabhan felt irritated with everyone. He did not feel like eating. He got up.

In his mind, Padmanabhan congratulated whoever was in charge of Achu's kitchen. The meal had been sumptuous. This was the way food should be sent to another house. There was plenty left after three of them had eaten. After Cheerupennu ate, there would still be enough for another two persons.

Narayani Amma was lying down on a mat she had spread on the floor in the patient's room. Kutti Narayanan poured two teaspoonfuls of cummin-seed water in which a tablet had been dissolved into the patient's mouth and he moaned feebly. Kutti Narayanan suddenly realised that Narayani Amma was sixty-eight years old. She had many ailments: diabetes, difficulty in passing urine, rheumatism. Since Achu could afford it, he used to get doctors to come and examine her on and off. Narayani Amma had removed her glasses and was lying on her side with her eyes open, gazing into the darkness under the bed. Kutti Narayanan thought, as he looked at her, that she would not last long.

The sick man looked as if he was sleeping peacefully. Seethalakshmi came in and sat at the foot of the bed. The boredom of having nothing to do was evident on her face.

Kutti Narayanan picked up a fan, gave it to her and said: 'Fan him now and then. He must be feeling hot inside.'

Kutti Narayanan went out. Those who had gone home to eat had not returned. When death arrived, there would be no one around, he thought. Except those who were indebted to him. But wait and see what it would be like after Master died—the house and compound would be full of people. That was how it was everywhere. Each one would talk about what he or she had done for the dead man. When someone was dying, only he, Kutti Narayanan, was needed. The Kutti Narayanan whom the Kizakkemuri folk called a drunkard, a ne'er-do-well. It was then he remembered. Was there a copy of the *Ramayanam* here, to read at dusk? He had lost the old copy he had bought at Guruvayoor, at the eastern shrine. Cheap copies were sure to be available at the Kunnamkulam bus station.

This was the right time to write a list. If only he could get a pencil and some paper.

Sandalwood pieces: there had better be two kilos, for Master was a great man. Then six yards of mull and a length of silk, two yards. Paddy, rice, coconut oil, a wooden rice-measure: these would be available in the house. The hand-woven towels called *thorthu mundus* were the most important item. They had to have twelve large ones. After all, Master had so many relatives.

The cheruman, Thami, walked into the courtyard. Kutti

Narayanan asked him by way of greeting: 'Don't you have work today?'

'I'm digging in the garden. How's the Thambran?'

'It's too early to say.'

He got down into the verandah and said:

'Not today. Tomorrow. But be ready. Don't fill yourself up with toddy at night and lie there dead to the world. Find two or three other people. Since it's not raining, it won't be hard to chop the wood.'

Whenever he went into the courtyard, Kutti Narayanan had always had noted the mango tree in the western corner. It was a huge one and would yield good firewood. Once the branches were bent, they would have to be bound with thick rope and pulled downwards to the north-east so as not damage the fence. He saw a woman wearing glasses walking up the hill with Achu. Wasn't that Vishalam? So the eldest daughter had arrived as well!

'We were wondering when you'd come. If you've not eaten, wash your hands and come. There's food ready.'

Achu said, 'She ate at home. She came straight there.'

Vishalam made a pretence of smiling at Kutti Narayanan and went in. Achu said,

'It's more convenient to park the car there.'

'Has she come by herself?'

'There's the driver.'

'And her husband?'

'He's gone to Bombay. He'll come later.'

'He can come at his convenience … Master would want all the children to be with him.'

Kutti Narayanan was happy that Vishalam was in a high position. The older daughter was more fair-skinned than the younger one. She had her late mother's complexion. She had large eyes, cheeks with a tinge of rose and luxuriant hair. Although Kutti Narayanan had been afraid of Master, he had hung around a lot near the river below the house. It had been such a pleasure to catch sight of Vishalam now and then even at a distance. If only the One above had drawn a fate line that had given him a little more education …

He went in, listened to the patient's breathing and gave him two teaspoonfuls of cummin-seed water.

Achu, who was standing at the door, said: 'The President was asking about you.'

'I wonder why.'

'I think it's his niece's engagement on Friday.'

The feast for an engagement ceremony at a Panchayat President's house would be like a small wedding feast in itself. The cook would be the Namboodiri who conducted the worship of the Goddess Bhagavati on the other bank of the river. But Kutti Narayanan would have to be there to co-ordinate everything. He had told the President openly once that though the Namboodiri performed the puja for the goddess regularly, he had stopped conducting some ancillary ceremonies, which was a mistake on his part. These were matters for which Kutti Naryanan could do something.

If the President's brother-in-law, who lived across the river, attended the engagement, a chicken was sure to be killed for the evening meal. They would have fun. An ounce of the stuff the man brought was worth two bottles of the adulterated toddy the Cherttala people sold.

'Which day is it, Achu? I hope it won't be before Friday.'

He'd be in a fix if it were the next day or the day after ...

'I didn't ask.'

There was a rumour that Achu did not get on well with the President since he had been in the running himself for the office. But that was a different matter. After all, a girl was getting a husband. It was up to Achu to organise the function, wasn't it?

What if there was a crisis by dusk and breathlessness set in? It would be most convenient. If only the son would come, everything could be finished by nine-thirty in the morning and those who had come from a distance could leave in the afternoon. If he wanted, he could attend the festival in the Perumkunnath temple. The Thiruvegappura team would play the *tayambaka* on the drums.

Having stood quite some time at the head of her father's bed, Vishalam came out and sat down on the chair next to the round table on the verandah. Seethalakshmi sat on the verandah ledge.

Kutti Narayanan started the conversation: 'When will he get back from Bombay?'

'In two days' time.'

Not a strand of Vishalam's hair had grown grey. Streaks of grey had begun to appear here and there in Seethalakshmi's hair and the shadows under her eyes had grown darker. Even now, Vishalam did not look more than thirty.

'Do you want something to drink?' asked Kutti Narayanan.

'No, nothing.'

Vishalam said, addressing no one in particular: 'I thought I'd be able to go back in the evening. The maidservant is on leave and the children are alone.'

Seethalakshmi did not say anything. Noting Kutti Narayanan's expression as he gazed adoringly at Vishalam, she said irritably: 'Kutti Narayanan Nair, go and attend to whatever Father needs.'

Embarrassed, he went in.

'Edathi, change if you want to, I have clothes in my suitcase.'

'I brought a suitcase too, since I wasn't sure what would happen. It's in the car, I'll get it later.'

Vishalam raised her head up and sighed. All her calculations had gone wrong.

That morning, as soon as her husband had left for the airport, she had telephoned Yamuna although she knew Yamuna had gone to Bangalore. Balagopalan had answered. He had known the call was not for Yamuna. As though to sound convincing, she had said she had telephoned to get a recipe Yamuna had promised her.

What if her fourteen-year-old daughter, Indu, was listening from somewhere inside?

'Why the recipe? Are you having a party?'

'Oh no. My husband's away. He took the first flight to Bombay this morning.'

He was being cautious too.

'Oh, he'd promised to give me a new video tape.'

'You can look for it here on your way back from the office. I don't know which one it is.'

'I may. Around seven.'

If he came in the evening for the video or a book, she would offer him a drink as a matter of courtesy. By the time they got to the second drink it would be late. The children would greet him and go off to the study. She would tell them to have dinner and join him for the third drink. They were on the brink of some happening. That day, she had given Indu and Sunny permission to go for an evening show of a film, pretending that they had insisted on going. The maidservant had gone to find out about her mother's illness and would return only the following day. 'I'll show you a film when the children are not around, 'Strictly for adults.' It had been a promise. They had a clear three hours, all the loopholes had been closed. What attractive quality had his grey eyes seen in her that Yamuna, who was so much younger, did not possess? It was then that the long-distance telephone call had come unexpectedly from her village.

The cowdung used to plaster the sun-drenched courtyard had begun to flake off. The waves of heat rising from it flowed into the verandah. Cursing everyone because she was so upset, Vishalam got up and said: 'I've got a bad headache, Seetha, I'm going to lie down.'

Seethalakshmi said to herself: 'The two of us came together, my husband and I. This headache! I've heard that some people who use hair dye have a perpetual headache.'

The sick man swallowed four or five spoons of kanji at night. The doctor came again at nine o'clock and examined him. He decided there was no need for an injection. Vishalam opened her purse as he was leaving but Seethalakshmi had already given him fifteen rupees by then.

'I would have given it,' said Vishalam.

'What does it matter who gives it?'

Kutti Narayanan asked all of them to go to bed. 'I'm not going to sleep. I'll call you if it's necessary.'

He sat down in the sick man's room, reading the *Ramayanam* in a soft voice.

Achu asked the cheruman, Thami, to sleep on the verandah so that he could run up to his house with a message if there was any change and made ready to leave.

'Do you want me to send any mattresses?'

Seethalakshmi said, 'No.'

Narayani Amma spread out a mat near the bed and lay down. Vishalam tried to persuade her to sleep in comfort in one of the other rooms.

Kutti Narayanan opened the *Ramayanam* at random at the Sundara Kandam. It was tough to read and he stopped after a while. He leaned against the wall and closed his eyes. If he felt sleepy, he thought, he would make some black tea. Later.

Vishalam could not sleep. There were no mosquitoes but she still felt suffocated because there was no fan. A month of planning, of exchanging glances and meaningful telephone calls—and then, when the opportunity arrived, everything had gone wrong. When would it happen again? If she hadn't had the car, she could have asked him to escort her home as soon as the long distance call came. But when she had the car and the driver, what would people think if she arrived with her husband's assistant? She should have mixed some gin and cordial and packed it into her briefcase. These people would never recognize the smell. At least it would have made it easier for her to fall asleep.

'Are you asleep, Edathi?'

'H'm...'

Seethalakshmi said, spreading her mat on the floor, 'I'll sleep here.'

'No, sleep on the other side.' Seethalakshmi made her bed, pretending she had not heard.

Vishalam placed her elbow over her eyes and shut her eyes tight. Her husband would have to go on many more official tours. The problem was to clear all the obstacles in their way—Yamuna, the children, the servant maid.

Seethalakshmi turned the light off. Vishalam felt the darkness was a relief. She thought she had a strip of Calmpose tablets in her handbag, but could not find it. Should she look once again, she wondered. She decided not to.

'Are you looking for a suitable match for Indu?'

'In two or three years. She's studying, after all.'

Indu was only seventeen. Maybe Seetha wanted Indu to be married off so that she could watch her older sister become a grandmother. Seetha asked her something else but she didn't answer. Let her think I'm trying to sleep, thought Vishalam.

Seethalakshmi tossed from side to side on her mat, unable to sleep. Were there things crawling over it? The mat had been rolled up and kept in the room used to store paddy. With her father in this condition, Seethalakshmi did not want to sleep in her husband's room lest it upset her sister. That's why she had found a mat and spread it here

'I wonder what these things are that are biting me,' said Seethalakshmi, sitting up and scratching her neck and back.

She got up, went out, gently closing the door behind her and made her way to Padmanabhan's room. She saw that Kutti Narayanan was dozing, leaning against the wall, and her aunt was asleep.

Seethalakshmi sat down on the bed and Padmanabhan moved nearer the wall to make room for her.

'Are you asleep?'

He grunted, 'H'm…'

All his problems would be solved if he was given charge of the project. He would certainly have to appoint some people on the strength of recommendations from the ministers. But he could take money from all the others. The Brahmin, Dharmalingam, would manage it efficiently if he were given a small share. And if enquiries were ever made at a later date, he could always plead ignorance. He had never demanded anything from anyone, he would say. No one who had got into the Company would dare make a complaint until he was confirmed. By that time, he would have gone back.

He would wait until the next evening. After that, if this situation continued, Seetha could stay back. He would leave for Palghat by the State Transport bus in the evening. If news of the death came to him while the M.D. was still in the office, he could go straight to his room and inform him. He had to do that. He had to tell the M.D. he could not stay any longer and that he would undertake any duties the M.D. was pleased to entrust him with. Then he would walk out with a sad face. It would be a moment replete with drama. News of a death would perhaps benefit him more than a gift of Black Label whisky. He moved Seethalakshmi's hand which was lying on his chest and tried to get some sleep.

Kutti Narayanan got up as the crows began to caw. He wiped off the spittle that had oozed from the patient's lips and called him softly: 'Master, would you like something to drink?'

A low grunt, like a reply. Kutti Narayanan went out and performed his ablutions, first below the palm tree at the boundary of the compound and then at the well. Then he boiled some water and made black coffee for himself. He mixed some Horlicks for the sick man. Well, there were plenty of women around. Let them make breakfast, he thought. He parted the patient's lips and poured in two teaspoonfuls of Horlicks.

Narayani Amma sat up.

'See if you can get him to swallow four teaspoonsful,' he said to her, then opened the front door and went out into the courtyard. It was the time when the days were growing shorter. The sun would not rise till later. He woke up the cheruman, Thami, and asked him to fetch the milk. They would probably not make anything for breakfast. It would be just as well to send for some food from the other house.

Achu came in, flashing a five-battery torch. He had a boy with him.

'Nothing special ...?'

'No.'

'I got up when Raju arrived. Didn't sleep after that.'

'This is Bhaskaran's ...'

'... second son.'

Kutti Narayanan smiled at Raju.

'I must have seen you as a small boy. Isn't your father coming?'

'He said to find out the news and telephone him.'

'Go in and see him.'

As soon as Raju went in, Achu said, 'Today's another busy day. I have to meet the M.P. when he comes to the Travellers' Bungalow. Then go to the Executive Engineer's office. What car I do?'

Kutti Naryanan consoled him. 'Go along. Nothing will happen in the daytime. Don't expect anything until after nightfall.'

When day had broken and the sick man's room became bright, Kutti Naryanan went up to him and gave him a close look. Was there a change in the rhythm of the breathing? He said to Seethalakshmi, who came in sleepily, 'There's a slight change.'

Padmanabhan came in as he was explaining the change in the rhythm of breathing that only he could detect. Seethalakshmi looked at Padmanabhan straight in the eye and said, 'Kutti Narayanan says there's a change.'

Padmanabhan looked at Kutti Narayanan questioningly and he nodded in assent.

'There'll be a complete change after sunset, that's what today will be like.'

Vishalam came in by then. It gave Seethalakshmi an inner satisfacion to see Vishalam looking dishevelled. Now she really looked older than her. Look at the dark circles under her eyes, thought Seethalakshmi. And the wrinkles on her face. It was the husbands who let their wives spend half their salary on cosmetics who were to be blamed.

Vishalam asked Raju: 'Won't your father come?'

'He asked me to find out how he is and telephone.'

Seethalakshmi suddenly realised she had not paid Raju any attention. She smiled and placed her hand on his shoulder. 'Did you come by bus or by train?' she asked.

'By train. Then I caught the last bus from Kuttippuram.'

Achu came to the door and asked the women: 'Shouldn't we get the doctor again?'

No one replied directly. Narayani Amma said to Kutti

Narayanan, 'He finds it hard to pass urine. If that were corrected, it would be a great relief to him.'

Kutti Narayanan found a reason: 'He has to drink some fluid first.'

'Let the doctor come and see him, Achu, for our satisfaction.' She massaged the sick man's hand gently. All we want, my Lord Guruvayoorappa, is that he shouldn't linger long and suffer.'

'Mother, go home if you like. You can come back later.' His mother did not reply. When Padmanabhan came in, Achu said: 'I'm going out. There's been a boundary dispute and the Circle Inspector is expected. Then our M.P. is coming this way. He'll be upset if he doesn't see me.'

'Achu, if you're going home, tell them to send the refreshments if they're ready.'

Achu cut Kutti Narayanan short and said angrily: 'Look Nair, tea, snacks, meals: they'll all be here on time. All we need is for you to stay with Uncle. The women will see to the kitchen.'

Kutti Narayanan no longer dared to ask about the Panchayat President's daughter's engagement after hearing this outburst. Which side of the bed had the man got up on, he wondered.

By the time the women finished their baths, one by one, and came out, a huge vessel filled with three layers of food had arrived from the ancestral house.

The patient swallowed six teaspoonsful of kanji at noon. But he did not open his eyes.

'He's swallowing fluids all right,' said Padmanabhan, sounding surprised. Kutti Narayanan grunted, then whispered: 'But his breathing. Did you see the way he's breathing?'

Padmanabhan led Kutti Narayanan out of the room.

'What if I leave at five? Sita can stay behind.'

Kutti Narayanan pondered. 'No, if you ask my opinion, I think it will all be over tonight. You can leave tomorrow at midday after everything is finished.'

'I have hundereds of things to attend to there, Kutti Narayanan Nair.'

'Be patient for one more night.'

When Padmanabhan left, Raju came up to him, smiling. He had Bhaskaran's big, broad teeth.

'Isn't it enough to join in the seventh-day ceremonies?'

'Yes, that's enough.'

'Someone said if you're at the cremation, you have to stay until the fourteenth day.'

'No, that's not necessary.'

'I have to go on an excursion the day after tomorrow, at night.'

'So you have to reach Coimbatore the day after. You can easily do that.'

There were some visitors who came to see the sick man. Dignitaries from the village. They stood at his door for a while.

'The President's not here?' asked Kutti Narayanan by way of greeting.

'He'll come.'

Nambiar, the farmer with a tractor, poked Kutti Narayanan playfully in his stomach.

'No exercise and endless eating—that's why you have this potbelly!'

They sat in the portico and asked Padmanabhan about the daily wage rate in Palghat. They argued about the reasons for the wages having risen to seventeen rupees in Kizhakkemuri.

As they were about to leave, Kutti Narayanan put in an appearance again as the representative of the household.

'It would be good if this weather holds and it doesn't rain, isn't that so, Kutti Narayana?'

At dusk, the sound of the drums from the Shiva temple in the distance wafted in with the western wind that blew down the slope of the hill. The Thiruvegappura drummers. Was it Achu or Raman? If it was Raman, there would be some fun at the finish. It was not for nothing he had attached himself to Raman at the temple festival last year.

Seethalakshmi lit the oil lamp at dusk. Narayani Amma began to chant her prayers loudly. Kutti Narayanan washed his hands and legs, smeared vibhuti over his forehead, sat down by the lamp and opened the *Ramayanam*.

It was a good augury, the book fell open at the page where the salvation of the bird, Jatayu, was described. He read two lines, closed his eyes, said a prayer. Then he opened his eyes and looked around him. Only Narayani Amma was there. He looked closely at her to find out whether she had grasped the significance of what he had read. Narayani Amma sat there, massaging her legs, swaying to and fro, her eyes shut.

Kutti Narayanan went in and checked the patient's breathing. He was very restless. Maybe this was a sign that the last breath would soon be drawn. Was there any Ganga water in the house, he wondered.

The sick man groaned. A blue jay cried out from a tree in the yard. He saw Narayani Amma's look reaching out towards him from behind her thick glasses. She understood that language. And so did he.

Kutti Narayanan went up to Master and stroked his forehead. He massaged his limbs.

The sick man was struggling to say something.

'What do you want? What is it? What?'

Narayani Amma came up to him too. Master's words could barely be made out through his groans.

'I want to get up.'

Narayani Amma shouted excitedly: 'Achu! Rajasekharan!'

Everyone came running into the room.

'Let's make him sit up,' said Kutti Narayanan.

'Should we?'

'We must.'

Together, the men lifted Master and propped him up against the wall on his pillow.

'Water ...' groaned Master.

A steel glass containing Horlicks was brought to his lips. Kutti Narayan noticed Master's hands going slowly up towards the glass.

Master opened his eyes slowly, moaning all the time. They

were all there before him. Seethalakshmi, who had been standing behind Rajasekharan, came forward.

'Father, Father ... it's I ...'

Master's tired eyes looked around, focusing on no one in particular.

Master moved the glass away from his lips.

Kutti Narayanan said, 'I am Kutti Narayanan.'

Master muttered, between groans: 'It's not hot, heat it up.'

Kutti Narayanan thought to himself, as he walked to the kitchen, he'll never give up his obstinacy. He felt confused. This was a strange kind of change. Maybe it was possible—a stage just preceding death when everything altered. Maybe there were only moments left now for the end. The senior most member of the Poothottil family, the village headman's father and Kalathil Kurup: Kutti Narayanan recalled the same thing having taken place in all three cases.

The next morning, the children stood around the sick man who was seated with his back resting against the wall.

Vishalam said, 'If there's anything you need, Father, just ask Achu Ettan to call me.'

The old man did not say anything.

'I'll drop Seetha at the junction before I go.'

Master nodded slowly.

Seetha touched her father's forehead. 'We can go when you're recovered. We'll have the eye surgery done there.'

Vishalam hesitated for a while, then said, 'I am leaving, Father.'

Master nodded.

Kutti Narayanan accompanied the women on their way out.

His hope that they would give him something was futile. Murmuring something to each other, they stepped into the courtyard, ignoring him completely even though he followed them like a shadow.

When he came back, Raju was standing at the door of the room, looking confused.

'I'm going. Please tell Grandfather, Kutti Narayanan.'

'Go up to him, child, and tell him.'

Raju went up to the bed. Master saw him stand there hesitantly and asked, 'Time to go?'

'H'm...'

'Get going then.'

Relieved, Raju left. Kutti Narayanan waited uncertainly. Then he said to Narayani Amma, 'I'm going out. I'll be back.'

He went out without waiting for a reply, his mind seething with anger at all the people who had united to deceive him.

Master gazed at Narayani Amma who was seated on the floor with her legs stretched out.

'Don't you want to go?'

Narayani Amma grunted in reply.

'Where's Achu?'

'He's gone out. He'll be back.'

Master cleared the phlegm in his throat and said softly: 'Are you listening? If I fall seriously ill again, don't send for the children. They've hundreds of things to do. No telegrams, no phone calls. Don't inform them till you're sure it's all over.'

His words trailed off as he gasped for breath.

Master looked at a distant point outside the window and murmured: 'Let whoever is free come after that. Tell Achu as well.'

Narayani Amma looked at her brother. The eyes dulled with age that gazed out through the window were filled with tears.

'You're crying, Ettan!'

'No, of course not ... My head feels hot, that's why my eyes are watering ...'

Master rubbed his eyes. 'You can go too.'

His sister did not answer. She kept chanting in her mind: 'Narayana! Narayana!'

Kadugannawa: A Travel Note

He had been twenty-two when he wandered through the Himalayan foothills with a shoulder bag that contained two sets of clothes and a camera. He had ridden a horse over a narrow path that went from Ijat Nagar to Almora. He had drunk bhang mixed with milk, gone to sleep and woken up to find himself lying on a boulder overlooking a chasm. That was long ago. Now, he avoided journeys. He seldom spent a night in a strange place. Even if he climbed a few steps, it took him three or four minutes to recover his breath. It was a nuisance carrying around pills for his blood pressure and tubes of insulin for injections. Nevertheless, he accepted the invitation to visit Sri Lanka. Although he did not have anything significant to say about the role newspapers could play in the development of Southeast Asia. He agreed because the invitation was from Sri Lanka. There was a place there that he had always wanted to see. Kadugannawa.

His colleagues at the Madras office had told him that he needed to be at the airport only two hours before departure. No one observed the rule that passengers to foreign countries had to report three hours in advance. But he got there very early. There was a time when he used to arrive only after everyone had checked in and his name was being announced and had run up the ladder just before it was removed. Now, if he did anything in a hurry, the thudding of his heart would grow very loud.

The departure lounge was almost empty. The plane would

leave on time. A group of Sri Lankans suddenly trooped in with bags and bundles and the lounge was full.

When taking class for new recruits to journalism, they always said, keep your eyes and ears open. A story worth reporting could happen any minute somewhere around you.

Were these people refugees? They couldn't be, refugees were being sent back by sea. These people were carrying back not only mixers and grinders, but even fresh vegetables from Madras. Maybe he could strike up a conversation with a couple of them—about comparative prices, or their new President. He could even ask them for their reaction—albeit delayed—to the news of the assassination of our former Prime Minister. No, he was not going to write a report of any kind.

There were women among the Sri Lankans. He suddenly thought of his mother. She used to call them Shingalathis. Sri Lanka was the land of the Shingalas and Shingalathis.

The last to join them were two *bhikshus*, Buddhist monks. He looked at them attentively when they sat down on two seats near him—one was a woman, a *bhikshuni*.

He had planned to make this trip in 1981. Pereira, a journalist friend from Goa who worked with *The Ceylon Observer*, had offered to make arrangements to take him wherever he wanted to go. He had even been ready to write an article on "An Investigation made by an Indian Journalist." But three days before he was due to leave, a rebellion broke out in Sri Lanka and a state of emergency was declared. Pereira called and asked him to postpone his journey. He agreed—the country was nearby after all, he could go there any time he wanted. But it was a mistake to have delayed the trip so long.

They announced that boarding had started on the plane to Sri Lanka. The tourists rushed to the gate, not bothering to form a queue. Even the saffron-clad bhikshuni forced her way forward like the rest.

A young man standing beside him laughed and said: 'Look at that!'

He laughed too.

'To Calambo?'

'Yes.'

'What's the climate like there?'

Which climate did he mean? The insurgency or the weather?

'I don't know.'

He made a note mentally: you did not say "Colombo", it was "Calambo".

Although he had a window seat, his view was blocked by the wing of the plane. It did not matter. He was not going to write a travelogue. He had sometimes written about countries he had visited in order to justify trips that were supposed to be on duty. He had often started them with the first thing he saw as the plane landed.

He glanced at his watch. Just as he calculated that it would take ten more minutes to land, the first announcement was made. He hurriedly filled up the immigration form and opened his briefcase again. The passport, the ticket, the letters and fax messages from the organisers of the seminar, were all there. Needless anxieties and fears filled one's mind as one grew older. Otherwise, why did he always check that the door had been bolted at night even after his daughter had told him that she had bolted it?

Dr Ramachandran had said: 'Mr Venugopalan, people get like that when they grow old.'

Air India had once made a mistake about the date and there had been no one to receive him when he walked out at Tokyo airport. He had gone by taxi to the Asia Centre. In a few hours he had knocked on the door of the friend and his astonished wife, who had been expecting him only the next day. The spirit of adventure had been his constant companion in those days.

Wouldn't the organisers of the seminar be waiting for him? He began to feel anxious.

While waiting for his baggage, he remembered: hadn't a bomb exploded here once, killing a number of people? When had it been? President Premadasa had died a few months ago. In a bomb blast in the middle of the city. He thought of how the Buddha had come to this island, which had been ruled by asuras and demons who had slaughtered and murdered.

When a bloodthirsty gang surrounded him, the Buddha smiled. Violent winds blew and lightning flashed. The demons trembled in fear.

'Give me a place where I can sit down,' said the Buddha.

'Deliver us from fear and we will give you this whole island.'

'You will no longer experience fear.'

He rebuked himself: do not be afraid. Life is only an interlude after one has made a treaty with death. He thought of the game of chess in Bergman's "Seventh Seal". He read about Vedanta and Buddhism nowadays in order to achieve freedom from fear.

One had to understand that danger lurked here all the time. Maybe that was why the Chief Editor, who never refused an invitation from abroad, had chosen him to take part in this seminar. He had not told the Chief Editor about the secret of Kadugannawa.

What a relief! A young man was waiting for him, holding a placard with his name on it. He went up to him, dragging his suitcase.

'I am P.K. Venugopal.' The young man took charge of his suitcase. They walked out.

At last he had come to the country he had thought he would never visit. Although late, Sri Lanka had invited him.

As the taxi sped forward, he looked at the kiosks and the small workshops on the roadside and thought they look like the shops in Changaramkulam, at home. He had not realised the airport was so far from the city. It took thirty-five minutes. As he signed the hotel register:

'Welcome, Mr Venugopal! I am Ashley Gunatilake.'

They had talked over the telephone twice. He had round, protuberant eyes, and the hint of a small beard that looked as if it had been left by mistake on his chin. He thought the man resembled some old black singer whose name he could not remember. He seemed to be bathed in sweat beneath his black suit.

He could see a bit of the sea from the fourth-floor room. There was a building opposite with a flag flying on top. He looked at the helicopter circling above it. Gunatilake said, 'Security—that's the President's office.'

Gunatilake parted the window curtains. 'Look, there are naval boats on guard in front.'

He told Gunatilake that it was his first visit to Sri Lanka. He had wanted to come earlier but had not been able to. He thought he would not mention the old connections now.

'It's been a very busy day, so I couldn't come to the airport.'

'That's all right. After all, you're here now, Mr Gunatilake.'

'Call me Ashley. Let's have a drink.'

He took out two cans of beer from the small refrigerator.

Venugopalan declined.

'Orange juice? Coke?'

No, he didn't want anything. He did not want to tell Gunatilake that he had to take forty units of insulin a day.

'With your permission.' Ashley gulped down his first beer straight from the can in a minute. He opened the second one, poured the contents into a glass and lit a cigarette.

'That's a relief. What a day!'

'What's the situation like now? Are things calm?'

'It's always calm. But danger can strike any moment. Do you see that roof that looks like a steeple? The bomb that killed Premadasa exploded beneath it.' What Kennedy said was right: "If someone wants to kill me, no security network can prevent it. All it needs is that one man be ready to give up his life to take mine!"

Ashley Gunatilake was an official in the Ministry of Information. He could not be more than thirty-five. Venugopalan felt that his tone held the maturity of an elder statesman.

'The LTTE recruits twelve-year-old children now. After the massacre in the military camp, fifteen-year-old teenagers queue up every day in our recruiting offices, eager to take revenge. Have you heard what Shelley said?'

'Who?'

'Shelley. P.B. Shelley, the English poet. "War is an

entertainment for rulers, a blessing for priests, a matter of logic for practitioners of law, a trade for mercenaries."'

In the space of five minutes, the man had quoted Kennedy and Shelley. He must thank his stars that he had Ashley as his host.

'Mr Ashley, I wrote that I wanted to visit certain places ...'

'After the seminar tomorrow, we've set apart Saturday and Sunday for sight-seeing. There's so much to see in this country. There'll be a person from the Department of Tourism with you.'

'Please, Mr Ashley. Come with me.'

'Let's see. I never tire of looking at historical monuments. Let's see. Any particular places you want to see?'

'Kandy.'

'Everyone goes there. The fourteenth-century capital. Three hours from here. What else?'

He said hesitantly, 'I think it's somewhere near there. Kadugannawa.'

'Oh, Kadugannawa? I know the place, it's on our way.'

Ashley's father-in-law was from there. He had moved to Colombo about ten years ago.

'He is now ...'

'He died last December.'

He thought Gunatilake would ask, what importance could Kadugannawa have for an elderly journalist from Kerala? He had decided to say that relatives of his used to live there.

Ashley looked at his watch and got up.

'The seminar is at five tomorrow. It will do if you're ready by four.' He held out his visiting card. 'Have a good rest.'

He placed the empty beer cans on top of the refrigerator and left.

A little later, Venugopalan went down to the hotel lobby. He browsed through the books and stationery in the shops. Compared to India, the prices were higher.

He stood outside the hotel for a while. The lights on the long road along the seashore came on suddenly. There was a military checkpost right in front. He went back to his room, called room service and ordered his meal for seven. Then he changed into a checked lungi and relaxed on the sofa.

What had it looked like, the face of the little girl seated on a steel trunk, twirling a bunch of keys? The face of the little Shingalathi girl? There had been two calendars at home at the time. Did one have a picture of baby Saroja? Or of Ashwathamma? Someone in the movies, anyway. The other one had Sri Krishna. Whenever he opened Amma's four-legged wooden box to examine its contents, Sri Krishna's reddish eyes used to stare accusingly at him. He was certain that the girl from Ceylon had a prettier face than the movie actress. She had a squarish face and shoulder-length hair. He had only a hazy picture of her in his mind now.

Venugopalan had gone to Devi Oppu's house only after he had decided on this trip. Devi Oppu was his father's niece. He had gone there to tell her that he would not be able to attend her youngest daughter's wedding.

'Once this is over, I'll be relieved. It was just our good fortune that this proposal came through,' said Devi Oppu.

He told her he was not sure he could attend the wedding. 'The children will come. I'll be in Ceylon at that time.'

Devi Oppu was upset.

'It's office work—a journalists' conference. And then, since it's in Ceylon ...'

'Haven't you been to Ceylon, Venu?'

'No. I planned to go a number of times but never made it.'

Devi Oppu remembered that Venu's older brothers, Kuttettan and Rajettan, had lived in Ceylon when they were children. His mother had returned to India before Appu was born.

Some of their relatives dropped by to ask about the wedding arrangements.

'Ah, Venu, it's quite a while since we saw you.'

Devi Oppu said to them: 'Venu is going to Ceylon, so he can't come for the wedding. He can visit the place Uncle worked in, can't you, Venu?'

He smiled. 'Maybe. I'll try.'

'What was the name of the place where Uncle worked? I can't remember ...'

'Kadugannawa.'

He would never forget the name. His older brothers used to write the address on the letters Amma wrote and he used to be the one who posted them.

Their neighbour, Visalakshi Amma, asked: 'Didn't a child come from there once, Devi?'

Devi Oppu said, 'Who knows whether they are still alive! It was such a long time ago. Her name was Leela.'

Venugopalan had made calculations earlier. The Shingalathi who was said to have lived with his father was not likely to be alive now. If she was, she would be at least ninety.

'Leela was my age. She might be alive.'

Venugopalan was astonished. He used to speak about her often, it was an intriguing story. A mother with four sons. She wanted a daughter very much. Then her husband came home from abroad after many years and there was a little girl with him. A rumour arose that she was his daughter and there was a violent quarrel in the house.

For some reason, Venugopalan had thought the child was younger than him.

'Devi Oppu, wasn't she ... wasn't that girl younger than me?'

'Oh no! You were nine then. She had her first period when we were playing in the yard of Marathattu. I remember it very well.'

He had heard the story of what happened when the girl went with Father to his ancestral house. For two whole days she had sat next to the wooden grain chest in the southern room. She did not even have a bath or go to the toilet. Devi Oppu and her mother had tried their best, then they had gone to Father very hesitantly and told him about her. It was only after that that the girl began going out to play with the other children.

'She must have been twelve or thirteen at the time, I'm sure of that. She had a very well-developed body.'

He had not known that the girl from Ceylon had had her

first period then. Venugopalan calculated. She must be sixty-two or sixty-three now.

He remembered the celebration the night Father came home. Two chickens were killed in the northern yard. His older brother had played records on the gramophone that Father had brought. Father had entertained their uncles and the village bigwigs in a room upstairs. They heard the Tamil songs played there late into the night. At some time during the night, after the guests left, Mother and Father had had a quarrel. He had woken up from sleep with a start hearing his mother talk loudly. The uncle who had come with Father had spoken of the Shingalathi.

Father left the next morning for Vanneri, his own village, taking the child with him. They stayed there three months and then left for Ceylon.

None of Father's children went to Vanneri, though all of them, especially the youngest, Venugopalan, liked going there. They always served tasty snacks for evening tea in Father's place. Their speciality was a pancake made with powdered country dates and rayi grass. Ammu Oppu, who presided over the kitchen, knew a secret recipe for making sweet payasam with mathok flour. She often gave the children roasted ayini seeds.

But Mother would tell everyone: 'Stay here and eat what you get. You needn't go anywhere.'

The waiter removed the dinner dishes. Venugopalan stood at the window, looking out. He could still hear the helicopter. The gunboats were not visible now. Now and then, he saw the fiery eye of a lighted cigarette in the booth on the roadside where soldiers stood guard.

The traffic had almost stopped but the town was still not asleep. He parted the curtains to let in the light of dawn and went to bed.

He called Ashley in the morning. No one picked up the phone. He got through at the third attempt.

'Did you sleep well?'

'Yes, very well.'

Did the paper for the seminar have to be distributed in

advance? No. The man from Bangladesh had not arrived. Patel from Bombay had come ...

'Ashley, the sight-seeing trip?'

'Don't worry, I'll arrange it. The car will come at four. Be ready.'

It was possible that some of the Malayalees still left in the country would come for the seminar conducted by the journalists of the SAARC if they knew that a P.K. Venugopalan Nair was one of the speakers. If any of the older people remembered Father ...

His older brother had said that Father had had a certain standing among the Ceylon Malayalees. He had seen the photograph taken at a reception given to the High Commissioner in Ceylon, who was a Malayalee, in Father's suitcase. He had been sure that Father was among those who stood in the back row.

His other brother, Rajettan, had been, as usual, sceptical. But the older brother had argued: "Isn't Father's address proof enough that he was well-known—K.M. Nair, Kadugannawa, Ceylon."

He had a faint hope that he would meet some elderly Malayalees at the seminar.

When he arrived at the seminar hall with the paper he had written laboriously over three days, there were only about fifteen people there. He waited outside. No, there was no one who had come because he had seen a Malayalee's name on the list.

There were six people on the dais. Venugopalan pretended to listen with interest to the Sri Lankan official who inaugurated the conference with a speech on the conflict between established powers and newly-awakened ones.

The conference was over sooner than he had expected.

Ashley had been in the audience. He said they could start at eight the next morning. They would spend the night at Anuradhapura. They would travel as the guests of the Department of Tourism, in a car they would provide.

'Ashley, you must come with me.'

'I'll try.'

'Don't say that, you must come.'

It may have been because he had communicated with Ashley through phone calls and letters that he looked upon him now as a close friend.

It rained at night but the morning sky was clear and bright.

Ashley arrived at eight thirty in a car from the Department of Tourism.

As they drove along, he asked Ashley about his family. He had two daughters and his wife worked in a bank. He had been educated in London and had worked there for two years in the Ceylon High Commission.

Ashley knew the history and legends of Ceylon and remembered dates accurately. As they walked around, looking at the historic monuments, Ashley described the age of Devanampriya Tissa. The first Buddha Vihara, Mihinthale. It was Emperor Asoka's son, Mahendra, who came here with the message of the Buddha. Mihinthale was named after Mahendra. Asoka's daughter, Sanghamitra, brought a branch of the bodhi tree and planted it there. 'Take it down if you want to—Sanghamitra, third century B.C. The wall around it was put up by Vikramaraja Simha ...'

He made some notes to satisfy Ashley.

There was a military camp outside the boundary wall. Once, a tourist bus that seemed to be carrying pilgrims had pulled up at the spot. The passengers had got down and pulled out AK-47s from beneath their saffron robes. They were Tamil militants. Sixty-seven people had died in the shooting that followed. There had been devotees and vendors who sold flowers at the roadside among the dead. It was after that that the military camp had been set up to guard the place.

Ashley bought a flower-tray from the mandapam in front of the bodhi tray, placed five white flowers on it and prayed for a minute.

'Ashley, you're ...'

'I'm a Buddhist.'

During the British rule, many people had taken Christian names in order to get admission in schools. The names continued to be used through generations. Ashley's grandfather was also an Ashley.

Ashley said, as they were looking at the shrine of the Buddha in samadhi and the Copper Palace:

'The king who embraced the religion of the Buddha disbanded the army. The soldiers dug wells and ponds and began to cultivate the land. Two men who came from Tamil Nadu to sell horses saw this country without an army and made their plans. They went back, returned with six boatloads of soldiers and captured the land. That is the story of the first invasion.'

'You are the people who always looked out for opportunities to invade,' said Ashley, smiling.

Venugopalan was feeling tired, walking around the ruins of the old viharas.

They had arranged to spend the night at the rest house on the banks of the Nuwara Mewa lake.

Ashley took out a bottle of "Old Arrack" and said, 'I prefer this to foreign whisky.'

Venugopalan mentioned his ailments and declined a drink. It had grown dark outside.

'It is new moon tomorrow.'

Venugopalan was anxious to know what the next day's programme was.

'You remember what I told you, Ashley?'

'Oh, yes. Kadugannawa. We're going that way. It's a pleasant place. The view from the top is beautiful. But there's nothing else there.'

Venugopalan said hesitantly: 'My father worked there for some time. And some other people from my village. An uncle ...'

'That's incredible! We'll go there.'

Venugopalan pretended to listen to the stories Ashley was telling with interest, while he remembered that it was after he finished college that his father had returned home for good. Their relatives and the villagers presumed that he would bring home plenty of money after having worked in Ceylon for thirty-one years. Venugopalan's mother had died by then. Father had come twice while she was still alive. He would come home in the morning and go back to Vanneri in the evening. Amma would arrange for two extra vegetable preparations and scrambled eggs to be made, but would not appear before him. When it was time to eat, she would ask one of the children to tell him that the leaves had been laid. Meenakshi Edathi, who helped Amma in the kitchen, would serve the food.

Devi Oppu's brother who was Father's eldest nephew made discreet enquiries about Father's savings and told them the money had been deposited in a bank.

The important people in the village came visiting every evening. Brandy bottles brought from Ceylon were opened and Vijayettan sent scrambled eggs and fried pappadams upstairs. When the bottles from Ceylon were finished, Vijayettan got some more from Thrissur. At the end of ten days, Father placed bottles of arrack distilled by Unneeri before his guests and said:

'You know our Unneeri. No foreign liquor can be compared to the liquor he distils.' His guests nodded agreement. From the next evening, Father found himself alone.

When the "Old Arrack" bottle was half empty, Ashley got up. Sweat was running down his forehead. He wanted to speak about a romantic interlude in his life in London, but postponed it to the next day.

Ashley was silent while they ate in the dining hall. He stumbled while they went back upstairs and laughed when Venugopalan put out his hand to steady him.

'Never mind. The Old Arrack's giving me a good kick!'

Venugopalan had to help him open the door of his room.

'Goodnight.'

'Goodnight.'

Once alone in his own room, Venugopalan took off his shoes. His feet felt free. It was clear that he was no longer fit for long journeys.

Vijayettan, who read detective novels day and night, seemed to have taken on the role of a detective himself, with the blessings of the womenfolk. He would waylay the postman before he reached the house and take away the letters addressed to Father. He would take them to the kitchen, steam them open, read them and then reseal them and hand them over to Father. However, he did not gather any fresh information. Father always kept his keys with him. Vijayettan found some old keys and managed to open Father's trunk after many attempts. He did not find any documents or old records. There was only an old Kozhikode Imperial Bank passbook, cancelled after transactions had been discontinued. He did not even get hold of Madhava Ammama's address.

When Vijayettan died, Venugopalan was working in the Delhi office of the newspaper. On his next visit home, he went to see his father's sisters in Vanneri. They told him old stories about Vijayettan and wept. Then they recounted his exploits as a detective and laughed.

'Venu, do you know why Father did not bring anything back with him?'

Father had had financial difficulties from the moment he came back. He began to borrow money from the man to whom they sold the yield from the coconut trees. His younger brother, who had looked after the household till then, said: 'My elder brother is here now. He can look after things,' and moved to his wife's house, some distance away. He lived on the income he made from the property there.

After many years, Vijayettan seemed to have found out the truth somehow. Father had owned a rubber estate when he came away. He had given it to the daughter he had by the Shingalathi and arranged a marriage for her before he returned.

This was news to Venugopalan. 'How did he find that out?'

'Vijayettan wrote to several people in Ceylon. He must have got the information through them.'

Father's younger sister said: 'Let her live in comfort. Whether she's one of us or not, she's a woman, isn't she?' Venu was distressed. Even when he earned a salary of three hundred rupees, he used to send a hundred to Father. Father used to tell everyone he met that his sons were not looking after him properly. There was the rubber estate he had gifted. And money as well, Venu did not know how much. Distress turned into anger.

The next morning, Ashley knocked on his door, dressed in jeans and a bright red T-shirt.

'Ready, Mr Venu?'

He was not yet ready.

They went to Polaneruwa. To the Parakrama Sagar lake that King Parakrama Bahu had made. Then there was Nishangamallan, who had woken up his workers in the middle of the night and made them chisel accounts of his great and noble deeds on stone.

'When will we reach Kadugannawa?'

'Our next stop in Kandy. We'll have lunch there. Kadugannawa is nearby. Don't you want to see Sigiriya?'

He did not show much interest. Ashley told him the story of the fifth century king, Dasasena, who had fought the Tamil invaders eighteen times. His nephew and the son he had had by his concubine joined forces and took him prisoner. The son he had had by his queen ran away to India. Kashyapan, who had taken the king prisoner, was upset when he found no gold or jewels in the palace. He asked his father: 'Where is all the wealth?'

Venugopalan was suddenly interested in Dasasena's story. All through the ages, there had been children who became furious when they could not find the wealth their fathers had amassed.

'And then?'

'The king said he would show him where the wealth was if he was taken to the large lake he had made. He was taken there in a chariot. The king stepped into the lake eagerly and drank water. He swam around for a while. Then, splashing in the water, he said: 'Here, this is my treasure!' The story goes that Kashyapan buried the king alive in a stone chamber.

Venugopalan decided to visit Sigiriya. It was an isolated, rocky hill in the middle of a forest. All around it lay the ruins of ramparts and trenches. Afraid of the Crown Prince who had gone away to India, Kashyapan built a palace on top of the hill. There was only one entrance—through the mouth of a lion carved in stone. Only one person could pass at a time through it. And so he ruled, from the top of the hill.

'Mogallanan, the Crown Prince, came back with an army and challenged Kashyapan, who came downhill to fight him. When he was defeated, Kashyapan plunged a sword into his neck and killed himself.'

Venugopalan stood before the steps leading into the lion's mouth. The left foreleg of the gigantic sculpture of the lion still stood, and three claws. Ashley stood between them and said, 'Look, the claw comes up to my knee. You can guess how huge the lion was!'

On the sides of the steps that led to the top were the figures of ten beautiful women. On the opposite side, on a wall polished like a mirror were graffiti scrawled by visitors.

'Come!'

Venugopalan climbed up with difficulty.

Ashley read out some of the things people had written. 'Saw the Lion King below. Do not want to see the palace of the King on top.'

Ashley stood there for a long time, reading and enjoying the words.

'Look, this is a ninth century line. He must have been a poet. "I found here the sky of my dreams."' Mogallanan's army must have lined up below, the place where rocks were strewn around.

'What were Kashyapan's soldiers doing while they climbed nearer?'

Ashley explained that the army had reached there on the night of the new moon.

We reached Kandy at noon. Ashley prayed with five white flowers at the great temple where the Buddha's tooth was kept.

Pointing to the gardens beside the lake and the Queens' bath-houses, Ashley said, 'Lawrence came here. D.H. Lawrence. In 1922.'

Lawrence had been angry with the dancers who performed before the Prince of Wales. The British prince had sat there indifferently while the Kandyan artistes tried hard to please him.

'1922! Look, Ashley, it was in 1922 that my father came to Ceylon.'

'He must have made plenty of money,' said Ashley, patting Venugopalan's shoulder.

Venugopalan told Ashley the story he had heard: his father had had some property here. An estate and a couple of shops. What they said at home was that he had given all of it to a girl here. A girl in Kadugannawa.

'Was she your father's … daughter?'

'Yes, there was a rumour like that as well. Her mother lived with Father for a long time, anyway.'

'Right! We'll find out. Like Mogallanan, we'll stand in the front yard and challenge them, I am entitled to a share of the property! Hey, it is the night of the new moon!'

With great enthusiasm, he took out a can of beer from his shoulder bag and opened it.

'March to Kadugannawa! Get ready, Mr Mogallanan!' Venu could not share his laughter. He wondered why he had told him that old story. He should have just seen the place …

It was Ashley who was eager to see the botanical gardens and the orchids.

They left the town and took the mountain road. They went through two ghat sections and reached the top. Ashley asked the chauffeur to stop.

'Do you know the meaning of the word, "Kadugannawa"? A wayside rest-house.' The tiled roofs of the houses on the border of Kandy were visible from there and so was a curve of the Mahabali river which skirted Kandy.

They stopped in the middle of a small bazaar and Ashley said, 'This is Kadugannawa.'

He got down slowly from the car. A small bazaar with not more than thirty shops. Only two buildings were of concrete. The rest had tiled roofs.

'This is it?'

'Yes.'

There were tea estates on the distant slopes. Beyond them was the forest.

'Your father's name?'

'K.M. Nair.'

Three taxis were parked under a banyan tree. Ashley spoke to the drivers, then walked towards the shops.

Venu was astonished. Was this the town where Father had made a great name? Padinhare Angadi, the bazaar at home, was bigger than this.

Father was supposed to have owned two shops. Above both of them, on the first floor, were lodgings for the workers who had been brought from his village. Venu looked around uneasily. There were only two buildings with two storeys. There were small wooden railings under the blackened tiles.

Ashley came back after quite a while. He had with him an old man wearing a collarless shirt and a checked lungi. He had a big moustache and gentle eyes.

'This man knew my father-in-law. Ask him whatever you want. I'll interpret for you.'

'Ask him about the Malayalees who used to live here. Whether any of them are still…'

Ashley talked to the man at length. Then he said:

'Venu, he says there are no Kochiyans here now. They call you people Kochiyans.'

'Not now. Long ago. About forty years ago …?'

Ashley and the man talked some more.

'There used to be a merchant. Then there was a *kattadia*—a magic-man, who cured people of their diseases with magic potions and incantations.' The building he pointed to was single-storeyed, a tiled, three-roomed structure.

When Ashley set out to explore the place again with the moustached man, Venugopalan said, 'No, Mr Ashley, let's go back.'

'But all these magic-men were your people.'

Perhaps …

One of Amma's brothers had worked with Father for a while. They had fallen out with each other and parted company. Venugopalan had heard that he had worked with a Shingalathi widow, looking after her affairs. And that he had practiced magic for a while. He had never gone back to Kerala.

Ashley brought someone else. A young man in jeans with a cigarette dangling from his lips. Dragging his slippers on the ground, he followed Ashley, nodding agreement to everything he said. Venu felt there was a tinge of mockery in his smile. Ashley told him to get into the front seat of the car. He threw away the stub of his cigarette and lit another one. He offered one to the driver, who refused it.

'Where are we going now?' asked Venu impatiently.

'Would Mogallanan have gone back without making full enquiries? Mr Venu, are you sure this is the name of the place?'

Venugopalan grasped at this route of escape: 'No, I'm uncertain about it now. Let's go back, Ashley.'

'Let's have a look at the place he's talking about. It's quite nearby. He says there are some people there connected to a Kochiyan.'

They stopped the car in five minutes. Ashley and the young man got down and Venu followed reluctantly. As they turned into the lane, he saw white banners with something written on them tied to the coconut palms. Ashley explained that they were tributes offered to a dead person by relatives and friends and that it was the custom to put them up in the vicinity of the dead person's house.

Venu thought of a story he had once read in which a person goes in search of someone and finds ... a dead body.

'Are we ... are we going to a house where a death has taken place?' asked Venu in consternation.

'No. It's the third house from that one.'

There were a number of bicycles and scooters parked near the house where the death had occurred and people stood in groups on the roadside. One of them, who knew the young man, asked him something. The house they entered was very small. The space between the lane and the door of the house was full of shrubs. There was a pond by the side of the house and a man sat by the edge, gathering up the scum with a long pole. He wore a knee-length lungi and his face was not visible. The bones on his brown-skinned body stood out.

Ashley and the young man went up to him. Venu waited on the first step leading to the house. They kept asking the man questions, but he did not turn round or answer. His entire attention was concentrated on scooping up the scum. It looked as if he was not even aware of the two people standing next to him.

Ashley raised his voice and it sounded as if he was on the verge of a heated exchange of words. The man shifted the pole from his right hand to the left and slowly turned towards the visitors. The stubble on his face had patches of grey. Venu thought he saw anger blazing in his eyes. He spat at them and the spittle almost touched their feet. Then he looked up and said something loudly.

After that he turned back and continued to gather up the scum with the tip of his pole.

Ashley waited a few minutes, then walked back. The young man offered the man a cigarette, but when he went on with his work, unmoving, he joined Ashley, smiling.

Ashley said, 'Poor fellow, he's mad!'

As they walked back to the car, the young man kept talking. When they came up to the road, Ashley shook the young man's hand and thanked him.

When the two of them were alone in the car, Venu wanted to ask Ashley two things. One was the old man's name. But it was the second question he asked first.

'What was he doing? Wasn't it scum that he was collecting?'

'Yes, it was. Some people boil the scum and eat it. People who are very poor.'

Venu decided not to ask him the man's name.

After a while, Ashley said: 'It appears this man's mother was a Kochiyan's daughter. The people in the bazaar said she died a long time ago. The Kochiyan had a small shop. No one remembers his name.'

Venu tried to console himself. This could not be the town

where Father used to run a business connected with tea estates. It could not have been here that he made a great name.

'I asked him his mother's name, his father's name, his maternal grandfather's name, but he wouldn't say a word. When I shouted at him, he finally said something. A classic statement.'

'Yes ...?'

'That all Kochiyans are thieves!' Ashley laughed.

Venu made a feeble attempt to laugh with him.

'The woman who was supposed to be your father's daughter ... what was her name?'

Venu hesitated, then said, without meeting his eyes: 'I don't know.'

'What a shame! My father-in-law has some other friends in this area. It would have been easy to find out if you knew her name. This is the place, isn't it?'

'I don't know, Ashley. Perhaps ... perhaps I got the name wrong. It could be some other name like Kadugannawa ... Some of your place names ...'

'The next place we should visit is Sardiyel where there is a memorial to policemen who were slaughtered by a notorious gangster. Or Medovelayil, where there's a harvest festival. Or else ...'

'No, that's enough. I'm tired. Let's go back to Colombo.'

'Calambo, not Colombo. Let's go then.'

Ashley looked out. 'It gets dark early on the hills. And then it's new moon today.'

Ashley burst out laughing for no reason at all.

Venu felt that the voice describing the scenes by the side of the road came from very faraway. He lay back on the seat pretending to listen to everything, pretending to look at everything. While he kept repeating to himself:

'Yes, I mistook the name. The name of the place. I'm sure ... it's not Kadugannawa. It's some other name ... some other ...'

The Deluge

It was good that the door had been kept open. It was a Sunday, so it would be convenient for people to come. They could sit down wherever there was space. Vivek Joshi said that though the rain had stopped, the roads were still water-logged. Uncle Joshi and his family used to creep along in their thirty-year-old car at a snail's pace even in normal times.

Another group had arrived. Ramesh's family from Andheri. Ramesh had come early and gone out to supervise some arrangements.

Bhaskarettan was sitting on the sofa, his eyes half closed, running his fingers over his forehead. Some of the visitors placed their hands on his shoulder and murmured words of sympathy. When it grew crowded inside, some people came out. It was on occasions like these that the small front yard between the house and the outer wall proved useful.

More people would come. Bhaskarettan had lived in the city for forty years and had many friends and acquaintances.

The unseasonal rains and floods were a constant topic of conversation among the vistors. Someone described how he had been trapped in his car on Friday evening in Dadar. Hundreds of cars had been caught in the rising waters, unable to move forward or go back.

'Finally, do you know what I did? I didn't look in front of

me or behind, I just opened the door and pissed! What else could I do?'

Only two or three people sniggered, listening to Bhonsle Sahib's feat.

'Have the children been informed?' A newcomer repeated the question many others before him had asked.

'I don't think it's possible to wait until they come. It's difficult for them to come at such short notice anyway. I spoke to them.' Ten years ago, there had been heavy rains in the city for three days continuously. The newspapers had estimated it as the heaviest rainfall in a hundred years. No one had estimated how heavy it was this time although many parts of the city were completely under water.

It had started raining on Thursday night. I had woken up to the sound of incessant rain. I had fallen into the habit of waking up at about two in the morning. I would drink a glass of water, go to the toilet and lie down again. I would wake up again only when the milkman rang the bell at five thirty. Just as I thought to myself that the rain that had started at night had not stopped. I noticed that water was splashing in through the tear in the wire netting fixed on the window to keep out mosquitoes.

Bhaskarettan groaned in his sleep.

'Such heavy rain! The water's splashing in.' I wondered whether Bhaskarettan had heard me.

I drew aside the plastic curtain and made an attempt to stop the rain splashing in by pressing on the torn wire netting.

'Come in, come in. Find yourself a place to sit.'

Ramesh, a friend of the family, had assumed the duties of a host. Now that he was there, Kadiri Sahib and Uncle Joshi went out. Playing host was not easy, especially on such occasions. Topics of conversation were hard to find. The floods in the city came in handy. The Malabari teashop owner who served tea free to people stranded in their cars in Dadar became a good subject for conversation.

'Move up a bit. You can sit here.'

There had been a bigger crowd here eleven years ago.

Remember? It was Ramesh who took over the arrangements that time as well. Our twenty-fifth wedding anniversary. The children insisted that we celebrate our silver wedding. The food was served in the hall of the colony club. A shamiana was put up outside for cocktails. Food was ordered for a hundred guests. The children calculated later that a hundred and forty people had come.

'Look, I bought the mobile phone reluctantly. That salesman bullied me into buying it. I really discovered how useful it is during these floods. Many people stranded on the way made good use of it.' That was Gangaram, who had set up a construction company after he retired.

When I got up on Friday morning I realised that the rain had not stopped. I did not think then that the incessant rain would become a flood.

There were no morning papers, no packets of milk in the plastic bags hanging on the front door. Water had stagnated in the yard outside the small verandah. A foul odour hung in the air, probably because the gutters were overflowing.

When I closed the door and turned, Bhaskarettan had turned on the light above the wash basin and begun to shave.

'So early ...?'

'I have to go out.'

'In this rain? Where?'

Bhaskarettan usually woke up to the whistle of the milk cooker. He would have three cups of tea one after the other, read three newspapers in full, make phone calls. At nine, he would go into the bathroom. He was very methodical about everything. In the old days, this routine used to change only if he had to take a morning flight.

He had taken charge of the advertisement division of a small newspaper four years ago. He had been the manager of a large advertising agency and had stayed idle for two years after he left it. He had had a large office staff, a car and driver at his disposal. Two or three dinners a week. For Deepavali, the house would be filled with gift parcels and there would be a sizeable bonus as well.

'Do you want to join this small newspaper?' I had expressed a doubt.

'I said I would help them for a short time. I'll try it for a year.' One year had become four. I had never asked what they would pay him. We never used to talk about his income. At the time we got married, he used to tell me everything without being asked. 'This is all I'll get in hand. We'll have to live within those limits.'

'It doesn't matter. I get about three hundred after all.'

'No—'

'What ...?'

'You mustn't go to work anymore. We should be able to manage.'

I did not argue. I did not find it difficult to manage in the one-room flat.

It was Shanta Bhat and Chandrika Patel who told me about this colony, an hour's journey from the city. Their husbands had already booked flats there. I told him about it with some trepidation. He did not say anything.

'Think about it if it's feasible. We have two growing children.'

When the family property in the village had been divided, my elder sister had made me sign some papers and given me ten thousand rupees. The thought that it was in the bank gave me courage.

As the years passed, conversation at home had dwindled to bare essentials. But when we went to other people's houses for dinner, Bhaskarettan talked a great deal. He would crack jokes and make fun of me before his friends, calling me "the home department" or "boss". A mockery I enjoyed since it was loaded with affection.

The house had brought luck. I firmly believed that the change in his job and the rise in social status had happened after we came here. I prided myself secretly that it was the sale of the property in Vellinezhi and the ten thousand rupees I received for it that was the start of all this. Although I did not tell anyone that.

After the children were married, the house became very silent. They came once in two years and never stayed more than a week. They would pack a month's activity into that one week.

There were more people for the silver wedding than for the children's weddings. The congratulatory speeches made on the occasion were really worth hearing. The power behind Bhaskarettan's rise in his profession … a symbol of silent service. What were the words? Once they had emptied three or four glasses and had a mike in their hands, the words tumbled out of their mouths. All the same, there was sincerity and goodwill behind all of it.

Bhaskarettan was always moderate, even at cocktail parties. Only I knew that the first glass he picked up would last him until the end. But he never failed to observe the rules, the courtesies. He would be full of laughter and witticisms. He had started life working in London for a year and a half. His friends used to say that he had acquired his pleasing manners there.

Bhaskarettan used to talk a lot the year before we got married. He would call up my office at the appointed time, to make sure when I would leave. He would arrive at the bus stop in front of Bierce and Company at least five minutes ahead of time. What a pleasure it had been to listen to the ceaseless chatter of this man who had become so miserly with words now. How often we used to burst out laughing during the two hours we spent together before we parted company at dusk at the gate of the hostel.

The children wanted to celebrate my sixtieth birthday. I evaded their requests. Bhaskarettan had neither agreed or disagreed with the idea.

The milkman had not come, so I quickly made some black tea.

'Where are you off to?'

He had come out in jeans, contrary to his usual practice.

'Jeans …?' I smiled.

He did not seem to like my question.

'Why, are they prohibited?'

'No, no. Where are you going?'

'To Pune.'

'I wish you'd told me yesterday. Saroja's always been asking me to go to Pune.'

Saroja and Nambiar had been our neighbours when we stayed in the one-room flat in Matunga.

'I'm going on office work.'

I had seen the jeans in his suitcase six months ago when he returned from a business trip to Ahmedabad. I had watched him put it away carefully in the wardrobe and laughed to myself.

'I met the son of an old friend, a computer engineer. He insisted on buying it for me.'

'Which friend? Are there any of our old friends there?'

He had not replied to that.

Outside, the rain had not abated at all.

'What a downpour!'

'A car will come for me.' Bhaskarettan came to the door and looked out.

'Will you have breakfast? I can make some toast quickly.'

'There are three or four of us from the office. We've arranged to have breakfast at Lonavala.'

As the driver of the private taxi tried to decipher the door number in the rain, Bhaskarettan waved to him. He started to walk towards the car and I said,

'Wait. I'll bring an umbrella.'

He did not wait. He was quite wet by the time he got into the car.

The car had left by the time I could ask him when he would be back.

The milkman, his hair dripping wet in spite of the plastic sheet covering his head, got off his bicycle.

'The rain is terrible. There are all the signs of a real flood.'

The servant woman who swept the floor and cleaned the vessels had not yet come. It did not seem likely that she would come in this heavy rain.

There was water beneath the cot in the bedroom. I went to the bathroom when I was sure the rain had abated slightly. After my bath, I changed the wick in the small bronze lamp in front of the picture of Guruvayoorappan kept on a shelf hanging on the wall, lighted it and made an obeisance. As usual, I said my prayers in my mind. I had bought the picture and the lamp when we began to live in the flat in Matunga. I had intended to make the small room a puja room, but when Vasanthi had insisted that she have a room of her own, I had moved the picture, the lamp and the bowl of holy ash to a shelf on the wall.

When I went to the drawing room, I saw through the window that the rain had increased in intensity.

Normally, I would have made some semolina *uppuma* and ground some chutney to go with it. But I did not feel up to it. I ate three slices of bread.

When there had first been a hint of diabetes, I had reduced my intake of food. On Mondays, I ate nothing in the daytime. There was a saying in our villages that fasting on Mondays was good for a long married life. Luckily, Bhaskarettan had no ailments to speak of. Doctor Nadkarni said that regular food habits and half a tablet a day were all he needed. Bhaskarettan came with me to the doctor's once. The doctor suggested examining him and checking his blood pressure.

'I've no ailments of any kind, Doctor,' he said. Still, why don't you have yourself examined, I muttered in Malayalam.

'Why should I?'

Suddenly, he had looked angry. It's precisely because you lose your temper like this over small things that I felt the doctor should examine you, I said to myself.

For some time, I had used the face cream the children had brought before going to bed. Later, I stopped. When my hair started to grow grey, I used to go to the beauty parlour once a month and have it dyed. Then I thought, what use was it? The bill came to a hundred and twenty-five and there was the auto-rickshaw fare as well. At fifty or fifty-five, one turned grey anyway. How long could it be dyed black? After two of my teeth were removed, my cheeks had grown hollow. They would never be full again. Whether you were a man or a woman, you had to accept your age sometime. Wasn't I good-looking when I was young? That was enough. Now I was married and had two children. And they had three children of their own. That was good enough. I felt like telling Ramesh's wife all this whenever I saw her coarse, artificially blackened hair.

Bhaskarettan was a shade darker than me. And an inch taller. Nevertheless, his face looked young. Even now, women liked to hover around him at dinners and receptions. He was full of witticisms and old sayings twisted neatly to suit each occasion. Actually, even at this age, his face would be suffused with radiance when he laughed.

Someone once told me in the strictest confidence that Bhaskarettan had had a love affair before he got married. Not someone—it was the late Sharmaji's wife. I was already aware of this. He had stayed in her house as a paying guest when he returned from England. He had told me all about it. Her father was a Malayalee and her mother a Marathi. The girl had begun to take undue liberties with him. When he realised that her parents were encouraging her, he moved out. 'It was not a serious affair,' Mrs Sharma.

In a manner of speaking, you could say such things about me as well. Some evenings, I've walked with Satish Kumar, who works in the Radio Station. I've gone with him to the cinema and to coffee places. We've held hands as we walked. But I swear nothing else happened. Then there was Bhagavandas, personal assistant to the General Manager of my company. It was fun at that age to have many people say pleasant things and hover around me. It would be a lie not to admit that. I had gone to the record room to pick up a file. This Bhagavandas came up suddenly from behind and put his arms around me. I turned my face away, so his lips touched a spot below my ear. I felt the earth reeling around me. I was frightened. I stopped going to the record room alone. If I saw the fellow coming towards me while I waited for a bus, I would quickly withdraw into the crowd. When I saw Bhagavandas last year, I could hardly recognise him. He had become a grandfather many times over. I found it hard not to laugh when I recalled how crazy he had been over me once.

No one takes the minor involvements of youth seriously.

A woman once told me in great confidence: 'Rugmini, this is only for your ears. Bhaskarettan had a serious affair once.'

'Really?'

'It's the truth. He had a child by her. It was after that that he married you. It was a son. He looks exactly like Bhaskaran. Ditto.'

I wanted to tell that Sindhi woman that back in our village they would have described the child as the living image of the father.

My friends pitied me quite a bit when I got married. Rugmini was tall, fair-skinned, beautiful—she could have got someone with a better personality. She was carried away by the fact that he had worked in England.

Who knew what sort of a job he had had there?

To start with, Indians found jobs as porters and sweepers in England.

I had gone up to them quickly, to prevent them passing any more comments. All this gossip was being exchanged at the telephone operator, Girija's wedding.

I knew that it was because they had never heard him talk that they thought of Bhaskarettan's shortness of stature and dark complexion as problems.

Do you know, he wears trousers and a full-sleeved shirt even when he's alone at home? He changes into pyjamas only when he sits down to dinner.

When we started our life together, I used to ask him jokingly, 'Why are you all dressed-up? We're not expecting anyone.' Bhaskarettan would smile. 'In the African jungle, the white man shaves, polishes his shoes, changes for dinner. When he was asked the same question, the white man said: "I do this for my own satisfaction." You haven't seen that film of Chaplin where, starving and hungry, he boils and eats his shoes for Christmas, wearing a three-piece suit and using a knife and fork. Chaplin films are shown in the mornings. Watch them.'

Once, after attending a wedding, I said to him: 'The girl is no match for him at all. I wonder what he saw in her.'

We were on his scooter. Bhaskarettan said: 'Look, that whole area is a slum. You must look at it at night from a plane as it lands. It's beautiful! The glow of a thousand bulbs. It's the same place. Beauty and ugliness depend upon the person who sees, the point from where he looks ...'

He spoke in English. His pronunciation of English was different, wonderful. You could never tire of listening.

Wasn't it the Friday after the heavy rains started that I was talking about? The second day of the unseasonal rains. I used to telephone Ammini and Sarojiniedathi around noon. After that I would call Bhaskarettan at the office.

If I did not call Ammini, she would call me, just before she took a nap. I put a handful of rice in the cooker and warmed up the previous day's curry. It continued to rain outside. A soundless rain, without a wind, that filled me with a terrible dread. I thought it would never end. I had only heard of the flood that would occur at Kalpantham, when the world would end.

I dialed Ammini's number but could not get through. Ammini sometimes made kalan, a vegetable preparation with curd, and sends it across. Bhaskarettan was very fond of it. I had tried making it according to the recipe Ammini gave me but it did not turn out right. It was difficult to satisfy the tastes of a person who said he was thinking of writing a book on Kerala cookery.

I could not get Ammini's number. I tried Sarojiniedathi's. Sarojiniedathi had continued to stay in Bombay after her husband died. By herself. She was seventy now. Once a year, she organised the women's group dance, the Kaikottikkali, for the Onam festival. I used to take part in it until about six years ago. The rehearsals used to start four or five months in advance. Critical comments about the performance continued for three months after it was over. It seemed as if Sarojiniedathi stayed alone in the city only to arrange kaikottikkali once a year.

I could not get her number either. I tried Bhaskarettan's direct line at the office. The telephone had gone out of order because of the heavy rain.

Suddenly, the phone made a faint, whining sound.

'Hullo, is it Mrs Bhasker?'

'Yes, yes.'

'Oh, you don't know me. But I know you. I'm Mrs Gadgil, Shefali's mother. Shefali ... Bhaskar Saab's secretary.'

'Yes, I know her, though I didn't know her name was Shefali. I know of her as Miss Gadgil. She had called here a couple of times. I think I saw her once, in the office car. What is it, Mrs Gadgil?'

'We haven't met but I know all about you from Bhaskar Saab. How is your health now?'

'I'm all right.'

'Dolly's gone with Bhaskar Saab. We call her Dolly at home. Did he go by train or by car?'

'I don't know.'

He would get angry if I asked questions like that. Would he go to Pune by taxi or get off at the station? I didn't know.

'The rain is terrible. In the fifty-three years of my life, I've never seen such rains in Bombay. The radio said that there have been three landslides on the road to Pune.'

'Is that so? I don't listen to the radio.'

'They'll have trouble if they go by car. I was in the bathroom when she left. If you can ring up the office ...'

'Mrs Gadgil, I can't get outside numbers on my telephone. The only call I've had so far is this one from you. If you could call, Mrs Gadgil and let me know ...'

'I'm Mrinal. Call me that, Rugminiji. We know all about you. About your daughter in Dubai, your daughter in America, their children ... Saab has told us everything.'

'I'm glad, Mrinal. Mrinal must be short for Mrinalini, no?'

She laughed, sounding happy. When she put the phone down, I wondered whether I had the same kind of pain in my chest as I had once had when I had an attack of breathlessness.

Bhaskarettan had never told me that he had visited his secretary's house.

How old would Shefali be? The mother was fifty-three. She had mentioned her age, being a decent sort. The daughter could be twenty or thirty then, or somewhere in between.

I served out some rice and curry and placed the plate on the table. The phone rang. Maybe Mrinalini had some news. What a relief, it was Ammini.

'Ammini, why didn't you call? I can't get through to anyone.'

I felt I was on the verge of tears.

'I've been dialing your number for quite a while.'

It was raining as heavily there. Her husband had not gone out. The ground floor of his office was a godown and it was flooded.

'Ammini, don't hang up. I can't make outgoing calls. Bhaskarettan has gone to Pune. I don't know whether he's gone by car or by train.'

'Rugmini, how could anyone go out in this rain? Is he touched in the head?'

'If it was an official matter that had been fixed earlier, even an earthquake would not have deterred him. Don't you know how he is, Ammini? Someone called just now to say that there have been landslides.'

'Then they'll come back, what else? Don't worry so much.'

'Just call Bhaskarettan's office. Find out how they went to Pune, where they're staying and all that. Tell them I can't get through from here. And then call me, Ammini. You'll call back for sure, won't you?'

Ammini was my only connection with the outside world.

I felt relieved after I spoke to her. I ate a handful of rice. Suddenly, darkness filled the house. A wind which had been lying quiet somewhere came to life and joined the fury of the rain. When I saw the neem trees outside bend and sway, I realised how strong the wind was. I closed and bolted all the windows which were open. Although it was afternoon, it was pitch dark inside. I turned on the domed light in the centre of the room. The phone rang. I picked it up thinking it was Ammini. It was Mrinal Gadgil.

'Look, Mrs Mrinal Gadgil, didn't I tell you I can't make any calls from here? Call up the office and find out where they've booked rooms.'

'But Rugminiji, how will they reach Pune? They say nearly a thousand vehicles are stranded at Khandala. I called the office. They don't have any information. Bhaskar Saab is not a type who talks to everyone in the office. But don't be upset, Rugminiji. Bhaskar Saab is so mature, such a man of the world, so why worry?'

That was true. He was a type who would not lose his self-confidence even if he were surrounded by danger on all sides.

'If there's been a landslide, he'll find another route.'

I continued to listen to her. Let Mrinal Gadgil talk away, I thought. It was a comfort to listen to someone's voice.

'Hadn't the company decided to send Shefali out because she couldn't handle computers? It was Bhaskar Saab who insisted that she be confirmed.'

'Yes, he's a very kind-hearted person.'

'Her father and I separated when she was two. Bhaskar Saab is like a god to her.'

'Oh!'

'He's very fond of her too. When he went to Ahmedabad, she was the only one he took from the office.'

To Ahmedabad? He said the Circulation Manager and the Finance Manager were going with him. He had not mentioned the secretary at all.

'Didn't you like the jeans she bought him as a gift, Rugminiji?'

'Eh—what?'

'The jeans—'

'Oh!' I laughed heartily. 'I liked them very much. It must be because Shefali insists on it that he wears jeans at his age.'

'Isn't it the youthfulness of our minds that determines age, Rugminiji? I thought you would come for Shefali's birthday ...'

'I ...' What explanation could I give?

'Saab said you had a sudden dizziness and nausea. Saab was the only guest apart from a few relatives. It's the watch Saab gave her that day that she wears regularly now. You get whatever foreign articles you want here now, don't you?'

'Oh yes, in plenty.'

'Anyway, Rugminiji, what problem do you have to get them? With both your daughters living abroad ... It's difficult if you can't make a telephone call. I'll call again. I'm not worried at all since it's Bhaskar Saab ...' She laughed aloud and went on talking. Then she put the phone down.

For years now, I had had to remind him about my birthday very tactfully. When the children were with us, they used to each give me a card and say, "Many happy returns." Although Bhaskarettan was keen on observing the customs and formalities of the white men, he never bothered about remembering birthdays and wedding anniversaries.

Was the violent wind outside circling inside my mind as well? I prayed silently. I rebuked myself. It must have upset Bhaskarettan when both the girls got married and went abroad. It was not astonishing that her humility had awoken his affection. I scolded myself: why had I not realised he was a sixty-seven year old man who needed sympathy?

Mrinal's words, that I had not listened to properly, claimed my attention.

'He may be old in years, but he's young at heart, isn't he, Rugminiji?'

What had I said in reply? Had I grunted assent? Or laughed it off? I remembered the days when we were both young in body and heart. Years ago. A time when he had made onslaughts on my body night and day, to the point of exhaustion.

I walked up slowly to the closed window, opened it and peered out. The banana trees were bent double and almost touched the ground. The branch of a neem tree had snapped and hung down. The angry wind had not abated, nor the rain.

The phone did not ring again until dusk. When he went somewhere faraway, he used to call me as soon as he reached his destination. Later, he would call to say when he would start back.

If there had been a landslide at Khandala, he would have to come back. He used to go often to Pune when he was in the old company. I remembered that while his companions stayed in a hotel, Bhaskarettan always stayed in a guest house. Was it at the Agricultural College or the University? I recalled that he had told me he stayed there because they had large grounds where he could take a walk in the morning. He said the guest houses were more comfortable than big hotels.

The phone rang. To my relief, it was Ammini.

I asked her petulantly: 'How long you took, Ammini! Don't you know I can't make any calls?'

I held back my tears. We had at least a hundred close friends in this city. Couldn't they have called me from time to time? I was a prisoner in this small house, trapped between the storm and the flood.

'Look, Ammini, there's a place where he generally stays. A guest house. At the Agricultural College or the University. One of the two. Find out the number somehow. Sankarettan must have friends in Pune. Find out somehow if he's reached there. If you get him, ask him for all the news and call me. Won't you call me, Ammini? I am ...'

Ammini's voice changed. Was I making a nuisance of myself? She said she would try and put the phone down.

The darkness inside the house deepened. I turned on two more lamps. The rain continued to pour down with vengeful obstinacy. Mahalakshmi, the Goddess of Wealth and Prosperity, who presided over this city, must be disgusted, I thought. People had become so wicked. All one heard of every day was looting, murder, rape and kidnapping. Mahalakshmi must have allowed the city to be punished.

I had a wash, changed the wick of the lamp in front of the picture of Guruvayoorappan, poured in oil and lighted it. God, Bhagavan, may he come back safe.

He used to tell me in advance if he was not coming back at night. He would arrange for Krishna's daughter or Mrs Chatterji's houseboy to spend the night here. But he had gone to Ahmedabad saying he would return in three days and came back only on the fifth day. Krishna's daughter had come over and watched T.V. until midnight while I slept. There was nothing to fear even if I was alone. The houses were close to one another since it was a colony. There was a watchman at the gate. Still, it was a comfort to have someone inside the house.

I opened the front door slightly and looked out. When the wind swept in rain drops and dry leaves, I closed the door.

Mrinal Gadgil telephoned again.

'I've been trying your number for a long time but I couldn't get through. How are you, Rugminiji?'

'Oh, I'm all right.'

'If you have wheezing, it grows worse when it rains. I hope you are all right. You had angina earlier, didn't you? And now?'

'No, Mrinal, I'm fine.'

'You must have plenty of houses around since it's a colony. We live in an old flat, but there's a lot of space. The only problem is that we are on the fourth floor.'

It was a great comfort to hear a human voice from outside. But I wished she would not call again.

'Any news?'

'No, Dolly didn't call.'

I put the phone down. I turned on the T.V. The news was over. They were playing film songs. The girl who was singing was wiggling her hips and romancing with a young man. It was at least thirty years since I had gone to see a film. When a Malayalam film was shown here for journalists and they invited us, we went to see it. That was—let me see, in eighty or eighty-one. It was while I was expecting Vasanthi that we last bought tickets to see a film. Some film about an elephant. The elephant saves the hero. There is a fight in the jungle. The elephant dies, the hero looks at its carcass and sings a long song. I couldn't remember the name of the film.

It was wet, humid and cold. Even so, I felt thirsty. I drank three glasses of water. I wondered whether to make chapathies or warm up the leftover rice. I was not at all hungry.

I had no idea what time it was. The wall clock had stopped since the battery had not been changed. Where was my watch—in the cupboard or the drawer of the table? I used it only on rare occasions when I went out.

The phone rang, startling me.

It was Ammini.

'Look, Rugmini, Sankarettan called Pune. Guess what? It hasn't rained at all there!'

I remembered what my grandmother used to say. That at the end of the Kali Yuga, at the time of the Apocalypse, the Rain God would divide the country up and it would rain only in certain parts.

'And then?'

'Why didn't you tell me Vinitha is here?'

'But Vinitha is in Dubai.'

'Then who is it? Vasanthi? The Guest House Manager said that Bhaskar Saab has taken a room there and that his daughter was with him. It was I who spoke.'

I did not say anything.

'I didn't get Bhaskarettan. They were in the restaurant when I called. They asked me to call in half an hour. I'll call and then ...'

'Don't bother, Ammini. We know now that he's there. I'm relieved.'

I rang off.

I wandered aimlessly through the drawing room and bedrooms. I opened the windows. I thought there was a rhythmic cadence in the howling of the wind. I opened the front door and the water on the verandah swept into the drawing room. It spread over the carpet in the centre, changing the hue of the faded green.

The phone tinkled. When I lifted it, there was silence. The instrument was dead. No more outside calls would come to this house.

Standing at the front door, I was drenched. The chill tickled me. I could hear the rippling of the water that had collected in the front yard.

I stepped into the veranda. Darkness and the lapping of the water. The wind sounded as if someone was blowing through a hollow bamboo. Suddenly, the lights went out, even those at the gate and along the footpaths. I felt comfortable now that it was pitch dark. This was the deluge. When everything was submerged in the floods, didn't Bhagavan float over the water on a banyan leaf? What peace there must have been then.

I stretched out on the verandah, resting my head on the threshold. Cold fingers of water crept up from under my ribs to my back. Mischievous fingers that tried to turn me on my side, wet fingers that tried to tickle me. I imagined the city entirely engulfed in water and myself floating on the surface and laughed to myself. I was relieved, my mind was at rest, I was not afraid.

It was Sunday today. Those who were seated inside made room for the newcomers. Let everyone sit or stand in whatever space there is.

It's Shefali who has just come in. Yes, the figure I had seen in the office car is standing there unbuckling her sandals. Bhaskarettan sees her, sits up straight and looks at her. She sees a familiar face, walks towards her with relief and says something in a low voice. Bhaskarettan continues to look at her. So that, when she comes nearer to say something, he can open the floodgates of the tears he has been suppressing.

She looks around and says, 'I'll be back. I have to go to the airport, my uncle is coming at eleven.'

She goes up to Bhaskarettan before she leaves.

'I'm leaving.'

That's when something really funny happens. A wordless bit of fun. Only I can understand it. Bhaskarettan looks at her sorrowfully as if to say, you are all I have. She replies with a look. Shefali's eyes say, while the old woman was alive, it was great fun. But if you think I'm going to shoulder the burden of looking after an old man, forget about it! Then she walks out. Everyone there knows she won't come back. What can be funnier? I want to burst out into a raucous laugh. At least in order to wipe out the pleading look on Bhaskarettan's face. But I can't. They've moved the dining table and sofas to make space, covered my body and laid me out.

Had they brought in the dead body silently, with their heads lowered, murmuring something now and then, as we do in the villages in Kerala? When I came to North India, there were many local customs I could not reconcile myself to. But their funerals are good. They beat drums, shout "Ram Nam Sat Hai!" and treat the walk to the cremation ground as a celebration.

Let there be a celebration around my dead body. Ram Nam Sat Hai. Weren't most of the people who had come to the house North Indians? So the northern rituals and customs must be observed. Ram Nam Sat Hai!

Insight

It was a mistake to have assumed that the news would not have reached here.

She used to come by herself to her home in the village from time to time. No one used to be surprised by this.

She had a bath and breakfast and came and sat down in the verandah. Amma, her mother, went up to her and asked without any preliminaries: 'Sudha Kutty, is what we heard true?'

'What did you hear?' She gave her mother a harsh look, deliberating on how to build a wall of words around herself.

Amma closed her eyes and said softly: 'That you and Prabhakaran are separating ...' Amma had always had this habit of closing her eyes if she had something embarrassing to say. Sudha decided it was better to be aggressive than give her a direct answer.

'And who sends you news like this with telegraphic regularity?'

Amma sat down some distance away, stretching her legs out on the stone steps at the entrance. 'Sreedevi came to Narayanankutty's place the day before yesterday. Her Devu's husband is in Madras, isn't he?'

So her younger sister's mother-in-law was diffusing bits and pieces of news among the relatives.

'The news was in Visalam's letter yesterday as well.'

Once Chandri got the news from her elder sister, she would of course write to her mother.

Sudha stepped into the yard. It was only ten in the morning, but it was terribly hot. She kept close to the shade of the wall as she walked. As her pace quickened, her rubber slippers made a sound, tapping against her heels.

She often found excuses to come to this old house where her mother stayed by herself in search of solace. There was no telephone to disturb her. She did not have to dress up to entertain guests. She did not have to stay awake until Prabhakaran's executive friends left at midnight, listening to their jokes with a hostess's artificial smile clinging to her face. But then, she used to be given permission to come here only once in a while. And that, for three or four days.

The first question Amma asked was always: 'When do you have to go back?' This time, she had not asked. As she walked back to the verandah, Amma said, 'People keep saying all sorts of things. What really happened?'

She did not reply.

'As far as I could make out …' Amma stopped.

'It's true, Amma. It's better for us to separate.'

Amma bent her head and stared at the steps.

The girl who helped in the kitchen came and asked her something and Amma got up and went in.

Sudha had taken leave for fifteen days from the bank. A few people at the bank had an inkling of what was happening. She had spoken frankly only to Nirmala Srinivasan, the Cashier. It was Nirmala who had arranged a room for her at the Y.W.C.A.

She had felt that Amma liked to live on her own. Amma did not encourage relatives or friends to visit her. If the children did not go and see her, she never complained. She wrote letters on inland letter-forms once a month to her three children, regardless of whether they replied or not. She always had a young girl from one of the neighbouring houses to help her. When Sudha came the previous year, Amma had told her that the girl who was then working with her was going to get married. She was going to give her a gold chain weighing a sovereign.

'All three of you must give her whatever you can. You can send a money order in Kuttiraman's name. Or in mine.'

Visalam and Chandri were to send three hundred rupees each and Sudha four hundred. Sudha was being asked to give more since both of them worked and they had no children.

When the girl left, her younger sister had come to help Amma in the kitchen.

Visalaedathi was anxious about Amma staying here alone. She had a large house in Thiruvananthapuram and many servants.

It was on an occasion when they had all gathered at home. 'If Amma falls ill, there's not even a doctor nearby,' Visalaedathi had said.

'I'm not going to fall ill,' was Amma's reply.

A black hen and her brood of chickens came hesitantly into the yard from the banana grove through a gap in the wall. They ran along the sides of the yard pecking at morsels.

Sudha heard Amma say: 'It's a wildfowl. It comes here every day at this hour. God knows where it comes from!'

Sudha looked at them, amused. The mother hen was frightened when she saw people in the house. Sudha moved towards them softly to take a closer look, keeping to the shadows. The mother hen clucked a warning and ran into the garden, followed by the chicks.

Amma did not say anything while they had lunch.

Sreedharettan, her younger sister's husband's elder brother, came in the evening. He was the Headmaster of the local High School and an important person in the village.

Sudha readied herself for a cross examination based on rumours he had heard. Pretending nothing had happened, she asked about his wife and children and complained about the absence of a breeze in summer.

'How many days leave do you have, Sudha Kutty?'

'A week.'

Amma interrupted. 'I don't have any milk, Sreedhara, to make you some tea.'

'I don't want any.'

Sudha was at a loss when small talk ran out. But Sreedharan began to talk about the oppressive heat in Madras, the wealth Jayalalitha had amassed, Karunanidhi's rule … Sudha listened, contributing nothing of her own. When the conversation petered out, he got up to leave.

She had heard that this man's horoscope had also been considered at the time when marriage proposals were being discussed for her.

A swarm of dragonflies began to buzz around by evening. As a child, she had heard that dragonflies hovering low over the ground was a sign of rain. She wished it would rain. The heat in the month of Meenam here was no less that of the Vaikashi summer in Madras. Since they were still arguing about who would pay for them, there were no fans in the house.

'Sleep in the southern room at night. There'll be at least a faint breeze there,' said Amma as she served dinner.

'I can sleep anywhere.'

There was a rusty old table fan in Amma's room that Achan had bought years ago.

Sudha had not brought anything to read, nor had she picked up a book on the way. Achan's old books lay in a heap on the round table in Amma's room. Amma usually read for a while at night. There were no new books though. She glanced at the book that Amma had kept open on a copy of *A History of the World*. It was *Hima Giri Vihara* (Discourses from a Snow-capped Mountain).

A bed had been made in the southern room. She changed into a nightgown and looked at the time. Eight forty-five. In the city, Prabhakaran would be going back home after a game of rummy and two beers.

Amma walked in. 'You can bring that table fan in here if you want. It's a bit noisy, but it still works.'

'No, I don't need it.'

She sat down on the bed as if she was about to lie down, so that Amma would go away quickly.

'Still …' Amma wanted to talk.

'Tell me.'

'Separating after having lived together for five years'

She did not say anything.

'What will people think when they come to know?'

She turned slightly so that she did not have to see Amma's face.

Relieved to have found a topic to speak about, she asked, 'How can you make a phone call from here if you need to?'

'There's a booth now in the room next to the pharmacy. You can call anywhere you want.'

She was drained of words again.

'What have you decided to do?'

'I'm thinking it over.'

'Do you want me to come and speak to Prabhakaran?'

Sudha said hastily, 'No, no.'

Amma gave her a pitying look. Trying to suppress her anger, Sudha said: 'There's no need to try to bring about a compromise, Amma.'

Amma went out.

Sudha knew Amma would not speak of this matter again. Silent acquiescence was part of her nature. Achan had died after a paralytic stroke had confined him to bed for a year and a half. Amma had never spoken to anyone of her suffering, of the cruel fate she had been subjected to. She had not heard Amma protest even when people had murmured to each other about how a stepsister had snatched away Achan's entire earnings.

Amma said to Sudha the next morning: 'Your Valiamma at Cholayil has sent word that she would like to see you.'

Sudha hesitated.

'The old woman heard the news from Janu, who brings milk here from the house next to Valiamma's.'

'I'll go and see her.'

'You said you'd go last time as well but you didn't.'

'All right, I'll go.'

'She's eighty-four. Who knows how long she'll last. She can't see a thing. But she's quite fit otherwise.'

Valiamma of Cholayil was Sudha's grandmother's older sister. Because Amma called her Valiamma, Sudha did too.

Valiamma used to come here to visit her younger sister. She used to like doing Visaledathi's hair in different ways. At dusk, she used to make the three children sit down and recite their evening prayers loudly.

Muthassi, her grandmother, would give Valiamma the bed and lie down on the floor. Valiamma liked telling the children stories. It was Sudha Kutty she always caught hold of. Visalaedathi would dodge her and Chandri would fall asleep. Sudha thought Muthassi too was half-asleep as she listened.

There was the story of how Unniyamma hid Palat Koman behind her long, flowing tresses while she bathed in a pond. Then there was the story of Kovalan and Kannagi. Later, when she visited Madurai, she had recalled this story that Valiamma had narrated. Valiamma had described how Kannagi had plucked out her breast, thrown it at the city and set the place on fire as if she had stood watching it happen.

She had wanted to buy a gift for Valiamma. But she had quarrelled with Prabhakaran about something just as she was about to go shopping and had lain down in the hotel room in protest until it was time for the train.

She had last seen Valiamma the day before her wedding, when she had gone to receive her blessing. That was more than five years ago. Even while her grandmother was alive, she had somehow been more fond of Valiamma. She had come home seven times in those five years. Yes, seven. Prabhakaran had been with her on two occasions. Valiamma used to ask for her every time. She lived hardly three furlongs away and yet, every time, she had not been able to visit her for one reason or other.

The wildfowl and her chicks came into the yard that day as well. They did not seem to be as frightened as they had been the previous day. She went a little closer. Yes, they were a mother and her chicks all right. She watched the specks of sunlight glint against their black, shining feathers and scatter on the ground.

'Here are some visitors ...' The chicks scurried away hearing the voice.

Sreedevi Amma and her younger sister stood in the yard. Observing courtesies, Amma was asking them to sit down, telling

Janu to make some tea. Giving Sudha an uneasy look, Amma went in. The look said: 'You'll hear a bellyful.'

'Sit down, Sudha. You mustn't take offence if I speak frankly.'

She did not sit down. She made an effort to smile and failed.

'Do speak.'

'Why beat about the bush? I have to speak out. If what I heard is true, things are pretty bad.'

Sudha managed a smile and said nonchalantly, 'It's bad, but there's no way out.'

Sreedevi Amma's face darkened. She looked meaningfully at her younger sister who took the hint and said, 'What Narayanan Kutty wrote is right. It will bring shame to the family.'

Sudha stood there silently.

'To live together for five years and then put an end to ...'

Sreedevi Amma looked at her sister as if hinting to her to go on.

'I'm sure there were faults and mistakes on his side, but you have to accept them. That's what marriage means. The things your mother endured!'

Sudha attempted to smile. What she had wanted to say at first was: 'The fault is mine, Sreedevi Amma, not Prabhakaran's.' But she decided not to say anything.

They kept talking. Even as a child, Sudha had mastered the astonishing capacity to shut her ears to conversations that she was not interested in. As she began to search for forgotten names, characters in novels, the topography of places she had seen when younger, the voices would suddenly grow distant.

Sreedevi Amma asked as they were leaving: 'Do you think everything I said was futile?'

She smiled. 'No.'

'Don't you think there's some truth in what I said?'

'Yes.'

She sighed in relief. 'What have you decided then?'

Sudha smiled and said: 'Let me think it over.'

Parting her lips in a wide grin to express her satisfaction at having succeeded in her mission, Sreedevi Amma left, followed by her younger sister.

Amma asked: 'When are you going to Cholayil to see Valiamma?'

'I'll go.'

Valiamma too must be getting ready to give her advice.

Sumathi, who had been with her in High School, came in the afternoon with her three-year-old daughter. She used to wait for Sudha every day near the area where the carpenters worked. The wart below her nose seemed to have grown bigger. She had been married before she finished her tenth standard.

Sudha pressed her to sit down but she would not.

'How are you Sumathi?'

'Oh, getting along.'

She wore a glittering saree of blue, violet and red. Her husband, who was working in the Gulf, must have brought it. He came home on leave for two months every two years. A heady fragrance enveloped Sumathi and gold ornaments covered her neck and arms.

'I heard you'd come. Will you be here for some time?'

'Yes, a few days.'

The following Monday, there would be a house-warming ceremony at Sumathi's new house. 'You must come for it, Sudha Kutty.'

'I'll come if I'm still here.'

The child was tracing flower patterns on her mother's saree with her fingers. Stroking the little one's hair, Sudha said, 'I've forgotten her name.'

'Karthika.'

Holding the child's hand, Sudha tried to draw her closer but the child whimpered and clung to her mother.

Sumathi came right up to Sudha and said confidentially: 'I heard there was something wrong …'

'Oh, so you heard too …'

'Shankarettan who comes to lay the mosaic tiles … when his wife told me, I didn't believe her.'

Sudha grunted.

'Is it true, Sudha Kutty.'

She smiled. 'Yes, in a way.'

Sumathi's eyes widened in anxiety. Bending forward so that her forehead almost touched Sudha's, she said very softly: 'Don't assume that I'm advising someone who is more educated and knowledgeable than me. It's better in every way to be reconciled to living together.'

Sudha tapped her hand. 'Let me think it over.'

'It was a mistake to have decided not to have children now. Whether they were boys or girls, you would not have had these evil thoughts then.'

Sudha looked at Sumathi in surprise. And made a note in her mind of a good colloquial expression, "evil thoughts".

Sumathi left.

When Janu brought milk that evening, she said that Cholayil Valiamma had asked for Sudha again.

'You'd better go,' said Amma.

'I'll go tomorrow.'

'She's not in need of money. But give her something all the same. Visalam gave her fifty rupees when she went and the old lady told everyone she met about it for days on end.'

Amma laughed. This was the first time since she arrived that she had seen the gloom lift from Amma's face.

What if she said she was not going to compete with Visalaedathi?

She decided to leave on Monday. She would not wait for the two weeks to be over. There had been enough unpleasantness in the three days she had been here.

Should she call Hyderabad, she wondered. She had noted down the mobile number in the book in her handbag. And the direct number of his office in her mind.

There was no one to send to book her ticket. She would get into the ladies compartment. After all, it was only an overnight journey.

He had told her to call even from the village. 'If possible,' he had added.

The next day, after breakfast, she said, 'I'll go and see Valiamma.'

'Take Janu with you.'

'No, I don't need to.'

She first dropped in at the new house in the carpenters' work-area. Sumathi was so astonished and delighted, she did not know what to do. Two men were varnishing the windows under the supervision of the carpenter, Narayanan.

She walked around inside.

'Both bedrooms have attached bathrooms,' said Sumathi proudly.

Sudha found it difficult to evade the invitation to have something to drink.

'He's written to say he's coming in July.'

'Ask him to take you to Dubai. You can see the place too.'

'That won't happen. He said only people with high salaries can afford that.'

All the same, Sumathi was very happy.

'I must leave now, Sumathi. I want to drop in at Valiamma's place.'

'Remember what I told you?'

'Of course.'

She turned and smiled.

Once she had passed the cluster of bamboos, she saw the stream, now run dry. There used to be bramble thickets on both sides. Water used to flow plentifully through the stream all the year round. In the rainy season, it used to overflow into the channel below and form a minor tributary of the river.

The house had been built in Valiachan's, her great-grandfather's, time. There was a bamboo stile now in place of the gatehouse. Sudha went up the steps into the front yard. There was no one around. Pepper had been spread out to dry on a bamboo mat. As she stood there hesitantly, Thankedathi came into the verandah.

'Look who's here! Achamma was complaining this morning that you were going to leave without seeing her.'

Thankedathi insisted that she sit down on the chair that was placed next to the wooden ledge with a back-rest, and began to talk about her family. Both her sons were studying and had gone back the week before to the hostel because they had practical examinations. Her youngest, a girl, was in the ninth standard. When their mother died, her younger sisters had taken their share of the property, built houses in their husbands' village and settled down there.

'They palmed off this crumbling old house on me. There was no one to speak for me.'

Her voice trembled in customary tribute to her husband's death. She wiped her dry eyes.

'Where is Valiamma?'

'In the northern room. She can't see at all. And she doesn't like anyone leading her by the hand. Who knows when and where she's going to stumble and fall.'

Sudha heard Valiamma's voice at the door: 'No one's going to have trouble on my account.'

Valiamma placed both her hands on the door frame and put out her foot accurately onto the verandah. Sudha hurried up to her. At eighty four, Valiamma held herself erect, without the slightest trace of a stoop. Her blouse and upper cloth were pristine white. Starch glistened on her bordered mundu. The radiance Sudha remembered from childhood had not dimmed at all. Sudha looked particularly at the thickness of the knot of grey hair. Whenever she listened to the story of Unniyamma, she used to imagine that it was Valiamma herself who undid her hair and hid Komappan inside it.

Thankedathi was about to pull up a chair but Valiamma said: 'No, I'll sit here. Sit down, Sudha Kutty.'

Valiamma's hand stretched out more or less exactly towards her arm. She sat down next to Valiamma on the wooden ledge.

'You've put on weight, Sudha Kutty!'

Sudha looked at her own arms. It was true, she had put on weight.

'You were gasping when you took a few steps towards me. I can guess even without seeing you, from your breathing.'

Valiamma smiled. There was no life in her eyes, but her face was free of wrinkles. Age had furrowed only her neck.

'Thankam, make some tea. And if there's any jackfruit, fry some.'

Sudha said, 'No, I don't want anything. Just half a glass of tea.'

Valiamma was obviously waiting for Thankam to go into the kitchen.

'What have you decided, child?' Valiamma's question was very sudden. Sudha felt confused.

'Don't worry. I didn't send for you to scold you or find fault with you. It's four or five years, isn't it, since we met?'

Sudha felt relieved.

'All these creatures here grin when I speak of what I see. They wonder what a person both of whose eyes are clouded with cataract can see. Can they see as much as I can?'

She had raised a voice a bit, probably so that Thankedathi could hear her from the kitchen.

Valiamma lowered her voice again. 'What have you decided?'

Sudha suddenly felt disturbed. Her breathing quickened.

'If you feel you've had enough of him, you should put an end to it. Marriage is a personal matter. There's no point acting out a charade just to convince the people around you.'

Sudha sighed, drew up her legs and sat facing Valiamma. Valiamma moved her head closer.

'My first husband none of you would have seen him.'

'Amma's seen him. He was a music teacher, wasn't he, a *bhagavathar*?'

'That was the problem. His music classes were at the Pisharoty's place. And he ate in our house. He was a fine singer. Wore ear studs set with red stones and had a sandal paste *tilakam* on his forehead. You can take it that I too found him attractive.'

Valiamma ran her fingers through her hair and chuckled.

'He went away before a year was over.'

'Yes, Amma told me.'

'He didn't go because he wanted to. I told him to go,'

murmured Valiamma. She smiled, fixing her sightless eyes on a spot in the distance.

'He didn't have anything material to give me. I could have overlooked that. But he would act coy and speak with a lisp, like a woman. Shouldn't men be smart and lively? I told him to his face that it was better to end the relationship, there was no other way.'

Sudha had heard about Valiamma's first marriage, but had not known the details.

Then Grandfather, her Valiachan, had come along. He worked for the Salt Department. They had had three children. Valiachan had died and all the three children died too. Valiamma still survived.

'You've seen Valiachan, haven't you? He wasn't handsome or good-looking or anything like that, was he?'

'I've seen him when I was a child. He was ill and confined to bed.'

'There was no one like him in this whole area. He would be right in front for the festival procession. If the elephant ran amuck, they needed Madhavan Nair. Only he could deal with fireworks that burst into eighteen levels of colour!'

Thankedathi brought the tea. Valiamma maintained a serious expression while she stood there. As soon as Thankedathi turned to go in, Valiamma laughed.

'Those who looked at him from outside saw him as a fierce cobra. He would lose his temper, quarrel and scold. Only I knew how soft and gentle he was. I only had to say I had a cold and he would be concerned and anxious.'

Valiamma's laugh grew louder.

Sudha forgot the problems she had been trying to keep at bay. She heard what Valiamma was saying with the same pleasure she used to feel when listening to her narrate stories long ago.

'Having no worries at all can be upsetting. It was after I had Kuttyarayan ...'

'What?'

'An upheaval ... An obsession for a man. I told myself,

control yourself, wretch. But it was no use, you understand. Still ...'

Valiamma opened her mouth wide and laughed, without completing the sentence. Sudha realised that she had lost only her grinders, all her other teeth were intact.

'I was just your age then.' Valiamma sighed.

'Is he still alive, Valiamma?'

Valiamma's face dimmed.

'He's gone. They're all gone. I'm the only one left. I have to wait until I'm called. One can't make oneself die ...'

Valiamma shook her head as if she was trying to get rid of something, slid back and rested her head against the wall.

'The other person. Who is it, Sudha Kutty?'

Sudha was startled. 'What?'

'You saw a man. You liked him. You decided it was him you wanted to live with. Isn't this what happened?'

'Who told you?'

Valiamma drew up her knees. 'No one has to tell me these things. Who is it, child?'

She found it difficult not to show how embarrassed she was.

'Is it someone you work with?'

'No.'

She would not be able to explain it to Valiamma. She had met him at a dinner organised to say goodbye to Janardan Rao, the manager who had been transferred. Janardan Rao, who claimed to be a singer, was singing a ghazal. The chief guest, the organisers and the clients who had been invited were all drunk. He was standing by himself at the other end of the room with a glass of orange juice in his hand. He looked at her from time to time, then slowly made his way towards her. She said to herself, her mind full of fear, 'God, these footsteps are coming straight into my heart.'

She was happy when he told her that he spent ten days in Madras every month. He saw people coming towards them and said, 'I guess I can call you at the bank.'

She nodded. She could not ask him why he wanted to call.

Valiamma asked: 'Is he married?'

'No.'

'Does Prabhakaran know?'

She paused for a while before answering. 'He knows something.'

'Then you should separate. He'll find another woman. That's not a serious matter. You must separate.'

Sudha was amused.

'It's not as easy to separate as it used to be in the old days, Valiamma.'

'If you don't want each other, that's the end of it. Isn't it?'

The confidence to explain without feeling embarrassed came back to her.

'It's not like that. The couple have to file a joint petition. The Judge will summon them after six months and ask whether they still wish to separate. If they say they do, they have to wait another six months.

She saw anger spread slowly over Valiamma's face.

'If two people love each other and want to live together, does the Judge have to give his consent?'

'That's the law, Valiamma.'

Valiamma was not satisfied at all.

'True, if there are children, arrangements must be made to maintain them. But what has the Judge to do with people who want to live together?'

'That's the law.'

'Law indeed! Don't provoke me to speak my mind.'

Thankedathi came to fetch the empty glasses. Valiamma kept muttering soundlessly to herself. Thankedathi said: 'Until last year, Achamma could make us out as shadows. Now she doesn't see even that much.'

Sudha said: 'An operation will restore your vision. A lot of people do it even at your age. I can take you to Madras if you want.'

Valiamma's laugh was bitter.

'No, no. Why should I get back my vision? I've seen enough, my child!'

Sudha got up to go.

Thankedathi said: 'Have your lunch here.'

'Oh no. Amma would have cooked for me.'

'The rice is on the boil. You must drop in next time you come, Sudha Kutty.'

Thankedathi went in. A fourteen-year-old girl arrived at the bamboo stile and moved it. Valiamma's eyes went to the entrance. The girl removed her slippers just below the verandah, looked at Sudha, smiled and went in, her head bent, not making a sound. When she was at the door, Valiamma asked:

'Where have you been?'

The girl trembled. 'To the Pisharoty's place, to get a book from Sarada.'

'And do you have to get dolled up in a silk skirt to go there?'

The girl went pale and scurried in fearfully.

Valiamma turned towards Sudha. 'She didn't have a book in her hand, did she?'

'No, she didn't.'

'The moment I heard it rustle, I knew it was a silk skirt.'

'She's only a child after all, Valiamma.'

'She's too grown-up for her age. I can see ...'

'I'll go now.'

Valiamma stood up.

Sudha remembered what Amma had said and quietly opened the purse in her hand.

'No. You're going to give me some money. Don't. What need has Valiamma for money?'

Taken aback, Sudha shut her purse.

'When you come ... when you come next ...' Valiamma's voice broke. 'If I'm alive, you must come and see me. That's all I ask.'

She saw Valiamma's lustreless eyes fill with tears. Tears filled her eyes too, she could not hold them back. She bent down and touched Valiamma's feet, seeking her blessing. Remembering that she had done the same thing five years ago.

Valiamma placed her hands gently on Sudha's bent head.

'May it turn out well this time at least.'

She walked out. As soon as she reached the bazaar, she noticed the board of the S.T.D. booth in the distance.

She murmured both the telephone numbers to herself. She had to check the mobile number from her notebook before she called. If she hurried home after the call, she would not miss seeing the wildfowl and her chicks come into the yard.

She quickened her pace.

Glossary

Achamma	father's mother
Achan	father
Ammaman	uncle
Bhagavathar	music teacher
Bhagavathi	the goddess
Bhikshu	Buddhist monk
Bhikshuni	female Buddhist monk
Brahmarakshas	the spirit of a dead Brahmin who died a gruesome death
Chandu	a paste used to make a round mark on the forehead
Chechi	older sister
Cheruman	farmhand (also called pulaya in Malayalam)
Chovva	evil that occurs when the planet Mars falls on certain signs of the zodiac
Edathi	older sister
Ettan	older brother
Flood of '99	is the Malayalam Era 1099 which is equal to 1924
Illam	traditional Namboothiri household
Kadumanga	a pickle made with small mangoes
Kalan	a curry made with vegetables and curd
Kanji	rice gruel

Kanni	second month on the Malayalam calendar, approximately September to October
Kaikottikkali	a group dance by women
Kasturyadi	Ayurvedic tablet for easing breathing trouble
Koothu	a narrative usually performed only within temple premises (given by *Chakyar*, the narrator-performer)
Kothankallu	a game played with small pebbles or stones
Meenam	eighth month on the Malayalam calendar, approximately from mid March to mid April
Mundu	a cloth worn round the waist
Muthassi	grandmother
Nallukettu	a sunken courtyard in the centre of a house with wooden pillars at the corners
Oppa	older brother
Pativrata	chaste woman
Payasam	a sweet made with milk and rice
Pottu	spot; the round mark, usually, on a woman's forehead
Prasadam	sandalwood paste, flowers etc. received from temple; this is sometimes accompanied by fruits and other offerings as well
Sindooram	coloured powder used to make a mark on the forehead
Taravad	extended family; also used for the house in which the family lives
Tayambaka	a rhythmic display exclusively of drums; a very special temple art form
Thorthu mundu	longish towel, sometimes worn instead of a *mundu* by workmen
Thirovonam	the tenth day of the Chingam month, commemorating the return of Mahabali (Maveli of the legend)
Thulam	third month on the Malayalam calendar, approximately October to November
Thilakam	a mark made on the forehead

Vaidyar	practioner of indigenous medicine
Vaikashi	from May to June
Valiachan	father's older brother
Valiamma	mother's older sister
Velichappadu	a dancer in the Bhagavathi temple. He becomes possessed by the Goddess and functions as an oracle
Veshti	a cloth worn over the shoulder (the 'second' *mundu*)
Vibhuti	holy ash
Vrischikam	name of the fourth month on the Malayalam calendar, approximately November to December